Girls' Night Out

Twenty-nine Female Vampire Stories

Selected by
Stefan Dziemianowicz,
Robert Weinberg, and Martin H. Greenberg

Barnes
& Noble
Books
New York

1997 Barnes & Noble Books

ISBN 0-7607-0424-4

Book design by Leah Lococo

Printed and bound in the United States of America

97 98 99 00 01 M 9 8 7 6 5 4 3 2 1

BVG

CONTENTS

❦

INTRODUCTION

❦

A S ANY READER OF HORROR FICTION WILL TELL YOU, vampires are ubiquitous in our world. They come in all shapes and sizes and inhabit all niches of society. They live in brooding Gothic castles remote from familiar human haunts, and they work in the cubicle right next to yours. They wear distinctive black capes and flash their overgrown incisors—all of them, that is, except the ones who dress and look just like you and me. Many live to drink your blood, although many others—possibly more than you will ever be aware of—might just want to co-exist peacefully with human beings and not call attention to their alternative existence.

In the century since Bram Stoker's *Dracula* was published, vampires have assumed so many different guises in literature that it is impossible to find a single pigeonhole that will accommodate them all. Nevertheless, when we think of a vampire, the image that comes to most readers' minds is that of a predatory creature who is menacing, malevolent—and invariably male.

Sexist? Perhaps. Myopic? No doubt. Understandable? Certainly within reason.

The narrowness of our imaginations where vampires are concerned can be blamed largely on the forcefulness of Stoker's. *Dracula* is the most influential vampire novel ever written because it strikes the reader on an instinctive level. It is, in essence, a story about power and the control that it imparts. In Stoker's society, power resided with men, and Count Dracula was its most intense expression. To be sure, there are female vampires in *Dracula*, and they outnumber the male vampires four to one. But it is Dracula who emerges as the novel's most convincingly drawn vampire, in no small part because his ruthlessness seems perfectly consistent with his maleness.

It may come as a surprise to some readers, then, that one of the models for the fictional Count Dracula was a female vampire who was his equal in evil. Shortly before the publication of his novel in 1897, Stoker excised a chapter from the opening section (later published as the short story "Dracula's Guest") that evokes the name of "Countess Dolingen of Gratz in Styria." The reference is an oblique homage to Joseph Sheridan Le Fanu's novella "Carmilla," which had been published in 1871 and which Stoker had read. Carmilla, a centuries-old vampire who beguiles her way into households throughout Europe and preys upon their young women, embodies many of the attributes that we think of as common to all literary vampires. Although Dracula was an actual historical figure who had given rise to vampire myths long before the end of the nineteenth century, it is assumed that Stoker embellished his fictional vampire partly with elements borrowed from Le Fanu's story.

"Carmilla" was not the first treatment of a female vampire in literature, but Le Fanu's story is recognized today as a groundbreaking work that alerted writers to the rich potential of the female vampire theme. *Girls' Night Out* celebrates the legacy it helped inaugurate by gathering together 29 vampire tales written in the wake of Le Fanu's achievement. Each features a female vampire who can hold her own against her male counterparts and who is usually more than a match for her human prey. As a unit, these stories shed light on a tradition that developed parallel to the male vampire paradigm, and which often penetrated into territories off-limits to the sons of Dracula.

Three of the selections predate the publication of Stoker's novel and each occupies a seminal place in the canon of vampire fiction. Julian Hawthorne's "Ken's Mystery" (1883) and Anne Crawford's "A Mystery of the Campagna" (1887) both feature *femmes fatales* who seduce and destroy (or nearly destroy) their male victims. The vampires in these stories set the pattern for most depictions of the female vampire that have followed: unlike Dracula, who overpowers his victims by brute force, these vampires exploit a weakness in human beings, namely the power to love. No doubt, both Hawthorne and Crawford were simply paying lip service to the sexual politics of their time when they created female vampires whose methods seemed "gentler" than those of their masculine counterparts. But consciously or not, they also produced stories with marked emotional depth that explore what makes us human as much as what makes vampires inhuman.

Building on the foundation laid by Hawthorne and Crawford, horror writers of the past century have established an enduring literary tradition in which the female vampire's ability to arouse love, passion, obsession, and lust in her victims illuminates the darkest corners of the human psyche. *Girls' Night Out* features many different treatments of this inherently sexual aspect of female vampirism, ranging from Robert Bloch's "The Scent of Vinegar," in which vampire prostitutes embody the puritanical moral that the wages of sin are death, to K. W. Jeter's "The First Time," in which the loss of childhood innocence concomitant with sexual initiation into adulthood is likened to a vampiric death and resurrection. The selections vary in their portrayal of vampire allure as either an unspeakable abomination or the ultimate irresistible temptation, and ask readers to choose for themselves which type of victim they identify with most closely: the reluctant love-smitten suitor of Hugh B. Cave's "The Brotherhood of Blood," or the hero of C. L. Moore's "Shambleau," who is as attracted to as he is repulsed by the taboo sexuality of its vampiric monster.

The relationship of the vampire to its victim is one of the most fertile areas for development in all horror fiction, and the female vampire has proved a particularly dependable vehicle for exploring it. Mary Elizabeth Braddon's "Good Lady Ducayne," which we include here, was published just one year before *Dracula* and is recognized as one of the first stories to suggest that there are vampiric undercurrents in any dependent relationship. Its nonsupernatural vampire, who victimizes through her wealth and preys upon the youth of her female companions, set a precedent for some of the unconventional incarnations of the vampire that readers will find in the stories that follow: a helpless woman who saps the vitality out of her caretakers in Mary E. Wilkins-Freeman's "Luella Miller," an actress who cannibalizes her profession in Chet Williamson's "...To Feel Another's Woe," even a voracious consumer culture that feeds on subliminal human desires in Fritz Leiber's "The Girl with the Hungry Eyes."

Ultimately, the stories chosen for *Girls' Night Out* challenge reader preconceptions of what distinguishes female from male vampires. There are no boundaries that their undead damsels do not transgress. They fit as comfortably in science fiction settings as in the milieu of gothic horror. They walk the backroads of rural folklore and the mean streets of the modern city. They divide their attentions equally between men and women, and they can do good as easily as evil. And no matter who they are, or where they go, they always hold up a mirror in which men and women alike see their own reflections.

The tales you are about to read represent a liberation, both sexual and creative. It is our hope that their variety and diversity will expand perceptions of the vampire tale, and linger in the memory as fiction that transcends both gender and genre.

—STEFAN DZIEMIANOWICZ
New York, 1997

THE INSUFFICIENT ANSWER

ROBERT AICKMAN

OUR ART CRITIC HAD FOR SOME REASON NOT TURNED up at the office that day, so it was young Symes whom the London Editor sent to notice the new exhibition at Benson's Gallery near the Irving statue. As Symes, a worthy young chap fresh from six years drudgery on a local weekly in the Midlands, knew nothing of art, artists, or art dealers, he was unaware that the small round man standing in the door of the office just beyond the entrance to the Gallery was Benson himself. It being less than half an hour before closing time (Symes had left the assignment rather to the last), the premises were empty of visitors, who are seldom to be found in art galleries except simultaneously at the busiest hour. Benson was of that type, not uncommon in his profession, who treat the whole world indiscriminately as confidants, commonly adding to the good effect by a genially dramatic opening, savouring not in the least of condescension. His apparent lack of suavity and subtlety was unusual; but his knowledge of his business more than compensated. As Symes's slightly unassured professional creep round the exhibition neared the half-way mark and Benson's office door, Benson spoke.

'It's not good enough. It just won't do.'

Symes, feeling this to be some sort of challenge to his critical capacity, hastily temporized. 'Oh, it's surely not as bad as that. No. 42 I thought rather good. "Drunk Seaman", you know.'

'This,' said Benson heartily. 'Read it.'

He thrust out a piece of paper. It was a cablegram. Symes read it. 'Regret your proposal impossible. Cannot leave with harvest impending. Hastings.'

'Who's Hastings?'

'Lola Hastings. She makes excuse after excuse. All pretty weak.'

Symes tried for time to recall what he knew about Lola Hastings. 'What do you want her to do?' he asked.

'She hasn't been in England for fifteen years now.'

'As long as that?'

'We've gone on selling her stuff all this time, but there's an end to it. Hers is not the kind of thing you can sell for ever without people seeing her every now and then.'

'You mean it's not good enough?'

'It's far too good. You know what it's like trying to sell really good work by a living artist.'

'Very difficult.' That seemed probable.

'We've always managed to sell Lola Hastings's work none the less, and get good prices too. In fact, between you and me, she's always been our best seller so to speak.'

'Oh, yes,' said Symes.

'Simply because people have gone on remembering her. When she was here, she sold on her personality. You know what she was like. There was no one like her. But, as I say, we're nearing a full stop. I know the signs. She's got to come and show herself off a bit or her income's gone west, and ours too.'

'Why do you suppose she refuses?'

'I haven't a notion and no one can tell me. I've been angling for her for eighteen months now. As you know, she lives in Slovenia. You can't ring her up. You can only write. I've written again and again. She never does more than cable back saying "No". And what makes it worse, she always gives the most damn fool excuses. Harvest! Last time it was building a new studio, and the time before just snow. I ask you!'

'They do get a lot of snow in Slovenia, surely? Wolves and all that.'

'It's eyewash. It just won't do as an answer.'

'What about her work? If you go on selling it, how does she get it to you?'

'She manages that all right. It comes in packing cases in the usual way. Though every now and then there's a head missing—broken off, you know. Still it's not too bad. She must take a hell of a lot of trouble with the packing.'

Symes now recollected vaguely. 'I don't really know much about her. But I remember an article I read once called "Sculptress Friend of Kings". She had political influence in the days before the T.U.C.?'

'She had every kind of influence. No one ever did a thing without asking Mrs. Hastings first. And what an artist all the time! Now if that had been why she left . . .' Benson broke off. 'Have a cigarette?' He stepped back and lifted the large coloured box from his desk.

'Thank you very much,' said Symes. 'Why did she leave?'

'I think she was generally fed up.'

'Socialism?'

'Probably. And marriage. Her marriage to Hastings was a flop. There's no secret about that. God knows why she ever took him on! Though he was never the same man after she left him.'

'He was one of the early aviators, wasn't he?'

'Crossed some ocean or desert or bus station before anyone else. Couldn't care less myself. Had a brain like a carburettor. Handsome man though. He had that. And came to a bad end, poor fellow. Flew his plane into a mountain. That was ten or twelve years ago. I wonder if she cared?'

'Have you never considered going out to see her? I mean about her coming back to England. Or sending someone.'

'We tried it once but she cabled back the usual "No". Rather more firmly than usual. And it's no place to go visiting on spec. It's the absolute back of beyond. God awful spot I should say.'

'I asked because I've an idea. Just a thought.'

'Splendid!'

'Will you still be here if I finish looking round the rest of the exhibition first? You close at any minute, I believe.'

'We'll hold it for you after the doors shut. We're always pleased to do that for people who are really interested.'

'I'm the press. It's an assignment.'

'What paper?' Symes told him. 'Didn't Harris come to the press show?'

'He missed that day.'

'And this one?'

'And this one.'

'So much the better for me if you've an idea for netting Lola Hastings. Come inside my office.' He seated Symes in the armchair used for buyers. A naturally warm-hearted man, Benson was thoroughly used to receiving valuable help of all kinds from strangers.

'We're running a series just now: Women Who've Made as Good as Men.'

'Lola Hastings isn't a Red Cross nurse or a band leader. As a matter of fact, she made all her men competitors look silly, and that's not what your public want, I fancy.'

'She did marry a handsome airman, you say. I think she'd do very nicely. The mystery angle would be a novelty too. There's not much of that around most successful women.'

'It's your livelihood. You should know. What do you suggest, then?'

'Let me put the idea up to my editor. If he likes it, he'll send a special correspondent. For a little bit extra there'll be an additional private report for you. You can see the man before he goes, and tell him what to look for and what questions to ask.'

'He'll never get to Lola.'

'Then he'll never clock in with the old man again.'

'Do you suppose that no other journalist has had the idea? Lola's probably put up bars.'

'I do suppose that no other journalist has. The lady hardly sounds red hot news, you know. Isn't that just the trouble?'

Benson rose, opened an ormolu cabinet, and found two long drinks.

Later, after another minute or two in the exhibition, Symes was leaving the muffled carpeted rooms. 'Our motto: Bring 'em back alive!' he exclaimed, as pressmen do. He wrung Benson's hand, as pressmen do. Benson looked at him doubtfully for three seconds. Then he locked up the Gallery, and returned to look over the day's transactions.

It was Cust to whom the editor gave the assignment: not because he had contributed any of the earlier articles to the series. The editor had had a word with the proprietor, who, having played some part in society, was acquainted with the fact that a particularly close friend of the expatriate sculptress had been the Right Honourable Leo Cust, a former Home Secretary, well known for his advocacy of ecclesiastical reunion and a national lottery.

'Tell him to play his uncle,' his lordship had advised his editor, referring to his young employee.

Waiting for the first glimpse of the sun to make possible the start of a rough day on horseback, Cust hated himself for the warmly personal letter he had dutifully written to Mrs. Hastings; and not less in the light of her subsequent unexpectedly prompt and cordial reply and invitation. Not for the first or hundredth time, a feeling of distaste reached through him as he thought how much he hated his job; hated the whole journalistic system and the social upheaval which had made him its slave. He also hated riding; and he was now faced with a long day and a half on a horse, through dull looking country and accompanied by a solitary male escort not a word of whose remarks he could understand. In her letter, Mrs. Hastings had apologized for the absense of her 'truck', which, she said, had broken a back axle. 'The repair should take at least six months if I judge (as I always do) by precedent.' In this vehicle, Cust supposed, must periodically be transported the crates of sculpture spoken of by Symes and at the later uneasy interview with Benson. It was beyond belief that a single piece survived the dreadful mountain track intact. To walk more than a few yards among those large white stones was distressing. Cust hoped their horses were tough. To ask was impossible and would also, no doubt, be useless.

A crude yellow light was to be seen after ten or fifteen minutes of shivering inaction. The escort made a further unintelligible observation and Our Special Correspondent set out.

Journalists, whatever the legend about them, are used to comfort; Cust, despite his other oddities, being herein no exception. By four o'clock the next day, therefore, as their destination came into sight, he was in the most despondent of bad tempers. It was late autumn and at no hour of the twenty-four really warm. The country was every bit as dreary as it had promised: rocky, uncoloured, almost naked of development. The escort fed himself badly and his charge no better. Cust's horse had touches of rheumatism, and the other horse apparently resented a strange rider.

The Schloss Marcantonio, the form of address which continued to head the writing-paper of its tenant, despite the demise of the Hapsburg Empire, appeared a brownish-yellow outcrop in the grey landscape, being built presumably of transported stone. (Cust learned later that the transport was reputed to have been provided by Lucifer.) It straggled about a small steep-sided plateau, and was encompassed by a ramifying system of more or less concentric curtain walls, the lowest of which surrounded the base of the entire castle rock, where it rose from the uneven plain between two ranges of crumbling mountains. The walls, like the castle, were of yellowish-brown alien stone. The castle, like the walls, seemed largely ruinous. The ensemble was far from enlivening: remote but without grandeur.

They passed the two outermost walls simply through gaps in the uneven masonry, and began to ascend a zigzag cliff path designed primarily for defence. At every acute angle was a bastion, linked by a wall to the next bastion above and below it. A short way up, Cust dismounted, but the escort took no notice and rode to the summit as to the manner born. Cust toiled up, leading his invalid horse, and found the man still mounted and awaiting his charge's arrival. They were at the closed double gates of the outer bailey, and the escort dragged at the heavy rattling bellpull. A distant tinny response led to clogs or metal-soled shoes clattering across the stones of the court inside; and both the solid iron gates began to open simultaneously, operated by a crank turning a primitive system of gears. Before the gates were half opened, the escort rode in without a word, looking, as he passed beneath the battered arch, not unlike a bandit in a realistic film, tenacious but not picturesque. Cust followed him, noticing that the old woman who had worked the crank was hot after her brief labours, notwithstanding the chilliness of the autumn uplands. The gears began to groan once more and the gates fell shut with a sudden clang. Cust supposed that the mechanism was designed to shut the gates automatically: another defence measure, no doubt.

Inside was a large paved expanse surrounding another line of walls containing a similar pair of gates. Somewhat unusually situated between the two lines of fortification and near the centre of the yard between them, was a large structure built not in the imported, but in the local stone: possibly a guardhouse, though the comparatively big and frequent windows (now all closed and apparently uncurtained) somewhat belied the suggestion. On the battlemented summit of this erection, not much smaller, Cust reflected, than many a Cotswold manor, could be seen the wild heads of several motionless and staring children. Several more children darted from the entrance to the building as Cust and the escort appeared. They seemed interested but oddly silent. The escort rode through them past the isolated building without a word or sign. He rode straight into a long high ramshackle erection of wood which extended along the walls of the inner bailey to the left of the entry, and which Cust supposed to be stables. Was that not the common site for the stables in a medieval fortress?

The advancing children took the bridle of Cust's horse, and led the animal after his fellow, three of the urchins having silently mounted his back. Their interest in Cust himself appeared slight; but as he neared the building from which the children had come, another figure advanced towards him out of the doorway. A tall woman, of middle age, and wearing ugly but presentable clothes of British provincial cut, extended her hand and said: 'How do you do, Mr. Cust? I'm so glad you've managed to get here today. We always consider the journey takes forty-eight clear hours without the truck.'

Good heavens! thought Cust conventionally, taking in the unexpected figure. He said, 'How do you do? I was wondering where you *keep* the truck.'

'In a shed we've made out of a cave at the bottom of the rock. Right round the other side,' she replied. 'Mrs. Hastings cannot stand noise.'

'Forgive me, but I had supposed that you were Mrs. Hastings?'

'Indeed no, Mr. Cust. I am Miss Franklin, Mrs. Hastings's private secretary.'

'It must be an unusual life, Miss Franklin, living up here. A little grim at times, I should say.'

'It is unusual, Mr. Cust, and many would find it grim enough also. But it is not grim for me. I love my job.' Coming from an Englishwoman, the last remark might mean anything or nothing.

'There's certainly no harm in doing something off the beaten track—particularly nowadays; or living off it either for that matter,' said Cust amicably. 'I must admit that this is as far off it as I have been. How any of Mrs. Hastings's works survive that road I cannot imagine. Can you, honestly?'

For the first time she smiled. 'Well, Mr. Cust,' she said, 'I can. I pack them. I drive them down in the truck. If a single piece were even so much as cracked, Mrs. Hastings would never forgive me. Never, I assure you.'

To this Cust, to whom the bewailing Benson had shown warriors without legs and nymphs beheaded into valuelessness, could not at once find a rejoinder. The children, however, now reappeared. They emerged from the wooden sheds carrying his small pieces of baggage. There was still not a sound or cry to be heard from them.

'What very silent children!' remarked Cust. 'Particularly for peasants.'

'Mrs. Hastings won't allow anyone to speak within the Schloss precincts,' answered Miss Franklin. 'Unless she or I speak to them first, of course. The rule naturally does not apply to me.'

'Do they put up with it?'

'They have no alternative, Mr. Cust. The Schloss had been a deserted ruin for generations before Mrs. Hastings came. All the peasants were starving, literally starving, horrible to see. Mrs. Hastings has changed all that. It is a small price to pay, mere silence, when everyone knows Mrs. Hastings so much dislikes noise.'

Looking about him, Cust did not altogether see that the changes in question could amount to so much. But he only said: 'What about me? Must I go Trappist too?'

'Oh no, Mr. Cust,' she replied. 'Quite the contrary. Mrs. Hastings naturally expects our few guests to talk most freely. She is wholly dependent on them for all her news of the outside world. The newsboy doesn't call upon *us* every evening, you know.'

The tousled, ragged children now surrounded them.

'The peasants all sleep and live out here,' Miss Franklin continued, indicating, presumably, the manor-like building. 'Only Mrs. Hastings and I, and, of course, our occasional guests, sleep in the Schloss itself.' Suddenly she made some rapid and fairly lengthy utterance in the tongue of the country. The group of children silently dispersed and raced across to the great inner gates, through which they seemed to pass by a wicket, for almost at once they had disappeared and the gates looked as shut as ever in the now imperfect light. They had taken Cust's things with them.

'It's a language I find I can't manage at all,' said Cust ruefully. 'I'm not too good at languages, I'm afraid. How long did it take you to pick it up?'

'I only know enough to give simple orders. That doesn't take one long to learn. One naturally does not require general conversation.'

'Don't you sometimes find yourself rather short of that all the same?'

'Never, Mr. Cust,' she answered quietly and earnestly. 'Not only is Mrs. Hastings the most wonderful talker—her reputation will be known to you, but for me there is as well always nature. Nature always means so much to us English people, don't you think, Mr. Cust?' And after his cordial assent she continued: 'But I must show you your room. The peasant children have already taken your luggage there ahead of you. Then I must take you to Mrs. Hastings.'

'I'm looking forward to that,' said Cust as he walked across the other half of the yard beside the figure of Miss Franklin in her pale-blue woollen dress.

'The thingummygigs are out of order,' said Miss Franklin as they neared the inner gates. 'You can't open these like the others. There's no one here knows anything about machinery and the whole thing's been allowed to rust up. I should say it's beyond repair by this time.' A small wicket now became visible among the studs and straps of the vast iron gates. To it Miss Franklin administered a full back push. They clambered through, Miss Franklin remarking: 'It's all right this way. It's the other way that gives trouble, when you can't push.'

Ten yards beyond them rose the keep, the last defensible position. A large part seemed as usual in ruins, and no part showed any signs whatever of occupation in the least recent.

Through another door, opening at the top of a steep external stair, they entered a congerie of cold stone halls, closets, and corridors: yellow-brown, coldly stuffy, void of all but the crowding echoes. They walked a long way in silence. It was very dark, nightfall being near.

Miss Franklin, stopping at an ancient wooden door, indistinguishable, so far as Cust could see, from many others, opened it, and preceded him into the room within. This, his bedroom, was large and vaulted. Being lighted only by several archery slits with quatrefoil apertures cut in their centres, it would by now have been completely dark had it not been for a blazing fire in a vast ancient fireplace. (Cust felt relief that the fire was not smoking medievally in the apartment's centre.) The stone floor was largely covered with huge brightly coloured mats of peasant pattern. There were a narrow black bed, several hard black chairs, a massive black table, and at least three black-doored cupboards or the like let into the thickness of the stone. By one of the last Miss Franklin was standing. She wrenched open the door, the wood screaming along the stone floor to drag Cust's heart up to his throat. 'The garde-robe,' said Miss Franklin in neutral accents.

'Yes, I see. Thank you,' replied Cust, feeling a complete fool. 'And is there any means of lighting?'

'Torches,' said Miss Franklin, pointing to a mysterious, rather witch-like heap beside the fireplace. 'The peasants make them. There's a heap in every room. You stick the end in the fire and you'll be surprised how long they last.' She did this and stood with the flaming faggot in her extended arm. Cust, who in the gathering cold had drawn towards the fire, retreated a step.

'Don't be frightened,' said Miss Franklin, still in neutral tones. 'You'll soon get used to them. And there are brackets in most of the rooms.' She lifted the torch above her head, disclosing iron projections on each side of the chimney. Into one of them she inserted the torch; then with a quick circular motion thrust a second blazing torch into the other. Cust could most truly say that he had never seen anything like the shadowy stronghold room lighted by the two bundles of flame high above Miss Franklin's unremarkable head, commonplace features, and customary dress.

'You'll soon get used to it all,' she said. 'Now I'll just give you a few minutes to yourself, and then you must meet Mrs. Hastings.'

'How shall I find you?' asked Cust.

'I'll just hang about in the passage outside,' she answered. 'You come out when you're ready.'

When she had left, Cust took a minute or two to examine the room in more detail. The remaining doors, hitherto unaccounted for, admitted to bare, rather dusty cells. The garde-robe seemed medieval in more than name; and water was confined to a battered metal jug. There were no shelves, drawers, or adornments of any kind. Unpacking seemed bootless, and Miss Franklin was an urgent spectre outside. Cust opened the door.

'Bring a torch,' said Miss Franklin, who apparently had been waiting in almost total darkness. Cust started, but gingerly did as he was bid. The slight draught in the passage made the adventure doubly perilous.

'Now I will take you to Mrs. Hastings,' said Miss Franklin.

❨   ❨   ❨

On the north side of the keep a small postern door opened from a large hall. It had once given access to the yard; now it admitted to Mrs. Hastings's studio. When Miss Franklin knocked, a voice inside bade them go in. Cust entered a big room, lighted on three sides by long windows, through one of which the sunset still gave more than half light. The studio was the first recent addition Cust had noticed to the structure of the castle. At one end blazed another vast fire. A row of small, apparently coloured, figures stood along a wide curving shelf extending from one side of the fire, round the angle of the room, and half way to the door. At the opposite end of the room a dark-haired girl reclined on a dais, her only clothing a bright peasant blanket laid loosely across her loins. In the centre the sculptress half crouched, half lay on the floor, working in this uncomfortable posture upon a large vague figure. Lola Hastings had grey hair, neither short nor long, neither dressed nor wild; fine bones and the smooth pale skin of a woman no older than forty. Her features were in the antique mould, impressive but not hard or over-defined. Her large eyes were further magnified by enormous tortoise-shell-rimmed glasses. She wore dark brown trousers of the most ordinary pattern, but expensive brown shoes; a shirt of heavy dark-brown drill, open at the neck, and with sleeves rolled to the elbows, showing to much advantage the perfectly shaped hands and forearms.

When Miss Franklin introduced Cust, Mrs. Hastings indicated a large woolsack-like object for him to sit on, and asked to be excused from rising. The girl on the dais took no notice whatever. 'What about tea, Miss Franklin?' asked Mrs. Hastings in the most conventional manner; and Miss Franklin began to potter and clink in the chimney corner as if the scene were a Kensington life class.

'How do you manage with so little light?' asked Cust conversationally.

'Long experience, hard work, necessity—all the usual things,' Mrs. Hastings replied. 'Talent too, I fancy. I can work without light, if necessary.'

'I expect you're thinking of painters,' said Miss Franklin to Cust rather crushingly.

'Nonsense, Miss Franklin,' said Mrs. Hastings. 'Our guest's surprise is perfectly natural.'

'But you *paint* too, Mrs. Hastings,' said Miss Franklin. 'You can't do that in the dark.'

'I'm learning, Miss Franklin. I'm learning.'

This reply seemed perceptibly to shake the previously assured Miss Franklin. She stopped spooning out tea from a battered black tin and said: 'But you can't *paint* in the dark?' She seemed serious.

Mrs. Hastings took no notice of her but remarked: 'I'm glad you've come, Mr. Cust. Your uncle was a close friend of mine. You must tell me the news. All the news.'

Conventional conversation merged into a conventional studio tea party. Mrs. Hastings rose from the floor, disclosing her build to be muscular rather than slender, and her height to be slightly in excess of Cust's. Miss Franklin ignited several torches from the apparently usual heap by the fireplace, and raised them flaming into brackets. At a word from the sculptress, the silent girl joined them round the fire, having first twisted her long coloured blanket into the semblance of a robe to cover her nakedness.

Mrs. Hastings began to talk about her work. She was experimenting with coloured statues, she said, citing the painted marbles of Hellas, and the crude but tenacious colouring on many an Elizabethan tombstone effigy. She pointed to the row of little figures on the curved shelf. 'Look at them,' she said. 'Tell me what you think.'

Cust obediently put down his tea-cake and crossed to the shelf. The figures were very curious: a black-garbed, white-faced, indeterminate but manifestly female subject depicted in a range of slightly differing attitudes. An astonishing variety of facial and bodily expression, of emotions felt by the same person on different occasions, was conveyed by the completely unelaborated plaster planes. Cust had never seen anything like it and said so.

'Use of varying colour washes is the secret,' said Mrs. Hastings. 'That's only the experimental stage. You wait for the finished product.'

'I shall. Eagerly.' He resumed his tea-cake.

'Will it reinstate me with the London critics? Will people once more fight to buy my work?'

Cust hesitated for a moment. The treachery of his letter weighed on him more than ever. 'Are you not satisfied with London?' he asked.

She stared at him, the expression in her huge eyes behind the glasses puzzling him completely.

'You must know perfectly that I am not,' she answered. 'You are a man of the world, you move in artistic circles. You are a Cust. Cust!' she repeated raising her voice and with, it seemed, more irony than appeared upon the surface, as if the word itself, and not only a person named, had for her some special bitter meaning.

'I meant only that I did not know whether what London thinks is still important to you,' Cust said quickly, his wits rushing to dam the social breach, like blood to a wound.

'Your refuge leaves you more exposed than ever,' was the astonishing reply. 'Why have you come here?'

Cust began a careful lying explanation.

'You have heard talk,' she interrupted him. 'I am surrounded by talk. It reaches everywhere.' Cust thought of the silent retainers, one of them not four feet from him now.

'I have heard no talk,' he replied.

'Am I wrong about you?' she asked with passion. 'Please tell me the truth.'

Cust again fatally hesitated.

'I see,' she said bitterly. There was a pause. Miss Franklin had stopped eating some time ago and was staring at Cust venomously. The model looked merely bored. Models are the same everywhere.

'I've changed my mind,' said Mrs. Hastings at last, still bitterly, but wearily also. 'I was going to ask you to leave. But you can stay if you want to. You were to have stayed a week. You can stay a week.'

A sound seemed to come from the rigid Miss Franklin.

'Why have we no hot water?' asked Mrs. Hastings. Miss Franklin filled the kettle out of a large uncoloured jar of great weight. She set the water to boil.

'I am completely in the dark, you know,' said Cust warily. 'But you are all too right about me. I should like to tell you exactly why I came. May I? Now that my motives have changed, as it were. I assure you they have.'

She nodded gravely, fixing him all the time with her unwinking eyes.

'Times have changed in England, you know,' he began.

She nodded again.

'I am a journalist.' He had to pause for a moment. Yet once more she nodded. Her lack of surprise was anti-climactic.

'I have been sent to interview you.'

'About what?'

'About your work and why you live here and your life in general.'

'I live here so as not to be interviewed. I want not to be interviewed because of my work on the one hand, and my life in general on the other.'

'So I supposed.'

'Ah. Had you any other reason for coming?'

'Two others.'

'Curiosity?'

'My uncle told me something about you. From time to time before he died. You knew he was dead? It only happened recently.'

'I have visitors, like yourself, who bring me the news.'

'Then Mr. Benson is very worried about you. You appear to know that the sales of your work are falling. He says you will soon be ruined. He will too: or so he asserts. He believes that the only thing would be for you to come to England. But you put him off with insufficient reasons. Or so he regards them.'

'I entirely understand,' said Mrs. Hastings. 'Thank you for telling me so much.'

'I have told you everything,' replied Cust.

The kettle began to boil over and Miss Franklin foolishly scalded her left hand while attempting to deal with it.

During the conversation which occupied the next hour or so, nothing which seemed to Cust out of the ordinary occurred (though Cust's standard of the ordinary had modified since entering the Schloss Marcantonio) until he had occasion again to remark on Mrs. Hastings's extraordinary knowledge of dull happenings in the outside world.

'It was my husband who told me all about that particular thing,' she replied; and when Cust presumably allowed some hint of bewilderment to appear, continued: 'We separated years before his death, but he came to see me here on two occasions.'

'Indeed?' said Cust, aiming at the tone of polite interest.

'He landed his plane in the Schloss yard. An impossible thing to do, of course. Particularly in those days. But he was an impossible man. Later he took off successfully from the same place: something even more impossible.'

'He didn't try it the second time?'

'The second time was *completely* impossible. Even for him.' And it was only after a moment, and remembering what Benson had told him of Hastings's death, that Cust realized what she meant.

The model had been sent home to the Grange outside, as Cust now heard Mrs. Hastings call it, and Miss Franklin had departed from the studio ludicrously bearing a torch, like a schoolmistress in a village pageant of more than customary realism, when Mrs. Hastings invited Cust for a walk round the Schloss walls. 'I only leave the studio after dark,' she said without explanation. 'But I badly need exercise.' That was the last thing Cust needed after his interminable hours in the saddle, but he accompanied her up many winding steps and through narrow doorways out on to the parapet walk.

'Won't you be cold?' he asked, as the air struck him, sudden and frozen.

'I'm used to the night air,' she answered. 'I'll keep warm somehow.'

Cust, far more heavily clad, was shivering all over. The Balkan winter was near.

The way had always been medievally irregular, varying in width and height above the yard below, frequently interrupted with steps of uneven rise: now it was rough, jagged and precarious; the steps had been worn inwards by the years, like chalk cliffs by the sea. Frequently Cust found himself required to creep in the darkness along eighteen inches of lumpy stonework with an unrailed drop of thirty feet to the right of him, a six-foot rampart to the left; sometimes to scramble painfully across a litter of dislodged masonry. From time to time Mrs. Hastings briefly warned him of an actual gap. She herself glided and leapt with a precise bounding grace apparent even in the night.

When they had completed the circuit, Mrs. Hastings said: 'Shall we go round again, or would you care for a game of fives? There's a court in the cellars.' Cust, shivering and panting simultaneously, his suit dusty and his hair disordered, felt himself a ridiculous figure before her almost absurd serenity. 'Do you play fives?' she enquired politely.

Cust had once, with his partner, reached the semi-final of his House Championship, and his House was considered the fives House of the School. Without entering into these particulars, he answered merely that he had not played for years. 'Besides, I haven't the clothes,' he added.

'If you'd care for a game, I'll lend you some clothes,' she replied. 'We're about the same size.'

Re-entering the keep, they soon reached the door of her bedroom. 'Come in a moment,' she said.

The room, though considerably larger, resembled his own: there were the same blazing fire, the same sparse black furniture, including a big square bed, perfectly plain and apparently very old. Over the head hung a picture covered with two dull brown curtains: an eikon, Cust supposed, speculating that Mrs. Hastings, like so many of her profession, probably treasured the insignia of devotion. The eikon seemed a crude piece to serve as the sole ornament of an artist's bedroom: without gilt, embroidery, cross or other emblem, the brown coverings recalled the veil before the face of a leper. By the light of several torches already flaming from their sconces when Mrs. Hastings had entered the room, Cust saw that the long wall opposite the fireplace was dimly coloured from floor to ceiling with books. The line of the shelves was several times broken and continued round triangular recesses in the wall. The total effect in the flickering fiery light was slightly evil: as if Cust saw the devil-lent library of an alchemist. 'What a fine collection!' he said.

'It's very mixed,' replied Mrs. Hastings. 'When I came here, I ransacked my London house for books and brought them all. I thought I should have a lot of time for reading.'

Cust pulled out a volume at random and peered at the title page. '*Corridor With Mirrors*,' he read out, 'by Chris Massie.'

'Can't remember that one,' said Mrs. Hastings. 'I haven't had so much time to read as I supposed.'

But Cust was looking round. Only at the last infinitesimum of time before the words broke from him, did he restrain himself from saying something probably foolish. The room contained no mirror. Nor, he seemed now to recall, did his own.

Mrs. Hastings had pulled back one of the low-coloured curtains, tall and narrow, which had been drawn before the dark fortress windows. In the embrasure, reaching to the sill of the dark window, was disclosed a large press with drawers. One drawer, being opened, proved to be filled with clothes similar to those Mrs. Hastings was wearing.

'Help yourself,' she said. 'You can change in here.' Opening a small door to the side of the fireplace, she passed through it with a torch. Inside was a small closet. 'My husband used this as his dressing-room when he visited me,' said Mrs. Hastings. To Cust the room seemed cold for such a purpose.

Their game of fives was his last. The unsatisfactory light given by torches, though there was a battery of them arranged as effectively as possible, was doubtless partly to blame for his poor performance; also the fact that he had been used mainly to playing doubles, with a partner to rescue him in many moments of difficulty. But he doubted whether even had he been in practice and the light that of day, he would ever have competed on even terms with Mrs. Hastings, short-sighted though she possibly was as she played in her big glasses. Mortifying thoughts crawled like earwigs through his brain as he struggled away: how characteristic that he should have come in the intervening years almost to regard himself as having played for the School itself, almost to have won the Kinnaird Cup! How unwise that he should have disregarded the marked element of danger in the game even when played by experts in full training! Cust knew that his days for this most energetic of sports were over (though he must have been about fifteen years younger than Mrs. Hastings, long-sighted rather than short, and, of course, a man).

After he had resumed his own clothes, they dined in the studio. The food, though of peasant type, was not unlike that favoured by many artists nearer London. The meals at least at the Schloss Marcantonio seemed unsurprising. They were waited on by a silent ugly male peasant, whom the women addressed as Fischer. Miss Franklin seemed to be starting a slight cold. 'It's the days drawing in,' she said.

When the meal had concluded with the servant bringing strong black coffee and a large round tray of halva, Mrs. Hastings began to talk, and to Cust, lying aching and tired, time passed from thought in the unending Balkan night. Never before in all his life had he heard a good talker; never before had he entered the sublime state of simultaneous, equal, and deep self-loss and self-awareness which good talk alone can bring. No one can remember good talk when it is ended, for such conversation overrides the emotional jailers who keep watch during daily life. There remained in Cust's head only a few phrases and partial anecdotes, some of them as irrelevant to common experience as the single futile sentences occasionally recovered by drug takers from their paradises, and carefully noted in the instant of waking.

At some point Miss Franklin had retired, blowing excuses from her inadequate handkerchief. It was impossible to say how much later it was when Cust himself reached his bedroom, guided to the door by Mrs. Hastings (as the Castle geography was still a cause of difficulty to him), and feeling like a god, so clarified and enlarged by her utterances.

He sat for several minutes on the side of his bed. Like many men, he had difficulty in beginning to undress immediately he entered his bedroom. Then, gathering together the situation and disliking the prospect of having to 'live in his suitcase' (a very small one), while feeling reluctant to leave his possessions strewed about the room, he began more closely than before to investigate the unpromising accommodation. Opening the door of one of the two cupboards, he saw lying on the floor within a black lump. It had not been there, he thought, at the time of his previous inspection. Gingerly examining it, he found it to be a woman's handbag. It was open and gave the air of having been thrown into the corner of the cupboard rather as a pickpocket throws away the purse.

Leaving the cupboard door open, Cust crossed the room to where near the end furthest from the fire a torch burned more brightly than the rest. With his back to the fire he examined the bag. It was neither cheap nor expensive; neither large nor small. A middle-class handbag, concluded Cust. It bore the initial F in not very attractive modern lettering. It appeared to be empty.

Cust turned towards the warmth, exasperated and, unreasonably, a little frightened. Then the bag fell to the stone floor, and a tearing pain seemed to amputate his heart as he saw a young woman standing by the fire, with one arm reaching up to the high mantelpiece. She had smooth black hair hanging straight to her shoulders. She wore a black evening dress, cut low and reaching to the ground. Her face looked full and pale, her mouth soft and black, in the torchlight.

'Forgive me, forgive me,' she said. Her accents were soft and urgent.

The handbag and the presence of (presumably) its owner combined in an obvious suggestion.

'I am in the wrong room. I get lost in this place. I haven't learnt my way about yet. . . .'

But Lola had led him to the door: and there, moreover, on the floor were the initials on his suitcase. Momentarily he stood looking at them.

'I have been waiting for you. Please forgive me,' she said. Her voice, though pleasantly low, was certainly in the mode of the London middle class. Her tentative gesture of appeal was more individual and touching.

Cust rallied. 'What can I do for you? Would you like to sit down?'

She sat on a little black stool. 'How much do you know?'

'I know less than ever since I arrived at the Schloss,' replied Cust amiably. 'What should I know?'

'Hasn't she mentioned me?'

'I don't think so. Perhaps it depends who you are. Who are you?'

'Hasn't she mentioned Felicity?'

'No. Are you Felicity?'

'She will. But you mustn't believe anything she says.'

'I take it you are referring to Mrs. Hastings?'

'Poppy's even worse.'

'Who's Poppy?'

'Poppy Franklin. She stops at nothing. *I* believe she's mad.'

'Oh nonsense,' said Cust more amiably than ever. He was not so different from others of his sex as to be wholly superior to the pleasure derivable from such a conversation with a young, attractive, and well-dressed woman.

'You only came today.'

'When did *you* come?'

'If I told you truthfully, you wouldn't believe me.'

Cust looked at her. There was nothing of coyness in her tone. He considered for a moment. 'How did you get in here?'

'I might have hidden in one of the cupboards.'

The initial on the handbag stared him in the face. 'Is this yours?' He held it out to her.

She took it, but laid it indifferently on the floor beside her stool. 'It comes and goes,' she said. She did not thank Cust.

'As I said before,' he enquired, 'what can I do for you?'

'Will you help me?'

'To do what?'

'To get away. Those two women. They hate each other, of course, but they both want to keep me here. Each for her own reason.'

At this point, most unexpectedly, Cust perceived something new. 'Those statuettes in the studio,' he said. 'They're you.' The resemblance was beyond doubt.

'Yes. I'm Lola's raw material all right.' Cust was uncertain what her tone implied. 'Her only raw material for some time now.'

'But that at least can't be right,' Cust answered. 'There was a peasant girl modelling in the studio this very afternoon.'

'Was she like me?'

'Not in the least.' Cust found the question silly.

The other replied with a short laugh which left Cust more at a loss than ever. Then she said: 'The goose who lays the golden eggs.'

Not following this in the least Cust replied: 'Fewer golden eggs than there were. The market's falling away. Mrs. Hastings should pay a visit to England.'

Again the effect was unexpected. The girl leant violently towards him crying: 'No, no. Not that. Please. I beg of you.'

Her concern struck Cust as rather forced. Either Felicity was what she accused Miss Franklin of being, mad; or else her motives were too involved to be worth elucidating by a dog-tired man at an uncertain hour of the early morning. His voice sounded near boredom as he said, 'Hadn't we better call it a day? What about resuming tomorrow?'

But she answered very soberly: 'I'm sorry. I've already asked you to forgive me. If I tell you very quickly what I want, will you listen? You said you'd help me.'

Cust hadn't; but fatigue was overcoming him, excluding alike remonstrance and wonder. 'Very well then.'

She leaned back a little, extending her high-heeled shoes towards him. 'I came here on a visit. Poppy Franklin brought me. I met her at a party. She goes back to England every now and then, you know; for one reason and another. I was rather run down. You know what London is. Poppy said three weeks at the Schloss Marcantonio would be just right for me. I thought no harm could come to me with an old bag like Poppy.' She paused.

'You were Miss Franklin's friend first then?' said Cust to fill the gap.

'She said quite openly that she was lonely here. She said it was impossible not to be sometimes. Well, that's true enough. But immediately I met Lola, the whole situation changed. Those bloody little statues. Forgive my language. Do women still talk like that in London? "Only a phase", my mother used to say, "only a phase".' She seemed to expect an answer.

'Women still say bloody in London,' said Cust half-quizzically, half-yawning.

'Good.' Then she repeated more affirmatively. 'Good . . . Well, anyway I was just what Lola had been looking for, just the model she wanted, just right in every way. The long and the short of it is that I've been here ever since. You know what it's like getting here. You just can't get away without their help. There's nothing you can do. Still in the end I did try to make a bolt for it.' She was now beginning to seem agitated.

'What happened?' The wild story seemed disquietingly assured.

'This is the point. Promise me you won't tell anyone? If they're not talking about me, they have their reasons. Promise me. Oh, promise me.' There was a soft sane earnestness about this appeal which suddenly moved Cust very deeply.

'I promise,' he said. 'I promise faithfully.'

'Thank you,' she replied with delightful simplicity.

'Tell me,' said Cust gently, as she said nothing further.

'They got my notecase,' she continued very low. She was shuddering slightly. 'All my money was in it—I had enough of the local money to get me back if I could find anyone to help me. My passport too. Everything. Poppy threw my passport on the fire. There's always a fire burning in here, all the year round. They threw my handbag into that cupboard where you found it.'

'It wasn't there when I first entered the room,' interrupted Cust. But she took no notice. Her eyes were alight, her skin moist.

'This was *my* room then. The room they kept for visitors. When they'd thrown away my things, they put me in the room below. There's a way down from here. The room below's a prison. They make me dress like this night and day. It helps to hold me here. They've hidden all my other clothes. It's easy to hide things in the Schloss Marcantonio. All kinds of things are hidden so well they'll never be found again.' She was standing now and gesticulating wildly. All the torches were burning very low, making the shadows of her thick and sluggish.

'If it's a prison, how did you get up here?'

'I've learned how to get out. They don't know about it. You've promised not to tell them. You've promised.'

'I've promised.'

'Poppy comes round at a different hour every night and looks in at me.'

Cust had been subconsciously groping and here was his chance. 'Might it not be safer then if you were to go back now, and tomorrow we could talk about what to do? I'll think things over carefully in the meantime. Please don't worry. I'm quite sure I'll be able to help you. Everything will be all right.' However indifferent in other respects his journalistic performance, Cust had at least learnt that ideas which come at night are to be discarded in the morning.

Felicity, however, appeared in embarrassingly deep distress. Her shadowy figure was withdrawn into the dark corner of the vast overmantel. Her whole mien seemed to direct disappointment at Cust. Almost certainly she was weeping.

He could hear her tears coming in little gusts and panting cries. Then another sound became audible. Feet were running down the stone paved passage outside the room, with the rapid tapping step of a woman. Cust could not be certain whether the little cries were inside or outside the darkening chamber. They were dreadfully distressing. They urged to relief.

A brief rush of courage took him to the door. The events of the day had scattered all other feeling in him. Felicity was now barely visible.

Outside all was complete darkness. The racing steps had passed his door. There now seemed no doubt that the anguishing cries came from the runner.

After an uncertain number of seconds there was a single immense metallic clash, which seemed to shake even the rock the castle stood upon. There was no further sound.

Cust found himself stupidly thinking: 'And she so much dislikes noise!'

Withdrawing from the doorway back into the room, and carefully closing the door, he found the torches almost burnt to the sconces and in process of collapsing to the floor. He had to peer hard before he could decide that Felicity had gone. It was only later, after he had ignited new torches, that he realized the handbag was gone also.

Too tired for any further mental effort, he spent no time investigating the cupboards or looking for a secret stair from below. Having locked the door, he flung off his clothes and dragged back the window curtains.

Beyond the quatrefoil apertures was daylight.

The day following proved one of anti-climax: almost of ennui.

At an hour which his watch suggested was ten o'clock, Cust was awakened by Fischer pounding clamorously on his locked door. On being admitted, he proved to be bearing a simple breakfast. Sleepily Cust made some slight attempt to lead the man into talk, as he repaired and reinvigorated the still surviving fire. The attempt was unsuccessful; but later Fischer returned with a large brass can of boiling water, warm towels, and a wide earthenware bowl. Having silently removed the remains of breakfast, he left Cust to dress.

By this time Cust had the gravest doubts concerning the objectivity of what had seemed to take place the previous night. Still badly lacking sleep, he was in a state to believe any other evil hallucinatory. But he looked in the various empty cupboards, prowled round the solid walls, and half-heartedly stamped in several places on the unresponding floor. He had no idea what to do next, even of what he was expected to do next. Fischer did not again reappear. Lola and Miss Franklin, he felt, might be anywhere. Should he make his bed?

Not knowing very clearly how to make a bed, particularly an ancient bed of alien pattern, he collected his possessions into his suitcase, which he locked, and, placing it rather foolishly under his bed, advanced tentatively down the passage outside his room. No one was in evidence. The silence was complete. Having reached the large hall outside Lola's studio, he stood for a moment, then crossed it and knocked on the studio door. The sound echoed tumultuously, but there was no answer. After a longer period of irresolution, Cust tried the modern handle. The door seemed locked. Prowling on down the corridor, he reached a stair which he remembered having descended from the floor above and Lola's bedroom. Continuing further, down a part of the passage he had not previously traversed, he turned a corner to find further progress barred by an antique door which not only appeared locked but as if it had been locked for generations. Cust attempted to peer through the keyhole, but the instant emergence of a scuttling spider made him draw back. The spider stopped and remained quite still as if gummed to the woodwork.

Retreating, Cust climbed the winding stair. At Lola's door he paused for a longer period still. Then he knocked. His need for instruction in what to do with himself was so great that, despite the rattling echoes, he knocked three times: three times with no response. This time he did not try the handle, but strayed off uncertainly down the passage. On this higher level, the passage went in one direction only: in the other was merely a mass of stonework. Soon Cust reached the little doorway through which he had passed with Lola on to the rampart walk. Then he had not noticed a door, but now he saw there was one and that it was closed. This door also proved to be locked. The little windows lighting this part of the structure offered a view of the small inner courtyard. It was dirty, derelict, and deserted. At a distance beyond the inner courtyard wall could be seen the top of the servants' grange. The day was windy and overcast. Clouds in a rather beautiful wild grey were being dragged across the prospect. Cust continued along the passage until it suddenly and somewhat dangerously broke off in a sheer drop down to the large hall outside Lola's studio. On the far side of the hall, high under the vaulting, Cust could just make out what he took to be an aperture corresponding to that in which he stood. Once there must have been a wooden bridge or gallery, high above the floor of the hall, and linking the two sections of passage. The other section could now only be accessible, if at all, by a staircase of its own.

Further progress being apparently impossible, Cust returned towards his bedroom. On the way were several doors, one no doubt belonging to the Castle kitchen. He had been along the passage in the opposite direction, both when he had first entered the building and when he had descended with Lola to the torch-lit fives court. But the steps had seemed to run that way in his dream, and it was from that quarter that the alarming metallic crash had seemed to come: Cust therefore hesitated for a moment. Then he went on, and, ignoring the steps down to the fives court, which apparently occupied a large dungeon, soon reached the door through which he had originally followed Miss Franklin from the world outside. It was when he found this door locked that he was forced to consider that Felicity was no dream. She had said, and on the whole so quietly and plausibly, that she was a prisoner. What was he?

He would investigate further and with all possible resolution. Felicity had spoken of a room beneath his own. He would try to discover whether there was such a room, and whether he could reach it. If he could and it was empty, or if the room did not exist, he had indeed been suffering the night before from gross over-fatigue. He would seek an explanation of that iron tumult.

A little further on, the passage reached a corner corresponding to that, on the other side of the building, at which Cust had been routed by the spider. This time the passage suddenly ended in a large window, while to the left a flight of wide stone stairs descended into gloom. The window, which was filled with a single sheet of poor quality glass, poorly puttied at the edges, the workmanship of both glass and fitting doubtless reflecting local standards, was by far the largest Cust had yet seen in the Castle. Upon gazing through it (no part of it being made to open), Cust saw a possible explanation of its size. The window looked along the crumbling south wall of the Castle; but below it and below that wall was a precipice of rock he estimated to be at least three hundred feet high. That particular front of the Castle had needed less defence. Fortification had been less important. About half way up from the ground below, the rock appeared actually to bulge outwards. Cust supposed a concavity beneath, which would have made scaling finally impossible. The level of the plain only came into his view at some distance from the Castle rock. He wondered none the less what had formerly filled that large rent in the stronghold's body. Even situated where it was, it would hardly have been left totally unprotected. The glass had presumably been inserted at the time the studio was added. Staring through it Cust could see no life of any kind in the yellow rocky plain which extended before him to the foot of not distant yellower rockier mountains. There were not even birds.

He could see that any apartment below his own might well be a cell cut from the rock. The stair beside him might bring him to it. But that he would find down there the oddly clad young woman of the previous night was comfortingly improbable. Besides he would need a light; and could think of nothing but one of those brands which so abounded in the Castle, but which he hesitated to bear at nearly midday down ways in which he had no legitimate business. 'I am rescuing Felicity' could not be considered a viable answer to challenge.

Suddenly he remembered that his conversation with Felicity had seemed to end in a promise by him of further deliberation between them the next night, and an expression of his confidence in being able to aid her. He returned to his room, fired a torch, retraced his steps, and firmly descended the stair. At the bottom was the usual passage parallel with the two above, but this time pitch dark and rather damp. Advancing along it, Cust came on his left to a door, followed after a short interval by another. The second door was considerably larger than the first and its lintel seemed to bear worn carvings of some kind. Cust found it impossible to determine whether either could have given access to an apartment immediately beneath his own; but either might have done. Neither door seemed particularly suited to a place of detention, both being apparently less substantial and of later date than many others Cust had seen on the floors above. None the less Cust, determined to see his dream through to the end, to trample out the last ashes of possibility, immediately knocked upon each, and, obtaining as usual no answer, first announced his identity, then vigorously sought to enter. These doors also were locked, but rattled back and forth in a way quite unlike any others he had tried that day and so as to suggest that any even reasonably determined prisoner could readily have made a way out. Through the keyholes, moreover, light was unexpectedly though dimly visible. Cust supposed the rooms to be for stores, lighted by small orifices bored high up in the Castle rock. To give access to these rooms alone, it would hardly have seemed worth while to go to the great trouble of making, with primitive implements, the long rock conduit in which he stood. Perhaps, however, it had been intended to construct more of these underground compartments; perhaps they gave especially secure storage. Perhaps the passage led to something further and more significant . . . Then, cogitating outside the second door, Cust noticed that he was standing amidst a dense litter of cigarette ends. They were by no means all mere butts. Many were less than half-smoked. Both Lola and Miss Franklin had smoked on the previous night, the latter alternating, as so many smokers do, cigarettes with complaints about her catarrh and the state of her throat.

Cust was saved from renewed importunities at the door by the further discovery that the Castle well lay just beyond him; the unaccustomed torchlight and his preoccupation with the doors having prevented him from previously observing it. The well explained not only the laborious construction of the passage, but also the cigarettes, as water was still obviously drawn from it. A new galvanized bucket of cheap quality was visible at the end of the drawn-up rope; several more fairly new buckets lay on the rock floor; recently slopped water and recently imprinted footmarks had made mire of the slight soil deposit which had drifted to the end of the passage. His wits renewed, Cust could see the whole picture: while the bucket was slowly lowered (there was no knowing how far), filled, and raised, probably by a retainer, one lighted a cigarette; later one abandoned it in the exigencies of carrying water underground and in the dark. Moreover, the chance was great of his being at any moment discovered by someone seeking water. After all, absurd though the thought seemed, possibly luncheon was in preparation. Fleeing an embarrassing explanation, Cust was soon once more in his room with the torch safely extinguished.

There being apparently nothing else to do, he reopened his suitcase and groped for a book. From the entangling shirts he dragged a volume which had been given him by a friend who had seen him off. It was some General's war memoirs which that week had covered the bookstalls. After his unwonted experiences, Cust found the General surprisingly soothing: the General's assumptions about life were the common assumptions; the General's sincere and unremitted work for the cause of peace in his time made him seem a better chap than Cust had taken him to be. After a time there was a knock on the door and Lola entered full of apologies.

'I don't get up before midday. I told Miss Franklin to look after you, but this morning she hasn't got up either. I'm afraid she's rather ill. I'm so sorry that you've been neglected.'

'It's perfectly all right. I've been glad to take things easy. What's the matter with Miss Franklin?'

'Her cold seems to have become suddenly worse. She's covered with sweat, so I suppose she must have a temperature. She seemed to me delirious. She hardly understood what I said. I know nothing whatever about illness. I haven't even got a thermometer. It's very tiresome of her and quite unnecessary, as you saw for yourself. I suppose *you* can't help in any way? Have you any idea what to do in these cases?'

'Very little, I fear,' said Cust. 'Only the usual things. Keep her warm, don't give her too much to eat. Oh, and keep her bowels moving, I believe.'

'She'll have to do that for herself. We don't keep the Schloss bunged up with laxatives. This isn't British suburbia. But I'll tell Fischer to double stoke her fire and cut down on her diet. She never eats anyway.'

Lola's attitude was inconsistent with that which the General had so warmly praised in the nurses attached to his command.

'I suppose it's almost impossible to get a doctor up here?' asked Cust, despite everything a little sorry for Miss Franklin.

'There's one in practice down on the coast. Naturally he's useless. Not more so than the average G.P., of course. The people here don't go in for medicine. The priests have a down on it. We have had him more than once, but it's always been Miss Franklin who motored down for him and brought him back. Now the truck's out of order, as you know. Besides four journeys between here and the coast's a tall order just because that silly creature can't look after herself properly. Still it doesn't arise. We're cut off to all intents and purposes until the brigand who brought you here comes in five days' time to take you back. I'm so sorry to trouble you with all this. Lunch?'

Until dinner the rest of the day passed in what Cust had to admit to himself was boredom. It was difficult indeed to see what Miss Franklin could have done to help matters even had she been in robust health and up at her usual hour. Lola appeared excessively to resemble that multitude of hostesses who having collected guests leave them not only unoccupied but without possibility of occupation. Remembering the game of fives, however, and pondering other aspects of her character, Cust was glad that she did not resemble that other multitude of hostesses who, born organizers, never allow their guests any opportunity for private enterprise.

During luncheon, Lola appeared too pre-occupied for general conversation. Possibly she was in the toils of inspiration, for she spent the afternoon silently at work in the studio, with the girl of the day before as model, and with Cust turning the pages of his General.

By tea-time it was apparent that Miss Franklin's indisposition was wrecking the household. Fischer had to be brought in to make tea as best he could, and about Lola's manner to Cust was the faintest hint of regret that in the circumstances he could not be returned whence he came before five days. Cust's boredom and resentment were not diminished either by his lack of sleep or by the growing apprehension, the clarification of memory, which came with the gathering darkness. After a while he was fearing intensely the night before him.

Between tea and dinner Lola also read a book, the title of which Cust could not see. 'Really,' he reflected, 'one might be back with one's aunt.' Then a young peasant whom Cust had not previously seen knocked and entered.

'My fives partner,' said Lola. 'Will you come and watch us?' She made no reference to their own ineffective match.

Lack of other occupation and distaste also for solitude with his thoughts, took Cust once more to the underground court ablaze with torches.

'Can one play without speaking to one's opponent?' he asked as they descended. The young peasant had gone leaping ahead like an eager mongrel. This particular tyranny of Lola's was one which was beginning to irritate him. The Englishman's liking for the under-dog was being roused in him.

'We do the best we can,' she answered. 'I can't speak their language. I'm incapable of learning languages of any kind. And they're certainly incapable of learning mine. What could be worse than a perpetual mutual babel! I hate noise of any kind.' Cust's fear stirred sharply in its sleep. 'Besides if we could really understand one another, all would be over.'

'Is that a universal rule?' Cust had time to ask. But she had drawn on her gloves and plunged into the game.

For more than a hour Cust looked on completely absorbed. It was plain enough why Lola had not sought a second game with him. The young peasant played with the unremitting verve of an American professional: Lola like an elemental from mythology, graceful, unbelievably concentrated, murderous. For more than an hour there was silence except for the roaring crackle of the torches, the rattling and banging of the flying ball. The players neither relaxed their intensity nor paused for one instant between games. Then suddenly Lola brought the contest to a close: 'Go and draw six buckets of water,' she said to her opponent. 'Then boil it. Let me know when it's hot.' The man scurried away. Cust had noticed that orders given in English appeared to be perfectly understood. He wondered how far the linguistic incapacity alleged by Lola really extended. He resolved to be careful what he said. 'Buckets of hot water,' Lola was remarking, 'are the nearest I can offer to a bath. Would you like one tomorrow morning?'

'I expect I should,' Cust replied. 'Thank you. Where do you get your water? A well, I suppose?'

'An underground well. I think my predecessor thought it safer beyond reach of attack.'

'Being underground must make water-getting difficult. The quantity you want now, for instance? I suppose often it's literally all hands to the pumps?'

'Fischer and the man you just saw do all the water-carrying,' she answered.

Cust at this moment recalled the speed and insight with which she had penetrated his subterfuges upon their first meeting. She did not now seem to suspect his enquiries, but he deemed it best to desist from them. The litter of cigarettes had again become something of a mystery; but, on the other hand, it was improbable that in that vast structure, a place for imprisonment would be selected on the route to the well.

'The wretched creature seems worse,' announced Lola, rejoining Cust where he awaited her company for dinner in the studio. She was belated; in consequence, she apologized, of having bathed. Outside the rooms with fires, the Castle was freezing cold, but Lola never seemed to require additional clothing, even against the perils following a hot bath. 'Miss Franklin complains now that she awoke in the middle of the night and hasn't had any sleep since.'

'Does she say what woke her?'

Lola looked at Cust for a moment. But the question probably was a slightly odd one. Then she said: 'The onset of the fever, I suppose. Feverish people are always described as restless. I've had little to do with diseases. I've never encouraged them in my various households. Let's start eating.'

'I've some sleeping tablets in my case,' said Cust. 'Miss Franklin is welcome to a dose if she would like it.'

Lola considered for a moment. Then she said: 'Would you very much mind administering them? Knowing nothing about them, and knowing that Miss

Franklin knows nothing about them, I think there'd better be no chances taken. If you carry sleeping tablets about with you, you must be used to them.'

'Certainly,' said Cust. 'Of course I'll do all I can to help.' Her callous attitude to the sick Miss Franklin made him add: 'You have never suffered from insomnia?'

'I manage not to succumb to it,' she answered quite politely.

After dinner she took Cust, provided with a phial from his luggage, to Miss Franklin's bedroom; which proved to be in that part of the upper storey of the building which he had failed to reach that morning, and to be entered, as he had supposed, by a separate stair.

The room was in its contents completely unlike any other he had seen in the Castle. It even contained a small table mirror. The furniture was of the familiar type, simple, black, and wooden; but the apartment was packed with it, as if the occupant had collected together pieces from all over the building. There was a jumble of small tables all covered with objects personal to any elderly professional companion; the wall cupboards were unshut and bulging; vague pieces of half-finished textile craftsmanship hung upon the many chairs and lay about the floor. Miss Franklin appeared to make clothes, cushion-covers, and bedspreads; to embroider ineffectively; to knit, to operate a Singer machine, even halfheartedly to weave. The pathetic ingatherings of a lifetime lay scattered about, left exposed to the general gaze solely because cupboard and cabinet space was entirely insufficient to house them. Miss Franklin seemed to own nothing which would have been in the least strange at home; nothing in the least harmonious with where she now found herself. The severe figure of Lola appeared completely incongruous in the bedroom of the companion on whom she clearly depended for much: Cust might have been visiting a dying spinster aunt.

For dying, Miss Franklin, at least to the untrained eye of Cust, certainly appeared to be. She was grey, haggard, and palpably distraught with a very high fever indeed. Her hair was loose and tangled. Her conventional clothes and underclothes lay scattered unappetizingly around the bed. She was clawing the bedding, which lay half upon the floor, and dangerously near to the fire. She muttered incessantly: memories, Cust thought, of earlier days in Yorkshire. The name Whitby occurred several times during the short period he was in the room.

It was painfully obvious that no one had taken the smallest interest in her welfare since she fell ill.

Filled with this last reflection, which was indeed the strongest and most obvious the room could promote, Cust noticed lying half under Miss Franklin's shoulder an enormous bunch of keys.

'I'm far from sure whether sleeping pills should be given to a patient in that state,' said Cust. 'We really must at all costs get a doctor.'

'If I were to go down myself,' said Lola, who, Cust noticed, remained only just inside the door, appearing to find the room repugnant, 'if I were to go down myself, it would be at least four days before a doctor could be brought here, as you know from your own journey. I'm inclined to think that unless she's better before then, there'll be no need for a doctor. Don't you agree?'

Looking at Miss Franklin, Cust, from his almost total lack of medical knowledge, found it hard to differ. But he said: 'We must do what we can all the same.'

'Of course,' replied Lola from the door. 'And I think we'd better give her some sleep. Surely the risk can't be greater than letting her continue like that without any?'

Cust hesitated. He was standing with his back to Lola looking down at Miss Franklin's face. The illness made her witch-like. The whole course of events since he entered the Schloss, tore through his mind like a wisp of demons. Felicity's words about 'Poppy' took a prominent place in the pageant.

He regarded with profoundest aversion the task of forcing sleeping tablets between Miss Franklin's withered lips, dried up also with illness. Her jaws were opening and shutting with the fever. He was sure she had false teeth.

He had always understood that four of these tablets was a dangerous dose. Two was the number he himself was accustomed to take. One tablet was probably enough for a beginner in the habit. A single tablet would also be less repellent to administer.

Opening the bottle, he laid three tablets on the palm of his hand. 'I always find three the best quantity,' he said over his shoulder to Lola. Miss Franklin proved not so delirious as to be unable to understand what was required of her. The administration proved less grim than Cust had feared. Miss Franklin swallowed the tiny objects without demur or difficulty. Now she should more than sleep the clock round.

As the last tablet went down, Cust, under the show of replumping Miss Franklin's pillows, succeeded in pocketing the enormous bunch of keys. Lola seemed conscious of being out of her depths with the problems in that congested little room. The sounds of the fire and the two blazing torches, of Miss Franklin's breathings and mutterings also, gave him cover in the dim and flickering light. It was patent that no one cared what happened to any possession of Miss Franklin's.

When they had left the invalid and returned to the studio, Lola, as on the previous night, began to talk. Brilliant stories, new opinions, strange comments poured forth in a golden torrent. Whatever the other recommendations to her of the Schloss Marcantonio, it seemed clear enough to Cust that she lacked an audience. Charms and entertainments which might have been spread over a year, had been dammed up for his sole delight. Upon the unaccustomed listener, the effect was hypnotic and dreamlike.

Occasion arose for Cust to enquire what was the large work she was engaged upon, for which the peasant girl sat as model.

'It is called "The Soul",' said Lola. 'It will be a problem for Miss Franklin to get it down to the coast without a smash.'

'The statuettes too will be a problem. They must be pretty fragile,' said Cust.

'When I've perfected the technique, I'm not doing any more of them,' replied Lola.

'Not even if they're popular? As I'm sure they will be.'

'I shall start something else. I shall make that equally popular. Bonaparte said that men are governed by toys. Speaking of Bonaparte, though—"

The long curved line of figures stood staring at Cust while Lola made some apt remarks upon the deficiencies of the Corsican as a subject for the artist. 'Too obviously a democrat,' she concluded.

It occurred to Cust that so many images of the same person might well make a man dream of that person, especially when the images were so mysteriously animate, and the man so grossly over-exercised.

None the less Cust was taking no chances; and perhaps the day's supreme anti-climax was when he drugged himself into the quickest possible slumber, having carefully noted nothing in the least unusual in the few moments occupied in undressing.

'How's Miss Franklin?' Cust asked Fischer the next morning.

There was no reply. Fischer laid breakfast beside the bed.

'When will Mrs. Hastings be about?'

The question was unworthy. It did not merit a reply. It did not get one.

Things were not made easier by the General falling entirely into the hot water as Cust tried to read while shaving. In that room the light was never adequate at the best of times for such an enterprise.

Immediately he was dressed, he drew Miss Franklin's keys from under his bolster, placed them in his jacket pocket, ignited a torch, and crept towards the passage to the well. The keys being all unlabelled, opening the first of the two doors proved a slow job. When he had managed it he found himself in a stuffy little cell, ill-lighted by an irregular hole in the rock crudely glazed. The unsavoury place was filled with spiders, mould, and trunks. It might have been any family box-room. But Cust noted with interest and relief the names upon several of the boxes: there was one group inscribed in large black lettering 'Brue Hastings'; but the other group sported faded paper tags upon which were written in ancient ink 'Miss Lilian Franklin'. Cust took in the Christian name with perhaps excess of appetite. Then he relocked the door.

The second door opened to the first key Cust applied. At first this seemed strange to him, a cause for some uneasiness; then he realized that he had instinctively used the next key on the bunch. The door grated a little beneath its primitively carved lintel. At once Cust realized two things: the reason for the unsmoked cigarettes, and that he was not alone. The apartment was a chapel; and Lola, an even more unimagined fact, was there before him.

In the middle of the floor, somewhat huddled together, were several rows of the black peasant chairs. Lola was seated in the centre of the hindmost row with her head lying on her arm, which rested upon the back of the chair in front. Her attitude recalled that favoured by many worshippers as an alternative to kneeling. Cust stood for at least a minute regarding her and totally unable to move. Then his legs began to tremble, and the distress slowly encompassed his entire body.

Supposing Lola, however, to be so deeply engaged in devotions as to be unaware of his advent or indifferent to it (he knew little of such matters, but had
noticed the behaviour of certain persons in various churches), he began cautiously to look around him. The apartment upon closer examination was not so
certainly a chapel after all. The resemblance seemed to derive from three circumstances: the closely packed group of chairs; a corner behind Lola, curtained off
in the same dark fabric that Cust had noticed above Lola's bed, the general effect
being somewhat that of a vestry; and a collection of emblems ranged along a
wide stone abutment which continued along the length of the wall towards
which Lola was facing. The abutment was more or less the height of the various
altars Cust had seen; but the emblems, simple abstractions in polished wood,
were in forms totally unknown to him and beyond his comprehension. They recalled neither Christian ritual in any liturgy Cust had encountered; nor the para-
phernalia of diabolism he had once been introduced to in a house near Swiss
Cottage. He thought them more unconventionalized than the former can ever
be; more wholesome and appealing than the latter. Raking quickly through his
memories, he recalled an exhibition he had once been sent to criticize of Oriental Religious Art. The emblems did not in the least resemble anything in it.

While he had been puzzling himself, Lola had made no movement. Cust
modified his original hazy notions to the extent of recollecting notices intimat-
ing that certain portions of churches were 'Reserved for Private Prayer Only',
and requesting the silence, or even absence, of those otherwise preoccupied. He
wondered whether his entry was a discourteous, perhaps blasphemous, intrusion.
He looked hard at Lola's sprawling figure. Her attitude suggested extreme dis-
comfort. Her trousers were twisted, her limbs cramped. Then he looked more
narrowly still. He was almost certain that she slept. He tiptoed up to her. Her
breathing, the sagging in her every joint, were confirmation. There was something about her which suggested she had been asleep for hours: Cust knew the
subtle symptoms from experience with an uncle who often unintentionally spent
the night in an armchair at home, a learned book open upon his knees.

Convinced, Cust crept backwards to the curtained-off corner. Lifting one of
the curtains apart without a sound he had his most horrible experience yet. Inside was a large tomb in white marble, shining but entirely plain, on the top of
which lay what Cust first thought to be the body of Felicity, but immediately re-

alized to be a more than ordinarily realistic life-size figure of her. Cust dropped the curtain with a slight clink of the ring upon the rod above. Then he raised it again. The figure was as if Felicity lay on her back, though more perhaps as a corpse would lie than a living woman. She was wearing the same black evening dress, low cut and reaching to the feet. The impression of a corpse was increased by the drawn pallor of the features against the black hair. It was almost as if the full lips had been reddened after death. The finger nails, Cust noticed, were a matching dark crimson. The brilliantly suggestive use of the slightest traces of colour left Cust in no doubt whose hand had made this masterpiece. When he perceived that the figure was a simulacrum, the shining white box which was the rest of the tomb gave him a further disturbing thought: it was as if the sides were very thin, almost transparent and luminous; as if any moment the occupant, who certainly could not have been interred in the rock but must lie immediately within, would be likely to push out. Among his cascading thoughts, Felicity's advent into his room had been momentarily forgotten; he had for a minute or two lost sight of *why* the idea of her had become so momentous to him. He became filled with a fearful apprehension that she would return to him in the aspect she must present within that waxy sarcophagus. . . .

He withdrew cautiously from the chapel, locking the door behind him. Apparently Lola elected to be locked in. Presumably she must have keys of her own. Naturally she would have: knowing her, it would be ludicrous to suppose otherwise. It was clammy in this castle basement. Lola seemed never to take cold. This might be a good moment to enquire after Miss Franklin's health and return her keys. The household had been dislocated long enough.

When Cust knocked at Miss Franklin's door, she said: 'Come in': something else he had not expected, as it was the first time he had heard the words from behind any door in that castle.

He tried the handle. This time there was no change from precedent. The door was locked.

'Who's there?' sharply cried Miss Franklin.

'It's I. Mr. Cust. I wondered how you were and whether I could help in any way?'

'Thank you, Mr. Cust. I'm better. Please come in, if you wish. I'm decent.'

The last words should possibly have sounded pathetic, but Cust found them merely distasteful.

'The door seems to be locked,' he said.

'Wait a moment.' The intonation was absurdly characteristic of Miss Franklin's whole kind. But Cust was visualizing her increasingly frenzied searchings. Then she said: 'I think Mrs. Hastings must have taken my keys.'

'And left you a prisoner? Surely not?' said Cust.

'We always lock our doors,' replied Miss Franklin. 'This time there may have been some mistake.'

'Hasn't Mrs. Hastings keys of her own?' asked Cust through the door, lifting his eyes from the bunch in his hand.

'Oh, yes. But I wasn't at all well yesterday, as I imagine you know. Mrs. Hastings probably thought it best not to leave my keys lying about. They might have got into the wrong hands.' Though the conversation was being conducted under circumstances which made the obtaining of reliable impressions difficult, Cust seemed to detect the note not of loyal acceptance but of malicious innuendo.

'Well, what do we do now?' he asked.

'Don't you worry about me, Mr. Cust,' came through the door. 'I've learnt to find my way out.'

Cust instantly recalled that someone else had used those words. He had forgotten the precise expression. Remembering he nearly dropped the heavy bunch of keys.

It would not have mattered if he had. For suddenly there was a wrench, the door opened, and Miss Franklin stood before him, a short iron bar in her hand.

'I have no intention of being trapped,' she said.

Then her eyes fell upon the keys in Cust's hand. He had come intending to replace them, never supposing for one moment that their owner would be other than seriously ill, and probably insensible. Now, under her governess eye, he felt immeasurably foolish.

But she only hissed at him: 'How did you get them off her?'

'That's rather my business,' replied Cust, in part recovering his wits. 'Anyway here they are.' She took them from him quietly, still eyeing him. 'I'm delighted to see you're so much better.'

'Then you saw me when I was ill?'

There seemed no escape after all. 'Mrs. Hastings asked me to look at you yesterday. She thought I might be able to help. You looked rather bad. Unfortunately I was quite useless. I was afraid you might have pneumonia.'

'Pneumonia?' Cust might have said rabies.

'I recollected your cold when we last met.'

'Oh yes. That.' Miss Franklin laughed. 'I followed my sister Lilian's remedy.'

'Your sister Lilian?'

'Two heaped tablespoonsfull of salt in a tumbler of water piping hot and drink it down.'

'I see. It certainly seems to work like a charm.'

'Well, it works, Mr. Cust. Charms often don't and when they do you oftener wish they hadn't.' She still looked extremely ill and her hair was a disorganized heap; but she was fully dressed in an ugly brick-coloured frock.

'You know about charms?' enquired Cust lightly but, all recent events considered, fearing for the answer.

'I've been asleep for goodness knows how long. That's something I'm not used to at all. I think there must have been magic in the air.' The sentimental cliché sounded ludicrously sinister.

'You sleep badly then?' They were still standing with the open door between them, she with the keys in her hand.

'I do, Mr. Cust. It's a common thing when you're leaving your young days behind.'

Suddenly Cust stepped into the room and closed the door behind him. 'Miss Franklin,' he said, 'this place seems to me far from ideal for light sleepers. What was the noise that woke me up the night before last, a racket like all the foundry boilers in hell?'

She looked away from him, but only said, 'It's an iron shutter. There's a big window in the Castle which has an iron shutter. Sometimes when there's a wind, it flaps about. Like an ordinary shutter.'

'Does it protect the big window that overlooks the precipice? I thought it left the Castle somewhat vulnerable.'

'When the Schloss was in danger they closed the shutter. They shut themselves in.'

'Very snug I'm sure,' said Cust. 'But don't you and Mrs. Hastings often long to leave, all the same? It's a pretty wild spot and there's something to be said for home even nowadays.'

'Neither Mrs. Hastings nor I will ever leave. Rest assured of that, Mr. Cust. You are absolutely wasting your time. I advise you to go back to England as soon as possible. I seriously advise you.'

'Are you so devoted to Mrs. Hastings as all that? It can't be this place.'

After a second's silence, she turned to him and said very steadily: 'Mr. Cust, will you please leave my room, as I must prepare myself to resume charge of the domestic arrangements?'

'Tell me one thing before I go. Something different. Tell me: why did Mrs. Hastings come here in the first place? Why here?'

Again there was a moment's silence. Then she said: 'I should say it was simply to get away from the world of men.'

And there Cust had to leave it.

He had just opened the door when he noticed something lying on one of the many small tables that cluttered the room. Amid the usual litter was an unmistakable black object; which lay proclaiming to the world the initial of its owner.

Cust must have been staring at it, for Miss Franklin's eyes, averted since he had begun to question her, were now plainly upon him.

Neither of them spoke, and then Cust found that he was shutting himself out of the room.

Tragic was undoubtedly the word which had occurred to Cust as he had gazed upon the slumped sleeping figure of the sculptress. But perhaps about anyone so unbeautifully disposed would be a suggestion of defeat, of helplessness. Reappearing as usual at lunch-time, Lola seemed once more herself, in her normal daytime disposition: rather silent, rather dull, rather distant, rather regal. Even her trousers were pressed, and her heavy shirt was stiff with laundering. Her fine hair was closely ordered; her hands, as she peeled fruit, steady and vigorously graceful.

Half way through the first course, Miss Franklin entered, her appearance as depressing as ever.

'It's a good thing these attacks of yours don't last longer,' observed Lola.

'Everything goes to pieces without you. Still you always manage to get over it reasonably quickly.'

Miss Franklin made no reply, but, helping herself to food, began feebly to eat.

As the day pursued its indifferent course, the pace and tone set to serve the needs of genius, Cust came to wondering rather vacantly what more he could do. Too accustomed a journalist to feel curiosity where no story could result (and though Lola had not actually forbidden a story, it was hard indeed to see what story there was which could take its place adjoining the Football Results), he could fall back only upon wondering about Felicity. The whole rigmarole around him was also beyond him. He was virtually a prisoner until (presumably) his dreary escort returned and Lola chose to release him. But the secrets of the Schloss were secure from him every bit as effectively as he from the outside world (return to which, conceivably, in view of the total failure of his mission, would mean the sack). But there certainly remained Felicity. . . . In spite of everything, in spite even of that dreadful little curtained-off vestry, he almost wished he could see her again. . . . Though time and disfigurement may drive a man away, that little vestry in itself seemed not necessarily to do so. It was a strange situation.

None the less he was horribly frightened when, after an even more boring day, he was awakened in the small hours by Felicity apparently wrenching at his bedclothes. In the otherwise black darkness, he could just see her by the red light from the fire.

'I'm terribly, terribly sorry,' she said very softly, and drawing away a little as he awoke. 'But we must make a dash for it. They've got on to you. You may not know it, but they have.'

Cust was shaking and at the same time vastly half-yawning. So his voice sounded choked and alien. 'Where do you come from?' he asked very low.

'You gave yourself away in Poppy's bedroom,' she replied. 'I warned you about Poppy.'

'Do you mean that handbag of yours?'

'Poppy put that there to see what you did. I know her.'

'You seem to know everything.'

'It was the keys gave you away. You made a mess of that, you know.'

'Do you mean that Miss Franklin wasn't ill at all?'

Felicity laughed, very short and quiet. 'Oh no, I don't mean that. She was ill all right. She always is at these times.'

'These times?'

'Your boob was in not hanging on to the keys. Then we could have left through the door.'

'You know you don't really frighten me. Not now I'm awake. Not *you*.'

'Sh-sh-sh.' The sibilant was appealing. 'Poppy crawls about the Schloss all night. She never sleeps. Like a cat. She'll hear us. Lola never sleeps either. Lola's like a tiger.'

'She does sleep!' softly cried Cust before he could stop himself: then once more trembled momentarily as he wondered if he really knew.

But Felicity ignored him. 'Put on your clothes. Quickly. I won't watch. Anyway we can't risk a light.'

Cust thought for a moment.

'Quickly.'

Cust still thought.

'Oh quickly. *Please.* I do beg of you. It's for your sake now as well as mine. But it's for mine too.'

Suddenly Cust leapt from the bed towards her. You can't touch ghosts, he had suddenly remembered. She drew back from him and her tone was so natural and dismayed that he paused.

'What are you doing? How can you be so silly?'

It was so precisely what she would say that he withdrew half a pace, apologetic.

'Now come on. Dress quickly.'

He sat on the bed and said: 'Please tell me exactly what you want me to do? When I'm dressed.'

'I've told you. I know a way out of the Schloss. We can get away together. If you don't come with me, you'll never get away at all. Oh, please believe me.'

'What about *your* clothes? You won't get far as you are.'

'They've taken all *my* other clothes,' she replied desperately. 'I told you.'

Cust had reached a decision. 'I'll dress.'

She stood back in the darkness while he fumbled and groped with his garments.

'Are you ready?' she enquired much too soon. Cust, himself to the last, feared to look like a character in a thriller. There were always attractive young women in thrillers. They asked foolish men to do just the sort of thing that was now being demanded of him.

'Ready,' he replied none the less. 'What next?'

'You'll see.'

Now truly she seemed a wraith, as, only just visible, she glided to the door. Cust followed, half alert and curious, half drugged with obscure opiates.

'What about a torch?'

'Don't be a B.F.'

They began to creep down the passage in the direction away from the studio. For some seconds Cust stumbled along in total darkness. Then it seemed slightly less dark.

'Bloody hell!' came in a sharp vindictive whisper from in front of Cust. 'It must be Poppy. Oh, my God.' The last words were a cry of strangled misery.

Cust looked over his shoulder and saw a faint fiery glow. Was the Castle ablaze? Anything seemed possible. Then he supposed that it was someone approaching with a torch; but quite noiselessly. He waited.

'Don't you understand?' cried Felicity. 'It's Poppy.' There was still no other sound but her frightened whisper. 'Will you trust me? It's our last chance.'

Suddenly to Cust consideration like an angel came. 'You must do what you think best,' he said. 'But I'm facing it out. They're only two women.' He could see her faint shape shrink back and felt desperately pitiful. 'Good luck,' he added. 'Good luck to you always.'

He would have kissed her but she had gone and he embraced the dirty air. She could just be seen running in her black dress down the rosy stone tunnel.

The light was now quite strong and with an effort Cust turned towards its source. Of all his life's memories this was the most unforgettable: the figure not of Miss Franklin but of Lola; crazily staggering from side to side of the passage, but almost silently, her face as a set sculpture of all black agonies, her rigid left arm upholding a huge flaming torch against the background of grey vaulting and vast ill laid masonry.

She swayed quietly by him; a poor soul whom Cust's eyes could not leave, whom his feet had from pity to follow. As they neared the top of the stair to the well, Cust saw something else. In the big window a figure was dimly standing, a life-size image in a monstrous niche. Even in the confusing light it was plain that Felicity stood there, painfully, pathetically hesitating. Without thought Cust raised his hands to cover his ears; in a second the expected had happened. Felicity was gone, and that appalling clangour, for the second time since Cust arrived, filled the Schloss with echoes echoing echoes. There was no sound of breaking glass.

But there was a sound of laughter. Lola had ceased to move. She stood in the middle of the passage still holding the brand high above her head. In the steadier light, Cust could see what had previously been lost in shadow; the neat lady-like figure of Miss Franklin, standing at the top of the stair and to the side of the window. She was laughing, but her laughter was as ladylike as her raiment and bearing. She was not hysterical; she was amused.

Almost instantly Lola pulled herself together. The arm bearing the torch relaxed from its cataleptic rigour; the features more nearly approached the aspect of men and women who are in the presence of their kind; the voice was almost steady.

'I shan't be going to the sanctuary now, Miss Franklin.'

Miss Franklin stood staying nothing.

Then, turning to Cust, Lola remarked quite casually. 'What fools you must think us! We lock the Schloss to keep in what we lock our rooms to keep out. Be that as it may, I take it that the questions which brought you here are answered?'

'I am so very sorry,' was all that Cust could think of in reply.

'I don't think that either of us, Miss Franklin or I, would be particularly acceptable to London society at the present moment. We must absent ourselves from that felicity a while.'

She appeared fully in control of herself and the entire situation as she accompanied Cust back to the door of his room and bade him good night. Miss Franklin brought up the rear in silence.

The remaining days and nights passed in that uneventful but tense dullness which was the prevailing atmosphere of the place. No change whatever seemed to be made in the habitual way of life. The Schloss was still locked, the servants continued dumb, Lola seemed hard at work, Miss Franklin not too efficiently contrived the domesticities. One question Cust still burned to ask; but it was of Miss Franklin, for better for worse, that he asked it.

'The events of the other night,' he said, looking up from his book as she scrubbed a carpet sweeper up and down the studio floor, 'the events of the night. . . . Was that the last of them, do you suppose?'

The tone of her reply was by no means the least astonishing thing of all. 'Why do *you* suppose it should be?' she said in an accent of indignant contempt.

'Surely Mrs. Hastings would be glad if it were?' Cust exclaimed. Lola's face was continually before the eyes of his imagination.

'It is not a matter under Mrs. Hastings's control,' Miss Franklin replied.

'Nor yours, I suppose? . . .' Cust was for some reason prompted foolishly to enquire.

As on a previous occasion, Miss Franklin looked at him for a moment before replying. 'You suppose rightly, Mr. Cust.'

But this time all Felicity's fear and hatred of her, the constant references to her rather than to the sculptress, came back to him; and fond though he had almost thought himself of Felicity, nothing in the whole world would have persuaded him to continue the subject.

When the time came, they bade him conventional adieux still as if nothing unconventional had happened. The last he saw of either was the noble figure of Lola standing upon her battlement walk watching him ride away. She neither waved nor smiled. Miss Franklin had presumably gone about her domestic duties.

Three more things are worth record.

As the two horses bore their riders near the corner of the Castle rock, Cust contrived with difficulty to steer his mount a little aside. Looking back, he saw a large and ugly slab of deeply rusted ironwork. It appeared to be considerably overgrown with the vegetation which after years takes root in the most unlikely places, ultimately to cover the most inorganic matter with a vaguely living accumulation. Cust could not be sure of details: he had trouble in retaining his place in the saddle; the general colouration of the rocks all around him was not unlike that of iron; the whole picture was meshed with struggling plants.

Cust had left a suitcase down on the coast, larger than the small one which had accompanied him to the Schloss, bumping on the animal's side. Immediately he opened this larger suitcase upon his return, he found Felicity's handbag lying embedded in the clothes within it. As this time it remained with him, he took it back to England. It seemed useless to throw it away.

Cust did lose his job. His refusal to render any account whatever of his experiences to his editor or even his proprietor led them to think he lacked that first requisite of successful journalism, a nose for news. 'Overbred', was his lordship's comment, recalling Cust's uncle.

Nor was Benson, of Benson's Gallery near the Irving statue, notably more sympathetic.

MRS. AMWORTH

❦

E. F. BENSON

THE VILLAGE OF MAXLEY, WHERE, LAST SUMMER AND autumn, these strange events took place, lies on a heathery and pine-clad upland of Sussex. In all England you could not find a sweeter and saner situation. Should the wind blow from the south, it comes laden with the spices of the sea; to the east high downs protect it from the inclemencies of March; and from the west and north the breezes which reach it travel over miles of aromatic forest and heather. The village itself is insignificant enough in point of population, but rich in amenities and beauty. Half-way down the single street, with its broad road and spacious areas of grass on each side, stands the little Norman Church and the antique graveyard long disused: for the rest there are a dozen small, sedate Georgian houses, red-bricked and long-windowed, each with a square of flower-garden in front, and an ampler strip behind; a score of shops, and a couple of score of thatched cottages belonging to labourers on neighbouring estates, complete the entire cluster of its peaceful habitations. The general peace, however, is sadly broken on Saturdays and Sundays, for we lie on one of the main roads between London and Brighton and our quiet street becomes a race-course for flying motor-cars and bicycles.

A notice just outside the village begging them to go slowly only seems to encourage them to accelerate their speed, for the road lies open and straight, and there is really no reason why they should do otherwise. By way of protest, therefore, the ladies of Maxley cover their noses and mouths with their handkerchiefs as they see a motor-car approaching, though, as the street is asphalted, they need not really take these precautions against dust. But late on Sunday night the horde of scorchers has passed, and we settle down again to five days of cheerful and leisurely seclusion. Railway strikes which agitate the country so much leave us undisturbed because most of the inhabitants of Maxley never leave it at all.

I am the fortunate possessor of one of these small Georgian houses, and consider myself no less fortunate in having so interesting and stimulating a neighbour as Francis Urcombe, who, the most confirmed of Maxleyites, has not slept away from his house, which stands just opposite to mine in the village street, for nearly two years, at which date, though still in middle life, he resigned his Physiological Professorship at Cambridge University and devoted himself to the study of those occult and curious phenomena which seem equally to concern the physical and the psychical sides of human nature. Indeed his retirement was not unconnected with his passion for the strange uncharted places that lie on the confines and borders of science, the existence of which is so stoutly denied by the more materialistic minds, for he advocated that all medical students should be obliged to pass some sort of examination in mesmerism, and that one of the tripos papers should be designed to test their knowledge in such subjects as appearances at time of death, haunted houses, vampirism, automatic writing, and possession.

"Of course they wouldn't listen to me," ran his account of the matter, "for there is nothing that these seats of learning are so frightened of as knowledge, and the road to knowledge lies in the study of things like these. The functions of the human frame are, broadly speaking, known. They are a country, anyhow, that has been charted and mapped out. But outside that lie huge tracts of undiscovered country, which certainly exist, and the real pioneers of knowledge are those who, at the cost of being derided as credulous and superstitious, want to push on into those misty and probably perilous places. I felt that I could be of more use by setting out without compass or knapsack into the mists than by sitting in a cage like a canary and chirping about what was known. Besides, teaching is very bad for a man who knows himself only to be a learner: you only need to be a self-conceited ass to teach."

Here, then, in Francis Urcombe, was a delightful neighbour to one who, like myself, has an uneasy and burning curiosity about what he called the "misty and perilous places"; and this last spring we had a further and most welcome addition to our pleasant little community, in the person of Mrs. Amworth, widow of an Indian civil servant. Her husband had been a judge in the North-West Provinces, and after his death at Peshawar she came back to England, and after a year in London found herself starving for the ampler air and sunshine of the country to take the place of the fogs and griminess of town. She had, too, a special reason for settling in Maxley, since her ancestors up till a hundred years ago had long been native to the place, and in the old churchyard, now disused, are many gravestones bearing her maiden name of Chaston. Big and energetic, her vigorous and genial personality speedily woke Maxley up to a higher degree of sociality than it had ever known. Most of us were bachelors or spinsters or elderly folk not much inclined to exert ourselves in the expense and effort of hospitality, and hitherto the gaiety of a small tea-party, with bridge afterwards and goloshes (when it was wet) to trip home in again for a solitary dinner, was about the climax of our festivities. But Mrs. Amworth showed us a more gregarious way, and set an example of luncheon-parties and little dinners, which we began to follow. On other nights when no such hospitality was on foot, a lone man like myself found it pleasant to know that a call on the telephone to Mrs. Amworth's house not a hundred yards off, and an inquiry as to whether I might come over after dinner for a game of piquet before bed-time, would probably evoke a response of welcome. There she would be, with a comrade-like eagerness for companionship, and there was a glass of port and a cup of coffee and a cigarette and a game of piquet. She played the piano, too, in a free and exuberant manner, and had a charming voice and sang to her own accompaniment; and as the days grew long and the light lingered late, we played our game in her garden, which in the course of a few months she had turned from being a nursery for slugs and snails into a glowing patch of luxuriant blossoming. She was always cheery and jolly; she was interested in everything, and in music, in gardening, in games of all sorts was a competent performer. Everybody (with one exception) liked her, everybody felt her to bring with her the tonic of a sunny day. That one exception was Francis Urcombe; he, though he confessed he did not like her, acknowledged that he was vastly interested in her. This always seemed strange to me, for pleasant and jovial as she was, I could see nothing in her that could call forth conjecture or intrigued surmise, so healthy and unmysterious a figure did she present. But of the genuineness of Urcombe's interest there could be no doubt; one could see him watching and scrutinising her. In matter of age, she frankly volunteered the information that she was forty-five; but her briskness, her activity, her unravaged skin, her coal-black hair, made it difficult to believe that she was not adopting an unusual device, and adding ten years on to her age instead of subtracting them.

Often, also, as our quite unsentimental friendship ripened, Mrs. Amworth would ring me up and propose her advent. If I was busy writing, I was to give her, so we definitely bargained, a frank negative, and in answer I could hear her jolly laugh and her wishes for a successful evening of work. Sometimes, before her proposal arrived, Urcombe would already have stepped across from his house opposite for a smoke and a chat, and he, hearing who my intending visitor was, always urged me to beg her to come. She and I should play our piquet, said he, and he would look on, if we did not object, and learn something of the game. But I doubt whether he paid much attention to it, for nothing could be clearer than that, under that penthouse of forehead and thick eyebrows, his attention was fixed not on the cards, but on one of the players. But he seemed to enjoy an hour spent thus, and often, until one particular evening in July, he would watch her with the air of a man who has some deep problem in front of him. She, enthusiastically keen about our game, seemed not to notice his scrutiny. Then came that evening, when, as I see in the light of subsequent events, began the first twitching of the veil that hid the secret horror from my eyes. I did not know it then, though I noticed that thereafter, if she rang up to propose coming round, she always asked not only if I was at leisure, but whether Mr. Urcombe was with me. If so, she said, she would not spoil the chat of two old bachelors, and laughingly wished me good night.

Urcombe, on this occasion, had been with me for some half-hour before Mrs. Amworth's appearance, and had been talking to me about the mediæval beliefs concerning vampirism, one of those borderland subjects which he declared had not been sufficiently studied before it had been consigned by the medical profession to the dust-heap of exploded superstitions. There he sat, grim and eager, tracing, with that pellucid clearness which had made him in his Cambridge days so admirable a lecturer, the history of those mysterious visitations. In them all there were the same general features: one of those ghoulish spirits took up its abode in a living man or woman, conferring supernatural powers of bat-like flight and glutting itself with nocturnal blood-feasts. When its host died it continued to dwell in the corpse, which remained undecayed. By day it rested, by night it left the grave and went on its awful errands. No European country in the Middle Ages seemed to have escaped them; earlier yet, parallels were to be found, in Roman and Greek and in Jewish history.

"It's a large order to set all that evidence aside as being moonshine," he said. "Hundreds of totally independent witnesses in many ages have testified to the occurrence of these phenomena, and there's no explanation known to me which covers all the facts. And if you feel inclined to say 'Why, then, if these are facts, do we not come across them now?' there are two answers I can make you. One is that there were diseases known in the Middle Ages, such as the black death; which were certainly existent then and which have become extinct since, but for that reason we do not assert that such diseases never existed. Just as the black death visited England and decimated the population of Norfolk, so here in this very district about three hundred years ago there was certainly an outbreak of vampirism, and Maxley was the centre of it. My second answer is even more convincing, for I tell you that vampirism is by no means extinct now. An outbreak of it certainly occurred in India a year or two ago."

At that moment I heard my knocker plied in the cheerful and peremptory manner in which Mrs. Amworth is accustomed to announce her arrival, and I went to the door to open it.

"Come in at once," I said, "and save me from having my blood curdled. Mr. Urcombe has been trying to alarm me."

Instantly her vital, voluminous presence seemed to fill the room.

"Ah, but how lovely!" she said. "I delight in having my blood curdled. Go on with your ghost-story, Mr. Urcombe. I adore ghost-stories."

I saw that, as his habit was, he was intently observing her.

"It wasn't a ghost-story exactly," said he. "I was only telling our host how vampirism was not extinct yet. I was saying that there was an outbreak of it in India only a few years ago."

There was a more than perceptible pause, and I saw that, if Urcombe was observing her, she on her side was observing him with fixed eye and parted mouth. Then her jolly laugh invaded that rather tense silence.

"Oh, what a shame!" she said. "You're not going to curdle my blood at all. Where did you pick up such a tale, Mr. Urcombe? I have lived for years in India and never heard a rumour of such a thing. Some story-teller in the bazaars must have invented it: they are famous at that."

I could see that Urcombe was on the point of saying something further, but checked himself.

"Ah! very likely that was it," he said.

But something had disturbed our usual peaceful sociability that night, and something had damped Mrs. Amworth's usual high spirits. She had no gusto for her piquet, and left after a couple of games. Urcombe had been silent too, indeed he hardly spoke again till she departed.

"That was unfortunate," he said, "for the outbreak of—of a very mysterious disease, let us call it, took place at Peshawar, where she and her husband were. And—"

"Well?" I asked.

"He was one of the victims of it," said he. "Naturally I had quite forgotten that when I spoke."

The summer was unreasonably hot and rainless, and Maxley suffered much from drought, and also from a plague of big black night-flying gnats, the bite of which was very irritating and virulent. They came sailing in of an evening, settling on one's skin so quietly that one perceived nothing till the sharp stab announced that one had been bitten. They did not bite the hands or face, but chose always the neck and throat for their feeding-ground, and most of us, as the poison spread, assumed a temporary goitre. Then about the middle of August appeared the first of those mysterious cases of illness which our local doctor attributed to the long-continued heat coupled with the bite of these venomous insects. The patient was a boy of sixteen or seventeen, the son of Mrs. Amworth's gardener, and the symptoms were an anæmic pallor and a languid prostration, accompanied by great drowsiness and an abnormal appetite. He had, too, on his throat two small punctures where, so Dr. Ross conjectured, one of these great gnats had bitten him. But the odd thing was that there was no swelling or inflammation round the place where he had been bitten. The heat at this time had begun to abate, but the cooler weather failed to restore him, and the boy, in spite of the quantity of good food which he so ravenously swallowed, wasted away to a skin-clad skeleton.

I met Dr. Ross in the street one afternoon about this time, and in answer to my inquiries about his patient he said that he was afraid the boy was dying. The case, he confessed, completely puzzled him: some obscure form of pernicious anæmia was all he could suggest. But he wondered whether Mr. Urcombe would consent to see the boy, on the chance of his being able to throw some new light on the case, and since Urcombe was dining with me that night, I proposed to Dr. Ross to join us. He could not do this, but said he would look in later. When he came, Urcombe at once consented to put his skill at the other's disposal, and together they went off at once. Being thus shorn of my sociable evening, I telephoned to Mrs. Amworth to know if I might inflict myself on her for an hour. Her answer was a welcoming affirmative, and between piquet and music the hour lengthened itself into two. She spoke of the boy who was lying so desperately and mysteriously ill, and told me that she had often been to see him, taking him nourishing and delicate food. But to-day—and her kind eyes moistened as she spoke—she was afraid she had paid her last visit. Knowing the antipathy between her and Urcombe, I did not tell her that he had been called into consultation; and when I returned home she accompanied me to my door, for the sake of a breath of night air, and in order to borrow a magazine which contained an article on gardening which she wished to read.

"Ah, this delicious night air," she said, luxuriously sniffing in the coolness. "Night air and gardening are the great tonics. There is nothing so stimulating as bare contact with rich mother earth. You are never so fresh as when you have been grubbing in the soil—black hands, black nails, and boots covered with mud." She gave her great jovial laugh.

"I'm a glutton for air and earth," she said. "Positively I look forward to death, for then I shall be buried and have the kind earth all round me. No leaden caskets for me—I have given explicit directions. But what shall I do about air? Well, I suppose one can't have everything. The magazine? A thousand thanks, I will faithfully return it. Good night: garden and keep your windows open, and you won't have anæmia."

"I always sleep with my windows open," said I.

I went straight up to my bedroom, of which one of the windows looks out over the street, and as I undressed I thought I heard voices talking outside not far away. But I paid no particular attention, put out my lights, and falling asleep plunged into the depths of a most horrible dream, distortedly suggested no doubt, by my last words with Mrs. Amworth. I dreamed that I woke, and found that both my bedroom windows were shut. Half-suffocating I dreamed that I sprang out of bed, and went across to open them. The blind over the first was drawn down, and pulling it up I saw, with the indescribable horror of incipient nightmare, Mrs. Amworth's face suspended close to the pane in the darkness outside, nodding and smiling at me. Pulling down the blind again to keep that terror out, I rushed to the second window on the other side of the room, and there again was Mrs. Amworth's face. Then the panic came upon me in full blast; here was I suffocating in the airless room, and whichever window I opened Mrs. Amworth's face would float in, like those noiseless black gnats that bit before one was aware. The nightmare rose to screaming point, and with strangled yells I awoke to find my room cool and quiet with both windows open and blinds up and a half-moon high in its course, casting an oblong of tranquil light on the floor. But even when I was awake the horror persisted, and I lay tossing and turning. I must have slept long before the nightmare seized me, for now it was nearly day, and soon in the east the drowsy eyelids of morning began to lift.

I was scarcely downstairs next morning—for after the dawn I slept late— when Urcombe rang up to know if he might see me immediately. He came in, grim and preoccupied, and I noticed that he was pulling on a pipe that was not even filled.

"I want your help," he said, "and so I must tell you first of all what happened last night. I went round with the little doctor to see his patient, and found him just alive, but scarcely more. I instantly diagnosed in my own mind what this anæmia, unaccountable by any other explanation, meant. The boy is the prey of a vampire."

He put his empty pipe on the breakfast-table, by which I had just sat down, and folded his arms, looking at me steadily from under his overhanging brows.

"Now about last night," he said. "I insisted that he should be moved from his father's cottage into my house. As we were carrying him on a stretcher, whom should we meet but Mrs. Amworth? She expressed shocked surprise that we were moving him. Now why do you think she did that?"

With a start of horror, as I remembered my dream that night before, I felt an idea come into my mind so preposterous and unthinkable that I instantly turned it out again.

"I haven't the smallest idea," I said.

"Then listen, while I tell you about what happened later. I put out all light in the room where the boy lay, and watched. One window was a little open, for I had forgotten to close it, and about midnight I heard something outside, trying apparently to push it farther open. I guessed who it was—yes, it was full twenty feet from the ground—and I peeped round the corner of the blind. Just outside was the face of Mrs. Amworth and her hand was on the frame of the window. Very softly I crept close, and then banged the window down, and I think I just caught the tip of one of her fingers."

"But it's impossible," I cried. "How could she be floating in the air like that? And what had she come for? Don't tell me such—"

Once more, with closer grip, the remembrance of my nightmare seized me.

"I am telling you what I saw," said he. "And all night long, until it was nearly day, she was fluttering outside, like some terrible bat, trying to gain admittance. Now put together various things I have told you."

He began checking them off on his fingers.

"Number one," he said: "there was an outbreak of disease similar to that which the boy is suffering from at Peshawar, and her husband died of it. Number two: Mrs. Amworth protested against my moving the boy to my house. Number three: she, or the demon that inhabits her body, a creature powerful and deadly, tries to gain admittance. And add this, too: in mediæval times there was an epidemic of vampirism here at Maxley. The vampire, so the accounts run, was found to be Elizabeth Chaston . . . I see you remember Mrs. Amworth's maiden name. Finally, the boy is stronger this morning. He would certainly not have been alive if he had been visited again. And what do you make of it?"

There was a long silence, during which I found this incredible horror assuming the hues of reality.

"I have something to add," I said, "which may or may not bear on it. You say that the—the spectre went away shortly before dawn."

"Yes."

I told him of my dream, and he smiled grimly.

"Yes, you did well to awake," he said. "That warning came from your sub-conscious self, which never wholly slumbers, and cried out to you of deadly danger. For two reasons, then, you must help me: one to save others, the second to save yourself."

"What do you want me to do?" I asked.

"I want you first of all to help me in watching this boy, and ensuring that she does not come near him. Eventually I want you to help me in tracking the thing down, in exposing and destroying it. It is not human: it is an incarnate fiend. What steps we shall have to take I don't yet know."

It was now eleven of the forenoon, and presently I went across to his house for a twelve-hour vigil while he slept, to come on duty again that night, so that for the next twenty-four hours either Urcombe or myself was always in the room where the boy, now getting stronger every hour, was lying. The day following was Saturday and a morning of brilliant, pellucid weather, and already when I went across to his house to resume my duty the stream of motors down to Brighton had begun. Simultaneously I saw Urcombe with a cheerful face, which boded good news of his patient, coming out of his house, and Mrs. Amworth, with a gesture of salutation to me and a basket in her hand, walking up the broad strip of grass which bordered the road. There we all three met. I noticed (and saw that Urcombe noticed it too) that one finger of her left hand was bandaged.

"Good morning to you both," said she. "And I hear your patient is doing well, Mr. Urcombe. I have come to bring him a bowl of jelly, and to sit with him for an hour. He and I are great friends. I am overjoyed at his recovery."

Urcombe paused a moment, as if making up his mind, and then shot out a pointing finger at her.

"I forbid that," he said. "You shall not sit with him or see him. And you know the reason as well as I do."

I have never seen so horrible a change pass over a human face as that which now blanched hers to the colour of a grey mist. She put up her hand as if to shield herself from that pointing finger, which drew the sign of the cross in the air, and shrank back cowering on to the road. There was a wild hoot from a horn, a grinding of brakes, a shout—too late—from a passing car, and one long scream suddenly cut short. Her body rebounded from the roadway after the first wheel had gone over it, and the second followed. It lay there, quivering and twitching, and was still.

She was buried three days afterwards in the cemetery outside Maxley, in accordance with the wishes she had told me that she had devised about her interment, and the shock which her sudden and awful death had caused to the little community began by degrees to pass off. To two people only, Urcombe and myself, the horror of it was mitigated from the first by the nature of the relief that her death brought; but, naturally enough, we kept our own counsel, and no hint of what greater horror had been thus averted was ever let slip. But, oddly enough, so it seemed to me, he was still not satisfied about something in connection with her, and would give no answer to my questions on the subject. Then as the days of a tranquil mellow September and the October that followed began to drop away like the leaves of the yellowing trees, his uneasiness relaxed. But before the entry of November the seeming tranquillity broke into hurricane.

I had been dining one night at the far end of the village, and about eleven o'clock was walking home again. The moon was of an unusual brilliance, rendering all that it shone on as distinct as in some etching. I had just come opposite the house which Mrs. Amworth had occupied, where there was a board up telling that it was to let, when I heard the click of her front gate, and next moment I saw, with a sudden chill and quaking of my very spirit, that she stood there. Her profile, vividly illuminated, was turned to me, and I could not be mistaken in my identification of her. She appeared not to see me (indeed the shadow of the yew hedge in front of her garden enveloped me in its blackness) and she went swiftly across the road, and entered the gate of the house directly opposite. There I lost sight of her completely.

My breath was coming in short pants as if I had been running—and now indeed I ran, with fearful backward glances, along the hundred yards that separated me from my house and Urcombe's. It was to his that my flying steps took me, and next minute I was within.

"What have you come to tell me?" he asked. "Or shall I guess?"

"You can't guess," said I.

"No; it's no guess. She has come back and you have seen her. Tell me about it."

I gave him my story.

"That's Major Pearsall's house," he said. "Come back with me there at once."

"But what can we do?" I asked.

"I've no idea. That's what we have got to find out."

A minute later, we were opposite the house. When I had passed it before, it was all dark; now lights gleamed from a couple of windows upstairs. Even as we faced it, the front door opened, and next moment Major Pearsall emerged from the gate. He saw us and stopped.

"I'm on my way to Dr. Ross," he said quickly. "My wife has been taken suddenly ill. She had been in bed an hour when I came upstairs, and I found her white as a ghost and utterly exhausted. She had been to sleep, it seemed—but you will excuse me."

"One moment, Major," said Urcombe. "Was there any mark on her throat?"

"How did you guess that?" said he. "There was: one of those beastly gnats must have bitten her twice there. She was streaming with blood."

"And there's someone with her?" asked Urcombe.

"Yes, I roused her maid."

He went off, and Urcombe turned to me. "I know now what we have to do," he said. "Change your clothes, and I'll join you at your house."

"What is it?" I asked.

"I'll tell you on our way. We're going to the cemetery."

He carried a pick, a shovel, and a screwdriver when he rejoined me, and wore round his shoulders a long coil of rope. As we walked, he gave me the outlines of the ghastly hour that lay before us.

"What I have to tell you," he said, "will seem to you now too fantastic for credence, but before dawn we shall see whether it outstrips reality. By a most fortunate happening, you saw the spectre, the astral body, whatever you choose to call it, of Mrs. Amworth, going on its grisly business, and therefore, beyond doubt, the vampire spirit which abode in her during life animates her again in death. That is not exceptional—indeed, all these weeks since her death I have been expecting it. If I am right, we shall find her body undecayed and untouched by corruption."

"But she has been dead nearly two months," said I.

"If she had been dead two years it would still be so, if the vampire has possession of her. So remember: whatever you see done, it will be done not to her, who in the natural course would now be feeding the grasses above her grave, but to a spirit of untold evil and malignancy, which gives a phantom life to her body."

"But what shall I see done?" said I.

"I will tell you. We know that now, at this moment, the vampire clad in her mortal semblance is out; dining out. But it must get back before dawn, and it will pass into the material form that lies in her grave. We must wait for that, and then with your help I shall dig up her body. If I am right, you will look on her as she was in life, with the full vigour of the dreadful nutriment she has received pulsing in her veins. And then, when dawn has come, and the vampire cannot leave the lair of her body, I shall strike her with this"—and he pointed to his pick—"through the heart, and she, who comes to life again only with the animation the fiend gives her, she and her hellish partner will be dead indeed. Then we must bury her again, delivered at last."

We had come to the cemetery, and in the brightness of the moonshine there was no difficulty in identifying her grave. It lay some twenty yards from the small chapel, in the porch of which, obscured by shadow, we concealed ourselves. From there we had a clear and open sight of the grave, and now we must wait till its infernal visitor returned home. The night was warm and windless, yet even if a freezing wind had been raging I think I should have felt nothing of it, so intense was my preoccupation as to what the night and dawn would bring. There was a bell in the turret of the chapel, that struck the quarters of the hour, and it amazed me to find how swiftly the chimes succeeded one another.

The moon had long set, but a twilight of stars shone in a clear sky, when five o'clock of the morning sounded from the turret. A few minutes more passed, and then I felt Urcombe's hand softly nudging me; and looking out in the direction of his pointing finger, I saw that the form of a woman, tall and large in build, was approaching from the right. Noiselessly, with a motion more of gliding and floating than walking, she moved across the cemetery to the grave which was the centre of our observation. She moved round it as if to be certain of its identity, and for a moment stood directly facing us. In the greyness to which now my eyes had grown accustomed, I could easily see her face, and recognise its features.

She drew her hand across her mouth as if wiping it, and broke into a chuckle of such laughter as made my hair stir on my head. Then she leaped on to the grave, holding her hands high above her head, and inch by inch disappeared into the earth. Urcombe's hand was laid on my arm, in an injunction to keep still, but now he removed it.

"Come," he said.

With pick and shovel and rope we went to the grave. The earth was light and sandy, and soon after six struck we had delved down to the coffin lid. With his pick he loosened the earth round it, and, adjusting the rope through the handles by which it had been lowered, we tried to raise it. This was a long and laborious business, and the light had begun to herald day in the east before we had it out, and lying by the side of the grave. With his screw-driver he loosed the fastenings of the lid, and slid it aside, and standing there we looked on the face of Mrs. Amworth. The eyes, once closed in death, were open, the cheeks were flushed with colour, the red, full-lipped mouth seemed to smile.

"One blow and it is all over," he said. "You need not look."

Even as he spoke he took up the pick again, and, laying the point of it on her left breast, measured his distance. And though I knew what was coming I could not look away . . .

He grasped the pick in both hands, raised it an inch or two for the taking of his aim, and then with full force brought it down on her breast. A fountain of blood, though she had been dead so long, spouted high in the air, falling with the thud of a heavy splash over the shroud, and simultaneously from those red lips came one long, appalling cry, swelling up like some hooting siren, and dying away again. With that, instantaneous as a lightning flash, came the touch of corruption on her face, the colour of it faded to ash, the plump cheeks fell in, the mouth dropped.

"Thank God, that's over," said he, and without pause slipped the coffin lid back into its place.

Day was coming fast now, and, working like men possessed, we lowered the coffin into its place again, and shovelled the earth over it . . . The birds were busy with their earliest pipings as we went back to Maxley.

The Scent of Vinegar

⟨⟩

Robert Bloch

Every saturday night tim and bernie went bowling at the whorehouse.

"It didn't look like a whorehouse," Bernie said. "At least not any more than the places most of us lived in back then. And the damn thing was perched so high above Beverly Hills you'd have to look down to see King Vidor's spread." The old man glanced at Greg, the cigar in his hand semaphoring apology. "Sorry, I keep forgetting we're talking 1949. You've probably never even heard of the man."

"King Vidor." Greg paused. "He directed *The Big Parade*. And Bette Davis in *Beyond the Forest*, the picture where she says 'What a dump!' Right?"

Bernie aimed the cigar at Greg. "How old are you?"

"Twenty-six."

"I'm seventy-six." Bernie's eyes narrowed behind his hornrims. "Where'd you hear about Vidor?"

"Same place I heard about you," Greg said. "I'm a student of Hollywood history."

"And whorehouses." Bernie's dry chuckle rose, then ceased as pursed lips puffed on the cigar.

Greg Kolmer grinned. "They're part of Hollywood history too. The part I couldn't find in books."

Bernie was nodding. "In those days everything was hush-hush, and if you didn't keep your mouth shut, Howard Strickling shut it for you."

"Wasn't he publicity director at MGM?"

"Right again." Bernie's cigar gestured benediction. "He's the guy who said the first duty of a publicity man is to keep the news out of the paper." Another chuckle. "He knew everything. Including where Tim and I did our bowling."

"Was it really that big of a deal? I mean, all those stories about living it up out here—"

"—are true," Bernie said. "You think sex was invented by Madonna or some hot-dog computer hacks over at Cal Tech? Let me tell you, in the old days we had it all. Straights, gays, bi-, tri-: anything you wanted, you could get. You bring the ladder, we furnish the giraffe."

"Then why were you covering up?"

"Censorship. Simple as that. Everybody knew the rules and cooperated, or else. Tim and I were in management at the same studio; not top-level, but our names were on parking slots. So we weren't going to risk the 'or else' part, if you follow me."

Greg nodded, concealing his impatience. Because that was the only way to get Bernie to tell him what he really wanted to hear. And Bernie would tell him, sooner or later, because he had nothing else to do, sitting in this rundown old house on the wrong side of Wilshire with no friends to talk to, because you can't talk to the dead. Which is probably why he'd agreed to talk to Greg, was talking to him now.

"You take the stars," Bernie was saying. "The smart ones never fooled around with anybody under contract on their own lot. Getting involved with somebody you were liable to see every day was too risky; too much pressure, and you couldn't just walk away. So they patronized the hook-shops." Bernie's face crumpled in an old man's grin. "What do you suppose the folks in Peoria would say if they knew their favorite loverboy had to pay to play, just like the guy next door?"

"I doubt if many people in Peoria went to brothels in those days," Greg said.

"Maybe not." Bernie flicked cigar ash as he spoke. "But we did. Tim and I hung out at Kitty Earnshaw's. Great old broad, a million laughs."

Greg leaned forward. *At last. Now it's coming.* "The one who had this house up in the hills you were talking about?"

"Right. Kitty was the best. And her girls were user-friendly."

"Where was this place?"

Bernie spiraled his cigar in a northerly direction and more ash fell carpet-ward. "Way off Benedict Canyon somewhere, past Angelo. Been more than forty years since I've been up there, I don't remember—"

"Why'd you stop going?"

"Kitty Earnshaw retired, got married or religion or something. The new management was different, everyone Oriental. Not just Japs or Chinese, but girls from places like Burma, Singapore, Java, all over. Woman in charge never showed her face when I was there, but I heard stories. Marquess de Sade, that's what they called her."

"Marquis de Sade?"

"Marqu*ess*. A gag, I guess. But the place was getting a little too kinky for me. Like the night I met some drunk down at the bar and he says, 'You pick a girl yet? Take the one with the glass eye—she gives good socket.'"

Bernie shrugged. "Maybe that was a gag too, but I saw enough to make me start wondering. The chains and bondage scene—you know, with the little whips and the handcuffs on the bedposts, all four of them, and the Swiss Army knives. Anyhow, I stopped going there."

"And your friend Tim?"

"I don't know. Studio dropped him when television took over out here. What happened to him after that I can't say."

"Did you ever try to find out?"

The old man stubbed his cigar in the ashtray. "Look, Mr. Kolmer, I'm getting a little tired, so if you don't mind—"

"I understand, sir." Greg smiled. "And I want to thank you. You've been very helpful." He rose. "Just one other thing. The location of this place we've been talking about. If you could be more specific—"

Bernie frowned. "All I remember, it was east of Benedict. Dirt road, proba-bly been washed out for years now." He hesitated. "Come to think, the place must have been burned out in that big fire back in the Sixties."

"I could look it up," Greg said. "Fire Department records."

"Don't waste your time. The place wasn't even in Beverly Hills city limits, or L.A. either. Area up there is no-man's-land, which is why the house could operate. Nobody was sure who had jurisdiction."

"I see." Greg turned. "Thanks again."

The old man walked him to the door. "Don't do it," he said.

"Do what?"

"Don't try going up there. Look, it's none of my affair. But for your own good I'm telling you—"

"Telling me or warning me?"

"Call it advice. From somebody who knows."

"Knows what?"

The old man smiled, but his voice was somber. "That house up there is no place to take a bowling ball."

Greg didn't go up there with a bowling ball.

He didn't even take a Thomas map, because the place Bernie Tanner had told him about wasn't on the map. The area was blank, which meant there was no access unless Greg could locate that dirt road, which might or might not still exist.

It took Greg almost two hours of cursing up and down Benedict before he found the path. And it was scarcely more than that, at best a winding trail. The entrance was so overgrown with scrub that it couldn't be seen from the lane leading to it, and the stretch spiraling around the hillside was invisible from below, choked with weed and sage.

At first Greg wasn't sure it was wide enough even for his small car, but he had to chance it; chance the ruts and ridges and clumps of vegetation that punished tires and driver alike as the little hatchback went into a slow low. Without air-conditioning it was like trying to breathe with a plastic bag over your head, and by the time he was halfway up the hillside he wished he hadn't started.

Or *almost* wished. Only the thought of what might be on the summit kept him going, through the stifle of heat and the buzz of insect swarm.

The car stalled abruptly, and Greg broke into panic-ooze. Then the transmission kicked in again, and he sweated some more as a bump in the road sent the hatchback veering left, pitching Greg against the door. Beneath underbrush bordering a curve he caught a sudden sickening glimpse of the emptiness just beyond the edge, an emptiness ending in a tangle of treetops a thousand feet below.

Greg fought the wheel, and the car lurched back on an even course. The road must have been better in the old days; even so, it was one bitch of a trip to make just to go bowling. But that was Bernie Tanner's business and Bernie Tanner's road.

Greg's own road stretched back a lot farther than the bottom of this hill, all the way back to Tex Taylor, a onetime cowboy star at the Motion Picture Country Home. He had all those stories about the old days in Hollywood, and that's all Greg had wanted at first: just some kind of lead-in he could work up into a piece for one of those checkout-counter rags. He'd been selling that kind of stuff long enough to get used to the idea he'd never win a Pulitzer Prize.

But what the dying western wino told him gave sudden startling hope of another kind of prize—one that might have awaited presentation for nearly half a century up there at what Tex Taylor called the House of Pain. That's what he said its name was, after the Asian woman took over and began to give quality time to S-and-M freaks. Maybe it was all a crock, but it sounded possible, certainly worth a trip up there to find out.

Trouble was that Tex Taylor was borderline senile and couldn't remember exactly where this weirdo whorehouse was located. But he did, finally, come up with the name of somebody he'd seen there in the glory days. And that's how Greg got hold of Bernie Tanner.

Greg wondered if Bernie had any money. Today anything with a Beverly Hills address could probably fetch a mil or so on the current market. Maybe Bernie would pay him a mil or so just for old time's sake, just out of pride.

And there were others like Bernie still around, stars and directors and producers who were bankable way back when; some of them had saved their money or put it into real estate and led comfortable, quiet lives in Bel Air or Holmby Hills. If Bernie would pay a million, how much would all the others be willing to fork over, given the proper motivation?

Greg grinned at the thought. And then, as the car swung around the last curve, his grin widened.

He had reached the summit. And on the summit was the house.

Hey, it wasn't the Taj Mahal or Buckingham Palace or even the men's washroom at the Universal Tour. But the bottom line was it hadn't burned or gone down in an earthquake or been bulldozed by a developer. It was still here, standing in shadowy silhouette against the late afternoon sun.

Greg took a flashlight from the glove compartment and clipped it to his belt. Then he reached into the compartment again and found there was just enough left in the envelope for a little toot, enough to keep him bright-eyed and bushy-tailed while he did whatever he'd have to do up here. He waited for the rush, then got out and lifted the hood to let the steam escape. There'd be no water up here, and probably no gas or electricity; they must have had their own generator.

He stared up at the two-story structure. Frame, of course; nobody could have hauled machinery here for stone or concrete construction. The roof had lost its share of shingles, and paint peeled from boards that had once been white, but the building's bulk was impressive. Half a dozen boarded-up windows were ranked on either side of the front door: tall windows for a tall house. Greg closed his eyes and for a moment day was night and the windows blazed with the light of a thousand candles, the front door opened wide in welcome, the classic cars rolled up the driveway, headlights aglitter, wheels gleaming with chrome. And off behind the distant hills the moon was rising, rising over the House of Pain.

It was the toot, of course, and now moonlight shimmered into sunlight and he was back in the teeth of searing heat, radiator-boil, insect-buzz.

Greg walked over to the double door. Its weathered, sun-blistered surface barred intrusion, and at waist level the divided doors were secured by lock and chain. Both were rusty; too much to expect that he could just walk up and yank his way in.

But it happened. The chain gave, then came free in his fist, covering his palm and fingers with powdery particles of rust from the parted links. He tugged and the door swung outward. Hinges screeched.

Greg was in the house and the house was in him.

Its shadows entered his eyes, its silence invaded his ears, its dust and decay filled his lungs. How long had it been since these windows were first boarded, this door locked? How many years had the house stood empty in the dark?

Houses that once were thronged with people, throbbed to their pleasure and their pain—houses like this were hungry for life.

Greg withdrew the flashlight from his belt, flicking it on and fanning the beam for inspection. *What a dump!*

He was standing in a foyer with a solid wall directly ahead, archways opening at left and right. He moved right, along a carpet thickly strewn with dust long undisturbed, and found himself in a room that he imagined must take up most of this wing. A huge Oriental rug covered the floor; its design was obscured and fraying, but Greg thought he could detect the outline of a dragon. Sofas and chairs were grouped along three sides beneath gilt-framed paintings which, Greg noted, might have served as centerfolds for the *Kama Sutra.* Angled at the far corner was a piano, a concert grand. Once upon a time somebody had spent a lot of money furnishing this place, but right now it needed maid service.

Greg's flashlight crawled the walls, searching for shelves and bookcases, but there were none. The fourth side of the room was covered by a row of tattered drapes hung before the boarded-up windows. The drapery may also have displayed the dragon pattern, but outlines had faded; its fiery breath was long extinguished.

Greg crossed the foyer and went into the other wing. It turned out to be a bar, and at one time may have resembled Rick's place in *Casablanca,* but now the set was struck. The room was a tangle of up-ended tables and overturned wooden chairs, flanked by booths on two walls and tattered drapery on the third. Along the fourth wall was the bar, with a big mirror behind it, bordered on both sides by shelves and cupboards that had once displayed bottles and glasses but now held only heaps of shard. The mirror itself was cracked and mottled with mold. *Here's looking at you, kid.*

At one side of the bar a door led to what must have been the kitchen; on the other side an archway framed the base of a staircase beyond. Skirting the maze of tables and chairs, Greg headed for the archway.

Upstairs would be the bedrooms and maybe the private quarters of the Marquess or whatever she called herself. The place looked as if it had been abandoned in a hurry; the padlocked door and boarded-up windows may have been the results of a return visit. But why leave all the furnishings? Greg had no answer, but he hoped to find one. And find what else might also have been abandoned.

The stairs' worn padding muffled his footsteps, but creaking began when he reached the long hallway off the upper landing. It echoed again as he opened and closed the doors lining both sides of the corridor.

All led to bedrooms, each with its own indecorous decor. Here lay a round bed surrounded and surmounted by mirrors, but the sumptuous bedspread was riddled with moth-holes and the mirrors reflected only the light of Greg's flashlight beam. In another room stood a bare marble slab with metal cuffs and an assortment of chains hanging from ends and sides. The marble top was flecked, the metal attachments reddened with rust, not blood. And the whips on the wall rack dangled impotently; the case of knives and needles and surgical shears held pain captive through the empty years.

Empty years, empty rooms. Wall-mural obscenities turned into absurdities by the crisscross of cracks, the random censorship of fading over decades of decay.

But where were those private quarters: an office, someplace to keep the books, the files, the cash, and maybe—just maybe—what he was looking for? He hadn't gone through all this just to chase shadows. What the hell was he doing here anyway, prowling through a deserted whorehouse at sunset? The johns didn't come to these places looking for starkness and desolation; tricks were supposed to be welcomed. But what had he found except rot and ruin, a bar full of broken bottles, a parlor piano that grinned at him with keys like rows of yellowed teeth? Damn it, why didn't somebody tend to a customer? *Company, girls!*

Greg came to the end of the corridor, reached the last room on the left. There was nothing here now, and maybe never had been. Tex Taylor was lying, the old rummy had no proof, and he was just doing a number like the old ham he was, using Greg as an audience for the big deathbed-revelation scene. Who said people had to tell the truth just because they were dying?

He opened the door on a bedroom just like all the others, dark and deserted: bare walls and bare bureau top, empty chair and empty bed.

At least that's what he thought at first glance. But when he looked again he saw the shadow. A dark shadow, lying on the bed.

And now, in the flashlight's beam, the shadow turned to gold.

There was a golden girl lying on the bed, a golden girl with a jet-black halo of hair framing an almost feline face—slanted eyes closed in slumber above high cheekbones, coral curvature of lips relaxed in repose. The flashlight beam swept across her nudity, its light lending luster to the gold of her flesh.

Only one detail marred perfection. As Greg stared down he saw the spider. The big black spider, emerging from her pubic nest and crawling slowly upward across her naked belly.

Greg stifled his gasp as he realized the girl was dead.

She opened her eyes.

She opened her eyes and smiled up at him, opened her mouth and flicked a thin pink tongue in a sensual circle over the coral lips. Her smile widened, revealing twin razor-rows of teeth.

Now, still smiling, the girl sat up. She raised both arms, hands coming to rest on either side of the throat hidden by the dark tumble of her hair. The long fingers splayed, tightening their grip as if trying to wrench the head free.

Then the girl tugged, lifting her head off her neck.

She was still smiling.

And Greg was still gasping as he turned, stumbled from the room, down the hall and the stairs, through the littered bar below, the cobwebbed foyer. Then the door at last: *open fast, don't look back, slam it tight.*

The house had been dark, but now it was dark outside as well, and Greg was grateful he'd somehow managed to retain his flashlight. He ran to the car, keyed the ignition, sent the hatchback circling to the spot where the road wound down, down in the dark, around narrow curves, twisting trees. It didn't matter as long as he kept going down, going away from there, that place and that thing he'd seen—

Or *thought* he'd seen.

Someone doesn't just reach up and lift her head off her neck; nobody can do such a thing, loosening the red, blood-choked strands of the arteries and the darker filaments of veins all twined against the central cord of the esophagus with a flashlight beam shining on its coating of slime. You don't imagine details like that; you have to see them. And he *had* seen, it had happened, this was real.

But what was it?

Greg didn't know, but Bernie would. That had to be why the old man warned him about going up there, going to where it waited in the dark.

The clock on the dash told Greg it was 9:30. Most elderly people go to bed early, but a few stay up for the news. And tonight Bernie would be one of them, because Greg had news for him.

It took a half-hour to get down, but by the time he pulled up, parked and knocked on the front door his course was clear: this time he was going to get some answers.

The door opened on Bernie Tanner's startled stare. "Mr. Kolmer?" There was surprise in his voice, whisky on his breath.

"Didn't think I'd be back?" Greg said. "Thought she'd get me, is that it?"

"I don't know what you're talking about."

"Don't hand me that!" Greg's voice rose.

"Please, not so loud. I got neighbors—"

"You'll get new ones in Forest Lawn if you try to dump on me again." Greg tugged at the door. "Open up."

Bernie obeyed quickly, then closed the door even more quickly after his self-invited guest had entered. Turning, the old man lurched toward his chair. Greg noted the bottle on the table and the half-filled tumbler beside it. The old man picked up his glass and gestured. "Drink?"

"Never mind that." Greg seated himself on the sofa; its faded fabric reeked of alcohol and stale cigar smoke. "Let's have it," he said.

Bernie avoided his gaze. "Look, if something's wrong it's not my fault. I told you not to go up there."

"Sure. But it's what you didn't tell me that made trouble."

The old man shook his head. "I didn't think you'd go. I didn't think you or anyone else could find the place, even if it was still standing after—"

"After what?"

Bernie tried to push the question away with his hand. "Look, I told you all I can—"

"Maybe you'll have more to say after I steer the law up there to take a look around."

Bernie gulped air, then gulped the contents of his glass. "All right, I'll level. That place didn't close down because the madam got married. She got murdered."

"Keep talking."

The old man poured himself another drink. "This fella Tim, the one I told you used to go up there with me. I said I didn't know what became of him after I quit going. Well, I lied."

"Why?"

"I didn't want to get involved. It happened so long ago and it wouldn't do any good. You'd figure I was crazy, the way I figured Tim was when he told me."

"Told you what?"

"About the hookers up there, the Orientals the new madam brought in. He said they were some kind of vampires. If you dozed off, fell asleep, they'd suck your blood." The old man paused. "He showed me toothmarks on his neck."

"He should have gone to the police."

"Do you think they'd believe him any more than I did? Instead he went to Trenk, Ulrich Trenk—you wouldn't remember him, he did some horror flicks for the indies back then."

"*Blood of the Beast.*" Greg nodded. "*Crawlers.* I know the titles but I never saw them."

"Nobody did," Bernie said. "They got shelved before release. And so did Trenk. His stuff was too strong for those days. Trouble with him, he believed in what he did—not the lousy scripts, but the premises. Ghosts, vampires, werewolves, all that crap. And he believed Tim, because he'd heard some other things about the place up there, about the way bats flew around and—"

"Never mind that. Tell me what happened!"

Bernie reached for his drink. "Word was that Trenk went up there with Tim and three other guys who'd been customers and got suspicious; of what, God only knows. But there was some kind of hassle and the bottom line is the place closed down, everybody left, end of story."

"I thought you said the madam was murdered."

Bernie frowned. "Tim told me he'd been the one who killed her. He told me because he was dying down at the old Cedars of Lebanon hospital, with what they thought was some rare kind of blood disease. They'd only let me talk to him for five minutes; when I leaned on him for details he said to come back tomorrow."

"And—?"

"He died that same night." The old man swallowed his drink. "Maybe it's just as well I didn't hear the rest. Nobody else who went up with Tim ever said a word about it. Trenk went back to Europe, but he'd kept his mouth shut, too."

"What about those bats?"

"All I know is what Tim told me, and what he said didn't make much sense. Don't forget, he was dying, probably hallucinating."

"Probably," Greg said. He wondered if he should ask another question, but it wasn't worth the risk. The way Bernie talked, it didn't sound as if he even suspected, and if that was the case there was no sense giving him a clue.

The old man thought Tim was hallucinating. If Greg told him about the girl in the house, would he say that was a hallucination too?

Could be. After all, Greg did have himself a toot before going in, and it wasn't as little as he liked to tell himself it was. Maybe that washed-up cowboy actor was on something too—either that or just jiving him. But the cowboy was dead, Bernie's friend was dead, and Bernie looked as if he'd stayed up way past his bedtime.

Greg stood up. "I'll be going now," he said.

Bernie blinked. "Aren't you going to tell me what happened to you up there?"

"Nothing. It's just a spooky old house, and I guess I got carried away." Greg walked to the door, opened it, then glanced back at the old man slumped in his chair. "Just in case you've been worrying, let me relieve your mind. I didn't see any bats."

So much for his good deed for the day.

Now it was time to do a good deed for himself. It had been a long time since lunch. Driving off, Greg turned onto Olympic and headed for a mini-mall offering a choice of franchised junk food. He chose the place with the best grease-smells and wolfed down more than his diet dictated: two burgers with everything, extra fries, coffee and a shake. He hated pigging out like this, but right now it was all he could afford. If tonight had been different he might be eating at Morton's.

As it was, perhaps he ought to consider himself lucky just to be alive. There was no sense stewing about the rest.

Driving home he reached his decision before he reached his destination. Whether what he'd seen was real or the product of his imagination, one thing was certain: he didn't want to see it again.

When Greg pulled into his parking space under the apartment it was close to midnight. The close-to-witching hour when the unholy hosts rise from their graves—Leno, Letterman, Arsenio, reading their ad-libs to the cackling crowd, welcoming their guests with all the grace of Dracula greeting Renfield, then draining their blood—

Now where had all that come from? Riding the elevator up to the third floor, he had the answer. Damn Bernie and his vampire talk. And as for what Greg had seen, or thought he'd seen, there was an answer for that too—an answer he'd have to face sooner or later. And after tonight he knew it had better be soon. When the spiders come out of their hiding places and the sleeping beauties start taking off their heads, you'd better stop. Going up there had been enough of a bad trip in itself.

First thing he got into the apartment, he'd flush the rest of his little stash down the tube. If not, he'd be going down the tube himself one of these days. The time to think about it was over; this was *do it* time.

Only it didn't quite work out that way. When Greg opened the door and reached for the light-switch, a voice from the dark said "Freeze!" and that's what he did.

Footsteps sounded softly behind him and a faint gust of air fanned his neck as someone closed the front door.

Beside him a switch clicked on. Against the background of the cluttered little living room, the light of a lamp in the corner framed the outline of a man wearing jacket and jeans. But Greg's attention focused on the glint of a gun in the intruder's hand.

The gun gestured.

"Hands behind your head. That's right. Now move to the sofa and sit."

As Greg obeyed he got another glimpse of the gun. *Piece like that could blow your head off. God, what's happening? I need a fix.*

The intruder edged into a chair on the other side of the coffee table, and now the lamp highlighted eyes and cheekbones and skin tone.

For a moment Greg evoked an image of the golden girl he'd seen—or had he?—earlier this evening. But what he was seeing here was unquestionably real. A middle-aged man with coarse, close-cropped black hair: obviously an Asian or Asian-American, obviously not the friendly type. A man with an attitude, and a gun.

Just a snort, a sniff, anything—

The man's stare was cold. So was his voice. "Put your arms down. Both hands in your lap, palms up."

Greg complied and the man nodded. "My name is Ibraham," he said.

"Abraham?"

"Perhaps it was once, when Muslim rule began. But I'm called Ibraham in Kita Bharu."

"I don't know that country."

"It's a city. The capital of what used to be Kelanton, in Malaya." The man frowned. "I'm not here to give geography lessons."

Greg kept his palms up, his voice steady. "What are you here for?"

"I want you to take me to the house."

"House? I don't know—"

"Please, Mr. Kolmer. Your friend told me you went there earlier this evening."

"When did you see Bernie?"

"About an hour ago. He was kind enough to furnish your address, so when I found you were not home I took the liberty of inviting myself in."

The bathroom window, Greg told himself. *Why do I keep forgetting to lock it when I go out?*

That wasn't the question which needed answering at the moment. There was another one more important, so he asked it. "What did Bernie tell you?"

"Everything he knew." Ibraham's slight shrug didn't cause his aim to waver. "Enough for me to guess the rest." A nod didn't jar the gun either. "That story about researching an article—it's not true, is it, Mr. Kolmer? You went to that house looking for something you didn't find."

"How do you know?"

"If you found it you wouldn't have gone back to Tanner. Of course he didn't know what you were looking for, or he'd have told me that too." Ibraham lifted his gaze: eyes of onyx in slanted settings. "Tell me what you were after."

"I can't," Greg said. "Swear to God, I don't know."

"But you have some idea?" Ibraham leaned forward. "The truth—now."

Greg stared at the gun and its muzzle stared back. "The cowboy who told me about the place said there was a blackmail operation. This new madam was bugging rooms, getting pictures, filming with hidden cameras, using two-way mirrors and whatever else they had back in those days.

"There was a market then; magazines like *Confidential* paid plenty for such stuff, particularly if stars were involved. But nothing about the place ever showed up— I know, because I waded through library files. So my hunch was the material— photos, film, audio tape, whatever—never was submitted. Something happened to close the house down before the stuff could be peddled. Which meant—"

"It could still be there," Ibraham said, and nodded.

"How did you hear about all this?" Greg asked.

"From my mother. She was there when it happened."

"At the house?"

"She worked as a maid." For the first time there was a hint of amusement in Ibraham's eyes. "You must understand she was very young. The lady, the one they called the Marquess, adopted her after both my grandparents were killed in the war. When my mother came with her to this country she was only fifteen. Some of the other girls, the ones who did what was expected in such a place, weren't much older. But the Marquess protected my mother from everything, including full knowledge of what she was involved with. Of course she learned in time. But when she did, it was too late." Ibraham's eyes were somber now. "She was lucky. On the night everything happened she wasn't at the house. The Marquess' chauffeur had driven her down to a Westwood laundromat. I don't know how they found out about what took place, but news got to them somehow and they never went back. The chauffeur had a substantial bank account; he'd been the Marquess' lover. On the journey back to Kelanton he became my mother's lover as well. He died in a Johore brothel the day I was born.

"I never knew any of this until just before my mother died, several years ago. What she told me made me suspect the same thing you did, but I couldn't get over here immediately." Ibraham glanced at the gun. "In my country there is still a war going on."

"You're in the army?"

"The military became my career after I graduated from university in Singapore. Now I wish to retire."

Greg shifted cautiously. "Look, do you have to do this *shtick* with the gun?"

Ibraham lowered the weapon. "Probably not. After all, we're partners."

Greg fought for self-control, and lost. "No way!"

"It's the only way," Ibraham said. "You know how to find the house. And my mother told me what's hidden there. We go together. Tonight."

Greg shook his head. "Didn't Bernie tell you what happened to me—what I saw?"

"I know." Ibraham seemed to have no problem with self-control, Greg noted—but then, he had the gun. "My mother warned me. I know what to do."

Greg took a deep breath. "Maybe so. But do it tomorrow, when we can go up there in daylight."

"No. We can't afford delay."

"Do you think Bernie might start talking—"

"Only through an *ouija* board." Ibraham glanced down at his gun.

Fear iced Greg's spine. "Why?" he murmured.

"The old man was the only one who'd know where we were going. No sense taking chances."

"How can you say that, knowing what we might run into up there?"

"What we're going after is worth the risk. I'm sure you're aware of that or else you'd never have gotten into this in the first place. That house holds a fortune, and we're going to get it."

Greg glanced at the gun. "And when we get it, you'll get me," he said.

"I give you my word." Ibraham rose. "Either go with me or stay behind. Like Bernie."

Greg swallowed hard. "Look, man, I've had a rough night, you know? Let me get my medication—"

"What are you on?"

Greg told him, and Ibraham gestured quickly. "You're not going up there stoned," he said. "Could be bad for your health."

A muzzle moved to press against Greg's spine; that was bad for his health too.

"Move," said Ibraham.

And they did, in Greg's car, with him behind the wheel, Ibraham at his side, and the gun riding against his rib cage. The midnight air was humid; both men were perspiring moments after the car swung out into the deserted street.

"Roll down your window," Greg said.

"Don't you have an air conditioner?"

"Can't afford it."

"You can, after tonight."

Ibraham was smiling, but Greg frowned. "This thing I saw up there—what is it?"

"*Penangallan.* A kind of vampire, but not exactly."

"Meaning what?"

"A *penangallan* doesn't need to rest in grave-earth or coffin. Like your western vampires it seeks human blood for nourishment, but it can hibernate for years if necessary. Maybe the difference is in their metabolism. Vampires require a greater supply of energy to walk abroad each night. But the *penangallan* survives indefinitely in some sort of suspended animation. And when it does move, it flies."

Greg nodded. "You mean it turns itself into some kind of a bat."

Ibraham shook his head. "That's just superstition. The *penangallan* still retains human form—or part of its human form."

"I don't get it."

"These creatures can detach their heads from their bodies. And the head has the power of flight. When the head is removed, the stomach and intestines are pulled out and stay attached to it, receiving the blood it drinks."

The words triggered Greg's memory—just a flash, but enough. *The golden girl, sitting up and lifting her head from the open stump of the neck.* He'd seen it. It was true.

He felt a jarring movement and beside him Ibraham stirred in his seat. "Watch what you're doing," he said.

What Greg was doing was turning onto the concealed side road. Had they really come this far this quickly? Of course there was no traffic up here, no lights.

Strange how easy it was to locate the hidden opening this second time around, even in the dark. But then again, it was associated with something he wasn't likely to forget.

The car entered and moved upward in a tunnel formed by the overhanging trees lining the roadway. Greg switched headlights, but even the brights were of little help here. Then the trees thinned, but the underbrush thickened and the car began to lurch around the sharp curves.

"Watch it!" Ibraham warned.

But Greg had already warned himself with the memory of what lay ahead. *A head*—

"I can't cut it," he said. "We've got to wait. Tomorrow. We'll do it tomorrow."

"Now." The gun jabbed against his ribs; Ibraham's voice jabbed his ear. "You're going now. Either behind the wheel or dumped in the trunk."

"You're bluffing—"

"That's what the old man thought."

Greg's hands were wet on the wheel, but they stayed there as the car inched forward over the rutted roadway and climbed around a curve. Now he glanced at the Malayan. "Suppose we're wrong. Suppose we don't find anything there?"

"I told you what my mother said. It's there and we'll find it."

"One thing I don't understand," Greg said. "If the stuff they had on their customers was so valuable, why wasn't it used?"

"My mother wondered about that too, but she didn't learn the plan until later, from the Marquess' lover."

"Plan?"

"Bit by bit the pieces fit together. The Marquess had bought the place with more than just profit in mind. Back in Kelanton she had a reputation as a *pawang*—a sorceress, you'd call it—and she gathered together and brought the *penangallans*, which she controlled for her own purposes. Which were to use blackmail money to take over other vice operations and gradually gain political power in the area. The *penangallans* would deal with those who stood in her way. She was ready to carry out her plan when the end came. You know the rest."

Greg frowned. "Your mother could have gone to the police—"

"She was a fifteen-year-old girl, an illegal immigrant with forged papers, who spoke almost no English. Even if she'd found a way to contact the authorities—do you think anyone would go along with what she said about hookers who remove their heads, and all the rest of it?"

Greg had no answer for that, only another question as they angled up the torturous trail. "The thing I saw," he said. "Why would it still be there after all these years? Why didn't it leave the place when the Marquess was killed?"

"The *penangallan* flies low," Ibraham said. "It can't soar like a bat, and it must protect its dangling stomach sac and intestines from harm. In Malaysia, homes are often guarded by garlands of *Jenyu* leaves hung on doors and windows. The *penangallan* fears the *Jenyu* plant's sharp thorns." He glanced at the looming pines and the clumps of underbrush clustered beneath them. "Here your hillsides are covered with cacti and all kinds of spiky vegetation. It would rip the creatures' guts if they tried to escape."

"But they wouldn't have to fly," Greg said. "They could go down staying in their bodies just as they did up there."

Ibraham shrugged. "A *penangallan* preserves its body by drinking fresh blood. Without it the body will decay just like any other corpse. So if they did try to come down in human form before decay set in, there'd be problems. I don't think they'd last very long if word got out that human heads were flying around Beverly Hills and sucking blood in Bel Air. Besides, they'd have to have a place to hide. And to store the vinegar."

"Vinegar?"

"If the *penangallan* flies, its entrails swell up when exposed to the open air. So afterward it must soak its lower parts in a jar or vat of vinegar to shrivel the stomach and bowels to normal size. Then it fits them back into the body when the head is replaced."

No way, Greg told himself. *Either this guy is crazy or I am. There are no such things, no such place, no house—*

They rounded the turn and there it was.

If the place had looked ghostly by day, it looked ghastly in the grayish shroud of moonlight filtering through lowering clouds. Its dark silhouette seemed to slant toward them as the hatchback halted amidst spirals of steam from the hood. Greg stared numbly at the house. If it was real, then what about the rest—

"Out," Ibraham said.

Greg hesitated, then took a deep breath. "Look, I've told you everything I know, everything that happened. There's no reason for me to go in again with you now."

"What about the material you were looking for?"

Greg took another deep breath. "I've changed my mind. I don't want any part of it."

"Afraid?"

"After what you told me? Damned right I am."

"You expect me to go in by myself?" Ibraham asked. "So you can drive off and leave me stranded?"

"I'll wait, I swear it. Hey, you can take my car keys—"

"I'm taking you."

The gun rose, and so did Greg. Ibraham tensed as Greg's hand went to the glove compartment, then relaxed as the younger man brought out his flashlight.

Together they left the car and moved to the entrance in silence. Even the sound of the wind had died; everything had died here.

Greg halted before the door, and his companion eyed the broken lock. "You're making a mistake," Greg said. "If what you told me is true, a gun won't protect us from that thing I saw."

"There are other ways," Ibraham said, raising the weapon as he spoke. "Inside."

Inside was pitch blackness pierced by the pinpoint flashlight beam. Greg adjusted it so that they stood in a wider circle of radiance, but the light was dim against the darkness beyond. The silence itself seemed more intense than outside; there was nothing to disturb it here, nothing until they came.

"Leave the front door open," Greg whispered. "We might want to get out of here in a hurry."

Ibraham shrugged. "As you wish." Moving forward, he peered toward the right archway. "What's in there?"

Greg described the parlor, and his captor nodded.

Now he glanced to his left. "And here?"

"The bar."

The two men halted just past the archway as the flashlight beam roamed the room.

"All that damage," Ibraham said. "This must be where the fighting took place." He peered at the stairs on the far side.

Greg spoke quickly. "You don't have to go up there. I told you there's nothing in those bedrooms."

"Except the last one," Ibraham countered. "That's reason enough. We've got to go up."

"You know what's there. You admitted your gun won't help."

Ignoring him, Ibraham scanned the tile shambles of the littered floor. His eyes swept over the toppled tables, overturned chairs and broken glass. His eyes halted. "This will do," he said.

Greg followed his gaze to a chair turned upside down, two of its legs wrenched half-free from the base of the seat. "What do you mean?"

Ibraham told him what he meant. He told him what to do, then watched, gun in hand, while Greg did it. Getting the chair leg loose wasn't difficult, and locating a sharp knife in a drawer behind the bar wasn't a problem for him either. The hard part was whittling away at the wooden chair leg until the end was trimmed into a tapering shaft with a narrow point. It was Ibraham, rummaging through shelving beneath the bar counter, who came up with the bung-starter.

"Good," he said. "We're ready."

Greg didn't feel ready. He felt he needed out of here. Ibraham had already goaded him to the base of the stairs, and it was there that he turned.

"Hey, man," he said. "I thought we came here to look for that stuff."

"We will."

"You're wasting your time. It's not upstairs."

"But something else is. And we won't be safe looking around here until we dispose of it."

The gun muzzle guided Greg up the staircase. In the upper hallway the floorboards creaked, and so did the doors as Ibraham opened them in turn. But it was the sound of his own heartbeat that Greg heard as they reached the end of the hall and stood before the last door on the left.

It was Greg who opened the door, but Ibraham was the one who gasped as the flashlight beam encircled the burnished golden beauty of the naked girl on the bed.

Her eyes were closed, and this time she did not stir. Ibraham gestured impatiently, but Greg stood immobile at the bedside, staring down at the golden girl.

This was what he'd needed. Proof that he hadn't freaked out from dropping acid, that what he'd seen here before was real.

And if it was real, then so was the rest of what he'd seen, what had sent him screaming down the hillside. That's why he was standing here now, holding the sharpened stake. He knew what he must do, and this was the worst reality of all.

He took a step backward. He couldn't go through with this, no way, now was the time to get out of here—

The muzzle of the gun bit against his spine. Greg heard the faint click signaling the release of the safety catch.

The girl on the bed heard it too, for she stirred for a moment, stirred but didn't awaken.

Once she did, once she opened her eyes, it would be too late. Greg remembered the rows of pointed teeth, remembered the hands that tugged the head away from the neck swiftly, so very swiftly. Which meant he had to be swift too.

He belted the flashlight.

He lifted the stake with both hands.

Gasping with effort, he plunged it down into the cleft between the golden breasts.

Then her eyes did open, wide. Her lips retracted and he saw the teeth, saw the talons rise to slash at his face, claw at his wrists as he held the stake fast.

Snakelike she squirmed, and like a snake she hissed, but Ibraham was standing on the other side of the bed and he brought the broad head of the bung-starter down, driving the stake deep.

The golden hands tore frantically at the shaft imbedded between the golden breasts, but Greg's grip remained unbroken. He held the stake firmly as Ibraham hammered it home. There was a single shattering shriek as a gout of crimson geysered upward, then sudden silence.

Talons loosened their hold; the golden face fell back on the pillow, its slant-eyed stare veiled by the billowing black hair. No sound issued from the open mouth, and the blood around the base of the stake ceased further flow. Mercifully, there was no movement or hint of movement to come. The golden girl was dead.

Greg turned away, panting after his exertion, filling his laboring lungs with the acrid odor of blood. His stomach cramped and for a moment he thought he might pass out. Then he became aware that Ibraham was speaking.

"—not finished yet. But it should be safe to go now."

Greg unhooked his flashlight. "Go where?"

"To get what we came for." Ibraham motioned him to the door, and Greg noticed that he was again holding the gun.

So nothing had changed, really. Except that they'd come here this crazy midnight to pound a stake into the heart of a dead girl or an undead girl; it didn't matter which, because she was dead now. *We killed her and the stake went in and the blood spurted out just like in those horror movies only this wasn't a movie just a horror, God I need a fix—*

But there was no fix, not in the hall or on the stairs or down at the bar.

Ibraham's gun urged him along to the hall before the mottled mirror on the back wall. "Should be just about here," Ibraham said. He reached out and ran his free hand across the inner edge of the bar, muttering, "If my mother was right." A panel under the bar slid back silently, revealing a black rectangular opening.

"She was," Ibraham said.

Greg's flashlight dipped toward the darkness. "Lower," his captor said. "Must be some stairs."

There were. Greg descended first, beam fanning forward until he reached the bare stone surface below the fourteenth step. Ibraham followed, but this time his gun wasn't aimed at Greg. Like the flashlight, it swerved and circled, as if seeking possible targets in the cavernous cellar before them.

The two men moved slowly, silently. Nothing to hear but the thud of their own footsteps, nothing to see but the beam tracing a path along the stone floor beneath their feet.

Here the air was cooler, but the odor it carried, a mingling of dust and decay, was almost stifling. There was another smell, faint but pungent, which Greg couldn't identify.

Now Ibraham identified it for him. "Vinegar," he said. "Remember, I told you the *penangallan* shrinks its entrails in vinegar in order to squeeze them back down into the body? I was wondering where they kept their supply."

"But we didn't find any others—"

"My mother thought there could be a dozen among the Marquess' girls."

Greg started to speak, but Ibraham waved him to silence. "The scent is almost undetectable here. Probably evaporated."

"I'm not worried about the goddamn smell," Greg said. "But if there are more of those things down here—"

Suddenly his foot struck something, something that clattered as he stumbled back. The flashlight beam dipped down toward the stone surface, sweeping over the sprawled length of arm and leg bones, the ridged rib cage and nacreous neck of the skeleton.

It had no skull.

The rush came so quickly that Greg almost dropped the flashlight. Its beam wavered because his hand was shaking. No skull. No head. It was one of them.

Ibraham moved forward; his harsh whisper echoed through darkness: "Here's another."

Greg raised the flashlight, semicircling its dim beam, then wished he hadn't.

The floor ahead was littered with bones. Some, heaped against the walls, were partially joined: a leg attached to a pelvis, a collarbone to a humerus, radius and ulna to the metacarpals. Two other skeletons were fully articulated but, like the first, they lacked skulls. Greg's stare swept across the scatter, but Ibraham's attention was elsewhere. He skirted the bonepile, threading his way between heaps and jumbles, then approached the makeshift wooden shed rising along the right side of the cellar. More skeletal fragments lay there, piled almost at random, amidst shreds of rotted cloth.

There was a door at the far end of the shed's wall, and Ibraham pulled it open slowly, revealing the wooden shelving ranged along the far side within.

"Get some light over here," he said. Greg started toward him, raising the flashlight. Its beam sought the shelves—long, low shelves bearing wide-mouthed, deep-bodied clay bowls. There were perhaps a dozen pots of them resting side by side like the pots in a florist's shop, but what bloomed in each were not flowers.

Greg stared at the rows of human skulls. And they grinned at him in greeting, grinned as though sharing some grisly secret that only the dead can know.

Ibraham moved beside him. "You see what's happened here? Those bowls must have been filled with vinegar."

"To shrink the intestines." Greg nodded. "But why didn't it work?"

"You can't store liquids in leaky containers," Ibraham explained. "And every one of these bowls is cracked."

Now, peering more closely, Greg could see what he meant. Most of the cracks were visible just above the base of each bowl to form a pattern, almost as though they'd been gouged out by some sharp tool or instrument.

Greg frowned. "Didn't they realize it was wrong to use these?"

"They had no other choice," Ibraham said. "She must have broken them after the raid. Probably that's how they escaped the madam's fate—they hid down here while the raid was going on. Maybe the raiding party killed the bartender too. Stands to reason they took the bodies away and got rid of them." He glanced down at the scattered bones. "But the *penangallans* were safe here. They must have stayed in hiding a long time, and when they came out they were hungry. And you know what happens when there's no food in the house."

Greg nodded. "You go out to eat."

"Exactly. They flew off to try their luck at hunting. But there's not much around, just birds and perhaps some small game. Since they couldn't fly down from here, that's all they could find. The only way they could survive was to hibernate." Ibraham gestured. "The one upstairs was smarter. She must have known how little success they'd have out there, because she didn't go. And when they returned and came down here she had a surprise for them."

"Like you said, she'd broken the bowls."

"That's what I figure. While their bodies rested out in the cellar, they settled their heads and entrails in the bowls here, but most of the vinegar leaked out quickly; before it could be effective it was gone. The girl we saw upstairs was gone too, after locking them in. She probably had her own bowl and vinegar supply tucked away somewhere upstairs, because she'd already planned what she was going to do."

"But what *could* she do?" Greg said.

"You still don't get it." Ibraham glanced down. "Don't these bones and skeletons tell their own story? The heads rested helplessly in those dried-out jars while the stomachs burst and rotted away. And trapped out here, the headless bodies, blind and squirming in the dark."

Greg grimaced. "And the thing upstairs—?"

"She ate them," Ibraham said. "That's what kept her alive all these years." He nodded at the skeletons and the piles of bones. "She didn't need to fly in search of food. Not with a dozen bodies down here, bodies that still moved, bodies filled with blood. She stripped the flesh from these bones bit by bit, sucked arteries and veins dry. It must have been done over a long period, and most of the while she slept, just as we found her."

Greg's stomach knotted convulsively. "I'm outta here," he panted, turning to seek the stairs.

"First we get what we came for." Ibraham's weapon pressed against Greg from behind as he climbed. And back upstairs the gun prodded Greg to the rear of the room.

"Take a look behind the staircase," Ibraham ordered. "The madam could have had her office under there."

Greg swore silently. Of course the office would be in some place like that, close to the action but not easy for outsiders to spot. If he'd only looked around more carefully before going upstairs on the first visit, chances are he might not have had to go upstairs at all. The office would be where the madam kept the stuff. If he'd used his head and thought things through, he wouldn't be here now in the middle of the night, middle of nowhere, this crazy house with that crazy thing upstairs and a crazy gook downstairs pushing a gun into him for half of what they'd find.

"Let's go," the crazy gook was saying. "I tell you it's got to be here."

And that's where they found it, under the stairs. The door was metal, closed but unlocked, and behind it was the office. Or had been, until the intruders burst in, tore the drawers out of desks and filing cabinets, smashed them with crowbars and an ax that still lay atop shelving wrenched from a battered bookcase on the right wall.

Across from it, on the left wall, was an open safe.

Open, and empty.

Greg blinked at the bare steel shelf. "Gone; those bastards took the stuff with them—"

"Take another look," Ibraham said softly.

Greg followed his gaze, traveled with it across the bare concrete floor to the center of the room. His eyes followed a paper trail—or a trail of what had once been paper. Now it was just a brownish-gray muddle of charred shreds speckled with tiny glints from flecks of burned photos. From the trail rose an odor, faint as the scent of vinegar: the reek of long-dead ashes in which all hope lay buried.

"Outta here," Greg whispered.

Ibraham shook his head. "You think I don't know how you feel? I want to forget it ever happened. But before we put it behind us, there's one more job. The *penangallan*—"

"It's dead," Greg said. "We killed it. You know that."

"Not so. Remember, the *penangallan* isn't like other bloodsuckers. As long as the head remains attached to the digestive tract it can still fly and feed. A stake is not enough."

"It's enough for me," Greg told him. "I'm not going to tangle with that thing."

"The stake probably paralyzes it, at least for a time," Ibraham said. "But we can't take chances. We must cut off the head."

"Forget it. I'm finished."

Ibraham ignored him, but his weapon did not.

Would he shoot? Greg thought of Bernie Tanner for a moment and he didn't need an answer. Instead he asked another question. "What do you want me to do?"

Ibraham nodded toward the toppled shelving at his right. "Over there," he said. "Get the ax."

Greg turned, imagining the impact of a bullet in his back. And perhaps it wouldn't have been imagination if they'd found that blackmail material intact. No reason for Ibraham not to shoot him then, kill him and take all the loot; nobody'd ever know. But that could still be true now. If they got rid of the *penangallan*, Ibraham would get rid of him too—because Greg was the only one who could tie him to Bernie Tanner's murder.

So there really wasn't much choice but for Greg to do exactly what he was told: reach out and pick up the ax. But it was his own idea to turn swiftly, raise the ax and bring it down right between Ibraham's eyes.

The gurgle was still dying in his victim's throat as Greg ran, reeling through the office doorway, the barroom, the hall, the open front door.

He squeezed into the car, fumbling for his keys, cursing the broken air conditioner but grateful for the breeze from the windows. The air was still warm and moist, but it was clean, free of must and dust, the scent of vinegar, the mingled odor of stale ashes and fresh blood.

Blood. He'd killed a man; he was a murderer. But nobody knew, nobody would ever know if he played it cool. Even if somebody wandered up to the house there was nothing to connect him with what they'd find. Get himself a set of tires tomorrow and the old tread marks wouldn't match the new. They might get prints off the doorknobs and ax handle, but they'd have nothing to match them with; he'd never been fingerprinted. And they wouldn't be looking for him in the first place, with nothing to go by.

So he was home free, would be now that the car had started, now that he was wheeling down the hillside, with every twist and turn taking him farther away from that damned house and that damned thing; taking him closer to the lights and the streets, streets where you could find a fast fix, find it and forget what had happened. It would just be like a bad trip, he didn't really kill anyone, and there wasn't really anything like that thing with the golden face and the almond eyes and the gleaming, pointed teeth in the crimson mouth he was seeing now in the rearview mirror, rising up from the back seat.

Greg screamed, and so did the brakes of the car as he spun the wheel, spun and lost because there was no way to win, no way to turn from that narrow, tangled trail.

And then the thing was hovering behind him, rising up and swooping forward, its viscera lashing and looping.

The slimy coils twirled and tightened around Greg's neck, and from the stalklike stem above it the golden face dipped, lips fastening on Greg's flesh as the fangs found his throat. Ibraham had been right, after all.

Now Greg knew why a stake through the heart was not enough.

GOOD LADY DUCAYNE

❧

MARY ELIZABETH BRADDON

I

BELLA ROLLESTON HAD MADE UP HER MIND THAT her only chance of earning her bread and helping her mother to an occasional crust was by going out into the great unknown world as companion to a lady. She was willing to go to any lady rich enough to pay her a salary and so eccentric as to wish for a hired companion. Five shillings told off reluctantly from one of those sovereigns which were so rare with the mother and daughter, and which melted away so quickly, five solid shillings, had been handed to a smartly-dressed lady in an office in Harbeck Street, London, W., in the hope that this very Superior Person would find a situation and a salary for Miss Rolleston. The Superior Person glanced at the two half-crowns as they lay on the table where Bella's hand had placed them, to make sure they were neither of them florins, before she wrote a description of Bella's qualifications and requirements in a formidable-looking ledger.

"Age?" she asked, curtly.

"Eighteen, last July."

"Any accomplishments?"

"No; I am not at all accomplished. If I were I should want to be a governess—a companion seems the lowest stage."

"We have some highly accomplished ladies on our books as companions, or chaperon companions."

"Oh, I know!" babbled Bella, loquacious in her youthful candor. "But that is quite a different thing. Mother hasn't been able to afford a piano since I was twelve years old, so I'm afraid I've forgotten how to play. And I have had to help mother with her needlework, so there hasn't been much time to study."

"Please don't waste time upon explaining what you can't do, but kindly tell me anything you can do," said the Superior Person, crushingly, with her pen poised between delicate fingers waiting to write. "Can you read aloud for two or three hours at a stretch? Are you active and handy, an early riser, a good walker, sweet tempered, and obliging?"

"I can say yes to all those questions except about the sweetness. I think I have a pretty good temper, and I should be anxious to oblige anybody who paid for my services. I should want them to feel that I was really earning my salary."

"The kind of ladies who come to me would not care for a talkative companion," said the Person, severely, having finished writing in her book. "My connection lies chiefly among the aristocracy, and in that class considerable deference is expected."

"Oh, of course," said Bella; "but it's quite different when I'm talking to you. I want to tell you all about myself once and forever."

"I am glad it is to be only once!" said the Person, with the edges of her lips.

The Person was of uncertain age, tightly laced in a black silk gown. She had a powdery complexion and a handsome clump of somebody else's hair on the top of her head. It may be that Bella's girlish freshness and vivacity had an irritating effect upon nerves weakened by an eight-hour day in that overheated second floor in Harbeck Street. To Bella the official apartment, with its Brussels carpet, velvet curtains and velvet chairs, and French clock, ticking loud on the marble chimney-piece, suggested the luxury of a palace, as compared with another second floor in Walworth where Mrs. Rolleston and her daughter had managed to exist for the last six years.

"Do you think you have anything on your books that would suit me?" faltered Bella, after a pause.

"Oh, dear, no; I have nothing in view at present," answered the Person, who had swept Bella's half-crowns into a drawer, absent-mindedly, with the tips of her fingers. "You see, you are so very unformed—so much too young to be companion to a lady of position. It is a pity you have not enough education for a nursery governess; that would be more in your line."

"And do you think it will be very long before you can get me a situation?" asked Bella, doubtfully.

"I really cannot say. Have you any particular reason for being so impatient— not a love affair, I hope?"

"A love affair!" cried Bella, with flaming cheeks. "What utter nonsense. I want a situation because mother is poor, and I hate being a burden to her. I want a salary that I can share with her."

"There won't be much margin for sharing in the salary you are likely to get at your age—and with your—very—unformed manners," said the Person, who found Bella's peony cheeks, bright eyes, and unbridled vivacity more and more oppressive.

"Perhaps if you'd be kind enough to give me back the fee I could take it to an agency where the connection isn't quite so aristocratic," said Bella, who—as she told her mother in her recital of the interview—was determined not to be sat upon.

"You will find no agency that can do more for you than mine," replied the Person, whose harpy fingers never relinquished coin. "You will have to wait for your opportunity. Yours is an exceptional case: but I will bear you in mind, and if anything suitable offers I will write to you. I cannot say more than that."

The half-contemptuous bend of the stately head, weighted with borrowed hair, indicated the end of the interview. Bella went back to Walworth—tramped sturdily every inch of the way in the September afternoon—and "took off" the Superior Person for the amusement of her mother and the landlady, who lingered in the shabby little sitting-room after bringing in the tea-tray, to applaud Miss Rolleston's "taking off."

"Dear, dear, what a mimic she is!" said the landlady. "You ought to have let her go on the stage, mum. She might have made her fortune as an actress."

II

BELLA WAITED AND HOPED, AND LISTENED FOR THE POST-man's knocks which brought such store of letters for the parlors and the first floor, and so few for that humble second floor, where mother and daughter sat sewing with hand and with wheel and treadle, for the greater part of the day. Mrs. Rolleston was a lady by birth and education; but it had been her bad fortune to marry a scoundrel; for the last half-dozen years she had been that worst of widows, a wife whose husband had deserted her. Happily, she was courageous, industrious, and a clever needlewoman; and she had been able just to earn a living for herself and her only child, by making mantles and cloaks for a West-end house. It was not a luxurious living. Cheap lodgings in a shabby street off the Walworth Road, scanty dinners, homely food, well-worn raiment, had been the portion of mother and daughter; but they loved each other so dearly, and Nature had made them both so light-hearted, that they had contrived somehow to be happy.

But now this idea of going out into the world as companion to some fine lady had rooted itself into Bella's mind, and although she idolized her mother, and although the parting of mother and daughter must needs tear two loving hearts into shreds, the girl longed for enterprise and change and excitement, as the pages of old longed to be knights, and to start for the Holy Land to break a lance with the infidel.

She grew tired of racing downstairs every time the postman knocked, only to be told "nothing for you, miss," by the smudgy-faced drudge who picked up the letters from the passage floor. "Nothing for you, miss," grinned the lodging-house drudge, till at last Bella took heart of grace and walked up to Harbeck Street, and asked the Superior Person how it was that no situation had been found for her.

"You are too young," said the Person, "and you want a salary."

"Of course I do," answered Bella; "don't other people want salaries?"

"Young ladies of your age generally want a comfortable home."

"I don't," snapped Bella: "I want to help mother."

"You can call again this day week," said the Person; "or, if I hear of anything in the meantime, I will write to you."

No letter came from the Person, and in exactly a week Bella put on her neatest hat, the one that had been seldomest caught in the rain, and trudged off to Harbeck Street.

It was a dull October afternoon, and there was a greyness in the air which might turn to fog before night. The Walworth Road shops gleamed brightly through that grey atmosphere, and though to a young lady reared in Mayfair or Belgravia such shop-windows would have been unworthy of a glance, they were a snare and temptation for Bella. There were so many things that she longed for, and would never be able to buy.

Harbeck Street is apt to be empty at this dead season of the year, a long, long street, an endless perspective of eminently respectable houses. The Person's office was at the further end, and Bella looked down that long, grey vista almost despairingly, more tired than usual with the trudge from Walworth. As she looked, a carriage passed her, an old-fashioned, yellow chariot, on cee springs, drawn by a pair of high grey horses, with the stateliest of coachmen driving them, and a tall footman sitting by his side.

"It looks like the fairy godmother's coach," thought Bella. "I shouldn't wonder if it began by being a pumpkin."

It was a surprise when she reached the Person's door to find the yellow chariot standing before it, and the tall footman waiting near the doorstep. She was almost afraid to go in and meet the owner of that splendid carriage. She had caught only a glimpse of its occupant as the chariot rolled by, a plumed bonnet, a patch of ermine.

The Person's smart page ushered her upstairs and knocked at the official door. "Miss Rolleston," he announced, apologetically, while Bella waited outside.

"Show her in," said the Person, quickly; and then Bella heard her murmuring something in a low voice to her client.

Bella went in fresh, blooming, a living image of youth and hope, and before she looked at the Person her gaze was riveted by the owner of the chariot.

Never had she seen anyone as old as the old lady sitting by the Person's fire: a little old figure, wrapped from chin to feet in an ermine mantle; a withered, old face under a plumed bonnet—a face so wasted by age that it seemed only a pair of eyes and a peaked chin. The nose was peaked, too, but between the sharply pointed chin and the great, shining eyes, the small, aquiline nose was hardly visible.

"This is Miss Rolleston, Lady Ducayne."

Claw-like fingers, flashing with jewels, lifted a double eyeglass to Lady Ducayne's shining black eyes, and through the glasses Bella saw those unnaturally bright eyes magnified to a gigantic size, and glaring at her awfully.

"Miss Torpinter has told me all about you," said the old voice that belonged to the eyes. "Have you good health? Are you strong and active, able to eat well, sleep well, walk well, able to enjoy all that there is good in life?"

"I have never known what it is to be ill, or idle," answered Bella.

"Then I think you will do for me."

"Of course, in the event of references being perfectly satisfactory," put in the Person.

"I don't want references. The young woman looks frank and innocent. I'll take her on trust."

"So like you, dear Lady Ducayne," murmured Miss Torpinter.

"I want a strong young woman whose health will give me no trouble."

"You have been so unfortunate in that respect," cooed the Person, whose voice and manner were subdued to a melting sweetness by the old woman's presence.

"Yes, I've been rather unlucky," grunted Lady Ducayne.

"But I am sure Miss Rolleston will not disappoint you, though certainly after your unpleasant experience with Miss Tomson, who looked the picture of health—and Miss Blandy, who said she had never seen a doctor since she was vaccinated—"

"Lies, no doubt," muttered Lady Ducayne, and then turning to Bella, she asked, curtly, "You don't mind spending the winter in Italy, I suppose?"

In Italy! The very word was magical. Bella's fair young face flushed crimson.

"It has been the dream of my life to see Italy," she gasped.

From Walworth to Italy! How far, how impossible such a journey had seemed to that romantic dreamer.

"Well, your dream will be realized. Get yourself ready to leave Charing Cross by the train deluxe this day week at eleven. Be sure you are at the station a quarter before the hour. My people will look after you and your luggage."

Lady Ducayne rose from her chair, assisted by her crutch-stick, and Miss Torpinter escorted her to the door.

"And with regard to salary?" questioned the Person on the way.

"Salary, oh, the same as usual—and if the young woman wants a quarter's pay in advance you can write to me for a check," Lady Ducayne answered, carelessly.

Miss Torpinter went all the way downstairs with her client, and waited to see her seated in the yellow chariot. When she came upstairs again she was slightly out of breath, and she had resumed that superior manner which Bella had found so crushing.

"You may think yourself uncommonly lucky, Miss Rolleston," she said. "I have dozens of young ladies on my books whom I might have recommended for this situation—but I remembered having told you to call this afternoon—and I thought I would give you a chance. Old Lady Ducayne is one of the best people on my books. She gives her companion a hundred a year, and pays all travelling expenses. You will live in the lap of luxury."

"A hundred a year! How too lovely! Shall I have to dress very grandly? Does Lady Ducayne keep much company?"

"At her age! No, she lives in seclusion—in her own apartments—her French maid, her footman, her medical attendant, her courier."

"Why did those other companions leave her?" asked Bella.

"Their health broke down!"

"Poor things, and so they had to leave?"

"Yes, they had to leave. I suppose you would like a quarter's salary in advance?"

"Oh, yes, please. I shall have things to buy."

"Very well, I will write for Lady Ducayne's check, and I will send you the balance—after deducting my commission for the year."

"To be sure, I had forgotten the commission."

"You don't suppose I keep this office for pleasure."

"Of course not," murmured Bella, remembering the five shillings entrance fee; but nobody could expect a hundred a year and a winter in Italy for five shillings.

III

"From Miss Rolleston, at Cap Ferrino, to Mrs. Rolleston, in Beresford Street, Walworth, London.

"*How I wish you could see this place, dearest; the blue sky, the olive woods, the orange and lemon orchards between the cliffs and the sea—sheltering in the hollow of the great hills—and with summer waves dancing up to the narrow ridge of pebbles and weeds which is the Italian idea of a beach! Oh, how I wish you could see it all, mother dear, and bask in this sunshine, that makes it so difficult to believe the date at the head of this paper. November! The air is like an English June—the sun is so hot that I can't walk a few yards without an umbrella. And to think of you at Walworth while I am here! I could cry at the thought that perhaps you will never see this lovely coast, this wonderful sea, these summer flowers that bloom in winter. There is a hedge of pink geraniums under my window, mother—a thick, rank hedge, as if the flowers grew wild—and there are Dijon roses climbing over arches and palisades all along the terrace—a rose garden full of bloom in November! Just picture it all! You could never imagine the luxury of this hotel. It is nearly new, and has been built and decorated regardless of expense. Our rooms are upholstered in pale blue satin, which shows up Lady Ducayne's parchment complexion; but as she sits all day in a corner of the balcony basking in the sun, except when she is in her carriage, and all the evening in her armchair close to the fire, and never sees anyone but her own people, her complexion matters very little.*

"*She has the handsomest suite of rooms in the hotel. My bedroom is inside hers, the sweetest room—all blue satin and white lace—white enamelled furniture, looking-glasses on every wall, till I know my pert little profile as I never knew it before. The room was really meant for Lady Ducayne's dressing-room, but she ordered one of the blue satin couches to be arranged as a bed for me—the prettiest little bed, which I can wheel near the window on sunny mornings, as it is on castors and easily moved about. I feel as if Lady Ducayne were a funny old grandmother, who had suddenly appeared in my life, very, very rich, and very, very kind.*

"*She is not at all exacting. I read aloud to her a good deal, and she dozes and nods while I read. Sometimes I hear her moaning in her sleep—as if she had troublesome dreams. When she is tired of my reading she orders Francine, her maid, to read a*

French novel to her, and I hear her chuckle and groan now and then, as if she were more interested in those books than in Dickens or Scott. My French is not good enough to follow Francine, who reads very quickly. I have a great deal of liberty, for Lady Ducayne often tells me to run away and amuse myself; I roam about the hills for hours. Everything is so lovely. I lose myself in olive woods, always climbing up and up towards the pine woods above—and above the pines there are the snow mountains that just show their white peaks above the dark hills. Oh, you poor dear, how can I ever make you understand what this place is like—you, whose poor, tired eyes have only the opposite side of Beresford Street? Sometimes I go no farther than the terrace in front of the hotel, which is a favorite lounging-place with everybody. The gardens lie below, and the tennis courts where I sometimes play with a very nice girl, the only person in the hotel with whom I have made friends. She is a year older than I, and has come to Cap Ferrino with her brother, a doctor—or a medical student, who is going to be a doctor. He passed his M.B. exam. at Edinburgh just before they left home, Lotta told me. He came to Italy entirely on his sister's account. She had a troublesome chest attack last summer and was ordered to winter abroad. They are orphans, quite alone in the world, and so fond of each other. It is very nice for me to have such a friend as Lotta. She is so thoroughly respectable. I can't help using that word, for some of the girls in this hotel go on in a way that I know you would shudder at. Lotta was brought up by an aunt, deep down in the country, and knows hardly anything about life. Her brother won't allow her to read a novel, French or English, that he has not read and approved.

"'He treats me like a child,' she told me, 'but I don't mind, for it's nice to know somebody loves me, and cares about what I do, and even about my thoughts.'

"Perhaps this is what makes some girls so eager to marry—the want of someone strong and brave and honest and true to care for them and order them about. I want no one, mother darling, for I have you, and you are all the world to me. No husband could ever come between us two. If I ever were to marry he would have only the second place in my heart. But I don't suppose I ever shall marry, or even know what it is like to have an offer of marriage. No young man can afford to marry a penniless girl nowadays. Life is too expensive.

"Mr. Stafford, Lotta's brother, is very clever, and very kind. He thinks it is rather hard for me to have to live with such an old woman as Lady Ducayne, but then he does not know how poor we are—you and I—and what a wonderful life this seems

to me in this lovely place. I feel a selfish wretch for enjoying all my luxuries, while
you, who want them so much more than I, have none of them—hardly know what
they are like—do you, dearest?—for my scamp of a father began to go to the dogs
soon after you were married, and since then life has been all trouble and care and
struggle for you."

THIS LETTER WAS WRITTEN WHEN BELLA HAD BEEN LESS than a month at Cap Ferrino, before the novelty had worn off the landscape, and before the pleasure of luxurious surroundings had begun to cloy. She wrote to her mother every week, such long letters as girls who have lived in closest companionship with a mother alone can write; letters that are like a diary of heart and mind. She wrote gaily always; but when the new year began Mrs. Rolleston thought she detected a note of melancholy under all those lively details about the place and the people.

"My poor girl is getting homesick," she thought. "Her heart is in Beresford Street."

It might be that she missed her new friend and companion, Lotta Stafford, who had gone with her brother for a little tour to Genoa and Spezia, and as far as Pisa. They were to return before February; but in the meantime Bella might naturally feel very solitary among all those strangers, whose manners and doings she described so well.

The mother's instinct had been true. Bella was not so happy as she had been in that first flush of wonder and delight which followed the change from Walworth to the Riviera. Somehow, she knew not how, lassitude had crept upon her. She no longer loved to climb the hills, no longer flourished her orange stick in sheer gladness of heart as her light feet skipped over the rough ground and the coarse grass on the mountain side. The odor of rosemary and thyme, the fresh breath of the sea, no longer filled her with rapture. She thought of Beresford Street and her mother's face with a sick longing. They were so far—so far away! And then she thought of Lady Ducayne, sitting by the heaped-up olive logs in the overheated salon—thought of that wizened-nutcracker profile, and those gleaming eyes, with an invincible horror.

Visitors at the hotel had told her that the air of Cap Ferrino was relaxing—better suited to age than to youth, to sickness than to health. No doubt it was so.

She was not so well as she had been at Walworth; but she told herself that she was suffering only from the pain of separation from the dear companion of her girlhood, the mother who had been nurse, sister, friend, flatterer, all things in this world to her. She had shed many tears over that parting, had spent many a melancholy hour on the marble terrace with yearning eyes looking westward, and with her heart's desire a thousand miles away.

She was sitting in her favorite spot, an angle at the eastern end of the terrace, a quiet little nook sheltered by orange trees, when she heard a couple of Riviera habitués talking in the garden below. They were sitting on a bench against the terrace wall.

She had no idea of listening to their talk, till the sound of Lady Ducayne's name attracted her, and then she listened without any thought of wrong-doing. They were talking no secrets—just casually discussing a hotel acquaintance.

They were two elderly people whom Bella only knew by sight. An English clergyman who had wintered abroad for half his lifetime; a stout, comfortable, well-to-do spinster, whose chronic bronchitis obliged her to migrate annually.

"I have met her about Italy for the last ten years," said the lady; "but have never found out her real age."

"I put her down at a hundred—not a year less," replied the parson. "Her reminiscences all go back to the Regency. She was evidently then in her zenith; and I have heard her say things that showed she was in Parisian society when the First Empire was at its best—before Josephine was divorced."

"She doesn't talk much now."

"No; there's not much life left in her. She is wise in keeping herself secluded. I only wonder that wicked old quack, her Italian doctor, didn't finish her off years ago."

"I should think it must be the other way, and that he keeps her alive."

"My dear Miss Manders, do you think foreign quackery ever kept anybody alive?"

"Well, there she is—and she never goes anywhere without him. He certainly has an unpleasant countenance."

"Unpleasant," echoed the parson, "I don't believe the foul fiend himself can beat him in ugliness. I pity that poor young woman who has to live between old Lady Ducayne and Dr. Parravicini."

"But the old lady is very good to her companions."

"No doubt. She is very free with her cash; the servants call her good Lady Ducayne. She is a withered old female Croesus, and knows she'll never be able to get through her money, and doesn't relish the idea of other people enjoying it when she's in her coffin. People who live to be as old as she is become slavishly attached to life. I daresay she's generous to those poor girls—but she can't make them happy. They die in her service."

"Don't say they, Mr. Carton; I know that one poor girl died at Mentone last spring."

"Yes, and another poor girl died in Rome three years ago. I was there at the time. Good Lady Ducayne left her there in an English family. The girl had every comfort. The old woman was very liberal to her—but she died. I tell you, Miss Manders, it is not good for any young woman to live with two such horrors as Lady Ducayne and Parravicini."

They talked of other things—but Bella hardly heard them. She sat motionless, and a cold wind seemed to come down upon her from the mountains and to creep up to her from the sea, till she shivered as she sat there in the sunshine, in the shelter of the orange trees in the midst of all that beauty and brightness.

Yes, they were uncanny, certainly, the pair of them—she so like an aristocratic witch in her withered old age; he of no particular age, with a face that was more like a waxen mask than any human countenance Bella had ever seen. What did it matter? Old age is venerable, and worthy of all reverence; and Lady Ducayne had been very kind to her. Dr. Parravicini was a harmless, inoffensive student, who seldom looked up from the book he was reading. He had his private sitting-room, where he made experiments in chemistry and natural science—perhaps in alchemy. What could it matter to Bella? He had always been polite to her, in his far-off way. She could not be more happily placed than she was—in this palatial hotel, with this rich old lady.

No doubt she missed the young English girl who had been so friendly, and it might be that she missed the girl's brother, for Mr. Stafford had talked to her a good deal—had interested himself in the books she was reading, and her manner of amusing herself when she was not on duty.

"You must come to our little salon when you are 'off,' as the hospital nurses call it, and we can have some music. No doubt you play and sing?" Upon which

Bella had to own with a blush of shame that she had forgotten how to play the piano ages ago.

"Mother and I used to sing duets sometimes between the lights, without accompaniment," she said, and the tears came into her eyes as she thought of the humble room, the half-hour's respite from work, the sewing machine standing where a piano ought to have been, and her mother's plaintive voice, so sweet, so true, so dear.

Sometimes she found herself wondering whether she would ever see that beloved mother again. Strange forebodings came into her mind. She was angry with herself for giving way to melancholy thoughts.

One day she questioned Lady Ducayne's French maid about those two companions who had died within three years.

"They were poor, feeble creatures," Francine told her. "They looked fresh and bright enough when they came to Miladi; but they ate too much, and they were lazy. They died of luxury and idleness. Miladi was too kind to them. They had nothing to do; and so they took to fancying things; fancying the air didn't suit them, that they couldn't sleep."

"I sleep well enough, but I have had a strange dream several times since I have been in Italy."

"Ah, you had better not begin to think about dreams, or you will be like those other girls. They were dreamers—and they dreamt themselves into the cemetery."

The dream troubled her a little, not because it was a ghastly or frightening dream, but on account of sensations which she had never felt before in sleep—a whirring of wheels that went round in her brain, a great noise like a whirlwind, but rhythmical like the ticking of a gigantic clock: and then in the midst of this uproar as of winds and waves she seemed to sink into a gulf of unconsciousness, out of sleep into far deeper sleep—total extinction. And then, after that black interval, there had come the sound of voices, and then again the whirr of wheels, louder and louder—and again the black—and then she awoke, feeling languid and oppressed.

She told Dr. Parravicini of her dream one day, on the only occasion when she wanted his professional advice. She had suffered rather severely from the mosquitoes before Christmas—and had been almost frightened at finding a wound upon her arm which she could only attribute to the venomous sting of one of these torturers. Parravicini put on his glasses, and scrutinized the angry mark on the round, white arm, as Bella stood before him and Lady Ducayne with her sleeve rolled up above her elbow.

"Yes, that's rather more than a joke," he said; "he has caught you on the top of a vein. What a vampire! But there's no harm done, signorina, nothing that a little dressing of mine won't heal. You must always show me any bite of this nature. It might be dangerous if neglected. These creatures feed on poison and disseminate it."

"And to think that such tiny creatures can bite like this," said Bella; "my arm looks as if it had been cut by a knife."

"If I were to show you a mosquito's sting under my microscope you wouldn't be surprised at that," replied Parravicini.

Bella had to put up with the mosquito bites, even when they came on the top of a vein, and produced that ugly wound. The wound recurred now and then at longish intervals, and Bella found Dr. Parravicini's dressing a speedy cure. If he were the quack his enemies called him, he had at least a light hand and a delicate touch in performing this small operation.

"Bella Rolleston to Mrs. Rolleston—April 14th.

"EVER DEAREST,

"Behold the check for my second quarter's salary—five and twenty pounds. There is no one to pinch off a whole tenner for a year's commission as there was last time, so it is all for you, mother, dear. I have plenty of pocket-money in hand from the cash I brought away with me, when you insisted on my keeping more than I wanted. It isn't possible to spend money here—except on occasional tips to servants, or sous to beggars and children—unless one had lots to spend, for everything one would like to buy—tortoise-shell, coral, lace—is so ridiculously dear that only a millionaire ought to look at it. Italy is a dream of beauty: but for shopping, give me Newington Causeway.

"You ask me so earnestly if I am quite well that I fear my letters must have been very dull lately. Yes, dear, I am well—but I am not quite so strong as I was when I used to trudge to the West-end to buy half a pound of tea—just for a constitu-

tional walk—or to Dulwich to look at the pictures. Italy is relaxing; and I feel what the people here call 'slack.' But I fancy I can see your dear face looking worried as you read this. Indeed, and indeed, I am not ill. I am only a little tired of this lovely scene—as I suppose one might get tired of looking at one of Turner's pictures if it hung on a wall that was always opposite one. I think of you every hour in every day—think of you and our homely little room—our dear little shabby parlor, with the armchairs from the wreck of your old home, and Dick singing in his cage over the sewing machine. Dear, shrill, maddening Dick, who, we flattered ourselves, was so passionately fond of us. Do tell me in your next letter that he is well.

"My friend Lotta and her brother never came back after all. They went from Pisa to Rome. Happy mortals! And they are to be on the Italian lakes in May; which lake was not decided when Lotta last wrote to me. She has been a charming correspondent, and has confided all her little flirtations to me. We are all to go to Bellaggio next week—by Genoa and Milan. Isn't that lovely? Lady Ducayne travels by the easiest stages—except when she is bottled up in the train deluxe. We shall stop two days at Genoa and one at Milan. What a bore I shall be to you with my talk about Italy when I come home.

"Love and love—and ever more love from your adoring, BELLA."

IV

HERBERT STAFFORD AND HIS SISTER HAD OFTEN TALKED of the pretty English girl with her fresh complexion, which made such a pleasant touch of rosy color among all those sallow faces at the Grand Hotel. The young doctor thought of her with a compassionate tenderness—her utter loneliness in that great hotel where there were so many people, her bondage to that old, old woman, where everybody else was free to think of nothing but enjoying life. It was a hard fate; and the poor child was evidently devoted to her mother, and felt the pain of separation—"only two of them, and very poor, and all the world to each other," he thought.

Lotta told him one morning that they were to meet again at Bellaggio. "The old thing and her court are to be there before we are," she said. "I shall be charmed to have Bella again. She is so bright and gay—in spite of an occasional touch of homesickness. I never took to a girl on a short acquaintance as I did to her."

"I like her best when she is homesick," said Herbert; "for then I am sure she has a heart."

"What have you to do with hearts, except for dissection? Don't forget that Bella is an absolute pauper. She told me in confidence that her mother makes mantles for a West-end shop. You can hardly have a lower depth than that."

"I shouldn't think any less of her if her mother made matchboxes."

"Not in the abstract—of course not. Matchboxes are honest labor. But you couldn't marry a girl whose mother makes mantles."

"We haven't come to the consideration of that question yet," answered Herbert, who liked to provoke his sister.

In two years' hospital practice he had seen too much of the grim realities of life to retain any prejudices about rank. Cancer, phthisis, gangrene, leave a man with little respect for the humanity. The kernel is always the same—fearfully and wonderfully made—a subject for pity and terror.

Mr. Stafford and his sister arrived at Bellaggio in a fair May evening. The sun was going down as the steamer approached the pier; and all that glory of purple bloom which curtains every wall at this season of the year flushed and deepened in the glowing light. A group of ladies were standing on the pier watching the arrivals, and among them Herbert saw a pale face that startled him out of his wonted composure.

"There she is," murmured Lotta, at his elbow, "but how dreadfully changed. She looks a wreck."

They were shaking hands with her a few minutes later, and a flush had lighted up her poor pinched face in the pleasure of meeting.

"I thought you might come this evening," she said. "We have been here a week."

She did not add that she had been there every evening to watch the boat in, and a good many times during the day. The Grand Bretagne was close by, and it had been easy for her to creep to the pier when the boat bell rang. She felt a joy in meeting these people again; a sense of being with friends; a confidence which Lady Ducayne's goodness had never inspired in her.

"Oh, you poor darling, how awfully ill you must have been," exclaimed Lotta, as the two girls embraced.

Bella tried to answer, but her voice was choked with tears.

"What has been the matter, dear? That horrid influenza, I suppose?"

"No, no, I have not been ill—I have only felt a little weaker than I used to be. I don't think the air of Cap Ferrino quite agreed with me."

"It must have disagreed with you abominably. I never saw such a change in anyone. Do let Herbert doctor you. He is fully qualified, you know. He prescribed for ever so many influenza patients at the Londres. They were glad to get advice from an English doctor in a friendly way."

"I am sure he must be very clever!" faltered Bella, "but there is really nothing the matter. I am not ill, and if I were ill, Lady Ducayne's physician—"

"That dreadful man with the yellow face? I would as soon one of the Borgias prescribed for me. I hope you haven't been taking any of his medicines."

"No, dear, I have taken nothing. I have never complained of being ill."

This was said while they were all three walking to the hotel. The Staffords' rooms had been secured in advance, pretty ground-floor rooms, opening into the garden. Lady Ducayne's statelier apartments were on the floor above.

"I believe these rooms are just under ours," said Bella.

"Then it will be all the easier for you to run down to us," replied Lotta, which was not really the case, as the grand staircase was in the center of the hotel.

"Oh, I shall find it easy enough," said Bella. "I'm afraid you'll have too much of my society. Lady Ducayne sleeps away half the day in this warm weather, so I have a good deal of idle time; and I get awfully moped thinking of mother and home."

Her voice broke upon the last word. She could not have thought of that poor lodging which went by the name of home more tenderly had it been the most beautiful that art and wealth ever created. She moped and pined in this lovely garden, with the sunlit lake and the romantic hills spreading out their beauty before her. She was homesick and she had dreams; or, rather, an occasional recurrence of that one bad dream with all its strange sensations—it was more like a hallucination than dreaming—the whirring of wheels, the sinking into an abyss, the struggling back to consciousness. She had the dream shortly before she left Cap Ferrino, but not since she had come to Bellaggio, and she began to hope the air in this lake district suited her better, and that those strange sensations would never return.

Mr. Stafford wrote a prescription and had it made up at the chemist's near the hotel. It was a powerful tonic, and after two bottles, and a row or two on the lake, and some rambling over the hills and in the meadows where the spring flowers made earth seem paradise, Bella's spirits and looks improved as if by magic.

"It is a wonderful tonic," she said, but perhaps in her heart of hearts she knew that the doctor's kind voice, and the friendly hand that helped her in and out of the boat, and the lake, had something to do with her cure.

"I hope you don't forget that her mother makes mantles," Lotta said warningly.

"Or matchboxes; it is just the same thing, so far as I am concerned."

"You mean that in no circumstances could you think of marrying her?"

"I mean that if ever I love a woman well enough to think of marrying her, riches or rank will count for nothing with me. But I fear—I fear your poor friend may not live to be any man's wife."

"Do you think her so very ill?"

He sighed, and left the question unanswered.

One day, while they were gathering wild hyacinths in an upland meadow, Bella told Mr. Stafford about her bad dream.

"It is curious only because it is hardly like a dream," she said. "I daresay you could find some commonsense reason for it. The position of my head on my pillow, or the atmosphere, or something."

And then she described her sensations; how in the midst of sleep there came a sudden sense of suffocation; and then those whirring wheels, so loud, so terrible; and then a blank, and then a coming back to waking consciousness.

"Have you ever had chloroform given you—by a dentist, for instance?"

"Never—Dr. Parravicini asked me that question one day."

"Lately?"

"No, long ago, when we were in the train deluxe."

"Has Dr. Parravicini prescribed for you since you began to feel weak and ill?"

"Oh, he has given me a tonic from time to time, but I hate medicine, and took very little of the stuff. And then I am not ill, only weaker than I used to be.

I was ridiculously strong and well when I lived at Walworth, and used to take long walks every day. Mother made me take those tramps to Dulwich or Norwood, for fear I should suffer from too much sewing machine; sometimes—but very seldom—she went with me. She was generally toiling at home while I was enjoying fresh air and exercise. And she was very careful about our food—that, however plain it was, it should be always nourishing and ample. I owe it to her care that I grew up such a great, strong creature."

"You don't look great or strong now, you poor dear," said Lotta.

"I'm afraid Italy doesn't agree with me."

"Perhaps it is not Italy, but being cooped up with Lady Ducayne that has made you ill."

"But I am never cooped up. Lady Ducayne is absurdly kind, and lets me roam about or sit in the balcony all day if I like. I have read more novels since I have been with her than in all the rest of my life."

"Then she is very different from the average old lady, who is usually a slave driver," said Stafford. "I wonder why she carries a companion about with her if she has so little need of society."

"Oh, I am only part of her state. She is inordinately rich—and the salary she gives me doesn't count. Apropos of Dr. Parravicini, I know he is a clever doctor, for he cures my horrid mosquito bites."

"A little ammonia would do that, in the early stage of the mischief. But there are no mosquitoes to trouble you now."

"Oh, yes, there are; I had a bite just before we left Cap Ferrino." She pushed up her loose lawn sleeve, and exhibited a scar, which he scrutinized intently, with a surprised and puzzled look.

"This is no mosquito bite," he said.

"Oh, yes it is—unless there are snakes or adders at Cap Ferrino."

"It is not a bite at all. You are trifling with me. Miss Rolleston—you have allowed that wretched Italian quack to bleed you. They killed the greatest man in modern Europe that way, remember. How very foolish of you."

"I was never bled in my life, Mr. Stafford."

"Nonsense! Let me look at your other arm. Are there any more mosquito bites?"

"Yes; Dr. Parravicini says I have a bad skin for healing, and that the poison acts more virulently with me than with most people."

Stafford examined both her arms in the broad sunlight, scars new and old.

"You have been very badly bitten, Miss Rolleston," he said, "and if ever I find the mosquito I shall make him smart. But, now tell me, my dear girl, on your word of honor, tell me as you would tell a friend who is sincerely anxious for your health and happiness—as you would tell your mother if she were here to question you—have you no knowledge of any cause for these scars except mosquito bites—no suspicion even?"

"No, indeed! No, upon my honor! I have never seen a mosquito biting my arm. One never does see the horrid little fiends. But I have heard them trumpeting under the curtains and I know that I have often had one of the pestilent wretches buzzing about me."

Later in the day Bella and her friends were sitting at tea in the garden, while Lady Ducayne took her afternoon drive with her doctor.

"How long do you mean to stop with Lady Ducayne, Miss Rolleston?" Herbert Stafford asked, after a thoughtful silence, breaking suddenly upon the trivial talk of the two girls.

"As long as she will go on paying me twenty-five pounds a quarter."

"Even if you feel your health breaking down in her service?"

"It is not the service that has injured my health. You can see that I have really nothing to do—to read aloud for an hour or so once or twice a week; to write a letter once in a while to a London tradesman. I shall never have such an easy time with anybody. And nobody else would give me a hundred a year."

"Then you mean to go on till you break down; to die at your post?"

"Like the other two companions? No! If ever I feel seriously ill—really ill— I shall put myself in a train and go back to Walworth without stopping."

"What about the other two companions?"

"They both died. It was very unlucky for Lady Ducayne. That's why she engaged me; she chose me because I was ruddy and robust. She must feel rather disgusted at my having grown white and weak. By-the-bye, when I told her about the good your tonic had done me, she said she would like to see you and have a little talk with you about her own case."

"And I should like to see Lady Ducayne. When did she say this?"

"The day before yesterday."

"Will you ask her if she will see me this evening?"

"With pleasure! I wonder what you will think of her? She looks rather terrible to a stranger; but Dr. Parravicini says she was once a famous beauty."

It was nearly ten o'clock when Mr. Stafford was summoned by message from Lady Ducayne, whose courier came to conduct him to her ladyship's salon. Bella was reading aloud when the visitor was admitted; and he noticed the languor in the low, sweet tones, the evident effort.

"Shut up the book," said the querulous old voice. "You are beginning to drawl like Miss Blandy."

Stafford saw a small, bent figure crouching over the piled up olive logs; a shrunken old figure in a gorgeous garment of black and crimson brocade, a skinny throat emerging from a mass of old Venetian lace, clasped with diamonds that flashed like fireflies as the trembling old head turned towards him.

The eyes that looked at him out of the face were almost as bright as the diamonds—the only living feature in that narrow parchment mask. He had seen terrible faces in the hospital—faces on which disease had set dreadful marks—but he had never seen a face that impressed him so painfully as this withered countenance, with its indescribable horror of death outlived, a face that should have been hidden under a coffin-lid years and years ago.

The Italian physician was standing on the other side of the fireplace, smoking a cigarette, and looking down at the little old woman brooding over the hearth as if he were proud of her.

"Good evening, Mr. Stafford; you can go to your room, Bella, and write your everlasting letter to your mother at Walworth," said Lady Ducayne. "I believe she writes a page about every wild flower she discovers in the woods and meadows. I don't know what else she can find to write about," she added, as Bella quietly withdrew to the pretty little bedroom opening out of Lady Ducayne's spacious apartment. Here, as at Cap Ferrino, she slept in a room adjoining the old lady's.

"You are a medical man, I understand, Mr. Stafford."

"I am a qualified practitioner, but I have not begun to practice."

"You have begun upon my companion, she tells me."

"I have prescribed for her, certainly, and I am happy to find my prescription has done her good; but I look upon that improvement as temporary. Her case will require more drastic treatment."

"Never mind her case. There is nothing the matter with the girl—absolutely nothing—except girlish nonsense; too much liberty and not enough work."

"I understand that two of your ladyship's previous companions died of the same disease," said Stafford, looking first at Lady Ducayne, who gave her tremulous old head an impatient jerk, and then at Parravicini, whose yellow complexion had paled a little under Stafford's scrutiny.

"Don't bother me about my companions, sir," said Lady Ducayne. "I sent for you to consult you about myself—not about a parcel of anemic girls. You are young, and medicine is a progressive science, the newspapers tell me. Where have you studied?"

"In Edinburgh—and in Paris."

"Two good schools. And know all the new-fangled theories, the modern discoveries—that remind one of the medieval witchcraft, of Albertus Magnus, and George Ripley; you have studied hypnotism—electricity?"

"And the transfusion of blood," said Stafford, very slowly, looking at Parravicini.

"Have you made any discovery that teaches you to prolong human life—any elixir—any mode of treatment? I want my life prolonged, young man. That man there has been my physician for thirty years. He does all he can to keep me alive—after his lights. He studies all the new theories of all the scientists—but he is old; he gets older every day—his brain-power is going—he is bigoted—prejudiced—can't receive new ideas—can't grapple with new systems. He will let me die if I am not on my guard against him."

"You are of an unbelievable ingratitude, Ecclenza," said Parravicini.

"Oh, you needn't complain. I have paid you thousands to keep me alive. Every year of my life has swollen your hoards; you know there is nothing to come to you when I am gone. My whole fortune is left to endow a home for indigent women of quality who have reached their ninetieth year. Come, Mr. Stafford, I am a rich woman. Give me a few years more in the sunshine, a few years more above ground, and I will give you the price of a fashionable London practice—I will set you up at the West-end."

"How old are you, Lady Ducayne?"

"I was born the day Louis XVI was guillotined."

"Then I think you have had your share of the sunshine and the pleasures of the earth, and that you should spend your few remaining days in repenting your sins and trying to make atonement for the young lives that have been sacrificed to your love of life."

"What do you mean by that, sir?"

"Oh, Lady Ducayne, need I put your wickedness and your physician's still greater wickedness in plain words? The poor girl who is now in your employment has been reduced from robust health to a condition of absolute danger by Dr. Parravicini's experimental surgery; and I have no doubt those other two young women who broke down in your service were treated by him in the same manner. I could take upon myself to demonstrate—by most convincing evidence, to a jury of medical men—that Dr. Parravicini has been bleeding Miss Rolleston after putting her under chloroform, at intervals, ever since she has been in your service. The deterioration in the girl's health speaks for itself; the lancet marks upon the girl's arms are unmistakable; and her description of a series of sensations, which she calls a dream, points unmistakably to the administration of chloroform while she was sleeping. A practice so nefarious, so murderous, must, if exposed, result in a sentence only less severe than the punishment of murder."

"I laugh," said Parravicini, with an airy motion of his skinny fingers; "I laugh at once at your theories and at your threats. I, Parravicini Leopold, have no fear that the law can question anything I have done."

"Take the girl away, and let me hear no more of her," cried Lady Ducayne, in the thin, old voice, which so poorly matched the energy and fire of the wicked old brain that guided its utterances. "Let her go back to her mother—I want no more girls to die in my service. There are girls enough and to spare in the world, God knows."

"If you ever engage another companion—or take another English girl into your service, Lady Ducayne, I will make all England ring with the story of your wickedness."

"I want no more girls. I don't believe in his experiments. They have been full of danger for me as well as for the girl—an air bubble, and I should be gone. I'll have no more of his dangerous quackery. I'll find some new man—a better man than you, sir, a discoverer like Pasteur, or Virchow, a genius—to keep me alive.

Take your girl away, young man. Marry her if you like. I'll write a check for a thousand pounds, and let her go and live on beef and beer, and get strong and plump again. I'll have no more such experiments. Do you hear, Parravicini?" she screamed, vindictively, the yellow, wrinkled face distorted with fury, the eyes glaring at him.

The Staffords carried Bella Rolleston off to Varese next day, she very loath to leave Lady Ducayne, whose liberal salary afforded such help for the dear mother. Herbert Stafford insisted, however, treating Bella as coolly as if he had been the family physician, and she had been given over wholly to his care.

"Do you suppose your mother would let you stop here to die?" he asked. "If Mrs. Rolleston knew how ill you are, she would come post haste to fetch you."

"I shall never be well again till I get back to Walworth," answered Bella, who was low-spirited and inclined to tears this morning, a reaction after her good spirits of yesterday.

"We'll try a week or two at Varese first," said Stafford. "When you can walk halfway up Monte Generoso without palpitation of the heart, you shall go back to Walworth."

"Poor mother, how glad she will be to see me, and how sorry that I've lost such a good place."

This conversation took place on the boat when they were leaving Bellaggio. Lotta had gone to her friend's room at seven o'clock that morning, long before Lady Ducayne's withered eyelids had opened to the daylight, before even Francine, the French maid, was astir, and had helped to pack a Gladstone bag with essentials, and hustled Bella downstairs and out of doors before she could make any strenuous resistance.

"It's all right," Lotta assured her. "Herbert had a good talk with Lady Ducayne last night, and it was settled for you to leave this morning. She doesn't like invalids, you see."

"No," sighed Bella, "she doesn't like invalids. It was very unlucky that I should break down, just like Miss Tomson and Miss Blandy."

"At any rate, you are not dead, like them," answered Lotta, "and my brother says you are not going to die."

☾   ☾   ☾

It seemed rather a dreadful thing to be dismissed in that offhand way, without a word of farewell from her employer.

"I wonder what Miss Torpinter will say when I go to her for another situation," Bella speculated, ruefully, while she and her friends were breakfasting on board the steamer.

"Perhaps you may never want another situation," said Stafford.

"You mean that I may never be well enough to be useful to anybody?"

"No, I don't mean anything of the kind."

It was after dinner at Varese, when Bella had been induced to take a whole glass of Chianti, and quite sparkled after that unaccustomed stimulant, that Mr. Stafford produced a letter from his pocket.

"I forgot to give you Lady Ducayne's letter of adieu!" he said.

"What, did she write to me? I am so glad—I hated to leave her in such a cool way; for after all she was very kind to me, and if I didn't like her it was only because she was too dreadfully old."

She tore open the envelope. The letter was short and to the point:—

> Goodbye, child. Go and marry your doctor. I enclose a farewell gift for your trousseau.
> —ADELINE DUCAYNE

"A hundred pounds, a whole year's salary—no—why, it's for a—. A check for a thousand!" cried Bella. "What a generous old soul! She really is the dearest old thing."

"She just missed being very dear to you, Bella," said Stafford.

He had dropped into the use of her Christian name while they were on board the boat. It seemed natural now that she was to be in his charge till they all three went back to England.

"I shall take upon myself the privileges of an elder brother till we land at Dover," he said; "after that—well, it must be as you please."

The question of their future relations must have been satisfactorily settled before they crossed the Channel, for Bella's next letter to her mother communicated three startling facts.

First, that the inclosed check for £1,000 was to be invested in debenture stock in Mrs. Rolleston's name, and was to be her very own, income and principal, for the rest of her life.

Next, that Bella was going home to Walworth immediately.

And last, that she was going to be married to Mr. Herbert Stafford in the following autumn.

"And I am sure you will adore him, mother, as much as I do," wrote Bella.

"It is all good Lady Ducayne's doing. I never could have married if I had not secured that little nest-egg for you. Herbert says we shall be able to add to it as the years go by, and that wherever we live there shall be always a room in our house for you. The word 'mother-in-law' has no terrors for him."

Sometimes Salvation

Pat Cadigan

Ginny's dad turned her out. Yeah, that's right—
it ain't an unusual story. Wish I had a dime for every little snipe turned out by
dear old dad or the equivalent. Spend a couple days down here and you'll get the
idea that that's all anyone's dad does is turn them out. And I don't know which
ones make me feel sicker, the girls or the boys. Maybe what makes me sickest of
all is that they're all down here with me.

Time was when you never saw a kid living rough and now you can't go ten
feet without stepping on one. What is that shit, you may wonder. Shit? Yeah,
that's right—you think about what'll make a kid rather sleep rough than stay
around home—"home," make that—and you'll think *shit* isn't a strong enough
word for it.

Do not, please, get me wrong. I am not St. Francis of Assisi of the street
children, my heart is not gold, and I do not want to do anything to improve society or the world. What I am and what I want to do are all very simple: I am a
drunk and I want to be drunk as much as possible as long as possible. Very dull
compared to what some other people want, or so I hear. Mainly from the kids.

Some of the kids think what I want is too easy, or not interesting enough. I
say to them, Yeah, that's right—going off with a john is a lot more interesting,
lotta extra challenges in there: will I live through this, is this the one who's gonna
give me AIDS. So I guess I can do without *interesting.*

❨　　❨　　❨

With all the kids coming and going all the time, I don't always notice them right away, and some ain't around long enough for me to notice them. But Ginny I noticed first thing.

She was trying to look like any other chronic troublemaking and repeat-offending dead-end type of kid, and she was good enough that any stupid-ass citizen-zombie would have been fooled. But I know the difference between a kid that got thrown away early and been processed by the sewage-treatment plant they call the juvenile justice system, and a kid who's spent most of her life eating regular and doing homework. Plus, she slipped up when Dropkick brought her around to meet me. Not that I was looking so all-fired up to par that day, it was just that her old civilized reflexes kicked in when the Dropper said, "This is May, she's been here the longest." She actually put out her hand and said, "How do you do."

Even the Dropper stared at her, and the Dropper learned enough manners to pass in polite society himself. Well, never let it be said that I ain't house-trained when I want to be—I invited them both for a drink. Yeah, that's right, I did. And what I gave them is pretty benign shit compared to what everyone else in the world was giving them. Besides which, alcohol is a disinfectant, so it probably killed a bunch of germs and viruses in their systems.

She had just a capful, sipped a little and made a little face. As I recall, I was on the last half of that bottle, so I was stretching it some and it didn't have a whole lot of kick to it. I've mellowed out a lot since the old days when I used to do that trick with a can of Sterno and a loaf of bread.

So I watched her, sitting there under my bridge with me and old Dropkick, and I saw how she was. She was real tall for thirteen, taller than Dropkick, which actually wasn't too hard, and I could tell that she didn't like being so dirty. She kept combing her fingers through her hair and wiping her hands on her jeans, which were pretty loose on her. This girl was, like, *skeletal*, I realized after a bit and I got kind of annoyed. I heard all about anorexics like anybody else and I hate them. Because while I am not St. Francis of the street kids or anything, I ain't completely heartless either, and thinking about how the kids I know don't eat regular, I got no pity in me for someone who's starving on purpose and throwing food away. Or worse, throwing it up. I mean, I am not one to talk but I think that must be one of the few things in the world I'd name a sin if someone asked me. But nobody *did* ask me, did they.

So I looked at her pretty closely then and without too much kindness. And then I thought that if she really was one of those, she probably wouldn't be sitting there sipping Old Overbolt, even watered-down Old Overbolt, because we all know how fattening booze is, right? (I'm laughing my head off at that one.) Finally I say to her, "You hungry?" just to see what she'll say.

And she looks at me with those big brown eyes and nods just ever so slightly. And I look over at Dropkick and say, "What kind of host are you? Go get some food."

Dropkick says, "This isn't *my* place."

And I say, "You know what I mean. You brought her here, I supplied the beverage, so go get us all some hors d'oeuvres."

That got a giggle out of her, and the Dropper obediently got up and went off to see what he could scrounge and left the two of us eyeing each other.

After a long moment of silence, she says, "So how long have you lived under the bridge here in the park?"

And I laugh and say, "You're not from around here, are you, girl."

And then she looks *ashamed*, of all things. So I say, "Yeah, that's right, you're not, but that ain't no big deal. Nobody *around* here is from around *here*. You don't think anyone'd live like this in their own hometown, do you?"

She giggled again and covered her mouth quick, like she'd done something wrong.

"Chill," I say. "It wasn't that funny." The brown eyes get that trapped-animal look. "Never mind, hon, I already got it figured. Only thing I can't figure is why an honor student like you didn't have nowhere else to go."

"Nobody would believe me," she said in that dead voice they all get when they're on about it.

"You know that for a fact?" I asked her.

"Pretty much. I've got three sisters. Two of them don't believe me. The third one knows for sure I'm telling the truth but she also tends to laugh a lot at nothing and she hears voices. She's older than me, and Dad used to like *her* best." She stared at me, daring me something—maybe not to believe her, or to be not squeamish enough to hear her out. Or maybe even both.

"Your mother know?"

"My mother *helped.*"

I nodded at her. "Old story around these parts. Plenty others can tell it in several variations, some of 'em even nastier than yours."

She looked a question at me and I shook my head. "Nah. My story's pretty simple. I like my booze and I don't want to be bothered. I don't want men and I don't want women and I sure don't want any kids." She got this defensive look at that one. "Come on, honey, none of you are kids anymore and you should also try not to take the world so personally anyway. I just like my booze, and it likes me. It's always there, it's always good, it don't criticize and it don't make demands. It just does what it says it's gonna do and I say when you got something like that in your life, you're coming out ahead. Think about it."

So then she looks down at the capful in her hands and up at me with this dizzy kind of expression. "Are you telling me I ought to become an alcoholic?"

"Shit, no, honey. I'm just telling you why I am. You go be whatever your heart tells you. While you still have a heart."

And that gave her a turn so that she went even paler than she already was. Yeah, that's right—I told you I am not St. Francis or anything like that, and I have seen them come and go over and over and I know what happens to them. The job that their parents start on them, the streets'll finish up, and if the streets don't do it, juvenile justice surely will.

Assuming none of them gets "saved," that is.

Yeah, that's right—"saved." They come in vans with sodas and coffee and bags full of burgers, blankets during the cold weather. They're all from God, usually, though they don't make the old mistake of trying to get the kids to pray and shit. Even the Salvation Army seems to have wised up to the old casting bread upon the waters gig—what it really is, you throw a bunch of your shit overboard and it sinks and you never see it again. You're gonna help somebody, that's what happens and you don't get your blanket back, okay? But hell, that's the nature of a gift, isn't it? And nobody asked them to come around with their stuff anyway.

But always, some budget somewhere gets cut, and the first thing that goes is the so-called street ministry (this is what they usually call it). Because they can't think of selling their fucking mahogany desks or their furniture or shit like that—they keep their *things* and let the kids go wanting, which is the way it's always been anyway. So it's not like the kids really hurt over it or anything.

But they really piss me off when they do that and it just makes me surer that I like booze better than anything or anyone. Like I said, it always does what it says it's gonna do, and it don't make any stupid promises it can't keep.

One day I woke up and Ronald Reagan was president. I thought for sure it was the DTs, and maybe it was, because the next time I looked, it was some other guy, but things weren't any better. I think they'd gotten a lot worse, as a matter of fact, because there were practically no rescue squads coming around. I'd never thought I'd actually miss Jesus people in a van with coffee and burgers, and *I* didn't. It was the kids that needed that stuff, and there was nobody coming around with it.

Just before Ginny showed up, though, times changed again, and the vans came back with new faces but the same old things going on—food, and promises of more food and some help if the kids would come to the shelters. I don't tell nobody to go and I don't tell nobody not to go, even if the kids ask me. I just tell them what I told Ginny: you do what your heart tells you to do, while you still have one. This is, I think, the only thing you should tell anybody when they ask you what they should do. Because really, all they're asking for is permission to do that, and if they feel like they gotta get somebody's permission, why the hell not give it to them?

Yeah, that's right—I had it all figured out, didn't I. Me and the booze, we had it all mapped out. And then something happened that made it all different.

Then *she* came along.

Now when I think about it, I'm surprised someone like her didn't show up sooner. The pickings here're pretty good for that kind. Plenty other kinds came around; besides the Jesus people, of course, we had all manner of pimps—no, excuse me, there's really only one kind of pimp, and they only got one thing they sell and some might think it's all kinds of this and all kinds of that but then, there's some so stupid they think fifteen-year-old boys blow strange, ugly men because they like sex, too.

When *she* showed, I thought at first she was another Jesus person. I was on my way home from a Dumpster run with not too bad pickings—expiration dates and shit like that mean that some of us on tighter budgets eat as well as anybody. So I was passing the old truck dock on my way down the hill to my end of the park, and there she was, handing out doggy bags and cans of soda. Now I was impressed with the canned sodas, though someone was probably gonna bleed over them. Recycle money can mean one less blow job, which is pretty serious stuff. So all the kids were there, it looked like, and her being a new face, I stopped to check.

Handing out like Jesus, smiling like a pimp. Yeah, that's right, I thought, what we needed around these parts was a pimp pretending to be Jesus. That would make everything perfect. Since most of the kids never got a smile that didn't come from a pimp anyway, she must have looked like just some nice lady with plenty of food to give away.

I had a couple swallows with me—don't leave home without it, especially when you don't actually have a home. See, the way it is, I got to drink as much as would get a regular person hammered just to get sober so I can go on from there and get drunk. So sometimes I have to dose up on the fly to keep straight. I know when I need some because I get a little taste of the DTs when it's been too long. That's what I figured I was getting standing there watching her with the kids because there she was with her pimp's smile and her pretty face and her shiny hair and suddenly I saw an animal.

Big eyes with slitted pupils, nasty teeth; hungry. Sniffing them kids, tasting the air around them to get their flavors. If you saw that, you'd reach for a fucking drink, too.

A couple swallows was all it took to make stuff look normal again. Mostly normal. Still had the pimp's smile, which made me think of the nasty teeth, but I didn't see any.

Then Dropkick pushes Ginny over to this woman and Ginny is trying not to go. The woman is holding a bag in one hand and a can in the other and her pimp's smile goes from sort of curious to outright—shit, how to describe this. You'd see that look on someone's face when they fall in love at first sight, I think, or if they find a wallet in the gutter with a thousand dollars in it. That kind of look, lust and greed and pure-ass delight. *Candy, little girl? Or a burger?*

I went as far as to take a step toward them. Yeah, that's right, I wasn't thinking. Mainly I think I wanted to get a better look at her, see if there was any look of the beast left to her now that I'd had my swallows.

And then her and Ginny both turn to me and I think, shit, the DTs are bad this time. They look *wrong*. Like a matched set, but *wrong*. That's all I know. Better hurry home and get outside of a bottle. Which it so happens I have, some not-so-bad stuff that I was intending to stretch. But my rule is, first prevent delirium tremens, and worry later.

Quite a bender. I disappeared down a black hole for a while. Weird visions and crazy dreams; I ain't too wild about that part of it. Everybody I ever met in my life came to visit me under the bridge in the park, and I think some of them might actually have been there. Dropkick, for example, and Ginny.

And some little kid I couldn't remember the name of; hadn't seen her for a long time. Little eleven-year-old throwaway. She'd been living rough for a while by the time she found her way to the old truck docks where most of the kids stayed. I was drinking hard a lot of the time she was around: the most I remembered about her was she was letting her hair go dread, like a Rastafarian, which doesn't look as weird as you might think on a pubescent white girl, at least not if you've seen half the shit I've seen, anyway.

But yeah, that's right, she came to see me in my bender visions. She was a little bit older, just the way she would have been in real life, but she was also dressed better, dressed up and no cheap shit out of some thrift shop. Overpriced denims from some store with an overcute name and a trend-color T-shirt with a little breast pocket barely big enough for an M&M. And still the dreads in her hair. Ms. Pimp came with her. The way they were both staring, I knew the little one had told Ms. Pimp about me and I tried to remember what she would have known. Maybe just that I was down here under the bridge, nobody's queen bee and nobody's mother and nothing like St. Francis.

She gave her pants a little tug to save the knees, just like a citizen, and squatted down to look at me closer. "You listened," she said. "Maybe you don't remember now, but I know you were listening then when I told you. I told you everything and you heard me and you didn't tell me I was bad, and you didn't try to tell me what I should do. All I wanted was to tell someone, just get it out."

I tried to focus on her, but somehow my vision went right past and fixed on Ms. Pimp behind her. The way I was and the position and all, she looked twenty feet tall. And she didn't squat down.

That head tilts to one side. The kids says, "Help her."

She says, "I haven't been invited." So then the little one says, "Well, *I* was, once."

Like that, I understand, and I pass out.

I woke up right after someone took the gym socks out of my mouth. It felt like, anyway. What sky I could see from where I was lying looked gray and blah. I didn't feel much like moving, so for a long time, I didn't. Eventually, I got a sense for how I was laying there on the ground—almost spread-eagle, with my neck bent over to my right. I think I must have looked kind of dreamy, actually, or I would have except nobody coming off a bender looks that good.

Nobody makes you do anything after a bender when you don't matter, so since there was nobody to make me move, I just laid there until I felt like doing something else.

And *then* it hurt. The top of my head caved in and went crashing through six floors of brain, a couple levels of throat bile and made a direct hit on my stomach so that the dry heaves bent me in half and I sat up without meaning to. There she was, slumped against the wall, deep asleep like she didn't have a care in the world. Except, of course, she did, lots of them, but I couldn't figure why she'd brought them to me.

I picked up a little pebble and tossed it at her. She just twitched. Took two more direct hits, one on the shoulder and the other on her forehead, before she woke for me. That last one must have stung like a hornet.

"What're you doin' here," I say to her.

Ginny yawns, covering her mouth politely, pushes her dark hair back. She's got wavy-curly hair that could go dread pretty easy. "Watching over you."

"I don't need nobody to watch over *me*," I tell her. "And if you think I want to work out a deal where we take care of each other, you're dumber'n I look, 'cause I thought it was pretty clear I ain't down here to be no mother."

Ginny gets that smile like certain drug counselors I have known. Very patronizing smile, even if none of them mean it that way, or think they do. "Don't you ever worry about what could happen to you while you're passed out?"

"No," I say, "why should I? I'm passed out, I won't feel it."

Now she gives a that's-not-funny laugh and rolls her eyes. "Suppose it's a rapist with AIDS?"

"I guess you got a point," I say after a moment, "but I don't understand why you want to make it." I got her confused now. "I mean, I *tol'* you what I wanted out of life. Why are you tryin' to worry me with rapists with AIDS when you know I don't give a good goddamn about most anything, and I'd appreciate the world returning the favor."

She pressed her knuckles together. "I think it's because when I first looked at you, I knew I could have been looking at my own future. And now that I have a chance to prevent that future, I want to go all the way and save you, too."

Save me? Did this little piece of chicken just say she wanted to *save me?* All I can do is stare at her.

"I guess it's because I'll feel like I've erased every chance of this happening to me if I can help you," she goes on. "The way she wants to help me."

Yeah, that's right: *she.* Tiny little push on that word as it comes out of her mouth lets me know she's talking about who I think she's talking about. "What's that pimp got in mind for you?" I asked her.

She gives another little laugh. "She's not a pimp. She's something entirely different. Something new."

"New? I doubt *that.* Ain't nothin' new that comes around *here.*"

"Well, yeah, okay, she's actually very old. *Very* old. But what she's doing, she's doing in a new way. A way that's never been done for us before."

"Us?" I feel like a stupid echo. Maybe that's what I've come down to under this bridge, just a stupid echo. That's okay, as long as I can still drink when I'm not doing my echo thing.

"Us women. Us females." She pushed herself up on her knees and leaned toward me, looking hard into my face. Considering the way I know I smelled, that was no cheap trick. "Don't you ever think about that? How we always have to work our way out of being some man's adjunct? That we all end up belonging to some man and have to break free of him?"

"You see any men around me here?" I said. "The only men *I* ever been in thrall to're Jack Daniels and Jim Beam, and they ain't the jealous type."

"It's *why* you drink," she insisted. "All we ever seem to do is fight to keep from being used one way or another. Or we try to dull the pain of having been used up and thrown away by using booze, drugs, things like that."

Now I'm getting it—this is not coming out of her own mouth, this is all shit the pimp put in her head. Sounds real good, sounds like what you'd think you'd want to hear. But it's also got this canned sound. Like this little Ginny, in spite of everything, she still isn't sold, she can't quite believe no matter how much she wants to, and she's even maybe still a little scared of what the fine print on this deal is gonna say when she finally reads it.

"What do you want?" I say to her finally. "What do you want to do, what do you want me to do?"

"I'll bring her to you. Tonight. You'll be here, won't you." Not a question. Off she goes, leaving me there to wonder if my brain really could be swelling up inside my skull the way it feels. My hands are shaking, too.

I really do not fucking want to see this pimp. This was another idea Ginny got put in her head for her and didn't think up by herself, and doesn't even know it. So what this pimp has in mind for me, I'm right to be scared about it.

Son of a bitch; you know, this is just why I took up drinking—so I didn't have to do shit I was afraid of.

So all I had to do was take off, right? Yeah, that's right. Obviously, you never been on a bender, if you don't know how sick you get after. I was maybe about able to crawl out from under the bridge and then collapse. I should probably have been in a hospital or a drying-out place with a hangover like this. I've shaken it out in some of those places on the morning after and what I can tell you is, you'll wish you were dead no matter where you are. But at least when you wake up under a bridge, there aren't any goddam moralizing medical types brutalizing you and calling it treatment, and then claiming you're just so screwed up that you can't stand them knocking you around.

But it's also generally a lot cleaner and better smelling than under a bridge, so there's that, too. It's all got its price, whatever you do. I had a lot of time to think about that, lying there staring at the underside of the bridge and listening to people's footsteps while they walked over. With any luck, this wouldn't be the day some cop got ambitious and decided to clean up the park by starting with me. Mostly that happened only in election years, but not being the most conscientious voter, I couldn't remember if this was one or not.

Sometime in the afternoon, when the sun had moved from one side of the bridge to the other, it comes to me that I'm a lot sicker than usual this time, sick and weak. But with the sound of people walking over the bridge and the distant traffic and sirens and junk noise a cityful of human beings tend to make, dead-of-night visitations don't look like anything more than the same old booze phantoms wearing new masks. And then you wonder for a moment, maybe, what booze phantoms really are, but you don't really know anything for sure.

Except I decided I *did* know, and I didn't like it, but there wasn't much I could do. The little one, what *was* her name? Had I ever known it while I—apparently—sat and listened to her spilling her guts. Drinking *real* hard those times. Sometimes the only way you can stand to hear any of it is while you're shitfaced.

Well, I *was, once.*

She was *what.* Invited; now I remember. Invited to what, though—a bottle party under a bridge? What did that entitle her to?

A drink. I offered her a drink. I offer all of them drinks, and they never turn them down. Maybe, I thought to myself, I should have been more specific about what they were drinking.

I just lay there all day, mostly because the hideous pain in my head wouldn't let me move anymore than a blink, and tried to feel the spot where she must have leeched on me. Past the pain in my head, though, I just plain hurt all over; even feeling all weak and faded wasn't so unusual.

And maybe I should have known something by that. All my little friends that came and went, and some of them even stopping to say good-bye to that crazy old lush, May. Did they ever take a good-bye sip I maybe didn't know about?

And while we're at it, what kind of blood cocktail did I make?

❨   ❨   ❨

I felt her coming. It must have been like a Friday or Saturday night because the park was still real busy and sometimes, when the wind was right, voices carried from 'way up the hill where the docks were. The kids having some kind of party, it sounded like. Maybe some new ones had come in. Weekends you can see new faces, especially when the weather's good and nobody minds sleeping outside. Although the docks are such good shelter that they're almost not outside. No trucks unload there anymore and I couldn't tell you what was in the building. Stolen shit, maybe, or drugs, or illegal guns. Or maybe just a lot of dust and an owner who didn't care except for the tax write-off. Nobody connected with the building ever bothered the kids, anyway, which was why they all stayed around there. And then at night, the chicken hawks would come around. They weren't much for noise.

And then it was like my mind flew out like a bird, out from under the bridge and up the hill to the docks. Jumble of images, kids' faces, other faces, in and out of the shadows and then turning away to the street, light streaks from the street-lamps, from cars passing with their brights on, to looking up at *her*. And her smiling down at what I know now must be my little friend who came to see me in my bender. Coming back, some kind of goon squad, except they're supposed to be on my side—

The little one stops, feeling me like I feel her. She's under the white light of a streetlamp, and it's swinging overhead like a yo-yo doing the around-the-world trick.

She stops looking around and I get this *gotta-do-it* sensation inside: the old need for a drink, *now*. Except it's not from me but from inside her. And so here they come, to have a drink from what's stashed under the bridge.

It makes my head hurt worse, but I shove away all those pictures that don't belong in my brain. I shove them down and away by making myself look at stuff, really *look*, and name what I see—what *I* see. Graffiti up above me, says *Eddie was here* and somebody else put *and sukked my kok GOOD* and a third person had added *with duck sauce*, which was good for a two-second laugh while I tried to get up.

I rolled over and managed to get on my hands and knees. On the ground in front of me was—

—the top of the hill; looking down into the park, and just walk a little further on, the bridge would come into view, though you couldn't see what was under it until you got further down, especially in summer, when the trees were so thick—

—a fucking *flyer* for a church pancake breakfast, all-you-can-eat pancakes and sausage, Knights of Columbus would be doing the cooking. "Yeah, that's right, swords into ploughshares," I muttered; except in urban areas, where they became spatulas. Get your red-hot flapjacks, get your red-hot cross buns. I could have used some of those, I thought, trying to get my feet under me so I could stand up. I crawled closer to the wall. It curved but I thought I might be able to walk my hands up it.

The image of the bridge jumps into my head and I stagger sideways, feeling my feet go like they're dancing, but somehow, I stayed up, hands scraping on the dirty wall. Pain keeps me awake, new pain. I have to catch my breath, launch myself out of here and if I can put enough distance between me and her, maybe I'll fade like a cheap AM station—

But now the three of them were standing there, just out of the shelter of the bridge, watching me stay up. The flashlight Ginny's carrying lights up the whole inside under here. I even get a look at my own startled, dirty face, wide-eyed like *I* was some kid making a few discoveries about life lived rough.

Ginny and *her* give the little one in the middle a gentle push forward, toward me. She looks great now. Like a sleek, strong animal in her expensive denim trousers—you can't call those jeans, they've got *creases*, chrissakes—and her neat white blouse and her tapestry vest. Fashion-magazine teenager. Dread hair, yeah, but when the style changes, cut it off. It grows back, or so I hear. Or is that a myth about hair and nails growing on corpses after they're dead?

She laughed at me. "I don't know about that, but *our* hair grows just fine, even if *we* never grow any older. Come on, my sister." She holds out a hand to me.

I look from her to Ginny. "It'd make more sense if it was you six months from now. But her I don't remember at all."

"You remember me a little bit," the girl says. "But that's okay, really. Come on, my sister. Let us help you now."

She lets me see myself standing in front of her like some kind of living rack for hanging rags on, with my arms almost straight over my head, hands shifting on the rough stone while I hold myself up on the low arch of the bridge. Vertigo strikes and I almost fall forward into her, *almost*, but I have been out here a long time and I have held myself up in some terrible states, benderized, tenderized, and deep in DTs I can't describe and can't forget. So I can hold myself up under the bridge facing this. For a little bit longer, anyway.

My head cleared and what she'd been saying finally got through. "Sister?" I said. "Not me."

She nodded, and behind her, they nodded, too. "We both have a thirst, don't we." I felt her need-a-drink along with my own, which had been running along like an engine on low idle all day long and was now starting to rev higher. "I know why you've been thirsty, what you really wanted. Now you can drink something that will really give it to you."

"Oh?" I croaked. "You bring me some vodka?"

"Better," she says, and starts to go on.

"Oh, don't say that," I interrupt, feeling her words taking shape in my own throat. "That's *so corny*. 'Dark wine.' Besides, I ain't no wino." Not unless I'm really desperate, but there was no law that I had to tell anyone that. Even if they already knew it.

She blinked at me. "You don't understand," she said. "This, too, will be your friend; it will love you and it won't be critical, and it will always do what it says it's going to. See? I remember what you told me, even if you don't remember what I told you. Come on. This is no way for a woman to live."

"Your way *is?*" I said, and laughed. I walked my hands down the wall and leaned against it with my neck bent due to the curve. My arms had been getting numb.

She nods. "For thousands of years, women have done what they've had to do to stay alive. Now we'll do what we *want* to do and flourish. We've been saved."

Where does she *get* this stuff? And finally I understand who's really doing the talking here.

"She turned you out real good. Better job than anyone else's done on you," I say, letting her see me look from *her* to the beast who did the deed. "Probably nobody else could do anything to make you say it's right to rape somebody, but she got you. I guess blood's the thickest stuff you can get, huh? Yeah, that's right."

"Women don't rape each other," she said, starting to get angry at me.

"Rapists rape anybody they wanna rape. Did you want it when she came at you with those fuckin' teeth and those beast eyes?"

"I didn't understand then," she said, but I see her wavering.

"Yeah, that's right," I say. "I guess you didn't see how it was for your own good, huh? How you was really gonna *like* it when you got going and even though it hurt like a bastard at first—am I right about that, was it painful?—even though it hurt like anything, you'd be happy afterward that you went through it, you'd want it again and again, and you'd wanna do it as much as you could. So what the hell, let's turn pro, right? Isn't that right?"

And now I look right at Ginny, who was gonna get turned out tonight along with me and I see that for the moment, whatever cloud came over her starting with a doggy bag of food and a canned soda, it's lifted up now, at least temporarily, and if anyone's gonna do anything, it's got to be now.

I throw myself down and the little one makes a jump at me, but then I come up with the only thing I can think of to back her off and I hope it works.

For once, I was right. The Knights of Columbus pancake breakfast, with a line drawing of the Sacred Heart of Jesus and its happy come-one-come-all-break-bread-together sentiments driving it—*that* gets her. Sometimes all salvation is is somebody who cares about feeding the hungry, not feeding on them. Exact opposite of a pimp. Or a rapist.

It sends her backing away from me, confused and scared that a dirty piece of paper I picked up off the ground has some power she can't handle and can't understand.

"May," Ginny says, stepping toward me, and she's looking at the other two and then at me and there are so many hard questions there.

"I already told you," I say, wishing it didn't hurt so much to kneel, wishing my head would just explode if that's what it was going to do, "you do what your heart tells you, for as long as you have a heart. How long did you want to keep it?"

The flashlight beam turns away from me, and the darkness feels suddenly so good and cool on my throbbing, burning head. And I must be on the verge of passing out or something, because I'm lost in the cool and soothing dark for I don't know how long before I hear Ginny say, "I won't stop you if you leave now."

And sometime after that, she comes and takes the paper out of my hands. I have been holding it up like St. George's shield or maybe like I was a Knight of Columbus myself. Ginny helps me sit down and she stays by me for a while.

I didn't understand why until I stopped shaking. First I knew of it.

Now you want to hear the happy talk about how I realized the error of my ways, that there was some even bigger evils out there and I decided to clean up, dry out, and join the holy war against them. And Ginny went with me; we found a safe place to stay and I learned I wanted to be a mommy after all and she learned to trust me. And pretty soon we had enough to buy a used van and a coffee urn and a bunch of old blankets.

This is because you're a fool. You can't help it. In your world, the cavalry always shows up on time. Out here in the rough lane, the cavalry deserted as soon as it was out of sight of the fort and it ain't coming back. And if Mommy and Daddy were in the cavalry when that happened, it means they're not coming back either. So get used to it.

I didn't want to think about what had happened, so I went back to drinking as soon as I could manage it. That same night, as a matter of fact. Dropkick came down to see what was going on because he'd seen the three of them trooping down this way. He owed me a favor, so I made him scrounge me a flask. It went down raw, but it went down and stayed down. I gave Ginny some, but only a little. It takes a lot more for me and I wasn't in a sharing mood especially.

She didn't like it but Dropkick took it off her hands for her. Then she just sat and watched me. The Dropper set up the flashlight with the paper so that it was like a lamp and we were lit up for as long as the battery held out. I knew she didn't understand, but I wasn't in an explaining mood, either. I was in a drinking mood.

I tried to get her to leave with Dropkick but she wouldn't go. So I knew I'd have to talk to her about it just to get her out of my hair, which, for all the neglect, wasn't going dread. Maybe dreads were a young woman's game and hell, I was practically thirty.

So she barely got the word *Why* out of her mouth before I said, "Only if you never ask me again." And she nodded and I said, "Really. Never again. Because I drink instead of do this shit, and that's the way I like it."

And she goes, "But they offered—"

"Yeah, yeah, yeah, that's right, isn't it. They offered. And I guess, you being a good educated girl, very smart and all, you see what they like to call parallels between their habits and mine. But I will remind you that there are some important differences, one of the big ones being that my choice of beverage doesn't have to be inside some other person before I can drink it. And the other being that I'm this way because I want to be.

"Yeah, that's right, I'm sure they told you that they chose their way to be, too. You believe that? Maybe it's true. But now they got no choice. There's no clinic they go to to kick the habit and get straight again. There's no meetings to help you stay quit. They're fuckin' *animals* now. I saw her, she's a beast. I'm a drunk and no good, but I'm still human. Sometimes that's all the salvation you get."

Ginny shook her head like someone had hit her and she was dazed. "Are you saying that you're gonna quit this someday, dry out, or whatever? Get straight?"

"Could if I wanted to. Don't really want to." I shrugged. "Listen, that creature that turns you out, that's a beast. Your heart tell you to be one, too?"

"I don't see how you can be here like this and say stuff like that," she said.

"Me, either," I said. "Mostly, I don't. Mostly, I drink. And I'd appreciate being left to it."

She stood up and then paused. "One for the road?"

I held up the flask to see what was left. "Okay, a little one. Make sure it's a little one or I might take a notion to suck it back out of you."

She laughed a little nervously and took a very small polite sip, not bothering to wipe the neck first. "Thanks, May. I don't know what I'm going to do now."

"That's good," I said.

Yeah, that's right; sometimes that's salvation, too. Think about it.

THE BROTHERHOOD OF BLOOD

HUGH B. CAVE

IT IS MIDNIGHT AS I WRITE THIS. LISTEN! EVEN NOW THE doleful chimes of the Old North Church, buried in the heart of this enormous city of mine, are tolling the funereal hour.

In a little while, when the city thinks itself immune in sleep, deep-cradled in the somber hours of night—I shall go forth from here on my horrible mission of blood.

Every night it is the same. Every night the same ghoulish orgy. Every night the same mad thirst. And in a little while—

But first, while there is yet time, let me tell you of my agony. Then you will understand, and sympathize, and suffer with me.

I was twenty-six years old then. God alone knows how old I am now. The years frighten me, and I have deliberately forgotten them. But I was twenty-six when she came.

They call me an author. Perhaps I was; and yet the words which I gave to the world were not, and could not be, the true thoughts which hovered in my mind. I had studied—studied things which the average man dares not even consider. The occult—life after death—spiritualism—call it what you will.

I had written about such things, but in guarded phrases, calculated to divulge only those elementary truths which laymen should be told. My name was well known, perhaps too well known. I can see it now as it used to appear in the pages of the leading medical journals and magazines devoted to psychic investigation.

"By—Paul Munn—Authority on the Supernatural."

In those days I had few friends; none, in fact, who were in harmony with my work. One man I did know well—a medical student at Harvard University, in Cambridge. His name was Rojer Threng.

I can remember him now as he used to sit bolt upright in the huge chair in my lonely Back Bay apartment. He filled the chair with his enormous, loosely-constructed frame. His face was angular, pointed to gaunt extremes. His eyes— ah, you will have cause to consider those eyes before I have finished!—his eyes were eternally afire with a peculiar glittering life which I could never fully comprehend.

"And you can honestly sit there, spilling your mad theories to the world?" he used to accuse me in his rasping, deep-throated voice. "Good Lord, Munn, this is the Twentieth Century—a scientific era of careful thought—not the time of werewolves and vampires! You are mad!"

And yet, for all his open condemnation, he did not dare to stand erect, with his face lifted, and *deny* the things I told him. That sinister gleam of his eyes; there was no denying the thoughts lurking behind it. On the surface he was a sneering, indifferent doubter; but beneath the surface, where no man's eyes penetrated, he *knew*.

He was there in my apartment when she came. That night is vivid even now. There we sat, enveloped in a haze of gray cigarette smoke. I was bent over the desk in the corner, hammering a typewriter. He lay sprawled in the great overstuffed chair, watching me critically, intently, as if he would have liked to continue the heated argument which had passed between us during the past hour.

He had come in his usual unannounced manner, bringing with him an ancient newspaper clipping from some forgotten file in the university. Thrusting the thing into my hand, he had ordered me to read it.

That clipping was of singular interest. It was a half-hearted account of the infamous vampire horror of the little half-buried village of West Surrey. You recall it? It was known, luridly, as the "crime of eleven terrors." Eleven pitiful victims, each with the same significant blood-marks, were one after the other the prey of the unknown vampire who haunted that little village in the heart of an

English moor. And then, when the eleventh victim had succumbed, Scotland Yard—with the assistance of the famous psychic investigator, Sir Edmund Friel—discovered the vampire to be the same aged, seemingly innocent old woman who had acted as *attendant nurse* to the unfortunate victims. A ghastly affair.

But Threng held the newspaper clipping up to me as a mere "trick" of journalism. He denounced it bitterly.

"What *is* a vampire, Munn?" he sneered.

I did not answer him. I saw no use in continuing a futile debate on a subject in which we had nothing in common.

"Well?" he insisted.

I swung around, facing him deliberately.

"A vampire," I said thoughtfully, choosing my words with extreme care, "is a creature of living death, dependent upon human blood for its existence. From sunset to sunrise, during the hours of darkness, it is free to pursue its horrible blood-quest. During the day it must remain within the confines of its grave—dead, and yet alive."

"And how does it appear?" he bantered. "As the usual skeletonic intruder, cowled in black, or perhaps as a mystic wraith without substance?"

"In either of two forms," I said coldly, angered by his twisted smile. "As a bat—or in its natural human substance. In either shape it leaves the grave each night and seeks blood. It obtains its blood from the throats of its victims, leaving two significant wounds in the neck from which it has drawn life. Its victims, after such a death, inherit the powers of their persecutor—and become vampires."

"Rot!" Threng exclaimed. "Utter sentimentality and imagination."

I turned back to my typewriter, ignoring him. His words were not pleasant. I would have been glad to be rid of him.

But he was persistent. He leaned forward in his chair and said critically:

"Suppose I wished to become a vampire, Munn. How could I go about it? How *does* a man obtain life after death, or life *in* death?"

"By study," I answered crisply. "By delving into thoughts which men like you sneer at. By going so deeply into such things that he becomes possessed of inhuman powers."

That ended our discussion. He could not conceive of such possibilities; and he laughed aloud at my statement. Bitterly resentful, I forced myself to continue the work before me. He, in turn, thrust a cigarette into his mouth and leaned back in his chair like a great lazy animal. And then—*she* came.

The soft knock on the door panel—so suggestive that it seemed from the world beyond—startled me. I swung about, frowning at the intrusion. Visitors at this hour of night were not the kind of guests I wished to face.

I went to the door slowly, hesitantly. My hand touched the latch nervously. Then I forced back the foolish fear that gripped me, and drew the barrier wide. And there I saw her for the first time—tall, slender, radiantly lovely as she stood in the half-light of the outer passage.

"You—are Mr. Paul Munn?" she inquired quietly.

"I am," I admitted.

"I am Margot Vernee. It is unconventional, I suppose, calling upon you at this hour; but I have come because of your reputation. You are the one man in this great city who may be able to—help me."

I would have answered her, but she caught sight, then, of Rojer Threng. Her face whitened. She stepped back very abruptly, fearful—or at least so I thought—that he might have overheard her.

"I—I am sorry," she said quickly. "I thought that you were alone, Mr. Munn. I—may I return later? Tomorrow, perhaps—when you are not occupied?"

I nodded. At that particular moment I could not find a voice to answer her; for she had inadvertently stepped directly beneath the bracket lamp in the wall, and her utter beauty fascinated me, choking the words back into my throat.

Then she went; and as I closed the door reluctantly, Rojer Threng glanced quizzically into my face and said dryly:

"Wants you to help her, eh? I didn't know you went in for that sort of thing, Munn. Better be careful!"

And he laughed. God, how I remember that laugh—and the cruel, derisive hatred that was inherent in it! But I did not answer him. In fact, his words were driven mechanically into my mind, and I hardly heard them. Returning to the typewriter, I attempted to force myself once more into the work that confronted me; but the face of that girl blurred the lines of my manuscript. She seemed to be still in the room, still standing near me. Imagination, of course; and yet, in view of what has happened since that night, I do not know.

She did not return as she had promised. All during the following day I awaited her coming—restless, nervous, unable to work. At eleven in the evening I was still pacing automatically back and forth across the floor when the doorbell rang. It was Rojer Threng who stepped over the threshold.

At first he did not mention the peculiar affair of the previous night. He took his customary place in the big chair and talked idly about medical topics of casual interest. Then, bending forward suddenly, he demanded:

"Did she return, Munn?"

"No," I said.

"I thought not," he muttered harshly. "Not after she saw me here. I—used to know her."

It was not so much the thing he said, as the complete bitterness with which he spoke, that brought me about with a jerk, confronting him.

"You—knew her?" I said slowly.

"I knew her," he scowled. "Think of the name, man. Margot Vernee. Have I never mentioned it to you?"

"No." And then I knew that he had. At least, the inflection of it was vaguely familiar.

"Her story would interest you," he shrugged. "Peculiar, Munn—very peculiar, in view of what you were telling me last night, before she came."

He looked up at me oddly. I did not realize the significance of that crafty look then, but now I know.

"The Vernee family," he said, "is as old as France."

"Yes?" I tried to mask my eagerness.

"The Château Vernee is still standing—abandoned—forty miles south of Paris. A hundred years before the Revolution it was occupied by Armand Vernee, noted for his occult research and communications with the spirit world. He was dragged from the château by the peasants of the surrounding district when he was twenty-eight years old and burned at the stake—for witchcraft."

I stared straight into Threng's angular face. If ever I noticed that unholy gleam in his strange eyes, it was at that moment. His eyes were wide open, staring, burning with a dead, phosphorescent glow. Never once did they flicker as he continued his story in that sibilant, half-hissing voice of his.

"After Armand Vernee's execution, his daughter Regine lived alone in the château. She married a young count, gave birth to a son. In her twenty-eighth year she was prostrated with a strange disease. The best physicians in the country could not cure her. She—"

"What—kind of disease?" I said very slowly.

"The symptoms," he said, sucking in his breath audibly, "baffled all those who examined her. Two small red marks at the throat, Munn—and a continual loss of blood *while she slept.* She confessed to horrible dreams. She told of a great bat which possessed her father's face, clawing at the window of her chamber every night—gaining admittance by forcing the shutters open with its claws—hovering over her."

"And—she died?"

"She died. In her twenty-eighth year."

"And then?" I shuddered.

"Her son, François Vernee Leroux, lived alone in the château. The count would not remain. The horror of her death drove him away—drove him mad. The son, François, lived—alone."

Threng looked steadily at me. At least, his *eyes* looked. The rest of his face was contorted with passion, malignant.

"François Vernee died when he was twenty-eight years of age," he said meaningly. "He, too, left a son—and *that* son died at the age of twenty-eight. Each death was the same. The same crimson marks at the throat. The same loss of blood. The same—madness."

Threng reached for a cigarette and held a match triumphantly to the end of it. His face, behind the sudden glare of that stick of wood, was horrible with exultation.

"Margot Vernee is the last of her line," he shrugged. "Every direct descendant of Armand Vernee had died in the same ghastly way, at twenty-eight years of age. *That* is why the girl came here for help, Munn. She knows the inevitable end that awaits her! She knows that she cannot escape the judgment which Armand Vernee has inflicted upon the family of Vernee!"

◖   ◖   ◖

Rojer Threng was right. Three weeks after those significant words had passed his lips, the girl came to my apartment. She repeated, almost word for word, the very fundamental facts that Threng had disclosed to me. Other things she told me, too—but I see no need to repeat them here.

"You are the only man who knows the significance of my fate," she said to me; and her face was ghastly white as she said it. "Is there no way to avert it, Mr. Munn? Is there no alternative?"

I talked with her for an eternity. The following night, and every night for the next four weeks, she came to me. During the hours of daylight I delved frantically into research work, in an attempt to find an outlet from the dilemma which faced her. At night, alone with her, I learned bit by bit the details of her mad story, and listened to her pleas for assistance.

Then came that fatal night. She sat close to me, talking in her habitually soft, persuasive voice.

"I have formed a plan," I said quietly.

"A plan, Paul?"

"When the time comes, I shall prepare a sleeping-chamber for you with but one window. I shall seal that window with the mark of the cross. It is the only way."

She looked at me for a long while without speaking. Then she said, very slowly:

"You had better prepare the room, Paul—soon."

"You mean—" I said suddenly. But I knew what she meant.

"I shall be twenty-eight tonight—at midnight."

God forgive me that I did not keep her with me that night! I was already half in love with her. No—do not smile at that. You, too, after looking into her face continually for four long weeks—sitting close to her—listening to the soft whisper of her voice—you, too, would have loved her. I would have given my work, my reputation, my very life for her; and yet I permitted her to walk out of my apartment that night, to the horror that awaited her!

She came to me the next evening. One glance at her and I knew the terrible truth. I need not have asked the question that I did, but it came mechanically from my lips, like a dead voice.

"It—came?"

"Yes," she said quietly. "It came."

She stood before me and untied the scarf from her neck. And there, in the center of her white throat, I saw those infernal marks—two parallel slits of crimson, an eighth of an inch in length, horrible in their evil.

"It was a dream," she said, "and yet I know that it was no dream, but vivid reality. A gigantic bat with a woman's face—my mother's face—appeared suddenly at the window of my room. Its claws lifted the window. It circled over my bed as I lay there, staring at it in mute horror. Then it descended upon me, and I felt warm lips on my neck. A languid, wonderfully contented feeling came over me. I relaxed—and slept."

"And—when you awoke?" I said heavily.

"The mark of the vampire was here on my throat."

I stared at her for a very long time, without speaking. She did not move. She stood there by my desk; and a pitiful, yearning look came into her deep eyes.

Then, of a sudden, I was gripped with the helplessness of the whole evil affair. I stormed about the room, screaming my curses to the walls, my face livid with hopeless rage, my hands clawing at anything within reach of them. I tore at my face. I seized the wooden smoking-stand and broke it in my fingers, hurling the shattered pieces into a grinning, maddening picture of the Creator which hung beside the door. Then I tripped, fell, sprawled headlong—and groped again to my feet, quivering as if some tropic fever had laid its cold hands upon me.

There were tears in Margot's eyes as she came toward me and placed her hands on my arm. She would have spoken, to comfort me. I crushed her against me, holding her until she cried out in pain.

"Merciful Christ!" I cried. And the same words spurted from my lips, over and over again, until the room echoed with the intensity of them.

"You—love me, Paul?" she said softly.

"Love you!" I said hoarsely. "*Love* you! God, Margot—is there no way—"

"I love you, too," she whispered wearily. "But it is too late, Paul. The thing has visited me. I am a part of it. I—"

"I can keep you away from it!" I shouted. "I can hide you—protect you—where the thing will never find you!"

She shook her head, smiling heavily.

"It is too late, Paul."

"It is never too late!"

God! The words sounded brave enough then. Since then I have learned better. The creature that was preying on her possessed the infernal powers of life-in-death—powers which no mortal could deny. I knew it well enough, even when I made that rash promise. I had studied those things long enough to know my own limitations against them.

And yet I made the attempt. Before I left her that night, I hung the sign of the cross about her lovely throat, over the crimson stain of the vampire. I locked and sealed the windows of my apartment, breathing a prayer of supplication at each barrier as I made it secure. And then, holding her in my arms for a single unforgettable moment, I left her.

The apartment above mine was occupied by a singular fellow who had more than once called upon me to discuss my work. He, too, was a writer of sorts, and we had a meager something in common because of that. Therefore, when I climbed the stairs at a quarter to twelve that night and requested that he allow me to remain with him until morning, he was not unwilling to accede to my request, though he glanced at me most curiously as I made it.

However, he asked no questions, and I refrained from supplying any casual information to set his curiosity at rest. He would not have understood.

All that night I remained awake, listening for signs of disturbance in the rooms below me. But I heard nothing—not so much as a whisper. And when daylight came I descended the stairs with false hope in my heart.

There was no answer to my knock. I waited a moment, thinking that she might be yet asleep; then I rapped again on the panels. Then, when the silence persisted in haunting me, I fumbled frantically in my pockets for my spare key. I was afraid—terribly afraid.

And she was lying there when I stumbled into the room. Like a creature already dead she lay upon the bed, one white arm drooping to the floor. The silken comforter was thrown back. The breast of her gown was torn open. Fresh blood gleamed upon those dread marks in her throat.

I thought that she was dead. A sob choked in my throat as I dropped down beside her, peering into her colorless face. I clutched at her hand, and it was cold—stark cold. And then, unashamed of the tears that coursed down my cheeks, I lay across her still body, kissing her lips—kissing them as if it were the last time that I should ever see them.

She opened her eyes.

Her fingers tightened a little on my hand. She smiled—a pathetic, tired smile.

"It—came," she whispered. "I—knew it would."

I will not dwell longer on the death of the girl I loved. Enough to recount the simple facts.

I brought doctors to her. No less than seven expert physicians attended her and consulted among themselves about her affliction. I told them my fears; but they were men of the world, not in sympathy with what I had to tell them.

"Loss of blood," was their diagnosis—but they looked upon me as a man gone mad when I attempted to *explain* the loss of blood.

There was a transfusion. My own blood went into her veins, to keep her alive. For three nights she lived. Each of those nights I stood guard over her, never closing my eyes while darkness was upon us. And each night the thing came, clawing at the windows, slithering its horrible shape into the room where she lay. I did not know, then, how it gained admittance. Now—God help me— I know all the powers of that unholy clan. Its nocturnal creatures know no limits of space or confinement.

And this thing that preyed upon the girl I loved—I refuse to describe it. You will know *why* I make such a refusal when I have finished.

Twice I fought it, and found myself smothered by a ghastly shape of fog that left me helpless. Once I lay across her limp body with my hands covering her throat to keep the thing away from her—and I was hurled unmercifully to the floor, with an unearthly, long-dead stench of decayed flesh in my nostrils. When I regained consciousness, the wounds in her throat were newly opened, and my own wrists were marked with the ragged stripes of raking claws.

I realized, after that, that I could do nothing. The horror had gone beyond human power of prevention.

The mark of the cross which I had given her—that was worse than useless. I *knew* that it was useless. Had she worn it on that very first night of all, before the thing had claimed her for its own, it might have protected her. But now that this infernal mark was upon her throat, even the questionable strength of the cross was nullified by its evil powers. There was nothing left—nothing that could be done.

As a last resort I called upon Rojer Threng. He came. He examined her. He turned to me and said in a voice that was pregnant with unutterable malice:

"I can do nothing. If I could, I *would* not."

And so he left me—alone with the girl who lay there, pale as a ghost, upon the bed.

I knelt beside her. It was eight o'clock in the evening. Dusk was beginning to creep into the room. And she took my hand in hers, drawing me close so that she might speak to me.

"Promise me, Paul—" she whispered.

"Anything," I said.

"In two years you will be twenty-eight," she said wearily. "I shall be forced to return to you. It is not a thing that I can help; it is the curse of my family. I have no descendants—I am the last of my line. You are the one dearest to me. It is *you* to whom I must return. Promise me—"

She drew me very close to her, staring into my face with a look of supplication that made me cold, fearful.

"Promise me—that when I return—you will fight against me," she entreated. "You must wear the sign of the cross—always—Paul. No matter how much I plead with you—to remove it—promise me that you will not!"

"I would rather join you, even in such a condition," I said bitterly, "than remain here alone without you."

"No, Paul. Forget me. Promise!"

"I—promise."

"And you will wear the cross always, and never remove it?"

"I will—fight against you," I said sadly.

Then I lost control. I flung myself beside her and embraced her. For hours we lay there together in utter silence.

She died—in my arms.

It is hard to find words for the rest of this. It was hard, then, to find any reason for living. I did no work for months on end. The typewriter remained impassive upon its desk, forgotten, dusty, mocking me night after night as I paced the floor of my room.

In time I began to receive letters from editors, from prominent medical men, demanding to know why my articles had so suddenly ceased to appear in current periodicals. What could I say to them? Could I explain to them that when I sat down at the typewriter, *her* face held my fingers stiff? No; they would not have understood; they would have dubbed me a rank sentimentalist. I could not reply to their requests. I could only read their letters over and over again, in desperation, and hurl the missives to the floor, as a symbol of my defeat.

I wanted to talk. God, how I wanted to! But I had no one to listen to me. Casual acquaintances I did not dare take into my confidence. Rojer Threng did not return. Even the fellow in the rooms above me, who shared his apartment with me that night, did not come near me. He sensed that something peculiar, something beyond his scope of reason, enveloped me.

Six months passed and I began, slowly at first, to return to my regular routine. That first return to work was agony. More than one thesis I started in the proper editorial manner, only to find myself, after the first half-dozen pages, writing about *her*—*her* words, *her* thoughts. More than once I wrenched pages from the roll of the typewriter, ripped them to shreds and dashed them to the floor—only to gather them together again and read them a hundred times more, because they spoke of her.

And so a year passed. A year of my allotted time of loneliness, before she should return.

Three months more, and I was offered an instructorship at the university, to lecture on philosophy. I accepted the position. There I learned that Rojer Threng had graduated from the medical school, had hung out his private shingle, and was well along the road to medical fame. Once, by sheer accident, I encountered him in the corridors of the university. He shook my hand, spoke to me for a few minutes regarding his success, and excused himself at the first opportunity. He did not mention *her.*

Then, months later, came the night of my twenty-eighth birthday.

That night I did a strange thing. When darkness had crept into my room, I drew the great chair close to one of the windows, flung the aperture open wide, and waited. Waited—and *hoped. I wanted* her to come.

Yet I remembered my promise to her. Even as I lowered myself into the chair, I hung a crucifix about my throat and made the sign of the cross. Then I sat stiff, rigid, staring into the black void before me.

The hours dragged. My body became stiff, sore from lack of motion. My eyes were glued open, rimmed with black circles of anxiety. My hands clutched the arms of the chair, and never relaxed their intense grip.

I heard the distant bell of the Old North Church tolling eleven o'clock; and later—hours and hours and hours later—it struck a single note to indicate the half-hour before midnight.

Then, very suddenly, a black, bat-like shape was fluttering in the open window. It had substance, for I heard the dead impact of its great wings as they struck the ledge in front of me; and yet it had *no* substance, for I could discern the definite, unbroken shape of the window frame *through* its massive body! And I sat motionless, transfixed—staring.

The thing swooped past me. I saw it strike the floor—heard it struggling erratically between the legs of the table. Then, in front of my eyes, it dissolved into a creature of mist; and another shape took form. I saw it rise out of the floor—saw it become tall and lithe and slender. And then—then *she* stood before me, radiantly beautiful.

In that moment of amazement I forgot my danger. I lurched up from the chair and took a sudden step toward her. My arms went out. Her arms were already out; and she was standing there waiting for me to take her.

But even as I would have clasped her slender body, she fell away from me, staring in horror at the crucifix that hung from my throat. I stopped short. I spoke to her, calling her by name. But she retreated from me, circling around me until she stood before the open window. Then, with uncanny quickness, she was gone—and a great black-winged bat swirled through the opening into the outer darkness.

For an eternity I stood absolutely still, with my arms still outstretched. Then, with a dry, helpless sob, I turned away.

Need I repeat what must already be obvious? She returned. Night after night she returned to me, taking form before me with her lovely, pleading arms outstretched to enfold me. I could not bring myself to believe that this utterly lovely, supplicating figure could wish to do me harm. For that matter, I could not believe that she was dead—that she had ever died. I wanted her. God, how I wanted her! I would have given my life to take her beautiful body once more in my arms and hold her close to me.

But I remembered my promise to her. The crucifix remained about my throat. Never once did she touch it—or touch me. In fact, never once did I see her for more than a single fleeting instant. She took birth before my eyes—stood motionless while I stumbled out of the chair and groped toward her—and then the awful power of the sign of the cross thrust her back. Always the same. One maddening moment—and hours upon hours of abject, empty loneliness that followed.

I did no work. All day, every day, I waited in agony for the hour of her coming. Then one day I sat by myself and thought. I reasoned with myself. I argued my personal desires against the truths which I knew to be insurmountable.

And that night, when she stood before me, I tore the crucifix from my throat and hurled it through the open window. I took her in my arms. I embraced her; and I was glad, wonderfully glad, for the first time in more than two years.

We clung to each other. She, too, was glad. I could see it in her face, in her eyes. Her lips trembled as they pressed mine. They were warm, hot—alive.

I am not sure of all that happened. I do not want to be sure. Even as her slender body quivered in my arms, a slow stupor came over me. It was like sleep, but more—oh, so much more desirous than mere slumber. I moved back—I was forced back—to the great chair. I relaxed. Something warm and soft touched my throat. There was no pain, no agony. Life was drawn out of me.

It was daylight when I awoke. The room was empty. The sunlight streamed through the open window. Something wet and sticky lay upon my throat. I reached up, touched it, and stared at my fingers dispassionately. They were stained with blood.

I did not need to seize upon a mirror. The two telltale marks of the vampire were upon my neck. I knew it.

She came the next night. Again we lay together, deliriously happy. I had no regrets. I felt her lips at my throat . . .

Next morning I lay helpless in the big chair, unable to move. My strength had been drawn from me. I had no power to rise. Far into the day I remained in the same posture. When a knock came at my door, I could not stand up to admit the visitor. I could only turn my head listlessly and murmur: "Come in."

It was the manager of the house who entered. He scuffed toward me half apologetically and stood there, looking down at me.

"I've been 'avin' complaints, sor," he scowled, as if he did not like to deliver his message. "The chap up above yer 'as been kickin' about the noise yer makes down 'ere o' nights. It'll 'ave ter stop, sor. I don't like to be tellin' yer—but the chap says as 'ow 'e's seen yer sittin' all night long in front o' yer winder, with the winder wide open. 'E says 'e 'ears yer talkin' ter some 'un down 'ere late at night, sor."

"I'm—very ill, Mr. Robell," I said weakly. "Will you—call a doctor?"

He blinked at me. Then he must have seen that significant thing on my throat, for he bent suddenly over me and said harshly:

"My Gawd, sor. You *are* sick!"

He hurried out. Fifteen minutes later he returned with a medical man whom I did not recognize. The fellow examined me, ordered me to bed, spent a long while peering at the mark on my neck, and finally went out—perplexed and scowling. When he came back, in an hour or so, he brought a more experienced physician with him.

They did what they could for me; but they did not understand, nor did I undertake to supply them with information. They could not prevent the inevitable; that I knew. I did not want them to prevent it.

And that night, as I lay alone, *she* came as usual. Ten minutes before the luminous hands of the clock on the table beside me registered eleven o'clock, she came to my bed and leaned over me. She did not leave until daylight was but an hour distant.

The next day was my last; and that day brought a man I had never expected to see again. It brought Rojer Threng!

I can see his face even now, as he paced across the room and stood beside my bed. It was repulsive with hate, masked with terrible triumph. His lips curled over his teeth as he spoke; and his eyes—those boring, glittering, living eyes—drilled their way into my tired brain as he glared into my face.

"You wonder why I have come, Munn?"

"Why—" I replied wearily. I was already close to eternity; and having him there beside me, feeling the hideous dynamic quality of his gaunt body, drew the last tongue of life out of me.

"She has been here, eh?" he grinned evilly.

I did not answer. Even the word *she* coming from his lips, was profanity.

"I came here to tell you something, Munn," he rasped. "Something that will comfort you on the journey you are about to take. Listen—"

He lowered himself into the great chair and hunched himself close. And I was forced to listen to his savage threat, because I could not lift my hand to silence him.

"I used to love Margot Vernee, Munn," he said. "I loved her as much as you do—but in a different way. She'd have none of me. Do you understand? She would have none of me! She despised me. She *told* me that she despised me. *She!*"

His massive hands clenched and unclenched, as if they would have twisted about my throat. His eyes flamed.

"Then she loved *you! You*—with your thin, common body and hoary brain. She refused me, with all I had to offer her, and accepted you! Now do you know why I've come here?"

"You can do nothing—now," I said heavily. "It is too late. She is beyond your power."

Then he laughed. God, that laugh! It echoed and reechoed across the room, vibrating with fearful intensity. It lashed into my brain like fire—left me weak and limp upon the bed. And there I lay, staring after him as he strode out of the room.

I never saw Rojer Threng again.

I wonder if you know the meaning of death? Listen . . .

They carried me that evening to a strange place. I say *they*, but perhaps I should say *he*, for Rojer Threng was the man who ordered the change of surroundings. As for myself, I was too close to unconsciousness to offer resistance. I know only that I was lifted from my bed by four strong arms, and placed upon a stretcher, and then I was carried out of my apartment to a private car which waited at the curb below.

I bear no malice toward the two subordinates who performed this act. They were doing as they had been told to do. They were pawns of Rojer Threng's evil mind.

They made me as comfortable as possible in the rear section of the car. I heard the gears clash into place; then the leather cushion beneath me jerked abruptly, and the car droned away from the curb.

I could discern my surroundings, and I took mental note of the route we followed, though I do not know that it matters particularly. I remembered crossing the Harvard Bridge above the Charles River, with innumerable twinkling lights showing their reflections in the quiet water below. Then we followed one of the central thoroughfares, through a great square where the noise and harsh glare beat into my mind. And later—a long time later—the car came to a stop in the yards of the university.

Once again I was placed upon a stretcher. Where they took me I do not know; except that we passed through a maze of endless corridors in the heart of one of the university's many buildings. But the end of my journey lay in a small, dimly lighted room on one of the upper floors; and there I was lifted from the stretcher and placed upon a comfortable brocaded divan.

It was dusk then, and my two attendants set about making my comfort more complete. They spooned broth between my lips. They turned the light out of my eyes. They covered my prostrate body with a silken robe of some deep red color.

"Why," I murmured, "have you—brought me here?"

"It is Doctor Threng's order, sir," one of them said quietly.

"But I don't want—"

"Doctor Threng fully understands the nature of your malady, sir," the attendant replied, silencing my protest. "He has prepared this room to protect you."

I studied the room, then. Had he not spoken in such a significant tone, I should probably never have given a thought to the enclosure; but the soft inflection of his words was enough to remove my indifference.

As I have said, it was a small room. That in itself was not peculiar; but when I say that the walls were broken by only *one* window, you too will realize something sinister. The walls were low, forming a perfect square with the divan precisely in the center. No hangings, no pictures or portraits of any kind, adorned the walls themselves; they were utterly bare. I know now that they were *not* bare;

but the infernal wires that extended across them were so nearly invisible that my blurred sight did not notice.

One thing I shall never forget. When the attendants left me, after preparing me for the night, one of them said deliberately, as if to console me:

"You will be guarded every moment of this night, sir. The wall facing you has been bored through with a spy-hole. Doctor Threng, in the next room asked me to inform you that he will remain at the spy-hole all night—and will allow nothing to come near you."

And then they left me alone.

I knew that she would come. It was my last night on earth, and I was positive that she would see it through by my side, to give me courage. The strange room would not keep her away. She would be able to find me, no matter where they secreted me.

I waited, lying limp on the divan with my face toward the window. The window was open. I thought then that the attendants had left it open by mistake; that they had overlooked it. I know now that it was left wide because of Rojer Threng's command.

An hour must have passed after they left me to myself. An hour of despair and emptiness for me. She did not come. I began to doubt—to be afraid. I knew that I should die soon—very soon—and I dreaded to enter the great unknown without her guidance. And so I waited and waited and waited, and never once took my eyes from the window which was my only hope of relief.

Then—it must have been nearly midnight—I heard the doleful howling of a dog somewhere down in the yard below. I knew what it meant. I struggled up, propping myself on one elbow, staring eagerly.

A moment later the faint square of moonlight which marked the window-frame was suddenly blotted out. I saw a massive, winged shape silhouetted in the opening. For an instant it hovered there, flapping its great body. Then it swooped into the room where I lay.

I saw again that uncanny transformation of spirit. The nocturnal spectre dissolved before my eyes and assumed shape again, rising into a tall, languid, divinely beautiful woman. And *she* stood there, smiling at me.

All that night she remained by my side. She talked to me in a voice that was no more than a faint whisper, comforting me for the ordeal which I must soon undergo. She told me secrets of the grave—secrets which I may not repeat here, nor ever wish to repeat. Ah, but it was a relief from the loneliness and restlessness of my heart to have her there beside me, sitting so quietly, confidently, in the depths of the divan. I no longer dreaded the fate in store for me. It meant that I should be with her always. You who love or ever have loved with an all-consuming tenderness—you will understand.

The hours passed all too quickly. I did not take account of them. I knew that she would leave when it was necessary for her to go. I knew the unfair limits that were imposed upon her very existence. Hers was a life of darkness, from sunset to sunrise. Unless she returned to the secrets of the grave before daylight crept upon us, her life would be consumed.

The hour of parting drew near. I feared to think of it. With her close to me, holding my hand, I was at peace; but I knew that without her I should lapse again into an agony of doubt and fear. If I could have died then with her near me, I think I should have been contented.

But it was not to be. She bent over to kiss me tenderly and then rose from the divan.

"I—must go back, beloved," she whispered.

"Stay a moment more," I begged. "One moment—"

"I dare not, Paul."

She turned away. I watched her as if she were taking my very soul with her. She walked very softly, slowly, to the window, I saw her look back at me, and she smiled. God, how I remember that last smile! It was meant to give me courage—to put strength into my heart.

And then she stepped to the window.

Even as she moved that last step, the horrible thing happened. A monstrous, livid streamer of white light seared across the space in front of her. It blazed in her face like a rigid snake, hurling her back. There, engraved upon the wall, hung the sign of the cross, burning like a thing possessed of life!

She staggered away from it. I saw the terror in her face as she ran to the opposite wall. Ten steps she took; and then that wall too shone livid with the cross. Two horrible wires, transformed into writhing reality by some tremendous charge of electricity, glowed before her.

She sought frantically for a means of escape. Back and forth she turned. The sign of the cross confronted her on every side, hemming her in. There *was* no escape. The room was a veritable trap—a trap designed and executed by the infernally cunning mind of Rojer Threng.

I watched her in mute madness. Back and forth she went, screaming, sobbing her helplessness. I have watched a mouse in a wire cage do the same thing, but this—this was a thousand times more terrible.

I called out to her. I attempted to rise from the divan and go to her, but weakness came over me and I fell back quivering.

She realized then that it was the end. She fought to control herself, and she walked to the divan where I lay, and knelt beside me.

She did not speak. I think she had no voice at that moment. I held her close against me, my lips pressed into her hair. Like a very small, pitiful leaf she trembled in my arms.

And then—even as I held her—the first gleam of dawn slid across the floor of that ghastly room. She raised her head and looked into my face.

"Goodbye—Paul——"

I could not answer her. Something else answered. From the spy-hole in the opposite wall of the room came a hoarse, triumphant cackle—in Rojer Threng's malignant voice.

The girl was dead—dead in my arms. And that uncouth voice from the wall, screaming its derision, brought madness to my heart.

I lunged to my feet, fighting against the torture that drove through my body. I stumbled across the room. I reached the wall—found the spy-hole with my frozen fingers—clawed at it—raged against it—

And there, fighting to reach the man who had condemned me to an eternity of horror—I died.

My story is finished. The chimes of the Old North Church have just tolled a single funereal note to usher in the hour. One o'clock . . .

It is many, many years since that fateful night when I became a creature of the blood. I do not dare to remember the number of them. Between the hours of sunrise and sunset I cling to the earth of my grave—where I refuse to stay, until I have avenged her. Then I shall write more, perhaps, pleading for your assistance that I may join her in the true death. A spike through the heart will do it . . .

From sunset until sunrise, throughout the hours of night, I am as one of you. I breathe, I drink; occasionally, as at this moment, I write—so that I may speak her name again and see it before me. I have attended social functions, mingled with people. Only one precaution must I take, and that to avoid mirrors, since my deathless body casts no reflection.

Every night—*every night*—I have visited the great house where Rojer Threng lives. No, I have not yet avenged her. The monster is too cunning, too clever. The sign of the cross is always upon him, to keep me from his throat. But sometime—*sometime*—he will forget. And then—ah, *then!*

When it is done, I shall find a way to quit this horrible brotherhood. I shall die the real death, as she did—and I shall find her.

A Mystery of the Campagna

Anne Crawford

I

*Martin Detaille's Account
of What Happened at the Vigna Marziali*

MARCELLO'S VOICE IS PLEADING WITH ME NOW, perhaps because after years of separation I have met an old acquaintance who had a part in his strange story. I have a longing to tell it, and have asked Monsieur Sutton to help me. He noted down the circumstances at the time, and he is willing to join his share to mine, that Marcello may be remembered.

One day, it was in spring, he appeared in my little studio amongst the laurels and green alleys of the Villa Medici. 'Come *mon enfant*,' he said, 'put up your paints'; and he unceremoniously took my palette out of my hand. 'I have a cab waiting outside, and we are going in search of a hermitage.' He was already washing my brushes as he spoke, and this softened my heart, for I hate to do it myself. Then he pulled off my velvet jacket and took down my respectable coat from a nail on the wall. I let him dress me like a child. We always did his will, and he knew it, and in a moment we were sitting in the cab, driving through the Via Sistina on our way to the Porta San Giovanni, whither he had directed the coachman to go.

I must tell my story as I can, for though I have been told by my comrades, who cannot know very well, that I can speak good English, writing it is another thing. Monsieur Sutton has asked me to use his tongue, because he has so far forgotten mine that he will not trust himself in it, though he has promised to correct my mistakes, that what I have to tell you may not seem ridiculous, and make people laugh when they read of Marcello. I tell him I wish to write this for my countrymen, not his; but he reminds me that Marcello had many English friends who still live, and that the English do not forget as we do. It is of no use to reason with him, for neither do they yield as we do, and so I have consented to his wish. I think he has a reason which he does not tell me, but let it go. I will translate it all into my own language for my own people. Your English phrases seem to me to be always walking sideways, or trying to look around the corner or stand upon their heads, and they have as many little tails as a kite. I will try not to have recourse to my own language, but he must pardon me if I forget myself. He may be sure I do not do it to offend him. Now that I have explained so much, let me go on.

When we had passed out of the Porta San Giovanni, the coachman drove as slowly as possible; but Marcello was never practical. How could he be, I ask you, with an opera in his head? So we crawled along, and he gazed dreamily before him. At last, when we had reached the part where the little villas and vineyards begin, he began to look about him.

You all know how it is out there; iron gates with rusty names or initials over them, and beyond them straight walks bordered with roses and lavender leading up to a forlorn little casino, with trees and a wilderness behind it sloping down to the Campagna, lonely enough to be murdered in and no one to hear you cry. We stopped at several of these gates and Marcello stood looking in, but none of the places were to his taste. He seemed not to doubt that he might have whatever pleased him, but nothing did so. He would jump out and run to the gate, and return saying, 'The shape of those windows would disturb my inspiration,' or, 'That yellow paint would make me fail my duet in the second Act'; and once he liked the air of the house well enough, but there were marigolds growing in the walk, and he hated them. So we drove on and on, until I thought we should find nothing more to reject. At last we came to one which suited him, though it was terribly lonely, and I should have fancied it very *agaçant* to live so far away from the world with nothing but those melancholy olives and green oaks—ilexes, you call them—for company.

'I shall live here and become famous!' he said, decidedly, as he pulled the iron rod which rang a great bell inside. We waited, and then he rang again very impatiently and stamped his foot.

'No one lives here, *mon vieux!* Come, it is getting late, and it is so damp out here, and you know that the damp for a tenor voice—' He stamped his foot again and interrupted me angrily.

'Why, then, have you got a tenor? You are stupid! A bass would be more sensible; nothing hurts it. But you have not got one, and you call yourself my friend! Go home without me.' How could I, so far on foot? 'Go and sing your lovesick songs to your lean English misses! They will thank you with a cup of abominable tea, and you will be in Paradise! This is *my* Paradise, and I shall stay until the angel comes to open it!'

He was very cross and unreasonable, and those were just the times when one loved him most, so I waited and enveloped my throat in my pocket-handkerchief and sang a passage or two just to prevent my voice from becoming stiff in that damp air.

'Be still! silence yourself!' he cried. 'I cannot hear if anyone is coming.'

Someone came at last, a rough-looking sort of keeper, or *guardiano* as they are called there, who looked at us as though he thought we were mad. One of us certainly was, but it was not I. Marcello spoke pretty good Italian, with a French accent, it is true, but the man understood him, especially as he held his purse in his hand. I heard him say a great many impetuously persuasive things all in one breath, then he slipped a gold piece into the *guardiano's* horny hand, and the two turned towards the house, the man shrugging his shoulders in a resigned sort of way, and Marcello called out to me over his shoulder—

'Go home in the cab, or you will be late for your horrible English party! I am going to stay here tonight.' *Ma foi!* I took his permission and left him; for a tenor voice is as tyrannical as a jealous woman. Besides, I was furious, and yet I laughed. His was the artist temperament, and appeared to us by turns absurd, sublime, and intensely irritating; but this last never for long, and we all felt that were we more like him our pictures would be worth more. I had not got as far as the city gate when my temper had cooled, and I began to reproach myself for leaving him in that lonely place with his purse full of money, for he was not poor at all, and tempting the dark *guardiano* to murder him. Nothing could be easier than to kill him in his sleep and bury him away somewhere under the olive trees or in some old vault of a ruined catacomb, so common on the borders of the Campagna. There were sure to be a hundred convenient places. I stopped the coachman and told him to turn back, but he shook his head and said something about having to be in the Piazza of St. Peter at eight o'clock. His horse began to go lame, as though he had understood his master and was his accomplice. What could I do? I said to myself that it was fate, and let him take me back to the Villa Medici, where I had to pay him a pretty sum for our crazy expedition, and then he rattled off, the horse not lame at all, leaving me bewildered at this strange afternoon.

I did not sleep well that night, though my tenor song had been applauded, and the English misses had caressed me much. I tried not to think of Marcello, and he did not trouble me much until I went to bed; but then I could not sleep, as I have told you.

I fancied him already murdered, and being buried in the darkness by the *guardiano*. I saw the man dragging his body, with the beautiful head thumping against the stones, down dark passages, and at least leaving it all bloody and covered with earth under a black arch in a recess, and coming back to count the gold pieces. But then again I fell asleep, and dreamed that Marcello was standing at the gate and stamping his foot; and then I slept no more, but got up as soon as the dawn came, and dressed myself and went to my studio at the end of the laurel walk. I took down my painting jacket, and remembered how he had pulled it off my shoulders. I took up the brushes he had washed for me; they were only half cleaned after all, and stiff with paint and soap. I felt glad to be angry with him, and *sacré'd* a little, for it made me sure that he was yet alive if I could scold at him. Then I pulled out my study of his head for my picture of Mucius Scaevola holding his hand in the flame, and then I forgave him; for who could look upon that face and not love it?

I worked with the fire of friendship in my brush, and did my best to endow the features with the expression of scorn and obstinacy I had seen at the gate. It could not have been more suitable to my subject! Had I seen it for the last time? You will ask me why I did not leave my work and go to see if anything had happened to him, but against this there were several reasons. Our yearly exhibition was not far off and my picture was barely painted in, and my comrades had sworn that it would not be ready. I was expecting a model for the King of the Etruscans; a man who cooked chestnuts in the Piazza Montanara, and who had consented to stoop to sit to me as a great favour; and then, to tell the truth, the morning was beginning to dispel my fancies. I had a good northern light to work by, with nothing sentimental about it, and I was not fanciful by nature; so when I sat down to my easel I told myself that I had been a fool, and that Marcello was perfectly safe: the smell of the paints helping me to feel practical again. Indeed, I thought every moment that he would come in, tired of his caprice already, and even was preparing and practising a little lecture for him. Someone knocked at my door, and I cried 'Entrez!' thinking it was he at last, but no, it was Pierre Magnin.

'There is a curious man, a man of the country, who wants you,' he said. 'He has your address on a dirty piece of paper in Marcello's handwriting, and a letter for you, but he won't give it up. He says he must see 'il Signor Martino.' He'd make a superb model for a murderer! Come and speak to him, and keep him while I get a sketch of his head.'

I followed Magnin through the garden, and outside, for the porter had not allowed him to enter, I found the *guardiano* of yesterday. He showed his white teeth, and said, 'Good day, signore,' like a Christian; and here in Rome he did not look half so murderous, only a stupid, brown, country fellow. He had a rough peasant-cart waiting, and he had tied up his shaggy horse to a ring in the wall. I held out my hand for the letter and pretended to find it difficult to read, for I saw Magnin standing with his sketch-book in the shadow of the entrance hall. The note said this: I have it still and I will copy it. It was written in pencil on a leaf torn from his pocketbook:

Mon vieux! I have passed a good night here, and the man will keep me as long as I like. Nothing will happen to me, except that I shall be divinely quiet, and I already have a famous *motif* in my head. Go to my lodgings and pack up some clothes and all my manuscripts, with plenty of music paper and a few bottles of Bordeaux, and give them to my messenger. Be quick about it!

Fame is preparing to descend upon me! If you care to see me, do not come before eight days. The gate will not be opened if you come sooner. The *guardiano* is my slave, and he has instructions to kill any intruder who in the guise of a friend tries to get in uninvited. He will do it, for he has confessed to me that he has murdered three men already.

(Of course this was a joke. I knew Marcello's way.)

When you come, go to the *poste restante* and fetch my letters. Here is my card to legitimate you. Don't forget pens and a bottle of ink! Your Marcello.

There was nothing for it but to jump into the cart, tell Magnin, who had finished his sketch, to lock up my studio, and go bumping off to obey these commands. We drove to his lodgings in the Via del Governo Vecchio, and there I made a bundle of all that I could think of; the landlady hindering me by a thousand questions about when the Signore would return. He had paid for the rooms in advance, so she had no need to be anxious about her rent. When I told her where he was, she shook her head, and talked a great deal about the bad air out there, and said 'Poor Signorino!' in a melancholy way, as though he were already buried, and looked mournfully after us from the window when we drove away. She irritated me, and made me feel superstitious. At the corner of the Via del Tritone I jumped down and gave the man a franc out of pure sentimentality, and cried after him, 'Greet the Signore!' but he did not hear me, and jogged away stupidly whilst I was longing to be with him. Marcello was a cross to us sometimes, but we loved him always.

The eight days went by sooner than I had thought they would, and Thursday came, bright and sunny, for my expedition. At one o'clock I descended into the Piazza di Spagna, and made a bargain with a man who had a well-fed horse, remembering how dearly Marcello's want of good sense had cost me a week ago, and we drove off at a good pace to the Vigna Marziali, as I was almost forgetting to say that it was called. My heart was beating, though I did not know why I should feel so much emotion. When we reached the iron gate the *guardiano* answered my ring directly, and I had no sooner set foot in the long flower-walk than I saw Marcello hastening to meet me.

'I knew you would come,' he said, drawing my arm within his, and so we walked towards the little grey house, which had a sort of portico and several balconies, and a sun-dial on its front. There were grated windows down to the ground floor, and the place, to my relief, looked safe and habitable. He told me that the man did not sleep there, but in a little hut down towards the Campagna, and that he, Marcello, locked himself in safely every night, which I was also relieved to know.

'What do you get to eat?' said I.

'Oh, I have goat's flesh, and dried beans and polenta, with pecorino cheese, and there is plenty of black bread and sour wine,' he answered smilingly. 'You see I am not starved.'

'Do not overwork yourself, *mon vieux*,' I said; 'you are worth more than your opera will ever be.'

'Do I look overworked?' he said, turning his face to me in the broad, outdoor light. He seemed a little offended at my saying that about his opera, and I was foolish to do it.

I examined his face critically, and he looked at me half defiantly. 'No, not yet,' I answered rather unwillingly, for I could not say that he did; but there was a restless, inward look in his eyes, and an almost imperceptible shadow lay around them. It seemed to me as though the full temples had grown slightly hollow, and a sort of faint mist lay over his beauty, making it seem strange and far off. We were standing before the door, and he pushed it open, the *guardiano* following us with slow, loud-resounding steps.

'Here is my Paradise,' said Marcello, and we entered the house, which was like all the others of its kind. A hall, with stucco bas-reliefs, and a stairway adorned with antique fragments, gave access to the upper rooms. Marcello ran up the steps lightly, and I heard him lock a door somewhere above and draw out the key, then he came and met me on the landing.

'This,' he said, 'is my workroom,' and he threw open a low door. The key was in the lock, so this room could not be the one I heard him close. 'Tell me I shall not write like an angel here!' he cried. I was so dazzled by the flood of bright sunshine after the dusk of the passage, that I blinked like an owl at first, and then I saw a large room, quite bare except for a rough table and chair, the chair covered with manuscript music.

'You are looking for the furniture,' he said, laughing; 'it is outside. Look here!' and he drew me to a rickety door of worm-eaten wood and coarse greenish glass, and flung it open on to a rusy iron balcony. He was right; the furniture was outside: that is to say, a divine view met my eyes. The Sabine Mountains, the

Alban Hills, and broad Campagna, with its mediaeval towers and ruined aque-
ducts, and the open plain to the sea. All this glowing and yet calm in the sunlight.
No wonder he could write there! The balcony ran round the corner of the house,
and to the right I looked down upon an alley of ilexes, ending in a grove of tall
laurel trees—very old, apparently. There were bits of sculpture and some ancient
sarcophagi standing gleaming against them, and even from so high I could hear
a little stream of water pouring from an antique mask into a long, rough trough.
I saw the brown *guardiano* digging at his cabbages and onions, and I laughed to
think that I could fancy him a murderer! He had a little bag of relics, which dangled to and fro over his sun-burned breast, and he looked very innocent when he
sat down upon an old column to eat a piece of black bread with an onion which
he had just pulled out of the ground, slicing it with a knife not at all like a dagger. But I kept my thoughts to myself, for Marcello would have laughed at them.
We were standing together, looking down at the man as he drank from his hands
at the running fountain, and Marcello now leaned down over the balcony, and
called out a long 'Ohé!' The lazy *guardiano* looked up, nodded, and then got up
slowly from the stone where he had been half-kneeling to reach the jet of water.

'We are going to dine,' Marcello explained. 'I have been waiting for you.'
Presently he heard the man's heavy tread upon the stairs, and he entered bearing
a strange meal in a basket.

There came to light pecorino cheese made from ewe's milk, black bread of
the consistency of a stone, a great bowl of salad apparently composed of weeds,
and a sausage which filled the room with a strong smell of garlic. Then he disappeared and came back with a dish full of ragged-looking goat's flesh cooked
together with a mass of smoking polenta, and I am not sure that there was not
oil in it.

'I told you I lived well, and now you see!' said Marcello. It was a terrible
meal, but I had to eat it, and was glad to have some rough, sour wine to help me,
which tasted of earth and roots. When we had finished I said, 'And your opera!
How are you getting on?'

'Not a word about that!' he cried. 'You see how I have written!' and he turned
over a heap of manuscript; 'but do not talk to me about it. I will not lose my
ideas in words.' This was not like Marcello, who loved to discuss his work, and I
looked at him astonished.

'Come,' he said, 'we will go down into the garden, and you shall tell me about the comrades. What are they doing? Has Magnin found a model for his Clytemnestra?'

I humoured him, as I always did, and we sat upon a stone bench behind the house, looking towards the laurel grove, talking of the pictures and the students. I wanted to walk down the ilex alley, but he stopped me.

'If you are afraid of the damp, don't go down there,' he said, 'the place is like a vault. Let us stay here and be thankful for this heavenly view.'

'Well, let us stay here,' I answered, resigned as ever. He lit a cigar and offered me one in silence. If he did not care to talk, I could be still too. From time to time he made some indifferent observation, and I answered it in the same tone. It almost seemed to me as though we, the old heart-comrades, had become strangers who had not known each other a week, or as though we had been so long apart that we had grown away from each other. There was something about him which escaped me. Yes, the days of solitude had indeed put years and a sort of shyness, or rather ceremony, between us! It did not seem natural to me now to clap him on the back, and make the old, harmless jokes at him. He must have felt the constraint too, for we were like children who had looked forward to a game, and did not know now what to play at.

At six o'clock I left him. It was not like parting with Marcello. I felt rather as though I should find my old friend in Rome that evening, and here only left a shadowy likeness of him. He accompanied me to the gate, and pressed my hand, and for a moment the true Marcello looked out of his eyes; but we called out no last word to each other as I drove away. I had only said, 'Let me know when you want me'; and he said, 'Merci!' and all the way back to Rome I felt a chill upon me, his hand had been so cold, and I thought and thought what could be the matter with him.

That evening I spoke out my anxiety to Pierre Magnin, who shook his head and declared that malaria fever must be taking hold of him, and that people often begin to show it by being a little odd.

'He must not stay there! We must get him away as soon as possible,' I cried.

'We both know Marcello, and that nothing can make him stir against his will,' said Pierre. 'Let him alone, and he will get tired of his whim. It will not kill him to have a touch of malaria, and some evening he will turn up amongst us as merry as ever.'

But he did not. I worked hard at my picture and finished it, but for a few touches, and he had not yet appeared. Perhaps it was the extreme application, perhaps the sitting out in that damp place, for I insist upon tracing it to something more material than emotion. Well, whatever it was, I fell ill; more ill than I had ever been in my life. It was almost twilight when it overtook me, and I remember it distinctly, though I forget what happened afterwards, or, rather, I never knew, for I was found by Magnin quite unconscious, and he has told me that I remained so for some time, and then became delirious, and talked of nothing but Marcello. I have told you that it was very nearly twilight; but just at the moment when the sun is gone the colours show in their true value. Artists know this, and I was putting last touches here and there to my picture and especially to my head of Mucius Scaevola, or rather, Marcello.

The rest of the picture came out well enough; but that head, which should have been the principal one, seemed faded and sunk in. The face appeared to grow paler and paler, and to recede from me; a strange veil spread over it, and the eyes seemed to close. I am not easily frightened, and I know what tricks some peculiar methods of colour will play by certain lights, for the moment I spoke of had gone, and the twilight greyness had set in; so I stepped back to look at it. Just then the lips, which had become almost white, opened a little, and sighed! An illusion, of course. I must have been very ill and quite delirious already, for to my imagination it was a real sigh, or, rather, a sort of exhausted gasp. Then it was that I fainted, I suppose, and when I came to myself I was in my bed, with Magnin and Monsieur Sutton standing by me, and a Sœur de Charité moving softly about among medicine bottles, and speaking in whispers. I stretched out my hands, and they were thin and yellow, with long, pale nails; and I heard Magnin's voice, which sounded very far away, say, 'Dieu Merci!' And now Monsieur Sutton will tell you what I did not know until long afterwards.

⊡ II ⊡

Robert Sutton's Account
of What Happened at the Vigna Marziali

I AM ATTACHED TO DETAILLE, AND WAS VERY GLAD TO BE OF use to him, but I never fully shared his admiration for Marcello Souvestre, though I appreciated his good points. He was certainly very promising—I must say that. But he was an odd, flighty sort of fellow, not of the kind which we English care to take the trouble to understand. It is my business to write stories, but not having need of such characters I have never particularly studied them. As I say, I was glad to be of use to Detaille, who is a thorough good fellow, and I willingly gave up my work to go and sit by his bedside. Magnin knew that I was a friend of his, and very properly came to me when he found that Detaille's illness was a serious one and likely to last for a long time. I found him perfectly delirious, and raving about Marcello.

'Tell me what the *motif* is! I know it is a *Marche Funèbre!*' And here he would sing a peculiar melody, which, as I have a knack at music, I noted down, it being like nothing I had heard before. The Sister of Charity looked at me with severe eyes; but how could she know that all is grist for our mill, and that observation becomes with us a mechanical habit? Poor Detaille kept repeating this curious melody over and over, and then would stop and seem to be looking at his picture, crying that it was fading away.

'Marcello! Marcello! You are fading too! Let me come to you!' He was as weak as a baby, and could not have moved from his bed unless in the strength of delirium.

'I cannot come!' he went on; 'they have tied me down.' And here he made as though he were trying to gnaw through a rope at his wrists, and then burst into tears. 'Will no one go for me and bring me a word from you? Ah! if I could know that you are alive!'

Magnin looked at me. I knew what he was thinking. He would not leave his comrade, but I must go. I don't mind acknowledging that I did not undertake this unwillingly. To sit by Detaille's bedside and listen to his ravings enervated me, and what Magnin wanted struck me as troublesome but not uninteresting to one of my craft, so I agreed to go. I had heard all about Marcello's strange seclusion from Magnin and Detaille himself, who lamented over it openly in his simple way at supper at the Academy, where I was a frequent guest.

I knew that it would be useless to ring at the gate of the Vigna Marziali. Not only should I not be admitted, but I should arouse Marcello's anger and suspicion, for I did not for a moment believe that he was not alive, though I thought it very possible that he was becoming a little crazy, as his countrymen are so easily put off their balance. Now, odd people are oddest late in the day and at evening time. Their nerves lose the power of resistance then, and the real man gets the better of them. So I determined to try to discover something at night, reflecting also that I should be safer from detection then. I knew his liking for wandering about when he ought to be in his bed, and I did not doubt that I should get a glimpse of him, and that was really all I needed.

My first step was to take a long walk out of the Porta San Giovanni, and this I did in the early morning, tramping along steadily until I came to an iron gate on the right of the road, with 'Vigna Marziali' over it; and then I walked straight on, never stopping until I had reached a little bushy lane running down towards the Campagna to the right. It was pebbly, and quite shut in by luxuriant ivy and elder bushes, and it bore deep traces of the last heavy rains. These had evidently been effaced by no footprints, so I concluded that it was little used. Down this path I made my way cautiously, looking behind and before me, from a habit contracted in my lonely wanderings in the Abruzzi. I had a capital revolver with me—an old friend—and I feared no man; but I began to feel a dramatic interest in my undertaking, and determined that it should not be crossed by any disagreeable surprises. The lane led me further down the plain than I had reckoned upon, for the bushy edge shut out the view; and when I had got to the bottom and faced round, the Vigna Marziali was lying quite far to my left. I saw at a glance that behind the grey casino an alley of ilexes ended in a laurel grove; then there were plantations of kitchen stuff, with a sort of thatched cabin in their midst, probably that of a gardener. I looked about for a kennel, but saw none, so there was no watchdog. At the end of this primitive kitchen garden was a broad patch of grass, bounded by a fence, which I could take at a spring. Now, I knew my way, but I could not resist tracing it out a little further. It was well that I did so, for I found just within the fence a sunken stream, rather full at the time, in consequence of the rains, too deep to wade and too broad to jump. It struck me that it would be easy enough to take a board from the fence and lay it over for a bridge. I measured the breadth with my eye, and decided the board would span it; then I went back as I had come, and returned to find Detaille still raving.

As he could understand nothing it seemed to me rather a fool's errand to go off in search of comfort for him; but a conscious moment might come, and moreover, I began to be interested in my undertaking; and so I agreed with Magnin that I should go and take some food and rest and return to the Vigna that night. I told my landlady that I was going into the country and should return the next day, and I went to Nazarri's and laid in a stock of sandwiches and filled my flask with something they called sherry, for, though I was no great wine-drinker, I feared the night chill.

It was about seven o'clock when I started, and I retraced my morning's steps exactly. As I reached the lane, it occurred to me that it was still too light for me to pass unobserved over the stream, and I made a place for myself under the hedge and lay down, quite screened by the thick curtain of tangled overhanging ivy.

I must have been out of training, and tired by the morning's walk, for I fell asleep. When I awoke it was night; the stars were shining, a dank mist made its way down my throat, and I felt stiff and cold. I took a pull at my flask, finding it nasty stuff, but it warmed me. Then I rang my repeater, which struck a quarter to eleven, got up and shook myself free of the leaves and brambles, and went on down the lane. When I got to the fence I sat down and thought the thing over. What did I expect to discover? What *was* there to discover? Nothing! Nothing but that Marcello was alive; and that was no discovery at all for I felt sure of it. I was a fool, and had let myself be allured by the mere stage nonsense and mystery of the business, and a mouse would creep out of this mountain of precautions! Well, at least, I could turn it to account by describing my own absurd behaviour in some story yet to be written, and, as it was not enough for a chapter, I would add to it by further experience. 'Come along!' I said to myself. 'You're an ass, but it may prove instructive.' I raised the top board from the fence noiselessly. There was a little stile there, and the boards were easily moved. I laid down my bridge with some difficulty, and stepped carefully across, and made my way to the laurel grove as quickly and noiselessly as possible.

There all was thick darkness, and my eyes only grew slowly accustomed to it. After all there was not much to see; some stone seats in a semi-circle, and some fragments of columns set upright with antique busts upon them. Then a little to the right a sort of arch, with apparently some steps descending into the ground, probably the entrance to some discovered branch of a catacomb. In the midst of the enclosure, not a very large one, stood a stone table, deeply fixed in the earth. No one was there; of that I felt certain, and I sat down, having now got used to the gloom, and fell to eat my sandwiches, for I was desperately hungry.

Now that I had come so far, was nothing to take place to repay me for my trouble? It suddenly struck me that it was absurd to expect Marcello to come out to meet me and perform any mad antics he might be meditating there before my eyes for my especial satisfaction. Why had I supposed that something would take place in the grove I do not know, except that this seemed a fit place for it. I would go and watch the house, and if I saw a light anywhere I might be sure he was within. Any fool might have thought of that, but a novelist lays the scene of his drama and expects his characters to slide about in the grooves like puppets. It is only when mine surprise me that I feel they are alive. When I reached the end of the ilex alley I saw the house before me. There were more cabbages and onions after I had left the trees, and I saw that in this open space I could easily be perceived by any one standing on the balcony above. As I drew back again under the ilexes, a window above, not the one on the balcony, was suddenly lighted up; but the light did not remain long, and presently a gleam shone through the glass oval over the door below.

I had just time to spring behind the thickest trunk near me when the door opened. I took advantage of its creaking to creep up the slanting tree like a cat, and lie out upon a projecting branch.

As I expected, Marcello came out. He was very pale, and moved mechanically like a sleepwalker. I was shocked to see how hollow his face had become as he held the candle still lighted in his hand, and it cast deep shadows on his sunken cheeks and fixed eyes, which burned wildly and seemed to see nothing. His lips were quite white, and so drawn that I could see his gleaming teeth. Then the candle fell from his hand, and he came slowly and with a curiously regular step on into the darkness of the ilexes, I watching him from above. But I scarcely think he would have noticed me had I been standing in his path. When he had passed I let myself down and followed him. I had taken off my shoes, and my tread was absolutely noiseless; moreover, I felt sure he would not turn around.

On he went with the same mechanical step until he reached the grove. There I knelt behind an old sarcophagus at the entrance, and waited. What would he do? He stood perfectly still, not looking about him, but as though the clockwork within him had suddenly stopped. I felt that he was becoming psychologically interesting, after all. Suddenly he threw up his arms as men do when they are mortally wounded on the battle-field, and I expected to see him fall at full length. Instead of this he made a step forward.

I looked in the same direction, and saw a woman, who must have concealed herself there while I was waiting before the house, come from out of the gloom, and as she slowly approached and laid her head upon his shoulder, the out-stretched arms clasped themselves closely around her, so that her face was hidden upon his neck.

So this was the whole matter, and I had been sent off on a wild-goose chase to spy out a common love affair! His opera and his seclusion for the sake of work, his tyrannical refusal to see Detaille unless he sent for him—all this was but a mask to a vulgar intrigue which, for reasons best known to himself, could not be indulged in in the city. I was thoroughly angry! If Marcello passed his time mooning about in that damp hole all night, no wonder that he looked so wretchedly ill, and seemed half mad! I knew very well that Marcello was no saint. Why should he be? But I had not taken him for a fool! He had had plenty of ro-mantic episodes, and as he was discreet without being uselessly mysterious, no one had ever unduly pried into them, nor should we have done so now. I said to myself that that mixture of French and Italian blood was at the bottom of it; French flimsiness and light-headedness and Italian love of cunning! I looked back upon all the details of my mysterious expedition. I suppose at the root of my anger lay a certain dramatic disappointment at not finding him lying mur-dered, and I despised myself for all the trouble I had taken to this ridiculous end: just to see him holding a woman in his arms. I could not see her face, and her fig-ure was enveloped from head to foot in something long and dark; but I could make out that she was tall and slender, and that a pair of white hands gleamed from her drapery. As I was looking intently, for all my indignation, the couple

moved on, and still clinging to one another descended the steps. So even the solitude of the lonely laurel grove could not satisfy Marcello's insane love of secrecy!
I kept still awhile; then I stole to where they had disappeared, and listened; but
all was silent, and I cautiously struck a match and peered down. I could see the
steps for a short distance below me, and then the darkness seemed to rise and
swallow them. It must be a catacomb as I had imagined, or an old Roman bath,
perhaps, which Marcello had made comfortable enough, no doubt, and as likely
as not they were having a nice little cold supper there. My empty stomach told
me that I could have forgiven him even then could I have shared it; I was in truth
frightfully hungry as well as angry, and sat down on one of the stone benches to
finish my sandwiches.

The thought of waiting to see this love-sick pair return to upper earth never
for a moment occurred to me. I had found out the whole thing, and a great hum-
bug it was! Now I wanted to get back to Rome before my temper had cooled, and
to tell Magnin on what a fool's errand he had sent me. If he liked to quarrel with
me, all the better!

All the way home I composed cutting French speeches, but they suddenly
cooled and petrified like a gust of lava from a volcano when I discovered that the
gate was closed. I had never thought of getting a pass, and Magnin ought to have
warned me. Another grievance against the fellow! I enjoyed my resentment, and
it kept me warm as I patrolled up and down. There are houses, and even small
eating-shops outside the gate, but no light was visible, and I did not care to at-
tract attention by pounding at the doors in the middle of the night; so I crept
behind a bit of wall. I was getting used to hiding by this time, and made myself
as comfortable as I could with my ulster, took another pull at my flask, and
waited. At last the gate was opened and I slipped through, trying not to look as
though I had been out all night like a bandit. The guard looked at me narrowly,
evidently wondering at my lack of luggage. Had I had a knapsack I might have
been taken for some innocently mad English tourist indulging in the mistaken
pleasure of trudging in from Frascati or Albano; but a man in an ulster, with his
hands in his pockets, sauntering in at the gate of the city at break of day as
though returning from a stroll, naturally puzzled the officials, who looked at me
and shrugged their shoulders.

Luckily I found an early cab in the Piazza of the Lateran, for I was deadbeat, and was soon at my lodgings in the Via della Croce, where my landlady let me in very speedily. Then at last I had the comfort of throwing off my clothes, all damp with the night dew, and turning in. My wrath had cooled to a certain point, and I did not fear to lower its temperature too greatly by yielding to an overwhelming desire for sleep. An hour or two could make no great difference to Magnin—let him fancy me still hanging about the Vigna Marziali! Sleep I must have, no matter what he thought.

I slept long, and was awakened at last by my landlady, Sora Nanna, standing over me, and saying, 'There is a Signore who wants you.'

'It is I, Magnin!' said a voice behind her. 'I could not wait for you to come!' He looked haggard with anxiety and watching.

'Detaille is raving still,' he went on, 'only worse than before. Speak, for Heaven's sake! Why don't you tell me something?' And he shook me by the arm as though he thought I was still asleep.

'Have you nothing to say? You must have seen something! Did you see Marcello?'

'Oh! yes, I saw him.'

'Well?'

'Well, he was very comfortable—quite alive. He had a woman's arms around him.'

I heard my door violently slammed to, a ferocious 'Sacré gamin!' and then steps springing down the stairs. I felt perfecty happy at having made such an impression, and turned and resumed my broken sleep with almost a kindly feeling towards Magnin, who was at that moment probably tearing up the Spanish Scalinata two steps at a time, and making himself horribly hot. It could not help Detaille, poor fellow! He could not understand my news. When I had slept long enough I got up, refreshed myself with a bath and something to eat, and went off to see Detaille. It was not his fault that I had been made a fool of, so I felt sorry for him.

I found him raving just as I had left him the day before, only worse, as Magnin said. He persisted in continually crying, 'Marcello, take care! no one can save you!' in hoarse, weak tones, but with the regularity of a knell, keeping up a peculiar movement with his feet, as though he were weary with a long road, but must press forward to his goal. Then he would stop and break into childish sobs.

'My feet are so sore,' he murmured piteously, 'and I am so tired! But I will come! They are following me, but I am strong!' Then a violent struggle with his invisible pursuers, in which he would break off into that singing of his, alternating with the warning cry. The singing voice was quite another from the speaking one. He went on and on repeating the singular air which he had himself called A Funeral March, and which had become intensely disagreeable to me. If it was one indeed, it surely was intended for no Christian burial. As he sang, the tears kept trickling down his cheeks, and Magnin sat wiping them away as tenderly as a woman. Between his song he would clasp his hands, feebly enough, for he was very weak when the delirium did not make him violent, and cry in heartrending tones, 'Marcello, I shall never see you again! Why did you leave us?' At last, when he stopped for a moment, Magnin left his side, beckoning the Sister to take it, and drew me into the other room, closing the door behind him.

'Now tell me exactly how you saw Marcello,' said he; so I related my whole absurd experience—forgetting, however, my personal irritation, for he looked too wretched and worn for anybody to be angry with him. He made me repeat several times my description of Marcello's face and manner as he had come out of the house. That seemed to make more impression upon him than the love-business.

'Sick people have strange intuitions,' he said gravely; 'and I persist in thinking that Marcello is very ill and in danger. *Tenez!*' And here he broke off, went to the door, and called '*Ma Sœur!*' under his breath. She understood, and after having drawn the bedclothes straight, and once more dried the trickling tears, she came noiselessly to where we stood, the wet handkerchief still in her hand. She was a singularly tall and strong-looking woman, with piercing black eyes and a self-controlled manner. Strange to say, she bore the adopted name of Claudius, instead of a more feminine one.

'*Ma Sœur,*' said Magnin, 'at what o'clock was it that he sprang out of bed and we had to hold him for so long?'

'Half-past eleven and a few minutes,' she answered promptly. Then he turned to me.

'At what time did Marcello come out into the garden?'

'Well, it might have been half-past eleven,' I answered unwillingly. 'I should say that three-quarters of an hour might possibly have passed since I rang my repeater. Mind you, I won't swear it!' I hate to have people try to prove mysterious coincidences, and this was just what they were attempting.

'Are you sure of the hour, *ma sœur?*' I asked, a little tartly.

She looked at me calmly with her great, black eyes, and said:

'I heard the Trinità de' Monti strike the half-hour just before it happened.'

'Be so good as to tell Monsieur Sutton exactly what took place,' said Magnin.

'One moment, Monsieur,' and she went swiftly and softly to Detaille, raised him on her strong arm, and held a glass to his lips, from which he drank mechanically. Then she came and stood where she could watch him through the open door.

'He hears nothing,' she said, as she hung the handkerchief to dry over a chair; and then she went on. 'It was half-past eleven, and my patient had been very uneasy—that is to say, more so even than before. It might have been four or five minutes after the clock had finished striking that he became suddenly quite still, and then began to tremble all over, so that the bed shook with him.' She spoke admirable English, as many of the Sisters do, so I need not translate, but will give her own words.

'He went on trembling until I thought he was going to have a fit, and told Monsieur Magnin to be ready to go for the doctor, when just then the trembling stopped, he became perfectly stiff, his hair stood up upon his head, and his eyes seemed coming out of their sockets, though he could see nothing, for I passed the candle before them. All at once he sprang out of his bed and rushed to the door. I did not know he was so strong. Before he got there I had him in my arms, for he has become very light, and I carried him back to bed again, though he was struggling, like a child. Monsieur Magnin came in from the next room just as he was trying to get up again, and we held him down until it was past, but he screamed Monsieur Souvestre's name for a long time after that. Afterwards he was very cold and exhausted, of course, and I gave him some beef-tea, though it was not the hour for it.'

'I think you had better tell the Sister all about it,' said Magnin turning to me. 'It is the best that the nurse should know everything.'

'Very well,' said I; 'though I do not think it's much in her line.' She answered me herself: 'Everything which concerns our patients is our business. Nothing shocks me.' Thereupon she sat down and thrust her hands into her long sleeves, prepared to listen. I repeated the whole affair as I had done to Magnin. She never took her brilliant eyes from off my face, and listened as coolly as though she had been a doctor hearing an account of a difficult case, though to me it seemed almost sacrilege to be describing the behaviour of a love-stricken youth to a Sister of Charity.

'What do you say to that, *ma sœur?*' asked Magnin, when I had done.

'I say nothing, monsieur. It is sufficient that I know it'; and she withdrew her hands from her sleeves, took up the handkerchief, which was dry by this time, and returned quietly to her place at the bedside.

'I wonder if I have shocked her, after all?' I said to Magnin.

'Oh, no,' he answered. 'They see many things, and a *sœur* is as abstract as a confessor; they do not allow themselves any personal feelings. I have seen Sœur Claudius listen perfectly unmoved to the most abominable ravings, only crossing herself beneath her cape at the most hideous blasphemies. It was late summer when poor Justin Revol died. You were not here.' Magnin put his hand to his forehead.

'You are looking ill yourself,' I said. 'Go and try to sleep, and I will stay.'

'Very well,' he answered; 'but I cannot rest unless you promise to remember everything he says, that I may hear it when I wake'; and he threw himself down on the hard sofa like a sack, and was asleep in a moment; and I, who had felt so angry with him but a few hours ago, put a cushion under his head and made him comfortable.

I sat down in the next room and listened to Detaille's monotonous ravings, while Sœur Claudius read in her book of prayers. It was getting dusk, and several of the academicians stole in and stood over the sick man and shook their heads. They looked around for Magnin, but I pointed to the other room with my finger on my lips, and they nodded and went away on tiptoe.

It required no effort of memory to repeat Detaille's words to Magnin when he woke, for they were always the same. We had another Sister that night, and as Sœur Claudius was not to return till the next day at midday, I offered to share the watch with Magnin, who was getting very nervous and exhausted, and who seemed to think that some such attack might be expected as had occurred the night before. The new sister was a gentle, delicate-looking little woman, with tears in her soft brown eyes as she bent over the sick man, and crossed herself from time to time, grasping the crucifix which hung from the beads at her waist. Nevertheless she was calm and useful, and as punctual as Sœur Claudius herself in giving the medicines.

The doctor had come in the evening, and prescribed a change in these. He would not say what he thought of his patient, but only declared that it was necessary to wait for a crisis. Magnin sent for some supper, and we sat over it together in the silence, neither of us hungry. He kept looking at his watch.

'If the same thing happens tonight, he will die!' said he, and laid his head on his arms.

'He will die in a most foolish cause, then,' I said angrily, for I thought he was going to cry, as those Frenchmen have a way of doing, and I wanted to irritate him by way of a tonic; so I went on—

'It would be dying for a *vaurien* who is making an ass of himself in a ridiculous business which will be over in a week! Souvestre may get as much fever as he likes! Only don't ask me to come and nurse him.'

'It is not the fever,' said he slowly, 'it is a horrible nameless dread that I have; I suppose it is listening to Detaille that makes me nervous. Hark!' he added, 'it strikes eleven. We must watch!'

'If you really expect another attack you had better warn the Sister,' I said; so he told her in a few words what might happen.

'Very well, monsieur,' she answered, and sat down quietly near the bed, Magnin at the pillow and I near him. No sound was to be heard but Detaille's ceaseless lament.

And now, before I tell you more, I must stop to entreat you to believe me. It will be almost impossible for you to do so, I know, for I have laughed myself at such tales, and no assurances would have made me credit them. But I, Robert Sutton, swear that this thing happened. More I cannot do. It is the truth.

We had been watching Detaille intently. He was lying with closed eyes, and had been very restless. Suddenly he became quite still, and then began to tremble, exactly as Sœur Claudius had described. It was a curious, uniform trembling, apparently in every fibre, and his iron bedstead shook as though strong hands were at its head and foot. Then came the absolute rigidity she had also described, and I do not exaggerate when I say that not only did his short-cropped hair seem to stand erect, but that it literally did so. A lamp cast the shadow of his profile against the wall to the left of his bed, and as I looked at the immovable outline which seemed painted on the wall, I saw the hair slowly rise until the line where it joined the forehead was quite a different one—abrupt instead of a smooth sweep. His eyes opened wide and were frightfully fixed, then as frightfully strained, but they certainly did not see us.

We waited breathlessly for what might follow. The little Sister was standing close to him, her lips pressed together and a little pale, but very calm. 'Do not be frightened, *ma sœur*,' whispered Magnin; and she answered in a business-like tone, 'No, monsieur,' and drew still nearer to her patient, and took his hands, which were stiff as those of a corpse, between her own to warm them. I laid mine upon his heart; it was beating so imperceptibly that I almost thought it had stopped, and as I leaned my face to his lips I could feel no breath issue from them. It seemed as though the rigour would last for ever.

Suddenly, without any transition, he hurled himself with enormous force, and literally at one bound, almost into the middle of the room, scattering us aside like leaves in the wind. I was upon him in a moment, grappling with him with all my strength, to prevent him from reaching the door. Magnin had been thrown backwards against the table, and I heard the medicine bottles crash with his fall. He had flung back his hand to save himself, and rushed to help me with blood dripping from a cut in his wrist. The little Sister sprang to us. Detaille had thrown her violently back upon her knees, and now, with a nurse's instinct, she tried to throw a shawl over his bare breast. We four must have made a strange group!

Four? *We were five!* Marcello Souvestre stood before us, just within the door! We all saw him, for he was there. His bloodless face was turned towards us un-moved; his hands hung by his side as white as his face; only his eyes had life in them; they were fixed on Detaille.

'Thank God you have come at last!' I cried. 'Don't stand there like a fool! Help us, can't you?' But he never moved. I was furiously angry, and, leaving my hold, sprang upon him to drag him forwards. My outstretched hands struck hard against the door, and I felt a thing like a spider's web envelop me. It seemed to draw itself over my mouth and eyes, and to blind and choke me, and then to flut-ter and tear and float from me.

Marcello was gone!

Detaille had slipped from Magnin's hold, and lay in a heap upon the floor, as though his limbs were broken. The Sister was trembling violently as she knelt over him and tried to raise his head. We gazed at one another, stooped and lifted him in our arms, and carried him back to his bed, while Sœur Marie quietly collected the broken phials.

'You saw it, *ma sœur?*' I heard Magnin whisper hoarsely.

'Yes, monsieur!' she only answered, in a trembling voice, holding on to her crucifix. Then she said in a professional tone—

'Will monsieur let me bind up his wrist?' And though her fingers trembled and his hand was shaking, the bandage was an irreproachable one.

Magnin went into the next room, and I heard him throw himself heavily into a chair. Detaille seemed to be sleeping. His breath came regularly; his eyes were closed with a look of peace about the lids, his hands lying in a natural way upon the quilt. He had not moved since we laid him there. I went softly to where Magnin was sitting in the dark. He did not move, but only said: 'Marcello is dead!'

'He is either dead or dying,' I answered, 'and we must go to him.'

'Yes,' Magnin whispered, 'we must go to him, but we shall not reach him.'

'We will go as soon as it is light,' I said, and then we were still again.

When the morning came at last he went and found a comrade to take his place, and only said to Sœur Marie, 'It is not necessary to speak of this night'; and at her quiet, 'You are right, monsieur,' we felt we could trust her. Detaille was still sleeping. Was this the crisis the doctor had expected? Perhaps; but surely not in such fearful form. I insisted upon my companion having some breakfast before we started, and I breakfasted myself, but I cannot say I tasted what passed between my lips.

We engaged a closed carriage, for we did not know what we might bring home with us, though neither of us spoke out his thoughts. It was early morning still when we reached the Vigna Marziali, and we had not exchanged a word all the way. I rang at the bell, while the coachman looked on curiously. It was answered promptly by the *guardiano*, of whom Detaille has already told you.

'Where is the Signore?' I asked through the gate.

'*Chi lo sa?*' he answered. 'He is here, of course; he has not left the Vigna. Shall I call him?'

'*Call him?*' I knew that no mortal voice could reach Marcello now, but I tried to fancy he was still alive.

'No,' I said. 'Let us in. We want to surprise him; he will be pleased.'

The man hesitated, but he finally opened the gate, and we entered, leaving the carriage to wait outside. We went straight to the house; the door at the back was wide open. There had been a gale in the night, and it had torn some leaves and bits of twigs from the trees and blown them into the entrance hall. They lay scattered across the threshold, and were evidence that the door had remained open ever since they had fallen. The *guardiano* left us, probably to escape Marcello's anger at having let us in, and we went up the stairs unhindered, Magnin foremost, for he knew the house better than I, from Detaille's description. He had told him about the corner room with the balcony, and we pretended that Marcello might be there, absorbed betimes in his work, but we did not call him.

He was not there. His papers were strewn over the table as though he had been writing, but the inkstand was dry and full of dust; he could not have used it for days. We went silently into the other chambers. Perhaps he was still asleep? But, no! We found his bed untouched, so he could not have lain in it that night. The rooms were all unlocked but one, and this closed door made our hearts beat. Marcello could scarcely be there, however, for there was no key in the lock; I saw the daylight shining through the key-hole. We called his name, but there came no answer. We knocked loudly; still no sign from within; so I put my shoulder to the door, which was old and cracked in several places, and succeeded in bursting it open.

Nothing was there but a sculptor's modelling-stand, with something upon it covered with a white cloth, and the modelling-tools on the floor. At the sight of the cloth, still damp, we drew a deep breath. It could have hung there for many hours, certainly not for twenty-four. We did not raise it. 'He would be vexed,' said Magnin, and I nodded, for it is accounted almost a crime in the artist's world to unveil a sculptor's work behind his back. We expressed no surprise at the fact of his modelling: a ban seemed to lie upon our tongues. The cloth hung tightly to the object beneath it, and showed us the outline of a woman's head and rounded-bust, and so veiled we left her. There was a little winding stair leading out of the passage, and we climbed it, to find ourselves in a sort of belvedere, commanding a superb view. It was a small, open terrace, on the roof of the house, and we saw at a glance that no one was there.

We had now been all over the casino, which was small and simply built, being evidently intended only for short summer use. As we stood leaning over the balustrade we could look down into the garden. No one was there but the *guardiano*, lying amongst his cabbages with his arms behind his head, half asleep. The laurel grove had been in my mind from the beginning, only it had seemed more natural to go to the house first. Now we descended the stairs silently and directed our steps thither.

As we approached it, the *guardiano* came towards us lazily.

'Have you seen the Signore?' he asked, and his stupidly placid face showed me that he, at least, had no hand in his disappearance.

'No, not yet,' I answered, 'but we shall come across him somewhere, no doubt. Perhaps he has gone to take a walk, and we will wait for him. What is this?' I went on, trying to seem careless. We were standing now by the little arch of which you know.

'This?' said he; 'I have never been down there, but they say it is something old. Do the Signori want to see it? I will fetch a lantern.'

I nodded, and he went off to his cabin. I had a couple of candles in my pocket, for I had intended to explore the place, should we not find Marcello. It was there that he had disappeared that night, and my thoughts had been busy with it; but I kept my candles concealed, reflecting that they would give our search an air of premeditation which would excite curiosity.

'When did you see the Signore last?' I asked, when he had returned with the lantern.

'I brought him his supper yesterday evening.'

'At what o'clock?'

'It was the Ave Maria, Signore,' he replied. 'He always sups then.'

It would be useless to put any more questions. He was evidently utterly unobserving, and would lie to please us.

'Let me go first,' said Magnin, taking the lantern. We set our feet upon the steps; a cold air seemed to fill our lungs and yet to choke us, and a thick darkness lay beneath. The steps, as I could see by the light of my candle, were modern, as well as the vaulting above them. A tablet was let into the wall, and in spite of my excitement I paused to read it, perhaps because I was glad to delay whatever awaited us below. It ran thus:

'Questo antico sepolcro Romano scoprì il Conte Marziali nell' anno 1853, e piamente conservò.' In plain English:

'Count Marziali discovered this ancient Roman sepulchre in the year 1853, and piously preserved it.'

I read it more quickly than it has taken time to write here, and hurried after Magnin, whose footsteps sounded faintly below me. As I hastened, a draught of cold air extinguished my candle, and I was trying to make my way down by feeling along the wall, which was horribly dark and clammy, when my heart stood still at a cry from far beneath me—a cry of horror!

'Where are you?' I shouted; but Magnin was calling my name, and could not hear me. 'I am here. I am in the dark!'

I was making haste as fast as I could, but there were several turnings.

'I have found him!' came up from below.

'Alive?' I shouted. No answer.

One last short flight brought me face to face with the gleam of the lantern. It came from a low doorway, and within stood Magnin, peering into the darkness. I knew by his face, as he held the light high above him, that our fears were realized.

Yes; Marcello was there. He was lying stretched upon the floor, staring at the ceiling, dead, and already stiff, as I could see at a glance. We stood over him, saying not a word, then I knelt down and felt him, for mere form's sake, and said, as though I had not known it before, 'He has been dead for some hours.'

'Since yesterday evening,' said Magnin, in a horror-stricken voice, yet with a certain satisfaction in it, as though to say, 'You see, I was right.'

Marcello was lying with his head slightly thrown back, no contortions in his handsome features; rather the look of a person who has quietly died of exhaustion—who has slipped unconsciously from life to death. His collar was thrown open and a part of his breast, of a ghastly white, was visible. Just over the heart was a small spot.

'Give me the lantern,' I whispered, as I stooped over it. It was a very little spot, of a faint purplish-brown, and must have changed colour within the night.

I examined it intently, and should say that the blood had been sucked to the surface, and then a small prick or incision made. The slight subcutaneous effusion led me to this conclusion. One tiny drop of coagulated blood closed the almost imperceptible wound. I probed it with the end of one of Magnin's matches. It was scarcely more than skin deep, so it could not be the stab of a stiletto, however slender, or the track of a bullet. Still, it was strange, and with one impulse we turned to see if no one were concealed there, or if there were no second exit. It would be madness to suppose that the murderer, if there was one, would remain by his victim. Had Marcello been making love to a pretty *contadina*, and was this some jealous lover's vengeance? But it was not a stab. Had one drop of poison in the little wound done this deadly work?

We peered about the place, and I saw that Magnin's eyes were blinded by tears and his face as pale as that upturned one on the floor, whose lids I had vainly tried to close. The chamber was low, and beautifully ornamented with stucco bas-reliefs, in the manner of the well-known one not far from there upon the same road. Winged genii, griffins, and arabesques, modelled with marvellous lightness, covered the walls and ceiling. There was no other door than the one we had entered by. In the centre stood a marble sarcophagus, with the usual subjects sculptured upon it, on the one side Hercules conducting a veiled figure, on the other a dance of nymphs and fauns. A space in the middle contained the following inscription, deeply cut in the stone, and still partially filled with red pigment:

D.M.
VESPERTILIAE•THC•AIMA-
TOΠΩTIΔOC•Q•FLAVIVS•
VIX•IPSE•SOSPES•MON•
POSVIT

'What is this?' whispered Magnin. It was only a pickaxe and a long crowbar, such as the country people use in hewing out their blocks of 'tufa', and his foot had struck against them. Who could have brought them here? They must belong to the *guardiano* above, but he said that he had never come here, and I believed him, knowing the Italian horror of darkness and lonely places; but what had Marcello wanted with them? It did not occur to us that archaeological curiosity could have led him to attempt to open the sarcophagus, the lid of which had evidently never been raised, thus justifying the expression, 'piously preserved.'

As I rose from examining the tools my eyes fell upon the line of mortar where the cover joined to the stone below, and I noticed that some of it had been removed, perhaps with the pickaxe which lay at my feet. I tried it with my nails and found that it was very crumbly. Without a word I took the tool in my hand, Magnin instinctively following my movements with the lantern. What impelled us I do not know. I had myself no thought, only an irresistible desire to see what was within. I saw that much of the mortar had been broken away, and lay in small fragments upon the ground, which I had not noticed before. It did not take long to complete the work. I snatched the lantern from Magnin's hand and set it upon the ground, where it shone full upon Marcello's dead face, and by its light I found a little break between the two masses of stone and managed to insert the end of my crowbar, driving it in with a blow of the pickaxe. The stone chipped and then cracked a little. Magnin was shivering.

'What are you going to do?' he said, looking around at where Marcello lay.

'Help me!' I cried, and we two bore with all our might upon the crowbar. I am a strong man, and I felt a sort of blind fury as the stone refused to yield. What if the bar should snap? With another blow I drove it in still further, then using it as a lever, we weighed upon it with our outstretched arms until every muscle was at its highest tension. The stone moved a little, and almost fainting we stopped to rest.

From the ceiling hung the rusty remnant of an iron chain which must once have held a lamp. To this, by scrambling upon the sarcophagus, I contrived to make fast the lantern.

'Now!' said I, and we heaved again at the lid. It rose, and we alternately heaved and pushed until it lost its balance and fell with a thundering crash upon the other side; such a crash that the walls seemed to shake, and I was for a moment utterly deafened, while little pieces of stucco rained upon us from the ceiling. When we had paused to recover from the shock we leaned over the sarcophagus and looked in.

The light shone full upon it, and we saw—how is it possible to tell? We saw lying there, amidst folds of mouldering rags, the body of a woman, perfect as in life, with faintly rosy face, soft crimson lips, and a breast of living pearl, which seemed to heave as though stirred by some delicious dream. The rotten stuff swathed about her was in ghastly contrast to this lovely form, fresh as morning! Her hands lay stretched at her side, the pink palms were turned a little outwards, her eyes were closed as peacefully as those of a sleeping child, and her long hair, which shone red-gold in the dim light from above, was wound around her head in numberless finely plaited tresses, beneath which little locks escaped in rings upon her brow. I could have sworn that the blue veins on that divinely perfect bosom held living blood!

We were absolutely paralyzed, and Magnin leaned gasping over the edge as pale as death, paler by far than this living, almost smiling face to which his eyes were glued. I do not doubt that I was as pale as he at this inexplicable vision. As I looked the red lips seemed to grow redder. They *were* redder! The little pearly teeth showed between them. I had not seen them before, and now a clear ruby drop trickled down to her rounded chin and from there slipped sideways and fell upon her neck. Horror-struck I gazed upon the living corpse, till my eyes could not bear the sight any longer. As I looked away my glance fell once more upon the inscription, but now I could see—*and read*—it all. 'To Vespertilia'—that was in Latin, and even the Latin name of the woman suggested a thing of evil flitting in the dusk. But the full horror of the nature of that thing had been veiled to Roman eyes under the Greek της αιματοπωτιδος, 'The blood-drinker, the vampire woman.' And Flavius—her lover—*vix ipse sospes*, 'himself hardly saved' from that deadly embrace, had buried her here, and set a seal upon her sepulchre, trusting to the weight of stone and the strength of clinging mortar to imprison for ever the beautiful monster he had loved.

'Infamous murderess!' I cried, 'you have killed Marcello!' and a sudden, vengeful calm came over me.

'Give me the pickaxe,' I said to Magnin; I can hear myself saying it still. He picked it up and handed it to me as in a dream; he seemed little better than an idiot, and the beads of sweat were shining on his forehead. I took my knife, and from the long wooden handle of the pickaxe I cut a fine, sharp stake. Then I clambered, scarcely feeling any repugnance, over the side of the sarcophagus, my feet amongst the folds of Vespertilia's decaying winding-sheet, which crushed like ashes beneath my boot.

I looked for one moment at that white breast, but only to choose the loveliest spot, where the network of azure veins shimmered like veiled turquoises, and then with one blow I drove the pointed stake deep down through the breathing snow and stamped it in with my heel.

An awful shriek, so ringing and horrible that I thought my ears must have burst; but even then I felt neither fear nor horror. There are times when these cannot touch us. I stopped and gazed once again at the face, now undergoing a fearful change—fearful and final!

'Foul vampire!' I said quietly in my concentrated rage. 'You will do no more harm now!' And then, without looking back upon her cursed face, I clambered out of the horrible tomb.

We raised Marcello, and slowly carried him up the steep stairs—a difficult task, for the way was narrow and he was so stiff. I noticed that the steps were ancient up to the end of the second flight; above, the modern passage was somewhat broader. When we reached the top, the *guardiano* was lying upon one of the stone benches; he did not mean us to cheat him out of his fee. I gave him a couple of francs.

'You see that we have found the signore,' I tried to say in a natural voice. 'He is very weak, and we will carry him to the carriage.' I had thrown my handkerchief over Marcello's face, but the man knew as well as I did that he was dead. Those stiff feet told their own story, but Italians are timid of being involved in such affairs. They have a childish dread of the police, and he only answered, 'Poor signorino! He is very ill; it is better to take him to Rome,' and kept cautiously clear of us as we went up to the ilex alley with our icy burden, and he did not go to the gate with us, not liking to be observed by the coachman who was dozing on his box. With difficulty we got Marcello's corpse into the carriage, the driver turning to look at us suspiciously. I explained we had found our friend very ill, and at the same time slipped a gold piece into his hand, telling him to drive to the Via del Governo Vecchio. He pocketed the money, and whipped his horses into a trot, while we sat supporting the stiff body, which swayed like a broken doll at every pebble in the road. When we reached the Via del Governo Vecchio at last, no one saw us carry him into the house. There was no step before the door, and we drew up so close to it that it was possible to screen our burden from sight. When we had brought him into his room and laid him upon his bed, we noticed that his eyes were closed; from the movement of the carriage, perhaps, though that was scarcely possible. The landlady behaved very much as I had expected her to do, for, as I told you, I know the Italians. She pretended, too, that the signore was very ill, and made a pretence of offering to fetch a doctor, and when I thought it best to tell her that he was dead, declared that it must have happened that very moment, for she had seen him look at us and close his eyes again. She had always told him that he ate too little and that he would be ill. Yes, it was weakness and that bad air out there which had killed him; and then he worked too hard. When she had successfully established this fiction, which we were glad enough to agree to, for neither did we wish for the publicity of an inquest, she ran out and fetched a gossip to come and keep her company.

So died Marcello Souvestre, and so died Vespertilia the blood-drinker at last.

There is not much more to tell. Marcello lay calm and beautiful upon his bed, and the students came and stood silently looking at him, then knelt down for a moment to say a prayer, crossed themselves, and left him for ever.

We hastened to the Villa Medici, where Detaille was sleeping, and Sister Claudius watching him with a satisfied look on her strong face. She rose noiselessly at our entrance, and came to us at the threshold.

'He will recover,' said she, softly. She was right. When he awoke and opened his eyes he knew us directly, and Magnin breathed a devout 'Thank God!'

'Have I been ill, Magnin?' he asked, very feebly.

'You have had a little fever,' answered Magnin, promptly; 'but it is over now. Here is Monsieur Sutton come to see you.'

'Has Marcello been here?' was the next question. Magnin looked at him very steadily.

'No,' he only said, letting his face tell the rest.

'Is he dead, then?' Magnin only bowed his head. 'Poor friend!' Detaille murmured to himself, then closed his heavy eyes and slept again.

A few days after Marcello's funeral we went to the fatal Vigna Marziali to bring back the objects which had belonged to him. As I laid the manuscript score of the opera carefully together, my eye fell upon a passage which struck me as the identical one which Detaille had so constantly sung in his delirium, and which I noted down. Strange to say, when I reminded him of it later, it was perfectly new to him, and he declared that Marcello had not let him examine his manuscript. As for the veiled bust in the other room, we left it undisturbed, and to crumble away unseen.

For the Blood Is the Life

F. Marion Crawford

W E HAD DINED AT SUNSET ON THE BROAD ROOF OF
the old tower, because it was cooler there during the great heat of summer. Besides, the little kitchen was built at one corner of the great square platform, which made it more convenient than if the dishes had to be carried down the steep stone steps, broken in places and everywhere worn with age. The tower was one of those built all down the west coast of Calabria by the Emperor Charles V. early in the sixteenth century, to keep off the Barbary pirates, when the unbelievers were allied with Francis I. against the Emperor and the Church. They have gone to ruin, a few still stand intact, and mine is one of the largest. How it came into my possession ten years ago, and why I spend a part of each year in it, are matters which do not concern this tale. The tower stands in one of the loneliest spots in Southern Italy, at the extremity of a curving rocky promontory, which forms a small but safe natural harbour at the southern extremity of the Gulf of Policastro, and just north of Cape Scalea, the birthplace of Judas Iscariot, according to the old local legend. The tower stands alone on this hooked spur of the rock, and there is not a house to be seen within three miles of it. When I go there I take a couple of sailors, one of whom is a fair cook, and when I am away it is in charge of a gnome-like little being who was once a miner and who attached himself to me long ago.

My friend, who sometimes visits me in my summer solitude, is an artist by profession, a Scandinavian by birth, and a cosmopolitan by force of circumstances. We had dined at sunset; the sunset glow had reddened and faded again, and the evening purple steeped the vast chain of the mountains that embrace the deep gulf to eastward and rear themselves higher and higher toward the south. It was hot, and we sat at the landward corner of the platform, waiting for the night breeze to come down from the lower hills. The colour sank out of the air, there was a little interval of deep-grey twilight, and a lamp sent a yellow streak from the open door of the kitchen, where the men were getting their supper.

Then the moon rose suddenly above the crest of the promontory, flooding the platform and lighting up every little spur of rock and knoll of grass below us, down to the edge of the motionless water. My friend lighted his pipe and sat looking at a spot on the hillside. I knew that he was looking at it, and for a long time past I had wondered whether he would ever see anything there that would fix his attention. I knew that spot well. It was clear that he was interested at last, though it was a long time before he spoke. Like most painters, he trusts to his own eyesight, as a lion trusts his strength and a stag his speed, and he is always disturbed when he cannot reconcile what he sees with what he believes that he ought to see.

"It's strange," he said. "Do you see that little mound just on this side of the boulder?"

"Yes," I said, and I guessed what was coming.

"It looks like a grave," observed Holger.

"Very true. It does look like a grave."

"Yes," continued my friend, his eyes still fixed on the spot. "But the strange thing is that I see the body lying on the top of it. Of course," continued Holger, turning his head on one side as artists do, "it must be an effect of light. In the first place, it is not a grave at all. Secondly, if it were, the body would be inside and not outside. Therefore, it's an effect of the moonlight. Don't you see it?"

"Perfectly; I always see it on moonlight nights."

"It doesn't seem to interest you much," said Holger.

"On the contrary, it does interest me, though I am used to it. You're not so far wrong, either. The mound is really a grave."

"Nonsense!" cried Holger, incredulously. "I suppose you'll tell me what I see lying on it is really a corpse!"

"No," I answered, "it's not. I know, because I have taken the trouble to go down and see."

"Then what is it?" asked Holger.

"It's nothing."

"You mean that it's an effect of light, I suppose?"

"Perhaps it is. But the inexplicable part of the matter is that it makes no difference whether the moon is rising or setting, or waxing or waning. If there's any moonlight at all, from east or west or overhead, so long as it shines on the grave you can see the outline of the body on top."

Holger stirred up his pipe with the point of his knife, and then used his finger for a stopper. When the tobacco burned well he rose from his chair.

"If you don't mind," he said, "I'll go down and take a look at it."

He left me, crossed the roof, and disappeared down the dark steps. I did not move, but sat looking down until he came out of the tower below. I heard him humming an old Danish song as he crossed the open space in the bright moonlight, going straight to the mysterious mound. When he was ten paces from it, Holger stopped short, made two steps forward, and then three or four backward, and then stopped again. I knew what that meant. He had reached the spot where the Thing ceased to be visible—where, as he would have said, the effect of light changed.

Then he went on till he reached the mound and stood upon it. I could see the Thing still, but it was no longer lying down; it was on its knees now, winding its white arms round Holger's body and looking up into his face. A cool breeze stirred my hair at that moment, as the night wind began to come down from the hills, but it felt like a breath from another world.

The Thing seemed to be trying to climb to its feet, helping itself up by Holger's body while he stood upright, quite unconscious of it and apparently looking toward the tower, which is very picturesque when the moonlight falls upon it on that side.

"Come along!" I shouted. "Don't stay there all night!"

It seemed to me that he moved reluctantly as he stepped from the mound, or else with difficulty. That was it. The Thing's arms were still round his waist, but its feet could not leave the grave. As he came slowly forward it was drawn and lengthened like a wreath of mist, thin and white, till I saw distinctly that Holger shook himself, as a man does who feels a chill. At the same instant a little wail of pain came to me on the breeze—it might have been the cry of the small owl that lives among the rocks—and the misty presence floated swiftly back from Holger's advancing figure and lay once more at its length upon the mound.

Again I felt the cool breeze in my hair, and this time an icy thrill of dread ran down my spine. I remembered very well that I had once gone down there alone in the moonlight; that presently, being near, I had seen nothing; that, like Holger, I had gone and had stood upon the mound; and I remembered how, when I came back, sure that there was nothing there, I had felt the sudden conviction that there was something after all if I would only look behind me. I remembered the strong temptation to look back, a temptation I had resisted as unworthy of a man of sense, until, to get rid of it, I had shaken myself just as Holger did.

And now I knew that those white, misty arms had been round me too; I knew it in a flash, and I shuddered as I remembered that I had heard the night owl then too. But it had not been the night owl. It was the cry of the Thing.

I refilled my pipe and poured out a cup of strong southern wine; in less than a minute Holger was seated beside me again.

"Of course there's nothing there," he said, "but it's creepy, all the same. Do you know, when I was coming back I was so sure that there was something behind me that I wanted to turn round and look? It was an effort not to."

He laughed a little, knocked the ashes out of his pipe, and poured himself out some wine. For a while neither of us spoke, and the moon rose higher, and we both looked at the Thing that lay on the mound.

"You might make a story about that," said Holger after a long time.

"There is one," I answered. "If you're not sleepy, I'll tell it to you."

"Go ahead," said Holger, who likes stories.

❨   ❨   ❨

Old Alario was dying up there in the village behind the hill. You remember him, I have no doubt. They say that he made his money by selling sham jewellery in South America, and escaped with his gains when he was found out. Like all those fellows, if they bring anything back with them, he at once set to work to enlarge his house, and as there are no masons here, he sent all the way to Paola for two workmen. They were a rough-looking pair of scoundrels—a Neapolitan who had lost one eye and a Sicilian with an old scar half an inch deep across his left cheek. I often saw them, for on Sundays they used to come down here and fish off the rocks. When Alario caught the fever that killed him the masons were still at work. As he had agreed that part of their pay should be their board and lodging, he made them sleep in the house. His wife was dead, and he had an only son called Angelo, who was a much better sort than himself. Angelo was to marry the daughter of the richest man in the village, and, strange to say, though the marriage was arranged by their parents, the young people were said to be in love with each other.

For that matter, the whole village was in love with Angelo, and among the rest a wild, good-looking creature called Cristina, who was more like a gipsy than any girl I ever saw about here. She had very red lips and very black eyes, she was built like a greyhound, and had the tongue of the devil. But Angelo did not care a straw for her. He was rather a simple-minded fellow, quite different from his old scoundrel of a father, and under what I should call normal circumstances I really believe that he would never have looked at any girl except the nice plump little creature, with a fat dowry, whom his father meant him to marry. But things turned up which were neither normal nor natural.

On the other hand, a very handsome young shepherd from the hills above Maratea was in love with Cristina, who seems to have been quite indifferent to him. Cristina had no regular means of subsistence, but she was a good girl and willing to do any work or go on errands to any distance for the sake of a loaf of bread or a mess of beans, and permission to sleep under cover. She was especially glad when she could get something to do about the house of Angelo's father. There is no doctor in the village, and when the neighbours saw that old Alario was dying they sent Cristina to Scalea to fetch one. That was late in the afternoon, and if they had waited so long, it was because the dying miser refused to allow any such extravagance while he was able to speak. But while Cristina was gone matters grew rapidly worse, the priest was brought to the bedside, and when he had done what he could he gave it as his opinion to the bystanders that the old man was dead, and left the house.

You know these people. They have a physical horror of death. Until the priest spoke, the room had been full of people. The words were hardly out of his mouth before it was empty. It was night now. They hurried down the dark steps and out into the street.

Angelo, as I have said, was away, Cristina had not come back—the simple woman-servant who had nursed the sick man fled with the rest, and the body was left alone in the flickering light of the earthen oil lamp.

Five minutes later two men looked in cautiously and crept forward toward the bed. They were the one-eyed Neapolitan mason and his Sicilian companion. They knew what they wanted. In a moment they had dragged from under the bed a small but heavy iron-bound box, and long before any one thought of coming back to the dead man they had left the house and the village under cover of the darkness. It was easy enough, for Alario's house is the last toward the gorge which leads down here, and the thieves merely went out by the back door, got over the stone wall, and had nothing to risk after that except the possibility of meeting some belated countryman, which was very small indeed, since few of the people use that path. They had a mattock and shovel, and they made their way here without accident.

I am telling you this story as it must have happened, for, of course, there were no witnesses to this part of it. The men brought the box down by the gorge, intending to bury it until they should be able to come back and take it away in a boat. They must have been clever enough to guess that some of the money would be in paper notes, for they would otherwise have buried it on the beach in the wet sand, where it would have been much safer. But the paper would have rotted if they had been obliged to leave it there long, so they dug their hole down there, close to that boulder. Yes, just where the mound is now.

Cristina did not find the doctor in Scalea, for he had been sent for from a place up the valley, half-way to San Domenico. If she had found him, he would have come on his mule by the upper road, which is smoother but much longer. But Cristina took the short cut by the rocks, which passes about fifty feet above the mound, and goes round that corner. The men were digging when she passed, and she heard them at work. It would not have been like her to go by without finding out what the noise was, for she was never afraid of anything in her life, and, besides, the fishermen sometimes come ashore here at night to get a stone for an anchor or to gather sticks to make a little fire. The night was dark, and

Cristina probably came close to the two men before she could see what they were doing. She knew them, of course, and they knew her, and understood instantly that they were in her power. There was only one thing to be done for their safety, and they did it. They knocked her on the head, they dug the hole deep, and they buried her quickly with the iron-bound chest. They must have understood that their only chance of escaping suspicion lay in getting back to the village before their absence was noticed, for they returned immediately, and were found half an hour later gossiping quietly with the man who was making Alario's coffin. He was a crony of theirs, and had been working at the repairs in the old man's house. So far as I have been able to make out, the only persons who were supposed to know where Alario kept his treasure were Angelo and the one woman-servant I have mentioned. Angelo was away; it was the woman who discovered the theft.

It is easy enough to understand why no one else knew where the money was. The old man kept his door locked and the key in his pocket when he was out, and did not let the woman enter to clean the place unless he was there himself. The whole village knew that he had money somewhere, however, and the masons had probably discovered the whereabouts of the chest by climbing in at the window in his absence. If the old man had not been delirious until he lost consciousness, he would have been in frightful agony of mind for his riches. The faithful woman-servant forgot their existence only for a few moments when she fled with the rest, overcome by the horror of death. Twenty minutes had not passed before she returned with the two hideous old hags who are always called in to prepare the dead for burial. Even then she had not at first the courage to go near the bed with them, but she made a pretence of dropping something, went down on her knees as if to find it, and looked under the bedstead. The walls of the room were newly whitewashed down to the floor, and she saw at a glance that the chest was gone. It had been there in the afternoon, it had therefore been stolen in the short interval since she had left the room.

There are no carabineers stationed in the village; there is not so much as a municipal watchman, for there is no municipality. There never was such a place, I believe. Scalea is supposed to look after it in some mysterious way, and it takes a couple of hours to get anybody from there. As the old woman had lived in the village all her life, it did not even occur to her to apply to any civil authority for help. She simply set up a howl and ran through the village in the dark, screaming out that her dead master's house had been robbed. Many of the people looked out, but at first no one seemed inclined to help her. Most of them, judging her by themselves, whispered to each other that she had probably stolen the money herself. The first man to move was the father of the girl whom Angelo was to marry; having collected his household, all of whom felt a personal interest in the wealth which was to have come into the family, he declared it to be his opinion that the chest had been stolen by the two journeyman masons who lodged in the house. He headed a search for them, which naturally began in Alario's house and ended in the carpenter's workshop, where the thieves were found discussing a measure of wine with the carpenter over the half-finished coffin, by the light of one earthen lamp filled with oil and tallow. The search party at once accused the delinquents of the crime, and threatened to lock them up in the cellar till the carabineers could be fetched from Scalea. The two men looked at each other for one moment, and then without the slightest hesitation they put out the single light, seized the unfinished coffin between them, and using it as a sort of battering ram, dashed upon their assailants in the dark. In a few moments they were beyond pursuit.

That is the end of the first part of the story. The treasure had disappeared, and as no trace of it could be found the people naturally supposed that the thieves had succeeded in carrying it off. The old man was buried, and when Angelo came back at last he had to borrow money to pay for the miserable funeral, and had some difficulty in doing so. He hardly needed to be told that in losing his inheritance he had lost his bride. In this part of the world marriages are made on strictly business principles, and if the promised cash is not forthcoming on the appointed day the bride or the bridegroom whose parents have failed to produce it may as well take themselves off, for there will be no wedding. Poor Angelo knew that well enough. His father had been possessed of hardly any land, and now that the hard cash which he had brought from South America was gone, there was nothing left but debts for the building materials that were to have been used for enlarging and improving the old house. Angelo was beggared, and the nice plump little creature who was to have been his turned up her nose at him in the most approved fashion. As for Cristina, it was several days before she was missed, for no one remembered that she had been sent to Scalea for the doctor, who had never come. She often disappeared in the same way for days together, when she could find a little work here and there at the distant farms among the hills. But when she did not come back at all, people began to wonder, and at last made up their minds that she had connived with the masons and had escaped with them.

❨   ❨   ❨

I paused and emptied my glass.

"That sort of thing could not happen anywhere else," observed Holger, filling his everlasting pipe again. "It is wonderful what a natural charm there is about murder and sudden death in a romantic country like this. Deeds that would be simply brutal and disgusting anywhere else become dramatic and mysterious because this is Italy and we are living in a genuine tower of Charles V. built against genuine Barbary pirates."

"There's something in that," I admitted. Holger is the most romantic man in the world inside of himself, but he always thinks it necessary to explain why he feels anything.

"I suppose they found the poor girl's body with the box," he said presently.

"As it seems to interest you," I answered, "I'll tell you the rest of the story."

The moon had risen high by this time; the outline of the Thing on the mound was clearer to our eyes than before.

❨   ❨   ❨

The village very soon settled down to its small, dull life. No one missed old Alario, who have been away so much on his voyages to South America that he had never been a familiar figure in his native place. Angelo lived in the half-finished house, and because he had no money to pay the old woman-servant she would not stay with him, but once in a long time she would come and wash a shirt for him for old acquaintance's sake. Besides the house, he had inherited a small patch of ground at some distance from the village; he tried to cultivate it, but he had no heart in the work, for he knew he could never pay the taxes on it and on the house, which would certainly be confiscated by the Government, or seized for the debt of the building material, which the man who had supplied it refused to take back.

Angelo was very unhappy. So long as his father had been alive and rich, every girl in the village had been in love with him; but that was all changed now. It had been pleasant to be admired and courted, and invited to drink wine by fathers who had girls to marry. It was hard to be stared at coldly, and sometimes laughed at because he had been robbed of his inheritance. He cooked his miserable meals for himself, and from being sad became melancholy and morose.

At twilight, when the day's work was done, instead of hanging about in the open space before the church with young fellows of his own age, he took to wandering in lonely places on the outskirts of the village till it was quite dark. Then he slunk home and went to bed to save the expense of a light. But in those lonely twilight hours he began to have strange waking dreams. He was not always alone, for often when he sat on the stump of a tree, where the narrow path turns down the gorge, he was sure that a woman came up noiselessly over the rough stones, as if her feet were bare; and she stood under a clump of chestnut trees only half a dozen yards down the path, and beckoned to him without speaking. Though she was in the shadow he knew that her lips were red, and that when they parted a little and smiled at him she showed two small sharp teeth. He knew this at first rather than saw it, and he knew that it was Cristina, and that she was dead. Yet he was not afraid; he only wondered whether it was a dream, for he thought that if he had been awake he should have been frightened.

Besides, the dead woman had red lips, and that could only happen in a dream. Whenever he went near the gorge after sunset she was already there waiting for him, or else she very soon appeared, and he began to be sure that she came a little nearer to him every day. At first he had only been sure of her blood-red mouth, but now each feature grew distinct, and the pale face looked at him with deep and hungry eyes.

It was the eyes that grew dim. Little by little he came to know that some day the dream would not end when he turned away to go home, but would lead him down the gorge out of which the vision rose. She was nearer now when she beckoned to him. Her cheeks were not livid like those of the dead, but pale with starvation, with the furious and unappeased physical hunger of her eyes that devoured him. They feasted on his soul and cast a spell over him, and at last they were close to his own and held him. He could not tell whether her breath was as hot as fire or as cold as ice; he could not tell whether her red lips burned his or froze them, or whether her five fingers on his wrists seared scorching scars or bit his flesh like frost; he could not tell whether he was awake or asleep, whether she was alive or dead, but he knew that she loved him, she alone of all creatures, earthly or unearthly, and her spell had power over him.

When the moon rose high that night the shadow of that Thing was not alone down there upon the mound.

Angelo awoke in the cool dawn, drenched with dew and chilled through flesh, and blood, and bone. He opened his eyes to the faint grey light, and saw the stars still shining overhead. He was very weak, and his heart was beating so slowly that he was almost like a man fainting. Slowly he turned his head on the mound, as on a pillow, but the other face was not there. Fear seized him suddenly, a fear unspeakable and unknown; he sprang to his feet and fled up the gorge, and he never looked behind him until he reached the door of the house on the outskirts of the village. Drearily he went to his work that day, and wearily the hours dragged themselves after the sun, till at last he touched the sea and sank, and the great sharp hills above Maratea turned purple against the dove-coloured eastern sky.

Angelo shouldered his heavy hoe and left the field. He felt less tired now than in the morning when he had begun to work, but he promised himself that he would go home without lingering by the gorge, and eat the best supper he could get himself, and sleep all night in his bed like a Christian man. Not again would he be tempted down the narrow way by a shadow with red lips and icy breath; not again would he dream that dream of terror and delight. He was near the village now; it was half an hour since the sun had set, and the cracked church bell sent little discordant echoes across the rocks and ravines to tell all good people that the day was done. Angelo stood still a moment where the path forked, where it led toward the village on the left, and down to the gorge on the right, where a clump of chestnut trees overhung the narrow way. He stood still a minute, lifting his battered hat from his head and gazing at the fast-fading sea westward, and his lips moved as he silently repeated the familiar evening prayer. His lips moved, but the words that followed them in his brain lost their meaning and turned into others, and ended in a name that he spoke aloud—Cristina! With the name, the tension of his will relaxed suddenly, reality went out and the dream took him again, and bore him on swiftly and surely like a man walking in his sleep, down, down, by the steep path in the gathering darkness. And as she glided beside him, Cristina whispered strange, sweet things in his ear, which somehow, if he had been awake, he knew that he could not quite have understood; but now they were the most wonderful words he had ever heard in his life. And she kissed him also, but not upon his mouth. He felt her sharp kisses upon his white throat, and he knew that her lips were red. So the wild dream sped on through twilight and darkness and moonrise, and all the glory of the summer's night. But in the chilly dawn he lay as one half dead upon the mound down there, recalling and not recalling, drained of his blood, yet strangely longing to give those red lips more. Then came the fear, the awful nameless panic, the mortal horror that guards the confines of the world we see not, neither know of as we know of other things, but which we feel when its icy chill freezes our bones and stirs our hair with the touch of a ghostly hand. Once more Angelo sprang from the mound and fled up the gorge in the breaking day, but his step was less sure this time, and he panted for breath as he ran; and when he came to the bright spring of water that rises half-way up the hillside, he dropped upon his knees and hands and plunged his whole face in and drank as he had never drunk before—for it was the thirst of the wounded man who has lain bleeding all night long upon the battle-field.

She had him fast now, and he could not escape her, but would come to her every evening at dusk until she had drained him of his last drop of blood. It was in vain that when the day was done he tried to take another turning and to go home by a path that did not lead near the gorge. It was in vain that he made promises to himself each morning at dawn when he climbed the lonely way up from the shore to the village. It was all in vain, for when the sun sank burning into the sea, and the coolness of the evening stole out as from a hiding-place to delight the weary world, his feet turned toward the old way, and she was waiting for him in the shadow under the chestnut trees; and then all happened as before, and she fell to kissing his white throat even as she flitted lightly down the way, winding one arm about him. And as his blood failed, she grew more hungry and more thirsty every day, and every day when he awoke in the early dawn it was harder to rouse himself to the effort of climbing the steep path to the village; and when he went to his work his feet dragged painfully, and there was hardly strength in his arms to wield the heavy hoe. He scarcely spoke to any one now, but the people said he was "consuming himself" for love of the girl he was to have married when he lost his inheritance; and they laughed heartily at the thought, for this is not a very romantic country. At this time, Antonio, the man who stays here to look after the tower, returned from a visit to his people, who live near Salerno. He had been away all the time since before Alario's death and knew nothing of what had happened. He has told me that he came back late in the afternoon and shut himself up in the tower to eat and sleep, for he was very tired. It was past midnight when he awoke, and when he looked out the waning moon was rising over the shoulder of the hill. He looked out toward the mound, and he saw something, and he did not sleep again that night. When he went out again in the morning it was broad daylight, and there was nothing to be seen on the mound but loose stones and driven sand. Yet he did not go very near it; he went straight up the path to the village and directly to the house of the old priest.

"I have seen an evil thing this night," he said; "I have seen how the dead drink the blood of the living. And the blood is the life."

"Tell me what you have seen," said the priest in reply.

Antonio told him everything he had seen.

"You must bring your book and your holy water to-night," he added. "I will be here before sunset to go down with you, and if it pleases your reverence to sup with me while we wait, I will make ready."

"I will come," the priest answered, "for I have read in old books of these strange beings which are neither quick nor dead, and which lie ever fresh in their graves, stealing out in the dusk to taste life and blood."

Antonio cannot read, but he was glad to see that the priest understood the business; for, of course, the books must have instructed him as to the best means of quieting the half-living Thing for ever.

So Antonio went away to his work, which consists largely in sitting on the shady side of the tower, when he is not perched upon a rock with a fishing-line catching nothing. But on that day he went twice to look at the mound in the bright sunlight, and he searched round and round it for some hole through which the being might get in and out; but he found none. When the sun began to sink and the air was cooler in the shadows, he went up to fetch the old priest, carrying a little wicker basket with him; and in this they placed a bottle of holy water, and the basin, and sprinkler, and the stole which the priest would need;

and they came down and waited in the door of the tower till it should be dark. But while the light still lingered very grey and faint, they saw something moving, just there, two figures, a man's that walked, and a woman's that flitted beside him, and while her head lay on his shoulder she kissed his throat. The priest has told me that, too, and that his teeth chattered and he grasped Antonio's arm. The vision passed and disappeared into the shadow. Then Antonio got the leathern flask of strong liquor, which he kept for great occasions, and poured such a draught as made the old man feel almost young again; and he got the lantern, and his pick and shovel, and gave the priest his stole to put on and the holy water to carry, and they went out together toward the spot where the work was to be done. Antonio says that in spite of the rum his own knees shook together, and the priest stumbled over his Latin. For when they were yet a few yards from the mound the flickering light of the lantern fell upon Angelo's white face, unconscious as if in sleep, and on his upturned throat, over which a very thin red line of blood trickled down into his collar; and the flickering light of the lantern played upon another face that looked up from the feast—upon two deep, dead eyes that saw in spite of death—upon parted lips redder than life itself—upon two gleaming teeth on which glistened a rosy drop. Then the priest, good old man, shut his eyes tight and showered holy water before him, and his cracked voice rose almost to a scream; and then Antonio, who is no coward after all, raised his pick in one hand and the lantern in the other, as he sprang forward, not knowing what the end should be; and then he swears that he heard a woman's cry, and the Thing was gone, and Angelo lay alone on the mound unconscious, with the red line on his throat and the beads of deathly sweat on his cold forehead. They lifted him, half-dead as he was, and laid him on the ground close by; then Antonio went to work, and the priest helped him, though he was old and could not do much; and they dug deep, and at last Antonio, standing in the grave, stooped down with his lantern to see what he might see.

His hair used to be dark brown, with grizzled streaks about the temples; in less than a month from that day he was as grey as a badger. He was a miner when he was young, and most of these fellows have seen ugly sights now and then, when accidents have happened, but he had never seen what he saw that night— that Thing which is neither alive nor dead, that Thing that will abide neither above ground nor in the grave. Antonio had brought something with him which the priest had not noticed. He had made it that afternoon—a sharp stake shaped from a piece of tough old driftwood. He had it with him now, and he had his heavy pick, and he had taken the lantern down into the grave. I don't think any power on earth could make him speak of what happened then, and the old priest was too frightened to look in. He says he heard Antonio breathing like a wild beast, and moving as if he were fighting with something almost as strong as himself; and he heard an evil sound also, with blows, as of something violently driven through flesh and bone; and then the most awful sound of all—a woman's shriek, the unearthly scream of a woman neither dead nor alive, but buried deep for many days. And he, the poor old priest, could only rock himself as he knelt there in the sand, crying aloud his prayers and exorcisms to drown these dreadful sounds. Then suddenly a small iron-bound chest was thrown up and rolled over against the old man's knee, and in a moment more Antonio was beside him, his face as white as tallow in the flickering light of the lantern, shoveling the sand and pebbles into the grave with furious haste, and looking over the edge till the pit was half full; and the priest said that there was much fresh blood on Antonio's hands and on his clothes.

❰   ❰   ❰

I had come to the end of my story. Holger finished his wine and leaned back in his chair.

"So Angelo got his own again," he said. "Did he marry the prim and plump young person to whom he had been betrothed?"

"No; he had been badly frightened. He went to South America, and has not been heard of since."

"And that poor thing's body is there still, I suppose," said Holger. "Is it quite dead yet, I wonder?"

I wonder, too. But whether it be dead or alive, I should hardly care to see it, even in broad daylight. Antonio is as grey as a badger, and he has never been quite the same man since that night.

I Vant to be Alone

❧

Barb D'Amato

It was that in-between time of day the french call *l'heure bleu*. There was a blue-gray haze of humid air over Central Park and a sooty haze over the rest of the city. From where I stood, I could see all the way across the park, and the buildings on the west might have been a charcoal sketch done on rough paper. No air stirred. New York was marinating in its own exhaust.

The Upper East Side was as hot as the rest of the city, despite being fashionable and expensive. Tonight was identical to a hundred other July evenings here, and yet night would never be the same again.

Yesterday, man had landed on the moon.

As I crossed Fifth Avenue, I looked at the sky. I wasn't sure whether this would be a night for a full moon or not. Because I had been doing background reading on my assignment, I had not had time to look up the phases of the moon, and it didn't matter anyway. What mattered was that night would never be the same. I stood on the pavement, a young earthbound man who might some day walk on the moon. The universe was less mysterious, perhaps, and to me more appalling.

I couldn't quite get a fix on how I felt about it. The human race had now gone far beyond the so-called discovery of the new world by the Europeans. After all, the new world was new only to the Europeans themselves, in their self-centeredness. The Maya, the Inca, the Eskimo, and the Native Americans had been there all along.

No, landing on the moon was far more than a giant step; it was wholly new.

And yet, there was something horrifying about it to me. Something dreadful—a metastasis of a sort. As if killer bees, previously confined to Africa, had come ashore in Florida in the luggage hold of an airliner. Or as if the beetle that carried Dutch elm disease were arriving in New York harbor in a piece of imported wood. Was mankind now to infect the entire universe?

For God's sake, what was the matter with me? I was on the verge of the scoop of my career, if I could bring it off. I was, as the British put it, "over the moon." That was an expression that would probably go by the wayside now, I guess, signifying, as it did, happiness beyond your wildest dreams.

Actually, I forgot about this peculiar angst and reverted to my normal personality when I stepped into the lobby of the building on the Upper East Side. Evening had darkened into night. The excitement of the upcoming interview bubbled in my blood, and the portentousness was added to by the elegance of the beautifully constructed building. Besides, I was young and feisty and hardheaded and pretty brash, too, the very model of the up-and-coming reporter. It was twenty-four years ago. I was twenty-seven.

Imagine being twenty-seven!

I had expected to be admitted by a butler in black or a maid dressed in gray with a white lace apron. Anything but what happened. The door was opened wide and there she stood.

That face, the enthralling face—as beautiful today at sixty-four as when she made *Anna Christie* at the age of twenty-five. Twenty-eight years since her last picture, and she was as famous as she had ever been. The deep-set eyes, the chiseled planes of cheek, that clean, firm line of chin. This was beauty that struck one dumb, and I couldn't speak. Me! Speechless!

"Mr. Briskman?" she said. Yes, the husky voice, slightly accented, very sensual.

"Hal Briskman, Miss Garbo."

She did not use my first name, though (callow youth!) I had half hoped she would. In fact, she didn't say anything at all, but stepped back, closed the door behind me, and led me into a wide living room.

"I have brought a tape recorder, Miss Garbo. Is that all right? I wanted to be precise when I quoted you."

"Quite all right."

She sat down and gestured to an adjacent chair. Then—nothing. She merely sat and watched me, watched intently and rather eagerly.

I was fully prepared, with three steno-pad pages of questions. I was always prepared in those days, knowing perfectly well I couldn't count on experience or craft.

"Uh—I don't especially want to go over parts of your personal history that have been written about frequently. Unless, that is, you want to tell me more about them. Add something." I looked at her. She merely watched. But she didn't object.

"Your father was an unskilled laborer, who died when you were young, I think?"

"Yes."

"You grew up in Stockholm." In a very poor district, but I didn't quite want to put it that way.

"Yes."

"Your first job was as a lather girl in a barber shop. Because someone noticed your beauty, you were given a role in an advertising film."

"Yes. It was sheer chance." She glanced from me to the room we sat in, reflecting, I suppose, that all this luxury was also the fruit of sheer chance. As was life, perhaps.

"Mauritz Stiller, the Swedish director, discovered you in 1924."

"Yes." For a moment I thought this would be another of her monosyllabic answers, but her eyes took on that hundred-mile gaze, like the last scene in *Queen Christina*, and she said, "He taught me everything. Everything."

She and he were always together; he was Svengali to her Trilby. He introduced her to artistic society, trained her dramatic skills, and even ran her professional business life.

"Then," I said, "Louis B. Mayer offered Stiller a Hollywood job in 1924, but Stiller insisted that you be given a contract as well."

"Yes."

"And you came together to the United States. Mayer, foolishly, didn't want to hire you, but he gave in."

Her head bent toward me. "Do you know what he said? Mayer said, 'American men don't like fat women.'"

"I heard about that."

"They wanted me ethereal, transparent. They thought I was big and awkward."

"But you filmed as ethereal."

"Yes, exactly. On the film," she said, her attention fixed closely on me.

"*The Torrent* showed how tremendously effective you were in front of the camera. But off-camera, in the midst of the Hollywood publicity storm, you were already developing a reputation for being noncommunicative."

"Yes. They believed it was because of my accent."

I waited in case she would tell me what the reason really was, if it wasn't the accent, but when the silence drew out, I finally said, "Then in 1927 Stiller went home to Sweden without you."

"Yes," she said, and those deep-sunken eyelids drooped.

How to ask about her romances? I said, "Your name was linked romantically with John Gilbert during the filming of *Flesh and the Devil*."

"Yes." Was that a faint smile?

"And later with Leopold Stokowski, and the director Rouben Mamoulian, even the famous health guru Gaylord Hauser and the photographer Cecil Beaton."

No answer at all. Now I was determined not to go on to the next question, to let the silence lengthen out until she *had* to say something, to give me a quotable line about one of the men.

But she didn't. After some time she said, "Do you know what someone called me? 'The dream princess of eternity.'"

She turned her face full to me and waited for my reaction.

I was stumped. Finally, thinking I sounded like a psychiatrist, I said, "Did you like it when they said that, or not?"

"Actually, I thought it was rather appropriate."

Another silence, not awkward really, but strung tight, like a filament of spiderweb.

"You were just about the only silent star who made a successful transition to sound. And you were spectacularly successful. For *Anna Christie*, as you know, of course, the ads were 'Garbo Talks!' Did it worry you, the change to sound?"

"No."

"And then *Ninotchka*. 'Garbo laughs!'"

"Yes."

Every aspect of her body—gestures, facial expressions, tone of voice—conveyed reticence. This didn't surprise me, as her shyness was legendary. And yet, she had agreed to the interview. What surprised me was a sort of hunger that went with the aloofness, an approach/avoidance. I put it down to her having been alone too long.

"Have you ever wanted to do another film?"

She took this very seriously, considering it for some time and answering more slowly than before. Finally she said, "Oh, no. I think I am now much too ethereal."

"You were twice voted best actress of the year by the New York film critics. Did you find that validating? Did it please you?"

"Somewhat."

"But you didn't receive an Oscar until 1954 when they gave you a special Oscar. Were you annoyed at being passed over earlier?"

"No."

I sighed. So many monosyllabic answers. I wasn't worried, really. I was here, in her apartment. I had spoken to the Enigma, the woman who went out, when she went out at all, heavily dressed in flowing coats and capes, with scarves over her head, the woman who had said she lived alone with a bar of soap and one toothbrush. Photographers and reporters descend upon her everywhere she goes, but none has ever gotten close enough for a close-up shot. People simply did not see her. But I had, only me, and it would be a coup, whatever she said. Still, I wanted some comment, some quote I could call my own.

I sighed again, shifted my weight, and may have made a move that looked like I was thinking of leaving.

At any rate, she seemed to realize that, if she was to keep my interest, she had to be more forthcoming. "Mauritz Stiller was the finest director I ever knew," she said.

"But he didn't stay on in Hollywood."

"No. What a shame that was. He was too impulsive. His directorial style was too changeable. The set was forever in an uproar. They had no idea how to tell whether he was getting the work done, although they should have known he would because he had in the past. He had made wonderful films. Hollywood wanted its movies produced like Fords, on a production line."

She moved closer, emphasizing her words with her eyes.

"Mauritz Stiller changed the whole direction of my life."

She was wearing something silk, I think, that brushed against itself with the sound that moth wings might make, on night air.

I said, "Why did you agree to talk with me?"

"It is pleasant to see someone young. Someone who is youthful and vigorous. I spend so much time with men and women who are gray and worn. Older people. It is pleasant to speak with someone who is so, so robust."

The lights took on an amber undertone. Like the color of honey. Her voice, an odd, quirky, low voice, held all the thick sweetness of honey. There was a humming in my ears.

I looked at my steno pad for reassurance. But how silly! Why did I need reassurance? There was my last major prepared question for her—indeed the Big Question. She had retired quite suddenly. She had never returned to film, nor even to public life. It had long been speculated that her retirement was the result not only of shyness, not only because she grew "tired of making faces," though she was certainly shy, but also because her last movie, *Two-Faced Woman*, made in 1941, was badly received by the critics and public both. I had left this for last for fear that she would be insulted and terminate the interview. I opened my mouth to ask her. I fully believed I was going to ask her that question.

Two-Faced Woman.

She moved closer to me.

"Well, thank you, Miss Garbo," was what my mouth said. "I don't want to exhaust my welcome." I rose abruptly to my feet.

She seemed puzzled. When I stood, she stood, too, and walked graciously with me to the door.

This was not a woman of impulse, and yet it seemed like an impulsive confidence when she said, "They wanted an ethereal woman. They wanted a woman who was young and ageless, too, and with the wisdom of ages."

❆   ❆   ❆

In a brief seventeen-year career of acting in American films, Greta Garbo had become the most famous of the screen goddesses. But she was always aloof, and always a mystery. And I have never, not so much as for one full day, ceased to wonder about that interview and about her. Who and what was she?

She said once, "I am a misfit in the world."

I'm fifty-one now; the next milestone will be sixty. I think more and more about the Isaac Watts line, "Time, like an ever rolling stream, bears all her sons away." I am being borne away, slowly, on a gentle river. And I wonder, sometimes.

What would a person do, what would a woman risk, to become an international star?

And would it be worth it?

The interview was, as I had expected, the coup of my career. Looking back on it, probably the foundation of my career. Because of that interview, just my unadorned report on how she looked and the literal reproduction of what she had said, I had a call to the *New York Times*, which gave me a boost to a higher position on the *Chicago Tribune*, which led finally to my present position, editor in chief at *Chicago Today*. Without that interview, I suspect none of this would have happened. Journalism is like a pyramid with a very wide bottom and a very narrow top. There are thousands and thousands of bright young reporters scrambling upward like termites, but they don't make it without at least one break.

Who was she? The Eternal Vamp.

An actress and a beautiful woman. That's all and that's enough.

I think, really, I was just in an odd frame of mind that night. There was in fact no subtext to our conversation, and my belief, fleeting even then, that she was—that she had another reality she was trying to tell me about—all that was a product of the oddness of that night. Man had walked on the moon, and I was primed for strangeness. The nature of the world had changed. I was moonstruck.

I'm really quite sure.

NELLIE FOSTER

⤳

AUGUST DERLETH

MRS. KRAFT CAME HURRIEDLY FROM THE HOUSE, closed the white gate behind her, and half ran across the dusty street. With one hand she held her long skirts clear of the walk; with the other she pressed a white handkerchief tightly to her lips. Her dark eyes were fixed on the green and white house at the end of the block, almost hidden in the shade of overhanging elms of great age.

The gate stood open, and Mrs. Kraft stepped quickly on to the lawn, forgetting to close the gate behind her. She avoided the low veranda, going around the side of the house, and entered the kitchen through the open door at the back.

Mrs. Perkins was leafing through her recipe book when the shadow of Mrs. Kraft momentarily darkened her door. She looked up and said, "How do, Mrs. Kraft? You're out early this morning." She smiled.

Mrs. Kraft did not smile. She stood quite still, her handkerchief still pressed tightly against her mouth, nodding curtly to acknowledge her neighbor's greeting.

Mrs. Perkins looked at her oddly. "What is it, Mrs. Kraft?" she asked a little nervously.

Mrs. Kraft took the handkerchief away from her mouth, clenching it tightly in her hand, and said, "It happened again last night."

Mrs. Perkins put her recipe book aside suddenly. "How do you know?" she asked breathlessly. Her eyes were unnaturally wide. "How do you know, Mrs. Kraft?"

Her visitor opened her hand jerkily. "It was my niece this time. She saw the woman, too. I didn't want Andrew to let the child go out last night, but she would have her way. She wanted to go to her Aunt Emmy's."

"Beyond the cemetery," breathed Mrs. Perkins. "But she came back before dark, surely?"

Mrs. Kraft shook her head. "No. At dusk, just before the street lights went on. The woman was there, standing in the road. The child was afraid, even when the woman took her hand and walked along with her."

"What did she do? Oh, I hope nothing serious happened!"

"The same as before. The woman kissed the child, and the little one went to sleep. This morning she is so weak, she couldn't get up. Loss of blood, the doctor said."

Mrs. Perkins clasped her hands helplessly in her lap. "What can we do, Mrs. Kraft? Nobody would believe us if we said what this must be."

Mrs. Kraft made an impatient movement with her head. Then she leaned forward, her dark eyes shining, speaking in a low voice. "The child knew the woman."

Mrs. Perkins started. "It wasn't . . . wasn't—"

Mrs. Kraft nodded. "Nellie Foster—not yet a month dead!"

Mrs. Perkins wove her fingers together nervously. She had gone pale, and her uneasiness was more pronounced than her visitor's.

"My niece is the third child, Mrs. Perkins. We must do something, or it will continue—and the children may die."

Mrs. Perkins said nothing. Her visitor went on.

"I'm going to do something, if you won't," she said. "Tonight I'm going to watch at the cemetery. There won't be another child to be taken like that."

"I don't know what I can do," murmured Mrs. Perkins quietly. "I get so nervous. If I saw Nellie Foster, I'd probably scream."

Mrs. Kraft shook her head firmly. "That would never do," she admitted.

"Did you go to the minister?" asked Mrs. Perkins.

Mrs. Kraft pressed her lips tightly together before she spoke. Then she said, "He said there were no such things. He said only ignorant people believed in vampires."

Mrs. Perkins shook her head in disapproval.

"He asked me how Nellie Foster could have become one, and I told him about the cat jumping over her coffin. He smiled, and wouldn't believe me." Mrs. Kraft stood up, nodding her head. "And I know it's Nellie Foster, because I was out to the cemetery this morning, and there were three little holes in the grave—like finger holes, going way down deep."

"What are you going to do?"

"I don't know yet. But I'll watch, and I won't let her get out of the cemetery."

"Maybe the men could do something," suggested Mrs. Perkins hopefully.

"It would be worse than telling the minister, to go to them. They'd laugh. If he wouldn't believe it, they wouldn't," said Mrs. Kraft scornfully. "It will be left for some one else to do."

"I wish I could help," said Mrs. Perkins.

Mrs. Kraft looked at her reflectively, her eyes hardening. "You can, if you want."

Mrs. Perkins nodded eagerly.

"If I'm to go to the cemetery, I've got to be protected."

The other woman nodded. Mrs. Kraft pursed her lips firmly. "I need something," she went on, "and I'd like to use that blessed crucifix your son brought from Belgium, the one Cardinal Mercier gave him, a very old one, he said it was."

For a moment Mrs. Perkins wavered. Her lips faltered a little. Then, quailing before the stern eyes of Mrs. Kraft, she moved noiselessly to get the crucifix.

Mrs. Kraft attached it to a black ribbon around her neck, and tucked it out of sight in the bosom of her black dress. Then she rose to go.

"I'll tell you what happened in the morning, Mrs. Perkins. And if I don't come"—Mrs. Kraft faltered—"then something's wrong. And if I'm not here before noon, you'd best go to the cemetery, perhaps, and look around a bit."

Mrs. Perkins quavered, "You don't think she'd go for you, Mrs. Kraft?"

"They don't only go for children, Mrs. Perkins. I've read about them. If they can't die, they have to have blood—and we've blood, too."

Nodding her head sagely, Mrs. Kraft went from the house, her lips still pursed, her hand still tightly clenching her handkerchief.

☾　　☾　　☾

Mrs. Kraft sat on the back porch with Mrs. Perkins a little after sunrise the next morning. The dew was not yet gone; it hung heavy on the hollyhocks and delphinium. The early sunlight threw long shadows across the garden.

Mrs. Kraft was talking. "I got there just after sunset and hid behind the oak tree near old Mr. Prince's grave, and watched for Nellie Foster. When the moon came up, I saw something on her grave, something gray. It was like a part of some one lying there, and it was moving. It was misty, and I couldn't see it well. Then I saw a hand, and then another, and after that a face," Mrs. Kraft coughed a little; Mrs. Perkins shuddered.

"And then?" prompted Mrs. Perkins. She leaned forward, fascinated.

"It was Nellie Foster," Mrs. Kraft went on in a low voice. "She was crawling out of her grave. I could see her plainly then in the moonlight. It was Nellie, all right. I'd know her anywhere. She pulled herself out—it was like mist coming out of those holes in the grave, those little holes."

"What did you do?"

"I think I was scared. I didn't move. When the mist stopped coming there was Nellie standing on the grave. Then I ran toward her, holding the cross in my hand. Before I could reach her, she was gone."

Mrs. Kraft's face twisted suddenly in pain. "This morning they found the little Walters girl, like the others. I should have watched beside the grave. I should have stopped Nellie. I shouldn't have let her get out. It's my fault that the little Walters girl was attacked. My fault. I could have stopped Nellie. I could have watched there all night. I should have gone forward before she got out of the grave."

She rose suddenly, disturbed. "I'm going now, Mrs. Perkins. Let me keep the cross a little longer. I'll need it tonight."

Mrs. Perkins nodded, and her visitor was gone, her black-clothed figure walking quickly across the road. Mrs. Perkins watched her go, wondering about Nellie Foster, hoping that soon something might be done to stop her coming from her grave. There was her own little Flory to think about. What if some day Nellie Foster should see her, and then they would find little Flory? Mrs. Perkins shuddered. "Oh Lord, give me power to do something," she thought. "Let me help." Then she thought, "And Nellie Foster was always such a nice girl! It's hard to believe." She went into the house, shaking her head.

She had intended to go over to see Mrs. Kraft just after dinner, to talk about doing something, but a sudden storm struck the town, and for six hours it raged, pouring rain, darkening the village. For six hours only lightning flashes brightened the darkness. Then, at seven o'clock, the sky cleared abruptly, and the setting sun came out to finish the July day in a blaze of rainbow glory.

Mrs. Perkins finished washing the supper dishes, saw her Flory go out to play until dark, and finally started for Mrs. Kraft's. Going out to the sidewalk, she saw an elderly man coming quickly down the street. Mr. Shurz, she thought. Seems in a hurry, too. She pondered this. Something on his mind, likely. She purposely slowed her pace.

At the gate she met him. He would have gone past had he not spied her suddenly. Then he stopped breathlessly. "Miz' Perkins, have y' heard the news?"

Mrs. Perkins shook her head. "Lightning strike somewhere?" she asked.

"If only 'twere that, Miz' Perkins, Ma'am." The old man shook his head dolefully. "The like of this we've never had in this town before, 'slong as I can remember. This afternoon during the storm, some one got into the cemetery and dug open Nellie Foster's grave!"

Mrs. Perkins leaned over the gate, her hands tightly clenched on the pointed staves. "What?" she whispered hoarsely. "What's that you say, Mr. Shurz?"

"'Tis just as I say, Miz' Perkins. Some one dug into Nellie Foster's grave, in all that storm, too, and opened the coffin, Miz' Perkins, Ma'am, *and druv a stake clean through her body!*"

"A stake . . . through her body!" She shook her head. "Just what Mrs. Kraft said should be done," she murmured to herself.

Mr. Shurz did not hear her. He nodded vehemently. "Clean through, Miz' Perkins, Ma'am. And a powerful lot of blood there were, too; 'twas a surprize to Doctor Barnes. A strange, unnatural thing, the doctor said."

"But surely the coffin was covered again?"

"Partly, only partly, Miz' Perkins. Seems the man got scared away."

"Oh . . . it was a man, then?"

Mr. Shurz looked at her, smiling vacuously. "'Course 'twas a man, Miz' Perkins."

"He was seen, then?"

Mr. Shurz shook his head. "Oh, no, he wasn't seen. No, ma'am, he wasn't seen. Too slick for that, he was."

Mrs. Perkins felt her heart pounding in her breast. She felt suddenly that she was stifling. She opened the gate and stepped on to the sidewalk at Mr. Shurz's side, walking along with him. She did not hear what he was saying.

Mrs. Kraft was out on her lawn. She was pale, dishevelled. Mrs. Perkins was thinking: I hope he won't notice anything; I hope he won't notice anything. Mr. Shurz stopped with Mrs. Perkins. Mrs. Perkins could hardly bring herself to say, "How do, Mrs. Kraft?"

Then, as Mr. Shurz was repeating his story to Mrs. Kraft, Mrs. Perkins' eyes fell on the stain of red clay on Mrs. Kraft's hands, a stain at first difficult to wash away. She wanted to look away from Mrs. Kraft's rough hands, but she could not. Then she noticed that Mr. Shurz had seen the stain, too.

"Bin diggin' in red clay, have you, Miz' Kraft?" He laughed hollowly. "Looks mighty like that clay they dug away off Nellie Foster's coffin, now." He wagged his head.

Mrs. Perkins felt faint. She heard him talking, rambling on. Deep down in her she wanted to say something, anything, to change the subject, but she could not. Then she heard Mrs. Kraft speaking.

"I've been digging in the garden, Mr. Shurz," she smiled politely, despite her white, drawn face. "This stain is mighty hard to get off your hands."

Mrs. Perkins heard herself saying, "That's right. I warned Mrs. Kraft not to touch the red clay when we were digging up her sweet william right after the storm, but she wouldn't listen." She was thinking, "Oh Lord, don't let him look into the garden; don't let him see how black the ground is there."

Mr. Shurz grinned broadly and shrugged his shoulders. "'Tis a good time to dig garden, after rain. Well, I must be off. We'll be catching him who meddled with Nellie Foster."

The women, standing one on each side of the fence, watched the old man go down the street. Mrs. Perkins was afraid to look at Mrs. Kraft. Then she heard her neighbor cough lightly, and turned.

Mrs. Kraft was holding out the crucifix. "I don't think I'll need it any more, Mrs. Perkins," she was saying.

MADELEINE

BARBARA HAMBLY

THE YOUNG MAN'S NAME WAS PHILIP. HE WAS A SOLICI-tor's clerk somewhere in the city, thin and very fair—Madeleine liked fair and slender young men. On winter evenings she would watch them from the shadows of an alleyway at one end of the street where all the firms had their offices. The lighted windows were like illuminated pictures in the city's cindery winter dusks; clerks in frock coats closing up the ledgers, returning deed boxes to high shelves. She pictured the movement of the muscles under their shirts, thought about the texture of the lips under those brave attempts at mustaches, imagined the taste, the freshness, of the soft skin between high celluloid collar and ear. They would come out into the gaslight of the narrow street, pulling on their gloves, chatter-ing with one another happily, about the matters dear to the hearts of young men: tobacco, boating, cards, girls.

Sometimes, Madeleine would follow one of them.

In the summer when the darkness did not fully come until nearly nine o'clock, she would lie in her coffin and stretch out her awareness, listening across the city for their voices, fragile and light as the voices of children playing in some other part of a great garden. She could trace them, every one, if she concen-trated; pick out a certain set of footsteps, the jaunty whistling of a popular waltz, through the clamoring of carriage wheels and hooves on cobbles, the yam-mering of costermongers trying to dispose of the day's stale wares and the whooping oompah of tavern bands; trace them sometimes each back to his own shabby rooms.

When full dark came, sweet with the gluey warmth of the city's summer, she would set forth in her glitter of lace and jet, to find the streets where they lived.

This was what she did with Philip.

She watched him for weeks, for young clerks were her hobby, her treat, rather than the staple of her nights.

He lived with a woman named Olivia, five or six years older than he, a sort of bluestocking who pursued studies in the Old Library at the university. Madeleine would see them through the lace curtains of her flat when the lights were up in the darkness, talking as they cooked supper, hands waving with the earnestness of lovers, brandishing sausages at one another on the end of forks; or else would listen to them make love, from where she stood on the flagway, or in the next street, or three blocks away, seeking out the sound through all the night sounds of the city, all the lovers, all the children playing on the night pavements, all the parents arguing over money or dreams. She knew how their breaths entwined, heard the words the woman said—surprisingly coarse for that tall, thin, old-maidish form, that narrow bespectacled face—and the soft little sound Philip would make, between a gasp and a whimper, at her touch.

It was that sound that decided Madeleine. That, and the fineness of his skin. She waited until Olivia departed on some journey of several days, then encountered Philip, as if by accident, in the street on his way back to his flat.

She took him that night, draining his blood until he collapsed, fainting, in her arms; stroking his face, his throat, his shoulders with her long glassy fingernails as he lay in the tangle of his bed-sheets gazing up at her with wonder and terror in his wandering brown eyes. She treasured him so much she left him a little alive, and when she lay at dawn in her coffin in the expensive and heavily secured town house that was hers, she sleepily, satedly probed out with her mind, to hear his labored gasps as he struggled for air, picturing him lying there in extremity, unable even to call for help. She took that picture down with her into the dreamless vampire sleep and hoped vaguely that he would live until night.

He was alive when she threw back the tall windows from his balcony again. It was clear to her that no one had come to him all day. He only just managed to turn his head on the pillows when she came in, and she treasured the moment of his exquisite despair. He had known all day that she would be back with the darkness.

She savored that, as much as she savored the blood that finally drew out his life.

Two nights later Madeleine went to the cemetery of St. Joseph, to see his tomb.

It was a family tomb, like a gray granite temple. He had been the younger son of some bourgeois with aspirations to the professions. In the warm gloom of the late spring evening the smell of mortar was sharp in the air, contrasting with the waxy pungence of funeral wreaths. Madeleine had killed on her way there, a carpet-seller in his grimy shop near the bank of the river, a man no one would miss, except perhaps his wife, if he had one . . . and probably not her, much. So she felt indulgent with the world, as she moved through the darkness of tombs and ivy and ornamental trees toward the place.

A veiled woman stood on the tomb's steps. But though Madeleine walked with a vampire's soundless, weightless stride, the woman seemed to hear, and raised her head, putting back her veil with hands gloved in shabby and mended black kid. Her spectacles flashed like all-seeing eyes in the dark.

"I thought that you would come here," she said.

Madeleine laughed. Men had told her—before they died, before they knew what she was and the extent of their danger—that she had a laugh like silver bells, like the cold tinkling of glass chimes. "Oh, it's one who knows, is it?" she mocked.

Olivia stood for some moments, regarding her in the near-total darkness beneath the trees. With the sight of night-walking things, Madeleine could see this woman quite clearly; not precisely beautiful, with her long, narrow face and those enormous gray eyes behind the thick rounds of glass, but oddly compelling. Her brown hair was piled on her head beneath the veiled black hat, and her hands, though narrow, were as long as a man's. *She must have the most dreadful time finding gloves*, thought the vampire, with detached amusement. *If her feet are anything like in proportion she probably hunts all over the city for shoes.* Madeleine's own hands and feet were small, exquisite in high-buttoned shoes handmade for her by an old man on the fringes of the financial district. The money she'd taken from the carpet-seller's shop—and from Philip's desk drawer—would probably go toward paying for another pair.

"Nobody will believe you, you know," she said, coming closer, dainty as a bisque doll in her small-waisted gown, the silk taffeta of her petticoats murmuring like last fall's leaves on the grass. "They never do. What did his family put it down that he'd died of, a 'wasting sickness'?"

Then she stopped, for Olivia was not backing away from her, not hiding her face. She only stood, looking at Madeleine with a kind of calm sadness, like, Madeleine thought in irritation, some placid cow observing her over a fence.

"And that is all that he was to you?" Olivia said.

"Darling, how can you say that?" Madeleine smiled dreamily. "He was a desperately sweet boy—as I'm sure you know, my dear. I've always had a terrible weakness for sweet boys." Her smile broadened, to make her white teeth gleam. She felt warm throughout, and powerful, the blood of the carpet-seller rich and sweet in her veins for all his unprepossessing appearance. *Sometimes one dines on caviar,* she thought, *and other times, on pot roast.* Her cheeks, she knew, would be rosy with the flush of stolen life, her lips dark crimson.

Olivia's face was as white as her own had been when she'd risen from her coffin with the coming of night.

"What, are you worried he'll turn into a wicked, wicked vampire like me?"

The woman shook her head. "No. I know that is not how vampires are made."

"Oooh." Madeleine formed a little moue with her lips. "A scholar, no less."

"After a fashion." Olivia stepped forward suddenly and lifted her hand. Madeleine scented the coldness of silver on her, a great deal of silver. Under that black mourning dress with its high collar and long sleeves she must have chains of it, circling her throat and her wrists, perhaps small discs sewn into the flounces of her petticoats, the cotton of her corset cover.

Madeleine stepped back, her flowerlike nostrils flaring. "Don't try it," she said, and her voice was suddenly a snarl. "I am warning you, my dear. Just because you know what I am doesn't mean you can do anything about it. The blood I have taken, the lives I have taken, are all within me, giving me strength. All your learning, and all your study, can't prevail against that."

"No," replied Olivia. "You took their blood, and you took their lives, uncaring of who they were and what they were, only to add to your own life and strength."

Madeleine laughed again, not the sweet silver-bell laugh of the lady now, but cruel and hard and scornful. "Who and what they were? They were *ordinary*, darling. Ordinary and common and dull. Like yourself, I'm afraid; are we really going to go through a sermon on how evil I am? I expected more of you."

"Is that why you came here?" Olivia spoke without irony, without trace of anger in her clear gray eyes. "Because you expected something of me? I'm sorry to disappoint you. You took their blood, and you took their lives, and so all I can do is charge you to be aware of what you have taken. To be aware fully. Then maybe you will not be so quick to do it again."

Madeleine was angry now, irritated at the argument and impatient to leave. She considered taking this woman, here and now, for the cemetery was utterly deserted, but her native caution prevailed. First, because Olivia had come prepared, her clothing thick with hidden silver, and Madeleine was not sure she could overpower the other woman without getting badly burned. Second, because the vampires of the city lived upon the city's poor. If too many young and handsome clerks died in too rapid succession, or if family members or lovers died too—even if not upon the very grave of the earlier victim—the police would begin to inquire. There were priests, and strange old scholars at the university, who knew things that other men scorned to believe, and it did not do to bring matters too much to their attention.

And third . . .

No, thought Madeleine, backing from Olivia until she was little more than a glitter of jet beads, like colorless fire within the smoke of her lace. *There is no third reason. This woman is only a stupid woman, praying and sniveling over a man she couldn't even keep.*

There was no third reason.

But she found no cutting remark, no perfect exit line, upon which to make her departure. So she had to content herself with saying, "Fool—a thousand times a fool," as she faded into the night.

Olivia, standing upon the steps of the granite tomb, did not move until she was gone.

Lying in her coffin at dawn, Madeleine let her mind rove through the city, tasting the final perfumes of the night. Mist rising from the river, the smell of the

hay barges coming in from the country, the voices of marketwomen at their bar-
rows. "'Ere, get 'em fresh, new from the country, cucumbers cool as ice!" Prostitutes gathering in the cafes for a final cup of coffee before going home. "Well,
I'll give 'im the money, if he wants to gamble so bad, but damned if I'll let that
bastard tell me what to do in me spare time." Small children waking and being
got ready for school. The wheels of milk wagons rocking over pavements beneath
chestnut trees, the self-satisfied purring of cats padding up stone steps for the
first cream of the day. Summer was coming, a bad time for vampires in northern
latitudes, but there was an enchantment in it, too; returning to her coffin long
before sleep was ready to come, and lying in its darkness for hours before it was
safe to rise, Madeleine walked through the city with her ears, with her mind. Frequently she chose her victims that way, only later trying to trace down their
voices, their footfalls, their smells.

It gave her amusement, and a sense of keenness to her hunt.

"So I says to my wife, I says, 'How you gonna deal with a man like that?' He
brings carpets in from the East, he says. . . ."

Madeleine twitched uncomfortably in her narrow coffin, as a memory from
last night's predawn dozing intruded into her mind. Whose voice was that?

Yes, the carpet-seller. A loud boor, and no loss to anyone. His voice grated
even yet in her memory.

"Them guys that go to Turkey all the time, buying up carpets, they gotta be
a little crazy, you know? You could get yourself killed, traveling around on some
cockamamie camel or donkey or whatever, carrying money 'cause they don't got
no banks there. . . ."

She tried to push the voice from her mind, tried to silence her thoughts. She
hadn't heard the old man's grating voice for more than a few minutes last night.
In her after-sunset rambles, looking almost at random for a victim in the swarm-
ing alleys of the riverside slums, she had heard it again and remembered it from
that half-dozing listening. Had heard it then and had smiled. She remembered
thinking, *His wife will probably thank me. . . .*

Why did she hear him say now, "Ruchel and me, thirty years we been married, you think she remembers which tie I always wear on Sabbath? Always she's
asking me, What tie you gonna wear to *shul*, Jakov, like she hasn't seen me put on
the red one every goddam Sabbath. . . ."

Shut UP, old man, Madeleine thought savagely, and turned her mind away, seeking the darkness of sleep, the quiet of dreams. But she was still awake when, long after sunrise, the day-duty policeman walked past the house whistling opera, and the gardener came to tend the place and make it look like it was lived in, though during the day none of the neighbors ever saw movement behind the locked doors, the drawn blinds.

When she slept, there was no quiet in her sleep.

Madeleine woke feeling somewhat refreshed, but only by careful concentration on the sounds outside could she avoid remembering what the carpet-seller's voice sounded like. For a time she lay, listening and breathing in the scents of the coming night, feeling her mind and senses stir, her blood and her hunger rise. She remembered, more than the carpet-seller, the woman Olivia, and felt a vicious desire to seek her out and kill her, though she knew that such a thing was out of the question for months, if ever.

Still, when she rose at last from her coffin, when she slipped out of the cloud of lace that was her negligee, and stroked her cold, slim, white body in the blood-orange glow of the lamplight, when she dressed carefully, in dove gray this time, all trimmed with black lace like a tabby cat, she found herself thinking she wanted a woman.

The woman she killed was tall and gawky and wore spectacles, though she was older than Olivia, and getting fat with the starchy diet of the working poor. She was a seamstress, stitching over lamplight to finish a client's order before some party tomorrow night. Madeleine was careful not to get blood on the shimmering apricot-colored silk, which she then held up to herself before the seamstress's long mirror. It was a little too big, but she took it anyway, liking the fabric. It would not take much, she told herself, to alter it to her own more fragile body.

That she had nearly thirty such dresses, taken in the confidence of alterations she had no concept of how to perform, did not cross her mind. All those were out of style by this time, anyway.

She did not even realize whose voice she heard in her mind, like the memory of an overheard conversation, as she was walking the dark streets, watching the night go by. "Poor Alicia was in labor with her for two days, no wonder the dear little thing was so sickly as a child," she seemed to hear a woman's gentle voice say. "But she was always smart as paint. Her father would never hear of her going with the other children to Sunday school to learn reading, but little Nicole, when she was four years old she slipped out of the house and ran away with her friend Lettice . . . You remember Lettice? That dear redheaded girl. . . ."

Madeleine shook her head angrily, her admiration of the ghostly shimmer of lights through river mist broken by that constant, murmuring recollection. . . .

". . . so I says to him, Morrie, I says. You want me to pay top price for a piece of carpet some Moslem heathen has had laying out in front of his shop for donkeys to walk over? Is that what you're telling me?"

Damn! thought Madeleine furiously. *Don't let that infernal carpet-seller start up again!*

She tried to turn her mind away, to think of something else, but all that would come to her was the woman's soft voice, talking about her children. Endlessly.

Madeleine usually didn't kill twice in a night, but she felt the desperate need for the intense concentration of the hunt to take her mind off those voices. She made her way to the poorest section of town and found a beggar, a wretched and whining specimen no one would miss and, because she needed excitement, let him see her, let him know her for what she was, with the seamstress's blood still on her mouth and the flames of hell gleaming in her eyes. She pursued the man through the dripping and filthy alleys, cutting him off easily when he tried to run to pubs and police stations where there were lights and people, driving him back into the garbage-smelling lanes that fronted the docks, feeling her own excitement rise with the stepped-up pounding of his heart, the frantic heat of his blood. The little man was sobbing, mumbling desperate prayers to a half-forgotten God, unable to run or even to stand anymore when she overtook him at last, and then she let him escape her, two or three times, pursuing him languidly, easily, in the dark.

When she was done she threw his body in the river and watched the tide take it out.

"I never had the chances other people got."

Madeleine woke up, broad awake, though she knew it was barely past noon.

"Ma, she always said we wasn't supposed to smoke her tobacco, so whenever any of her tobacco was missin', my brothers'd tell her it was me that took it, just me, not them or anything, and I'd be the one that got the buckle end of the belt. It was always the same. Look, I can't help it if I'm little. I can't help it if I had this twisted foot. . . ."

The swell of rage in her was like a heat about to blow the lid off the coffin.

". . . so you'd think a boy with opportunities like that, he'd go into business for his father, wouldn't you? Nice shop, good money, seat in *shul* by the eastern wall for High Holy Days. . . ."

"I wanted Elizabeth—that's my oldest—to have the best education, to have the best start in the world she can get. That's why I took in extra work, to get her proper schooling, though the nuns at St. Irene's are terribly expensive and I do have to make her extra clothing, because some of the other girls there are so unkind. Still, when I offered the Mother Superior to do the embroidery on the new altar cloth. . . ."

The heat was followed by cold, and the terrible, first sinking drop of fear. She understood whose those voices were, speaking chattily in her head.

That bitch! I'll kill her . . . I'll ram her sniveling voices down her throat!

Madeleine had never been awake in the daytime. Another time she might have savored the experience, the overpowering weight of languor that made even the movement of a hand into effort; might even have tracked the policeman by his whistling—Rossini and Verdi—back to his house, to call upon him some night on his way back from the pub. But now all she heard was the carpet-seller's diatribes on the shortcomings of his suppliers, the seamstress's gentle praise of her children, the beggar's complaints about his ill health, poverty, and misuse by his next-door neighbor's dog.

She did not sleep, from noon until the coming of dark.

Thanks to her double meal of the night before, she rose at last not hungry. As a general rule Madeleine spent considerable time in her town house preparing for the hunt, washing, curling her witch-black hair, sometimes only stroking her body, observing the trim perfection of the pink-tipped apples of her breasts, the slight, bony projections of hipbone and knee, running her hands down the small of her back to feel the tiny indentations there, one on either side of the spine, which only slender and perfect women had. Then she would stand naked before her huge armoires, holding up dress after dress, intent on matching each ensemble exactly with her mood of that night and the image she desired to portray. Would she be the gracious lady extending favors tonight? The mysterious dark beauty? The deadly serpent?

Tonight she pulled on a walking suit of black-shot red, like old blood. *She will see me in my rage,* she thought with bitter fury. *She will see the kind of danger she has tampered with. And she will rue the night she brought herself to MY attention.*

"You know, I see people passing me by every day, and you know, they could afford a couple of coins," whined a voice in her mind. "I don't ask for a lot, but I can't work—my constitution won't take the strain of a factory job, and I never had the education for one of the professions, though Father Benjamin at the church, he always said I had the brains for it . . ."

The windows of the flat that Olivia had shared with the beautiful Philip were dark when Madeleine reached the street. By the glow of the gaslights, she could see that the lace curtains which had hung there were gone.

The rooms were empty of everything save dust, and the faintly mealy smell of Olivia's books.

And Madeleine's rage had made her hungry.

Down in the street again she heard passing footfalls and looked around, her anger seeking the outlet of blood, the drugged satisfaction of the warming of her cold flesh. But she heard one of the women passing say to the other, in a voice that would have scratched glass, "Well, you know how he gets when he's drunk, and I wasn't gonna get me a black eye just for the satisfaction of breakin' a bottle over his greasy skull."

She thought about hearing that voice, over and over in her mind, and shuddered. But her hunger did not ease, and knowing that she could not immediately slake it, it became all she could think about. All she could think about, that is, in between what Ruchel's parents did on the occasion of last Passover and how Alicia had gotten married to Nicole's father in the first place.

You took their blood, and you took their lives, Olivia had said. *And so all I can do is charge you to be aware of what you have taken.*

Bitching, stinking, ordinary CATTLE! thought Madeleine furiously. *What the hell does she know about it? What the hell does she know about ME?*

But there was fear in her heart as she moved off through the city, to find others who might know what to do; others who had made her what she was, and had taught her the hidden ways, the little tricks, the secret joys. She went quickly, as if she were being pursued, but found that she could not outrace the voices in her mind.

"You hear their voices in your mind? Of your *victims?*" Sazerac burst into a whoop of delighted laughter.

"It isn't funny!" cried Madeleine furiously, but the cool, fine-boned face, white as silk by the gaslights of his parlor, convulsed with amusement, almost to tears.

"Good Lord, Count, what if you were forced to listen to yours?" chuckled Cecile, the master vampire's new favorite—taller than Madeleine and fuller of figure, and without her serpentine, dancer's grace. In an exaggerated nasal imitation of lower-class accents, the blonde vampire continued, "Gee, are you a real *count?* Like with a *castle?* Ooo, is that an honest-to-Christ *ruby?* Oh, *Count. . . ."*

Sazerac collapsed into renewed gales of mirth.

Cecile's eyes—pale blue and cold as sapphires—danced maliciously as she looked up at Madeleine. "What, darling, are you actually spending time *thinking* about their nasty little lives?" She, like Madeleine—for Sazerac had made and initiated them both—dressed for whatever role she planned to play in her hunt, and tonight she had evidently been a temptress. Flushed pale rose with the internal warmth of her kill, her breasts rose like thick cream above a low-cut gown of amber silk, intricately beaded on the bodice, so that in the warm half-light of Sazerac's town house parlor, she resembled a florid golden dragon in her lair.

"Not any more than I can help," gritted Madeleine.

"My darling, I'm sorry I laughed." Sazerac put out a hand to cup Madeleine's cheek, but his white lips still twitched with the effort not to giggle again. "Truly. Forgive me."

"What can I do?" begged Madeleine, trying not to sound as if she were begging. Not in front of Cecile. Possibly not in front of Sazerac. "The woman has left the city. Who can I go to, to remove this . . . this charge? This curse?"

"Try a priest," purred Cecile. "That way if he doesn't lift the curse at least you can hear mass all night afterward."

Nerves rubbed beyond endurance, Madeleine spun on her in a flash of fury, but Sazerac laid a reproving hand on the arm of each woman. "My darling," he said gently to Madeleine, "you need perspective on this. It's a dreadful thing, yes, but you know it's something that will fade. It must, simply with usage."

"Oh, I don't know." Cecile laid one white, rounded arm along the back of the green-black velvet settee which she shared with the vampire count. "One's love of new sensation doesn't. Or at least it hasn't for me, and you say it has not for you. One's . . . one's *relish* for the touch of every sunset, the taste of each new kill. Those don't fade."

"This is different," said Sazerac quickly. "And if not . . ." His face made a grab at sobriety and then dissolved into laughter again. "And if not, think what a time you'll have searching the city for a mute!"

Toward morning, driven by hunger, Madeleine killed a child. After seven and a half hours of listening to the little boy's unceasing—and utterly unvarying—complaint about the disappearance of his toy horse, she regretted it. She had forgotten how infuriatingly persistent children can be.

Whether she slept or not during that day, or the days following, she was not sure. If she did, the voices persisted into her dreams, until she was ready to swear that they were all sitting in the great, heavily curtained bedroom in a circle around her coffin, each yammering on about his or her own affairs, like hideously ill-mannered guests. She woke exhausted, her nerves scraped raw, the monologues intruding into her thoughts, preventing her from listening to the world outside. She spent the dark hours pacing the streets of the city, searching, listening, trying to stretch out her crippled senses to pick up the whisper of the woman Olivia's voice, the sound of her sensible-heeled shoes clacking on the pavement, the smell of her books, her bath powder, her hair.

She searched the Old Library, the university quarter with its steep, soot-black buildings jostling one another along the riverbank among ancient churches and crumbling fountains in half-forgotten squares. There were young men there, studying late by lamplight or tupping shopgirls in their garrets. She thought about killing one of them, for hunger was driving her frantic, but every time she listened to their conversations she drew back. *Dear God, don't let me get a law student! Or one who's having trouble with his girlfriend.*

They all seemed to be having trouble with their girlfriends. Or else they belonged to doctrinaire communist groups vociferously protesting the government's latest policies, or were having philosophical crises of conscience about the meaning of their lives.

Madeleine killed rats instead, though they did little for her hunger, and went hungry to bed; she woke feeling as if she had spent the day being dragged over broken bottles and cobblestones.

She grew thin and edgy. The voices did not fade with familiarity, as Sazerac had promised. Rather they grew, rehashing the old topics over and over endlessly. Sometimes she turned, positive Jakov the carpet-seller was walking along at her heels; it was as if their reality grew with feeding. There was no satisfaction to be had in the blood of animals. By two in the morning she felt that the only way to obtain relief, for even a few hours, was to hunt, to kill, as she had hunted the beggar. She stalked a dock-worker for hours and never heard him speak one word . . . not until after he was dead, and she was lying in her coffin once again, hearing his constant, muttered, foul-mouthed spew about his hatred of rich women and how he was going to beat the tar out of his nigger foreman if the asslicker ordered him around one more time.

She went two more nights without killing, listening to the voices unabated all around her. Hunger and the need for the kill clouded her mind, robbed her of whatever pleasure in life she had left. She tried killing a novelist, reflecting at least that his conversation should be interesting, and discovered that novelists' chief concerns are their royalties, and how their publishers and agents conspire to rob them, and whether their wives are cheating on them and with whom. The following week she killed a young woman of breeding and refinement and was driven nearly to the screaming point by meticulous speculations about glove length, the genealogies of acquaintances, and who should sit next to whom at dinner.

Sazerac and Cecile sought her out the night after that and warned her. "A sweet young man, or a tender girl, is all very well two, maybe three times a year," the master vampire said gravely, toying with the small cup of café noir in the blaze of gaslight at the Cafe New York. He inhaled deeply, savoring the perfumes of the ladies at the next tables, the expensive tobaccos which permeated the clothing of the fashionable gentlemen who strolled by on the flagway outside. In Madeleine's mind, the stevedore cursed at the bosses who cheated him and the pansy faggots who wouldn't even throw him a tip, the child cried shrilly, *David took my HORSE. David took my HORSE. He's going to break it. David took my HORSE.*

"But you mustn't make a habit of it, my dear Madeleine." He took her chin in his hand, gazed deep in her eyes, and there was no pity in his, only a dangerous, steely glint. "You had your fun with your little attorney's clerk. You know the rules. Too many deaths of a 'wasting sickness' will have the police wondering about the strange marks on the bodies, wondering about old legends. You have me, and Cecile, to think of as well, you know."

She whispered, "You don't understand."

The eyes did not soften one fraction with the smile that only moved the pale lips. "What, still fretting about your silly voices? I thought you were stronger than that."

Cecile rose, her eyes already following a dusky-skinned young waiter who was pocketing his tips, taking off his apron, joking with his friends about finding a girl on his way home. "Just see," she said, "that it doesn't happen again."

But of course it did. Those with some education, some style of living, at least did not have the obsessive narrowness, the foul-mouthed resentments common to so many of the poor. One hot morning as Madeleine lay tossing wretchedly in her coffin, she heard voices outside, hushed and grim, and knew them for detectives, heard a man's quiet voice say, "Have you ever wondered, gentlemen, why so many of the old legends all speak of the same things?"

She knew, as she listened to the sounds of the endless summer twilight, that she must shift her quarters, and shift them soon. But she had not fed properly in two nights, only cats and dogs, and it was difficult for her to think. Even more difficult, with the hectic clamor going on in her head, complaining, worrying, recounting old stories of loved ones, detailing conversations with friends and the minutiae of the lives she had stolen. She tried to concentrate on a letter to her house agent, on plans for emergency quarters, but her hunger made her insane with restlessness, and the voices would give her no peace. She ended by going out to hunt, with the high summer twilight barely gone from the sky and all the world smelling of lilacs and the river, and killed a young girl sitting alone on her balcony, speculating, it turned out, about whether Thomas or Louis, or perhaps George, loved her the most, and how she was going to get Andrew to propose to her, and whether she should get the shell-pink silk made up into a dress, or the oyster taffeta.

Madeleine heard about it all.

She was lying awake, gritting her teeth in fury and wretchedness, when she heard, beneath the cacophony of the voices, the crash of a rear window breaking, the snap of a latch. Her mind drugged and thick with lack of sleep, with the loginess of daytime, she thrust the lid of the coffin back, struggled to rise. Her limbs felt weighted, sodden, almost as if those who jangled and bickered in her head were clinging to her wrists, her negligee, her feet.

The room was pitch-black. She couldn't seem to open her eyes, couldn't keep them open. She fell, weak and muzzy with the daylight she knew had to be outside; in the depths of the house she heard men's footfalls, smelled their bodies, the sweat in their shirts and the mud on their shoes. Her mind reached out to hear their voices, to tell her what to flee, but all she heard was "... told Ruchel once I told her a thousand times, you can't trust those door-to-door salesmen for anything! That soap is worthless!"

Shut up, you old bastard. I'd kill you if I hadn't already. . . .

"... and do you know what that editor said to me? He said I didn't kill enough people in that story! He said, there's paper and a pen in the next room, and here's your manuscript, and you go in there right now and write me another death scene. . . ."

"David took my HORSE. . . ."

She blundered into a door, fumbled the knob, trying desperately to open her eyes. Rooms thickly curtained, lightless; why did she feel, when she pulled the door open, that the chamber was crowded with people, people all talking as they came toward her. . . .

"But if I seat Jeffrey next to Caroline, that will put Caroline across from Mr. Fontaine, and after what Mrs. Fontaine said about Caroline's sister we can't risk that, . . ."

GET AWAY FROM ME!

"Lousy no-good women, hump any man they see; I'd beat the lot of 'em with a strap, the filthy whores. . . ."

"I never was strong enough to join the army, you see. If I had been, my whole life would have been different. But they'd never take me because I'm small. . . ."

"GET AWAY FROM ME!" She wasn't aware she'd screamed it aloud until she heard footfalls in the stairwell, and then she wasn't even sure. For there seemed to be footfalls all around her, dark figures. . . . Her eyes felt gummed as she stumbled,

weaving like a drunken woman, seeking the hall, the back stairs, the cellar. Get away. . . . Get away. . . .

"So I said, Ruchel, I said, is it any shame to make a little money off *goyim* swine who'd just as soon burn my shop down as look at me, just because I'm a Jew?"

"David took my HORSE . . ." She could almost feel small hands clinging to the fragile stuff of her nightgown.

"But you see, if Andrew proposes to me, I'd have to accept him because if I turn him down this time he'll ask Violette, and I *can't* let him marry her, only I don't want to get married either, at least not to Andrew. . . ."

She fell against walls, stumbled, barking her knees on the sharp edges of stairs. Darkness everywhere, voices shouting behind her, less real to her than the jabbering in her head. *I charge you to be aware of what you have taken.* . . .

Their blood. And their lives.

Her hands groped at a door latch, her head lolling on her shoulders, her knees like water. For some reason the metal was warm under her hand. The cellar door . . . it had to be the cellar door.

Then she opened the door, and like a colorless moth bumping blindly from a cellar, staggered outside into the all-devouring blaze of light and heat.

The detectives and the priest buried what they found, the pile of bone and ash and rags still smoking on the threshold of the rear door. It took only a small space in the municipal potter's field. The priest, and the elderly scholar from the university who had been with them, came back later and mixed certain holy things in the earth of the grave, to give its inhabitant what rest they could.

The following night a woman came to the cemetery, veiled in black. She found the grave easily, by the voices that whispered around it in the warm night air.

"Who are you?" she asked the first voice. "What is your name?"

"My name is Jakov Bernstein," said the voice. "I sell carpets, down by the river. I have a wife, Ruchel. . . . Is she all right?"

"I will tell her," said Olivia, "that *you* are all right, now." And she told him, in the Yiddish that he best understood—for she had been a scholar of languages at the university, before her studies had led her into other and stranger paths—

how to find his way across to the world where he now must go, and how to release his hold on this one.

"And what is your name?" she asked again.

"I'm Emma Normand," said a woman's voice. "I'm Elizabeth's mother, and
Annette's, and little Gerard's. I've been so worried. . . ."

"They will be well," said Olivia. "As well as any can be in this world. Go
now, and be in peace."

So many, she thought, listening to the voices of the shades. But they were
fewer than the number of days that had passed since Philip had died. That was
something.

For a long time she stood, hearing their names, hearing what they said about
their concerns, their families, their lives; even the stevedore Finn, and the beggar
Lucius del Valle. When she had heard them out, she gave them such instructions
as she thought they would understand, and let them go. From the earth beneath
her feet came no sound, no whisper from the ashes and the bones.

It was almost dawn when she left Madeleine's grave, disappearing into the
luminous summer darkness, the silence like still water. As she passed out of sight
beneath the trees, almost hesitantly, a bird began to sing.

KEN'S MYSTERY

CRUD

JULIAN HAWTHORNE

O NE COOL OCTOBER EVENING—IT WAS THE LAST DAY
of the month, and unusually cool for the time of year—I made up my mind to
go and spend an hour or two with my friend Keningale. Keningale was an artist
(as well as a musical amateur and poet), and had a very delightful studio built
onto his house, in which he was wont to sit of an evening. The studio had a cavernous fire-place, designed in imitation of the old-fashioned fire-places of Elizabethan manor-houses, and in it, when the temperature out-doors warranted, he
would build up a cheerful fire of dry logs. It would suit me particularly well, I
thought, to go and have a quiet pipe and chat in front of that fire with my friend.

I had not had such a chat for a very long time—not, in fact, since Keningale
(or Ken, as his friends called him) had returned from his visit to Europe the year
before. He went abroad, as he affirmed at the time, 'for purposes of study',
whereat we all smiled, for Ken, so far as we knew him, was more likely to do anything else than to study. He was a young fellow of buoyant temperament, lively
and social in his habits, of a brilliant and versatile mind, and possessing an income of twelve or fifteen thousand dollars a year; he could sing, play, scribble,
and paint very cleverly, and some of his heads and figure-pieces were really well
done, considering that he never had any regular training in art; but he was not a
worker. Personally he was fine-looking, of good height and figure, active, healthy,
and with a remarkably fine brow, and clear, full-gazing eye. Nobody was surprised at his going to Europe, nobody expected him to do anything there except

amuse himself, and few anticipated that he would be soon again seen in New York. He was one of the sort that find Europe agrees with them. Off he went, therefore; and in the course of a few months the rumour reached us that he was engaged to a handsome and wealthy New York girl whom he had met in London. This was nearly all we did hear of him until, not very long afterward, he turned up again on Fifth Avenue, to every one's astonishment; made no satisfactory answer to those who wanted to know how he happened to tire so soon of the Old World; while, as to the reported engagement, he cut short all allusion to that in so peremptory a manner as to show that it was not a permissible topic of conversation with him. It was surmised that the lady had jilted him; but on the other hand, she herself returned home not a great while after, and, though she had plenty of opportunities, she has never married to this day.

Be the rights of that matter what they may, it was soon remarked that Ken was no longer the careless and merry fellow he used to be; on the contrary, he appeared grave, moody, averse from general society, and habitually taciturn and undemonstrative even in the company of his most intimate friends. Evidently something had happened to him, or he had done something. What? Had he committed a murder? or joined the Nihilists? or was his unsuccessful love affair at the bottom of it? Some declared that the cloud was only temporary, and would soon pass away. Nevertheless, up to the period of which I am writing, it had not passed away, but had rather gathered additional gloom, and threatened to become permanent.

Meanwhile I had met him twice or thrice at the club, at the opera, or in the street, but had as yet had no opportunity of regularly renewing my acquaintance with him. We had been on a footing of more than common intimacy in the old days, and I was not disposed to think that he would refuse to renew the former relations now. But what I had heard and myself seen of his changed condition imparted a stimulating tinge of suspense or curiosity to the pleasure with which I looked forward to the prospects of this evening. His house stood at a distance of two or three miles beyond the general range of habitations in New York at this time, and as I walked briskly along in the clear twilight air I had leisure to go over in my mind all that I had known of Ken and had divined of his character. After all, had there not always been something in his nature—deep down, and held in abeyance by the activity of his animal spirits—but something strange and separate, and capable of developing under suitable conditions into—into what? As I asked myself this question I arrived at his door; and it was with a feeling of relief that I felt the next moment the cordial grasp of his hand, and his voice bidding me welcome in a tone that indicated unaffected gratification at my presence. He drew me at once into the studio, relieved me of my hat and cane, and then put his hand on my shoulder.

'I am glad to see you,' he repeated, with singular earnestness—'glad to see you and to feel you; and tonight of all nights in the year.'

'Why tonight especially?'

'Oh, never mind. It's just as well, too, you didn't let me know beforehand you were coming; the unreadiness is all, to paraphrase the poet. Now, with you to help me, I can drink a glass of whisky and water and take a bit draw of the pipe. This would have been a grim night for me if I'd been left to myself.'

'In such a lap of luxury as this, too!' said I, looking round at the glowing fireplace, the low, luxurious chairs, and all the rich and sumptuous fittings of the room. 'I should have thought a condemned murderer might make himself comfortable here.'

'Perhaps; but that's not exactly my category at present. But have you forgotten what night this is? This is November-eve, when, as tradition asserts, the dead arise and walk about, and fairies, goblins, and spiritual beings of all kinds have more freedom and power than on any other day of the year. One can see you've never been in Ireland.'

'I wasn't aware till now that you had been there, either.'

'Yes, I have been in Ireland. Yes—' He paused, sighed, and fell into a reverie, from which, however, he soon roused himself by an effort, and went to a cabinet in a corner of the room for the liquor and tobacco. While he was thus employed I sauntered about the studio, taking note of the various beauties, grotesquenesses, and curiosities that it contained. Many things were there to repay study and arouse admiration; for Ken was a good collector, having excellent taste as well as means to back it. But, upon the whole, nothing interested me more than some studies of a female head, roughly done in oils, and, judging from the sequestered positions in which I found them, not intended by the artist for exhibition or criticism. There were three or four of these studies, all of the same face, but in different poses and costumes. In one the head was enveloped in a dark hood, overshadowing and partly concealing the features; in another she seemed to be peering duskily through a latticed casement, lit by a faint moonlight; a third showed her splendidly attired in evening costume, and jewels in her hair and ears, and sparkling on her snowy bosom. The expressions were as various as the poses; now it was demure penetration, now a subtle inviting glance, now burning passion, and again a look of elfish and elusive mockery. In whatever phase, the countenance possessed a singular and poignant fascination, not of beauty merely, though that was very striking, but of character and quality likewise.

'Did you find this model abroad?' I inquired at length. 'She has evidently inspired you, and I don't wonder at it.'

Ken, who had been mixing the punch, and had not noticed my movements, now looked up, and said: 'I didn't mean those to be seen. They don't satisfy me, and I am going to destroy them; but I couldn't rest till I'd made some attempts to reproduce—What was it you asked? Abroad? Yes—or no. They were all painted here within the last six weeks.'

'Whether they satisfy you or not, they are by far the best things of yours I have ever seen.'

'Well, let them alone, and tell me what you think of this beverage. To my thinking, it goes to the right spot. It owes its existence to your coming here. I can't drink alone, and those portraits are not company, though, for aught I know, she might have come out of the canvas tonight and sat down in that chair.' Then, seeing my inquiring look, he added, with a hasty laugh, 'It's November-eve, you know, when anything may happen, provided it's strange enough. Well, here's to ourselves.'

We each swallowed a deep draught of the smoking and aromatic liquor, and set down our glasses with approval. The punch was excellent. Ken now opened a box of cigars, and we seated ourselves before the fire-place.

'All we need now,' I remarked, after a short silence, 'is a little music. By-the-by, Ken, have you still got the banjo I gave you before you went abroad?'

He paused so long before replying that I supposed he had not heard my question. 'I have got it,' he said, at length, 'but it will never make any more music.'

'Got broken, eh? Can't it be mended? It was a fine instrument.'

'It's not broken, but it's past mending. You shall see for yourself.'

He arose as he spoke, and going to another part of the studio, opened a black oak coffer, and took out of it a long object wrapped up in a piece of faded yellow silk. He handed it to me, and when I had unwrapped it, there appeared a thing that might once have been a banjo, but had little resemblance to one now. It bore every sign of extreme age. The wood of the handle was honey-combed with the gnawings of worms, and dusty with dry-rot. The parchment head was green with mould, and hung in shrivelled tatters. The hoop, which was of solid silver, was so blackened and tarnished that it looked like dilapidated iron. The strings were gone, and most of the tuning-screws had dropped out of their decayed sockets. Altogether it had the appearance of having been made before the Flood, and been forgotten in the forecastle of Noah's Ark ever since.

'It is a curious relic, certainly,' I said. 'Where did you come across it? I had no idea that the banjo was invented so long ago as this. It certainly can't be less than two hundred years old, and may be much older than that.'

Ken smiled gloomily. 'You are quite right,' he said; 'it is at least two hundred years old, and yet it is the very same banjo that you gave me a year ago.'

'Hardly,' I returned, smiling in my turn, 'since that was made to my order with a view to presenting it to you.'

'I know that; but the two hundred years have passed since then. Yes; it is absurd and impossible, I know, but nothing is truer. That banjo, which was made last year, existed in the sixteenth century, and has been rotting ever since. Stay. Give it to me a moment, and I'll convince you. You recollect that your name and mine, with the date, were engraved on the silver hoop?'

'Yes; and there was a private mark of my own there, also.'

'Very well,' said Ken, who had been rubbing a place on the hoop with a corner of the yellow silk wrapper; 'look at that.'

I took the decrepit instrument from him, and examined the spot which he had rubbed. It was incredible, sure enough; but there were the names and the date precisely as I had caused them to be engraved; and there, moreover, was my own private mark, which I had idly made with an old etching point not more than eighteen months before. After convincing myself that there was no mistake, I laid the banjo across my knees, and stared at my friend in bewilderment. He sat smoking with a kind of grim composure, his eyes fixed upon the blazing logs.

'I'm mystified, I confess,' said I. 'Come; what is the joke? What method have you discovered of producing the decay of centuries on this unfortunate banjo in a few months? And why did you do it? I have heard of an elixir to counteract the effects of time, but your recipe seems to work the other way—to make time rush forward at two hundred times his usual rate, in one place, while he jogs on at his usual gait elsewhere. Unfold your mystery, magician. Seriously, Ken, how on earth did the thing happen?'

'I know no more about it than you do,' was his reply. 'Either you and I and all the rest of the living world are insane, or else there has been wrought a miracle as strange as any in tradition. How can I explain it? It is a common saying—a common experience, if you will—that we may, on certain trying or tremendous occasions, live years in one moment. But that's a mental experience, not a physical one, and one that applies, at all events, only to human beings, not to senseless things of wood and metal. You imagine the thing is some trick or jugglery. If it be, I don't know the secret of it. There's no chemical appliance that I ever heard of that will get a piece of solid wood into that condition in a few months, or a few years. And it wasn't done in a few years, or a few months either. A year ago today at this very hour that banjo was as sound as when it left the maker's hands, and twenty-four hours afterward—I'm telling you the simple truth—it was as you see it now.'

The gravity and earnestness with which Ken made this astounding statement were evidently not assumed. He believed every word that he uttered. I knew not what to think. Of course my friend might be insane, though he betrayed none of the ordinary symptoms of mania; but, however that might be, there was the banjo, a witness whose silent testimony there was no gainsaying. The more I meditated on the matter the more inconceivable did it appear. Two hundred years—twenty-four hours; these were the terms of the proposed equation. Ken and the banjo both affirmed that the equation had been made; all worldly knowledge and experience affirmed it to be impossible. What was the explanation? What is time? What is life? I felt myself beginning to doubt the reality of all things. And so this was the mystery which my friend had been brooding over since his return from abroad. No wonder it had changed him. More to be wondered at was it that it had not changed him more.

'Can you tell me the whole story?' I demanded at length.

Ken quaffed another draught from his glass of whisky and water and rubbed his hand through his thick brown beard. 'I have never spoken to any one of it heretofore,' he said, 'and I had never meant to speak of it. But I'll try and give you some idea of what it was. You know me better than any one else; you'll understand the thing as far as it can ever be understood, and perhaps I may be relieved of some of the oppression it has caused me. For it is rather a ghastly memory to grapple with alone, I can tell you.'

Hereupon, without further preface, Ken related the following tale. He was, I may observe in passing, a naturally fine narrator. There were deep, lingering tones in his voice, and he could strikingly enhance the comic or pathetic effect of a sentence by dwelling here and there upon some syllable. His features were equally susceptible of humorous and of solemn expressions, and his eyes were in form and hue wonderfully adapted to showing great varieties of emotion. Their mournful aspect was extremely earnest and affecting; and when Ken was giving utterance to some mysterious passage of the tale they had a doubtful, melancholy, exploring look which appealed irresistibly to the imagination. But the interest of his story was too pressing to allow of noticing these incidental embellishments at the time, though they doubtless had their influence upon me all the same.

'I left New York on an Inman Line steamer, you remember,' began Ken, 'and landed at Havre. I went the usual round of sight-seeing on the Continent, and got round to London in July, at the height of the season. I had good introductions, and met any number of agreeable and famous people. Among others was a young lady, a countrywoman of my own—you know whom I mean—who interested me very much, and before her family left London she and I were engaged. We parted there for the time, because she had the Continental trip still to make, while I wanted to take the opportunity to visit the north of England and Ireland. I landed at Dublin about the 1st of October, and, zigzagging about the country, I found myself in County Cork about two weeks later.

'There is in that region some of the most lovely scenery that human eyes ever rested on, and it seems to be less known to tourists than many places of infinitely less picturesque value. A lonely region too: during my rambles I met not a single stranger like myself, and few enough natives. It seems incredible that so beautiful a country should be so deserted. After walking a dozen Irish miles you come across a group of two or three one-roomed cottages, and, like as not, one or more of those will have the roof off and the walls in ruins. The few peasants whom one sees, however, are affable and hospitable, especially when they hear you are from that terrestrial heaven whither most of their friends and relatives have gone before them. They seem simple and primitive enough at first sight, and yet they are as strange and incomprehensible a race as any in the world. They are as superstitious, as credulous of marvels, fairies, magicians, and omens, as the men whom St Patrick preached to, and at the same time they are shrewd, sceptical, sensible, and bottomless liars. Upon the whole, I met with no nation on my travels whose company I enjoyed so much, or who inspired me with so much kindliness, curiosity, and repugnance.

'At length I got to a place on the sea-coast, which I will not further specify than to say that it is not many miles from Ballymacheen, on the south shore. I have seen Venice and Naples, I have driven along the Cornice Road, I have spent a month at our own Mount Desert, and I say that all of them together are not so beautiful as this glowing, deep-hued, soft-gleaming, silvery-lighted, ancient harbour and town, with the tall hills crowding round it and the black cliffs and headlands planting their iron feet in the blue, transparent sea. It is a very old place, and has had a history which it has outlived ages since. It may once have had two or three thousand inhabitants; it has scarce five or six hundred today. Half the houses are in ruins or have disappeared; many of the remainder are standing empty. All the people are poor, most of them abjectly so; they saunter about with bare feet and uncovered heads, the women in quaint black or dark-blue cloaks, the men in such anomalous attire as only an Irishman knows how to get together, the children half naked. The only comfortable-looking people are the monks and the priests, and the soldiers in the fort. For there is a fort there, constructed on the huge ruins of one which may have done duty in the reign of Edward the Black Prince, or earlier, in whose mossy embrasures are mounted a couple of cannon, which occasionally sent a practice-shot or two at the cliff on the other side of the harbour. The garrison consists of a dozen men and three or four officers and non-commissioned officers. I suppose they are relieved occasionally, but those I saw seemed to have become component parts of their surroundings.

'I put up at a wonderful little old inn, the only one in the place, and took my meals in a dining-saloon fifteen feet by nine, with a portrait of George I (a print varnished to preserve it) hanging over the mantel-piece. On the second evening after dinner a young gentleman came in—the dining-saloon being public property of course—and ordered some bread and cheese and a bottle of Dublin stout. We presently fell into talk; he turned out to be an officer from the fort, Lieutenant O'Connor, and a fine young specimen of the Irish soldier he was. After telling me all he knew about the town, the surrounding country, his friends, and himself, he intimated a readiness to sympathize with whatever tale I might choose to pour into his ear; and I had pleasure in trying to rival his own outspokenness. We became excellent friends; we had up a half-pint of Kinahan's whisky, and the lieutenant expressed himself in terms of high praise of my countrymen, my country, and my own particular cigars. When it became time for him to depart I accompanied him—for there was a splendid moon abroad—and bade him farewell at the fort entrance, having promised to come over the next day and make the acquaintance of the other fellows. "And mind your eye, now, going back, my dear boy," he called out, as I turned my face homeward. "Faith, 'tis a spooky place, that graveyard, and you'll as likely meet the black woman there as anywhere else!"

'The graveyard was a forlorn and barren spot on the hill-side, just the hither side of the fort: thirty or forty rough head-stones, few of which retained any semblance of the perpendicular, while many were so shattered and decayed as to seem nothing more than irregular natural projections from the ground. Who the black woman might be I knew not, and did not stay to inquire. I had never been subject to ghostly apprehensions, and as a matter of fact, though the path I had to follow was in places very bad going, not to mention a haphazard scramble over a ruined bridge that covered a deep-lying brook, I reached my inn without any adventure whatever.

'The next day I kept my appointment at the fort, and found no reason to regret it; and my friendly sentiments were abundantly reciprocated, thanks more especially, perhaps, to the success of my banjo, which I carried with me, and which was as novel as it was popular with those who listened to it. The chief personages in the social circle besides my friend the lieutenant were Major Molloy, who was in command, a racy and juicy old campaigner, with a face like a sunset, and the surgeon, Dr Dudeen, a long, dry, humorous genius, with a wealth of anecdotical and traditional lore at his command that I have never seen surpassed. We had a jolly time of it, and it was the precursor of many more like it. The remains of October slipped away rapidly, and I was obliged to remember that I was a traveller in Europe, and not a resident in Ireland. The major, the surgeon, and the lieutenant all protested cordially against my proposed departure, but, as there was no help for it, they arranged a farewell dinner to take place in the fort on Allhalloween.

'I wish you could have been at that dinner with me! It was the essence of Irish good-fellowship. Dr Dudeen was in great force; the major was better than the best of Lever's novels; the lieutenant was overflowing with hearty good-humour, merry chaff, and sentimental rhapsodies anent this or the other pretty girl of the neighbourhood. For my part I made the banjo ring as it had never rung before, and the others joined in the chorus with a mellow strength of lungs such as you don't often hear outside of Ireland. Among the stories that Dr Dudeen regaled us with was one about the Kern of Querin and his wife, Ethelind Fionguala—which being interpreted signifies "the white-shouldered". The lady, it appears, was originally betrothed to one O'Connor (here the lieutenant smacked his lips), but was stolen away on the wedding night by a party of vampires, who, it would seem, were at that period a prominent feature among the troubles of Ireland. But as they were bearing her along—she being unconscious—to that supper where she was not to eat but to be eaten, the young Kern of Querin, who happened to be out duck-shooting, met the party, and emptied his gun at it. The vampires fled, and the Kern carried the fair lady, still in a state of insensibility, to his house. "And by the same token, Mr. Keningale," observed the doctor, knocking the ashes out of his pipe, "ye're after passing that very house on your way here. The one with the dark archway underneath it, and the big mullioned window at the corner, ye recollect, hanging over the street as I might say—"

'"Go 'long wid the house, Dr Dudeen, dear," interrupted the lieutenant; "sure can't you see we're all dying to know what happened to sweet Miss Fionguala, God be good to her, when I was after getting her safe upstairs—"

'"Faith, then, I can tell ye that myself, Mr O'Connor," exclaimed the major, imparting a rotary motion to the remnants of whisky in his tumbler. "'Tis a question to be solved on general principles, as Colonel O'Halloran said that time he was asked what he'd do if he'd been the Dook o' Wellington, and the Prussians hadn't come up in the nick o' time at Waterloo. "Faith," says the colonel, "I'll tell ye—"

'"Arrah, then, major, why would ye be interruptin' the doctor, and Mr Keningale there lettin' his glass stay empty till he hears—The Lord save us! the bottle's empty!"

'In the excitement consequent upon this discovery, the thread of the doctor's story was lost; and before it could be recovered the evening had advanced so far that I felt obliged to withdraw. It took some time to make my proposition heard and comprehended; and a still longer time to put it in execution; so that it was fully midnight before I found myself standing in the cool pure air outside the fort, with the farewells of my boon companions ringing in my ears.

'Considering that it had been rather a wet evening indoors, I was in a remarkably good state of preservation, and I therefore ascribed it rather to the roughness of the road than to the smoothness of the liquor, when, after advancing a few rods, I stumbled and fell. As I picked myself up I fancied I had heard a laugh, and supposed that the lieutenant, who had accompanied me to the gate, was making merry over my mishap; but on looking round I saw that the gate was closed and no one was visible. The laugh, moreover, had seemed to be close at hand, and to be even pitched in a key that was rather feminine than masculine. Of course I must have been deceived; nobody was near me: my imagination had played me a trick, or else there was more truth than poetry in the tradition that Halloween is the carnival-time of disembodied spirits. It did not occur to me at the time that a stumble is held by the superstitious Irish to be an evil omen, and had I remembered it it would only have been to laugh at it. At all events, I was physically none the worse for my fall, and I resumed my way immediately.

'But the path was singularly difficult to find, or rather the path I was following did not seem to be the right one. I did not recognize it; I could have sworn (except I knew the contrary) that I had never seen it before. The moon had risen, though her light was as yet obscured by clouds, but neither my immediate surroundings nor the general aspect of the region appeared familiar. Dark, silent hill-sides mounted up on either hand, and the road, for the most part, plunged downward, as if to conduct me into the bowels of the earth. The place was alive with strange echoes, so that at times I seemed to be walking through the midst of muttering voices and mysterious whispers, and a wild, faint sound of laughter seemed ever and anon to reverberate among the passes of the hills. Currents of colder air sighing up through narrow defiles and dark crevices touched my face as with airy fingers. A certain feeling of anxiety and insecurity began to take possession of me, though there was no definable cause for it, unless that I might be belated in getting home. With the perverse instinct of those who are lost I hastened my steps, but was impelled now and then to glance back over my shoulder, with a sensation of being pursued. But no living creature was in sight. The moon, however, had now risen higher, and the clouds that were drifting slowly across the sky flung into the naked valley dusky shadows, which occasionally assumed shapes that looked like the vague semblance of gigantic human forms.

'How long I had been hurrying onward I know not, when, with a kind of suddenness, I found myself approaching a graveyard. It was situated on the spur of a hill, and there was no fence around it, nor anything to protect it from the incursions of passers-by. There was something in the general appearance of this spot that made me half fancy I had seen it before; and I should have taken it to be the same that I had often noticed on my way to the fort, but that the latter was only a few hundred yards distant therefrom, whereas I must have traversed several miles at least. As I drew near, moreover, I observed that the head-stones did not appear so ancient and decayed as those of the other. But what chiefly attracted my attention was the figure that was leaning or half sitting upon one of the largest of the upright slabs near the road. It was a female figure draped in black, and a closer inspection—for I was soon within a few yards of her— showed that she wore the calla, or long hooded cloak, the most common as well as the most ancient garment of Irish women, and doubtless of Spanish origin.

'I was a trifle startled by this apparition, so unexpected as it was, and so strange did it seem that any human creature should be at that hour of the night in so desolate and sinister a place. Involuntarily I paused as I came opposite her, and gazed at her intently. But the moonlight fell behind her, and the deep hood of her cloak so completely shadowed her face that I was unable to discern anything but the sparkle of a pair of eyes, which appeared to be returning my gaze with much vivacity.

'"You seem to be at home here," I said, at length. "Can you tell me where I am?"

'Hereupon the mysterious personage broke into a light laugh, which, though in itself musical and agreeable, was of a timbre and intonation that caused my heart to beat rather faster than my late pedestrian exertions warranted; for it was the identical laugh (or so my imagination persuaded me) that had echoed in my ears as I arose from my tumble an hour or two ago. For the rest, it was the laugh of a young woman, and presumably of a pretty one; and yet it had a wild, airy, mocking quality, that seemed hardly human at all, or not, at any rate, character-istic of a being of affections and limitations like unto ours. But this impression of mine was fostered, no doubt, by the unusual and uncanny circumstances of the occasion.

'"Sure, sir," said she, "you're at the grave of Ethelind Fionguala."

'As she spoke she rose to her feet, and pointed to the inscription on the stone. I bent forward, and was able, without much difficulty, to decipher the name, and a date which indicated that the occupant of the grave must have en-tered the disembodied state between two and three centuries ago.

'"And who are you?" was my next question.

'"I'm called Elsie," she replied. "But where would your honour be going November-eve?"

'I mentioned my destination, and asked her whether she could direct me thither.

'"Indeed, then, 'tis there I'm going myself," Elsie replied; "and if your hon-our'll follow me, and play me a tune on the pretty instrument, 'tisn't long we'll be on the road."

'She pointed to the banjo which I carried wrapped up under my arm. How she knew that it was a musical instrument I could not imagine; possibly, I thought, she may have seen me playing on it as I strolled about the environs of the town. Be that as it may, I offered no opposition to the bargain, and further intimated that I would reward her more substantially on our arrival. At that she laughed again, and made a peculiar gesture with her hand above her head. I un-covered my banjo, swept my fingers across the strings, and struck into a fantastic dance-measure, to the music of which we proceeded along the path, Elsie slightly in advance, her feet keeping time to the airy measure. In fact, she trod so lightly, with an elastic, undulating movement, that with a little more it seemed as if she might float onward like a spirit. The extreme whiteness of her feet attracted my eye, and I was surprised to find that instead of being bare, as I had supposed, these were incased in white satin slippers quaintly embroidered with gold thread.

'"Elsie," said I, lengthening my steps so as to come up with her, "where do you live, and what do you do for a living?"

'"Sure, I live by myself," she answered; "and if you'd be after knowing how, you must come and see for yourself."

'"Are you in the habit of walking over the hills at night in shoes like that?"

'"And why would I not?" she asked, in her turn. "And where did your honour get the pretty gold ring on your finger?"

'The ring, which was of no great intrinsic value, had struck my eye in an old curiosity-shop in Cork. It was an antique of very old-fashioned design, and might have belonged (as the vendor assured me was the case) to one of the early kings or queens of Ireland.

'"Do you like it?" said I.

'"Will your honour be after making a present of it to Elsie?" she returned, with an insinuating tone and turn of the head.

'"Maybe I will, Elsie, on one condition. I am an artist; I make pictures of people. If you will promise to come to my studio and let me paint your portrait, I'll give you the ring, and some money besides."

'"And will you give me the ring now?" said Elsie.

'"Yes, if you'll promise"

'"And will you play the music to me?" she continued.

'"As much as you like."

'"But maybe I'll not be handsome enough for ye," said she, with a glance of her eyes beneath the dark hood.

'"I'll take the risk of that," I answered, laughing, "though, all the same, I don't mind taking a peep beforehand to remember you by." So saying, I put forth a hand to draw back the concealing hood. But Elsie eluded me, I scarce know how, and laughed a third time, with the same airy, mocking cadence.

'"Give me the ring first, and then you shall see me," she said, coaxingly.

'"Stretch out your hand, then," returned I, removing the ring from my finger. "When we are better acquainted, Elsie, you won't be so suspicious."

'She held out a slender, delicate hand, on the forefinger of which I slipped the ring. As I did so, the folds of her cloak fell a little apart, affording me a glimpse of a white shoulder and of a dress that seemed in that deceptive semi-darkness to be wrought of rich and costly material; and I caught, too, or so I fancied, the frosty sparkle of precious stones.

'"Arrah, mind where ye tread!" said Elsie, in a sudden, sharp tone.

'I looked round, and became aware for the first time that we were standing near the middle of a ruined bridge which spanned a rapid stream that flowed at a considerable depth below. The parapet of the bridge on one side was broken down, and I must have been, in fact, in imminent danger of stepping over into empty air. I made my way cautiously across the decaying structure; but, when I turned to assist Elsie, she was nowhere to be seen.

'What had become of the girl? I called, but no answer came. I gazed about on every side, but no trace of her was visible. Unless she had plunged into the narrow abyss at my feet, there was no place where she could have concealed herself—none at least that I could discover. She had vanished, nevertheless; and since her disappearance must have been premeditated, I finally came to the conclusion that it was useless to attempt to find her. She would present herself again in her own good time, or not at all. She had given me the slip very cleverly, and I must make the best of it. The adventure was perhaps worth the ring.

'On resuming my way, I was not a little relieved to find that I once more knew where I was. The bridge that I had just crossed was none other than the one I mentioned some time back; I was within a mile of the town, and my way lay clear before me. The moon, moreover, had now quite dispersed the clouds, and shone down with exquisite brilliance. Whatever her other failings, Elsie had been a trustworthy guide; she had brought me out of the depth of elf-land into the material world again. It had been a singular adventure, certainly; and I mused over it with a sense of mysterious pleasure as I sauntered along, humming snatches of airs, and accompanying myself on the strings. Hark! what light step was that behind me? It sounded like Elsie's; but no, Elsie was not there. The same impression or hallucination, however, recurred several times before I reached the outskirts of the town—the tread of an airy foot behind or beside my own. The fancy did not make me nervous; on the contrary, I was pleased with the notion of being thus haunted, and gave myself up to a romantic and genial vein of reverie.

'After passing one or two roofless and moss-grown cottages, I entered the narrow and rambling street which leads through the town. This street a short distance down widens a little, as if to afford the wayfarer space to observe a remarkable old house that stands on the northern side. The house was built of stone, and in a noble style of architecture; it reminded me somewhat of certain palaces of the old Italian nobility that I had seen on the Continent, and it may very probably have been built by one of the Italian or Spanish immigrants of the sixteenth or seventeenth century. The moulding of the projecting windows and arched doorway was richly carved, and upon the front of the building was an escutcheon wrought in high relief, though I could not make out the purport of the device. The moonlight falling upon this picturesque pile enhanced all its beauties, and at the same time made it seem like a vision that might dissolve away when the light ceased to shine. I must often have seen the house before, and yet I retained no definite recollection of it; I had never until now examined it with my eyes open, so to speak. Leaning against the wall on the opposite side of the street, I contemplated it for a long while at my leisure. The window at the corner was really a very fine and massive affair. It projected over the pavement below, throwing a heavy shadow aslant; the frames of the diamond-paned lattices were heavily mullioned. How often in past ages had that lattice been pushed open by some fair hand, revealing to a lover waiting beneath in the moonlight the charming countenance of his high-born mistress! Those were brave days. They had passed away long since. The great house had stood empty for who could tell how many years; only bats and vermin were its inhabitants. Where now were those who had built it? and who were they? Probably the very name of them was forgotten.

'As I continued to stare upward, however, a conjecture presented itself to my mind which rapidly ripened into a conviction. Was not this the house that Dr Dudeen had described that very evening as having been formerly the abode of the Kern of Querin and his mysterious bride? There was the projecting window, the arched doorway. Yes, beyond a doubt this was the very house. I emitted a low exclamation of renewed interest and pleasure, and my speculations took a still more imaginative, but also a more definite turn.

'What had been the fate of that lovely lady after the Kern had brought her home insensible in his arms? Did she recover, and were they married and made happy ever after; or had the sequel been a tragic one? I remembered to have read that the victims of vampires generally became vampires themselves. Then my thoughts went back to that grave on the hill-side. Surely that was unconsecrated ground. Why had they buried her there? Ethelind of the white shoulder! Ah! why had not I lived in those days; or why might not some magic cause them to live again for me? Then would I seek this street at midnight, and standing here beneath her window, I would lightly touch the strings of my bandore until the casement opened cautiously and she looked down. A sweet vision indeed! And what prevented my realizing it? Only a matter of a couple of centuries or so. And was time, then, at which poets and philosophers sneer, so rigid and real a matter that a little faith and imagination might not overcome it? At all events, I had my banjo, the bandore's legitimate and lineal descendant, and the memory of Fionguala should have the love-ditty.

'Hereupon, having retuned the instrument, I launched forth into an old Spanish love-song, which I had met with in some mouldy library during my travels, and had set to music of my own. I sang low, for the deserted street re-echoed the lightest sound, and what I sang must reach only my lady's ears. The words were warm with the fire of the ancient Spanish chivalry, and I threw into their expression all the passion of the lovers of romance. Surely Fionguala, the white-shouldered, would hear, and awaken from her sleep of centuries, and come to the latticed casement and look down! Hist! see yonder! What light—what shadow is that that seems to flit from room to room within the abandoned house, and now approaches the mullioned window? Are my eyes dazzled by the play of the moonlight, or does the casement move—does it open! Nay, this is no delusion; there is no error of the senses here. There is simply a woman, young, beautiful, and richly attired, bending forward from the window, and silently beckoning me to approach.

'Too much amazed to be conscious of amazement, I advanced until I stood directly beneath the casement, and the lady's face, as she stooped toward me, was not more than twice a man's height from my own. She smiled and kissed her finger-tips; something white fluttered in her hand, then fell through the air to the ground at my feet. The next moment she had withdrawn, and I heard the lattice close.

'I picked up what she had let fall; it was a delicate lace handkerchief, tied to the handle of an elaborately wrought bronze key. It was evidently the key of the house, and invited me to enter. I loosened it from the handkerchief, which bore a faint, delicious perfume, like the aroma of flowers in an ancient garden, and turned to the arched doorway. I felt no misgiving, and scarcely any sense of strangeness. All was as I had wished it to be, and as it should be; the mediæval age was alive once more, and as for myself, I almost felt the velvet cloak hanging from my shoulder and the long rapier dangling at my belt. Standing in front of the door I thrust the key into the lock, turned it, and felt the bolt yield. The next instant the door was opened, apparently from within; I stepped across the threshold, the door closed again, and I was alone in the house, and in darkness.

'Not alone, however! As I extended my hand to grope my way it was met by another hand, soft, slender, and cold, which insinuated itself gently into mine and drew me forward. Forward I went, nothing loath; the darkness was impenetrable, but I could hear the light rustle of a dress close to me, and the same delicious perfume that had emanated from the handkerchief enriched the air that I breathed, while the little hand that clasped and was clasped by my own alternately tightened and half relaxed the hold of its soft cold fingers. In this manner, and treading lightly, we traversed what I presumed to be a long, irregular passageway, and ascended a staircase. Then another corridor, until finally we paused, a door opened, emitting a flood of soft light, into which we entered, still hand in hand. The darkness and the doubt were at an end.

'The room was of imposing dimensions, and was furnished and decorated in a style of antique splendour. The walls were draped with mellow hues of tapestry; clusters of candles burned in polished silver sconces, and were reflected and multiplied in tall mirrors placed in the four corners of the room. The heavy beams of the dark oaken ceiling crossed each other in squares, and were laboriously carved; the curtains and the drapery of the chairs were of heavy-figured damask. At one end of the room was a broad ottoman, and in front of it a table, on which was set forth, in massive silver dishes, a sumptuous repast, with wines in crystal beakers. At the side was a vast and deep fire-place, with space enough on the broad hearth to burn whole trunks of trees. No fire, however, was there, but only a great heap of dead embers; and the room, for all its magnificence, was cold—cold as a tomb, or as my lady's hand—and it sent a subtle chill creeping to my heart.

'But my lady! how fair she was! I gave but a passing glance at the room; my eyes and my thoughts were all for her. She was dressed in white, like a bride; diamonds sparkled in her dark hair and on her snowy bosom; her lovely face and slender lips were pale, and all the paler for the dusky glow of her eyes. She gazed at me with a strange, elusive smile; and yet there was, in her aspect and bearing, something familiar in the midst of strangeness, like the burden of a song heard long ago and recalled among other conditions and surroundings. It seemed to me that something in me recognized her and knew her, had known her always. She was the woman of whom I had dreamed, whom I had beheld in visions, whose voice and face had haunted me from boyhood up. Whether we had ever met before, as human beings meet, I knew not; perhaps I had been blindly seeking her all over the world, and she had been awaiting me in this splendid room, sitting by those dead embers until all the warmth had gone out of her blood, only to be restored by the heat with which my love might supply her.

'"I thought you had forgotten me," she said, nodding as if in answer to my thought. "The night was so late—our one night of the year! How my heart rejoiced when I heard your dear voice singing the song I know so well! Kiss me—my lips are cold!"

'Cold indeed they were—cold as the lips of death. But the warmth of my own seemed to revive them. They were now tinged with a faint colour, and in her cheeks also appeared a delicate shade of pink. She drew fuller breath, as one who recovers from a long lethargy. Was it my life that was feeding her? I was ready to give her all. She drew me to the table and pointed to the viands and the wine.

'"Eat and drink," she said. "You have travelled far, and you need food."

'"Will you eat and drink with me?" said I, pouring out the wine.

'"You are the only nourishment I want," was her answer. "This wine is thin and cold. Give me wine as red as your blood and as warm, and I will drain a goblet to the dregs."

'At these words, I know not why, a slight shiver passed through me. She seemed to gain vitality and strength at every instant, but the chill of the great room struck into me more and more.

'She broke into a fantastic flow of spirits, clapping her hands, and dancing about me like a child. Who was she? And was I myself, or was she mocking me when she implied that we had belonged to each other of old? At length she stood still before me, crossing her hands over her breast. I saw upon the forefinger of her right hand the gleam of an antique ring.

'"Where did you get that ring?" I demanded.

'She shook her head and laughed. "Have you been faithful?" she asked. "It is my ring; it is the ring that unites us; it is the ring you gave me when you loved me first. It is the ring of the Kern—the fairy ring, and I am your Ethelind—Ethelind Fionguala."

'"So be it," I said, casting aside all doubt and fear, and yielding myself wholly to the spell of her inscrutable eyes and wooing lips. "You are mine, and I am yours, and let us be happy while the hours last."

'"You are mine, and I am yours," she repeated, nodding her head with an elfish smile. "Come and sit beside me, and sing that sweet song again that you sang to me so long ago. Ah, now I shall live a hundred years."

'We seated ourselves on the ottoman, and while she nestled luxuriously among the cushions, I took my banjo and sang to her. The song and the music resounded through the lofty room, and came back in throbbing echoes. And before me as I sang I saw the face and form of Ethelind Fionguala, in her jewelled bridal dress, gazing at me with burning eyes. She was pale no longer, but ruddy and warm, and life was like a flame within her. It was I who had become cold and bloodless, yet with the last life that was in me I would have sung to her of love that can never die. But at length my eyes grew dim, the room seemed to darken, the form of Ethelind alternately brightened and waxed indistinct, like the last flickerings of a fire; I swayed toward her, and felt myself lapsing into unconsciousness, with my head resting on her white shoulder.'

Here Keningale paused a few moments in his story, flung a fresh log upon the fire, and then continued:

'I awoke, I know not how long afterward. I was in a vast, empty room in a ruined building. Rotten shreds of drapery depended from the walls, and heavy festoons of spiders' webs gray with dust covered the windows, which were destitute of glass or sash; they had been boarded up with rough planks which had themselves become rotten with age, and admitted through their holes and crevices pallid rays of light and chilly draughts of air. A bat, disturbed by these rays or by my own movement, detached himself from his hold on a remnant of mouldy tapestry near me, and after circling dizzily around my head, wheeled the flickering noiselessness of his flight into a darker corner. As I arose unsteadily from the heap of miscellaneous rubbish on which I had been lying, something which had been resting across my knees fell to the floor with a rattle. I picked it up, and found it to be my banjo—as you see it now.

'Well, that is all I have to tell. My health was seriously impaired; all the blood seemed to have been drawn out of my veins; I was pale and haggard, and the chill—Ah, that chill,' murmured Keningale, drawing nearer to the fire, and spreading out his hands to catch the warmth—'I shall never get over it; I shall carry it to my grave.'

REVELATIONS IN BLACK

༺❦༻

CARL JACOBI

I

T WAS A DREARY, FORLORN ESTABLISHMENT WAY DOWN ON Harbor Street. An old sign announced the legend: "Giovanni Larla—Antiques," and a dingy window revealed a display half masked in dust.

Even as I crossed the threshold that cheerless September afternoon, driven from the sidewalk by a gust of rain and perhaps a fascination for all antiques, the gloominess fell upon me like a material pall. Inside was half darkness, piled boxes and a monstrous tapestry, frayed with the warp showing in worn places. An Italian Renaissance wine cabinet shrank despondently in its corner and seemed to frown at me as I passed.

"Good afternoon, *Signor*. There is something you wish to buy? A picture, a ring, a vase perhaps?"

I peered at the squat, pudgy bulk of the Italian proprietor there in the shadows and hesitated.

"Just looking around," I said, turning my eyes to the jumble about me. "Nothing in particular. . . ."

The man's oily face moved in smile as though he had heard the remark a thousand times before. He sighed, stood there in thought a moment, the rain drumming and swishing against the outer pane. Then very deliberately he stepped to the shelves and glanced up and down them considering. I moved to his side, letting my eyes sweep across the stacked array of ancient oddities. At length he drew forth an object which I perceived to be a painted chalice.

"An authentic Sixteenth Century Tandart," he murmured. "A work of art, *Signor.*"

I shook my head. "No pottery," I said. "Books perhaps, but no pottery."

He frowned slowly. "I have books too," he replied, "rare books which nobody sells but me, Giovanni Larla. But you must look at my other treasures too."

There was, I found, no hurrying the man. A quarter of an hour passed, during which I had to see a Glycon cameo brooch, a carved chair of some indeterminate style and period, and a muddle of yellowed statuettes, small oils and one or two dreary Portland vases. Several times I glanced at my watch impatiently, wondering how I might break away from this Italian and his gloomy shop. Already the fascination of its dust and shadows had begun to wear off, and I was anxious to reach the street.

But when he had conducted me well toward the rear of the shop, something caught my fancy. I drew then from the shelf the first book of horror. If I had but known the terrible events that were to follow, if I could only have had a foresight into the future that September day, I swear I would have avoided the book like a leprous thing, would have shunned that wretched antique store and the very street it stood on like places accursed. A thousand times I have wished my eyes had never rested on that cover in black. What writhings of the soul, what terrors, what unrest, what madness would have been spared me!

But never dreaming the hideous secret of its pages I fondled it casually and remarked:

"An unusual book. What is it?"

Larla glanced up and scowled.

"That is not for sale," he said quietly. "I don't know how it got on these shelves. It was my poor brother's."

The volume in my hand was indeed unusual in appearance. Measuring but four inches across and five inches in length and bound in black velvet with each outside corner protected with a triangle of ivory, it was the most beautiful piece of book-binding I had ever seen. In the center of the cover was mounted a tiny piece of ivory intricately cut in the shape of a skull. But it was the title of the book that excited my interest. Embroidered in gold braid, the title read:

"Five Unicorns and a Pearl."

I looked at Larla. "How much?" I asked and reached for my wallet.

He shook his head. "No, it is not for sale. It is . . . it is the last work of my brother. He wrote it just before he died in the institution."

"The institution?" I queried.

Larla made no reply but stood staring at the book, his mind obviously drifting away in deep thought. A moment of silence dragged by. There was a strange gleam in his eyes when finally he spoke. And I thought I saw his fingers tremble slightly.

"My brother, Alessandro, was a fine man before he wrote that book," he said slowly. "He wrote beautifully, *Signor*, and he was strong and healthy. For hours I could sit while he read to me his poems. He was a dreamer, Alessandro; he loved everything beautiful, and the two of us were very happy.

"All . . . until that terrible night. Then he . . . but no . . . a year has passed now. It is best to forget." He passed his hand before his eyes and drew in his breath sharply.

"What happened?" I asked sympathetically, his words arousing my curiosity.

"Happened, *Signor?* I do not really know. It was all so confusing. He became suddenly ill, ill without reason. The flush of sunny Italy, which was always on his cheek, faded, and he grew white and drawn. His strength left him day by day. Doctors prescribed, gave medicines, but nothing helped. He grew steadily weaker until . . . until that night."

I looked at him curiously, impressed by his perturbation.

"And then————?" I urged.

Hands opening and closing, Larla seemed to sway unsteadily; his liquid eyes opened wide to the brows, and his voice was strained and tense as he continued:

"And then . . . oh, if I could but forget! It was horrible. Poor Alessandro came home screaming, sobbing, tearing his hair. He was . . . he was stark, raving mad!

"They took him to the institution for the insane and said he needed a complete rest, that he had suffered from some terrific mental shock. He . . . died three weeks later with the crucifix on his lips."

For a moment I stood there in silence, staring out at the falling rain. Then I said:

"He wrote this book while confined to the institution?"

Larla nodded absently.

"Three books," he replied. "Two others exactly like the one you have in your hand. The bindings he made, of course, when he was quite well. It was his original intention, I believe, to pen in them by hand the verses of Marini. He was very clever at such work. But the wanderings of his mind which filled the pages now, I have never read. Nor do I intend to. I want to keep with me the memory of him when he was happy. This book has come on these shelves by mistake. I shall put it with his other possessions."

My desire to read the few pages bound in velvet increased a thousandfold when I found they were unobtainable. I have always had an interest in abnormal psychology and have gone through a number of books on the subject. Here was the work of a man confined in the asylum for the insane. Here was the unexpurgated writing of an educated brain gone mad. And unless my intuition failed me, here was a suggestion of some deep mystery. My mind was made up. I must have it.

I turned to Larla and chose my words carefully.

"I can well appreciate your wish to keep the book," I said, "and since you refuse to sell, may I ask if you would consider lending it to me for just one night? If I promised to return it in the morning? . . ."

The Italian hesitated. He toyed undecidedly with a heavy gold watch chain. "No. I am sorry. . . ."

"Ten dollars and back tomorrow unharmed."

Larla studied his shoe.

"Very well, *Signor*, I will trust you. But please, I ask you, please be sure and return it."

That night in the quiet of my apartment I opened the book. Immediately my attention was drawn to three lines scrawled in a feminine hand across the inside of the front cover, lines written in a faded red solution that looked more like blood than ink. They read:

"Revelations meant to destroy but only binding without the stake. Read, fool, and enter my field, for we are chained to the spot. Oh wo unto Larla!"

I mused over these undecipherable sentences for some time without solving their meaning. At last, shrugging my shoulders, I turned to the first page and began the last work of Alessandro Larla, the strangest story I had ever in my years of browsing through old books, come upon.

"On the evening of the fifteenth of October I turned my steps into the cold and walked until I was tired. The roar of the present was in the distance when I came to twenty-six bluejays silently contemplating the ruins. Passing in the midst of them I wandered by the skeleton trees and seated myself where I could watch the leering fish. A child worshipped. Glass threw the moon at me. Grass sang a litany at my feet. And the pointed shadow moved slowly to the left.

"I walked along the silver gravel until I came to five unicorns galloping beside water of the past. Here I found a pearl, a magnificent pearl, a pearl beautiful but black. Like a flower it carried a rich perfume, and once I thought the odor was but a mask, but why should such a perfect creation need a mask?

"I sat between the leering fish and the five galloping unicorns, and I fell madly in love with the pearl. The past lost itself in drabness and————"

I laid the book down and sat watching the smoke-curls from my pipe eddy ceilingward. There was much more, but I could make no sense to any of it. All was in that strange style and completely incomprehensible. And yet it seemed the story was more than the mere wanderings of a madman. Behind it all seemed to lie a narrative cloaked in symbolism.

Something about the few sentences—just what I can not say—had cast an immediate spell of depression over me. The vague lines weighed upon my mind, hung before my eyes like a design, and I felt myself slowly seized by a deep feeling of uneasiness.

The air of the room grew heavy and close. The open casement and the out-of-doors seemed to beckon to me. I walked to the window, thrust the curtain aside, stood there, smoking furiously. Let me say that regular habits have long been a part of my make-up. I am not addicted to nocturnal strolls or late meanderings before seeking my bed; yet now, curiously enough, with the pages of the book still in my mind I suddenly experienced an indefinable urge to leave my apartment and walk the darkened streets.

I paced the room nervously, irritated that the sensation did not pass. The clock on the mantel pushed its ticks slowly through the quiet. And at length with a shrug I threw my pipe to the table, reached for my hat and coat and made for the door.

Ridiculous as it may sound, upon reaching the street I found that urge had increased to a distinct attraction. I felt that under no circumstances must I turn any direction but northward, and although this way led into a district quite un-known to me, I was in a moment pacing forward, choosing streets deliberately and heading without knowing why toward the outskirts of the city. It was a bril-liant moonlight night in September. Summer had passed and already there was the smell of frosted vegetation in the air. The great chimes in Capitol tower were sounding midnight, and the buildings and shops and later the private houses were dark and silent as I passed.

Try as I would to erase from my memory the queer book which I had just read, the mystery of its pages hammered at me, arousing my curiosity, dampen-ing my spirits. "Five Unicorns and a Pearl!" What did it all mean?

More and more I realized as I went on that a power other than my own will was leading my steps. It was absurd, and I tried to resist, to turn back. Yet once when I did momentarily come to a halt that attraction swept upon me as inex-orably as the desire for a narcotic.

It was far out on Easterly Street that I came upon a high stone wall flanking the sidewalk. Over its ornamented top I could see the shadows of a dark build-ing set well back in the grounds. A wrought-iron gate in the wall opened upon a view of wild desertion and neglect. Swathed in the light of the moon, an old courtyard strewn with fountains, stone benches and statues lay tangled in rank weeds and undergrowth. The windows of the building, which evidently had once been a private dwelling, were boarded up, all except those on a little tower or cupola rising to a point in the front. And here the glass caught the blue-gray light and refracted it into the shadows.

Before that gate my feet stopped like dead things. The psychic power which had been leading me had now become a reality. Directly from the courtyard it emanated, drawing me toward it with an intensity that smothered all reluctance.

❆　　❆　　❆

Strangely enough, the gate was unlocked; and feeling like a man in a trance I swung the creaking hinges and entered, making my way along a grass-grown path to one of the benches. It seemed that once inside the court the distant sounds of the city died away, leaving a hollow silence broken only by the wind rustling through the tall dead weeds. Rearing up before me, the building with its dark wings, cupola and façade oddly resembled a colossal hound, crouched and ready to spring.

There were several fountains, weather-beaten and ornamented with curious figures, to which at the time I paid only casual attention. Farther on, half hidden by the underbrush, was the life-size statue of a little child kneeling in position of prayer. Erosion of the soft stone had disfigured the face, and in the half-light the carved features presented an expression strangely grotesque and repelling.

How long I sat there in the quiet, I don't know. The surroundings under the moonlight blended harmoniously with my mood. But more than that I seemed physically unable to rouse myself and pass on.

It was with a suddenness that brought me electrified to my feet that I became aware of the real significance of the objects about me. Held motionless, I stood there running my eyes wildly from place to place, refusing to believe. Surely I must be dreaming. In the name of all that was unusual this . . . this absolutely couldn't be. And yet————

It was the fountain at my side that had caught my attention first. Across the top of the water basin were *five stone unicorns,* all identically carved, each seeming to follow the other in galloping procession. Looking farther, prompted now by a madly rising recollection, I saw that the cupola, towering high above the house, eclipsed the rays of the moon and threw *a long pointed shadow* across the ground *at my left.* The other fountain some distance away was ornamented with the figure of a stone fish, *a fish* whose empty eyesockets *were leering* straight in my direction. And the climax of it all—the wall! At intervals of every three feet on the top of the street expanse were mounted crude carven stone shapes of birds. And count-ing them I saw that *those birds were twenty-six bluejays.*

Unquestionably—startling and impossible as it seemed—I was in the same setting as described in Larla's book! It was a staggering revelation, and my mind reeled at the thought of it. How strange, how odd that I should be drawn to a portion of the city I had never before frequented and thrown into the midst of a narrative written almost a year before!

I saw now that Alessandro Larla, writing as a patient in the institution for the insane, had seized isolated details but neglected to explain them. Here was a problem for the psychologist, the mad, the symbolic, the incredible story of the dead Italian. I was bewildered, confused, and I pondered for an answer.

As if to soothe my perturbation there stole into the court then a faint odor of perfume. Pleasantly it touched my nostrils, seemed to blend with the moonlight. I breathed it in deeply as I stood there by the curious fountain. But slowly that odor became more noticeable, grew stronger, a sickish sweet smell that began to creep down my lungs like smoke. And absently I recognized it. Heliotrope! The honeyed aroma blanketed the garden, thickened the air, seemed to fall upon me like a drug.

And then came my second surprize of the evening. Looking about to discover the source of the irritating fragrance I saw opposite me, seated on another stone bench, a woman. She was dressed entirely in black, and her face was hidden by a veil. She seemed unaware of my presence. Her head was slightly bowed, and her whole position suggested a person deep in contemplation.

I noticed also the thing that crouched by her side. It was a dog, a tremendous brute with a head strangely out of proportion and eyes as large as the ends of big spoons. For several moments I stood staring at the two of them. Although the air was quite chilly, the woman wore no over-jacket, only the black dress relieved solely by the whiteness of her throat.

With a sigh of regret at having my pleasant solitude thus disturbed I moved across the court until I stood at her side. Still she showed no recognition of my presence, and clearing my throat I said hesitatingly:

"I suppose you are the owner here. I . . . I really didn't know the place was occupied, and the gate . . . well, the gate was unlocked. I'm sorry I trespassed."

She made no reply to that, and the dog merely gazed at me in dumb silence. No graceful words of polite departure came to my lips, and I moved hesitatingly toward the gate.

"Please don't go," she said suddenly, looking up. "I'm lonely. Oh, if you but knew how lonely I am!" She moved to one side of the bench and motioned that I sit beside her. The dog continued to examine me with its big eyes.

Whether it was the nearness of that odor of heliotrope, the suddenness of it all, or perhaps the moonlight, I did not know, but at her words a thrill of pleasure ran through me, and I accepted the proffered seat.

There followed an interval of silence, during which I puzzled my brain for a means to start conversation. But abruptly she turned to the beast and said in German:

"Fort mit dir, Johann!"

The dog rose obediently to its feet and stole slowly off into the shadows. I watched it for a moment until it disappeared in the direction of the house. Then the woman said to me in English which was slightly stilted and marked with an accent:

"It has been ages since I have spoken to any one. . . . We are strangers. I do not know you, and you do not know me. Yet . . . strangers sometimes find in each other a bond of interest. Supposing . . . supposing we forget customs and formality of introduction? Shall we?"

For some reason I felt my pulse quicken as she said that. "Please do," I replied. "A spot like this is enough introduction in itself. Tell me, do you live here?"

She made no answer for a moment, and I began to fear I had taken her suggestion too quickly. Then she began slowly:

"My name is Perle von Mauren, and I am really a stranger to your country, though I have been here now more than a year. My home is in Austria near what is now the Czechoslovakian frontier. You see, it was to find my only brother that I came to the United States. During the war he was a lieutenant under General Mackensen, but in 1916, in April I believe it was, he . . . he was reported missing.

"War is a cruel thing. It took our money; it took our castle on the Danube, and then—my brother. Those following years were horrible. We lived always in doubt, hoping against hope that he was still living.

"Then after the Armistice a fellow officer claimed to have served next to him on grave-digging detail at a French prison camp near Monpré. And later came a thin rumor that he was in the United States. I gathered together as much money as I could and came here in search of him."

Her voice dwindled off, and she sat in silence staring at the brown weeds. When she resumed, her voice was low and wavering.

"I . . . found him . . . but would to God I hadn't! He . . . he was no longer living."

I stared at her. "Dead?" I asked.

The veil trembled as though moved by a shudder, as though her thoughts had exhumed some terrible event of the past. Unconscious of my interruption she went on:

"Tonight I came here—I don't know why—merely because the gate was unlocked, and there was a place of quiet within. Now have I bored you with my confidences and personal history?"

"Not at all," I replied. "I came here by chance myself. Probably the beauty of the place attracted me. I dabble in amateur photography occasionally and react strongly to unusual scenes. Tonight I went for a midnight stroll to relieve my mind from the bad effect of a book I was reading."

She made a strange reply to that, a reply away from our line of thought and which seemed an interjection that escaped her involuntarily.

"Books," she said, "are powerful things. They can fetter one more than the walls of a prison."

She caught my puzzled stare at the remark and added hastily: "It is odd that we should meet here."

For a moment I didn't answer. I was thinking of her heliotrope perfume, which for a woman of her apparent culture was applied in far too great a quantity to manifest good taste. The impression stole upon me that the perfume cloaked some secret, that if it were removed I should find . . . but what? It was ridiculous, and I tried to cast the feeling aside.

The hours passed, and still we sat there talking, enjoying each other's companionship. She did not remove her veil, and though I was burning with a desire to see her features, I had not dared ask her to. A strange nervousness had slowly seized me. The woman was a charming conversationalist, but there was about her an indefinable something which produced in me a distinct feeling of unease.

It was, I should judge, but a few moments before the first streaks of dawn when it happened. As I look back now, even with mundane objects and thoughts on every side, it is not difficult to realize the dire significance, the absolute base-

ness of that vision. But at the time my brain was too much in a whirl to understand.

A thin shadow moving across the garden attracted my gaze once again into
the night about me. I looked up over the spire of the deserted house and started
as if struck by a blow. For a moment I thought I had seen a curious cloud formation racing low directly above me, a cloud black and impenetrable with two
wing-like ends strangely in the shape of a monstrous flying bat.

I blinked my eyes hard and looked again.

"That cloud!" I exclaimed, "that strange cloud! . . . Did you see————"
I stopped and stared dumbly.

The bench at my side was empty. The woman had disappeared.

During the next day I went about my professional duties in the law office with
only half interest, and my business partner looked at me queerly several times
when he came upon me mumbling to myself. The incidents of the evening before
were rushing through my mind in grand turmoil. Questions unanswerable hammered at me. That I should have come upon the very details described by mad
Larla in his strange book: the leering fish, the praying child, the twenty-six bluejays, the pointed shadow of the cupola—it was unexplainable; it was weird.

"Five Unicorns and a Pearl." The unicorns were the stone statues ornament-
ing the old fountain, yes—but the pearl? With a start I suddenly recalled the
name of the woman in black: *Perle* von Mauren. The revelation climaxed my train
of thought. What did it all mean?

Dinner had little attraction for me that evening. Earlier I had gone to the
antique-dealer and begged him to loan me the sequel, the second volume of his
brother Alessandro. When he had refused, objected because I had not yet returned the first book, my nerves had suddenly jumped on edge. I felt like a narcotic fiend faced with the realization that he could not procure the desired drug.
In desperation, yet hardly knowing why, I offered the man money, more money,
until at length I had come away, my powers of persuasion and my pocket-book
successful.

The second volume was identical in outward respects to its predecessor except that it bore no title. But if I was expecting more disclosures in symbolism I
was doomed to disappointment. Vague as "Five Unicorns and a Pearl" had been,

the text of the sequel was even more wandering and was obviously only the ramblings of a mad brain. By watching the sentences closely I did gather that Alessandro Larla had made a second trip to his court of the twenty-six bluejays and met there again his "pearl."

There was a paragraph toward the end that puzzled me. It read:

> *"Can it possibly be? I pray that it is not. And yet I have seen it and heard it snarl. Oh, the loathsome creature! I will not, I will not believe it."*

I closed the book with a snap and tried to divert my attention elsewhere by polishing the lens of my newest portable camera. But again, as before, that same urge stole upon me, that same desire to visit the garden. I confess that I had watched the intervening hours until I would meet the woman in black again; for strangely enough, in spite of her abrupt exit before, I never doubted but that she would be there waiting for me. I wanted her to lift the veil. I wanted to talk with her. I wanted to throw myself once again into the narrative of Larla's book.

Yet the whole thing seemed preposterous, and I fought the sensation with every ounce of will-power I could call to mind. Then it suddenly occurred to me what a remarkable picture she would make, sitting there on the stone bench, clothed in black, with the classic background of the old courtyard. If I could but catch the scene on a photographic plate. . . .

I halted my polishing and mused a moment. With a new electric flash-lamp, that handy invention which has supplanted the old mussy flash-powder, I could illuminate the garden and snap the picture with ease. And if the result were satisfactory it would make a worthy contribution to the International Camera Contest at Geneva next month.

The idea appealed to me, and gathering together the necessary equipment I drew on an ulster (for it was a wet, chilly night) and slipped out of my rooms and headed northward. Mad, unseeing fool that I was! If only I had stopped then and there, returned the book to the antique-dealer and closed the incident! But the strange magnetic attraction had gripped me in earnest, and I rushed headlong into the horror.

❰   ❰   ❰

A fall rain was drumming the pavement, and the streets were deserted. Off to the east, however, the heavy blanket of clouds glowed with a soft radiance where the moon was trying to break through, and a strong wind from the south gave promise of clearing the skies before long. With my coat collar turned well up at the throat I passed once again into the older section of the town and down forgotten Easterly Street. I found the gate to the grounds unlocked as before, and the garden a dripping place masked in shadow.

The woman was not there. Still the hour was early, and I did not for a moment doubt that she would appear later. Gripped now with the enthusiasm of my plan, I set the camera carefully on the stone fountain, training the lens as well as I could on the bench where we had sat the previous evening. The flash-lamp with its battery handle I laid within easy reach.

Scarcely had I finished my arrangements when the crunch of gravel on the path caused me to turn. She was approaching the stone bench, heavily veiled as before and with the same sweeping black dress.

"You have come again," she said as I took my place beside her.

"Yes," I replied. "I could not stay away."

Our conversation that night gradually centered about her dead brother, although I thought several times that the woman tried to avoid the subject. He had been, it seemed, the black sheep of the family, had led more or less of a dissolute life and had been expelled from the University of Vienna not only because of his lack of respect for the pedagogues of the various sciences but also because of his queer unorthodox papers on philosophy. His sufferings in the war prison camp must have been intense. With a kind of grim delight she dwelt on his horrible experiences in the grave-digging detail which had been related to her by the fellow officer. But of the manner in which he had met his death she would say absolutely nothing.

Stronger than on the night before was the sweet smell of heliotrope. And again as the fumes crept nauseatingly down my lungs there came that same sense of nervousness, that same feeling that the perfume was hiding something I should know. The desire to see beneath the veil had become maddening by this time, but still I lacked the boldness to ask her to lift it.

Toward midnight the heavens cleared and the moon in splendid contrast shone high in the sky. The time had come for my picture.

"Sit where you are," I said. "I'll be back in a moment."

Stepping quickly to the fountain I grasped the flash-lamp, held it aloft for an instant and placed my finger on the shutter lever of the camera. The woman remained motionless on the bench, evidently puzzled as to the meaning of my movements. The range was perfect. A click, and a dazzling white light enveloped the courtyard about us. For a brief second she was outlined there against the old wall. Then the blue moonlight returned, and I was smiling in satisfaction.

"It ought to make a beautiful picture," I said.

She leaped to her feet.

"Fool!" she cried hoarsely. "Blundering fool! What have you done?"

Even though the veil was there to hide her face I got the instant impression that her eyes were glaring at me, smoldering with hatred. I gazed at her curiously as she stood erect, head thrown back, body apparently taut as wire, and a slow shudder crept down my spine. Then without warning she gathered up her dress and ran down the path toward the deserted house. A moment later she had disappeared somewhere in the shadows of the giant bushes.

I stood there by the fountain, staring after her in a daze. Suddenly, off in the umbra of the house's façade there rose a low animal snarl.

And then before I could move, a huge gray shape came hurtling through the long weeds, bounding in great leaps straight toward me. It was the woman's dog, which I had seen with her the night before. But no longer was it a beast passive and silent. Its face was contorted in diabolic fury, and its jaws were dripping slaver. Even in that moment of terror as I stood frozen before it, the sight of those white nostrils and those black hyalescent eyes emblazoned itself on my mind, never to be forgotten.

Then with a lunge it was upon me. I had only time to thrust the flash-lamp upward in half protection and throw my weight to the side. My arm jumped in recoil. The bulb exploded, and I could feel those teeth clamp down hard on the handle. Backward I fell, a scream gurgling to my lips, a terrific heaviness surging upon my body.

I struck out frantically, beat my fists into that growling face. My fingers groped blindly for its throat, sank deep into the hairy flesh. I could feel its very breath mingling with my own now, but desperately I hung on.

The pressure of my hands told. The dog coughed and fell back. And seizing that instant I struggled to my feet, jumped forward and planted a terrific kick straight into the brute's middle.

"*Fort mit dir*, Johann!" I cried, remembering the woman's German command.

It leaped back and, fangs bared, glared at me motionless for a moment. Then abruptly it turned and slunk off through the weeds.

Weak and trembling, I drew myself together, picked up my camera and passed through the gate toward home.

Three days passed. Those endless hours I spent confined to my apartment suffering the tortures of the damned.

On the day following the night of my terrible experience with the dog I realized I was in no condition to go to work. I drank two cups of strong black coffee and then forced myself to sit quietly in a chair, hoping to soothe my nerves. But the sight of the camera there on the table excited me to action. Five minutes later I was in the dark room arranged as my studio, developing the picture I had taken the night before. I worked feverishly, urged on by the thought of what an unusual contribution it would make for the amateur contest next month at Geneva, should the result be successful.

An exclamation burst from my lips as I stared at the still-wet print. There was the old garden clear and sharp with the bushes, the statue of the child, the fountain and the wall in the background, but the bench—the stone bench was empty. There was no sign, not even a blur of the woman in black.

My brain in a whirl, I rushed the negative through a saturated solution of mercuric chloride in water, then treated it with ferrous oxalate. But even after this intensifying process the second print was like the first, focused in every detail, the bench standing in the foreground in sharp relief, but no trace of the woman.

I stared incredulously. She had been in plain view when I snapped the shutter. Of that I was positive. And my camera was in perfect condition. What then was wrong? Not until I had looked at the print hard in the daylight would I believe my eyes. No explanation offered itself, none at all; and at length, confused unto weakness, I returned to my bed and fell into a heavy sleep.

Straight through the day I slept. Hours later I seemed to wake from a vague nightmare, and had not strength to rise from my pillow. A great physical faintness had overwhelmed me. My arms, my legs, lay like dead things. My heart was fluttering weakly. All was quiet, so still that the clock on my bureau ticked distinctly each passing second. The curtain billowed in the night breeze, though I was positive I had closed the casement when I entered the room.

And then suddenly I threw back my head and screamed from the bottommost depths of my soul! For slowly, slowly creeping down my lungs was that detestable odor of heliotrope!

Morning, and I found all was not a dream. My head was ringing, my hands trembling, and I was so weak I could hardly stand. The doctor I called in looked grave as he felt my pulse.

"You are on the verge of a complete collapse," he said. "If you do not allow yourself a rest it may permanently affect your mind. Take things easy for a while. And if you don't mind, I'll cauterize those two little cuts on your neck. They're rather raw wounds. What caused them?"

I moved my fingers to my throat and drew them away again tipped with blood.

"I . . . I don't know," I faltered.

He busied himself with his medicines, and a few minutes later reached for his hat.

"I advise that you don't leave your bed for a week at least," he said. "I'll give you a thorough examination then and see if there are any signs of anemia." But as he went out the door I thought I saw a puzzled look on his face.

Those subsequent hours allowed my thoughts to run wild once more. I vowed I would forget it all, go back to my work and never look upon the books again. But I knew I could not. The woman in black persisted in my mind, and each minute away from her became a torture. But more than that, if there had been a decided urge to continue my reading in the second book, the desire to see the third book, the last of the trilogy, was slowly increasing to an obsession. It gripped me, etched itself deep into my thoughts.

At length I could stand it no longer, and on the morning of the third day I took a cab to the antique store and tried to persuade Larla to give me the third volume of his brother. But the Italian was firm. I had already taken two books, neither of which I had returned. Until I brought them back he would not listen. Vainly I tried to explain that one was of no value without the sequel and that I wanted to read the entire narrative as a unit. He merely shrugged his shoulders and toyed with his watch chain.

Cold perspiration broke out on my forehead as I heard my desire disregarded. Like the blows of a bludgeon the thought beat upon me that I must have that book. I argued. I pleaded. But to no avail.

At length when Larla had turned the other way I gave in to desperation, seized the third book as I saw it lying on the shelf, slid it into my pocket and walked guiltily out. I make no apologies for my action. In the light of what developed later it may be considered a temptation inspired, for my will at the time was a conquered thing blanketed by that strange lure.

Back in my apartment I dropped into a chair and hastened to open the velvet cover. Here was the last chronicling of that strange series of events which had so completely become a part of my life during the past five days. Larla's volume three. Would all be explained in its pages? If so, what secret would be revealed?

With the light from a reading-lamp glaring full over my shoulder I opened the book, thumbed through it slowly, marveling again at the exquisite handprinting. It seemed then as I sat there that an almost palpable cloud of intense quiet settled over me, a mental miasma muffling the distant sounds of the street. I was vaguely aware of an atmosphere, heavy and dense, in which objects other than the book lost their focus and became blurred in proportion.

For a moment I hesitated. Something psychic, something indefinable seemed to forbid me to read farther. Conscience, curiosity, that queer urge told me to go on. Slowly, like a man in a hypnotic trance wavering between two wills, I began to turn the pages, one at a time, from front to back.

Symbolism again. Vague wanderings with no sane meaning.

But suddenly my fingers stopped! My eyes had caught sight of the last paragraph on the last page, the final pennings of Alessandro Larla. I started downward as a terrific shock ripped through me from head to foot. I read, re-read, and read again those words, those blasphemous words. I brought the book closer. I traced each word in the lamplight, slowly, carefully, letter for letter. I opened and closed my eyes. Then the horror of it burst like a bomb within me.

In blood-red ink the lines read:

> *"What shall I do? She has drained my blood and rotted my soul. My pearl is black, black as all evil. The curse be upon her brother, for it is he who made her thus. I pray the truth in these pages will destroy them for ever.*
>
> *"But my brain is hammering itself apart. Heaven help me, Perle von Mauren and her brother, Johann, are vampires!"*

With a scream I leaped to my feet.

"Vampires!" I shrieked. "Vampires! Oh, my God!"

I clutched at the edge of the table and stood there swaying, the realization of it surging upon me like the blast of a furnace. Vampires! Those horrible creatures with a lust for human blood, fiends of hell, taking the shape of men, of bats, of dogs. I saw it all now, and my brain reeled at the horror of it.

Oh, why had I been such a fool? Why had I not looked beneath the surface, taken away the veil, gone farther than the perfume? That damnable heliotrope was a mask, a mask hiding all the unspeakable foulness of the grave.

My emotions burst out of control then. With a cry I swept the water-glass, the books, the vase from the table, smote my fist down upon the flat surface again and again until a thousand little pains were stabbing the flesh.

"Vampires!" I screamed. "No, no—oh God, it isn't true!"

But I knew that it was. The events of the past days rose before me in all their horror now, and I could see the black significance of every detail.

The brother, Johann—some time since the war he had become a vampire. When the woman sought him out years later he had forced this terrible existence upon her too. Yes, that was it.

With the garden as their lair the two of them had entangled poor Alessandro Larla in their serpentine coils a year before. He had loved the woman, had worshipped her madly. And then he had found the truth, the awful truth that had sent him stumbling home, stark, raving mad.

Mad, yes, but not mad enough to keep him from writing the facts in his three velvet-bound books for the world to see. He had hoped the disclosures would dispatch the woman and her brother for ever. But it was not enough.

Following my thoughts, I whipped the first book from the table stand and opened the front cover. There again I saw those scrawled lines which had meant nothing to me before.

"Revelations meant to destroy but only binding without the stake. Read, fool, and enter my field, for we are chained to the spot. Oh, wo unto Larla!"

Perle von Mauren had written that. Fool that I was, unseeing fool! The books had not put an end to the evil life of her or her brother. No, only one thing could do that. Yet the exposures had not been written in vain. They were recorded for mortal posterity to see.

Those books bound the two vampires, Perle von Mauren and her brother, Johann, to the old garden, kept them from roaming the night streets in search of victims. Only him who had once passed through the gate could they pursue and attack.

It was the old metaphysical law: evil shrinking in the face of truth.

Yet if the books had bound their power in chains they had also opened a new avenue for their attacks. Once immersed in the pages of the trilogy, the reader fell helplessly into their clutches. Those printed lines had become the outer reaches of their web. They were an entrapping net within which the power of the vampires always crouched.

That was why my life had blended so strangely with the story of Larla. The moment I had cast my eyes on the opening paragraph I had fallen into their coils to do with as they had done with Larla a year before. I had been lured, drawn relentlessly into the tentacles of the woman in black. Once I was past the garden gate the binding spell of the books was gone, and they were free to pursue me and to————

A giddy sensation rose within me. Now I saw why the scientific doctor had been puzzled. Now I saw the reason for my physical weakness. Oh, the foulness of it! She had been—feasting on my blood!

With a sobbing cry I flung the book to a far corner, turned and began madly pacing up and down the room. Cold perspiration oozed from every pore. My heart pounded like a runner's. My brain ran wild.

Was I to end as Larla had ended, another victim of this loathsome being's power? Was she to gorge herself further on my life and live on? Were others to be preyed upon and go down into the pits of despair? No, and again no! If Larla had been ignorant of the one and only way in which to dispose of such a creature, I was not. I had not vacationed in south Europe without learning something of these ancient evils.

Frantically I looked about the room, took in the objects about me. A chair, a table, a taboret, one of my cameras with its long tripod. I stared at the latter as in my terror-stricken mind a plan leaped into action. With a lunge I was across the floor, had seized one of the wooden legs of the tripod in my hands. I snapped it across my knee. Then, grasping the two broken pieces, both now with sharp splintered ends, I rushed hatless out of the door to the street.

A moment later I was racing northward in a cab bound for Easterly Street.

"Hurry!" I cried to the driver as I glanced at the westering sun. "Faster, do you hear?"

We shot along the cross-streets, into the old suburbs and toward the outskirts of town. Every traffic halt found me fuming at the delay. But at length we drew up before the wall of the garden.

Tossing the driver a bill, I swung the wrought-iron gate open and with the wooden pieces of the tripod still under my arm, rushed in. The courtyard was a place of reality in the daylight, but the moldering masonry and tangled weeds were steeped in silence as before.

Straight for the house I made, climbing the rotten steps to the front entrance. The door was boarded up and locked. Smothering an impulse to scream, I retraced my steps at a run and began to circle the south wall of the building. It was this direction I had seen the woman take when she had fled after I had tried to snap her picture. The twenty-six bluejays on the wall leered at me like a flock of harpies.

Well toward the rear of the building I reached a small half-open door leading to the cellar. For a moment I hesitated there, sick with the dread of what I knew lay before me. Then, clenching hard the two wooden tripod stakes, I entered.

Inside, cloaked in gloom, a narrow corridor stretched before me. The floor was littered with rubble and fallen masonry, the ceiling interlaced with a thousand cobwebs.

I stumbled forward, my eyes quickly accustoming themselves to the half-light from the almost opaque windows. A maddening urge to leave it all and flee back to the sunlight was welling up within me now. I fought it back. Failure would mean a continuation of the horrors—a lingering death—would leave the gate open for others.

At the end of the corridor a second door barred my passage. I thrust it open—and stood swaying there on the sill staring inward. A great loathing crept over me, a stifling sense of utter repulsion. Hot blood rushed to my head. The air seemed to move upward in palpable swirls.

Beyond was a small room, barely ten feet square, with a low-raftered ceiling. And by the light of the open door I saw side by side in the center of the floor—two white wood coffins.

How long I stood there leaning weakly against the stone wall I don't know. There was a silence so profound the beating of my heart pulsed through the passage like the blows of a mallet. And there was a slow penetrating odor drifting from out of that chamber that entered my nostrils and claimed instant recognition. Heliotrope! But heliotrope defiled by the rotting smell of an ancient grave.

Then suddenly with a determination born of despair I leaped forward, rushed to the nearest coffin, seized its cover and ripped it open.

Would to heaven I could forget the sight that met my eyes. There lay Perle von Mauren, the woman in black—unveiled.

That face—how can I describe it? It was divinely beautiful, the hair black as sable, the cheeks a classic white. But the lips—oh God! those lips! I grew suddenly sick as I looked upon them. They were scarlet, crimson . . . and sticky with human blood.

I moved like an automaton then. With a low sob I reached for one of the tripod stakes, seized a flagstone from the floor and with the pointed end of the wood resting directly over the woman's heart, struck a crashing blow. The stake jumped downward. A sickening crunch—and a violent contortion shook the coffin. Up to my face rushed a warm, nauseating breath of rot and decay.

I wheeled and hurled open the lid of her brother's coffin. With only a flashing glance at the young masculine Teutonic face I raised the other stake high in the air and brought it stabbing down with all the strength in my right arm. Red blood suddenly began to form a thick pool on the floor.

For an instant I stood rooted to the spot, the utter obscenity of it all searing its way into my brain like a hot sword. Even in that moment of stark horror I realized that not even the most subtle erasures of Time would be able to remove that blasphemous sight from my inner eye.

It was a scene so abysmally corrupt—I pray heaven my dreams will never find it and re-vision its unholy tableau. There before me, focused in the shaft of light that filtered through the open door like the miasma from a fever swamp, lay the two white caskets.

And within them now, staring up at me from eyeless sockets—two gray and moldering skeletons, each with its hideous leering head of death.

The rest is but a vague dream. I seem to remember rushing madly outside, along the path to the gate and down the street, down Easterly, away from that accursed garden of the jays.

At length, utterly exhausted, I reached my apartment, burst open the door and staggered in. Those mundane surroundings that confronted me were like balm to my burning eyes. But as if in mocking irony there centered into my gaze three objects lying where I had left them, the three volumes of Larla.

I moved across to them, picked them up and stared down vacantly upon their black sides. These were the hellish works that had caused it all. These were the pages that were responsible. . . .

With a low cry I turned to the grate on the other side of the room and flung the three of them onto the still glowing coals.

There was an instant hiss, and a line of yellow flame streaked upward and began eating into the velvet. I watched the fire grow higher . . . higher . . . and diminish slowly.

And as the last glowing spark died into a blackened ash there swept over me a mighty feeling of quiet and relief.

THE FIRST TIME

K. W. JETER

HIS FATHER AND HIS UNCLE DECIDED IT WAS ABOUT time. Time for him to come along. They went down there on a regular basis, with their buddies, all of them laughing and drinking beer right in the car, having a good time even before they got there. When they left the house, laying a patch of rubber out by the curb, he'd lie on his bed upstairs and think about them—at least for a little while, till he fell asleep—think about the car heading out on the long straight road, where there was nothing on either side except the bare rock and dirt and the dried-brown scrubby brush. With a cloud of dust rolling behind them, his uncle Tommy could just floor it, one-handing the steering wheel, with nothing to do but keep it on the dotted line all the way down there. He lay with the side of his face pressed into the pillow, and thought of them driving, making good time, hour after hour, tossing the empties out the window, laughing and talking about mysterious things, things you only had to say the name of and everybody knew what you were talking about, without another word being said. Even with all the windows rolled down, the car would smell like beer and sweat, six guys together, one of them right off his shift at the place where they made the cinder blocks, the fine gray dust on his hands and matted in the dark black hair of his forearms. Driving and laughing all the way, until the bright lights came into view—he didn't know what happened after that. He closed his eyes and didn't see anything.

And when they got back—they always got back late at night, so even though they'd been gone nearly the whole weekend, and he'd gotten up and watched television and listened to his mom talking to her friends on the phone, and had something to eat and stuff like that, when his father and his uncle and their buddies got back, the noise of the car pulling up, with them still talking and laughing, but different now, slower and lower-pitched and satisfied—it was like it woke him up from the same sleep he'd fallen into when they'd left. All the other stuff was just what he'd been dreaming.

"You wanna come along?" His father had asked him, turning away from the TV. Just like that, no big deal, like asking him to fetch another beer from the fridge. "Me and Tommy and the guys—we're gonna go down there and see what's happening. Have a little fun."

He hadn't said anything back for a little while, but had just stared at the TV, the colors fluttering against the walls of the darkened room. His father hadn't had to say anything more than *down there*—he knew where that meant. A little knot, one he always had in his stomach, tightened and drew down something in his throat.

"Sure," he'd finally mumbled. The string with the knot in it looped down lower in his gut. His father just grunted and went on watching the TV.

He figured they'd decided it was time because he'd finally started high school. More than that, he'd just about finished his first year and had managed to stay out of whatever trouble his older brother had gotten into back then, finally causing him to drop out and go into the army and then god knew what—nobody had heard from his brother in a long time. So maybe it was as some kind of reward, for doing good, that they were going to take him along with them.

He didn't see what was so hard about it, about school. What made it worth a reward. All you had to do was keep your head down and not draw attention to yourself. And there was stuff to do that got you through the day: he was in the band, and that was okay. He played the baritone sax—it was pretty easy because they never got any real melodies to play, you just had to fart around in the background with everybody else. Where he sat was right in front of the trombone section, which was all older guys; he could hear them talking, making bets about which of the freshman girls would be the next to start shaving her legs. Plus they had a lot of jokes about the funny way flute players made their mouths go when they were playing. Would they still look that funny way when they had something else in their mouths? It embarrassed him because the flute players were right across from the sax section, and he could see the one he'd already been dating a couple of times.

One time, when they'd been alone, she'd given him a piece of paper that she'd had folded up in the back pocket of her jeans. The paper had gotten shaped round, the same shape as her butt, and he'd felt funny taking it and unfolding it. The paper was a mimeographed diagram that her minister at her Episcopalian youth group had given her and the rest of the girls in the group. It showed what parts of their bodies they could let a boy touch, at what stage. You had to be engaged, with a ring and everything, before you could unhook her bra. He'd kept the piece of paper, tucked in one of his books at home. In a way, it'd been kind of a relief, just to know what was expected of him.

It was what worried him about going down there, with his father and his uncle and the other guys—he didn't know what he was supposed to do when they got there. He lay awake the night before, wondering. He turned on the light and got out the piece of paper the girl who played the flute had given him, and looked at the dotted lines that made a sort of zone between the diagram's throat and navel, and another zone below that, that looked like a pair of underpants or the bottom half of a girl's two-piece swimsuit. Then he folded the paper back up and stuck it in the book where he kept it. He didn't think the diagram was going to do him any good where he was going.

"All right—let's get this show on the road." His uncle Tommy leaned out of the driver's-side window and slapped the door's metal. They always went down there in Tommy's car because it was the biggest, an old Dodge that wallowed like a boat even on the straightaways. The other guys chipped in for the gas. "Come on—let's move on out." Tommy's big yellow grin was even looser; he'd already gotten into the six-pack stowed down on the floor.

For a moment, he thought they'd all forgotten about taking him along. There were already five guys in the car when it'd pulled up in front of the house, and his father would make the sixth. He stood on the porch, feeling a secret hope work at the knot in his gut.

"Aw, man—what the hell were you guys thinking of?" The voice of one of the guys in the car floated out, across the warm evening air. It was Bud, the one who worked at the cinder block factory. "There's no way you can stick seven of us in here, and then drive all the way down there."

The guy next to Bud, in the middle of the backseat, laughed. "Well, hell—maybe you can just sit on my lap, then."

"Yeah, well, you can just sit on this." Bud gave him the finger, then drained the last from a can of beer and dropped it onto the curb. Bud pushed the door open and got out. "You guys just have a fine old time without me. I got some other shit to take care of."

Tommy's grin grew wider. "Ol' Bud's feeling his age. Since that little sweetheart last time fucked up his back for him."

"Your ass."

From the porch, he watched Bud walking away, the blue glow of the streetlights making the cinder block dust on Bud's workshirt go all silver. He couldn't tell if Bud had been really mad—maybe about him coming along and taking up space in the car—or if it was just part of the joke. A lot of the time he couldn't tell whether his father and his buddies were joking or not.

"Come on—" His father had already gotten in the car, up front, elbow hanging over the sill of the door. "What're you waiting for?"

He slid in the back. The seat had dust from Bud's shirt on it, higher up than his own shoulders. "Here we go," said his father, as his head rocked back into the cinder block dust. The guy next to him, his father's buddy, peeled a beer off a six-pack and handed it to him. He held it without opening it, letting the cold seep into his hands as the streets pivoted around and swung behind the car, until they were past the last streetlight and onto the straight road heading for the southern hills.

All the way down there, they talked about baseball. Or football, shouting over the radio station that Tommy had turned up loud. He didn't listen to them, but leaned his shoulder against the door, gulping breath out of the wind, his face stung red. For a long while he thought there was something running alongside the car, a dog or something, but faster than a dog could run, because his uncle Tommy had the car easily wound up to over seventy. The dog, or whatever it was, loped in the shadows at the side of the road, a big grin like Tommy's across its muzzle, its bright spark eyes looking right at him. But when another car came along, going the other way, the headlights making a quick scoop over the road, the dog wasn't there. Just the rocks and brush zooming by, falling back into the dark behind them. He pushed his face farther out into the wind, eyes squinted, the roar swallowing up the voices inside the car. The dog's yellow eyes danced like coins out there, keeping alongside and smiling at him.

"All *right*—we have uh-*rived.*" His uncle Tommy beat an empty beer can against the curve of the steering wheel, then pitched it outside.

He looked up ahead, craning his neck to see around his father in the front seat. He could see a bridge, with lights strung up along it. And more lights beyond it, the town on the other side. He dropped back in his seat, combing his hair down into place with his fingers.

The lights, when they got across the bridge, were like Christmas lights, strings of little colored bulbs laced over the doorways of the buildings and even across the street, dangling up above, pushing back the night sky. There were other lights, too, the kind you'd see anywhere, blinking arrows that pointed to one thing or another, big yellow squares with the plastic strips for the black letters to stick on, covered in chicken wire to keep people's hands off.

Tommy let the car crawl along, inching through the traffic that had swallowed them up soon as they'd hit the town. So many other cars, all of them moving so slow, that people crossing the street, going from the lit-up doorways on one side to those on the other, just threaded their way through. Or if they were young guys, and the cars were bumper to bumper, they'd slap their hands down on a hood and a trunk lid and just vault over, with a little running step on the ridge of the bumpers halfway across, and just laughing and shouting to each other the whole time.

Even though it was so loud in the street—with all the car radios blaring away, with everybody's windows rolled down, and the even louder music thumping out of the doorways—he felt a little drowsy somehow. He'd drunk the beer his father's buddy had given him, and a couple more after that, and had gone on staring out at the dark rolling by the whole way down here. Now the street's noise rolled over him like the slow waves at the ocean's surface, far above him.

"Bail out, kid—let's go!" The guy beside him, in the middle of the backseat, was pushing him in the arm. His head lolled for a moment, neck limp, before he snapped awake. He looked around and saw his father and his uncle and the other guys all getting out of the car. Rubbing his eyes, he pushed the door open and stumbled out.

He followed them up the alley where they'd parked, out toward the lights and noise rolling in the street. It wasn't as bright and loud at this end; they'd left most of the action a couple of blocks back.

His father and his uncle were already down the street, laughing and swapping punches as they went, little boxing moves with feints and shuffles, like a couple of teenagers or something. His uncle Tommy was always carrying on, doing stuff like that, but he'd never seen his father so wild and happy. They had their arms around each other's shoulders, and their faces and chests lit up red as they stepped into one of the doorways, his father sweeping back a curtain with his hand. The light that had spilled out into the street blinked away as the curtain fell back into place. He broke into a run to catch up with the others.

Some kind of a bar—that was what it looked like and smelled like, the smell of spilled beer and cigarette smoke that had soaked into everything and made the air a thick blue haze around the lights. The others were already sitting around a table, one of the booths at the side; they'd left room for him at the end, and he slid in beside his uncle Tommy.

The man came around from behind the bar with a tray of beers, squat brown bottles sweating through the crinkly foil labels. He didn't know whether his father had already ordered, or whether the bartender already knew what they wanted, from all the times they'd been here before. He wasn't sure he'd get served, but it didn't seem to matter here how young he was; the bartender put a beer down in front of him, too. He took a pull at it as he looked around at the empty stage at one end of the room, with heavy red curtains draped around it and big PA speakers at the side. The other booths, and some of the tables in the middle, were crowded with bottles, men elbowing them aside as they leaned forward and talked, dropping the butts of their cigarettes into the empties.

Somebody poked him—it felt like a broom handle—and he looked around and saw a face grinning at him. A man short enough to look him straight in the eye where he sat; the grin split open to show brown teeth, except for two in front that were shining gold. The little man poked him again, with two metal tubes that had wires hooked to them, running back to a box that hung from a strap around the man's neck.

"Yeah, yeah—just take 'em." His father waggled a finger at the tubes, while digging with the other hand into his inside coat pocket. "Just hold on to 'em now. This is how they make you a man in these parts." His father came up with a dollar bill from a roll in the coat pocket and handed it over to the little man.

The tubes were about the size of the inside of a toilet paper roll, but shiny, and hard and cold to the touch. He looked at them sitting in his hands, then glanced up when he saw the little man turning a crank at the side of the box hanging around his neck.

An electric shock jumped out of the tubes, stinging his palms. He dropped them and jerked away. He looked around and saw his father and his buddies all roaring with laughter. Right beside him, his uncle Tommy was slapping the table with one hand, turning red and choking on a swallow of beer.

"Here—give 'em here." His father traded another dollar bill for the tubes, the wires dangling between the bottles as he took them from the little man. "Let 'er rip."

The little man turned the crank on the box, digging into it to make it go round faster and faster. His father winced with the first surge, then squeezed the tubes harder, hands going white-knuckled, teeth gritting together, lips drawn back. The crank on the box went around in a blur, until his father's hands flew open and the tubes clattered onto the table, knocking over one of the bottles. Beer foamed out and dribbled over the edge.

"Whoa! Jesus fucking Christ!" His father shook his hands, loose at the wrist. The guy sitting next over stuck out a palm and his father slapped it, grinning in triumph. The little man with the box did a kind of dance, laughing to show all the brown and gold teeth and pointing with a black-nailed finger. Then squatting down, the short legs bowing out, and cupping a hand to his crotch, acting like there was some cannonball-sized weight hanging there. The little man laughed and pointed to the man sitting in the booth again, then took another dollar bill and trotted away with the box and the tubes to another table.

He was looking at his father putting the roll of bills back into the coat pocket. His own hands still stung, and he wrapped them around the wet bottle in front of him to cool them.

"Yessir—that fucker'll sober you right up." His father signaled to the bartender. "I'm gonna need a couple more after that little bastard."

Somebody came walking over to the booth, but it wasn't the bartender. He looked up and saw one of the guys, one of his father's buddies—the guy hadn't been there the whole time they'd been messing around with the little man with the box.

"Lemme out." His uncle Tommy nudged him. "I think it's just about my turn."

He didn't know what his uncle meant, but he stood up and let Tommy slide out of the booth. The other guy took his place, sorting through the bottles on the table for the one that had been there before, that he hadn't finished.

Before he sat back down, he watched his uncle Tommy walking across the bar, squeezing past the backs of the chairs circled around the tables. There was a door in the corner with one of those wordless signs, a stick figure to indicate the men's room. But Tommy didn't head off toward that. His uncle pulled back the curtain hiding a doorway off to the side and disappeared behind it. He sat back down, but kept looking over at the curtain as he sipped at the beer that had grown warm in his hands.

Then—he didn't know how long it was—his uncle Tommy was back. Standing beside him, at the outside of the booth.

"Come on, fella—" Across the table, his father stabbed a thumb up in the air a couple of times. "Get up and let your old uncle siddown."

His uncle smelled different, sweat and something else. He got up, stepping back a little bit—the scent curled in his nostrils like something from an animal—and let his uncle slide into the booth.

He sat back down. His uncle Tommy had a big grin on his face. Around the table, he saw a couple of the other guys give a slow wink to each other, then tilt their beers up again.

Tommy glanced sidelong at him, then leaned over the table and spewed out a mouthful of blood. Enough of it to swamp across the tabletop, knocking the empty bottles over in the flood.

And he wasn't sitting in the booth then, next to his uncle. He'd jumped out of the booth, the way you would from the door of a rolling car; he stumbled and almost fell backward. Standing a couple of feet away, he listened to the men pounding the table and howling their laughter, louder than when the man with the box had shocked him.

"Tom, you shit-for-brains—" His father was red-faced, gasping for breath.

His uncle Tommy had a dribble of red going down his chin, like the finger of blood that had reached the edge of the table and dribbled over. Pretty drunk, his uncle smiled as he looked around the booth at the guys, pleased with the joke. His uncle turned and smiled at him, red seeping around the teeth in the sloppy grin.

The laughter dwindled away, the men shaking their heads and rubbing tears from the corners of their eyes. They all took long pulls at their beers. That was when he saw that there wasn't any room in the booth for him. They'd all shifted a little bit and taken up all the room; his uncle was sitting right at the end where he'd been.

They didn't say anything, but he knew what it meant. He turned around and looked across the bar, to the curtain that covered the doorway over there. It meant it was his turn now.

The woman ran her hand along the side of his neck. "You haven't been around here before, have you?" She smiled at him. Really smiled, not like she was laughing at him.

"No—" He shook his head. Her hand felt cool against the heat that had come rushing up under his skin. He pointed back over his shoulder. "I came with my dad, and his friends."

Her gaze moved past his eyes, up to where her fingers tangled around in his hair. "Uh-huh," she said. "I know your daddy."

She got up from the bed. He sat there watching her as she stood at a little shelf nailed to the wall. The shelf had a plastic-framed mirror propped up on it, and a towel and a bar of soap. She watched herself taking off her dangly earrings, gold ones, drawing the curved hooks out. She laid them down in front of the little mirror.

"Well, you don't have to worry none." She spoke to the mirror. "There's always a first time. Then it's easy after that." She rubbed a smudge away from the corner of her eye. "You'll see."

When he'd pulled aside the curtain and stepped into the dark—away from the bar's light, its noise of laughing and talking falling behind him—he hadn't even been able to see where he was, until he'd felt the woman take his hand and lead him a little farther along, back to where the doors to a lot of little rooms were lit up by a bulb hanging from the hallway's ceiling. One of the doors had opened and a man had come out and shoved past him in the narrow space, and he'd caught a whiff of the smell off the man, the same as had been on his uncle Tommy when he'd come back out to the booth.

When the woman had closed the door and come over to the bed to sit close by him, he'd held his breath for a moment, because he thought the scent would be on her too, that raw smell, like sweat, only sharper. But she smelled sweet, like something splashed on from a bottle, the kind women always had on their dressers. That made him realize that she was the first woman, the first female thing, he'd been near, for what seemed like days. All the way down here—in the car with his father and his uncle and their buddies, packed up tight with them as they'd gone barreling along in the night, and then crowded around the table in the booth, the same night rolling through the street outside, until their sweat was all he could smell, right down into his throat.

"Here—you don't want to get that all mussed up." The woman had on a white slip—it shone in the dim light as she came back toward the bed. "Let's take it off." She bent down, her dark hair brushing against his face, and started unbuttoning his shirt.

He felt cold, the sweat across his arms and shoulders chilling in the room's air. The woman sat down and leaned back against the bed's pillow, dropping his shirt to the floor. "Come a little closer." She stretched out her arms toward him.

"You see . . . there's nothing to be afraid of." Her voice went down to a whisper, yet somehow it filled the little room; it ate up all the space, until there was just the bed and her on it.

"We'll go real slow, so you won't get scared." She smiled at him, her hand tracing down his rib cage. She was a lot older than him; this close to her, he could see the tiny wrinkles around her eyes, the skin that had gone soft and tissuey around the bone, dark underneath it. The sweet smell covered up something else; when he breathed her breath, it slid down his throat and stuck there.

"Look . . ." She took his hand and turned his arm around, the pale skin underneath showing. She drew a fingernail along the blue vein that ran down to the pulse ticking away in his wrist.

She dropped his hand and held out her own arm. For just a second—then she seemed to remember something. She lifted her hips to pull the slip up, then shimmied the rest of the way out of it like a quick snakeskin. She threw it on the floor with his shirt.

"Now look . . ." She traced the vein in her arm. Her fingernail left a long thin mark along it. She did it again, the mark going deeper. Then a dot of red welled up around her nail, in the middle of her forearm. She dug the nail in deeper, then peeled back the white skin, the line pulling open from the inside of her elbow to her wrist.

"Look," she whispered again. She held the arm up to his face. The room was so small now, the ceiling pressing against his neck, that he couldn't back away. "Look." She held the long slit open, her fingers pulling the skin and flesh back. The red made a net over her hand, collecting in thicker lines that coursed to the point of her elbow and trickled off. A red pool had formed between her knee and his, where their weight pressed the mattress down low.

The blue line inside her arm was brighter now, revealed. "Go on," she said. "Touch it." She leaned forward, bringing her mouth close to his ear. "You have to."

He reached out—slowly—and lay his fingertips on the blue line. For a moment he felt a shock, like the one the man in the bar had given him. But he didn't draw his hand away from the slit the woman held open to him. Under his fingertips he felt the tremble of the blood inside.

Her eyelids had drawn down, so that she looked at him through her lashes. Smiling. "Don't go . . ." He saw her tongue move across the edges of her teeth. "There's more . . ."

She had to let go of the edges, to guide him. The skin and flesh slid against his fingers, under the ridge of his knuckles. He could still see inside the opening, past her hand and his.

She teased a white strand away from the bone. "Here . . ." She looped his fingers under the tendon. As his fingers curled around it, stretching and lifting it past the glistening muscle, the hand at the end of the arm, her hand, curled also. The fingers bent, holding nothing, a soft gesture, a caress.

He could barely breathe. When the air came into his throat, it was heavy with the woman's sweet smell, and the other smell, the raw, sharper one that he'd caught off his uncle.

"See?" The woman bent her head low, looking up through her lashes into his eyes. Her breasts glowed with sweat. Her hair trailed across her open arm, the ends of the dark strands tangling in the blood. "See—it's not so bad, is it?"

She wanted him to say no, she wanted him to say it was okay. She didn't want him to be frightened. But he couldn't say anything. The smell had become a taste lying on his tongue. He finally managed to shake his head.

Her smile was a little bit sad. "Okay, then." She nodded slowly. "Come on."

The hand at the end of the arm had squeezed into a fist, a small one because her hands were so small. The blood that had trickled down into her palm seeped out from between the fingers and thumb. With her other hand, she closed his fingers around the white tendon tugged up from inside. She closed her grip around his wrist and pulled, until the tendon snapped, both ends coming free from their anchor on the bone.

She made him lift his hand up, the ends of the tendon dangling from where it lay across his fingers. She had tilted her head back, the cords in her throat drawn tight.

"Come on . . ." She leaned back against the pillow. She pulled him toward her. One of her hands lay on the mattress, palm upward, open again, red welling up from the slit in her arm. With her other hand she guided his hand. His fingers made red smears across the curve of her rib cage. "Here . . ." She forced his fingertips underneath. "You have to push hard." The skin parted and his fingers sank in, the thin bone of the rib sliding across the tips.

"That's right . . ." She nodded as she whispered, eyes closed. "Now you've got it. . . ."

Her hand slid down from his, down his wrist and trailing along his forearm. Not holding and guiding him any longer, but just touching him. He knew what she wanted him to do. His fingers curled around the rib, the blood streaming down to his elbow as the skin opened wider. He lifted and pulled, and the woman's rib cage came up toward him, the ones higher snapping free from her breastbone, all of them grinding softly against the hinge of her spine.

His hand moved inside, the wing of her ribs spreading back. Her skin parted in a curve running up between her breasts. He could see everything now, the shapes that hung suspended in the red space, close to each other, like soft nestled stones. The shapes trembled as his hand moved between them, the webs of sinew stretching, then peeling open, the spongy tissue easing around his hand and forearm.

He reached up higher, his body above hers now, balancing his weight on his other hand hard against the mattress, deep in the red pool along her side. Her knees pressed into the points of his hips.

He felt it then, trembling against his palm. His hand closed around it, and he saw it in her face as he squeezed it tight into his fist.

The skin parted further, the red line dividing her throat, to the hinge of her jaw. She lifted herself up from the pillow, curling around him, the opening soft against his chest. She wrapped her arm around his shoulders to hold him closer to her.

She tilted her head back, pressing her throat to his mouth. He opened his mouth, and his mouth was full, choking him until he had to swallow. The heat streaming across his face and down his own throat pulsed with the trembling inside his fist.

He swallowed again now, faster, the red heat opening inside him.

It was lying on the bed, not moving. He stood there looking at it. He couldn't even hear it breathing anymore. The only sound in the little room was a slow dripping from the edge of the mattress onto the floor.

He reached down, fingertip trembling, and touched its arm. Its hand lay open against the pillow, palm upward. Underneath the red, the flesh was white and cold. He touched the edge of the opening in its forearm. Already, the blue vein and the tendon had drawn back inside, almost hidden. The skin had started to close, the ends of the slit becoming a faint white line, that he couldn't even feel, though he left a smeared fingerprint there. He pulled back his hand, then he turned away from the bed and stumbled out into the hallway with the single light bulb hanging from the ceiling.

They looked up and saw him as he walked across the bar. He didn't push the empty chairs aside, but hit them with his legs, shoving his way past them.

His uncle Tommy scooted over, making room for him at the booth. He sat down hard, the back of his head striking the slick padding behind him.

They had all been laughing and talking just before, but they had gone quiet now. His father's buddies fumbled with the bottles in front of them, not wanting to look at him.

His father dug out a handkerchief, a blue checked one. "Here—" A quiet voice, the softest he'd ever heard his father say anything. His father held out the handkerchief across the table. "Clean yourself up a little."

He took the handkerchief. For a long time, he sat there and looked down at his hands and what was on them.

They were all laughing again, making noise to keep the dark pushed back. His father and his uncle and their buddies roared and shouted and pitched the empties out the windows. The car barreled along, cutting a straight line through the empty night.

He laid his face into the wind. Out there, the dog ran at the edge of the darkness, its teeth bared, its eyes like bright heated coins. It ran over the stones and dry brush, keeping pace with the car, never falling behind, heading for the same destination.

The wind tore the tears from his eyes. The headlights swept across the road ahead, and he thought of the piece of paper folded in the book in his bedroom. The piece of paper meant nothing now, he could tear it into a million pieces. She'd know, too, the girl who played the flute and who'd given the piece of paper to him. She'd know when she saw him again, she'd know that things were different now, and they could never be the same again. They'd be different for her now, too. She'd know.

The tears striped his face, pushed by the wind. He wept in rage and shame at what had been stolen from him. Rage and shame that the woman down there, in the little room at the end of the street with all the lights, would be dead, would get to know over and over again what it was to die. That was what she'd stolen from him, from all of them.

He wept with rage and shame that now he was like them, he was one of them. He opened his mouth and let the wind hammer into his throat, to get out the stink and taste of his own sweat, which was just like theirs now.

The dog ran beside the car, laughing as he wept with rage and shame. Rage and shame at what he knew now, rage and shame that now he knew he'd never die.

GIRL'S NIGHT OUT

KATHE KOJA AND
BARRY N. MALZBERG

Annie: Thirty-six years old and already her breasts had begun to sag, accept the truth: faint erotic droop now that in ten years, five, would be less appetizing and more ominously maternal, then urged by gravity into the pendulous collapse of the old. Soft shell of flesh behind the high-buttoned shirt, not a place to cry in climax now but a place to merely cry, fall to the woes, the sheer brutality of her city. Around Annie's waist the slightest roll of fat, still mere pudge, but she did not believe in exercising, working out, had passed the physical when she came on duty at twenty-five and that was the end of that. Plenty of working out on the job, she thought; what a job. Up and down the corridors of the city, pad out, looking for knowledge, one by one the secrets of the city disclosed—unwillingly, unwillingly—to her.

Marvin: the cop's boyfriend. Oh, God, poor Annie, thirty-six and forty-two and they were *boyfriend* and *girlfriend*, what kinds of names were those for what they did, for what they were to one another? Sucking it up and putting it back, night after week after night again and the name for what they did could be as cute (*playing house, hide the salami*) as the boyfriend-girlfriend business. Marvin, half-bald and with his own spreading pudge, Marvin who had recently opened a CopyCopy franchise with borrowed money, most of it hers, had all kinds of names for her job, for what she did. "It's all shit," he told her, arm crooked about her shoulder, her head uncomfortable on his chest (which bore at times a resemblance to hers: but no use pointing that out), "just shit, just lies and more lies.

They lie to you, you lie to the lieutenant, the lieutenant lies to the chief who lies to the mayor. Who lies to the people. Who lie to you. Get it?"

Well, yes, she supposed she did get it. "Thank you for pointing that out," Annie said. Her back was aching again; she shifted against the sheets, squirmed for comfort, tried to stay out of the wet spot which always seemed to be on her side of the bed. "Now you can explain what's so noble about running a copy place." *With my money,* she thought, *and about five hundred from the bank.* "At least I'm trying to make a contribution, trying to extend—"

"Trying to *what*? Extend, lady, was that what I heard?" He leaned toward her, his gaze keen and persuasive, persuasive Marvin, casting back like CopyCopy refractory images of himself, little shades of Marvin on the wall, reproductions of Marvin in her vision: infinitely reproducible, eternally dead. —Well, maybe that was too harsh; you couldn't have this much energy, this much assurance and be dead, could you? "Make a difference," he said, and smiled in the way that he would only *after* he had gotten himself off, a don't-care, no-excuses smile. "Is that why you became a cop? A *detective*, excuse me, I don't mean to forget the promotion, is that why? What are you detecting these days, anyway? Kids who go off on one another in alleyways? Fathers who do things broadside to their daughters, nickel and dime window thieves hustling crap down back alleys? Oh, that's a major contribution to society, isn't it. Of course we don't talk much about the job," he said, "you aren't exactly forthcoming. Which is okay by me, but if you're talking about difference, Annie, what exactly is the point? All you're trying to do is solve what can't be solved; a pension can't be worth this."

It makes a difference to me, she wanted to say to this one example of the Marvins who lay beside her in the bed, but instead she said nothing, turning again in his loose grasp to face away from him, face the wall: bare wall, bare space for Marvin after that second divorce, three years ago and still no pictures, posters, nothing on his walls but a CopyCopy calendar with the old franchiser's name obliterated and his markered in. The least he could do was make up some calendars of his own. The least he could do was be halfway decent to her, she had been screwing him for five years, even before that miserable divorce, had put up with his crying and complaints; the least he could do was shut up, that would have been a decent thing under the circumstances but they never did, did they?

"Now what are you doing?" he said. "Busy, busy, always on the move, can't let it lie, detective, can't rest can you? But what now for God's sake, it's after midnight."

"I'm going home," she said. "I'm going home, there's work to do."

"Annie, come on, what the hell work could you have to do? at this hour?" *You're lying,* his gaze said, intense and subtle that gaze and he could muster more intensity, more sheer *eroticism* for argument than he could ever manage in fucking when the eyes, open only intermittently, said (and not to her but to the silent refracted self, the self inside): *come on, come on, get it over with now, I have to finish, have to get it done,* oh the wives had loved it, hadn't they? Well, maybe. No accounting for taste or the power of misguided pity and anyway with Marvin getting it over with fast was a blessing. "You're lying to me, Annie," he said. "You, too. See what I mean? All in a circle and little Annie out there in the alleys taking notes, but you ought to break the chain; or would that make too much of a difference?"

"No," she said, "as a matter of fact I'm not lying. I've got paperwork." Her panty hose were loose and baggy; she did not put them on. Buttoning her shirt, off-duty shirt that looked after all like the on-duty attire, uniform, uniform, no private place for Annie. *I have to go detect some paperwork, Marvin, that's what I have to do. I have to get away from you,* she almost said but let it go, said it instead with her gaze at the bare walls, past the bare walls into the bare space of their time together: boyfriend and girlfriend, sorrow and waste, Annie and Marvin and the wet spot always on her side. *I have to go someplace where I don't think about you,* she thought, *where I can't think about you. Good-bye.* "Good-bye," she said, standing, looking for her shoes. "Be in touch. Don't be a stranger."

"Annie," the man who had taken her money without giving her a note because if two people were close enough to make love they should not let paper come between them (and she had fallen for that, had let herself fall), "Annie, this is stupid. We don't have to talk, we don't have to sleep either if you don't want, we could just watch TV or something. Or if you're not satisfied down there, I could try to—"

"I can sleep at home," she said, "or watch TV or do that other thing myself without help. All right?" and to the door, out the door and, *What a sweetheart,* she thought, *what a wonderful generous guy. If I'm not satisfied down there, he'll help me.* No perp had ever made her a better or more sincere offer. The closed door was silent and she realized she had left her gloves inside. *Screw it,* she thought, *I'll get them next time, or buy some downtown if it's cold tomorrow.* Brown gloves with furry white lining, like the whores wear, the whores beckoning imperious as traffic cops to the patrollers downtown. In her early years she had worked entrapment detail a few times, been a whore with furry gloves on the winter streets, had tricked the tricks right into her circle: the best of the detail, even with the cold. She had always had a talent for connecting fast and she had—so young then—loved to hear the johns whimper with terror and sudden, stunning knowledge as the uniforms arrived. All the bullshit, all the come-ons and the hey-babys gone, gone, down the drain, all their smiles to silence as she sat and stroked her gloved hands against her knees: waiting as they did for the uniforms, waiting with a pleased and pleasant smile.

It was brutal outside, the cold hurt, the air small slivering knives in her harsh, uneven respiration; hard to breathe; *cold inside,* cold Annie now cold as a corpse, as a body in the street. She could no longer remember the first dead person she had ever seen—that was a myth, about never forgetting the first one— but she did remember the dead whore she found frozen in a bus stop shelter, sheltered from nothing, eyes open and hands in her pockets; she had had no gloves either, nothing to keep her warm. That, too, had been in the first year, when she was still riding patrol, riding with men who disdained or actively hated her or tried to come on to her all at the same time; until after the hearings and more bad publicity, it was apparently not all right to harass policewomen (although calling them "cunt" or "bitch" was not specifically harassment, it was all the same sort of good-natured hazing all the new officers had to put up with, and you were a bitch, a cunt anyway if you complained). So first-year Annie, still passionate, had argued with the dead whore's pimp at the morgue, too new to understand his display of decency by responding to her call, came in but that was as far as he had been willing to take it. She had tried to shame him into at least taking custody of the body, at least giving the body her proper name.

"She's listed as a Jane Doe, Bobby," she had said, her back aching, her eyes burning. "For God's sake, the least you can do is give us her real name for the death certificate. She had *your* name in her pocket, that's why I called you. You must owe her something for that."

Pettishly, pulling on his gloves, expensive leather driving gloves: "I don't fucking *know* her real name, all right?" They give themselves names and are gone, and

Jane Doe the whore was buried, buried in the frozen ground but being frozen herself probably didn't mind too much, did she? Did she? Or was that another lie and was the afterlife a CopyCopy franchise *too* and you just kept on feeling everything just as you had before, the same stuff infinitely replicated, again and again and again *and* again, all the way down to dust? Merciful, unfeeling dust but who knew even then? There were no takers, no statements from the opposition here.

So: away, now, from Marvin, driving one-handed, the other in her pocket but cold, still so cold and her bed back there was cold, too, the sheets austere and pale green: pictures of the forest on her walls, the forest in autumn, Bambi's lair in early spring. When Annie was a little girl, she had wanted to be a botanist. Study plants: play with flowers. Growing things. Did the plants feel what it was like to grow, roots moving slow as death itself underground? And did they feel the coming of the cold, when they shriveled in winter, when they fell into the darkness, did they know what was happening?

Herself under blankets later, cold and cold, two sleeping pills and she did not remember passing the cusp, going into the darkness, did not remember when the alarm she had routinely set rang, and rang, and rang, ejecting her if only temporarily from that darkness, startling her, starting her, beginning the next of Annie's days.

Which lurched ahead, no meaning, even on the new night shift she tried to keep her days full, tried not to make of herself an invalid, striking at sleep against the day, against the drawn shades: she read, she watched television, she thought of her life, she thought of essences and chronology draining in her sterile, functional little civil servant's apartment. Of course no call from Marvin, no call *to* Marvin, to hell with Marvin and his wet spots and his certainty of lives, and she took herself out to dinner, a late dinner for the midnight shift. Bloomington was a college town, but one could hardly infer this from the bleak restaurant and its neighborhood and the hard, lost people who sat one by one or in pairs in the dining room or at the bar and did not say anything to her and little more to each other. *Here it is,* she thought, *this is it, this is life,* and a man laughed, watching the waitress walk away he laughed, and said something to the woman with whom he shared the table; who did not laugh in return but made the brief smile of the unwilling accomplice; what had the man said? Nice ass? What's the blue plate special and do you come with it? It was the kind of thing Marvin would have said.

After the restaurant, it was still too early to check into work, but Annie did not want to go home, did not know exactly what she wanted (had she ever?) and so drove the old car around Bloomington's downtown and then to the university, barren and vacant now, the exuberant children done in perhaps by weather, colder still tonight. She rubbed at the windshield with her ungloved palm, the defroster working only in small clear islands leaving the larger, clotted patches of white. Cold fingers on cold glass, it had been stupid not to go back for her gloves, but nothing, *nothing* was going to put her back into contact with Marvin unless he called first, he could keep the gloves, he could keep the loan, too, could stiff her for seventy-five hundred dollars; it was worth it not to feel that she had *bought* this terrible man for that amount.

New shift: still only the second week. Midnight was all the same, they told her, she would adapt. She shrugged, did not particularly care, day or night, night and day what did it matter? Marvin was right on that issue: everything was a circle, lie up, lie down, lie all around and: It's not for long, they told her, just a routine reassignment to balance off staff levels, wait until after the election and the pressure will come off, which as Marvin could have told her was another lie; but she did not need Marvin to figure that one out any more than she needed Marvin to have an orgasm; and it had been a long time, hadn't it, Miss Eagle-Eye, Miss Marple, Miss Tracer of Lost Knowledge? Had been a long, long time, not that Marvin had noticed or—and here was some measure of her plunge—*she* had taken account of it, until now. You burrowed deep into the blanket of your life, the coverlet and the folds covered you, inside and outside ceasing to contrast, differentiation gone forever and wasn't she too young to be having thoughts like this? No, she guessed, having them proved evidently she was not.

Her night was quiet: reports on a high school hanging (and weren't they surprised to find the girl dangling in the faculty bathroom, stretched out and blue at the end of a rope; a pregnancy? AIDS? lost love? Seventeen; who knew) which appeared to be suicide; a mutual husband-and-wife asphyxiation when the Medicare benefits had run out, chronic nephritis the dry-eyed son had said in his statement, they would have gone broke paying the bills (and her insane urge to pat his hand, say, *This way is better, isn't it?* just to see him, just to see his face; funny how you could always, always tell the bastards; like Marvin: two words and you knew); a few problems with the chronic prostitution at the south end which had picked up apparently in the long, continuing absence of Miss Eagle-Eye, she supposed. When the cat's away. Or something. Cold sifting air beneath the desk, the broken space heater squatting miserable as a pet beside her ankles, her only pet and companion in the room: thin staff at night, most of them cruising, warmer in the squad cars than in here. Paperwork: that was the lie that was no lie. Working her way through it, the pile deep as a pile of leaves, some botanist: signing her name over and over, *Annie, Annie, Annie, Annie* here and here and here. When her shift ended, she shuffled outside, hands in pockets to her car: and saw the color, bright scarf, something, hanging from the dumpster.

Of course, she had to look against her sudden cool revulsion, that was her profession, it was nothing, but she had to look: who throws away a brand-new scarf? Across the parking lot, cold inside and out and inside the dumpster, pillowed with trash, frozen garbage and broken boxes and half of a busted crate, dead rats: and a dead woman, curled like a fetus, one end of the scarf still soft, gripping her neck.

Another Jane Doe, another whore maybe, too, but it was hard to tell: she was almost too pretty to be a whore, too clean-looking, too expensive-looking. Long dark hair, model's pallor, very pretty this one and her clothes were pretty too, as pretty as she was dead. Annie gasped, the impact of the dead woman, the sight of the dead woman, and each was the same, the same as the first time, as the last time: and with the sick feeling of replication she reached toward the dead, pretty woman in the dumpster, the absolute pallor of those features locking that face into the remoteness, the falsely gentle artifice of portraiture and in her exposed pectoral, Annie could now see the small fissure, the cradling stamp of blood which told the story and the bullet somewhere within the skin, smashed toward the bone. Reaching to touch her, to confirm the mortality of the ruin there before she went back inside to report this, begin the tedious motions of official discovery which would keep her there for hours, hours and hours and maybe longer than that, reaching toward the corpse she felt in the instant of touch, the moment of communion that dead hand and the leap, the instant spring of the cold as if on tendrils, little tendrils and strings of cold grasping her, and in that grasp and spring the pressure, small squeezing pressure of that hand on her own

and, *She's alive, this one is alive,* as the whickering cold passed through her wrist, pulsing with the rhythm of life and the moving eyes of the corpse, woman now,
rolling in slow arctic motion as the pressure of cold fingers, tendrils, strings became enormous, hard enough to bruise.

As Annie dragged her hand free, as she stumbled back toward the building
only fifty yards away: *She's alive.* Get help, get a doctor, and still stumbling in cold
astonishment that they did not respond to her screams, only stared at her as she
fell deadweight on the crash bar, as she cried out her knowledge, until she became
aware that all of this was strangling in her throat, she had made no sound at all:
and then in the language of panic, of gesture her swooping arm: *Hurry!* and then
they moved, uncertain, but they moved and *"Get her to a hospital,"* she said that
aloud, she was sure she had heard herself speak: her own voice but lower, higher,
something, different, as if the cold regained, metal box and tin like a coffin, a
body in garbage had gifted her with her own true voice: not the burble of shock,
not the blank laconic accent of the law, the streets, the criminal justice system
but her own true voice, calling, testifying, directing as: *Yes* in the dumpster, *yes* in
the scarf and movement, *yes,* as they returned from the parking lot, the cold to
summon the white wagon, the paramedics, as they turned to her as if to listen to
what her new voice had to say.

St. Luke's, the statue just to the left of the heavy red EMERGENCY sign: apostle
and healer and the staff had offered Annie no real resistance. "This is a criminal
investigation," she could have said. "I must have access," but no one said much of
anything, no challenge, no confrontation as she walked into and then cleared
Sylvia's room: "We are entitled to privacy during questioning," she could have
said, or, simply: "Finders keepers," but it was unnecessary. They responded to her
without heat, they left her and the woman alone: Sylvia.

Sylvia, that was the woman's name, one of the first things she had said when
she returned to a consciousness roped in running plastic, tubes in and out, veins
and nostrils but no identification, only a halting and then stammering line of
questions: her name was Sylvia and she did not know what she was doing here.
What had happened? What had happened to her? She remembered nothing but
the screams near the dumpster and then her slow arc toward light; she did not
know from where she had come or what all of this meant; she knew her name,

that she had been lying badly hurt yet somehow untouched, some cold and central part of her inviolate and without pain.

Lying there, morgue-beautiful still with her gown and her tubes, upper lip dry against her teeth and she reached out to Annie, grasped her again in that cold tendentious fashion, the little tendrils now with faint blood-heat and in the breathing silence created by this touch she and Annie looked at one another for a long time, blood past pallor in that face now, the swimming aura of life and implication. "I don't remember," Sylvia said, "I don't know what happened. I saw light, and then you were touching me. I don't remember anything before. My name is Sylvia; I don't know where I live or who I am. I only know that somehow I deserve to be here."

Her gown, blue printed high and modest around that throat and with her free hand Annie reached, gently tugged it down, lower, to stare at the place where the hole had been: and could not know its presence.

"I deserve to be here," Sylvia said again.

"*No,*" Annie said, squeezing the hand she held, "don't say that. Someone hurt you: that was wrong. It wasn't your fault, do you understand? Someone *shot* you, Sylvia, I saw it, I saw the wound—" and Annie touched it, touched the place where the hole had been "—and it *wasn't your fault.*"

"No one hurt me," Sylvia said; incredibly she was smiling, dry lip across dry teeth, flesh against smooth enamel; "they just don't understand," she said. She put her hand atop Annie's hand, the one at her gown; their other hands were still connected. "They thought I was one thing," she said, "but I was really something else."

Annie said nothing; felt as if in amazement that cold vitality, that feeling of blood beneath the skin; how smooth Sylvia's hands were. The terrible wound already closing over when the attendants had begun to load her onto the stretcher, and in its place the smooth, smooth skin.

"What do you think?" Sylvia said.

Annie's hands without motion; the tubes going in and out. A little light above the bed began to blink, red and out, red and out.

Marvin: and it was she who called him after all, called him from her apartment, from the pale end of the morning after the dark had gone. Crouched on the chair, arms stiff somehow as if she could still feel those tendrils, that cold: "She's an amnesiac," Annie said, holding the phone to her mouth as if Marvin were there beside her, or on the other end of the world and only this instrument could make bearable any conversation they might share. "She doesn't remember anything. Who shot her, how she might have gotten there, anything."

"Why haven't you called?" he said. "That was some way you walked out last week, I never saw you act that way before. I don't know who you think you are or what you're doing but that's not the kind of thing you should do, I won't be—"

"She just doesn't know," Annie said. "Don't you get it? But it isn't her fault; none of it is. I told her that, I said, Sylvia, it's not your—"

"Listen, Annie, I don't know what the hell you're talking about and I can't stay on the phone all day, I'm busy. I have a business to run down here, there's people in the shop and I don't have time for this. You just be over tonight, I should be back around midnight, and if I'm not, you wait for me. You understand? Annie, are you listening?"

She smelled dust; she smelled her whole life around her, bereft of conscious odor, of sweat or burning, of gasoline or cosmetics or blood. Dust, everywhere, dust on the phone as she put it down, dust on the coffee table, dust in the air. None of the rooms contained real color, beige walls, brown carpets: only the testament of muted greens, bedsheets and calendar, her closet filled with businesslike clothing, her shoes in tired piles, brown and black. Sylvia was an amnesiac; it was not and never could be her fault.

At the hospital it was easy, easy: how could they stop this? how declare it was not feasible? Sylvia was sane, she was healthy (*the closed wound, the open door*) and there was no way, no way whatsoever Annie knew that they could keep Sylvia in the hospital or prevent her from staying with the detective who had found her. She was amnesiac, certainly, but as certainly competent to make decisions; her condition left her both vulnerable and closed off, nowhere else for her to go, nowhere else where she might have been taken, no one else hovering on the perimeters of her life; all of it easier than Annie could have imagined, first the thought, then the circumvention, then the plan working itself with a kind of uncoiling ease which confirmed everything which Marvin had said to her that night: lies, it was all lies, she lied to the staff who lied to headquarters who lied to the chief who lied to the press by denying it all and soon enough Annie, in a kind of thrall she could not have imagined, would be sitting in her rooms with Sylvia, just the two of them in a kind of confidentiality which Annie had intimated but never known, guessed without experiencing, longed for without identifying. And then Sylvia would, from the very vacancy of her history, begin telling all her secrets, one by one by one while Annie, detecting, would be absorbing those secrets in a kind of attention and rigor she could not have imagined she would possess. "*She was dead*," she could have told them. "*She had no vitals when I found her in that dumpster*," but somewhere between the cold and the rescuing ambulance those tendrils, those pointing streaks had become warmth, a strange, clinging warmth which rose through Sylvia and arced into Annie, together now through the process of circumstance into what had become an absolute. Looking at Sylvia dressing now in Annie's own clothes, chosen with care, carried to the hospital, Annie could see not so much the woman herself, either dumpster corpse or restored simulacrum of that corpse later, but something else: she saw replications of herself, CopyCopies, layers upon layers of Annies which were being sent back to her through those same tendrils which first had carried the cold, then the warmth: Annie's blouse and blue jeans, Annie's socks and shoes, Annie's silence and silent acceptance: but why reject for Sylvia that which she seemed— through her job, her wretched relations with Marvin—to have accepted for herself? Annie's old ski jacket, zippered against the cold; smooth hands, bare as Annie's were bare. In the car Sylvia said nothing, sat gazing calmly out the window, watching Bloomington pass by; the heater wheezed and blew dust, warm air into their faces; in the apartment the dust settled, and was still.

Neither of them asked the obvious questions: *Why am I here? Who are you? Where do you come from?* Sylvia sat quietly, looking out the window, gazing past the blinds; Annie went back to work. When she came home, Sylvia was still in the chair; she might not have moved once; she was still wearing the blouse, the jeans, the shoes. Slowly Annie approached her, set down her purse, pulled off her coat. Slowly she sat beside her, sat on the floor as Sylvia turned slightly in the chair so that Annie was almost touching, was closer still. Annie's head against Sylvia's knee; silence between them, detective and victim, woman and woman.

"Are you a prostitute?" Annie said.

Sylvia shrugged. "I suppose," she said. "I suppose I could have been. You're a policewoman," she said, "a detective; aren't you?"

"Yes," Annie said.

They sat for a long time that way. Annie could feel her own blood, moving through her body, moving through the silent chambers of her heart, whisk of ventricle, stutter of motion. Inside Sylvia's body everything was still, its inner noises denied by that greater silence, the envelope of flesh, not of mystery but memory: the body, and how it hurts: the body and how it heals. Replication, and disaster; flesh, and blood.

"Men like me," Sylvia said, smiling her dry-lipped smile. "They like me a lot. But they're never as smart as they think they are, or should be."

"I don't understand," Annie said, "I don't understand anything. I know this man—" and stopped. Sylvia waited. Annie leaned her head against Sylvia's knee, pressed it there strongly, the denim of the jeans strangely cool against her face. She said nothing; Sylvia said nothing. Both were waiting. Finally Annie said, without moving, barely moving her lips, "Why?" That was the question which it seemed she had wanted from the first to ask, but trapped within her own re-straint, her panic and dismay could not: an absurd solemnity and shyness which piece by piece Sylvia, her nearness, her silence, had stripped from her: "Why are they like that? What do they think they are? What do they want of us? Or is it really us they want," she could have asked, "or the casting image which they seek, some huge, idealized image of themselves tossed up and over the screen of or-gasm, some answer to a question they are too self-absorbed to ask? What is it, what do they want from us?" and she had never conceived that she would even be asking such questions, conditional or otherwise, of anyone, let alone an amnesiac shooting victim yanked first from a dumpster and then a hospital bed. She had not even known that these questions were important to her or that it was pos-sible to frame them, but now she knew nothing else, was nothing but a swirl of disorder and pain around those seeking questions and it was possible to wonder, memory in mind of that smooth, vacant place on Sylvia's body, the hole that was not a hole, if Sylvia had any kind of objective reality or had merely appeared in response to Annie's questions, Annie's needs, a need pasted together of the shards of her own confused insight and Marvin's contempt, of her midnight shift and her *own* contempt for what she had become: through her fault, her silent and grievous fault.

"Sylvia," she said, leaning harder into that knee, that bone, that stalk of flesh, no tendrils now but the smooth, desperate connection established in the cleaving silence. "Please," she said, "tell me. Who else can I ask? Who else can you tell? I need this, Sylvia," she said, "it's just us and I need to know."

"Yes," Sylvia said, looking at her: and the two of them seemed to conjoin, conflate in the agony of Annie's need: "yes," she said, "I'll tell you, I'll tell you all about them, I'll tell you what they are and what *we* are too. I'll teach you: and then I'll show you what to do." Lustrous eyes, and the slow, dreamy caress of her breath, so soft it stirred no dust, woke no echoes, displaced no memories or agonies of same: the silence of the apartment, the feel of denim, the arc of defiance, submission, those looping strophes in the light.

The phone: and she called him, of course she called him, they would not speak otherwise for why should *he* call *her?* "Marvin," she said when he answered, Copy-Copy loud, loud behind him, "Marvin, I want you to meet someone, Sylvia, she's my new friend, I want you to come and see us together, we've been busy, but now I want you to come."

"Is that right?" Marvin said, "you want me to come calling? After you ignore me, you don't call for a week, two weeks, and you expect me to come when you call? Forget it, Annie," he said, "just forget it. If I have any time later on this week, *I'll* call *you*, but otherwise you can just forget——"

and Sylvia in the corner, winking. "You don't have to take that," she said by her posture, the curve of her lips, "he's nothing to you, you never have to listen to anything like that from him again."

"No," Annie said, "no, Marvin, I don't think you understand, I don't think you understand your position and while we're talking, Marvin, where's that seventy-five hundred you borrowed?"

Silence. The sounds of replication, of one and another, and another, and another. "Listen here," Marvin said, although more quietly, "listen, Annie, we don't need——"

"You didn't even give me a note," Annie said, gazing at Sylvia who gazed back at her, "so I guess I'll have to take it out of you personally instead of looking for the courts to do it, and I will, I will, you have no idea how sure I am about this." He said nothing over the phone, seemed to be breathing, shaking his head, the sound of teeth, then clicking. "I want you to come over here, Marvin," Annie said, "I have my rights too, this cuts both ways."

"I'm busy," he said, "I'm busy down here. This is a job you know."

and Sylvia laughed, the sound of her laughter present somehow through the wire, through the made connection and

Marvin said, "Now look here—" and Annie said, "No, no, *you* look. As soon as you close, you come down, you come over here," and put the phone down, determined, smashing the connection, smashing Marvin, and then looking over at Sylvia. "Was that all right?" she wanted to say, "did I do it the right way?" But she did not say that because there was no need to say it, Sylvia gave her the answer unbidden, streams of further laughter and then she flung the phone high in the air, watched it hit the wall, then bounce to the floor, and Annie said, "It was always that easy, wasn't it? It was never that much of a problem, anytime we wanted we could have done this?"

"Yes," Sylvia said, "yes, we could have done it, they lie helpless to us, to our touch." In her tone, her voice their utter fragility, their vulnerable posturing, their torment: and the laughter again. Annie laughing harder now and all of their sounds gathering, the crash of the dumpster, clatter of the ambulance, whicker and clash of the copy machines, dim sounds of sirens or solicitation: all of it present, all of it just.

Later: Marvin: but not too much later, he had closed the store early, and perhaps responded to something in Annie's voice. Marvin: Marvin in the room, coming through the door with his own key, looking at Annie and then at Sylvia, at them together in confusion and then with a slow, gathering attention which might have been apprehension.

"What is this?" he said, "what's going on? Is this what you wanted me to see?" And Annie, smiling, came upon him.

"Go ahead," Sylvia said in the darkness, the deep shadows concealing her, taking her from the frame of vision, no reference in the room. "Go ahead: do this. I've taught you what they are," Sylvia said, "and now you know exactly what to do."

Oh, the luster of Sylvia's eyes and the slow, dreamy caress of her assent, the imparted knowledge between them fire, and she came toward Marvin. Astonished, he retreated, one step, two: "Annie," he said, "*Annie*," and she came closer again, he was against the wall, hammered against the wall in the way that she had been pressed against the bed, as indifferently, as carelessly he had fucked her and, "Here," Annie said, "here's what you want," and oh, *oh* that slow connection, the arc of defiance, submission, the looping strophes; the thin and greedily suspired little rivulets of blood, taking in the blood as she took him in against all of the circumstances, the loops and strangled lines of her new necessities.

Sylvia, laughing in the dark.

"Is this what you wanted? Is *this* what you wanted?"

"Oh, yes, oh, yes," she said, gasping with the flow, more and more and she felt herself beginning to suffocate, closure of the breath, closure of the wound and fought to breathe even as she would not release that connection, oh, no, *oh*, no: no release, no closure, the fullness of the fluid, the fullness of her stink, the keening and the roaring and the wheedling, greedy, gulping little sounds of her ingestion; oh, yes. Oh, Marvin, and all of the Marvins, a hundred copied Marvins plunging beneath Annie ascendant, her history calamitously restored: in state, in passion, in frieze atop her prey, that broken man beneath restored now as well, pure as an original and Annie atop whispering, "I am Sylvia I am Sylvia I am Sylvia," detecting no longer, prostituting nothing but the attitudes of those feeble copies left behind now, drained empty now, dusty-dry in silence on the floor: "I *am* Sylvia," she said, mouth sore, throat heavy with what lay inside her, the squared confines of the dumpster as deep and icy as the replicating night.

NIGHT LAUGHTER

ELLEN KUSHNER

THE THING IS, IT'S JUST THAT YOU START TO HATE
the daytime. All the bad things happen during the day: rush hour, lines at the
bank, unwanted phone calls, junk mail, overworked people being rotten to each
other. Night is the time for lovers, for reading alone by lamplight, for dancing,
for cool breezes. It doesn't matter if your blood is hot or cold; it's the time for
you.

"Come on," I say, tugging at his wrist, "come on, let's have fun!" He holds
back, reluctant. "Come on, let's dance!"

All over the city the lights are blinking off and on all the time. Night laughter. "Come on into the night!"

"Crazy," he says, "that's what you are."

Rich nighttime laughter bubbles in me. I let a little of it show in the corners
of my mouth to scare him. He's scared. He says, "You wanna dance?"

I turned away, shrug nonchalantly. "Nah, not really."

"You wanna . . . go for a ride?"

"Nah," I lick my lips, trite, unmistakable. "Let's go for a walk. In the park."

"No one's in the park at this hour."

"We'll be. Just the two of us, alone. With the long paths all to ourselves."

He rises, follows. The night is like that.

He's wearing a good suit, the best he's got. The night's the time for dressing
up, dressing high, dressing fine. Your real night clothes, those are the pressed

black and starched white that a gentleman wore, with maybe a touch of gold or a bright ribbon sash setting it off. And a woman was always sleek and bright, lean and clean as a new machine, streamlined as a movie queen. My dress is like that; it clings and swirls so smooth, so long. I stride along beside him in my spiky heels, like a thoroughbred horse with tiny goat's hoofs. Long ago, in Achaea, God wore goat's hoofs and played the pipes all night long. Pipes of reed, like the mouth of a saxophone, blowing long and lonely down the wind between the standing trees.

The trees of the park are sparse, hanging over us in ordered rows, dark and tall as the street lamps between them, but under the tree is shadow. The circles of light, when you come to them, are bright enough to read by. Little insects buzz and flutter against their haloes.

Bums are asleep on the benches; poor guys, don't even know if it's night or day. I always avoid them. The only thing they want is money; they never knew how to have a good time, or they've forgotten how. I knew someone once who couldn't bear the light of day, quite right. He'd get out of his white jacket and into a velvet dressing gown, put on dark glasses and retire from the sunrise like poison, while we watched the lights going out in strings across the park, and he'd be making his jokes about what to do with the waking birds and their noise. Owl, I called him, and he called me Mouse. But finally we couldn't take it anymore, he took to sucking red life out of a wine bottle with thick glass, green as sunshades, and he lost the taste for real life altogether; now for all I know he's one of the bums on the benches. They know they're safe: we won't touch them if we don't have to.

This man I'm with, he keeps darting his eyes left and right, as if he's looking for a cop or a junkie or a mugger. I take his arm, press up against him. "You're cold," he says.

I flip my silver scarf twice around my throat. "No, I'm not."

Lights from the passing cars streak our path. I tilt my head back, eyes veiled against the glare of sky, the light bouncing off the clouds.

He says, "I think I see my office. There, over the trees."

I lead him deeper into the darkness, toward the boat pond.

He says, "Y'know it's really dangerous in here," coming all the time along with me.

I kick off my shoes, they go shooting up like silver rockets out over the old lake. My feet press the damp earth, soft and cool, perfect night feeling. Not just earth under them; there's old cigarette stubs moldering into clay and hard edges of glass and a little bird's bone.

Considerately I lean my back against a tree, unwrap my scarf and smile one of my dream smiles.

"Cigarette?" I ask huskily. He fumbles in his pocket, holds the white stick out to me; I just lean there, holding the pose, and finally he places the end between my polished lips. I look up sultry through my eyelashes, and he produces a light.

Oh, the gorgeousness of that tiny flame, orange and strong in the darkness! You don't get orange like that by daylight. I suck it to a perfect scarlet circle on the end of my cigarette, and then I give it back to him, trailing its ghostly wisp of smoke. Automatically he smokes it.

Automatic, still too nervous. He doesn't know how to have a good time! He was a mistake, a good-looking mistake. But then, not every night is perfect. I sigh so quietly only the wind hears me. Frogs are croaking in the pond, competing with crickets for airspace over the distant traffic roar. Another good night, opening itself to me. All you have to do is want it.

"C'mere," I say in my husky dusky cigarette voice. His tie so neatly tied, his shoes so clean they catch the little light on their rounded surface . . . He walks toward me. The expression on his face is steadier, more hopeful: here at last is something he thinks he'll understand. He buries his face in my neck. My white arms glow around his shoulders.

He's all pressed into me now, I'm like sandwich filling between him and the tree. There's a bubble of laughter in my throat; I'm thinking, What would happen if I swiftly stepped aside and all his hard softness were pressing against bark? But I just shift my weight, enjoying the way he picks up on it, shifting his body to conform to me. Now he likes the night. Now his hands have some life in them, running the maze between my dress and my skin. With my fingertips I touch his ears, his jaw, the rim of his collar, while he presses, presses, his breath playing like a brassy syncopated band, his life pulsing hard, trying to burst through his clothes. Owl always said, Let them do that.

He's working my dress up around my waist. His hands are hot. Ah, he's happy. He's fumbling with his buckle. I breathe on him and make him laugh.

"Fun?" I ask.

"Mm-hmm."

"You're having a good time now."

I tickle the base of his throat and he throws back his head, face joyous in the mercury-colored cloudlight. Night laughter rises in me, too strong anymore to be contained. It wells through my mouth and fixes on his throat, laughter hard and sharp as the edge of a champagne glass, wet and bright as a puddle in neon.

It's fun, it's wild, it's night-blooming orchid and splashing fountains and the fastest car you've ever been in, speeding along the coast . . . It's *life*.

He hardly weighs anything now. I leave him under the tree; the bums can have what he's got left. I take a pair of slippers out of my bag; it's after midnight, but I won't be running home barefoot, not like some unfortunate fairy-tale girl. Midnight's just the beginning for me.

In the distance a siren goes wailing by. Unsprung trucks speed across town, their trailers pounding as though they're beating the pavement to death. Moonlight and street light blend on the surface of the water.

I pass under the big statue of the hero on the horse, and walk jaunty and silent footed among his many lamplit shadows. Around the bend I see a white gleam, too white and sharp to be anything but a pressed evening jacket. For a moment I think that it is Owl again. But his face, when he turns to look at me, is different.

His jacket is a little rumpled but not dirty, and his black bow tie is perfectly in place. He is smiling. I catch up to him.

"Cigarette?" he says.

"No thanks, I just had one."

He takes one from a gold-plated case, lights it and inhales slowly and contentedly. Where his lips touched it I see a dark stain.

"Hungry?"

"Not a bit."

"Wonderful night," I say.

He nods, still smiling. "Let's go dancing," he says.

We'll have a good time.

La Dame

❧

Tanith Lee

'The game is done! I've won! I've won!'
Quoth she, and whistles thrice.
THE ANCIENT MARINER
COLERIDGE.

O F THE LAND, AND WHAT THE LAND GAVE YOU—WAR,
pestilence, hunger, pain—he had had enough. It was the sea he wanted. The sea
he went looking for. His grandfather had been a fisherman, and he had been
taken on the ships in his boyhood. He remembered enough. He had never been
afraid. Not of water, still or stormy. It was the ground he had done with, full of
graves and mud.

His name was Jeluc, and he had been a soldier fourteen of his twenty-eight
years. He looked a soldier as he walked into the village above the sea.

Some ragged children playing with sticks called out foul names after him.
And one ran up and said, "Give us a coin." "Go to hell," he answered, and the
child let him alone. It was not a rich village.

The houses huddled one against another. But at the end of the struggling,
straggling street, a long stone pier went out and over the beach, out into the water. On the beach there were boats lying in the slick sand, but at the end of the
pier was a ship, tied fast, dipping slightly, like a swan.

She was pale as ashes, and graceful, pointed and slender, with a single mast,
the yard across it with a sail the colour of turned milk bound up. She would take
a crew of three, but one man could handle her. She had a little cabin with a hollow window and door.

Birds flew scavenging round and round the beach; they sat on the house roofs between, or on the boats. But none alighted on the ship.

Jeluc knocked on the first door. No one came. He tried the second and third doors, and at the fourth a woman appeared, sour and scrawny.

"What is it?" She eyed him like the Devil. He was a stranger.

"Who owns the pale ship?"

"The ship? Is Fatty's ship."

"And where would I find Fatty?"

"From the wars, are you?" she asked. He said nothing. "I have a boy to the wars. He never came back."

Jeluc thought, Poor bitch. Your son's making flowers in the muck. But then, the thought, What would he have done here?

He said again, "Where will I find Fatty?"

"Up at the drinking-house," she said, and pointed.

He thanked her and she stared. Probably she was not often thanked.

The drinking-house was out of the village and up the hill, where sometimes you found the church. There seemed to be no church here.

It was a building of wood and bits of stone, with a sloping roof, and inside there was the smell of staleness and ale.

They all looked up, the ten or so fellows in the house, from their benches.

He stood just inside the door and said, "Who owns the pale ship?"

"I do," said the one the woman had called Fatty. He was gaunt as a rope. He said, "What's it to you?"

"You don't use her much."

"Nor I do. How do you know?"

"She has no proper smell of fish, or the birds would be at her."

"There you're wrong," said Fatty. He slurped some ale. He did have a fat mouth, perhaps that was the reason for his name. "She's respected, my lady. Even the birds respect her."

"I'll buy your ship," said Jeluc. "How much?"

All the men murmured.

Fatty said, "Not for sale."

Jeluc had expected that. He said, "I've been paid off from my regiment. I've got money here, look." And he took out some pieces of silver.

The men came round like beasts to be fed, and Jeluc wondered if they would set on him, and got ready to knock them down. But they knew him for a soldier. He was dangerous beside them, poor drunken sods.

"I'll give you this," said Jeluc to Fatty.

Fatty pulled at his big lips.

"She's worth more, my lady."

"Is that her name?" said Jeluc. "That's what men call the sea. *La Dame.* She's not worth so much, but I won't worry about that."

Fatty was sullen. He did not know what to do.

Then one of the other men said to him, "You could take that to the town. You could spend two whole nights with a whore, and drink the place dry."

"Or," said another, "you could buy the makings to mend your old house."

Fatty said, "I don't know. Is my ship. Was my dad's."

"Let her go," said another man. "She's not lucky for you. Nor for him."

Jeluc said, "Not lucky, eh? Shall I lower my price?"

"Some daft tale," said Fatty. "She's all right. I've kept her trim."

"He has," the others agreed.

"I could see," said Jeluc. He put the money on a table. "There it is."

Fatty gave him a long, bended look. "Take her then. She's the lady."

"I'll want provisions," he said. "I mean to sail over to the islands."

A grey little man bobbed forward. "You got more silver? My wife'll see to you. Come with me."

The grey man's wife left the sack of meal, and the dried pork and apples, and the cask of water, at the village end of the pier, and Jeluc carried them out to the ship.

Her beauty impressed him as he walked towards her. To another maybe she would only have been a vessel. But he saw her lines. She was shapely. And the mast was slender and strong.

He stored the food and water, and the extra things, the ale and rope and blankets, the pan for hot coals, in the cabin. It was bare, but for its cupboard and the wooden bunk. He lay here a moment, trying it. It felt familiar as his own skin.

The deck was clean and scrubbed, and above the tied sail was bundled on the creaking yard, whiter than the sky. He checked her over. Nothing amiss.

The feel of her, dipping and bobbing as the tide turned, gave him a wonderful sensation of escape.

He would cast off before sunset, get out on to the sea, in case the oafs of the village had any amusing plans. They were superstitious of the ship, would not use her but possibly did not like to see her go. She was their one elegant thing, like a madonna in the church, if they had had one.

Her name was on her side, written dark.

The wind rose as the leaden sun began to sink.

He let down her sail, and it spread like a swan's wing. It was after all discoloured, of course, yet from a distance it would look very white. Like a woman's arm that had freckles when you saw it close.

The darkness came, and by then the land was out of sight. All the stars swarmed up, brilliant, as the clouds melted away. A glow was on the tips of the waves, such as he remembered. Tomorrow he would set lines for fish, baiting them with scraps of pork.

He cooked his supper of meal cakes on the coals, then lit a pipe of tobacco. He watched the smoke go up against the stars, and listened to the sail, turning a little to the wind.

The sea made noises, rushes and stirrings, and sometimes far away would come some sound, a soft booming or a slender cry, such as were never heard on land. He did not know what made these voices, if it were wind or water, or some creature. Perhaps he had known in his boyhood, for it seemed he recalled them.

When he went to the cabin, leaving the ship on her course, with the rope from the tiller tied to his waist, he knew that he would sleep as he had not slept on the beds of the earth.

The sea too was full of the dead, but they were a long way down. Theirs was a clean finish among the mouths of fishes.

He thought of mermaids swimming alongside, revealing their breasts, and laughing at him that he did not get up and look at them.

He slept.

Jeluc dreamed he was walking down the stone pier out of the village. It was starlight, night, and the pale ship was tied there at the pier's end as she had been. But between him and the ship stood a tall gaunt figure. It was not Fatty or the grey man, for as Jeluc came near, he saw it wore a black robe, like a priest's, and a hood concealed all its skull face but for a broad white forehead.

As he got closer, Jeluc tried to see the being's face, but could not. Instead a white thin hand came up and plucked from him a silver coin.

It was Charon, the Ferryman of the Dead, taking his fee.

Jeluc opened his eyes.

He was in the cabin of the ship called *La Dame*, and all was still, only the music of the water and the wind, and through the window he saw the stars sprinkle by.

The rope at his waist gave its little tug, now this way, now that, as it should. All was well.

Jeluc shut his eyes.

He imagined his lids weighted by silver coins.

He heard a soft voice singing, a woman's voice. It was very high and sweet, not kind, no lullaby.

In the morning he was tired, although his sleep had gone very deep. But it had been a long walk he had had to the village.

He saw to the lines, baiting them carefully, and went over the ship, but she was as she should be. He cooked some more cakes, and ate a little of the greasy pork. The ale was flat and bitter, but he had tasted far worse.

He stood all morning by the tiller.

The weather was brisk but calm enough, and at this rate he would sight the first of the islands by the day after tomorrow. He might be sorry at that, but then he need not linger longer. He could be off again.

In the afternoon he drowsed. And when he woke, the sun was over to the west like a bullet in a dull dark rent in the sky.

Jeluc glimpsed something. He turned, and saw three thin men with ragged dripping hair, who stood on the far side of the cabin on the afterdeck. They were quite still, colourless and dumb. Then they were gone.

Perhaps it had been some formation of the clouds, some shadow cast for a moment by the sail. Or his eyes, playing tricks.

But he said aloud to the ship, "Are you haunted, my dear? Is that your secret?"

When he checked his lines, he had caught nothing, but there was no law which said he must.

The wind dropped low and, as yesterday, the clouds dissolved when the darkness fell, and he saw the stars blaze out like diamonds, but no moon.

It seemed to him he should have seen her, the moon, but maybe some little overcast had remained, or he had made a mistake.

He concocted a stew with the pork and some garlic and apple, ate, smoked his pipe, listened to the noises of the sea.

He might be anywhere. A hundred miles from any land. He had seen no birds all day.

Jeluc went to the cabin, tied the rope, and lay down. He slept at once. He was on the ship, and at his side sat one of his old comrades, a man who had died from a cannon shot two years before. He kept his hat over the wound shyly, and said to Jeluc, "Where are you bound? The islands? Do you think you'll get there?"

"This lady'll take me there," said Jeluc.

"Oh, she'll take you somewhere."

Then the old soldier showed him the compass, and the needle had gone mad, reared up and poked down, right down, as if indicating hell.

Jeluc opened his eyes and the rope twitched at his waist, this way, that.

He got up, and walked out on to the deck.

The stars were bright as white flames, and the shadow of the mast fell hard as iron on the deck. But it was all wrong.

Jeluc looked up, and on the mast of the ship hung a wiry man, with his long grey hair all tangled round the yard and trailing down the sail, crawling on it, like the limbs of a spider.

This man Jeluc did not know, but the man grinned, and he began to pull off silver rings from his fingers and cast them at Jeluc. They fell with loud cold notes. A huge round moon, white as snow, rose behind the apparition. Its hand tugged and tugged, and Jeluc heard it curse. The finger had come off with the ring, and fell on his boot.

"What do you want with me?" said Jeluc, but the man on the mast faded, and the severed finger was only a drop of spray.

Opening his eyes again, Jeluc lay on the bunk, and he smelled a soft warm perfume. It was like flowers on a summer day. It was the aroma of a woman.

"Am I awake now?"

Jeluc got up, and stood on the bobbing floor, then he went outside. There was no moon, and only the sail moved on the yard.

One of the lines was jerking, and he went to it slowly. But when he tested it, nothing was there.

The smell of heat and plants was still faintly about him, and now he took it for the foretaste of the islands, blown out to him.

He returned to the cabin and lay wakeful, until near dawn he slept and dreamed a mermaid had come over the ship's rail. She was pale as pale, with ash blonde hair, and he wondered if it would be feasible to make love to her, for she had a fish's tail, and no woman's parts at all that he could see.

Dawn was so pale it seemed the ship had grown darker. She had a sort of flush, her sides and deck, her smooth mast, her outspread sail.

He could not scent the islands anymore.

Rain fell, and he went into the cabin, and there examined his possessions, as once or twice he had done before a battle. His knife, his neckscarf, of silk, which a girl had given him years before, a lucky coin he had kept without believing in it, a bullet that had missed him and gone into a tree. His money, his boots, his pipe. Not much.

Then he thought that the ship was now his possession, too, *his* lady.

He went and stood in the rain and looked at her.

There was nothing on the lines.

He ate pork for supper.

The rain eased, and in the cabin, he slept.

The woman stood at the tiller.

She rested her hand on it, quietly.

She was very pale, her hair long and blonde, and her old-fashioned dress the shade of good paper.

He stood and watched her for some time, but she did not respond, although he knew she was aware of him, and that he watched.

Finally he walked up to her, and she turned her head.

She was very thin, her face all bones, and she had great glowing pale gleaming eyes, and these stared now right through him.

She took her hand off the tiller and put it on his shoulder, and he felt her touch go through him like her look, straight down his body, through his heart, belly and loins, and out at his feet.

He thought, She'll want to go into the cabin with me.

So he gave her his arm.

They walked, along the deck, and he let her pass into the cabin first.

She turned about, as she had turned her head, slowly, looking at everything, the food and the pan of coals, which did not burn now, the blankets on the bunk.

Then she moved to the bunk and lay down, on her back, calm as any woman who had done such a thing a thousand times.

Jeluc went to her at once, but he did not wait to undo his clothing. He found, surprising himself, that he lay down on top of her, straight down, letting her frail body have all his weight, his chest on her bosom, his loins on her loins, but separated by their garments, legs on her legs. And last of all, his face on her face, his lips against hers.

Rather than lust it was the sensuality of a dream he felt, for of course it was a dream. His whole body sweetly ached, and the centre of joy seemed at his lips rather than anywhere else, his lips that touched her lips, quite closed, not even moist nor very warm.

Light delicious spasms passed through him, one after another, ebbing, flowing, resonant, and ceaseless.

He did not want to change it, did not want it to end. And it did not end.

But eventually, he seemed to drift away from it, back into sleep. And this was so comfortable that, although he regretted the sensation's loss, he did not mind so much.

When he woke, he heard them laughing at him. Many men, laughing, low voices and higher ones, coarse and rough as if torn from tin throats and voice boxes of rust. "He's going the same way." "So he is too."

Going the way that they had gone. The three he had seen on the deck, the one above the sail.

It was the ship. The ship had him.

He got up slowly, for he was giddy and chilled. Wrapping one of the blankets about him, he stepped out into the daylight.

The sky was white with hammerheads of black. The sea had a dull yet oily glitter.

He checked his lines. They were empty. No fish had come to the bait, as no birds had come to the mast.

He gazed back over the ship.

She was no longer pale. No, she was rosy now. She had a dainty blush to her, as if of pleasure. Even the sail was like the petal of a rose.

An old man stood on the afterdeck and shook his head and vanished.

Jeluc thought of lying on the bunk, facedown, and his vital juices or their essence draining into the wood. He could not avoid it. Everywhere here he must touch her. He could not lie to sleep in the sea.

He raised his head. No smell of land.

By now, surely, the islands should be in view, up against those clouds there— But there was nothing. Only the water on all sides and below, and the cold sky above, and over that, the void.

During the afternoon, as he watched by the tiller for the land, Jeluc slept.

He found that he lay with his head on her lap, and she was lovely now, prettier than any woman he had ever known. Her hair was honey, and her dress like a rose. Her white skin flushed with health and in her cheeks and lips three flames. Her eyes were dark now, very fine. They shone on him.

She leaned down, and covered his mouth with hers.

Such bliss—

He woke.

He was lying on his back, he had rolled, and the sail tilted over his face.

He got up, staggering, and trimmed the sail.

Jeluc attended to the ship.

The sunset came and a ghost slipped round the cabin, hiding its sneering mouth with its hand.

Jeluc tried to cook a meal, but he was clumsy and scorched his fingers. As he sucked them, he thought of her kisses. If kisses were what they were.

No land.

The sun set. It was a dull grim sky, with a hole of whiteness that turned grey, yet the ship flared up.

She was red now, *La Dame*, her cabin like a live coal, her sides like wine, her sail like blood.

Of course, he could keep awake through the night. He had done so before. And tomorrow he would sight the land.

He paced the deck, and the stars came out, white as ice or knives. There was no moon.

He marked the compass, saw to the sail, set fresh meat on the lines that he knew no fish would touch.

Jeluc sang old songs of his campaigns, but hours after he heard himself sing, over and over:

"*She the ship*
"*She the sea*
"*She the she.*"

His grandfather had told him stories of the ocean, of how it was a woman, a female thing, and that the ships that went out upon it were female also, for it would not stand any human male to go about on it unless something were between him and—her. But the sea was jealous too. She did not like women, true human women, to travel on ships. She must be reverenced, and now and then demanded sacrifice.

His grandfather had told him how, once, they had had to throw a man overboard, because he spat into the sea. It seemed he had spat a certain way, or at the wrong season. He had had, too, the temerity to learn to swim, which few sailors were fool enough to do. It had taken a long while for him to go down. They had told the widow the water washed him overboard.

Later, Jeluc believed that the ship had eyes painted on her prow, and these saw her way, but now they closed. She did not care where she went. And then too he thought she had a figurehead, like a great vessel of her kind, and this was a woman who clawed at the ship's sides, howling.

But he woke up, in time.

He kept awake all night.

In the morning the sun rose, lax and pallid as an ember, while the ship burned red as fire.

Jeluc looked over and saw her red reflection in the dark water.

There was no land on any side.

He made a breakfast of undercooked meal cakes, and ate a little. He felt her tingling through the soles of his boots.

He tested the sail and the lines, her tiller, and her compass. There was something odd with its needle.

No fish gave evidence of themselves in the water, and no birds flew overhead.

The sea rolled in vast glaucous swells.

He could not help himself. He slept.

There were birds!

He heard them calling, and looked up.

The sky, pale grey, a cinder, was full of them, against a sea of stars that were too faint for night.

And the birds, so black, were gulls. And yet, they were gulls of bone. Their beaks were shut like needles. They wheeled and soared, never alighting on the mast or yard or rails of the ship.

I'm dreaming, God help me. God wake me—

The gulls swooped over and on, and now, against the distant diluted dark, he saw the tower of a lighthouse rising. It was the land, at last, and he was saved.

But oh, the lighthouse sent out its ray, and from the opposing side there came another, the lamp flashing out. And then another, and another. They were before him and behind him, and all round. The lit points of them crossed each other on the blank sombre sparkle of the sea. A hundred lighthouses, sending their signals to hell.

Jeluc stared around him. And then he heard the deep roaring in the ocean bed, a million miles below.

And one by one, the houses of the light sank, they went into the water, their long necks like Leviathan's, and vanished in a cream of foam.

All light was gone. The birds were gone.

She came, then.

She was beautiful now. He had never, maybe, seen a beautiful woman.

Her skin was white, but her lips were red. And her hair was the red of gold. Her gown was the red of winter berries. She walked with a little gliding step.

"Lady," he said, "you don't want me."

But she smiled.

Then he looked beyond the ship, for it felt not right to him, and the sea was all lying down. It was like the tide going from the shore, or, perhaps, water from a basin. It ran away, and the ship dropped after it.

And then they were still in a pale nothingness, a sort of beach of sand that stretched in all directions. Utterly becalmed.

"But I don't want the land."

He remembered what the land had given him. Old hurts, drear pains. Comrades dead. Wars lost. Youth gone.

"Not the land," he said.

But she smiled.

And over the waste of it, that sea of salt, came a shrill high whistling, once and twice and three times. Some sound of the ocean he had never heard.

Then she had reached him. Jeluc felt her smooth hands on his neck. He said, "Woman, let me go into the water, at least." But it was no use. Her lips were soft as roses on his throat.

He saw the sun rise, and it was red as red could be. But then, like the ship in his dream, he closed his eyes. He thought, But there was no land.

There never is.

The ship stood fiery crimson on the rising sun, that lit her like a bonfire. Her sides, her deck, her cabin, her mast and sail, like fresh pure blood.

Presently the sea, which moved under her in dark silk, began to lip this blood away.

At first, it was only a reflection in the water, but next it was a stain, like heavy dye.

The sea drank from the colour of the ship, for the sea too was feminine and a devourer of men.

The sea drained *La Dame* of every drop, so gradually she turned back paler and paler into a vessel like ashes.

And when the sea had sucked everything out of her, it let her go, the ship, white as a bone, to drift away down the morning.

THE GIRL WITH THE
HUNGRY EYES

༒

FRITZ LEIBER

ALL RIGHT, I'LL TELL YOU WHY THE GIRL GIVES ME the creeps. Why I can't stand to go downtown and see the mob slavering up at her on the tower, with that pop bottle or pack of cigarettes or whatever it is beside her. Why I hate to look at magazines any more because I know she'll turn up somewhere in a brassière or a bubble bath. Why I don't like to think of millions of Americans drinking in that poisonous half-smile. It's quite a story—more story than you're expecting.

No, I haven't suddenly developed any long-haired indignation at the evils of advertising and the national glamor-girl complex. That'd be a laugh for a man in my racket, wouldn't it? Though I think you'll agree there's something a little perverted about trying to capitalize on sex that way. But it's okay with me. And I know we've had the Face and the Body and the Look and what not else, so why shouldn't someone come along who sums it all up so completely, that we have to call her the Girl and blazon her on all the billboards from Times Square to Telegraph Hill?

But the Girl isn't like any of the others. She's unnatural. She's morbid. She's unholy.

Oh, these are modern times, you say, and the sort of thing I'm hinting at went out with witchcraft. But you see I'm not altogether sure myself what I'm hinting at, beyond a certain point. There are vampires and vampires, and not all of them suck blood.

And there were the murders, if they were murders. Besides, let me ask you this. Why, when America is obsessed with the Girl, don't we find out more about her? Why doesn't she rate a *Time* cover with a droll biography inside? Why hasn't there been a feature in *Life* or the *Post*? A profile in *The New Yorker*? Why hasn't *Charm* or *Mademoiselle* done her career saga? Not ready for it? Nuts!

Why haven't the movies snapped her up? Why hasn't she been on "Information, Please"? Why don't we see her kissing candidates at political rallies? Why isn't she chosen queen of some sort of junk or other at a convention?

Why don't we read about her tastes and hobbies, her views of the Russian situation? Why haven't the columnists interviewed her in a kimono on the top floor of the tallest hotel in Manhattan and told us who her boyfriends are?

Finally—and this is the real killer—why hasn't she ever been drawn or painted?

Oh no she hasn't. If you knew anything about commercial art, you'd know that. Every blessed one of those pictures was worked up from a photograph. Expertly? Of course. They've got the top artists on it. But that's how it's done.

And now I'll tell you the why of all that. It's because from the top to the bottom of the whole world of advertising, news, and business, there isn't a solitary soul who knows where the Girl came from, where she lives, what she does, who she is, even what her name is.

You heard me. What's more, not a single solitary soul ever sees her—except one poor damned photographer, who's making more money off her than he ever hoped to in his life and who's scared and miserable as hell every minute of the day.

No, I haven't the faintest idea who he is or where he has his studio. But I know there has to be such a man and I'm morally certain he feels just like I said.

Yes, I might be able to find her, if I tried. I'm not sure though—by now she probably has other safeguards. Besides, I don't want to.

Oh, I'm off my rocker, am I? That sort of thing can't happen in the Era of the Atom? People can't keep out of sight that way, not even Garbo?

Well, I happen to know they can, because last year I was that poor damned photographer I was telling you about. Yes, last year, when the Girl made her first poisonous splash right here in this big little city of ours.

Yes, I know you weren't here last year and you don't know about it. Even the Girl had to start small. But if you hunted through the files of the local newspapers, you'd find some ads, and I might be able to locate you some of the old displays—I think Lovelybelt is still using one of them. I used to have a mountain of photos myself, until I burned them.

Yes, I made my cut off her. Nothing like what that other photographer must be making, but enough so it still bought this whiskey. She was funny about money. I'll tell you about that.

But first picture me then. I had a fourth-floor studio in that rathole the Hauser Building, not far from Ardleigh Park.

I'd been working at the Marsh-Mason studios until I'd gotten my bellyful of it and decided to start in for myself. The Hauser Building was awful—I'll never forget how the stairs creaked—but it was cheap and there was a skylight.

Business was lousy. I kept making the rounds of all the advertisers and agencies, and some of them didn't object to me too much personally, but my stuff never clicked. I was pretty near broke. I was behind on my rent. Hell, I didn't even have enough money to have a girl.

It was one of those dark gray afternoons. The building was very quiet—I'd just finished developing some pix I was doing on speculation for Lovelybelt Girdles and Budford's Pool and Playground. My model had left. A Miss Leon. She was a civics teacher at one of the high schools and modeled for me on the side, just lately on speculation, too. After one look at the prints, I decided that Miss Leon probably wasn't just what Lovelybelt was looking for—or my photography either. I was about to call it a day.

And then the street door slammed four storys down and there were steps on the stairs and she came in.

She was wearing a cheap, shiny black dress. Black pumps. No stockings. And except that she had a gray cloth coat over one of them, those skinny arms of hers were bare. Her arms are pretty skinny, you know, or can't you see things like that any more?

And then the thin neck, the slightly gaunt, almost prim face, the tumbling mass of dark hair, and looking out from under it the hungriest eyes in the world.

That's the real reason she's plastered all over the country today, you know—those eyes. Nothing vulgar, but just the same they're looking at you with a hunger that's all sex and something more than sex. That's what everybody's been looking for since the Year One—something a little more than sex.

Well, boys, there I was, alone with the Girl, in an office that was getting shadowy, in a nearly empty building. A situation that a million male Americans have undoubtedly pictured to themselves with various lush details. How was I feeling? Scared.

I know sex can be frightening. That cold heart-thumping when you're alone with a girl and feel you're going to touch her. But if it was sex this time, it was overlaid with something else.

At least I wasn't thinking about sex.

I remember that I took a backward step and that my hand jerked so that the photos I was looking at sailed to the floor.

There was the faintest dizzy feeling like something was being drawn out of me. Just a little bit.

That was all. Then she opened her mouth and everything was back to normal for a while.

"I see you're a photographer, mister," she said. "Could you use a model?"

Her voice wasn't very cultivated.

"I doubt it," I told her, picking up the pix. You see, I wasn't impressed. The commercial possibilities of her eyes hadn't registered on me yet, by a long shot. "What have you done?"

Well, she gave me a vague sort of story and I began to check her knowledge of model agencies and studios and rates and what not and pretty soon I said to her, "Look here, you never modeled for a photographer in your life. You just walked in here cold."

Well, she admitted that was more or less so.

All along through our talk I got the idea she was feeling her way, like someone in a strange place. Not that she was uncertain of herself, or of me, but just of the general situation.

"And you think anyone can model?" I asked her pityingly.

"Sure," she said.

"Look," I said, "a photographer can waste a dozen negatives trying to get one halfway human photo of an average woman. How many do you think he'd have to waste before he got a real catchy, glamorous photo of her?"

"I think I could do it," she said.

Well, I should have kicked her out right then. Maybe I admired the cool way she stuck to her dumb little guns. Maybe I was touched by her underfed look. More likely I was feeling mean on account of the way my pictures had been snubbed by everybody and I wanted to take it out on her by showing her up.

"Okay, I'm going to put you on the spot," I told her. "I'm going to try a couple of shots of you. Understand it's strictly on spec. If somebody should ever want to use a photo of you, which is about one chance in two million, I'll pay you regular rates for your time. Not otherwise."

She gave me a smile. The first. "That's swell by me," she said.

Well, I took three or four shots, close-ups of her face since I didn't fancy her cheap dress, and at least she stood up to my sarcasm. Then I remembered I still had the Lovelybelt stuff and I guess the meanness was still working in me because I handed her a girdle and told her to go behind the screen and get into it and she did, without getting flustered as I'd expected, and since we'd gone that far, I figured we might as well shoot the beach scene to round it out, and that was that.

All this time I wasn't feeling anything particular one way or the other, except every once in a while I'd get one of those faint dizzy flashes and wonder if there was something wrong with my stomach or if I could have been a bit careless with my chemicals.

Still, you know, I think the uneasiness was in me all the while.

I tossed her a card and pencil. "Write your name and address and phone," I told her and made for the darkroom.

A little later she walked out. I didn't call any good-byes. I was irked because she hadn't fussed around or seemed anxious about her poses, or even thanked me, except for that one smile.

I finished developing the negatives, made some prints, glanced at them, decided they weren't a great deal worse than Miss Leon. On an impulse I slipped them in with the pictures I was going to take on the rounds next morning.

By now I'd worked long enough, so I was a bit fagged and nervous, but I didn't dare waste enough money on liquor to help that. I wasn't very hungry. I think I went to a cheap movie.

I didn't think of the Girl at all, except maybe to wonder faintly why in my present womanless state I hadn't made a pass at her. She had seemed to belong to a—well, distinctly more approachable social strata than Miss Leon. But then, of course, there were all sorts of arguable reasons for my not doing that.

Next morning I made the rounds. My first stop was Munsch's Brewery. They were looking for a "Munsch Girl." Papa Munsch had a sort of affection for me, though he razzed my photography. He had a good natural judgment about that, too. Fifty years ago he might have been one of the shoestring boys who made Hollywood.

Right now he was out in the plant, pursuing his favorite occupation. He put down the beaded schooner, smacked his lips, gabbled something technical to someone about hops, wiped his fat hands on the big apron he was wearing, and grabbed my thin stack of pictures.

He was about halfway through, making noises with his tongue and teeth, when he came to her. I kicked myself for even having stuck her in.

"That's her," he said. "The photography's not so hot, but that's the girl."

It was all decided. I wonder now why Papa Munsch sensed what the Girl had right away, while I didn't. I think it was because I saw her first in the flesh, if that's the right word.

At the time I just felt faint.

"Who is she?" he asked.

"One of my new models." I tried to make it casual.

"Bring her out tomorrow morning," he told me. "And your stuff. We'll photograph her here.

"Here, don't look so sick," he added. "Have some beer."

Well, I went away telling myself it was just a fluke, so that she'd probably blow it tomorrow with her inexperience, and so on.

Just the same, when I reverently laid my next stack of pictures on Mr. Fitch, of Lovelybelt's, rose-colored blotter, I had hers on top.

Mr. Fitch went through the motions of being an art critic. He leaned over backward, squinted his eyes, waved his long fingers, and said, "Hmm. What do you think, Miss Willow? Here, in this light, of course, the photograph doesn't show the bias cut. And perhaps we should use the Lovelybelt Imp instead of the Angel. Still, the girl. . . . Come over here, Binns." More finger-waving. "I want a married man's reaction."

He couldn't hide the fact that he was hooked.

Exactly the same thing happened at Budford's Pool and Playground, except that Da Costa didn't need a married man's say-so.

"Hot stuff," he said, sucking his lips. "Oh boy, you photographers!"

I hotfooted it back to the office and grabbed up the card I'd given her to put down her name and address.

It was blank.

I don't mind telling you that the next five days were about the worst I ever went through, in an ordinary way. When next morning rolled around and I still hadn't got hold of her, I had to start stalling.

"She's sick," I told Papa Munsch over the phone.

"She at a hospital?" he asked me.

"Nothing that serious," I told him.

"Get her out here then. What's a little headache?"

"Sorry, I can't."

Papa Munsch got suspicious. "You really got this girl?"

"Of course I have."

"Well, I don't know. I'd think it was some New York model, except I recognized your lousy photography."

I laughed.

"Well, look, you get her here tomorrow morning, you hear?"

"I'll try."

"Try nothing. You get her out here."

He didn't know half of what I tried. I went around to all the model and employment agencies. I did some slick detective work at the photographic and art studios. I used up some of my last dimes putting advertisements in all three papers. I looked at high school yearbooks and at employee photos in local house organs. I went to restaurants and drugstores, looking at waitresses, and to dime stores and department stores, looking at clerks. I watched the crowds coming out of movie theaters. I roamed the streets.

Evenings, I spent quite a bit of time along Pickup Row. Somehow that seemed the right place.

The fifth afternoon I knew I was licked. Papa Munsch's deadline—he'd given me several, but this was it—was due to run out at six o'clock. Mr. Fitch had already canceled.

I was at the studio window, looking out at Ardleigh Park.

She walked in.

I'd gone over this moment so often in my mind that I had no trouble putting on my act. Even the faint dizzy feeling didn't throw me off.

"Hello," I said, hardly looking at her.

"Hello," she said.

"Not discouraged yet?"

"No." It didn't sound uneasy or defiant. It was just a statement.

I snapped a look at my watch, got up and said curtly, "Look here, I'm going to give you a chance. There's a client of mine looking for a girl your general type. If you do a real good job you might break into the modeling business.

"We can see him this afternoon if we hurry," I said. I picked up my stuff. "Come on. And next time if you expect favors, don't forget to leave your phone number."

"Uh-uh," she said, not moving.

"What do you mean?" I said.

"I'm not going out to see any client of yours."

"The hell you aren't," I said. "You little nut, I'm giving you a break."

She shook her head slowly. "You're not fooling me, baby. You're not fooling me at all. They want me." And she gave me the second smile.

At the time I thought she must have seen my newspaper ad. Now I'm not so sure.

"And now I'll tell you how we're going to work," she went on. "You aren't going to have my name or address or phone number. Nobody is. And we're going to do all the pictures right here. Just you and me."

You can imagine the roar I raised at that. I was everything—angry, sarcastic, patiently explanatory, off my nut, threatening, pleading.

I would have slapped her face off, except it was photographic capital.

In the end all I could do was phone Papa Munsch and tell him her conditions. I knew I didn't have a chance, but I had to take it.

He gave me a really angry bawling out, said "no" several times and hung up.

It didn't worry her. "We'll start shooting at ten o'clock tomorrow," she said. It was just like her, using that corny line from the movie magazines.

About midnight Papa Munsch called me up.

"I don't know what insane asylum you're renting this girl from," he said, "but I'll take her. Come around tomorrow morning and I'll try to get it through your head just how I want the pictures. And I'm glad I got you out of bed!"

After that it was a breeze. Even Mr. Fitch reconsidered and, after taking two days to tell me it was quite impossible, he accepted the conditions too.

Of course you're all under the spell of the Girl, so you can't understand how much self-sacrifice it represented on Mr. Fitch's part when he agreed to forego supervising the photography of my model in the Lovelybelt Imp or Vixen or whatever it was we finally used.

Next morning she turned up on time according to her schedule, and we went to work. I'll say one thing for her, she never got tired and she never kicked at the way I fussed over shots. I got along okay, except I still had that feeling of something being shoved away gently. Maybe you've felt it just a little, looking at her picture.

When we finished I found out there were still more rules. It was about the middle of the afternoon. I started with her to get a sandwich and coffee.

"Uh-uh," she said, "I'm going down alone. And look, baby, if you ever try to follow me, if you ever so much as stick your head out of that window when I go, you can hire yourself another model."

You can imagine how all this crazy stuff strained my temper—and my imagination. I remember opening the window after she was gone—I waited a few minutes first—and standing there getting some fresh air and trying to figure out what could be behind it, whether she was hiding from the police, or was somebody's ruined daughter, or maybe had got the idea it was smart to be temperamental, or more likely Papa Munsch was right and she was partly nuts.

But I had my pictures to finish up.

Looking back, it's amazing to think how fast her magic began to take hold of the city after that. Remembering what came after, I'm frightened of what's happening to the whole country—and maybe the world. Yesterday I read something in *Time* about the Girl's picture turning up on billboards in Egypt.

The rest of my story will help show you why I'm frightened in that big, general way. But I have a theory, too, that helps explain, though it's one of those things that's beyond that "certain point." It's about the Girl. I'll give it to you in a few words.

You know how modern advertising gets everybody's mind set in the same direction, wanting the same things, imagining the same things. And you know the psychologists aren't so skeptical of telepathy as they used to be.

Add up the two ideas. Suppose the identical desires of millions of people focussed on one telepathic person. Say a girl. Shaped her in their image.

Imagine her knowing the hiddenmost hungers of millions of men. Imagine her seeing deeper into those hungers than the people that had them, seeing the hatred and the wish for death behind the lust. Imagine her shaping herself in that complete image, keeping herself as aloof as marble. Yet imagine the hunger she might feel in answer to their hunger.

But that's getting a long way from the facts of my story. And some of those facts are darn solid. Like money. We made money.

That was the funny thing I was going to tell you. I was afraid the Girl was going to hold me up. She really had me over a barrel, you know.

But she didn't ask for anything but the regular rates. Later on I insisted on pushing more money at her, a whole lot. But she always took it with that same contemptuous look, as if she were going to toss it down the first drain when she got outside.

Maybe she did.

At any rate, I had money. For the first time in months I had money enough to get drunk, buy new clothes, take taxicabs. I could make a play for any girl I wanted to. I only had to pick.

And so of course I had to go and pick . . .

But first let me tell you about Papa Munsch.

Papa Munsch wasn't the first of the boys to try to meet my model but I think he was the first to really go soft on her. I could watch the change in his eyes as he looked at her pictures. They began to get sentimental, reverent. Mama Munsch had been dead for two years.

He was smart about the way he planned it. He got me to drop some information which told him when she came to work, and then one morning he came pounding up the stairs a few minutes before.

"I've got to see her, Dave," he told me.

I argued with him, I kidded him, I explained he didn't know just how serious she was about her crazy ideas. I even pointed out he was cutting both our throats. I even amazed myself by bawling him out.

He didn't take any of it in his usual way. He just kept repeating, "But, Dave, I've got to see her."

The street door slammed.

"That's her," I said, lowering my voice. "You've got to get out."

He wouldn't, so I shoved him in the darkroom. "And keep quiet," I whispered. "I'll tell her I can't work today."

I knew he'd try to look at her and probably come busting in, but there wasn't anything else I could do.

The footsteps came to the fourth floor. But she never showed at the door. I got uneasy.

"Get that bum out of there!" she yelled suddenly from beyond the door. Not very loud, but in her commonest voice.

"I'm going up to the next landing," she said. "And if that fat-bellied bum doesn't march straight down to the street, he'll never get another picture of me except spitting in his lousy beer."

Papa Munsch came out of the darkroom. He was white. He didn't look at me as he went out. He never looked at her pictures in front of me again.

That was Papa Munsch. Now it's me I'm telling about. I talked around the subject with her, I hinted, eventually I made my pass.

She lifted my hand off her as if it were a damp rag.

"No, baby," she said. "This is working time."

"But afterward . . ." I pressed.

"The rules still hold." And I got what I think was the fifth smile.

It's hard to believe, but she never budged an inch from that crazy line. I mustn't make a pass at her in the office, because our work was very important and she loved it and there mustn't be any distractions. And I couldn't see her anywhere else, because if I tried to, I'd never snap another picture of her—and all this with more money coming in all the time and me never so stupid as to think my photography had anything to do with it.

Of course I wouldn't have been human if I hadn't made more passes. But they always got the wet-rag treatment and there weren't any more smiles.

I changed. I went sort of crazy and light-headed—only sometimes I felt my head was going to burst. And I started to talk to her all the time. About myself.

It was like being in a constant delirium that never interfered with business. I didn't pay any attention to the dizzy feeling. It seemed natural.

I'd walk around and for a moment the reflector would look like a sheet of white-hot steel, or the shadows would seem like armies of moths, or the camera would be a big black coal car. But the next instant they'd come all right again.

I think sometimes I was scared to death of her. She'd seem the strangest, most horrible person in the world. But other times. . . .

And I talked. It didn't matter what I was doing—lighting her, posing her, fussing with props, snapping my pictures—or where she was—on the platform, behind the screen, relaxing with a magazine—I kept up a steady gab.

I told her everything I knew about myself. I told her about my first girl. I told her about my brother Bob's bicycle. I told her about running away on a freight, and the licking Pa gave me when I came home. I told her about shipping to South America and the blue sky at night. I told her about Betty. I told her about my mother dying of cancer. I told her about being beaten up in a fight in an alley behind a bar. I told her about Mildred. I told her about the first picture I ever sold. I told her how Chicago looked from a sailboat. I told her about the longest drunk I was ever on. I told her about Marsh-Mason. I told her about Gwen. I told her about how I met Papa Munsch. I told her about hunting her. I told her about how I felt now.

She never paid the slightest attention to what I said. I couldn't even tell if she heard me.

It was when we were getting our first nibble from national advertisers that I decided to follow her when she went home.

Wait, I can place it better than that. Something you'll remember from the out-of-town papers—those maybe murders I mentioned. I think there were six.

I say "maybe" because the police could never be sure they weren't heart attacks. But there's bound to be suspicion when attacks happen to people whose hearts have been okay, and always at night when they're alone and away from home and there's a question of what they were doing.

The six deaths created one of those "mystery poisoner" scares. And afterward there was a feeling that they hadn't really stopped, but were being continued in a less suspicious way.

That's one of the things that scares me now.

But at that time my only feeling was relief that I'd decided to follow her.

I made her work until dark one afternoon. I didn't need any excuses, we were snowed under with orders. I waited until the street door slammed, then I ran down. I was wearing rubber-soled shoes. I'd slipped on a dark coat she'd never seen me in, and a dark hat.

I stood in the doorway until I spotted her. She was walking by Ardleigh Park toward the heart of town. It was one of those warm fall nights. I followed her on the other side of the street. My idea for tonight was just to find out where she lived. That would give me a hold on her.

She stopped in front of a display window of Everley's department store, standing back from the flow. She stood there looking in.

I remembered we'd done a big photograph of her for Everley's, to make a flat model for a lingerie display. That was what she was looking at.

At the time it seemed all right to me that she should adore herself, if that was what she was doing.

When people passed she'd turn away a little or drift back farther into the shadows.

Then a man came by alone. I couldn't see his face very well, but he looked middle-aged. He stopped and stood looking in the window.

She came out of the shadows and stepped up beside him.

How would you boys feel if you were looking at a poster of the Girl and suddenly she was there beside you, her arm linked with yours?

This fellow's reaction showed plain as day. A crazy dream had come to life for him.

They talked for a moment. Then he waved a taxi to the curb. They got in and drove off.

I got drunk that night. It was almost as if she'd known I was following her and had picked that way to hurt me. Maybe she had. Maybe this was the finish.

But the next morning she turned up at the usual time and I was back in the delirium, only now with some new angles added.

That night when I followed her she picked a spot under a streetlight, opposite one of the Munsch Girl billboards.

Now it frightens me to think of her lurking that way.

After about twenty minutes a convertible slowed down going past her, backed up, swung into the curb.

I was closer this time. I got a good look at the fellow's face. He was a little younger, about my age.

Next morning the same face looked up at me from the front page of the paper. The convertible had been found parked on a side street. He had been in it. As in the other maybe-murders, the cause of death was uncertain.

All kinds of thoughts were spinning in my head that day, but there were only two things I knew for sure. That I'd got the first real offer from a national advertiser, and that I was going to take the Girl's arm and walk down the stairs with her when we quit work.

She didn't seem surprised. "You know what you're doing?" she said.

"I know."

She smiled. "I was wondering when you'd get around to it."

I began to feel good. I was kissing everything good-bye, but I had my arm around hers.

It was another of those warm fall evenings. We cut across into Ardleigh Park. It was dark there, but all around the sky was a sallow pink from the advertising signs.

We walked for a long time in the park. She didn't say anything and she didn't look at me, but I could see her lips twitching and after a while her hand tightened on my arm.

We stopped. We'd been walking across the grass. She dropped down and pulled me after her. She put her hands on my shoulders. I was looking down at her face. It was the faintest sallow pink from the glow in the sky. The hungry eyes were dark smudges.

I was fumbling with her blouse. She took my hand away, not like she had in the studio. "I don't want that," she said.

☾   ☾   ☾

First I'll tell you what I did afterward. Then I'll tell you why I did it. Then I'll tell you what she said.

What I did was run away. I don't remember all of that because I was dizzy, and the pink sky was swinging against the dark trees. But after a while I staggered into the lights of the street. The next day I closed up the studio. The telephone was ringing when I locked the door and there were unopened letters on the floor. I never saw the Girl again in the flesh, if that's the right word.

I did it because I didn't want to die. I didn't want the life drawn out of me. There are vampires and vampires, and the ones that suck blood aren't the worst. If it hadn't been for the warning of those dizzy flashes, and Papa Munsch and the face in the morning paper, I'd have gone the way the others did. But I realized what I was up against while there was still time to tear myself away. I realized that wherever she came from, whatever shaped her, she's the quintessence of the horror behind the bright billboard. She's the smile that tricks you into throwing away your money and your life. She's the eyes that lead you on and on, and then show you death. She's the creature you give everything for and never really get. She's the being that takes everything you've got and gives nothing in return. When you yearn toward her face on the billboards, remember that. She's the lure. She's the bait. She's the Girl.

And this is what she said, "I want you. I want your high spots. I want everything that's made you happy and everything that's hurt you bad. I want your first girl. I want that shiny bicycle. I want that licking. I want that pinhole camera. I want Betty's legs. I want the blue sky filled with stars. I want your mother's death. I want your blood on the cobblestones. I want Mildred's mouth. I want the first picture you sold. I want the lights of Chicago. I want the gin. I want Gwen's hands. I want your wanting me. I want your life. Feed me, baby, feed me."

Dress of White Silk

❧

Richard Matheson

Quiet is here and all in me.

Granma locked me in my room and wont let me out. Because its happened she says. I guess I was bad. Only it was the dress. Mommas dress I mean. She is gone away forever. Granma says your momma is in heaven. I dont know how. Can she go in heaven if shes dead?

Now I hear granma. She is in mommas room. She is putting mommas dress down the box. Why does she always? And locks it too. I wish she didnt. Its a pretty dress and smells sweet so. And warm. I love to touch it against my cheek. But I cant never again. I guess that is why granma is mad at me.

But I amnt sure. All day it was only like everyday. Mary Jane came over to my house. She lives across the street. Everyday she comes to my house and play. Today she was.

I have seven dolls and a fire truck. Today granma said play with your dolls and it. Dont you go inside your mommas room now she said. She always says it. She just means not mess up I think. Because she says it all the time. Dont go in your mommas room. Like that.

But its nice in mommas room. When it rains I go there. Or when granma is doing her nap I do. I dont make noise. I just sit on the bed and touch the white cover. Like when I was only small. The room smells like sweet.

I make believe momma is dressing and I am allowed in. I smell her white silk dress. Her going out for night dress. She called it that I dont remember when.

I hear it moving if I listen hard. I make believe to see her sitting at the dressing table. Like touching on perfume or something I mean. And see her dark eyes. I can remember.

Its so nice if it rains and I see eyes on the window. The rain sounds like a big giant outside. He says shushshush so every one will be quiet. I like to make believe that in mommas room.

What I like almost best is to sit at mommas dressing table. It is like pink and big and smells sweet too. The seat in front has a pillow sewed in it. There are bottles and bottles with bumps and have colored perfume in them. And you can see almost your whole self in the mirror.

When I sit there I make believe to be momma. I say be quiet mother I am going out and you can not stop me. It is something I say I dont know why like I hear it in me. And oh stop your sobbing mother they will not catch me I have my magic dress.

When I pretend I brush my hair long. But I only use my own brush from my room. I didnt never use mommas brush. I dont think granma is mad at me for that because I never use mommas brush. I wouldnt never.

Sometimes I did open the box up. Because I know where granma puts the key. I saw her once when she wouldnt know I saw her. She puts the key on the hook in mommas closet. Behind the door I mean.

I could open the box lots of times. Thats because I like to look at mommas dress. I like best to look at it. It is so pretty and feels soft and like silky. I could touch it for a million years.

I kneel on the rug with roses on it. I hold the dress in my arms and like breathe from it. I touch it against my cheek. I wish I could take it to sleep with me and hold it. I like to. Now I cant. Because granma says. And she says I should burn it up but I loved her so. And she cries about the dress.

I wasnt never bad with it. I put it back neat like it was never touched. Granma never knew. I laughed that she never knew before. But she knows now I did it I guess. And shell punish me. What did it hurt her? Wasnt it my mommas dress?

What I like real best in mommas room is look at the picture of momma. It has a gold thing around it. Frame is what granma says. It is on the wall on top the bureau.

Momma is pretty. Your momma was pretty granma says. Why does she? I see momma there smiling on me and she *is* pretty. For always.

Her hair is black. Like mine. Her eyes are even pretty like black. Her mouth is red so red. I like the dress and its the white one. It is all down on her shoulders. Her skin is white almost white like the dress. And so are her hands. She is so pretty. I love her even if she is gone away forever. I love her so much.

I guess I think thats what made me bad. I mean to Mary Jane.

Mary Jane came from lunch like she does. Granma went to do her nap. She said dont forget now no going to your mommas room. I told her no granma. And I was saying the truth but then Mary Jane and I was playing fire truck. Mary Jane said I bet you havent no mother I bet you made up it all she said.

I got mad at her. I have a momma I know. She made me mad at her to say I made up it all. She said Im a liar. I mean about the bed and the dressing table and the picture and the dress even and every thing.

I said well Ill show you smarty.

I looked into granmas room. She was doing her nap still. I went down and said Mary Jane to come on because granma wont know.

She wasnt so smart after then. She giggled like she does. Even she made a scaredy noise when she hit into the table in the hall upstairs. I said youre a scaredy cat to her. She said back well *my* house isnt so dark like this. Like that was so much.

We went in mommas room. It was more dark than you could see. I said this is my mommas room I suppose I made up it all.

She was by the door and she wasnt smart then either. She didnt say any word. She looked around the room. She jumped when I got her arm. Well come on I said.

I sat on the bed and said this is my mommas bed see how soft it is. She didnt say nothing. Scaredy cat I said. Am not she said like she does.

I said to sit down how can you tell if its soft if you dont sit down. She sat down by me. I said feel how soft it is. Smell how sweet it is.

I closed my eyes but funny it wasnt like always. Because Mary Jane was there. I told her to stop feeling the cover. You said to she said. Well stop it I said.

See I said and I pulled her up. Thats the dressing table. I took her and brought her there. She said let go. It was so quiet and like always. I started to feel bad. Because Mary Jane was there. Because it was in my mommas room and momma wouldnt like Mary Jane there.

But I had to show her the things because. I showed her the mirror. We looked at each other in it. She looked white. Mary Jane is a scaredy cat I said. Am not am not she said anyway nobodys house is so quiet and dark inside. Anyway she said it smells.

I got mad at her. No it doesnt smell I said. Does so she said you said it did. I got madder too. It smells like sugar she said. It smells like sick people in your mommas room.

Dont say my mommas room is like sick people I said to her.

Well you didnt show me no dress and youre lying she said there isnt no dress. I felt all warm inside so I pulled her hair. Ill show you I said youre going to see my mommas dress and youll better not call me a liar.

I made her stand still and I got the key off the hook. I kneeled down. I opened the box with the key.

Mary Jane said pew that smells like garbage.

I put my nails in her and she pulled away and got mad. Dont you pinch me she said and she was all red. Im telling my mother on you she said. And anyway its not a white dress its dirty and ugly she said.

Its not dirty I said. I said it so loud I wonder why granma didnt hear. I pulled out the dress from the box. I held it up to show her how its white. It fell open like the rain whispering and the bottom touched on the rug.

It is too white I said all white and clean and silky.

No she said she was so mad and red it has a hole in it. I got more madder. If my momma was here shed show you I said. You got no momma she said all ugly. I hate her.

I have. I said it way loud. I pointed my finger to mommas picture. Well who can see in this stupid dark room she said. I pushed her hard and she hit against the bureau. See then I said mean look at the picture. Thats my momma and shes the most beautiful lady in the world.

Shes ugly she has funny hands Mary Jane said. She hasnt I said shes the most beautiful lady in the world!

Not not she said *she has buck teeth.*

I dont remember then. I think the dress moved in my arms. Mary Jane screamed. I dont remember what. It got dark and the curtains were closed I think. I couldnt see anyway. I couldnt hear nothing except buck teeth funny hands buck teeth funny hands even when no one was saying it.

There was something else because I think I heard some one call *dont let her say that!* I couldnt hold to the dress. And I had it on me I cant remember. Because I was grown up strong. But I was a little girl still I think. I mean outside.

I think I was terrible bad then.

Granma took me away from there I guess. I dont know. She was screaming god help us its happened its happened. Over and over. I dont know why. She pulled me all the way here to my room and locked me in. She wont let me out. Well Im not so scared. Who cares if she locks me in a million billion years? She doesn't have to even give me supper. Im not hungry anyway.

Im full.

SHAMBLEAU

❧

C. L. MOORE

MAN HAS CONQUERED SPACE BEFORE. YOU MAY BE
sure of that. Somewhere beyond the Egyptians, in that dimness out of which come echoes of half-myth-
ical names—Atlantis, Mu—somewhere back of history's first beginnings there must have been an
age when mankind, like us today, built cities of steel to house its star-roving ships and knew the
names of the planets in their own native tongues—heard Venus' people call their wet world "Sha-
ardol" in that soft, sweet, slurring speech and mimicked Mars' guttural "Lakkdiz" from the harsh
tongues of Mars' dryland dwellers. You may be sure of it. Man has conquered Space before, and out
of that conquest faint, faint echoes run still through a world that has forgotten the very fact of a civ-
ilization which must have been as mighty as our own. There have been too many myths and legends
for us to doubt it. The myth of the Medusa, for instance, can never have had its roots in the soil of
Earth. That tale of the snake-haired Gorgon whose gaze turned the gazer to stone never originated
about any creature that Earth nourished. And those ancient Greeks who told the story must have remembered, dimly and half believing, a tale of antiquity about some strange being from one of the
outlying planets their remotest ancestors once trod.

"Shambleau! Ha . . . Shambleau!" The wild hysteria of the mob rocketed from
wall to wall of Lakkdarol's narrow streets and the storming of heavy boots over
the slag-red pavement made an ominous undernote to that swelling bay, "Shambleau! Shambleau!"

Northwest Smith heard it coming and stepped into the nearest doorway,
laying a wary hand on his heat-gun's grip, and his colorless eyes narrowed.

Strange sounds were common enough in the streets of Earth's latest colony on Mars—a raw, red little town where anything might happen, and very often did. But Northwest Smith, whose name is known and respected in every dive and wild outpost on a dozen wild planets, was a cautious man, despite his reputation. He set his back against the wall and gripped his pistol, and heard the rising shout come nearer and nearer.

Then into his range of vision flashed a red running figure, dodging like a hunted hare from shelter to shelter in the narrow street. It was a girl—a berry-brown girl in a single tattered garment whose scarlet burnt the eyes with its brilliance. She ran wearily, and he could hear her gasping breath from where he stood. As she came into view he saw her hesitate and lean one hand against the wall for support, and glance wildly around for shelter. She must not have seen him in the depths of the doorway, for as the bay of the mob grew louder and the pounding of feet sounded almost at the corner she gave a despairing little moan and dodged into the recess at his very side.

When she saw him standing there, tall and leather-brown, hand on his heat-gun, she sobbed once, inarticulately, and collapsed at his feet, a huddle of burning scarlet and bare, brown limbs.

Smith had not seen her face, but she was a girl, and sweetly made and in danger; and though he had not the reputation of a chivalrous man, something in her hopeless huddle at his feet touched that chord of sympathy for the under-dog that stirs in every Earthman, and he pushed her gently into the corner behind him and jerked out his gun, just as the first of the running mob rounded the corner.

It was a motley crowd, Earthmen and Martians and a sprinkling of Venusian swampmen and strange, nameless denizens of unnamed planets—a typical Lakkdarol mob. When the first of them turned the corner and saw the empty street before them there was a faltering in the rush and the foremost spread out and began to search the doorways on both sides of the street.

"Looking for something?" Smith's sardonic call sounded clear above the clamor of the mob.

They turned. The shouting died for a moment as they took in the scene before them—tall Earthman in the space-explorer's leathern garb, all one color from the burning of savage suns save for the sinister pallor of his no-colored eyes in a scarred and resolute face, gun in his steady hand and the scarlet girl crouched behind him, panting.

The foremost of the crowd—a burly Earthman in tattered leather from which the Patrol insignia had been ripped away—stared for a moment with a strange expression of incredulity on his face overspreading the savage exultation of the chase. Then he let loose a deep-throated bellow, "Shambleau!" and lunged forward. Behind him the mob took up the cry again, "Shambleau! Shambleau! Shambleau!" and surged after.

Smith, lounging negligently against the wall, arms folded and gun-hand draped over his left forearm, looked incapable of swift motion, but at the leader's first forward step the pistol swept in a practised half-circle and the dazzle of blue-white heat leaping from its muzzle seared an arc in the slag pavement at his feet. It was an old gesture, and not a man in the crowd but understood it. The foremost recoiled swiftly against the surge of those in the rear, and for a moment there was confusion as the two tides met and struggled. Smith's mouth curled into a grim curve as he watched. The man in the mutilated Patrol uniform lifted a threatening fist and stepped to the very edge of the deadline, while the crowd rocked to and fro behind him.

"Are you crossing that line?" queried Smith in an ominously gentle voice.

"We want that girl!"

"Come and get her!" Recklessly Smith grinned into his face. He saw danger there, but his defiance was not the fool-hardy gesture it seemed. An expert psychologist of mobs from long experience, he sensed no murder here. Not a gun had appeared in any hand in the crowd. They desired the girl with an inexplicable bloodthirstiness he was at a loss to understand, but toward himself he sensed no such fury. A mauling he might expect, but his life was in no danger. Guns would have appeared before now if they were coming out at all. So he grinned in the man's angry face and leaned lazily against the wall.

Behind their self-appointed leader the crowd milled impatiently, and threatening voices began to rise again. Smith heard the girl moan at his feet.

"What do you want with her?" he demanded.

"She's Shambleau! Shambleau, you fool! Kick her out of there—we'll take care of her!"

"I'm taking care of her," drawled Smith.

"She's Shambleau, I tell you! Damn your hide, man, we never let those things live! Kick her out here!"

The repeated name had no meaning to him, but Smith's innate stubbornness rose defiantly as the crowd surged forward to the very edge of the arc, their clamor growing louder. "Shambleau! Kick her out here! Give us Shambleau! Shambleau!"

Smith dropped his indolent pose like a cloak and planted both feet wide, swinging up his gun threateningly. "Keep back!" he yelled. "She's mine! Keep back!"

He had no intention of using that heat-beam. He knew by now that they would not kill him unless he started the gun-play himself, and he did not mean to give up his life for any girl alive. But a severe mauling he expected, and he braced himself instinctively as the mob heaved within itself.

To his astonishment a thing happened then that he had never known to happen before. At his shouted defiance the foremost of the mob—those who had heard him clearly—drew back a little, not in alarm but evidently surprised. The ex-Patrolman said, "Yours! She's *yours?*" in a voice from which puzzlement crowded out the anger.

Smith spread his booted legs wide before the crouching figure and flourished his gun.

"Yes," he said. "And I'm keeping her! Stand back there!"

The man stared at him wordlessly, and horror and disgust and incredulity mingled on his weather-beaten face. The incredulity triumphed for a moment and he said again,

"*Yours!*"

Smith nodded defiance.

The man stepped back suddenly, unutterable contempt in his very pose. He waved an arm to the crowd and said loudly, "It's—his!" and the press melted away, gone silent, too, and the look of contempt spread from face to face.

The ex-Patrolman spat on the slag-paved street and turned his back indifferently. "Keep her, then," he advised briefly over one shoulder. "But don't let her out again in this town!"

Smith stared in perplexity almost open-mouthed as the suddenly scornful mob began to break up. His mind was in a whirl. That such bloodthirsty animosity should vanish in a breath he could not believe. And the curious mingling of contempt and disgust on the faces he saw baffled him even more. Lakkdarol was anything but a puritan town—it did not enter his head for a moment that his claiming the brown girl as his own had caused that strangely shocked revulsion to spread through the crowd. No, it was something deeper-rooted than that. Instinctive, instant disgust had been in the faces he saw—they would have looked less so if he had admitted cannibalism or *Pharol*-worship.

And they were leaving his vicinity as swiftly as if whatever unknowing sin he had committed were contagious. The street was emptying as rapidly as it had filled. He saw a sleek Venusian glance back over his shoulder as he turned the corner and sneer, "Shambleau!" and the word awoke a new line of speculation in Smith's mind. Shambleau! Vaguely of French origin, it must be. And strange enough to hear it from the lips of Venusians and Martian drylanders, but it was their use of it that puzzled him more. "We never let those things live," the ex-Patrolman had said. It reminded him dimly of something . . . an ancient line from some writing in his own tongue . . . "Thou shalt not suffer a witch to live." He smiled to himself at the similarity, and simultaneously was aware of the girl at his elbow.

She had risen soundlessly. He turned to face her, sheathing his gun, and stared at first with curiosity and then in the entirely frank openness with which men regard that which is not wholly human. For she was not. He knew it at a glance, though the brown, sweet body was shaped like a woman's and she wore the garment of scarlet—he saw it was leather—with an ease that few unhuman beings achieve toward clothing. He knew it from the moment he looked into her eyes, and a shiver of unrest went over him as he met them. They were frankly green as young grass, with slit-like, feline pupils that pulsed unceasingly, and there was a look of dark, animal wisdom in their depths—that look of the beast which sees more than man.

There was no hair upon her face—neither brows nor lashes, and he would have sworn that the tight scarlet turban bound around her head covered baldness. She had three fingers and a thumb, and her feet had four digits apiece too, and all sixteen of them were tipped with round claws that sheathed back into the flesh like a cat's. She ran her tongue over her lips—a thin, pink, flat tongue as feline as her eyes—and spoke with difficulty. He felt that that throat and tongue had never been shaped for human speech.

"Not—afraid now," she said softly, and her little teeth were white and pointed as a kitten's.

"What did they want you for?" he asked her curiously. "What had you done? Shambleau . . . is that your name?"

"I—not talk your—speech," she demurred hesitantly.

"Well, try to—I want to know. Why were they chasing you? Will you be safe on the street now, or hadn't you better get indoors somewhere? They looked dangerous."

"I—go with you." She brought it out with difficulty.

"Say you!" Smith grinned. "What are you, anyhow? You look like a kitten to me."

"Shambleau." She said it somberly.

"Where d'you live? Are you a Martian?"

"I come from—from far—from long ago—far country—"

"Wait!" laughed Smith. "You're getting your wires crossed. You're not a Martian?"

She drew herself up very straight beside him, lifting the turbaned head, and there was something queenly in the poise of her.

"Martian?" she said scornfully. "My people—are—are—you have no word. Your speech—hard for me."

"What's yours? I might know it—try me."

She lifted her head and met his eyes squarely, and there was in hers a subtle amusement—he could have sworn it.

"Some day I—speak to you in—my own language," she promised, and the pink tongue flicked out over her lips, swiftly, hungrily.

Approaching footsteps on the red pavement interrupted Smith's reply. A dryland Martian came past, reeling a little and exuding an aroma of *segir*-whisky, the Venusian brand. When he caught the red flash of the girl's tatters he turned his head sharply, and as his *segir*-steeped brain took in the fact of her presence he lurched toward the recess unsteadily, bawling, "Shambleau, by *Pharol!* Shambleau!" and reached out a clutching hand.

Smith struck it aside contemptuously.

"On your way, drylander," he advised.

The man drew back and stared, blear-eyed.

"Yours, eh?" he croaked. "*Zut!* You're welcome to it!" And like the ex-Patrolman before him he spat on the pavement and turned away, muttering harshly in the blasphemous tongue of the drylands.

Smith watched him shuffle off, and there was a crease between his colorless eyes, a nameless unease rising within him.

"Come on," he said abruptly to the girl. "If this sort of thing is going to happen we'd better get indoors. Where shall I take you?"

"With—you," she murmured.

He stared down into the flat green eyes. Those ceaselessly pulsing pupils disturbed him, but it seemed to him, vaguely, that behind the animal shallows of her gaze was a shutter—a closed barrier that might at any moment open to reveal the very deeps of that dark knowledge he sensed there.

Roughly he said again, "Come on, then," and stepped down into the street.

She pattered along a pace or two behind him, making no effort to keep up with his long strides, and though Smith—as men know from Venus to Jupiter's moons—walks as softly as a cat, even in spaceman's boots, the girl at his heels slid like a shadow over the rough pavement, making so little sound that even the lightness of his footsteps was loud in the empty street.

Smith chose the less frequented ways of Lakkdarol, and somewhat shame-facedly thanked his nameless gods that his lodgings were not far away, for the few pedestrians he met turned and stared after the two with that by now familiar mingling of horror and contempt which he was as far as ever from understanding.

The room he had engaged was a single cubicle in a lodging-house on the edge of the city. Lakkdarol, raw camp-town that it was in those days, could have furnished little better anywhere within its limits, and Smith's errand there was not one he wished to advertise. He had slept in worse places than this before, and knew that he would do so again.

There was no one in sight when he entered, and the girl slipped up the stairs at his heels and vanished through the door, shadowy, unseen by anyone in the house. Smith closed the door and leaned his broad shoulders against the panels, regarding her speculatively.

She took in what little the room had to offer in a glance—frowsy bed, rickety table, mirror hanging unevenly and cracked against the wall, unpainted chairs—a typical camp-town room in an Earth settlement abroad. She accepted its poverty in that single glance, dismissed it, then crossed to the window and leaned out for a moment, gazing across the low roof-tops toward the barren countryside beyond, red slag under the late afternoon sun.

"You can stay here," said Smith abruptly, "until I leave town. I'm waiting here for a friend to come in from Venus. Have you eaten?"

"Yes," said the girl quickly. "I shall—need no—food for—a while."

"Well——" Smith glanced around the room. "I'll be in sometime tonight. You can go or stay just as you please. Better lock the door behind me."

With no more formality than that he left her. The door closed and he heard the key turn, and smiled to himself. He did not expect, then, ever to see her again.

He went down the steps and out into the late-slanting sunlight with a mind so full of other matters that the brown girl receded very quickly into the background. Smith's errand in Lakkdarol, like most of his errands, is better not spoken of. Man lives as he must, and Smith's living was a perilous affair outside the law and ruled by the ray-gun only. It is enough to say that the shipping-port and its cargoes outbound interested him deeply just now, and that the friend he awaited was Yarol the Venusian, in that swift little Edsel ship the *Maid* that can flash from world to world with a derisive speed that laughs at Patrol boats and leaves pursuers floundering in the ether far behind. Smith and Yarol and the *Maid* were a trinity that had caused the Patrol leaders much worry and many gray hairs in the past, and the future looked very bright to Smith himself that evening as he left his lodging-house.

Lakkdarol roars by night, as Earthmen's camp-towns have a way of doing on every planet where Earth's outposts are, and it was beginning lustily as Smith went down among the awakening lights toward the center of town. His business there does not concern us. He mingled with the crowds where the lights were brightest, and there was the click of ivory counters and the jingle of silver, and red *segir* gurgled invitingly from black Venusian bottles, and much later Smith strolled homeward under the moving moons of Mars, and if the street wavered a little under his feet now and then—why, that is only understandable. Not even Smith could drink red *segir* at every bar from the *Martian Lamb* to the *New Chicago* and remain entirely steady on his feet. But he found his way back with very little difficulty—considering—and spent a good five minutes hunting for his key before he remembered he had left it in the inner lock for the girl.

He knocked then, and there was no sound of footsteps from within, but in a few moments the latch clicked and the door swung open. She retreated soundlessly before him as he entered, and took up her favorite place against the window, leaning back on the sill and outlined against the starry sky beyond. The room was in darkness.

Smith flipped the switch by the door and then leaned back against the panels, steadying himself. The cool night air had sobered him a little, and his head was clear enough—liquor went to Smith's feet, not his head, or he would never have come this far along the lawless way he had chosen. He lounged against the door now and regarded the girl in the sudden glare of the bulbs, blinding a little as much at the scarlet of her clothing as at the light.

"So you stayed," he said.

"I—waited," she answered softly, leaning farther back against the sill and clasping the rough wood with slim, three-fingered hands, pale brown against the darkness.

"Why?"

She did not answer that, but her mouth curved into a slow smile. On a woman it would have been reply enough—provocative, daring. On Shambleau there was something pitiful and horrible in it—so human on the face of one half-animal. And yet . . . that sweet brown body curving so softly from the tatters of scarlet leather—the velvety texture of that brownness—the white-flashing smile. . . . Smith was aware of a stirring excitement within him. After all—time would be hanging heavy now until Yarol came. . . . Speculatively he allowed the steel-pale eyes to wander over her, with a slow regard that missed nothing. And when he spoke he was aware that his voice had deepened a little. . . .

"Come here," he said.

She came forward slowly, on bare clawed feet that made no slightest sound on the floor, and stood before him with downcast eyes and mouth trembling in that pitifully human smile. He took her by the shoulders—velvety soft shoulders, of a creamy smoothness that was not the texture of human flesh. A little tremor went over her, perceptibly, at the contact of his hands. Northwest Smith caught his breath suddenly and dragged her to him . . . sweet, yielding brownness in the circle of his arms . . . heard her own breath catch and quicken as her velvety arms closed about his neck. And then he was looking down into her face, very near, and the green animal eyes met his with the pulsing pupils and the flicker of—something—deep behind their shallows—and through the rising clamor of his blood, even as he stooped his lips to hers, Smith felt something deep within him shudder away—inexplicable, instinctive, revolted. What it might be he had no words to tell, but the very touch of her was suddenly loathsome—so soft and velvet and unhuman—and it might have been an animal's face that lifted itself to his mouth—the dark knowledge looked hungrily from the darkness of those slit pupils—and for a mad instant he knew that same wild, feverish revulsion he had seen in the faces of the mob. . . .

"God!" he gasped, a far more ancient invocation against evil than he realized, then or ever, and he ripped her arms from his neck, swung her away with such a force that she reeled half across the room. Smith fell back against the door, breathing heavily, and stared at her while the wild revolt died slowly within him.

She had fallen to the floor beneath the window, and as she lay there against the wall with bent head he saw, curiously, that her turban had slipped—the turban that he had been so sure covered baldness—and a lock of scarlet hair fell below the binding leather, hair as scarlet as her garment, as unhumanly red as her eyes were unhumanly green. He stared, and shook his head dizzily and stared again, for it seemed to him that the thick lock of crimson had moved, *squirmed* of itself against her cheek.

At the contact of it her hands flew up and she tucked it away with a very human gesture and then dropped her head again into her hands. And from the deep shadow of her fingers he thought she was staring up at him covertly.

Smith drew a deep breath and passed a hand across his forehead. The inexplicable moment had gone as quickly as it came—too swiftly for him to understand or analyze it. "Got to lay off the *segir*," he told himself unsteadily. Had he imagined that scarlet hair? After all, she was no more than a pretty brown girl-creature from one of the many half-human races peopling the planets. No more than that, after all. A pretty little thing, but animal. . . . He laughed a little shakily.

"No more of that," he said. "God knows I'm no angel, but there's got to be a limit somewhere. Here." He crossed to the bed and sorted out a pair of blankets from the untidy heap, tossing them to the far corner of the room. "You can sleep there."

Wordlessly she rose from the floor and began to rearrange the blankets, the uncomprehending resignation of the animal eloquent in every line of her.

Smith had a strange dream that night.

He thought he had awakened to a room full of darkness and moonlight and moving shadows, for the nearer moon of Mars was racing through the sky and everything on the planet below her was endued with a restless life in the dark. And something . . . some nameless, unthinkable *thing* . . . was coiled about his throat . . . something like a soft snake, wet and warm. It lay loose and light about his neck . . . and it was moving gently, very gently, with a soft, caressive pressure that sent little thrills of delight through every nerve and fiber of him, a perilous delight—beyond physical pleasure, deeper than joy of the mind. That warm softness was caressing the very roots of his soul with a terrible intimacy. The ecstasy of it left him weak, and yet he knew—in a flash of knowledge born of this impossible dream—that the soul should not be handled. . . . And with that knowledge a horror broke upon him, turning the pleasure into a rapture of revulsion, hateful, horrible—but still most foully sweet. He tried to lift his hands and tear the dream-monstrosity from his throat—tried but half-heartedly; for though his soul was revolted to its very deeps, yet the delight of his body was so great that his hands all but refused the attempt. But when at last he tried to lift his arms a cold shock went over him and he found that he could not stir . . . his body lay stony as marble beneath the blankets, a living marble that shuddered with a dreadful delight through every rigid vein.

The revulsion grew strong upon him as he struggled against the paralyzing dream—a struggle of soul against sluggish body—titanically, until the moving dark was streaked with blankness that clouded and closed about him at last and he sank back into the oblivion from which he had awakened.

❨   ❨   ❨

Next morning, when the bright sunlight shining through Mars' clear, thin air awakened him, Smith lay for a while trying to remember. The dream had been more vivid than reality, but he could not now quite recall . . . only that it had been more sweet and horrible than anything else in life. He lay puzzling for a while, until a soft sound from the corner aroused him from his thoughts and he sat up to see the girl lying in a cat-like coil on her blankets, watching him with round, grave eyes. He regarded her somewhat ruefully.

"Morning," he said. "I've just had the devil of a dream. . . . Well, hungry?"

She shook her head silently, and he could have sworn there was a covert gleam of strange amusement in her eyes.

He stretched and yawned, dismissing the nightmare temporarily from his mind.

"What am I going to do with you?" he inquired, turning to more immediate matters. "I'm leaving here in a day or two and I can't take you along, you know. Where'd you come from in the first place?"

Again she shook her head.

"Not telling? Well, it's your own business. You can stay here until I give up the room. From then on you'll have to do your own worrying."

He swung his feet to the floor and reached for his clothes.

Ten minutes later, slipping the heat-gun into its holster at his thigh, Smith turned to the girl. "There's food-concentrate in that box on the table. It ought to hold you until I get back. And you'd better lock the door again after I've gone."

Her wide, unwavering stare was his only answer, and he was not sure she had understood, but at any rate the lock clicked after him as before, and he went down the steps with a faint grin on his lips.

The memory of last night's extraordinary dream was slipping from him, as such memories do, and by the time he had reached the street the girl and the dream and all of yesterday's happenings were blotted out by the sharp necessities of the present.

Again the intricate business that had brought him here claimed his attention. He went about it to the exclusion of all else, and there was a good reason behind everything he did from the moment he stepped out into the street until the time when he turned back again at evening; though had one chosen to follow him during the day his apparently aimless rambling through Lakkdarol would have seemed very pointless.

He must have spent two hours at the least idling by the space-port, watching with sleepy, colorless eyes the ships that came and went, the passengers, the vessels lying at wait, the cargoes—particularly the cargoes. He made the rounds of the town's saloons once more, consuming many glasses of varied liquors in the course of the day and engaging in idle conversation with men of all races and worlds, usually in their own languages, for Smith was a linguist of repute among his contemporaries. He heard the gossip of the spaceways, news from a dozen planets of a thousand different events; he heard the latest joke about the Venusian Emperor and the latest report on the Chino-Aryan war and the latest song hot from the lips of Rose Robertson, whom every man on the civilized planets adored as "the Georgia Rose". He passed the day quite profitably, for his own purposes, which do not concern us now, and it was not until late evening, when he turned homeward again, that the thought of the brown girl in his room took definite shape in his mind, though it had been lurking there, formless and submerged, all day.

He had no idea what comprised her usual diet, but he bought a can of New York roast beef and one of Venusian frog-broth and a dozen fresh canal-apples and two pounds of that Earth lettuce that grows so vigorously in the fertile canal-soil of Mars. He felt that she must surely find something to her liking in this broad variety of edibles, and—for his day had been very satisfactory—he hummed *The Green Hills of Earth* to himself in a surprizingly good baritone as he climbed the stairs.

The door was locked, as before, and he was reduced to kicking the lower panels gently with his boot, for his arms were full. She opened the door with that softness that was characteristic of her and stood regarding him in the semi-darkness as he stumbled to the table with his load. The room was unlit again.

"Why don't you turn on the lights?" he demanded irritably after he had barked his shin on the chair by the table in an effort to deposit his burden there.

"Light and—dark—they are alike—to me," she murmured.

"Cat eyes, eh? Well, you look the part. Here, I've brought you some dinner. Take your choice. Fond of roast beef? Or how about a little frog-broth?"

She shook her head and backed away a step.

"No," she said. "I can not—eat your food."

Smith's brows wrinkled. "Didn't you have any of the food-tablets?"

Again the red turban shook negatively.

"Then you haven't had anything for—why, more than twenty-four hours! You must be starved."

"Not hungry," she denied.

"What can I find for you to eat, then? There's time yet if I hurry. You've got to eat, child."

"I shall—eat," she said, softly. "Before long—I shall—feed. Have no—worry."

She turned away then and stood at the window, looking out over the moonlit landscape as if to end the conversation. Smith cast her a puzzled glance as he opened the can of roast beef. There had been an odd undernote in that assurance that, undefinably, he did not like. And the girl had teeth and tongue and presumably a fairly human digestive system, to judge from her human form. It was nonsense for her to pretend that he could find nothing that she could eat. She must have had some of the food concentrate after all, he decided, prying up the thermos lid of the inner container to release the long-sealed savor of the hot meat inside.

"Well, if you won't eat you won't," he observed philosophically as he poured hot broth and diced beef into the dish-like lid of the thermos can and extracted the spoon from its hiding-place between the inner and outer receptacles. She turned a little to watch him as he pulled up a rickety chair and sat down to the food, and after a while the realization that her green gaze was fixed so unwinkingly upon him made the man nervous, and he said between bites of creamy canal-apple, "Why don't you try a little of this? It's good."

"The food—I eat is—better," her soft voice told him in its hesitant murmur, and again he felt rather than heard a faint undernote of unpleasantness in the words. A sudden suspicion struck him as he pondered on that last remark—some vague memory of horror-tales told about campfires in the past—and he

swung round in the chair to look at her, a tiny, creeping fear unaccountably aris-
ing. There had been that in her words—in her unspoken words, that men-
aced. . . .

She stood up beneath his gaze demurely, wide green eyes with their pulsing
pupils meeting his without a falter. But her mouth was scarlet and her teeth were
sharp. . . .

"What food do you eat?" he demanded. And then, after a pause, very softly,
"Blood?"

She stared at him for a moment, uncomprehending; then something like
amusement curled her lips and she said scornfully, "You think me—vampire, eh?
No—I am Shambleau!"

Unmistakably there were scorn and amusement in her voice at the suggestion, but as unmistakably she knew what he meant—accepted it as a logical suspicion—vampires! Fairy-tales—but fairy-tales this unhuman, outland creature
was most familiar with. Smith was not a credulous man, nor a superstitious one,
but he had seen too many strange things himself to doubt that the wildest legend might have a basis of fact. And there was something namelessly strange
about her. . . .

He puzzled over it for a while between deep bites of the canal-apple. And
though he wanted to question her about a great many things, he did not, for he
knew how futile it would be.

He said nothing more until the meat was finished and another canal-apple
had followed the first, and he had cleared away the meal by the simple expedient
of tossing the empty can out of the window. Then he lay back in the chair and
surveyed her from half-closed eyes, colorless in a face tanned like saddle-leather.
And again he was conscious of the brown, soft curves of her, velvety—subtle
arcs and planes of smooth flesh under the tatters of scarlet leather. Vampire she
might be, unhuman she certainly was, but desirable beyond words as she sat submissive beneath his slow regard, her red-turbaned head bent, her clawed fingers
lying in her lap. They sat very still for a while, and the silence throbbed between
them.

She was so like a woman—an Earth woman—sweet and submissive and demure, and softer than soft fur, if he could forget the three-fingered claws and the
pulsing eyes—and that deeper strangeness beyond words. . . . (Had he dreamed

that red lock of hair that moved? Had it been *segir* that woke the wild revulsion he knew when he held her in his arms? Why had the mob so thirsted for her?) He sat and stared, and despite the mystery of her and the half-suspicions that thronged his mind—for she was so beautifully soft and curved under those revealing tatters—he slowly realized that his pulses were mounting, became aware of a kindling within . . . brown girl-creature with downcast eyes . . . and then the lids lifted and the green flatness of a cat's gaze met his, and last night's revulsion woke swiftly again, like a warning bell that clanged as their eyes met—animal, after all, too sleek and soft for humanity, and that inner strangeness. . . .

Smith shrugged and sat up. His failings were legion, but the weakness of the flesh was not among the major ones. He motioned the girl to her pallet of blankets in the corner and turned to his own bed.

From deeps of sound sleep he awoke, much later. He awoke suddenly and completely, and with that inner excitement that presages something momentous. He awoke to brilliant moonlight, turning the room so bright that he could see the scarlet of the girl's rags as she sat up on her pallet. She was awake, she was sitting with her shoulder half turned to him and her head bent, and some warning instinct crawled coldly up his spine as he watched what she was doing. And yet it was a very ordinary thing for a girl to do—any girl, anywhere. She was unbinding her turban. . . .

He watched, not breathing, a presentiment of something horrible stirring in his brain, inexplicably. . . . The red folds loosened, and—he knew then that he had not dreamed—again a scarlet lock swung down against her cheek . . . a hair, was it? a lock of hair? . . . thick as a thick worm it fell, plumply, against that smooth cheek . . . more scarlet than blood and thick as a crawling worm . . . and like a worm it crawled.

Smith rose on an elbow, not realizing the motion, and fixed an unwinking stare, with a sort of sick, fascinated incredulity, on that—that lock of hair. He had not dreamed. Until now he had taken it for granted that it was the *segir* which had made it seem to move on that evening before. But now . . . it was lengthening, stretching, moving of itself. It must be hair, but it *crawled;* with a sickening life of its own it squirmed down against her cheek, caressingly, revoltingly, impossibly. . . . Wet, it was, and round and thick and shining. . . .

She unfastened the last fold and whipped the turban off. From what he saw then Smith would have turned his eyes away—and he had looked on dreadful things before, without flinching—but he could not stir. He could only lie there on his elbow staring at the mass of scarlet, squirming—worms, hairs, what?—that writhed over her head in a dreadful mockery of ringlets. And it was lengthening, falling, somehow growing before his eyes, down over her shoulders in a spilling cascade, a mass that even at the beginning could never have been hidden under the skull-tight turban she had worn. He was beyond wondering, but he realized that. And still it squirmed and lengthened and fell, and she shook it out in a horrible travesty of a woman shaking out her unbound hair—until the unspeakable tangle of it—twisting, writhing, obscenely scarlet—hung to her waist and beyond, and still lengthened, an endless mass of crawling horror that until now, somehow, impossibly, had been hidden under the tight-bound turban. It was like a nest of blind, restless red worms . . . it was—it was like naked entrails endowed with an unnatural aliveness, terrible beyond words.

Smith lay in the shadows, frozen without and within in a sick numbness that came of utter shock and revulsion.

She shook out the obscene, unspeakable tangle over her shoulders, and somehow he knew that she was going to turn in a moment and that he must meet her eyes. The thought of that meeting stopped his heart with dread, more awfully than anything else in this nightmare horror; for nightmare it must be, surely. But he knew without trying that he could not wrench his eyes away—the sickened fascination of that sight held him motionless, and somehow there was a certain beauty. . . .

Her head was turning. The crawling awfulness rippled and squirmed at the motion, writhing thick and wet and shining over the soft brown shoulders about which they fell now in obscene cascades that all but hid her body. Her head was turning. Smith lay numb. And very slowly he saw the round of her cheek foreshorten and her profile come into view, all the scarlet horrors twisting ominously, and the profile shortened in turn and her full face came slowly round toward the bed—moonlight shining brilliantly as day on the pretty girl-face, demure and sweet, framed in tangled obscenity that crawled. . . .

The green eyes met his. He felt a perceptible shock, and a shudder rippled down his paralyzed spine, leaving an icy numbness in its wake. He felt the goose-flesh rising. But that numbness and cold horror he scarcely realized, for the green eyes were locked with his in a long, long look that somehow presaged nameless things—not altogether unpleasant things—the voiceless voice of her mind assailing him with little murmurous promises. . . .

For a moment he went down into a blind abyss of submission; and then somehow the very sight of that obscenity in eyes that did not then realize they saw it, was dreadful enough to draw him out of the seductive darkness . . . the sight of her crawling and alive with unnamable horror.

She rose, and down about her in a cascade fell the squirming scarlet of—of what grew upon her head. It fell in a long, alive cloak to her bare feet on the floor, hiding her in a wave of dreadful, wet, writhing life. She put up her hands and like a swimmer she parted the waterfall of it, tossing the masses back over her shoulders to reveal her own brown body, sweetly curved. She smiled, exquisitely, and in starting waves back from her forehead and down about her in a hideous background writhed the snaky wetness of her living tresses. And Smith knew that he looked upon Medusa.

The knowledge of that—the realization of vast backgrounds reaching into misted history—shook him out of his frozen horror for a moment, and in that moment he met her eyes again, smiling, green as glass in the moonlight, half hooded under drooping lids. Through the twisting scarlet she held out her arms. And there was something soul-shakingly desirable about her, so that all the blood surged to his head suddenly and he stumbled to his feet like a sleeper in a dream as she swayed toward him, infinitely graceful, infinitely sweet in her cloak of living horror.

And somehow there was beauty in it, the wet scarlet writhings with moonlight sliding and shining along the thick, worm-round tresses and losing itself in the masses only to glint again and move silvery along writhing tendrils—an awful, shuddering beauty more dreadful than any ugliness could be.

But all this, again, he but half realized, for the insidious murmur was coiling again through his brain, promising, caressing, alluring, sweeter than honey; and the green eyes that held his were clear and burning like the depths of a jewel, and behind the pulsing slits of darkness he was staring into a greater dark that held all things. . . . He had known—dimly he had known when he first gazed into those flat animal shallows that behind them lay this—all beauty and terror, all horror and delight, in the infinite darkness upon which her eyes opened like windows, paned with emerald glass.

Her lips moved, and in a murmur that blended indistinguishably with the silence and the sway of her body and the dreadful sway of her—her hair—she whispered—very softly, very passionately, "I shall—speak to you now—in my own tongue—oh, beloved!"

And in her living cloak she swayed to him, the murmur swelling seductive and caressing in his innermost brain—promising, compelling, sweeter than sweet. His flesh crawled to the horror of her, but it was a perverted revulsion that clasped what it loathed. His arms slid round her under the sliding cloak, wet, wet and warm and hideously alive—and the sweet velvet body was clinging to his, her arms locked about his neck—and with a whisper and a rush the unspeakable horror closed about them both.

In nightmares until he died he remembered that moment when the living tresses of Shambleau first folded him in their embrace. A nauseous, smothering odor as the wetness shut around him—thick, pulsing worms clasping every inch of his body, sliding, writhing, their wetness and warmth striking through his garments as if he stood naked to their embrace.

All this in a graven instant—and after that a tangled flash of conflicting sensation before oblivion closed over him. For he remembered the dream—and knew it for nightmare reality now, and the sliding, gently moving caresses of those wet, warm worms upon his flesh was an ecstasy above words—that deeper ecstasy that strikes beyond the body and beyond the mind and tickles the very roots of the soul with unnatural delight. So he stood, rigid as marble, as helplessly stony as any of Medusa's victims in ancient legends were, while the terrible pleasure of Shambleau thrilled and shuddered through every fiber of him; through every atom of his body and the intangible atoms of what men call the soul, through all that was Smith the dreadful pleasure ran. And it was truly dreadful. Dimly he knew it, even as his body answered to the root-deep ecstasy, a foul and dreadful wooing from which his very soul shuddered away—and yet in the innermost depths of that soul some grinning traitor shivered with delight. But deeply, behind all this, he knew horror and revulsion and despair beyond telling, while the intimate caresses crawled obscenely in the secret places of his soul—knew that the soul should not be handled—and shook with the perilous pleasure through it all.

And this conflict and knowledge, this mingling of rapture and revulsion all took place in the flashing of a moment while the scarlet worms coiled and crawled upon him, sending deep, obscene tremors of that infinite pleasure into every atom that made up Smith. And he could not stir in that slimy, ecstatic embrace—and a weakness was flooding that grew deeper after each succeeding wave of intense delight, and the traitor in his soul strengthened and drowned out the revulsion—and something within him ceased to struggle as he sank wholly into a blazing darkness that was oblivion to all else but that devouring rapture. . . .

The young Venusian climbing the stairs to his friend's lodging-room pulled out his key absent-mindedly, a pucker forming between his fine brows. He was slim, as all Venusians are, as fair and sleek as any of them, and as with most of his countrymen the look of cherubic innocence on his face was wholly deceptive. He had the face of a fallen angel, without Lucifer's majesty to redeem it; for a black devil grinned in his eyes and there were faint lines of ruthlessness and dissipation about his mouth to tell of the long years behind him that had run the gamut of experiences and made his name, next to Smith's, the most hated and the most respected in the records of the Patrol.

He mounted the stairs now with a puzzled frown between his eyes. He had come into Lakkdarol on the noon liner—the *Maid* in her hold very skillfully disguised with paint and otherwise—to find in lamentable disorder the affairs he had expected to be settled. And cautious inquiry elicited the information that Smith had not been seen for three days. That was not like his friend—he had never failed before, and the two stood to lose not only a large sum of money but also their personal safety by the inexplicable lapse on the part of Smith. Yarol could think of one solution only: fate had at last caught up with his friend. Nothing but physical disability could explain it.

Still puzzling, he fitted his key in the lock and swung the door open.

In that first moment, as the door opened, he sensed something very wrong. . . . The room was darkened, and for a while he could see nothing, but at the first breath he scented a strange, unnamable odor, half sickening, half sweet.

And deep stirrings of ancestral memory awoke within him—ancient, swamp-born memories from Venusian ancestors far away and long ago. . . .

Yarol laid his hand on his gun, lightly, and opened the door wider. In the dimness all he could see at first was a curious mound in the far corner. . . . Then his eyes grew accustomed to the dark, and he saw it more clearly, a mound that somehow heaved and stirred within itself. . . . A mound of—he caught his breath sharply—a mound like a mass of entrails, living, moving, writhing with an unspeakable aliveness. Then a hot Venusian oath broke from his lips and he cleared the door-sill in a swift stride, slammed the door and set his back against it, gun ready in his hand, although his flesh crawled—for he *knew.* . . .

"Smith!" he said softly, in a voice thick with horror. "Northwest!"

The moving mass stirred—shuddered—sank back into crawling quiescence again.

"Smith! Smith!" The Venusian's voice was gentle and insistent, and it quivered a little with terror.

An impatient ripple went over the whole mass of aliveness in the corner. It stirred again, reluctantly, and then tendril by writhing tendril it began to part itself and fall aside, and very slowly the brown of a spaceman's leather appeared beneath it, all slimed and shining.

"Smith! Northwest!" Yarol's persistent whisper came again, urgently, and with a dream-like slowness the leather garments moved . . . a man sat up in the midst of the writhing worms, a man who once, long ago, might have been Northwest Smith. From head to foot he was slimy from the embrace of the crawling horror about him. His face was that of some creature beyond humanity—dead-alive, fixed in a gray stare, and the look of terrible ecstasy that overspread it seemed to come from somewhere far within, a faint reflection from immeasurable distances beyond the flesh. And as there is mystery and magic in the moonlight which is after all but a reflection of the everyday sun, so in that gray face turned to the door was a terror unnamable and sweet, a reflection of ecstasy beyond the understanding of any who have known only earthly ecstasy themselves. And as he sat there turning a blank, eyeless face to Yarol the red worms writhed ceaselessly about him, very gently, with a soft, caressive motion that never slacked.

"Smith . . . come here! Smith . . . get up . . . Smith, Smith!" Yarol's whisper hissed in the silence, commanding, urgent—but he made no move to leave the door.

And with a dreadful slowness, like a dead man rising, Smith stood up in the nest of slimy scarlet. He swayed drunkenly on his feet, and two or three crimson tendrils came writhing up his legs to the knees and wound themselves there, supportingly, moving with a ceaseless caress that seemed to give him some hidden strength, for he said then, without inflection,

"Go away. Go away. Leave me alone." And the dead, ecstatic face never changed.

"Smith!" Yarol's voice was desperate. "Smith, listen! Smith, can't you hear me?"

"Go away," the monotonous voice said. "Go away. Go away. Go—"

"Not unless you come too. Can't you hear? Smith! Smith! I'll—"

He hushed in mid-phrase, and once more the ancestral prickle of race-memory shivered down his back, for the scarlet mass was moving again, violently, rising. . . .

Yarol pressed back against the door and gripped his gun, and the name of a god he had forgotten years ago rose to his lips unbidden. For he knew what was coming next, and the knowledge was more dreadful than any ignorance could have been.

The red, writhing mass rose higher, and the tendrils parted and a human face looked out—no, half human, with green cat-eyes that shone in that dimness like lighted jewels, compellingly. . . .

Yarol breathed "Shar!" again, and flung up an arm across his face, and the tingle of meeting that green gaze for even an instant went thrilling through him perilously.

"Smith!" he called in despair. "Smith, can't you hear me?"

"Go away," said that voice that was not Smith's. "Go away."

And somehow, although he dared not look, Yarol knew that the—the other—had parted those worm-thick tresses and stood there in all the human sweetness of the brown, curved woman's body, cloaked in living horror. And he felt the eyes upon him, and something was crying insistently in his brain to lower that shielding arm. . . . He was lost—he knew it, and the knowledge gave him that courage which comes from despair. The voice in his brain was growing, swelling, deafening him with a roaring command that all but swept him before it—command to lower that arm—to meet the eyes that opened upon darkness—to submit—and a promise, murmurous and sweet and evil beyond words, of pleasure to come. . . .

But somehow he kept his head—somehow, dizzily, he was gripping his gun in his upflung hand—somehow, incredibly, crossing the narrow room with averted face, groping for Smith's shoulder. There was a moment of blind fumbling in emptiness, and then he found it, and gripped the leather that was slimy and dreadful and wet—and simultaneously he felt something loop gently about his ankle and a shock of repulsive pleasure went through him, and then another coil, and another, wound about his feet. . . .

Yarol set his teeth and gripped the shoulder hard, and his hand shuddered of itself, for the feel of that leather was slimy as the worms about his ankles, and a faint tingle of obscene delight went through him from the contact.

That caressive pressure on his legs was all he could feel, and the voice in his brain drowned out all other sounds, and his body obeyed him reluctantly—but somehow he gave one heave of tremendous effort and swung Smith, stumbling, out of that nest of horror. The twining tendrils ripped loose with a little sucking sound, and the whole mass quivered and reached after, and then Yarol forgot his friend utterly and turned his whole being to the hopeless task of freeing himself. For only a part of him was fighting, now—only a part of him struggled against the twining obscenities, and in his innermost brain the sweet, seductive murmur sounded, and his body clamored to surrender. . . .

"*Shar! Shar y'danis . . . Shar mor'la-rol*———" prayed Yarol, gasping and half unconscious that he spoke, boy's prayers that he had forgotten years ago, and with his back half turned to the central mass he kicked desperately with his heavy boots at the red, writhing worms about him. They gave back before him, quivering and curling themselves out of reach, and though he knew that more were reaching for his throat from behind, at least he could go on struggling until he was forced to meet those eyes. . . .

He stamped and kicked and stamped again, and for one instant he was free of the slimy grip as the bruised worms curled back from his heavy feet, and he lurched away dizzily, sick with revulsion and despair as he fought off the coils, and then he lifted his eyes and saw the cracked mirror on the wall. Dimly in its reflection he could see the writhing scarlet horror behind him, cat face peering out with its demure girl-smile, dreadfully human, and all the red tendrils reaching after him. And remembrance of something he had read long ago swept incongruously over him, and the gasp of relief and hope that he gave shook for a moment the grip of the command in his brain.

Without pausing for a breath he swung the gun over his shoulder, the reflected barrel in line with the reflected horror in the mirror, and flicked the catch.

In the mirror he saw its blue flame leap in a dazzling spate across the dimness, full into the midst of that squirming, reaching mass behind him. There was a hiss and blaze and a high, thin scream of inhuman malice and despair—the flame cut a wide arc and went out as the gun fell from his hand, and Yarol pitched forward to the floor.

Northwest Smith opened his eyes to Martian sunlight streaming thinly through the dingy window. Something wet and cold was slapping his face, and the familiar fiery sting of *segir*-whisky burnt his throat.

"Smith!" Yarol's voice was saying from far away. "N. W.! Wake up, damn you! Wake up!"

"I'm—awake," Smith managed to articulate thickly. "Wha's matter?"

Then a cup-rim was thrust against his teeth and Yarol said irritably, "Drink it, you fool!"

Smith swallowed obediently and more of the fire-hot *segir* flowed down his grateful throat. It spread a warmth through his body that awakened him from the numbness that had gripped him until now, and helped a little toward driving out the all-devouring weakness he was becoming aware of, slowly. He lay still for a few minutes while the warmth of the whisky went through him, and memory sluggishly began to permeate his brain with the spread of the *segir*. Nightmare memories . . . sweet and terrible . . . memories of——

"God!" gasped Smith suddenly, and tried to sit up. Weakness smote him like a blow, and for an instant the room wheeled as he fell back against something firm and warm—Yarol's shoulder. The Venusian's arm supported him while the room steadied, and after a while he twisted a little and stared into the other's black gaze.

Yarol was holding him with one arm and finishing the mug of *segir* himself, and the black eyes met his over the rim and crinkled into sudden laughter, half hysterical after that terror that was passed.

"By *Pharol!*" gasped Yarol, choking into his mug. "By *Pharol*, N. W.! I'm never gonna let you forget this! Next time you have to drag me out of a mess I'll say——"

"Let it go," said Smith. "What's been going on? How——"

"Shambleau." Yarol's laughter died. "Shambleau! What were you doing with a thing like that?"

"What was it?" Smith asked soberly.

"Mean to say you didn't know? But where'd you find it? How——"

"Suppose you tell me first what you know," said Smith firmly. "And another swig of that *segir*, too, please. I need it."

"Can you hold the mug now? Feel better?"

"Yeah—some. I can hold it—thanks. Now go on."

"Well—I don't know just where to start. They call them Shambleau——"

"Good God, is there more than one?"

"It's a—a sort of race, I think, one of the very oldest. Where they come from nobody knows. The name sounds a little French, doesn't it? But it goes back beyond the start of history. There have always been Shambleau."

"I never heard of 'em."

"Not many people have. And those who know don't care to talk about it much."

"Well, half this town knows. I hadn't any idea what they were talking about, then. And I still don't understand, but——"

"Yes, it happens like this, sometimes. They'll appear, and the news will spread and the town will get together and hunt them down, and after that—well, the story doesn't get around very far. It's too—too unbelievable."

"But—my God, Yarol!—what was it? Where'd it come from? How——"

"Nobody knows just where they come from. Another planet—maybe some undiscovered one. Some say Venus—I know there are some rather awful legends of them handed down in our family—that's how I've heard about it. And the minute I opened that door, awhile back—I—I think I knew that smell. . . ."

"But—what *are* they?"

"God knows. Not human, though they have the human form. Or that may be only an illusion . . . or maybe I'm crazy. I don't know. They're a species of the vampire—or maybe the vampire is a species of—of them. Their normal form must be that—that mass, and in that form they draw nourishment from the—I suppose the life-forces of men. And they take some form—usually a woman form, I think, and key you up to the highest pitch of emotion before they—begin. That's to work the life-force up to intensity so it'll be easier. . . . And they give, always, that horrible, foul pleasure as they—feed. There are some men who, if they survive the first experience, take to it like a drug—can't give it up—keep the thing with them all their lives—which isn't long—feeding it for that ghastly satisfaction. Worse than smoking *ming* or—or 'praying to *Pharol*'."

"Yes," said Smith. "I'm beginning to understand why that crowd was so surprized and—and disgusted when I said—well, never mind. Go on."

"Did you get to talk to—to it?" asked Yarol.

"I tried to. It couldn't speak very well. I asked it where it came from and it said—'from far away and long ago'—something like that."

"I wonder. Possibly some unknown planet—but I think not. You know there are so many wild stories with some basis of fact to start from, that I've sometimes wondered—mightn't there be a lot more of even worse and wilder superstitions we've never even heard of? Things like this, blasphemous and foul, that those who know have to keep still about? Awful, fantastic things running around loose that we never hear rumors of at all!

"These things—they've been in existence for countless ages. No one knows when or where they first appeared. Those who've seen them, as we saw this one, don't talk about it. It's just one of those vague, misty rumors you find half hinted at in old books sometimes. . . . I believe they are an older race than man, spawned from ancient seed in times before ours, perhaps on planets that have gone to dust, and so horrible to man that when they are discovered the discoverers keep still about it—forget them again as quickly as they can.

"And they go back to time immemorial. I suppose you recognized the legend of Medusa? There isn't any question that the ancient Greeks knew of them. Does it mean that there have been civilizations before yours that set out from Earth and explored other planets? Or did one of the Shambleau somehow make its way into Greece three thousand years ago? If you think about it long enough you'll go off your head! I wonder how many other legends are based on things like this—things we don't suspect, things we'll never know.

"The Gorgon, Medusa, a beautiful woman with—with snakes for hair, and a gaze that turned men to stone, and Perseus finally killed her—I remembered this just by accident, N. W., and it saved your life and mine—Perseus killed her by using a mirror as he fought to reflect what he dared not look at directly. I wonder what the old Greek who first started that legend would have thought if he'd known that three thousand years later his story would save the lives of two men on another planet. I wonder what that Greek's own story was, and how he met the thing, and what happened. . . .

"Well, there's a lot we'll never know. Wouldn't the records of that race of—of *things*, whatever they are, be worth reading! Records of other planets and other ages and all the beginnings of mankind! But I don't suppose they've kept any records. I don't suppose they've even any place to keep them—from what little I know, or anyone knows about it, they're like the Wandering Jew, just bobbing up here and there at long intervals, and where they stay in the meantime I'd give my eyes to know! But I don't believe that terribly hypnotic power they have indicates any superhuman intelligence. It's their means of getting food—just like a frog's long tongue or a carnivorous flower's odor. Those are physical because the frog and the flower eat physical food. The Shambleau uses a—a mental reach to get mental food. I don't quite know how to put it. And just as a beast that eats the bodies of other animals acquires with each meal greater power over the bodies of the rest, so the Shambleau, stoking itself up with the life-forces of men, increases its power over the minds and the souls of other men. But I'm talking about things I can't define—things I'm not sure exist.

"I only know that when I felt—when those tentacles closed around my legs—I didn't want to pull loose, I felt sensations that—that—oh, I'm fouled and filthy to the very deepest part of me by that—pleasure—and yet—"

"I know," said Smith slowly. The effect of the *segir* was beginning to wear off, and weakness was washing back over him in waves, and when he spoke he was half meditating in a low voice, scarcely realizing that Yarol listened. "I know it—much better than you do—and there's something so indescribably awful that the thing emanates, something so utterly at odds with everything human—there aren't any words to say it. For a while I was a part of it, literally, sharing its thoughts and memories and emotions and hungers, and—well, it's over now and I don't remember very clearly, but the only part left free was that part of me that was all but insane from the—the obscenity of the thing. And yet it was a pleasure so sweet—I think there must be some nucleus of utter evil in me—in everyone—that needs only the proper stimulus to get complete control; because even while I was sick all through from the touch of those—things—there was something in me that was—was simply gibbering with delight. . . . Because of that I saw things—and knew things—horrible, wild things I can't quite remember— visited unbelievable places, looked backward through the memory of that—creature—I was one with, and saw—God, I wish I could remember!"

"You ought to thank your God you can't," said Yarol soberly.

His voice roused Smith from the half-trance he had fallen into, and he rose on his elbow, swaying a little from weakness. The room was wavering before him, and he closed his eyes, not to see it, but he asked, "You say they—they don't turn up again? No way of finding—another?"

Yarol did not answer for a moment. He laid his hands on the other man's shoulders and pressed him back, and then sat staring down into the dark, ravaged face with a new, strange, undefinable look upon it that he had never seen there before—whose meaning he knew, too well.

"Smith," he said finally, and his black eyes for once were steady and serious, and the little grinning devil had vanished from behind them, "Smith, I've never asked your word on anything before, but I've—I've earned the right to do it now, and I'm asking you to promise me one thing."

Smith's colorless eyes met the black gaze unsteadily. Irresolution was in them, and a little fear of what that promise might be. And for just a moment Yarol was looking, not into his friend's familiar eyes, but into a wide gray blankness that held all horror and delight—a pale sea with unspeakable pleasures sunk beneath it. Then the wide stare focused again and Smith's eyes met his squarely and Smith's voice said, "Go ahead. I'll promise."

"That if you ever should meet a Shambleau again—ever, anywhere—you'll draw your gun and burn it to hell the instant you realize what it is. Will you promise me that?"

There was a long silence. Yarol's somber black eyes bored relentlessly into the colorless ones of Smith, not wavering. And the veins stood out on Smith's tanned forehead. He never broke his word—he had given it perhaps half a dozen times in his life, but once he had given it, he was incapable of breaking it. And once more the gray seas flooded in a dim tide of memories, sweet and horrible beyond dreams. Once more Yarol was staring into blankness that hid nameless things. The room was very still.

The gray tide ebbed. Smith's eyes, pale and resolute as steel, met Yarol's levelly.

"I'll—try," he said. And his voice wavered.

My Dear Emily

✑

Joanna Russ

San Francisco, 188—

I am so looking forward to seeing my dear Emily at last, now she is grown, a woman, although I'm sure I will hardly recognize her. She must not be proud (as if she could be!) but will remember her friends, I know, and have patience with her dear Will who cannot help but remember the girl she was, and the sweet influence she had in her old home. I talk to your father about you every day, dear, and he longs to see you as I do. Think! a learned lady in our circle! But I know you have not changed . . .

EMILY CAME HOME FROM SCHOOL IN APRIL WITH HER bosom friend Charlotte. They had loved each other in school, but they didn't speak much on the train. While Emily read Mr. Emerson's poems, Charlotte examined the scenery through opera-glasses. She expressed her wish to see "savages."

"That's foolish," says Emily promptly.

"If we were carried off," says Charlotte, "I don't think you would notice it in time to disapprove."

"That's very foolish," says Emily, touching her round lace collar with one hand. She looks up from Mr. Emerson to stare Charlotte out of countenance, properly, morally, and matter-of-course young lady. It has always been her style.

"The New England look," Charlotte snaps resentfully. She makes her opera-glasses slap shut.

"I should like to be carried off," she proposes; "but then I don't have an engagement to look forward to. A delicate affair."

"You mustn't make fun," says Emily. Mr. Emerson drops into her lap. She stares unseeing at Charlotte's opera-glasses.

"Why do they close?" she asks helplessly.

"I beg your pardon?" blankly, from Charlotte.

"Nothing. You're much nicer than I am," says Emily.

"Look," urges Charlotte kindly, pressing the toy into her friend's hand.

"For savages?"

Charlotte nods, Emily pushes the spring that will open the little machine, and a moment later drops them into her lap where they fall on Mr. Emerson. There is a cut across one of her fingers and a blue pinch darkening the other.

"They hurt me," she says without expression, and as Charlotte takes the glasses up quickly, Emily looks with curious sad passivity at the blood from her little wound, which has bled an incongruous passionate drop on Mr. Emerson's clothbound poems. To her friend's surprise (and her own, too) she begins to cry, heavily, silently, and totally without reason.

He wakes up slowly, mistily, dizzily, with a vague memory of having fallen asleep on plush. He is intensely miserable, bound down to his bed with hoops of steel, and the memory adds nausea to his misery, solidifying ticklishly around his bare hands and the back of his neck as he drifts towards wakefulness. His stomach turns over with the dry brushy filthiness of it. With the caution of the chronically ill, he opens his eyelids, careful not to move, careful even to keep from focusing his gaze until—he thinks to himself—his bed stops holding him with the force of Hell and this intense miserable sickness goes down, settles . . . Darkness. No breath. A glimmer of light, a stone wall. He thinks: *I'm dead and buried, dead and buried, dead and*— With infinite care he attempts to breathe, sure that this time it will be easy; he'll be patient, discreet, sensible, he won't do it all at once—

He gags. Spasmodically, he gulps, cries out, and gags again, springing convulsively to his knees and throwing himself over the low wall by his bed, laboring as if he were breathing sand. He starts to sweat. His heartbeat comes back, then pulse, then seeing, hearing, swallowing . . . High in the wall a window glimmers, a star is out, the sky is pale evening blue. Trembling with nausea, he rises to his feet, sways a little in the gloom, then puts out one arm and steadies himself against the stone wall. He sees the window, sees the door ahead of him. In his tearing eyes the star suddenly blazes and lengthens like a knife; his hands over his face, longing for life and strength to come back, the overwhelming flow of force that will crest at sunrise, leaving him raging at the world and ready to kill anyone, utterly proud and contemptuous, driven to sleep as the last resort of a balked assassin. But it's difficult to stand, difficult to breathe: *I wish I were dead and buried, dead and buried, dead and buried— But there!* he whispers to himself like a charm, *There, it's going, it's going away.* He smiles slyly round at his companionable, merciful stone walls. With an involuntarily silent, gliding gait he moves toward the door, opens the iron gate, and goes outside. Life is coming back. The trees are black against the sky, which yet holds some light; far away in the West lie the radiant memories of a vanished sun. An always vanished sun.

"Alive!" he cries, in triumph. It is—as usual—his first word of the day.

Dear Emily, sweet Emily, met Martin Guevara three days after she arrived home. She had been shown the plants in the garden and the house plants in stands and had praised them; she had been shown the sun-pictures and had praised *them;* she had fingered antimacassars, promised to knit, exclaimed at gaslights, and passed two evenings at home, doing nothing. Then in the hall that led to the pantry Sweet Will had taken her hand and she had dropped her eyes because you were supposed to and that was her style. Charlotte (who slept in the same room as her friend) embraced her at bedtime, wept over the handtaking, and then Emily said to her dear, dear friend (without thinking):

"Sweet William."

Charlotte laughed.

"It's not a joke!"

"It's so funny."

"I love Will dearly." She wondered if God would strike her dead for a hypocrite. Charlotte was looking at her oddly, and smiling.

"You mustn't be full of levity," said Emily, peeved. It was then that Sweet William came in and told them of tomorrow's garden-party, which was to be composed of her father's congregation. They were lucky, he said, to have acquaintances of such position and character. Charlotte slipped out on purpose, and Will, seeing they were alone, attempted to take Emily's hand again.

"Leave me alone!" Emily said angrily. He stared.

"I said leave me alone!"

And she gave him such a look of angry pride that, in fact, he did.

☾   ☾   ☾

Emily sees Guevara across the parlor by the abominable cherry-red sofa, talking animatedly and carelessly. In repose he is slight, undistinguished, and plain, but no one will ever see him in repose; Emily realizes this. His strategy is never to rest, to bewilder, he would (she thinks) slap you if only to confuse you, and when he can't he's always out of the way and attacking, making one look ridiculous. She knows nobody and is bored; she starts for the door to the garden.

At the door his hand closes over her wrist; he has somehow gotten there ahead of her.

"The lady of the house," he says.

"I'm back from school."

"And you've learned—?"

"Let me go, please."

"Never." He drops her hand and stands in the doorway. She says:

"I want to go outside."

"Never."

"I'll call my father."

"Do." She tries and can't talk; I wouldn't *bother*, she thinks to herself, loftily. She goes out into the garden with him. Under the trees his plainness vanishes like smoke.

"You want lemonade," he says.

"I'm not going to talk to you," she responds. "I'll talk to Will. Yes! I'll make him—"

"In trouble," says Mr. Guevara, returning silently with lemonade in a glass cup.

"No thank you."

"She wants to get away," says Martin Guevara. "I know."

"If I had your trick of walking like a cat," she says, "I could get out of anything."

"I *can* get out of anything," says the gentleman, handing Emily her punch, "out of an engagement, a difficulty. I can even get *you* out of anything."

"I loathe you," whispers Emily suddenly. "You walk like a cat. You're ugly."

"Not out here," he remarks.

"Who has to be afraid of lights?" cries Emily energetically. He stands away from the paper lanterns strung between the trees, handsome, comfortable and collected, watching Emily's cut-glass cup shake in her hand.

"I can't move," she says miserably.

"Try." She takes a step towards him. "See; you can."

"But I wanted to go *away!*" With sudden hysteria she flings the lemonade (cup and all) into his face, but he is no longer there.

"What are you doing at a church supper, you hypocrite!" she shouts tearfully at the vacancy.

Sweet William has to lead her in to bed.

"You thought better of it," remarks Martin, head framed in an evening window, sounds of footsteps outside, ladies' heels clicking in the streets.

"I don't know you," she says miserably, "I just don't." He takes her light shawl, a pattern in India cashmere.

"That will come," he says, smiling. He sits again, takes her hand, and squeezes the skin on the wrist.

"Let me go, please?" she says like a child.

"I don't know."

"You talk like the smart young gentlemen at Andover; they were all fools."

"Perhaps you overawed them." He leans forward and puts his hand around the back of her neck for a moment. "Come on, dear."

"What are you talking about!" Emily cries.

"San Francisco is a lovely city. I had ancestors here three hundred years ago."

"Don't think that because I came here——"

"She doesn't," he whispers, grasping her shoulder, "she doesn't know a thing."

"God damn you!"

He blinks and sits back. Emily is weeping. The confusion of the room—an over-stuffed, over-draped hotel room—has gotten on her nerves. She snatches for her shawl, which is still in his grasp, but he holds it out of her reach, darting his handsome, unnaturally young face from side to side as she tries to reach round him. She falls across his lap and lies there, breathless with terror.

"You're cold," she whispers, horrified, "you're cold as a corpse." The shawl descends lightly over her head and shoulders. His frozen hands help her to her feet. He is delighted; he bares his teeth in a smile.

"I think," he says, tasting it, "that I'm going to visit your family."

"But you don't—" she stumbles—"you don't want to . . . sleep with me. I know it."

"I can be a suitor like anyone else," he says.

That night Emily tells it all to Charlotte, who, afraid of the roué, stays up and reads a French novel as the light drains from the windows and the true black dark takes its place. It is almost dawn and Charlotte has been dozing, when Emily shakes her friend awake, kneeling by the bed with innocent blue eyes reflecting the dying night.

"I had a terrible dream," she complains.

"Hmmmm?"

"I dreamed," says Emily tiredly. "I had a nightmare. I dreamed I was walking by the beach and I decided to go swimming and then a . . . a thing, I don't know . . . it took me by the neck."

"Is that all?" says Charlotte peevishly.

"I'm sick," says Emily with childish satisfaction. She pushes Charlotte over in the bed and climbs in with her. "I won't have to see that man again if I'm sick."

"Pooh, why not?" mumbles Charlotte.

"Because I'll have to stay home."

"He'll visit you."

"William won't let him."

"Sick?" says Charlotte then, suddenly waking up. She moves away from her friend, for she has read more bad fiction than Emily and less moral poetry.

"Yes, I feel awful," says Emily simply, resting her head on her knees. She pulls away in tired irritation when her friend reaches for the collar of her nightdress. Charlotte looks and jumps out of bed.

"Oh," says Charlotte. "Oh—goodness—oh—" holding out her hands.

"What on earth's the matter with you?"

"He's—" whispers Charlotte in horror, "he's—"

In the dim light her hands are black with blood.

❨　　❨　　❨

"You've come," he says. He is lying on his hotel sofa, reading a newspaper, his feet over one arm and a hand trailing on the rug.

"Yes," she answers, trembling with resolution.

"I never thought this place would have such a good use. But I never know when I'll manage to pick up money—"

With a blow of her hand, she makes a fountain of the newspaper; he lies on the sofa, mildly amused.

"Nobody knows I came," she says rapidly. "But I'm going to finish you off. I know how." She hunts feverishly in her bag.

"I wouldn't," he remarks quietly.

"Ah!" Hauling out her baby cross (silver), she confronts him with it like Joan of Arc. He is still amused, still mildly surprised.

"In your hands?" he says delicately. Her fingers are loosening, her face pitiful.

"My dear, the significance is in the feeling, the faith, not the symbol. You use that the way you would use a hypodermic needle. Now in your father's hands—"

"I dropped it," she says in a little voice. He picks it up and hands it to her.

"You can touch—" she says, her face screwing up for tears.

"I can."

"Oh my God!" she cries in despair.

"My dear." He puts one arm around her, holding her against him, a very strong man for she pushes frantically to free herself. "How many times have I said that! But you'll learn. Do I sound like the silly boys at Andover?" Emily's eyes are fixed and her throat contracts; he forces her head between her knees. "The way you go on, you'd think I was bad luck."

"I—I—"

"And you without the plentiful lack of brains that characterizes your friend. She'll be somebody's short work and I think I know whose."

Emily turns white again.

"I'll send her around to you afterwards. Good God! What do you think will happen to her?"

"She'll die," says Emily clearly. He grasps her by the shoulders.

"Ah!" he says with immense satisfaction. "And after that? Who lives forever after that? Did you know that?"

"Yes, people like you don't die," whispers Emily. "But you're not people—"

"No," he says intently, "no. We're not." He stands Emily on her feet. "We're a passion!" Smiling triumphantly, he puts his hands on each side of her head, flattening the pretty curls, digging his fingers into the hair, in a grip Emily can no more break than she could break a vise.

"We're passion," he whispers, amused. "Life is passion. Desire makes life."

"Ah, let me go," says Emily.

He smiles ecstatically at the sick girl.

"Desire," he says dreamily, "lives; *that* lives when nothing else does, and we're desire made purely, desire walking the Earth. Can a dead man walk? Ah! If you want, want, want . . ."

He throws his arms around her, pressing her head to his chest and nearly suffocating her, ruining her elaborate coiffure and crushing the lace at her throat. Emily breathes in the deadness about him, the queer absence of odor, or heat, or presence; her mouth is pressed against the cloth of his fashionable suit, expensive stuff, a good dollar a yard, gotten by—what? But his hands are strong enough to get anything.

"You see," he says gently. "I enjoy someone with intelligence, even with morals; it adds a certain— And besides—" here he releases her and holds her face up to his— "we like souls that come to us; these visits to the bedrooms of unconscious citizens are rather like frequenting a public brothel."

"I abhor you," manages Emily. He laughs. He's delighted.

"Yes, yes, dear," he says, "but don't imagine we're callous parasites. Followers of the Marquis de Sade, perhaps—you see Frisco has evening hours for its book-stores!—but sensitive souls, really, and apt to long for a little conscious partnership." Emily shuts her eyes. "I said," he goes on, with a touch of hardness, "that I am a genuine seducer. I flatter myself that I'm not an animal."

"You're a monster," says Emily, with utter conviction. Keeping one hand on her shoulder, he steps back a pace.

"Go." She stands, unable to believe her luck, then makes what seems to her a rush for the door; it carries her into his arms.

"You see?" He's pleased; he's proved a point.

"I can't," she says, with wide eyes and wrinkled forehead . . .

"You will." He reaches for her and she faints.

❬   ❬   ❬

Down in the dark where love and some other things make their hidingplace, Emily drifts aimlessly, quite alone, quite cold, like a dead woman without a passion in her soul to make her come back to life.

She opens her eyes and finds herself looking at his face in the dark, as if the man carried his own light with him.

"I'll die," she says softly.

"Not for a while," he drawls, sleek and content.

"You've killed me."

"I've loved."

"Love!"

"Say 'taken' then, if you insist."

"I do! I do!" she cries bitterly.

"You decided to faint."

"Oh the hell with you!" she shouts.

"Good girl!" And as she collapses, weeping hysterically, "Now, now, come here, dear . . ." nuzzling her abused little neck. He kisses it in the tenderest fashion with an exaggerated, mocking sigh; she twists away, but is pulled closer and as his lips open over the teeth of inhuman, dead desire, his victim finds—to her surprise—that there is no pain. She braces herself and then, unexpectedly, shivers from head to foot.

"Stop it!" she whispers, horrified. "Stop it! Stop it!"

But a vampire who has found a soul-mate (even a temporary one) will be immoderate. There's no stopping them.

Charlotte's books have not prepared her for *this*.

"You're to stay in the house, my dear, because you're ill."

"I'm not," Emily says, pulling the sheet up to her chin.

"Of course you are." The Reverend beams at her, under the portrait of Emily's dead mother which hangs in Emily's bedroom. "You've had a severe chill."

"But I have to get out!" says Emily, sitting up. "Because I have an appointment, you see."

"Not now," says the Reverend.

"But I *can't* have a severe chill in the *summer!*"

"You look so like your mother," says the Reverend, musing. After he has gone away, Charlotte comes in.

"I have to stay in the damned bed," says Emily forcefully, wiggling her toes under the sheet. Charlotte, who has been carrying a tray with tea and a posy on it, drops it on the washstand.

"Why, Emily!"

"I have to stay in the damned bed the whole damned day," Emily adds.

"Dear, why do you use those words?"

"Because the whole world's damned!"

After the duties of his employment were completed at six o'clock on Wednesday, William came to the house with a doctor and introduced him to the Reverend and Emily's bosom friend. The street lamps would not be lit for an hour but the sun was just down and a little party congregated in the garden under remains of Japanese paper lanterns. No one ever worried that these might set themselves on fire. Lucy brought tea—they were one of the few civilized circles in Frisco—and over the tea, in the darkening garden, to the accompaniment of sugar-tongs and plopping cream (very musical) they talked.

"Do you think," says the Reverend, very worried, "that it might be consumption?"

"Perhaps the lungs are affected," says the doctor.

"She's always been such a robust girl." This is William, putting down the teapot which has a knitted tube about the handle, for insulation. Charlotte is stirring her tea with a spoon.

"It's very strange," says the doctor serenely, and he repeats "it's very strange" as shadows advance in the garden. "But young ladies, you know—especially at twenty—young ladies often take strange ideas into their heads; they do, they often do; they droop; they worry." His eyes are mild, his back sags, he hears the pleasant gurgle of more tea. A quiet consultation, good people, good solid people, a little illness, nothing serious—

"No," says Charlotte. Nobody hears her.

"I knew a young lady once—" ventures the doctor mildly.

"No," says Charlotte, more loudly. Everyone turns to her, and Lucy, taking the opportunity, insinuates a plate of small-sized muffins in front of Charlotte.

"I can tell you all about it," mutters Charlotte, glancing up from under her eyebrows. "But you'll *laugh*."

"Now, dear—" says the Reverend.

"Now, miss—" says the doctor.

"As a friend—" says William.

Charlotte begins to sob.

"Oh," she says, "I'll—I'll tell you about it."

Emily meets Mr. Guevara at the Mansion House at seven, having recovered an appearance of health (through self-denial) and a good solid record of spending the evenings at home (through self-control). She stands at the hotel's wrought-iron gateway, her back rigid as a stick, drawing on white gloves. Martin material-izes out of the blue evening shadows and takes her arm.

"I shall like living forever," says Emily, thoughtfully.

"God deliver me from Puritans," says Mr. Guevara.

"What?"

"You're a lady. You'll swallow me up."

"I'll do anything I please," remarks Emily severely, with a glint of teeth.

"Ah."

"I will." They walk through the gateway. "You don't care two pins for me."

"Unfortunately," says he, bowing.

"It's not unfortunate as long as *I* care for me," says Emily, smiling with great energy. "Damn them all."

"You proper girls would overturn the world." Along they walk in the evening, in a quiet, respectable rustle of clothes. Halfway to the restaurant she stops and says breathlessly:

"Let's go—somewhere else!"

"My dear, you'll ruin your health!"

"You know better. Three weeks ago I was sick as a dog and much you cared; I haven't slept for days and I'm fine."

"You look fine."

"Ah! You mean I'm beginning to look dead, like you." She tightens her hold on his arm, to bring him closer.

"Dead?" says he, slipping his arm around her.

"Fixed. Bright-eyed. Always at the same heat and not a moment's rest."

"It agrees with you."

"I adore you," she says.

When Emily gets home, there's a reckoning. The Reverend stands in the doorway and sad William, too, but not Charlotte, for she is on the parlor sofa, having had hysterics.

"Dear Emily," says the Reverend. "We don't know how to tell you this—"

"Why, Daddy, *what?*" exclaims Emily, making wide-eyes at him.

"Your little friend told us—"

"Has something happened to Charlotte?" cries Emily. "Oh tell me, tell me, what happened to Charlotte?" And before they can stop her she has flown into the parlor and is kneeling beside her friend, wondering if she dares pinch her under cover of her shawl. William, quick as a flash, kneels on one side of her and Daddy on the other.

"Dear Emily!" cries William with fervor.

"Oh sweetheart!" says Charlotte, reaching down and putting her arms around her friend.

"You're well!" shouts Emily, sobbing over Charlotte's hand and thinking perhaps to bite her. But the Reverend's arms lift her up.

"My dear," says he, "you came home unaccompanied. You were not at the Society."

"But," says Emily, smiling dazzlingly, "two of the girls took all my hospital sewing to their house because we must finish it right away and I have not—"

"You have been lying to us," the Reverend says. *Now,* thinks Emily, *Sweet William will cover his face.* Charlotte sobs.

"She can't help it," says Charlotte brokenly. "It's the spell."

"Why, I think everyone's gone out of their minds," says Emily, frowning. Sweet William takes her from Daddy, leading her away from Charlotte.

"Weren't you with a gentleman tonight?" says Sweet Will firmly. Emily backs away.

"For shame!"

"She doesn't remember it," explains Charlotte; "it's part of his spell."

"I think you ought to get a doctor for *her,*" observes Emily.

"You were with a gentleman named Guevara," says Will, showing less ten-derness than Emily expects. "Weren't you? Well—weren't you?"

"Bad cess to you if I was!" snaps Emily, surprised at herself. The other three gasp. "I won't be questioned," she goes on, "and I won't be spied upon. And I think you'd better take some of Charlotte's books away from her; she's getting downright silly."

"You have too much color," says Will, catching her hands. "You're ill but you don't sleep. You stay awake all night. You don't eat. But look at you!"

"I don't understand you. Do you want me to be ugly?" says Emily, trying to be pitiful. Will softens; she sees him do it.

"My dear Emily," he says. "My dear girl—we're afraid for you."

"Me?" says Emily, enjoying herself.

"We'd better put you to bed," says the Reverend kindly.

"You're so kind," whispers Emily, blinking as if she held back tears.

"That's a good girl," says Will, approving. "We know you don't understand. But we'll take care of you, Em."

"*Will* you?"

"Yes, dear. You've been near very grave danger, but luckily we found out in time, and we found out what to do; we'll make you well, we'll keep you safe, we'll—"

"Not with *that* you won't," says Emily suddenly, rooting herself to the spot, for what William takes out of his vest pocket (where he usually keeps his watch) is a broad-leaved, prickle-faced dock called wolfsbane; it must distress any vampire of sense to be so enslaved to pure superstition. But enslaved they are, nonetheless.

"Oh, no!" says Emily swiftly. "That's silly, perfectly silly!"

"Common sense must give way in such a crisis," remarks the Reverend gravely.

"You bastard!" shouts Emily, turning red, attempting to tear the charm out of her fiancé's hand and jump up and down on it. But the Reverend holds one arm and Charlotte the other and between them they pry her fingers apart and William puts his property gently in his vest pocket again.

"She's far gone," says the Reverend fearfully, at his angry daughter. Emily is scowling, Charlotte stroking her hair.

"Ssssh," says Will with great seriousness. "We must get her to bed," and be-tween them they half-carry Emily up the stairs and put her, dressed as she is, in the big double bed with the plush headboard that she has shared so far with Charlotte. Daddy and fiancé confer in the room across the long, low rambling hall, and Charlotte sits by her rebellious friend's bed and attempts to hold her hand.

"I won't permit it; you're a damned fool!" says Emily.

"Oh, Emmy!"

"Bosh."

"It's true!"

"Is it?" With extraordinary swiftness, Emily turns round in the bed and rises to her knees. "Do you know anything about it?"

"I know it's horrid, I—"

"Silly!" Playfully Emily puts her hands on Charlotte's shoulders. Her eyes are narrowed, her nostrils widened to breathe; she parts her lips a little and looks archly at her friend. "You don't know anything about it," she says insinuatingly.

"I'll call your father," says Charlotte quickly.

Emily throws an arm around her friend's neck.

"Not yet! Dear Charlotte!"

"We'll save you," says Charlotte doubtfully.

"Sweet Charrie; you're my friend, aren't you?"

Charlotte begins to sob again.

"Give me those awful things, those leaves."

"Why, Emily, I *couldn't!*"

"But he'll come for me and I have to protect myself, don't I?"

"I'll call your father," says Charlotte firmly.

"No, I'm *afraid.*" And Emily wrinkles her forehead sadly.

"Well—"

"Sometimes I—I—" falters Emily. "I can't move or run away and everything looks so—so strange and *horrible*—"

"Oh, here!" Covering her face with one hand, Charlotte holds out her precious dock leaves in the other.

"Dear, dear! Oh, sweet! Oh thank you! Don't be afraid. He isn't after you."

"I hope not," says the bosom friend.

"Oh no, he told me. It's me he's after."

"How awful," says Charlotte, sincerely.

"Yes," says Emily. "Look." And she pulls down the collar of her dress to show the ugly marks, white dots unnaturally healed up, like the pockmarks of a drug addict.

"Don't!" chokes Charlotte.

Emily smiles mournfully. "We really ought to put the lights out," she says. "Out!"

"Yes, you can see him better that way. If the lights are on, he could sneak in without being seen; he doesn't mind lights, you know."

"I don't know, dear—"

"I do." (Emily is dropping the dock leaves into the washstand, under cover of her skirt.) "I'm afraid. Please."

"Well—"

"Oh, you must!" And leaping to her feet, she turns down the gas to a dim glow; Charlotte's face fades into the obscurity of the deepening shadows.

"So. The lights are out," says Emily quietly.

"I'll ask Will—" Charlotte begins . . .

"No, dear."

"But, Emily—"

"He's coming, dear."

"You mean Will is coming."

"No, not Will."

"Emily, you're a—"

"I'm a sneak," says Emily, chuckling, "Sssssh!" And, while her friend sits paralyzed, one of the windows swings open in the night breeze, a lead-paned window that opens on a hinge, for the Reverend is fond of culture and old architecture. Charlotte lets out a little noise in her throat; and then—with the smash of a pistol shot—the gaslights shatter and the flame goes out. Gas hisses into the air, quietly, insinuatingly, as if explaining the same thing over and over. Charlotte screams with her whole heart. In the dark a hand clamps like a vice on Emily's wrist. A moment passes.

"Charlotte?" she whispers.

"Dead," says Guevara.

Emily has spent most of the day asleep in the rubble, with his coat rolled under her head where he threw it the moment before sunrise, the moment before he staggered to his place and plunged into sleep. She has watched the dawn come up behind the rusty barred gate, and then drifted into sleep herself with his face before her closed eyes—his face burning with a rigid, constricted, unwasting vitality. Now she wakes aching and bruised, with the sun of late afternoon in her face. Sitting against the stone wall, she sneezes twice and tries, ineffectually, to shake the dust from her silk skirt.

Oh, how—she thinks vaguely—*how messy.* She gets to her feet. *There's something I have to do.* The iron gate swings open at a touch. *Trees and gravestones tilted every which way. What did he say? Nothing would disturb it but a Historical Society.*

Having tidied herself as best she can, with his coat over her arm and the address of his tailor in her pocket, she trudges among the erupted stones, which tilt crazily to all sides as if in an earthquake. Blood (Charlotte's, whom she does not think about) has spread thinly on to her hair and the hem of her dress, but her hair is done up with fine feeling, despite the absence of a mirror, and her dress is dark gray; the spot looks like a spot of dust. She folds the coat into a neat package and uses it to wipe the dust off her shoes, then lightens her step past the cemetery entrance, trying to look healthy and respectable. She aches all over from sleeping on the ground.

Once in town and having ascertained from a shop window that she will pass muster in a crowd, Emily trudges up hills and down hills to the tailor, the evidence over her arm. She stops at other windows, to look or to admire herself; thinks smugly of her improved coloring; shifts the parcel on her arm to show off her waist. In one window there is a display of religious objects—beads and crosses, books with fringed gilt bookmarks, a colored chromo of Madonna and Child. In this window Emily admires herself.

"It's Emily, dear!"

A Mrs. L——— appears in the window beside her, with Constantia, Mrs. L———'s twelve-year-old offspring.

"Why, dear, whatever happened to you?" Mrs. L———, noticing no hat, no gloves, and no veil.

"Nothing; whatever happened to you?" says Emily cockily. Constantia's eyes grow wide with astonishment at the fine, free audacity of it.

"Why, you look as if you'd been—"

"Picknicking," says Emily, promptly. "One of the gentlemen spilled beer on his coat." And she's in the shop now and hanging over the counter, flushed, counting the coral and amber beads strung around a crucifix.

Mrs. L——— knocks doubtfully on the window-glass.

Emily waves and smiles.

Your father—form Mrs. L———'s lips in the glass.

Emily nods and waves cheerfully.

They do go away, finally.

"A fine gentleman," says the tailor earnestly, "a very fine man." He lisps a little.

"Oh very fine," agrees Emily, sitting on a stool and kicking the rungs with her feet. "Monstrous fine."

"But very careless," says the tailor fretfully, pulling Martin's coat nearer the window so he can see it, for the shop is a hole-in-the-wall and dark. "He shouldn't send a lady to this part of the town."

"I was a lady once," says Emily.

"Mmmmmm."

"It's fruit stains—something awful, don't you think?"

"I cannot have this ready by tonight," looking up.

"Well, you must, that's all," says Emily calmly. "You always have and he has a lot of confidence in you, you know. He'd be awfully angry if he found out."

"Found out?" sharply.

"That you can't have it ready by tonight."

The tailor ponders.

"I'll positively stay in the shop while you work," says Emily flatteringly.

"Why, Reverend, I saw her on King Street as dirty as a gypsy, with her hair loose and the wildest eyes and I *tried* to talk to her, but she dashed into a shop—"

The sun goes down in a broad belt of gold, goes down over the ocean, over the hills and the beaches, makes shadows lengthen in the street near the quays where a lisping tailor smooths and alters, working against the sun (and very uncomfortable he is, too), watched by a pair of unwinking eyes that glitter a little in the dusk inside the stuffy shop. (*I think I've changed,* meditates Emily.)

He finishes, finally, with relief, and sits with an *ouf!* handing her the coat, the new and beautiful coat that will be worn as soon as the eccentric gentleman comes out to take the evening air. The eccentric gentleman, says Emily incautiously, will do so in an hour by the Mansion House when the last traces of light have faded from the sky.

"Then, my dear Miss," says the tailor unctuously, "I think a little matter of pay—"

"You don't think," says Emily softly, "or you wouldn't have gotten yourself into such a mess as to be this eccentric gentleman's tailor." And out she goes.

Now nobody can see the stains on Emily's skirt or in her hair; street lamps are being lit, there are no more carriages, and the number of people in the streets grows—San Francisco making the most of the short summer nights. It is perhaps fifteen minutes back to the fashionable part of the town where Emily's hatless, shawlless state will be looked on with disdain; here nobody notices. Emily dawdles through the streets, fingering her throat, yawning, looking at the sky, thinking: *I love, I love, I love—*

She has fasted for the day but she feels fine; she feels busy, busy inside as if the life inside her is flowering and bestirring itself, populated as the streets. She remembers—

I love you. I hate you. You enchantment, you degrading necessity, you foul and filthy life, you promise of endless love and endless time . . .

What words to say with Charlotte sleeping in the same room, no, the same bed, with her hands folded under her face! Innocent sweetheart, whose state must now be rather different.

Up the hills she goes, where the view becomes wider and wider, and the lights spread out like sparkles on a cake, out of the section which is too dangerous, too low, and too furtive to bother with a lady (or is it something in her eyes?), into the broader bystreets where shore-leave sailors try to make her acquaintance by falling into step and seizing her elbow; she snakes away with unbounded strength, darts into shadows, laughs in their faces: "I've got what I want!"

"Not like me!"

"Better!"

This is the Barbary Coast, only beginning to become a tourist attraction; there are barkers outside the restaurants advertising pretty waiter girls, dance

halls, spangled posters twice the height of a man, crowds upon crowds of people, one or two guides with tickets in their hats, and Emily—who keeps to the
shadows. She nearly chokes with laughter: *What a field of ripe wheat!* One of the
barkers hoists her by the waist onto his platform.

"Do you see this little lady? Do you see this—"

"Let me go, God damn you!" she cries indignantly.

"This angry little lady—" pushing her chin with one sun-burned hand to
make her face the crowd. "This—" But here Emily hurts him, slashing his palm
with her teeth, quite pleased with herself, but surprised, too, for the man was
holding his hand cupped and the whole thing seemed to happen of itself. She es-
capes instantly into the crowd and continues up through the Coast, through the
old Tenderloin, drunk with self-confidence, slipping like a shadow through the
now genteel streets and arriving at the Mansion House gate having seen no family spies and convinced that none has seen her.

But nobody is there.

Ten by the clock, and no one is there, either; eleven by the clock and still no
one. *Why didn't I leave this life when I had the chance!* Only one thing consoles Emily,
that by some alchemy or nearness to the state she longs for, no one bothers or
questions her and even the policemen pass her by as if in her little corner of the
gate there is nothing but a shadow. Midnight and no one, half-past and she
dozes; perhaps three hours later, perhaps four, she is startled awake by the sound
of footsteps. She wakes: nothing. She sleeps again and in her dream hears them
for the second time, then she wakes to find herself looking into the face of a lady
who wears a veil.

"What!" Emily's startled whisper.

The lady gestures vaguely, as if trying to speak.

"What is it?"

"Don't—" and the lady speaks with feeling but, it seems, with difficulty
also—"don't go home."

"Home?" echoes Emily, stupefied, and the stranger nods, saying:

"In danger."

"Who?" Emily is horrified.

"He's in danger." Behind her veil her face seems almost to emit a faint light
of its own.

"You're one of them," says Emily. "Aren't you?" and when the woman nods, adds desperately, "Then you must save him!"

The lady smiles pitifully; that much of her face can be seen as the light breeze plays with her net veil.

"But you must!" exclaims Emily. "You know how; I don't; you've got to!"

"I don't dare," very softly. Then the veiled woman turns to go, but Emily— quite hysterical now—seizes her hand, saying:

"Who are you? Who are you?"

The lady gestures vaguely and shakes her head.

"Who are you!" repeats Emily with more energy. "You tell me, do you hear?"

Sombrely the lady raises her veil and stares at her friend with a tragic, digni- fied, pitiful gaze. In the darkness her face burns with unnatural and beautiful color.

It is Charlotte.

Dawn comes with a pellucid quickening, glassy and ghostly. Slowly, shapes emerge from darkness and the blue pours back into the world—twilight turned backwards and the natural order reversed. Destruction, which is simple, logical, and easy, finds a kind of mocking parody in the morning's creation. Light has no business coming back, but light does.

Emily reaches the cemetery just as the caldron in the east overflows, just as the birds (*idiots!* she thinks) begin a tentative cheeping and chirping. She sits at the gate for a minute to regain her strength, for the night's walking and worry have tried her severely. In front of her the stones lie on graves, almost completely hard and real, waiting for the rising of the sun to finish them off and make com- plete masterpieces of them. Emily rises and trudges up the hill, slower and slower as the ground rises to its topmost swell, where three hundred years of peaceful Guevaras fertilize the grass and do their best to discredit the one wild shoot that lives on, the only disrespectful member of the family. Weeping a little to herself, Emily lags up the hill, raising her skirts to keep them off the weeds, and mur- derously hating in her heart the increasing light and the happier celebrating of the birds. She rounds the last hillock of ground and raises her eyes to the Gue- varas' eternal mansion, expecting to see nobody again. There is the corner of the building, the low iron gate—

In front of it stands Martin Guevara between her father and Sweet Sweet Will, captived by both arms, his face pale and beautiful between two gold crosses that are just beginning to sparkle in the light of day.

"We are caught," says Guevara, seeing her, directing at her his fixed, white smile.

"You let him go," says Emily—very reasonably.

"You're safe, my Emily!" cries Sweet Will.

"Let him go!" She runs to them, stops, looks at them, perplexed to the bottom of her soul.

"Let him go," she says. "Let him go, let him go!"

Between the two bits of jewelry, Emily's life and hope and only pleasure smiles painfully at her, the color drained out of his face, desperate eyes fixed on the east.

"You don't understand," says Emily, inventing. "He isn't dangerous now. If you let him go, he'll run inside and then you can come back any time during the day and finish him off. I'm sick. You—"

The words die in her throat. All around them, from every tree and hedge, from boughs that have sheltered the graveyard for a hundred years, the birds begin their morning noise. A great hallelujah rises; after all, the birds have nothing to worry about. Numb, with legs like sticks, Emily sees sunlight touch the top of the stone mausoleum, sunlight slide down its face, sunlight reach the level of a standing man—

"I adore you," says Martin to her. With the slow bending over of a drowning man, he doubles up, like a man stuck with a knife in a dream; he doubles up, falls—

And Emily screams; what a scream! as if her soul were being haled out through her throat; and she is running down the other side of the little hill to regions as yet untouched by the sun, crying inwardly: I need help! help! help!—She knows where she can get it. Three hundred feet down the hill in a valley, a wooded protected valley sunk below the touch of the rising sun, there she runs through the trees, past the fence that separates the old graveyard from the new, expensive, cast-iron-and-polished-granite—

There, just inside the door (for they were rich people and Charlotte's mother's sister lived in Frisco) lies Emily's good friend, her old friend, with her hat and cloak off and her blonde hair falling over the bier to her knees—Charlotte in a white wrap like a slip. Emily stops inside the door, confused; Charlotte regards her fixedly.

"There's not much time," says Charlotte.

"Help him!" whispers Emily.

"I can't; he's already gone."

"Please—please—" but Charlotte only rises glidingly on her couch, lifting her beautiful bare shoulders out of the white silk, fixedly regarding her friend with that look that neither time nor age will do anything to dim.

"I won't," says Emily, frightened, "I don't think—" taking a few unwilling steps towards the coffin, "I don't think that now—"

"You only have a moment," says Charlotte. Emily is now standing by her friend and slowly, as if through tired weakness, she slips to her knees.

"Quickly," says Charlotte, scarcely to be heard at all. Looping one arm around her friend's neck, she pulls her face up to hers.

"But not without him"—Emily is half suffocated—"Not without him! Not this way!" She tries to break the grip and cannot. Charlotte smiles and dips her head.

"Not without him," her voice dying away faintly, "Not without him . . . not without . . . without . . ."

Sunlight touches the door, a moment too late.

AMERICAN GOTHIC

༄

RAY RUSSELL

┌───┐
│ I │
└───┘

YOU WANT TO HEAR TELL ABOUT THE CONJURE WOMAN and that murder we had us in these parts? Well, she was a powerful conjure woman, that's for certain-sure, knew a heap of strange words and all, but the whole thing happened a long time ago. Still, I told the story so many times I don't guess it'll hurt me none to tell it again.

I expect I better start out with the little old gal we had us out to the farm that summer. She was a foreign gal, from Hungaria or Poland or Pennsylvania or some such place. About fifteen. Awful dumb. But kind of fetching, with yellow pigtails and cornflower eyes and a pair of real well-developed chests on her. She had just about the prettiest little sitter I ever saw, too. Well, my son Jug's eyeballs lit on her one day when she was hunkered down feeding the chickens, first or second day she worked for us I think it was, and that was the day Jug became a man, you might say.

Only thing was, he didn't know how to go about it. Hell's bells, he was only fourteen. All he knew was, when she was squatted down on her haunches like that, with her meal-sack dress stretched tight across her sitter, he got this feeling in his jeans, like if by magic. He didn't know why. There it was. So what he did was, he sauntered over to her and looked her straight in the eye and unbuttoned himself. "Looky here," he said. "You ever seen the like of this before?"

Well, she didn't know what to say. Her mouth just fell open like a steam shovel. She couldn't hardly speak a word of English anyway. She just *run*.

But she run in the wrong direction. She run for the barn. That was her big mistake. I was all the way in the house, drinking coffee in the kitchen, and I heard her even in there. Squealed like a stuck pig.

But the pair of them got on like a house afire, after that.

Jug's maw, she died when he was born, poor little lady. Right fond of her, I was. She's buried out in the rear pasture, underneath the big slippery elm. I raised Jug myself. Maybe that's why he turned out so wild, no maw to gentle him and teach him proper ways. Jug wasn't his real name. I called him that on account of his ears.

One day, the hired gal came to me and, in that broken English of hers, told me she couldn't hardly get no work done, Jug was always after her. I talked to the boy, but he said, "Paw, when I see that gal just walk past me in that thin dress of hers and her legs all bare and everything, that durn thing just stands straight up like a skunk's tail and ain't a dang thing I can do about it except grab that gal and let her have it."

Just then, she walked past the window, carrying a pail, and the way her sitter moved under that dress, I saw what he meant. It was a chilly morning, and her nipples poked out the cloth like a couple of shotgun shells.

"You run along and feed the hogs," I told the boy, "and I'll talk to the gal."

So he took off, and then I took off. After the gal. Caught up to her out by the pump and told her to take a rest for herself, come back to the house and have a cup of coffee.

She was setting there in the kitchen, drinking her coffee, and I got to thinking about my life, and how lonely it was. Kept looking at them straight smooth fifteen-year-old legs. Them chests. Them big dumb blue eyes.

"Child," I said, "I think you could use a bath." She could, too. So I heated up some water on the stove and filled the big washtub right there in the middle of the kitchen floor. Told her to take off that dress. She didn't want to at first, but I guess she thought she could trust me because I was like a father or something, must have seemed like an old man to her. So she took it off, and Judas priest what a body that gal had. I just could hardly believe it. I told her to step in the tub, then I got a big bar of brown soap and I knelt down next to the tub and started soaping her up real good. I washed her back, I washed her front. I washed her legs. By this time, I was pretty near crazy.

When she stepped out of the tub all shiny and wet and smelling of soap, I just couldn't help myself. Right there on the kitchen floor, on a big towel, I plowed her, and I mean to tell you it was like a soft ripe plum all warm from the sun and so full of sweet juice it's split up the middle. It was a long time since I'd had a woman, and it was all over before you could say turkey buzzard.

After that, I wrapped the big towel around her and took her up to the bedroom and did it again, slow and easy.

Of course, this didn't solve the problem none. It added to it. Instead of having one jasper after her, now she had two. Any time Jug wasn't plowing her, I was. She didn't really complain, but she didn't get any chores done neither. The farm sure went to hell. Not that it was ever much of a farm. Just a few acres. It was my wife's farm, actually. She inherited it from her father, and it just naturally got handed down to me when she died. But, like I said, it went plumb to hell. The plowing got neglected because of the other plowing. Pigs got so skinny we figured it would be a mercy to slaughter them all for bacon before they got any skinnier. Never seemed to be enough time to feed them. Jug and me was always too tuckered out. But I was firm with the boy.

"Jug," I said one day, "you get out there and milk the cow. Then hitch up the horse to that plow. And there's a whole lot of hay that needs pitching. And—"

"Paw," he said, "you can just go climb a goose. If they is any work to be done on this farm, then we are going to divvy it up. I ain't about to bust my butt out there all day while you stay in here servicing the hired gal."

"Son, you talk respectful to your paw."

"Aw, shoot, Paw, don't hand me that crap."

Well, we divvied up the work, just like he said. We did the gal's work, too. It didn't seem right to make her work while she was taking such good care of us the other way. Of course, as long as she wasn't working, we stopped paying her. But she didn't mind. She had her board and keep. She did do the cooking for us, though. And she was a worse cook than Jug, which is going some. But we knew when we was well off—we ate what she fixed.

One day we had a visit from the preacher, Reverend Simms. Tall, skinny fellow with a squint, dressed all in black. About my age. Had a wife with a face just like George Washington on the dollar bill. But he left her at home that day, thanks for small mercies. Come chugging and shaking out to the farm in his old flivver one evening when I was setting on the back porch smoking my pipe and watching the sun get red.

"Brother Taggott," he said.

"Evening, Reverend," I said.

"There is some peculiar talk going round," he said. "Seems you got yourself a little foreign gal out here on the farm."

"That's right. From Pennsylvania or such."

"Well, Brother, I don't mean no offense, because I know you're a Godly man, but somehow it don't seem proper. I mean to say, you don't have no other women folk here to take care of the gal. Just you and your son. And your son, well, he is getting close to the age when he'll be noticing the gal. And here she is, out here all alone with you men folk on the farm, no one to protect her or tell her what's right and what's wrong."

"What do you think we should do, Reverend?"

"The gal is a minor. She belongs in the county orphanage. They'll put her to work there and teach her moral principles."

"How they going to do that? She can't hardly talk English."

"They'll teach her that, too. Brother Taggott, it's the only decent way. My wife give me the idea, and I've never known her to be wrong in matters of morality and propriety."

"Well, Reverend," I said, "I reckon you and your missus are right."

"I'm glad you see it that way."

"Only thing is, the gal may not hanker to go to no orphanage. She likes it here."

"That don't matter. It's for her own good."

"I know that. But how am I going to explain that to her? She can't hardly talk English, and she's dumb as a goat besides."

"Faith can move mountains, Brother."

"Amen. You know, I think you better be the one to talk to her."

"Good idea."

"I mean, you being a man of the cloth and all."

"Right, Brother. I agree. So if you will kindly take me in to her, I'll set things straight."

"Come right in, Reverend." I took him into the kitchen and poured him out a cup of coffee. "You set for a minute, Reverend, and I'll just go try and tell the gal you're here."

Well, she was upstairs in the bedroom, resting up, and I told her, best I could, about the Reverend and what he come for. You see, it wasn't exactly true anymore about her not talking English—when me and Jug got to know her better, we all got to understand each other some, what with her learning some English and us learning a word or two of her foreign talk, and sign language and such, we could all talk together pretty good by now. So I made her understand what the preacher was up to, and then I went back down to the kitchen.

"You'll find her up yonder, Reverend, waiting for you. She's all yours."

"Thank you, Brother Taggott. You're being very decent about this."

"I just want to do what's right."

So off he went, upstairs.

He was up there about a half an hour. When he come down, the gal wasn't with him.

"Ain't she going with you?" I said.

"Brother Taggott," he said, "the ways of the Lord are wondrous."

"Amen."

"A little child shall lead them."

"It's the gospel truth."

"That simple, unaffected child upstairs has taught me, in her untutored way, that there is a law higher than man's law. It is God's law, and it is the law of Love."

"Hallelujah."

"Now, man's law says that the child belongs in the orphanage. But can a cold institution like that offer her Love? Can it give her the simple human warmth she is getting here in your home?"

"It sure can't," I said.

"Right, Brother. It can't. And so it is my decision that the child should stay here, under your guidance."

"Anything you say, Reverend."

"But I must impose a condition."

"What's that?"

"It's true that you can provide her with most of the necessities of life. A home. Shelter from the storm. Food for her body. And that all-important Love of which I have just made reference. But the one thing you cannot provide her with, Brother Taggott, is religious counsel. So I say that I will allow the gal to stay here with you, *provided* that I may come by to visit with her, in private, as her spiritual advisor. Shall we say once a week?"

"How about Friday evenings, just after supper?"

"That will be fine. That will be just fine."

But as he was walking out the door, I remembered something, and I said, "Reverend? What about Mrs. Simms?"

"You leave her to me," he said, and left.

Things went along pretty smooth after that, for a while. Me and Jug was happy. The hired gal wasn't complaining. Every Friday, spank after supper-time, the Reverend would come by and he would take her aside someplace and spiritual-advise her for about twenty minutes or thereabouts. Life just seemed to slide by like water in a crick.

Then one day, Mrs. Simms drove out to the farm in that flivver. Drove right up to me and looked straight at me with those chips of co-cola-bottle glass she used for eyes. Now, I don't mean to say that she was ugly. That face of hers might have looked right handsome on a man. But on a woman it just didn't set right.

"Mr. Taggott," she said. Had a voice like Dewey Elgin, the bass singer in the church choir.

"Ma'am," I said.

"This little bit my husband has been spiritual-advising."

"Yes, ma'am."

"I want to see her."

"Why, surely. I'll take you in to her directly."

She climbed down off the flivver and followed right behind me as I headed for the house. I was just a mite worried about what she would see there. If the hired gal was upstairs with Jug, that wouldn't hurt none because I'd have time to shoo Jug out the side door and get the gal spic-and-spanned before the Reverend's wife clapped eyes on her. But if she was standing round the kitchen washing the dishes or cleaning the stove, she just might be buck naked, don't you see.

She'd took to going around like that in the house half the time. Can't say I blame her. Didn't seem hardly worth the trouble getting into a dress, the way things were with her and Jug and me.

So I high-tailed it up onto the back porch and into the kitchen ahead of Mrs. Simms. But it was all right. The gal had a dress on. Even had shoes on. Wondered where she got them until I remembered they used to belong to Jug's maw. They were a pair of town shoes she bought once. Shiny red, with heels about two inches high and a place for the toes to peek out. The gal's bare legs looked even better than usual in them shoes, and I was about to tell her to kick them off and shove them under the sink when I heard the screen door slam shut behind me and felt those cold, cold eyes on the back of my neck.

"Why, here's Mrs. Simms come to see you, gal," I said. "Right friendly of her, don't you think?"

Mrs. Simms looked her over from head to foot. I declare, it was like a snake watching a bird. "What's your name, missy?" she said. The gal told her. "You like it here on the Taggott farm?" The gal just nodded. Mrs. Simms drilled holes clean through her with her eyes. Then she grabbed the gal's arm. "There's meat on *your* bones," she said. "I don't guess they're starving you. But *you* look mighty peak-ed, Mr. Taggott . . ."

Well, I was, for a fact. Peak-ed and skinnied-down, me and Jug both, just like them pigs that got so pitiful skinny because the two of us were always too tuckered out to feed them.

Then Mrs. Simms said something real peculiar. All mixed in with some foreign-sounding words, not the hired gal's foreign words, but more like they might be that Frenchy talk, the sort my old Uncle Maynard brought back from the world's war, Madamazell from Armenteers parly-voo, and all. What Mrs. Simms said sounded like "La Bell Dom Sawn Mare See." And then she said it again, "La Bell Dom Sawn Mare See hath thee in thrall. God help you."

"Amen," I said, because that's what I always say when God is brought up, specially by a preacher or a preacher's wife. Not that I knew what she was talking about. Something from Scripture, I expect. She was a right well educated woman.

"Good day to you, Mr. Taggott," she said to me, then she turned and left, slamming the screen door.

I sure breathed a lot easier when I heard that flivver start up and rattle itself down the road.

The trouble started soon after.

$$II$$

THE GAL TOLD ME, AFTER SUPPER A FEW DAYS LATER, THAT she was in the family way.

"*What?*" I said.

She nodded.

"You sure?" I said.

She did some of that sign language.

"Jesus Christ on a mountain," I said. Then I said, "Whose is it?"

She didn't catch my meaning.

"Father. Pappy. Daddy. Papa. Paw. Me? Jug? *Who?*"

The gal just shrugged. I was plumb upset.

I found Jug out in the barn, sound asleep in the hay. Kicked him in the sitter, and sit he did, straight up. "Paw, what the hell!" he hollered.

"The gal's got a duck in the oven," I told him.

"That's good—I'm hungry enough to eat a bear, claws and all."

"You damn fool, she's pregnant!"

"Jesus Christ on a mountain," he said.

"What are we going to do?"

"You asking *me?* I'm just a young'un!"

"You're old enough to plow the hired gal!"

"And *you're* old enough to know better!"

"Get it through your head, boy. Someone is going to have to marry up with her."

"Shoot, Paw, *I* don't want to get married!"

"You think I do? Bad enough I had to marry your maw after she clicked with you. I ain't about to get caught a second time."

"That's just it, Paw—you're already broke to the double harness! It won't hurt you none!"

"It won't hurt you none, neither. Every man ought to get himself married up once in his life. But two times is one time too many. I already done my hitch. It's your turn now."

"Damn it, Paw, the young'un might be yours! That would make him my own half-brother!"

"And if I married up with her and the young'un was yours, it'd be my own grandchild! Either way, we got ourselfs a mess on our hands."

Just then, I heard the Reverend's flivver. "What the hell day is this?" I said.

"Friday," said Jug.

"Let's get back to the house. We got to have a talk with that preacher."

Reverend Simms wasn't too eager to talk to us—wanted to get off with the gal and start in on his spiritual-advising—until we told him our news. Then he took his hand off the gal's shoulder like it was a red hot stove.

"I see," he said. "Well, what do you aim to do?"

"Reverend," I said, "there ain't no two ways about it. You're going to have to marry the gal."

"*Me???*"

"I mean, marry her to one of us, all legal and proper in the church."

"Yes," he said, like all the straw was knocked out of him. He been looking that way for weeks, anyway.

"But which one of us?" I said.

"Which one? Why, the one who ... who ..." Then he broke off and scratched his head. "I see the problem," he said.

We all stood around there in the kitchen for a spell, not saying anything. Then I got down a jug of corn liquor. I poured out a glass of the stuff for the Reverend, clear as water it was, and another glass for myself.

"Can't I have none, Paw?" Jug said.

"You're just a young'un," I said. The preacher and me, we lifted our glasses and threw the stuff down our necks and shuddered and waited for it to hit us. After about five seconds, it did. Like a couple of horse shoes falling on our heads. "Son of a bitch," I said. "Lordy Lordy," said the Reverend.

After he got his wind back, he said, "The gal will have to decide."

So we asked her. But all she did was shrug and look dumb.

"Then," said the preacher, "why don't you toss a coin?"

"That don't seem right," I said. "Leaves it up to luck. Ought to be something more like a game, with some skill to it."

The preacher said, "You got a pack of cards in the house?"

"No."

"Dice?"

"No."

"I'm mighty pleased to hear you don't have those instruments of the Devil in your house, Brother Taggott, but how in tarnation you going to decide?"

Jug spoke up. "There's them games they play at the county fair. Sack races. Greased pig."

"I'm too old for a sack race," I said. "You'd beat me."

"But you ain't too old to catch a greased pig, Paw. I seen you do it just last year."

I said, "The boy's right. We're both a caution with a greased pig."

"Then it would be a fair contest," said Reverend Simms.

"I reckon."

"Only thing is," said Jug, "we ain't got no pigs."

"No *pigs?*" said the preacher.

"Butchered the last one a week ago," I said, snapping my fingers. I'd plumb forgot that.

"I declare," said the preacher. "The problems increase and multiply. Could we have another drop of that refreshment, Brother? It might help jog the brain."

I poured out another two glasses from the jug, and we gulped them down. "Lordy Lordy," I said. "Son of a bitch," said the Reverend.

The corn didn't jog *our* brains none, but it seemed to jog Jug's, just the smell of it maybe. Because he said, "Reverend? Why don't we grease the hired gal?"

Now, I'll say right here and now that if the preacher and me was cold sober, that idea of Jug's wouldn't have got no further than that. But we each had about a pint of powerful moonshine in our guts by that time, and the idea didn't sound so bad. It sounded even better after we swallowed another couple of glasses. Like the Reverend said, it was kind of fitting. After all, it was the gal who was the prize, so to speak, so why shouldn't she be the one to get greased?

Well, we all went outside behind the barn. The sun had gone down by that time, but there was a full moon, so we could see pretty good. One thing we had plenty of was pig fat, so Jug went and got a barrel of it. We tried to tell the gal what we was doing, but I don't know if she rightly understood. She was a good gal, though, and just stood there while me and Jug took off her dress and greased her from her chin down to her foot soles. If you ain't never smeared grease all over a buck naked, strapping gal with your bare hands, then I'm here to tell you you've missed something. Pretty soon, the gal was slippery as a fresh-caught carp.

"You reckon she's about ready, Reverend?" I said.

"I reckon."

A peculiar feeling came over me then, all shivery-like, for no reason at all. Might be it was the way the moon made everything look cold and blue—it was pretty near to full that time of the month. Even the gal, all naked like that and shining like a fish, looked cold.

But might be it was some other thing. Because I recollect thinking—looking at Jug and the Reverend standing there so peak-ed and sucked-dry looking in the moonlight and knowing I didn't look no better—I recollect thinking about that grease on my hands, the grease I done smeared all over the gal, and how it come from the pigs we slaughtered before their time because they got so skinny on account we never got round to feeding them because Jug and me was always tuckered out from forever plowing the gal . . .

And, do you see, it was like that little old gal had sucked *all* of us dry in one way or t'other, wore down me and Jug and the preacher to a frazzle, and even wore down the pigs, you might say, until they had to be slaughtered and rendered down into fat to smear all over her. She was the only one on the farm who was still sleek and healthy, with meat on her bones . . .

But fool thoughts like that got blowed away when the Reverend said, "Yes, Brother Taggott, I reckon that gal has soaked up all the pig fat her sweet little body can accommodate."

"Then let's get started, Paw!" said Jug. "I'm just hankering to get my arms locked around that gal and pin her to the ground! I'm hankering fit to bust!"

"But first," said the preacher, "we got to set up some rules. Now, ordinarily, the fellow who catches the pig wins it. But seeing as how neither of you are exactly eager to win this gal in marriage, you might not try very hard to catch her. So we have to turn the rules clear around. The one who catches her *loses* her. The one who *don't* catch her *wins* her. And marries her."

That put a crimp in my scheme, because that was just what I was aiming to do—let her slip away on purpose. But the preacher was one jump ahead of me.

"Reverend?" said Jug. "To make it all the more fair and square, don't you think me and Paw ought to strip down ourselfs?"

"Aw, hell, Jug," I said, "I'm too old for such goings on. Besides, there's a snap in the air."

"The boy's got a point, Brother," said the preacher. "If you are both Adam-naked, then nobody can say the winner's clothes were rougher than the loser's. It would equalize things."

So Jug and me stripped down to the buff and stood there in the moonlight like a pair of damn fools.

The preacher said, "Brother Taggott, your years entitle you to the first try."

"All right," I said, "but only if we put more grease on her after my turn. I ain't fool enough to get all the grease rubbed off on me just so's Jug can have an easy time of it."

The preacher nodded. "I will even help with the re-greasing," he said.

"I thought you would."

He took out a big watch from his pocket. "This here timepiece," he said, "was owned by a gambling man. Used it to clock horses. When he saw the error of his ways and was saved, he presented it to me out of gratitude. Each of you will have exactly sixty seconds to catch the gal. Before we begin, Brother, I suggest we signalize the occasion by taking another snort from that jug which I notice you brought out here with you."

I handed him the jug and he hoisted it up to his mouth and poured about a half a pint down his gullet. When he handed it back to me, I did the same. Jug asked again if he could wet his whistle and I told him no he couldn't.

"Ready, Brother Taggott?" said the preacher.

"I'm ready."

He looked down at his watch. "Then—*go get her!*"

The gal run and I was right behind her. When we turned the corner by the pig trough, I grabbed her shoulder but it slipped clean away from me. Next time, as we went past the wood pile, I got her around the waist and threw her down. She hopped out of my arms like a frog. I clutched at her chests, but they popped right out of my hands like they was a couple of skinned peaches. Dug my fingers into her sitter, but it squirmed away, both parts of it. Tried to grab her thighs, but my hands just slid all the way down her legs to her knees, and then down to her ankles, and then she was gone.

"Time's up!" yelled Reverend Simms.

I was covered with pig fat from head to foot. More of it on me than on the gal.

"You win, Paw!" said Jug.

"Not yet I don't," I said. "It might turn out to be a draw. Let's get the girl greased up again."

The preacher pitched in and helped us, and this time the gal got to seeing the fun of it, and she giggled and squealed the whole time we was greasing her.

"You ready, Jug?" the Reverend said when we was through.

"Oh, yes *sir,* Reverend, I sure am!" He sure was, too. You'd of had to be blind not to see that.

The Reverend looked at that watch of his. "*Go, boy!*" he yelled.

He took after her like a hound dog after a rabbit. She gave him a good run for his money, all the way around the outhouse and back toward the rear pasture. Then she tripped on a root and went face down and Jug was right on top of her. Held on to her for dear life. Squirm and squiggle? I'm here to tell you she did! Almost got away from him one time—but then we heard her squeal like a stuck pig and I figured Jug really *had* pinned her to the ground just like he said he'd do.

It was all that good corn liquor, don't you see. Made me so numb I couldn't hold on to her. But Jug hadn't touched a drop of white lightning.

"Time's up and she's still down," said the Reverend. "I reckon the boy wins. I mean loses." She was still squealing fit to bust.

"Jug!" I called out. "You let that gal up right now, y'hear?"

"In a . . . minute . . . Paw . . ." he said, all gaspy-like.

"Right *now!*" I yelled back. "That little lady is my future wife!"

"I respectfully suggest a very short engagement," said the preacher.

"How does tomorrow morning suit you?"

"Ten o'clock? Don't come no earlier because I'm baptizing the Geer baby at nine."

"Jed Geer? I thought he had everything shot off in the war."

"I said it before and I'll say it again, Brother Taggott. The ways of the Lord are wondrous."

"Amen. *Jug? You hear me? Let that little gal up!*"

"Yes, Paw. Here . . . I . . . *come!*"

Anyway, that's how I got engaged to the hired gal. But the wedding was something else again.

Bright and early next morning, we all got ourselfs scrubbed pink and shiny. Jug was going to be my best man. He was big enough to wear my stripy blue Sunday suit, and I wore an old black suit with tails hanging down in the back that used to belong to Jug's maw's paw. I inherited it with the farm. Wore it only two times before, to my first wedding and when I buried Jug's maw. Aimed to be buried in it myself. We squeezed the hired gal into an old white dress of Jug's maw. It was like stuffing two pounds of feed into a one pound bag. Jug's maw was a skinny little thing, and the hired gal sure wasn't. It was all right, long as she didn't sit down, bend over, or breathe. Put those red shoes on her, too. She looked right pretty.

"Good enough to eat," said Mrs. Simms, when she saw her standing in the kitchen in her wedding clothes.

The Reverend's wife come over to bring the gal to the church in the flivver and give her away. Me and Jug was supposed to get there in the buckboard. Wasn't proper for all of us to arrive together at the same time, she said, or some such folderol. So I hitched up the horse to the buckboard, and me and Jug started for the church.

When we got to the church, the Reverend Simms was standing outside waiting for us. "Morning, Brother Taggott," he said. "You look as fancy as a Christmas goose."

"Why, thank you kindly."

"But where is your blushing bride?"

"Your missus is toting her over here in your flivver, Reverend. Me and Jug, we come in the buckboard."

"Why, Mrs. Simms didn't tell me she was aiming to do that," he said. "But I expect they'll be along any minute."

A half an hour later it was, before the flivver come clattering and smoking up to the church. Mrs. Simms climbed out—but no hired gal. I was all steamed up from waiting so long, and when I saw the gal wasn't with her, I just rared back and hollered, "Where in tarnation is that little gal?"

"Where the moon don't shine, Mr. Taggott," she said, "nor the sun, neither. Husband: a word with you." She led the Reverend into the church, and left me and Jug a-standing there like a pair of just-born calves.

Later on, the Reverend explained it all to me. I didn't understand the half of it, but maybe you will. Seems like his missus knew what we was all up against the minute she first laid eyes on the gal. Knew she wasn't like regular folk. Foreign trash, don't you see. Mrs. Simms knew about those things, her being a powerful conjure woman like I told you, and she said the gal was a suck-you-something-or-t'other, said they had a lot of them over yonder where the gal came from, there was whole books writ about them, and poems, too, like that La Bell Dom Sawn Mare See. She was just sucking the life out of me and Jug and the Reverend. The only way to get rid of one of them is to pound a stake right through its heart, she said. So that's what she did, and buried the gal out on my place, in the rear pasture, next to my wife, underneath the big slippery elm. So I never did have to get married up again, after all.

And Mrs. Simms said she didn't even come from Pennsylvania like we thought. It was some other place, called Transylvania, I believe.

But some times at night, even now, do you know that I still miss that little old gal? When I get to feeling lonely, I think on her something fierce, and I recollect how the moonlight glowed all blue on her bare body, and it don't matter a hill of beans if she was what Mrs. Simms said she was or not.

Of course, the Sheriff didn't credit a word of it, and charged Mrs. Simms with murder. Motive was the Reverend spiritual-advising the gal once a week thataway. Not guilty for reason of insanity, they said, and she went to the asylum. If she wasn't insane when she went in, she surely was when she died there ten years later.

I didn't make up any of this out of my head.

THE PEARLS OF THE VAMPIRE QUEEN

MICHAEL SHEA

I

To Taramat Light-Touch
Sow-and-Farrow Inn
Karkmahn-Ra

WARMEST SALUTATIONS, O PRINCE OF SCOUNDRELS! DEAR
deft-fingered felon, Paragon of Pilferers, Nabob of Knaves—good morrow, good day, or good night, whichever suits the hour this finds you! Do you
guess who I am that greets you thus? Eh? Of course you do. Who else but your
own nimble, narrow-built, never-baffled Nifft—inimitable Nifft of the knife-
keen wits!

Has it been two years since we've been out of touch? That much and more,
by the Black Crack! I'm sure you thought me dead or something like it, and I
promise you, Taramat, I came close to it, for the haul that Barnar and I made in
Fregor Ingens has taken us all of twenty-six months of breakneck squandering
to dissipate, and if it had been just a jot richer, we would certainly have died of
our vices before we'd wasted it all.

Haul? In Fregor? But of course—you don't know about it yet! Stupid of
me . . . suppose I write you a nice long letter telling you all about it? It's raining
here in Chilia where we're visiting Barnar's family. I've got lots of time on my
hands, and we won't be getting back down your way till late this spring. So it's
agreed then, and I assure you it's no trouble at all, for I love to reminisce about
exploits, especially remarkable ones. Just be sure to share this with Ellen if you
see her—you know how she dotes on me and relishes keeping abreast of what
I'm doing. ·

Well, it was swamp pearls, Taramat—*five hundred apiece.* Yes. You may well gape (as I know you're doing). You know their value, I'm sure, but have you ever seen one? Black as obsidian, twelve-faceted (the runts have six), and big as your thumb. They are dazzling to behold—nothing less—and we never doubted that obtaining some was worth risking the vampire queen's wrath.

Now we knew that Queen Vulvula's divers go down after them in threes— one pearl-picker and two stranglers. But this is because they are anxious not to kill the pearl-bearing polyps. With a pair of heavies, the thing's palps can be pinned and the picker left free to take its pearls. They attack the polyp's strangling-node only as a last resort, to free one of their team from a lethal grip of one of the palps. But a diver can get sufficient diversion from just one strangler if the man is strong enough and goes straight for the strangling-node and squeezes to kill. You try to be quick and not leave the thing dead, as their corpses make a good trail for the archer-boats, but to get by with one strangler, he can't be shy about damaging the things. You know Barnar's strength. I was content to risk the picking with him strangling solo, and he was willing to try it if I was. So we signed up as men-at-arms on a Chilite skirmisher to get passage to Cuneate Bay, and spent three days there in Draar Harbor getting provisions. Then we headed south.

With good mounts the swamps are about ten days' journey inland. It's bad country, but our luck was good right up through the eighth day. Then, on the eighth night, it went bad. We were in the salt marshes near the mountains that flank the swamps when three huge salt beetles attacked us. Luckily, though wood is scarce there, we'd kept enough of a fire going to give us a little light to fight by. We killed them all, but not before they'd killed our mounts. Worse, their caustic blood destroyed both our spear shafts. We still had our bows and blades, but we would rather have lost these than the spears, which would be the only really useful weapons in the swamps. When you're swimming you can't use a bow, so it's no help against lurks, and it's scant help against ghuls because they're so tough-bodied in all but a few places. And swords bring you far closer than you ever want to be, either to a lurk or a ghul.

The swamps begin to the south of the Salt Tooth Mountains. As soon as we reached the upper passes of this range, we were looking across a plain of clouds that seemed to have no end. The range forms a wall the clouds can't pass, and the plains below have been a sump of rains for thousands of years.

Descending the range's swamp side, we were deep in cottony fog most of the way down, but just as we neared the plain we entered a zone of clear air between the clouds and the swamp. In the cold gray light between the cloud ceiling and the watery floor, we could see for miles across the pools and thickly grown mudbars that concealed our illicit fortune-to-be. The bars and ridges of silt are mazelike, turning the waters, which look jet black from a distance, into a puzzle of crazy-shaped lagoons. But the growth on these bars, though thick, is not as lush as you'd expect. It's mainly shrubs and flowers; big trees are rare. The question of cover would be tricky as a result. The place offered many avenues of vision down which a man standing on a flatboat could overlook a dozen lagoons at a glance.

But when we stood on the bog's very rim, pausing before we entered the waters, Barnar snuffed softly and said to me: "It's got that smell, Nifft. There could be a great prize waiting for us here." He was right, too. It had that peculiar stink of threat about it. You looked at that low-riding cloud cover, looking torn and dirty as a stable floor, and then at those endless unclean waters, and you knew that obscene riches lay ripening out there, riches so encumbered with danger that their guards had ceased to believe that they could ever be stolen, not in any big way.

II

THE WATERS ONLY LOOKED UNCLEAN. ONCE YOU WERE IN them, you were amazed to be able to see all the way down to your feet—and down to the bottom of most of the pools, none of which, even of the broader ones, was very deep. The reason is the soil of the swamps. If you dive for a handful of bottom silt and squeeze the water out, you'll find it hefts like iron, and if you kick at the bottom, you set up a low boil of mud that sinks down very fast. I've been told since that the polyps need this dense earth to nourish the growth of their pearls. While the light was still at its strongest, gray and bleached though that was, we made haste to cut our teeth in this business.

In half an hour we were swimming, nudging our packs before us with one hand and holding our drawn swords before us underwater with the other. We had put cork inside our packs and wrapped them in oilskin, and our sword blades were heavily greased. The best way to survive in the swamps is to turn into a water rat and stay in the water for the whole of your working day, and to crawl out onto the bars only to sleep. For one thing, it keeps your water-adjusted reflexes in top readiness. The clarity gives you a few seconds' warning when a lurk comes off the bottom at you, but if you're in and out, your underwater eye will get fuddled and you'll be too slow to take one of those warnings. For another thing, the lagoons are so interconnected that if you swim a mazy path you can go anywhere and almost never risk the visibility of crossing a bar of land.

The first polyp we found grew alone in a small pool. It stood as tall as a man, its palp-tips almost touching the surface. Neither of us knew if this was big or average. It would have been beautiful, standing there in the pool, its blurred redness seeming to burn, if we hadn't had to fight the thing. The palps began to writhe with exploring gestures the minute we paddled into the pool. Keeping out of range, we sank underwater to view it. Down at the base of its anchor-stalk, right below where the bouquet of its arms began, was the small cluster of exposed fibers that is called the strangling-node, from the use men put it to. At the same point on the stalk, but on the other side of it, were two large lumps—pearl blisters for sure.

We surfaced. "Get well breathed, Ox," I said. "I'll hit the blisters the instant you touch the node and draw its arms out of the way. Breathe up."

Barnar nodded. He tied his sword to his floating pack. I wore mine for lurks, but Barnar was going to have both hands full. He emptied his lungs and filled them, each time more deeply. I did the same. We nodded our readiness, and went under.

We swam toward the polyp, dividing to hit it from opposite sides. I had to hang back till Barnar had drawn all its palps, and I watched as he swam in low and seized the node. All those blood-red palps whipped together and grabbed for him, faster than you'd believe anything could move underwater. It bent like a bush that's suddenly lashed by a storm wind, and it had him by the neck, trunk, and leg so suddenly that he could keep only one hand on the node and had to use the other to free his throat.

I went in. My contact with the thing was brief, but still it made my skin crawl—for the thing was like stone that lived and moved. This toughness is what makes one's work so hard, for the things are unpierceable by any weapon. I pressed on either side of one of the blisters, and the pearl popped out into the water like a seed squeezed from the ripe fruit. I tried to grasp it, but it kept squirting out of my fingers. Something hit me like a hammer between the shoulders. Catching the pearl with a lucky grab, I crawfished madly through the mud, took two more bone-cracking blows on the shoulder, and was clear. I came up starving for air.

Barnar was still down there, a huge blur in the silt where the red arms were striking like thresher's flails. I pocketed the pearl, took air, and went down. The two of them were deadlocked, because Barnar's one-hand grip on the node distracted just enough palps that he could bear, for a few moments, the assault of the rest. His hands are enormously strong. In the steppes he had taken a piece of rock salt and crushed it in one hand—it was as big as a road-apple. But his lungs were surely fit to crack by now, while the polyp was not weakening. I swam in beside him and added both my hands to the node. It was just enough pain to loosen the rest of the thing's grip on my friend. We scrambled backward. Something tore flesh from my face, and then I was free. Barnar boomed like a whale as he broke back into the air. We swam weakly to the mud bar and rested our upper bodies on it. I showed him the pearl. His face was torn in two places, the kind of raw, nasty wound one gets from rocks. My left cheek was a ruin. I still bear the scar of it.

"Well," said Barnar, "high pay, hard work."

"True," I said. "Still, friend, this may be the hardest work I've ever done." And then we heard a movement, distinct, but perhaps a lagoon or two distant. We drew our swords and towed our bundles round into the adjoining pool. Some bushes atop the farther bar were still shaking. From the lagoon beyond came a flat striking sound, the tearing of water, and the grunts and panting of a man.

We swam to the bar and looked over. A smallish man was thrashing on the surface of the water, driving a spear beneath him against the bottom. Even as we watched, his thrusts grew more methodical and he calmed down. A thick fluid, denser than the water and green in color, was boiling up around him, mixed with bubbles.

I began to think I knew the man. He turned his spear round to prod something down there with its butt—and the head he thus exposed showed a viscous green smear of lurk blood. Then he cursed, spat, and swam to the bar, where some bundles lay on the mud and a sword hung in the bushes. I then remembered he had been at the trade fair at Shapur, where I had first learned of the pearl swamps. He had been in the room where a small group of friends of mine had been talking about poaching. He seemed not to have learned more of the matter than was spoken there, to judge by his spread-out gear. Your goods on a bank are like a promise to any archer-squad that happens on them that you yourself are somewhere nearby, and they'll hound you out, even if you've managed to duck them first. As for the sword, even in the dull swamplight its sheath of chased bronze was as good as a signpost.

"I think I know him," I told Barnar. "Best join with him, eh? The work would be easier for three, and if he's not instructed he'll draw patrols into the area."

"All right," my friend said. "But he gets only a quarter share till he shapes up. Obvious amateur. I think he's just lost a partner."

He had indeed, as we saw upon swimming into his lagoon. We made gestures of peace. He turned his spearhead toward us and waited warily. Then we had eyes only for what lay under the water.

First, we saw that our polyp had been a small one. This pool was dominated by a nine-footer. Held in its palps was the body of another man, a big one. It was not the polyp, though, that had killed the man—and it was probably not his or his partner's inexperience either, but just bad luck. For a lurk as big as a mastiff also lay on the bottom, its fangs still hooked into the man's leg, its flat eye-knobbed head broken and giving off a green cloud of body fluids. Lurks look just like spiders, except the rear part of them isn't a fat, smooth sac—it's plated and ribbed, instead, like a beetle's body. Their poison balloons a man up a good one-and-a-half times his size. Even allowing for that, the pale sausage of a man down there must have been big enough in life to make Barnar look normal.

Of the three things on that pond bottom, only the polyp lived, and we learned something further in watching it as we swam past: the things have, amidst their palps, mouthparts for animal prey, and if left with a sufficiently inert body in their grip, they will devour it, though with a disgusting slowness. The polyp had the dead man's arm hugged tight in its arms and was working on the flesh with a slow rasping and plucking movement.

The little man's name was Kerkin. He remembered our meeting and knew my name without being told, be it said with due modesty. He was no less impressed with the difficulties of this task than we were, and we reached partnership promptly. Kerkin's hopes would have been defeated without us, and he accepted a quarter share with humility. We gave him some cork and helped him remake his bundle.

"Look there!" he cried. The great polyp was thrashing convulsively. It had more purple in it to begin with than ours had—we were to learn that that was generally the color of the big ones. But now it was amazingly pale, almost white, and its rhythmic stiffening had a helpless, purposeless quality, as of sheer pain. In a short time, it slowed, and ceased to move at all.

"The lurk poison!" said Barnar. Of course that was it. The polyp's toughness would have laughed at the biggest lurk's direct assault. But the poison entered the creature handily through its tainted meal. The thing had four blisters, three of which had full-sized pearls in them, the fourth a runt.

For a while we had a perfect poaching implement. We dragged the body of Kerkin's friend—his name had been Hasp—to several more lagoons. We found that if a polyp was jabbed forcibly in the node, it would attack and ultimately feed on the corpse we thrust into its arms. We took more than a dozen pearls this way, and then Hasp began to come to pieces—due not to the nibblings of the polyps, but to the lurk poison. The skeleton began to fragment and the skin to dissolve with terrible suddenness, filling the water with unwholesome stringy clouds of corroded flesh. In a few moments the whole lagoon was transformed into a disgusting broth from which we swam with desperate haste, keeping our faces clear of the water. It killed two small polyps growing there, but we did not dive for their pearls.

The real labor recommenced. While the takings were so easy, Kerkin had begun to whine. After all, the profitable Hasp had been *his* partner, not ours, and we should share even thirds. Now that it was again a wrestling game he dropped this theme readily. We took three more pearls in the same time we had taken to make our first dozen. We climbed up onto a broad bar in the evening, too tired to eat the jerky in our packs. We worked our way into the bushes and lay like the dead—that is, Barnar and I. Kerkin had the first watch, and in his excitement over the wealth we had already made, sleep was far from him. He would not even let me take mine, but insisted on talking. He showed his eagerness like an amateur, but I couldn't help seeing him with a friendly eye—he might have been a stupider version of myself at that age. So I talked with him awhile.

"Not a single flatboat did we see all day," he crowed. "So few people realize, Nifft, how clear it gets here for poaching at this season—of course if it got around, they'd get poached so hard in the fall that they'd take action and the easy times would be over. But we are here now, that's the great thing!"

"You said it's the Year King ceremony that caused it," I said. "So what's that all about then, friend Kerkin?"

Kerkin was eager to talk of this. In matters of the Queen's government his information far exceeded ours, and every man likes to be expert in something.

"The ceremony's called the god-making of the Year King. It means that the Queen ends his year's reign by immortalizing him, as they say." He paused and chuckled, and so I played along and asked:

"And how does she do that for him?"

"How else? She drains his body of every last drop of his blood, before the eyes of her assembled people. She's very thorough too, for she has to get all of it. If even a cup is lost to her, the charm of the blood is imperfect and its magic fails."

"And what is its magic for her, Kerkin?"

"It erases from her body the entire year's aging! Of course like all great magic it carries a terrible penalty for failure in its execution. Starting from the sacred night, for every single night that she is in default of the Year King's blood, she will age an entire year. And this aging, if subsequently she repairs the charm, can never be erased; thereafter, the Year King's blood will restore her only to the age to which she advanced while in default. A month's default, you see, would then make a hag of her, and a hag she would stay ever after, even with the charm reinstated."

Kerkin was a river of information, and I encouraged him to flow on—it does not hurt to gather what one can, when it's being offered free. The Queen's feeding was not confined to this yearly rite alone, though this was the bare minimum essential to her needs. She fed sporadically on random subjects—seldom fatally, except where some punishment was due. The natives of the swamp had received her as their ruler for over three hundred years now, because she had provided the necessary sorcery to expel the ghul, who are also originals of the swamp, and with whom the swampfolk have been immemorially at war.

Kerkin grew warm with his tale. We should kill a ghul, or take the lurk he'd killed, and go to Vulvula's palace to collect the bounty, he said. The great pyramid at the swamp's heart would be alive with folk. Think of the spectacle, and of the jest of being there with a fortune in poached pearls under our doublets! We could sneak a look at the doomed Year King in his chamber before the godmaking, for the guards routinely granted a peek for a small bribe—it was almost a tradition. He rattled on, describing the labyrinthine interior of Vulvula's palace as if he knew it at first hand.

Poor Kerkin didn't live past noon of the next day. He fell behind us as we were seeking the day's second polyp. The first had taken all morning, nearly tired us to death, and yielded only a runt. Kerkin didn't have our stamina, and swam in a tired daze. Having lost sight of us, he took a side channel by mistake, and drifted off his guard into a pool he thought we had crossed ahead of him. The violent splashing he made in his misfortune brought us back. We were stunned by what we found. He had blundered into a very deep pool where grew a grandfather polyp so big it raised the hair of my nape—at least fifteen feet from root to palp-tips. And seemingly it hadn't waited provocation, but had seized Kerkin's dangling leg in palps thicker than his body. We got there just as it pulled him under. It enfolded his head between two immense palps and wrenched violently.

Kerkin's whole body spasmed as if lightning was going through it, then he hung from the thing's grip like a sodden log, and the polyp began to feed with a tearing and grinding that bared his arm bone in a sickening few seconds. We did not even try to get the pearls off his body. We swam to a silt bar and crawled onto the mud.

We felt glum as a northern winter. Now our labors must increase, and we'd begun to appreciate the full range of accidents that could befall a man here. We counted our pearls again. We had enough to live well on for a year—enough to buy expensive magic from the best sorcerers; enough to buy women of the rarest accomplishments. But there was so much *more* all around us. You know the feeling. I was racked by it once before. I had just robbed the Earl of Manxlaw and was passing through his seraglio on my way out of his villa, in the dead of night. I was beckoned by a lovely thing. Reckless with success, I paused to serve her with a will. But as soon as I rose, a half-dozen others had wakened, and they hotly persuaded me in whispers. I was profoundly moved. I felt filled with the power to stay there and serve them all. But I had a king's ransom in my bag, and left with a wrenching of the heart.

This was worse. The pearls are worth far more than gold by weight—a fortune of them is so marvelously portable for a man who lives on the move! Still, we stared at the dirty clouds and each of us waited for the other to be the first to suggest that we rest content with what we had.

"Well," I sighed, just to be saying something, "we have to thank the Queen for making this place as safe as it is. Think if we had ghuls here too!"

"At least they breathe air and have blood," Barnar growled. "They're not this nasty mud-crawling kind of thing. Polyps, lurks, *pah!*" I was only half seeing him as he spoke, for at that moment a plan was being born in my mind. This plan was a thing of unspeakable beauty and finesse; I was almost awed by my own ingenuity.

"By the Black Crack," I said quietly. "Barnar, I have an idea that will make us staggeringly rich. We must get that lurk Kerkin killed, and we must kill a ghul as well, and take them both to the pyramid of the Queen in time for the god-making of the Year King. Kerkin said that would be in five days. We can get there two days early at the least, and that will be perfect!"

YOU MIGHT PAY ME HIGH AND PRESS ME HARD, BUT I couldn't say which was worse—killing a lurk in a lagoon with a seven-foot spear, or hunting a ghul in the black hills west of the swamps. We had to do both.

What? you'll say, we couldn't find that lagoon again? No, we found it fast enough. Our polyp had turned black, with half its palps fallen off. The lurk was there too. Unfortunately, its whole hind section had been eaten away. We were saved the trouble at least of hunting out another lurk, because it *was* another lurk that had eaten the dead one's body away, and it was still right there. I hope my fate never again puts such a sight as that before my eyes, black as the mud it crouched on, and looking half as big as the whole pond bottom. I was swimming lead because I was quicker with the spear, and that thing came straight up off its meal at me.

Now as to the spear, it was luck we'd met Kerkin and had it at all, but two feet should have been sawn off its haft and the thing should have been rebalanced for aquatic use. As it was, the weapon was too unwieldy, what with the water's drag. If I hadn't been carrying it head-down under water, despite the way it slowed my swimming, I would have died right there. That lurk's fangs were as long as my forearms, and before I could even react they were close enough to my thighs for me to count the thorny hairs they were covered with. I had time only to brace my arms—the lurk's own thrust carried him up and pushed the spearhead through the flat part of his body, amongst all those black knobby eyes. I clung to that spear-haft like an ant to straw in a hurricane, and the buck of that big hell-spider lifted me so far out of the water that I was standing on top of it for an instant.

A handy thing about lurks is that all their hard parts are outside, and these by themselves are not very heavy. They will even moult like snakes, and when they do they leave entire perfect shells of themselves, light as straw. This lurk was a monster, big as a pony, but when we'd bled it we reduced it to half its weight. We milked the bulk of its poison out too—the bushes where it splattered yellowed and died before our eyes.

We towed the carcass out of the swamps to the foothills we had entered from the day before, and scrounged enough dead scrub to make a fire in an arroyo. We found that by slitting the abdomen and shoving coals and heated rocks inside, the rest of its guts could be liquefied and drained out. We worked over it the rest of the day and finally had reduced both parts of the body to a bare husk, mere shells of a tough, flexible stuff that was too dark to reveal its hollowness. The whole thing now weighed no more than a small man, though it was unwieldy. Lashed to the spear, it could be carried between us like game. We carried it all night, moving toward the hills in the west.

By dawn we had reached them. Here the ghuls have retreated, to lurk near the swamp, just outside the reach of Vulvula's sorcery. We hid the lurk in a gully and covered it with stones, even though nothing will eat a lurk but another lurk, and they seldom leave the water. We found a place to sleep nearby, well hidden, though ghuls never come out in the day. They hunt at night, and we slept till then, for that's the time they must be hunted too.

The things can only be pierced through the sternum, which is narrow, while their backward-folding knees give them the quickness and dodging power of hares. You know me as a man who'll take your money at any kind of a javelin match, but for ghuls I ask a good clear set and a chance to launch before it knows I'm there.

We tried an unusual approach. It was Barnar's plan, and a lovely piece of wit it was. He spun it out of the well-known melancholy of ghuls. They frequently commit suicide by flinging themselves against Vulvula's barriers—one finds them, it's said, hanging dead in midair, snared in the Queen's invisible nets of power, and crawling with the blue worms that her spell engenders in its victims. Barnar reasoned that given this sad temperament, a ghul would believe a man claiming to have come to him seeking death.

We found one high in the hills by the light of its cook fire. We studied it carefully from among the rocks. It had a man's leg and haunch on a spit—the skin was flaking away in ash, and the thigh-muscle swollen with its juices. The rest of the man lay in pieces by its side, limbs and head pulled from the trunk like a torn fowl's—for ghuls use neither steel nor stone. The huge hands that had done the tearing were crusted with black blood.

Let's say you were to take our friend Grimmlat. Leave his arms the same length but start his hands at his mid-forearms, and crowd all his muscles into the shortened arm that's left. Give him feet of the same proportions with toes like fingers and knees jutting backward. Double the size of his poppy eyes, under-sling his jaw an inch, and give him haggle teeth as long as your thumb, and you've got a ghul.

I picked my position in the shadows. Barnar heaved a loud sigh and called out: "Hail there! Is that a ghul?" He trudged noisily into the ghul's camp, and under the cover of his noise I moved up into the spot I'd picked. The ghul sprang up at Barnar's entry.

"May I sit down, friend ghul?" my friend asked. "I want you to do me the service of ending my life."

Ghuls, for all their ugliness, have a profoundly sad expression due to the way their great eyes droop at the corners, and you rather feel for them when you're not involved. This one was in a defensive crouch, otherwise I would have had my shot at once. In almost all postures the things keep their shoulders folded forward, with their breastbone sunk in between their chest-muscles. They're only vulnerable at the moment of attack. That was the point of Barnar's scheme. He sat down cross-legged, like a man who means to stay. Anger began to replace wariness in the ghul's face.

"Are you deaf?" snapped Barnar. "Why do you hang drooling like an idiot? Kill me!"

The ghul didn't like this. It snorted and sat down again, and resumed turning the spit with a stubborn glare.

"Why should I?" it said. They have small spidery voices, like a hag's.

"Why not?" boomed Barnar. "You could eat me! Are you so stupid you can't see that I'm a man like the one you're cooking there?" He gestured indignantly at the head that lay on its side by the ghul. The man had had an enviable black mustache. "You'd kill me quick enough if I didn't ask—you make no sense!" Barnar complained.

"I'm no idiot, you're one," the ghul quavered bitterly. "You'd rot before I got hungry again. Don't you know anything? And anyway I'll do whatever I please and I won't take orders from you, you big sack of horse-flop!" And it licked its ragged teeth loudly to drive the insult home.

"Insults!" cried Barnar, "and I thought I'd be doing you service for service." He heaved a great sigh and rested his forehead on his hands. The ghul looked interested now.

"Why do you want to die?" it asked grudgingly.

"Why?" Barnar's head came up in disbelief. "The world so gray and spongy and futile and cold as it is—life so short and nasty and poor and hemmed in on all sides by destruction—and you ask why? I've had enough of it all, that's why!"

The ghul looked musingly. It stood up slowly and took its supper's head in its hand—the hand was big enough for the head to roll several times over from the blood-black claws to the heel of the shovel-wide palm. It rolled the head thoughtfully for a moment, and then drew back its arm to throw. That was my shot.

I pinned it so solid that half the haft reemerged from its spine, but ghul vitality is terrible, and it actually finished the throw with my spear in it. Barnar moved in time, and the head struck the rock behind him so hard that it flew in pieces like a burst earthen jar.

We took the ghul back to where we had cached the lurk, getting there by dawn. Now we had to build up the lurk's body. We were sure it could be considerably collapsed, and with some experimenting we found how to fold back the legs over the head part, and flatten and fold the back part. We tied it snugly into this reduced position with thongs, and wrapped the whole thing in oilskin. The finished bundle was about the size of a small man who has folded himself up to sleep. We bled the ghul, too, but didn't prepare it any more than by tying the wrists and ankles together. Barnar slung it crosswise over his shoulder and back, and we entered the swamp again. We walked the mudbars openly now, hustling the lurk through the water where we had to, making fairly quick time.

We soon struck one of the marked routes to the pyramid, a series of yellow poles that followed an almost continuous system of mudbars. We stayed with this, and late in the evening we came in sight of the pyramid. It is truly immense, tall enough to join the flat, dark waters with the ragged cloud ceiling. We laid ourselves down atop a broad bar amidst the bushes. We found it easy to sleep.

IN THE MORNING WE WEIGHTED THE BUNDLED LURK AND sank it in a pool by the sixth route-marker out from the palace—more than a mile out. Then we headed for the palace.

I've taken these eyes of mine to many places, and have been no jack-out-of-the-way, but I'll tell you I had sense enough to be impressed by that pyramid. It had to be a good three hundred feet high to thrust its upper tiers into the clouds as it did. It was a mighty, terraced hill of a palace. It had quays and docking berths all around its skirts, for it stood in the center of a lake, and water unbroken by solid ground spread half a mile around it on all sides. The lower two-thirds was all of stone, but its upper tiers were built of wood. Those great beams were as massive-looking as the monumental stone under them, and could have come from no nearer than the Arbalest Forest, on the fringe of the Iron Hills. One could read the wet of the fog up at the summit from the wood's deep blackness.

By the time we got to the fringe of the palace's great lake, we'd been passed by several inbound boats. The lake was alive with taxi rafts, for it's quickest to get from one side to another of the palace by sailing round it. The interior is a master maze of corridors and chambers. We saw only one archer-squad going out to patrol. They gave us a wave. Bountymen are liked there, and to be traveling palaceward with a dead ghul over one's shoulder is to go with as much guarantee of welcome as a stranger may expect. At our signal a taxicraft came promptly away from the palace's bustling perimeter.

Our pilot liked bountymen but seemed to think they were a bit stupid for taking on such a hard job. A man never gives away more than when he speaks in friendly contempt. We wore no teeth or fangs and thus had to be beginners, and this gave countenance to very particular questions about the pyramid's interior and the god-making rite. The answers confirmed Kerkin's tale.

"We hear the whole top of it is made of big beams," Barnar said with yokelish awe. We were drawing near. Light leaked down the sides of the pyramid from rifts in the cloud, but it was weak light that was itself just leakage from higher clouds. Still, anything so huge, and alive, and old, raised by the hands of man, must fill you with awe—that's my view. The pilot spat in the water to say it all wasn't that wondrous if you knew it like he did.

"You should see the beams in the vaulted ceilings at the top, where the King begins his pilgrimage," he said. "Some of them weigh a ton each, yet are groined and dovetailed just as neat as a fly's whiskers."

The pilot was most reassuring on every important point. From his description a man could move through the entire top level among the ceiling beams, and never touch or be seen from the floor. And the guard on the King's door was two spearmen, no more—for the King was administered a paralytic beverage in his preparation for the preritual vigil. He sat, immobile and awake, in his windowless cell. And even though the level just below would be sealed off on the night before the rite, barring access to the top, the guard up there would not be added to. For it is part of the ceremonial assumption that the King awaits his godmaking eagerly, and that his guard is just an honor guard.

We got off at the west quay, by far the most public one. The Queen's Cabinet uses the entire east quay for military and economic business, while the terraces on the north and south sides are interrupted by several water-level exits—channels let into the palace's foundation, to permit the launching of craft directly from its interior. On the west are all the major markets and bazaars, and more than half of the inns and wineshops.

We loitered in the plazas, browsed at the scarf makers and swordsmith's stalls, and had wine at several different places. We got ourselves seen and made chat with merchants—fitting in. Feeling the mood of the place, and establishing our role, you see. The ghul on Barnar's shoulder was an excellent introduction. Most showed us the condescending warmth the pilot had. Bounty hunting is a common way for the rustic youths of the northern hills to get their first look at the metropolis, and folk are used to finding them sufficiently simple. A man whose eye is awake would have been alerted by our mature age, but as we know, most people don't look at things very closely. At one winestall the tapster overcharged us for the amusement of the other customers, then stopped me as I paid up, smiling, and revealed the joke. We all had a good laugh, and when we left I was able to steal the lidded goblet I'd had my wine in. It was just what we would need.

Next we bought rope and bowstrings. We needed quite a few yards of each; we split up to make the purchases, and both of us went to several different places to make up our halves of the quota. Less professional men would have been lulled by the holiday extravagances all around them, and the amazing number of people. It seemed the whole northern swamp—the drier part where most of the population lived—had joined the already large resident population in the palace. But we knew that all you need is to raise a few doubts in a few chance souls to have your best-laid plans buggered and blasted.

At noon we went to the Audiences, held in the central chamber of the pyramid's water-level. The Queen presided here, tirelessly, most of the year. She was now in her seven days' retirement in the catacombs under the foundations, below even the swamp waters. There she communed with the mummies of Year Kings past. She would ceremonially rise from thence on the eve of the god-making, and at the same time the King would be brought down from his cell on the pinnacle, which was called the "heaven" station of his ritual "pilgrimage." The pair would meet in the same Chamber of Audiences that we now entered. After their meeting, the King's body would be taken down to the catacombs—the "night" station of his pilgrimage—there to join the other Year Kings. There they stand in the dark, all gods together—gods of Night, you understand.

The chamber was vast. There must have been a thousand litigants there, and they did not begin to fill the place. Dozens of underjudges handled lesser cases in stalls round the room's perimeter, while royal causes were heard in the room's center by a tribunal of three of the Queen's priestesses. Theirs was a job normally handled by Vulvula alone—such was her wit and memory and clarity of judgment. And let it be said here: no one we talked with ever denied the Queen's justice is thorough and scrupulous, treating the great as strictly as the small. True, in her domain some dozens of people each year wake sick and groggy after horrible dreams, and must keep to their beds a month after, and a dozen or so others each year do not wake at all one morning. Still, fair rule is only had at a cost, eh?

Routine matters like tax payments had their own designated tribunals, and we found the one for bounty payments. The clerk there assigned us a skinner. The man rose from a bench where he sat with two other dirty-aproned men. He led us out of the chamber and through a good half mile of corridors. The building is fascinating. You get no sense of pattern at all, even after moving through it for a quarter of an hour. The ceiling heights vary, and some halls are short with many rooms, while others are long with doorways that are few and large. Residents here—and the halls thronged with them—rarely know more than their immediate "neighborhoods" very well. We came out of the municipal quay on the east side.

The man brought the whole skin off in one piece, so fast I couldn't follow his moves. They make parchment from it, and clothiers use it for rich men's slippers and ladies' dagger-sheaths. The guts and bones he threw in a bin on a raft, to be used for baiting the lurk-traps around the lake's perimeter. The head he threw in also, after breaking the jaws with a sledge and removing the teeth for us. It had ten—big grinders with cutting edges. He gave us a runt-pearl in payment.

On the same quay an old coppersmith sat on a stool. He offered to bind our teeth with wire for wearing round the neck. His work was cheap and quick, and we came away wearing our trophies—a five-tooth row apiece. This established our role, with a small disadvantage. Accomplished bountymen wear "jaws"— ten-tooth strings, row under row. They tend to be rough with novices of their own guild—they give them the treatment that greenness gets everywhere, and a bit more besides, if you see my meaning. There were surely some ace bountymen in this convocation. It would just have to be taken as it came.

We did next precisely what a pair of bumpkins *would* have: we went up to the peak of the pyramid to bribe the guards for a gawk at the Year King in his cell.

$$\boxed{V}$$

A S I'VE SAID, THE PYRAMID'S TOP IS IN THE CLOUDS. FROM its outer terraces you can't see anything but sweating-cold whiteness—above, below, all around. Standing there gave you a desperately lonely feeling. That blind whiteness made it a place without time, a kind of Death. You felt as if you might have been dead without realizing it, that all your busy actions had been grave-dreams, and you yourself a skeleton, a rack of hard white bones that had stood there without moving for a thousand years. We went inside and ascended to the last and highest level, which can only be reached from inside the second-to-last.

There were others coming and going, but the custom of peeking at the King still had enough of the illicit about it to keep people brisk and quiet up here. As rustics turned bountymen, we had some countenance for moving slower and staring around us.

The place was perfect—it alone of all the levels was simple in plan: a hollow square of halls with three doors to a side. A Year King must not have his vigil in a predecessor's cell before twelve years of purification have passed. Each year therefore the King waits in a different room. The halls were gloomy. They had very deeply vaulted ceilings because the tier is built to adorn the pyramid with an elegantly roofed crown, though it's never clear enough for this to be seen from below.

Our greatest encouragement was to see the two guards posted at the end room of a corridor, near a corner. Barnar muttered to me:

"I can do it. I'll want a catwalk of ropes from just over the door and running round the corner and sixty feet up that next hall."

"I'll string it tonight then," I said.

We looked the guards over as we waited our turn at the door's barred window. They were scarred veterans—blank, observant-eyed, and ready of movement underneath their practiced immobility. They would be good men. The post was lucrative, and the palace guard had elimination bouts just before the rite to determine who would get the King's Watch. I paid one of them, and we took our turn at the window—we'd already noted the door had no lock.

The cell was windowless, the plainest little box of bare wood you could imagine. By the far wall was a heap of cushions. A young man sat on the floor with his upper body leaned back on them. His legs were sprawled loosely on the floor with his lower body. He wore only a breechclout and moccasins. The garments were silver, signifying moonlight and Night, of which he was soon to be a deity. He was well made, muscled like a runner. It was eerie to see a body so molded, ridged and knotted with the habit of life and activity, yet lying so unstrung and strengthless. He seemed powerless even to sit upright. His eyes moved slowly and without aim, but for some reason he suddenly fixed them on our faces at the bars. He knit his brow, and his hand stirred from the cushions as if to reach up and touch his own face, but fell back before it could. I wonder now what kind of dreams or portents we were to him. If he had known the truth, he would have known that we would neither harm nor help him.

We came back down to the lake-level without directions. It cost us two extra hours of blundering around, but it sharpened our wits to the place and it taught us a fairly direct route in a way that guaranteed our remembering it. I didn't come out onto the quay with Barnar. In a dark turning I transferred to his pack all my share of the bowstring we'd bought, and all my gear except for my rope. He gave me all the rope he had. We had already chosen the wineshop where we would meet later that night. He went off to find an apothecary. I retraced the route we had just figured out, and returned to the upper levels.

I found an inn and killed an hour with wine and smoked eel. It was full dark when I reentered the dim halls of the Year King's vigil. They call me Nifft the Lean nowadays, but when I first earned myself a name, I was called Nifft the Nimble. I did the hardest work of this whole glorious nab right there in the next two hours. Right at the door where I entered, I slung up a line I had weighted with my dagger, and hauled myself up among the ceiling beams. I did it with a gaggle of revelers climbing the stairs just behind me, and several others, to judge by the footfalls, just about to round the next corner of the hallway. I was up in a blink, and my line after me.

I moved through the beams to within fifty yards of the guarded door, perfecting my movements and learning the pattern of the joists and rafters. Then I sat down to prepare my ropes. I suited them to the beam intervals where I was, which of course would be the same everywhere. I tripled the ropes, braided them loosely, and knotted them, three knots per interval. The finished hundred feet of catwalk, when I had it coiled round my shoulder, was half my own bulk. Now came the true feat. I proceeded toward the King's door, and coming directly over the guards, I began to anchor the catwalk.

I strung it high, with two levels of beams between me and them. Though the regular spacing of the beams made me visible enough to anyone who was looking, I was well in the shadow and being seen was not the danger. The risk was in the fact that a mere fifteen feet of empty air separated me from the ears of those guards. I worked slower than a miser's hand moving to his purse to pay. Gawkers at the King came steadily, and I managed to coincide the loudest part of my work with the advent and the murmurs of these. This was the knot tightening, for the catwalk must not sag and creak when Barnar used it, as then the halls would be barred to visitors and the silence complete. But rope noise being sharp, and the noises of the visitors subdued, it took agonizingly long to get even one knot firm.

The pressure eased as I got round the corner and down the next hall, but I was soon sweating so hard I was amazed it didn't drizzle down into the corridor and give me away. By the Black Crack, there's no work like hanging frozen for indefinite periods, again and again, unpredictably. It's lizard's work, to tell the truth. But when I had done, I'd left a catwalk up there neatly paralleling one of the longitudinal beams, such that with one foot on that beam and the other on the ropes, Barnar could move along a good broadstance support with both hands free for his special task.

The palace is mortal cold, and drenched as I was I nearly took a chill on my way down. A noisy fit of rheum would have ruined our next night's work. I hurried to stay warm, and at the wineshop out on the quay, where I found Barnar sitting, I ordered a hot posset.

Barnar gave me his afternoon's purchase: a healing gum used by pearl divers to seal wounds that might draw lurks to them. It was twisted in a scrap of ghul skin. I pocketed it and ordered a second posset, feeling much better. I began to observe that our table was getting respectful clearance from other customers, and interested looks. Barnar explained in a murmur:

"When I've gone you may inherit a quarrel. A pair of bountymen, with two jaws apiece. Biggish men—the one with a pair of lurk fangs over his jaws is the troubleseeker. I didn't quite break his right arm, thought it would bring too much notice if the man had to be carried off. People will tell them you're with me, and if they underestimate you, you'll be getting trouble."

"All right," I said, "any hints for procedure?"

"He's on the strong side, but very slow. His friend plays the jackal, follows him up."

Barnar's mention of leaving told me that he had not yet accomplished the most important errand that fell to his share today. We had rather expected that it would have to be done tonight, as sorcerers are a nocturnal breed.

"You found no one to consult, then?" I asked.

"Just getting a name was much," he rumbled. "It takes a lot of drinking around and rumor-gathering to begin to get a fix on someone reliable. There seems to be a consensus about a certain swamp-witch. I'm going to her now—she lives in the northern swamp. I've hired my guide, and he's standing ready with his raft."

"Then you'll go from her to get the lurk?"

"Yes. I'll see you just after dawn at the dock we landed at this morning."

"Good luck, Ox. Bargain hard. If you offer more than one pearl, she'll take you for green and pass you off with nonsense."

I sought out an inn almost as soon as he left, meaning to be out of trouble's way. I was spotted and followed even so, it seems. They were the truest kind of cutthroat, waiting for the dead of night, so at least I had a couple hours' sleep—it was in a great barracks of an inn, with more than thirty pallets—before I was wakened. A heavy boot-toe kicked me hard against the soles of my feet.

I had laid the spear, which Barnar had returned to me before leaving, along my right side under the blanket, with the head at my heel. This is the way you should do it, so you can lift it straight into action against anyone attacking from your bed's foot, which they must do if you've lain with your head to the wall, as I did. After the kick, it took me one second to sort out the two shapes in the darkness, and another to be sure of the rattle and gleam of teeth at their chests.

Then one further second passed during which the man who kicked me said the word "*Get*" in a fierce whisper, very distinct. He probably meant to say more than just "*Get*," but the passage of my spearhead through his heart supervened.

I used just enough thrust to strike heart-deep and no more, because I knew I'd have to have my spear free again quick; a man doesn't get to be a two-jaw bountyman by being slow on his feet. Sure enough, the other bolted quick as a rat. I used one and the same jerk to free my spear and pull myself to my feet. That man was fast. It took all my force to cock and throw before he got to the door, and I pinned him through the side of his rib cage below his arm just as he was sprinting through it. My spear was just sinking into him before the first man I'd stabbed hit the floor—I swear I was just in time to catch him and kill the noise. I laid him on my pallet, and went quietly after the second one. Some people were awake but feigning sleep, seeing that the scuffle was already settled. I carried the second bountyman back to my pallet, laid him by his colleague, and covered them both with my blanket. I took up my things, wiped my spearhead, and left. At another inn I caught three more hours' sleep.

E ARLY MORNING IS A GRAVEYARD KIND OF HOUR IN THE swamps—there's no clear air under the clouds then, because the mist is rising from the waters. It moves in slow, torn columns across the quays, and if you're standing at the waterside, you can't even see the pyramid. I found Barnar at the dock. We carried the bundled lurk across the terrace, and into the palace.

Inside there was some activity—here and there a tavern door opened, and you could see the tapster within kindling the public-room fire. We went as quickly as we could without running, and feared no questions. Since the Chamber of Audiences would be closed now until the god-making, bountymen arriving with a catch would be expected to wrap it up and take it to an inn for the duration.

But at the highest levels there were neither inns nor taverns, and outlanders ascending here with a large burden would draw scrutiny from any guardsman. Here we went even quicker, prepared to kill, counting on the hour to spare us the necessity. We met no one, and gained the outside staircase leading up to the second level from the top.

From the head of these stairs I crept to the door. Inside there was a guard strolling down the corridor, at the end of which was the staircase to the King's level. He passed the door and turned the corner. He was followed by another walking the same way about twenty seconds later. So it went—I watched five more minutes, but there was no gap in their circuit long enough for us to get to that staircase unseen. We would have to kill one.

I conferred with Barnar, then memorized the face of the next guard who passed. We took the one who followed. Barnar seized him from behind as he turned the corner and broke his neck. We hauled him back out to the staircase. We were going to tie his body to its underside, but I found a flask on him, so we chose a less mystery-creating plan. We drenched his beard and doublet with the liquor, replaced the flask in his belt, and Barnar lifted him high overhead. There was a gardened terrace about six levels down—invisible now, but I remembered its location and directed my friend. He heaved, grunting softly. The guard arched outward, seeming to hang sprawled in the fog, staring upward openmouthed, and then was swallowed in the whiteness. After a moment there was a soft crash of broken shrubbery. Barnar, as a last touch, wrenched the staircase's heavy bannister loose and left it hanging. When the guard whose face I had memorized passed, we entered and dashed down the hall with our load.

I got into the rafters, and Barnar threw up the lurk so that it landed across a beam. He came up, and we pulled our line after us. The level below would be sealed off by a full guard at midmorning, to begin the King's two-day preritual isolation, and just after the breakfast hour there would be a last-minute rush of gawkers. We rested, saving our work for that noisy hour.

When the folk began arriving, we carried the lurk within fifty yards of the King's door, and unwrapped it. I inserted crossed sticks into its body through the slit in its abdomen, and this swelled it out perfectly. Barnar prepared three thirty-foot lengths of bowstring and hooked one end of each into the body—one to the rear part, and one to either side of the flat head part, amid the base joints of the legs. Then, with as little left to do as possible, we carried it to just above the King's cell. We stretched it lengthwise atop a beam, tying its forelegs and rear body to two daggers pushed into the wood. It would have a whole day to lose the last of its creases. We laid the coiled bowstrings on top of it, and got out of there.

I have the trick of sleeping to kill time, and Barnar had been up all night. We found perches two full corridors away, in case we made sleep-noises.

When we woke, my time sense told me we had an hour or so to wait until our chosen time, the pit of night. The guards were under oaths of silence during this part of the vigil, but they ignored them. We listened to the small shapeless sounds that were all that was left of their conversation by the time it reached us. Their talk wavered feebly, like the flame of an ill-made candle in a gusty room. You could read their oppression of spirit in the way their voices blurred, ceased, and then, doggedly, started again. Barnar and I traded our thoughts with a look: they would be jumpy, all right.

It was a man like themselves they guarded, and he lay at the threshold of a grisly journey. When humankind make covenants with the more-than-human, or the less-than-human, you may buttress them with traditions and rites as you will, but there remains an unacknowledged horror that is never quieted in men's hearts. At last we moved, and as we came closer, our movements got as deft and still as the creeping of rats, minus even their tiny noise of nails. We entered the perilous silence above the King's door, and looked down upon the two polished domes of the guards' helmets. Their talk had stopped again. You could almost feel their gloom. They were ripe for our game.

We undid the lurk from the daggers—it had straightened nicely. Barnar took the coils of bowstring and tucked them under his arms, then picked up the lurk by the three lines, holding them near the hooks. I crouched on one side of the gap in the beams and fastened a line to a rafter. Barnar stood on the other side of the gap, one foot on the catwalk and the other on the beam, and poised the lurk over the opening. Remember the weight of the thing, my friends! He looked to me, and I nodded that I was ready. He began to pay out line through his fingers, letting the legs drop foremost and bringing the whole thing almost flush with the wall, so that it looked like it was crawling down it. It appeared real enough to stir your hair, its black legs flung out in their six-foot spread, its jointed barrel of a body taut and poised behind. If I had been standing twelve hours in the empty half-dark gnawed at by unhealthy thoughts, and had turned to see such a thing a foot above my shoulder, I would have done just what the guards did.

This is not to detract from Barnar's masterful handling. When he had the thing positioned, he let it drop a good four feet and scuff the wall as it did so. This brought their faces up at just the right instant to see the monster lurch to a murderous poised halt an arm's length above them. They peeled themselves from the doorway and spilled across the corridor, one man losing his spear as he sprawled. Barnar was already hauling the lurk back upward with a marvelous smooth speed that made it seem to be scuttling in reverse motion up the wall.

Holding the lurk straight-armed before him, he danced along the beam and catwalk to the next large gap in the rafters, and cast it down through. The throw was perfect. The skeleton struck with a rattling splash right next to the men, who were just struggling to their feet. He was playing dangerously near them, for the bowstrings were far from invisible, but his speed and timing were such that the men were kept in a state of maximum panic. The second throw sent them stumbling round the corner. I had dropped my line, slid down and entered the King's cell before I heard the sound of Barnar's third cast down the next hallway. Things couldn't be better—they had only one spear and so they wouldn't risk a cast with it, and Barnar could play them several moments more while they gathered their wits and the puppet's reality was put to a test.

I moved as quick as a dodging, darting fly. I had cup, salve, and poniard out, and the King by the ankle in an instant. I cut him under the bump of the ankle, where you'll get a good half-cup of blood and the bleeding will then peter out. I pocketed the goblet, wiped the wound clean, and sealed it with the salve. I scarcely spared a glance for the King's face—he was staring at me with strange sad intensity, as if he knew me and I had somehow disappointed him. Then I was shutting the door, shinning up the rope, and drawing it after me.

I rushed along the catwalk past the corner and signaled through the beams. Barnar was just drawing up the lurk. He unhooked the lines and set the great spider-thing on a beam so that its forelegs hung down into the guards' range of vision. Then Barnar was with me and we were dancing through those beams almost as fast as a man can jog on level ground, going the opposite way round the square of halls from the point where the reinforcements would be entering. Our two guards had been shouting for them for some time—for it was death for them to leave their post on this floor—and we heard boots thundering on the stairs already.

We had left our plans vague at this point, counting on turmoil but unable to foresee its precise form. We had included the possibility of revealing ourselves as practical jokers, since there would be enough guards there who were jealous of our two victims' special post to raise a laugh and some sympathy for our game. But this being the eve of the god-making, and the swamp-folks' prime night of revel out of the whole year, when the pyramid was alive with drinkers and singers from top to bottom, we'd seen at least a good chance for a cleaner escape. This we got. The downstairs guards flooded up into the hall where their colleagues were, and after a brief interval a stampede of more miscellaneous footfalls came pounding up the stairs. We got down from rafters in time to be in the hall as the red-faced citizenry rushed in. They eddied at the head of the stairs, prevented from entering the hall where the action was by the crowd of guards there. We jumped from round the corner and waved excitedly.

"This way! We can get through over here!" I shouted. Threescore of men and women cried out and pounded after us. We let the crowd overtake and surround us, falling back into it as we all rushed round the other way. As they rounded the last corner before the King's cell, we dropped out of the rear of the rout and ran back to the stairs.

N THE NEXT NIGHT WE STOOD BY THE DAIS IN THE center of the Chamber of Audiences. It had cost us our runt-pearl from the ghul to buy this place from one of the chamber guards. Those near us had paid as much. The whole vast hall was packed with folk, hot and close, from wall to wall. We had taken our place hours early, and heard the tale of the "puppet-show upstairs" passed among the folk around us, variously distorted. People enjoyed it hugely. A new jocose tradition might have gotten started, had we not spoiled the humor of the idea for the Queen a short time later.

She appeared in the great doorway at midnight. Lines of guards held clear a broad aisle from the doorway to the dais, where the altar stood, and she remained in the doorway at the end of this aisle, not moving for a long time. She wore a coarse white robe that covered her entire body. Her long black hair was unbound, and her face had a terrible beauty, meaning both those words. It was a northron face—nose large and strong, eyes set both shadowy deep and wide apart, a marvelous wide mouth with lips of infinite expression.

There was a weight and power in the way she stood, a *realness* that made that whole human multitude seem a shadowy and passing thing. She stood in her straightness and silence and six hundred years of life—for she was ancient when she came to this place—and all of our thousands surrounding her seemed brief, fugitive, whispering—like a host of dead leaves. Truly my friends, aren't our lives as quick in their passing as a thief's shadow across a wall? Queen Vulvula's hand moved to her throat, and her robe fell from her nakedness. She moved forth down the aisle.

She had a body to stir and stiffen you: big guava breasts, hanging-ripe; thighs round and strong; hips like a bulging vase for milk or scented oil. But as she drew near the dais, we saw it was an autumnal body. The breasts were frost-nipped, beginning to dwindle from within as apples will. Her thighs moved with a chilled slowness, and the veins were beginning to map themselves out on the backs of her hands. And as she mounted toward the altar we saw that at the corners of her plump and flexible mouth dark nets of wintery erosion were spreading out across her jaw.

As she stood on the dais I felt her presence fully, like a gust from the icy gulf of her heart. She looked over us as a harvester looks over a great stubborn field that he has made to yield him fruit. She knew her alienness in her people's minds; their unspoken horror and the danger she lived in because of it. And she relished it. The risk and care of empire gratified her centuries-deep mind. She smiled very slightly. Looking at her mouth, you knew that it would have a small frosty atmosphere all its own around it, and that its kiss would suck your soul out in a blaze of cold fire. She moved to the head of the altar.

Literally its head, for the altar was a big statue of a man in a wrestler's bridge, that is, supporting himself on his feet and hands but face upward, so that his thighs, stomach, and chest formed a long level surface. The Queen spoke some words in a language I have never heard. Her voice was mellower than you expected, soft at the edges. Effortlessly it filled the whole hall. As she spoke she pointed overhead, then to the altar, and then floorward, meaning the catacombs below, no doubt. Then she spoke for our understanding:

> *"Your sons have fattened in my rule.*
> *Your rafts go laden with peaceful trade.*
> *There's no man's wife need fear the ghul.*
>
> *Your pearls are spared the poacher's raid—*
> *They're farmed by laws that spread their worth,*
> *And keep ensheathed war's wasteful blade.*

> *You've had what good men get on earth—*
> *Now grant your Queen does nothing cruel*
> *Who, dead with craving, ends her dearth.*
>
> *Her year-long lord, with year-long Heaven paid,*
> *Comes now to her to see her thirst allayed."*

The King appeared in the doorway, borne on a litter by two bearers. He slouched, still strengthless, in the seat, but the set of his head showed his wits more awake than before. He wore a sacrificial fillet of graven bronze round his brow, and as they carried him forward, you could see his eyes moving restlessly under its line.

The bearers set the litter before the altar. They were powerful men, of Barnar's type. One grasped the King's wrists and the other his ankles. The Queen spoke again, and there was a tenderness in her voice:

> *"Rise to me now, my love, a king,*
> *And descend from me as a God.*
>
> *You will sit in Eternity with your line,*
> *And rule the ever-after-living hosts.*
> *You will wield the scepter of the shadow-kind,*
> *You will be judge and shepherd of the ghosts.*
>
> *Rise to me now, my love, a king,*
> *And descend from me as a God."*

When she had said this, they lifted the King onto the altar. He looked to this side and that as they pressed his legs against the stone legs, his back against the stone chest, his arms and shoulders against the arms and shoulders of stone. And as he looked here and there, I thought for a moment that he looked at me, and smiled, ever so faintly. I don't insist on this—I half think it was a dream myself—the air was so charged, and the silence crawled all over the skin of the multitude like a swarm of ants. But do you suppose he understood what had been done, and took some last small comfort, some revenge in the thought?

She knelt beside him, and her face was taut, refined by a tension of icy love, made younger before our eyes by her passionate anticipation. She lowered her face—worshipfully, kissing—to the muscled juncture of his neck and shoulder. And then there was a crisp, liquid sound of horrible distinctness, her hands clutched his shoulders, and the King's body rose and convulsed upon the stone with the raw coiling power of a speared eel.

The two giants holding him grunted with strain, and the Queen's head rode with the youth's surging body as if it were a part of it. He hammered the rock like a beached dolphin pounds the wet sand, slowing with suffocation, and as he stilled, the Queen clutched and nuzzled with a weasel's self-forgetting lust. Her shoulders worked like pumps as she sucked, and her hands kneaded his torso as if it were a great udder of blood. She almost drowned herself in her hunger, and had to tear her face up from its feeding to breathe with all the desperate speed of a diver breaking the surface. She reared her crazed glass-eyed face before the crowd—her lips smeared, her chin drizzling red. Her breasts were actually fuller now—they jutted youthfully, and I saw a thin thread of blood-red leakage from both her nipples. She leaned and drank again. The King barely moved. His skin tightened over the muscles, while the muscles themselves seemed to be slowly dissolving.

She grew calmer, methodical. She drank from both his wrists next, and then from inside of both his thighs, to empty him efficiently. She licked her mouth clean, then cupped and lifted her breasts and licked her nipples. A priestess ascended the dais with a silver laver in which she washed herself a second time, and then drank off the water. Another priestess brought her a robe of scarlet. She put it on and, flanked by the priestesses, stepped down. It was done.

When she had exited, the littermen laid the King's husk on the litter and bore it from the hall. The Queen would spend the night above, in the King's cell, where the priestesses would install for her a large mirror framed in gold. The King would go to the catacombs, where other priestesses waited with the sacred taxidermy tools.

VIII

THE NEXT MORNING, ON THE WESTERN QUAY, WE WAITED for the expected to befall. We had hired a taxi raft, and had it standing by. Then the commotion came boiling out of the palace, borne by scores of hurrying folk. The Queen had been heard to waken, rise, and a moment later, scream.

We boarded at once. An hour later we had reached a certain great mudbar near the fringe of the swamp—one so large it amounted to an island. Here we waited, sending the pilot back well paid and at double speed with a small scroll for the Queen. We'd chosen a shrewd man who would have the savvy to get himself into the Queen's hearing in an uproar like the one you would expect in the pyramid. The scroll's marking would help. We had written on the outside: "Concerning the Year King's Missing Blood." A glance at this added vigor to his plying of the stern oar, and he was soon out of sight.

This was the most ticklish step of all. Having two thousand prime swamp pearls put into our hands was going to be a simple matter now. But remaining alive for even an instant after the King's blood was back in the Queen's control—this was going to strain both wit and nerve to accomplish.

Barnar's interview with the swamp-witch was made with this difficulty in mind. If you're going to guarantee your safety with sorcerers—and the vampire queen was a very great one—you've got to get them to protect you with their own thaumaturgy. The trick is to make them give you magic that they cannot themselves afterward over-pass. You've got to ask for the best thing in their repertory.

The swamp-witch was no Vulvula. But it was worthwhile having her professional opinion as to what is the fastest thing that wizardry can call to the aid of a man. I would have guessed, all by myself and without paying a pearl, the answer that she gave my friend. Still, it was something to have a confirmation. She told Barnar that the fastest being, in the upper world and the subworlds alike, is a basiliscus. I can almost see you nodding wisely, Taramat. Read on a bit.

So we demanded, along with the pearls, a ring charmed to command the service of a basiliscus. Then we sat down, had a bit of jerky and wine, and waited.

The priestess of the Queen came almost impossibly soon. When we saw she had two archers on the raft with her, I quickly waded into the water. The King's blood had dried into a grayish biscuit, full of little holes like lava-rock. I held it up and called out:

"Throw your bows in the water—double quick! Otherwise the Queen is going to have to drink this whole swamp to save her youth!"

The bows went overboard. The men kept their spears, but this was fair, as we had one, and we couldn't expect them to risk our robbing them. The raft came up to the islet. We gestured the soldiers back. The priestess stepped ashore with two leathern bags and stood staring at us, rage in her eyes, her mouth impassive. I stayed in the water, as the soldiers were so near. Barnar said:

"Time is short, woman. Give us the ring. We'll make the exchange when we're on the creature's back." She nodded wordlessly, and tossed him a small silver ring. Barnar put it on his smallest finger and raised his hands. The spell the witch had taught him was brief. He intoned it with great verve and authority. First there was a long silence.

Then the earth began to wrinkle and crack, like pottery glaze, along a thirty-foot seam that crossed the width of the islet. The cracks darkened and grew, the fragmented clay began to buckle, and even I, standing in the water, felt a giant mass jerking and slithering underfoot. A lizard-foot that could have held me like a doll reached out of the tormented mire. A second followed, as a polished scaly snout appeared. The seam bulged and gaped, and the vast reptile heaved clear, hurling blocks of clay to all sides and raising waves from which I was barely quick enough to save the blood-cake. With imperial self-absorption the basiliscus hauled itself into the water on the other side of the islet, and unfolded its wings to bathe them. They were no bigger, fanned out, than the raft the soldiers stood on—curiously stunted-looking, given the body's bulk. In its own good time it crawled back into the islet and aimed its obsidian eye, big as a target-shield, attentively at Barnar.

The basiliscus isn't a true demon because it can barely use speech at all, but it falls under the compulsions of the Great Age of Thaumaturgy and is part of our inheritance of power from our forebears. You tell it where you want to go. It takes you there and you feed it the ring in payment, allowing it to return to the subworlds. And you'd better feed it the ring, and ask no further trips. Magic compels it just so far, and then its nature asserts itself. Into its ragged pit of an earhole, Barnar whispered the name of our destination, then mounted its back. I jumped from the water and vaulted on behind him, keeping the blood-cake poised for a throw at the lagoon.

The priestess approached and opened the mouths of both bags for our inspection. I don't know which felt more unreal, to be sitting on the back of that lizard or to be looking at the oily luster of two thousand perfect swamp pearls. The priestess stepped nearer, the bags in one hand, the other extended for the blood. I made the exchange with pickpocket deftness, hugged the bags to me, and Barnar shouted: "Away!"

A slow gale of breath entered the cavelike chest under us. For a moment nothing happened, and fleetingly it bothered me that in that time, neither the priestess nor the soldiers stirred. They didn't make a move, and yet had time enough, if they were good, to spear us both from our mount. Then we were fifty yards away.

The basiliscus's scales were big as flagstones and smooth as wax. Luckily there was room in their interstices for you to sink half your hand in, because its back was far too broad to grip with your legs. It took exactly three running leaps, crossing lakelets like puddles and using big mudbars as stepping-stones. Its wings hammered once, twice, and then suddenly they were winnowing cottony fog, and there was no swamp to be seen.

We swam thundering up through clouds and mist for several moments, knuckles cracking with the strain of our climbing speed, and then we were in clear sky, with the clouds a level white broth below, hemmed in a bowllike rim of ragged peaks. Beyond the hills, where we were headed, the salt steppes lay parching under the hot blue emptiness. Then, through the rush of wind and the creaking leathery toil of the vast wings, we heard a whine far to our rear.

We looked back, and learned in one glance that there *is* something faster than a basiliscus. Whatever its name is—for that we never learned—there was one of them bursting from the cloud-broth just where we had exited. It had one human rider. Even at that moment I marveled that any man should venture to sit astride the spiny neck of such a thing.

I have seen its kind in little—stilt-legged bugs with long bodies and two forelegs it uses as arms, barbed along their insides for piercing what they snatch. Their flat triangular heads have two globelike eyes and dainty greedy mouths, whose hunger the barbed arms must constantly serve. This one's head was big enough for a man to dance on, and it was dead white all over. Only the furious power of its wings—two shining blurs at its sides—set off its form against the white background of clouds. The thing was big enough to kill our basiliscus, though it probably wouldn't be able to eat more than two-thirds of him. Of course it would start with us.

There was no hurrying our mount, which sped its maximum as a matter of course. Meanwhile, the Queen's rider guided the huge pale insect into a long sloping climb that would intersect our course, for we had leveled off. I remembered seeing the lightning deftness of the little cousins of this thing—they can snatch a spider out of its web without leaving a tremor among the silk threads. This thing would have a fifteen-foot reach if an inch, and to cap the mess, I could only defend our rear with one hand; it was imperative for both of us to keep one hand dug into the lizard's scales, or the wind of our passage would sweep us off.

We were over the steppes now. Hopelessly I chose a stabbing-grip on our spear with my free hand. The look of the hell-bug as it rose behind us was all fragility and grace. Its two lower pairs of legs hung trailing in dainty curves under its long body, which looked as smooth and balanced as the war-canoes of the southeastern savages. It was getting so near you could make out the faceting of its eye-globes, a taunting reminder of the pearls in our bags. I could even see the face of the soldier guiding the thing.

It's strange to see a man's face through the screaming wind of that speed, with the whole sky around you and the whole world beneath, a barren floor, and still to get as clear a feel for his past and his character, as if the two of you were sitting at mugs in a cozy tavern. But I did feel I knew the man in that glance— plain sense said that it would be a tough and tried soldier, for an important mission like this. The face said that and more—the scars above and below the steady bright eyes, squinted against the wind, the mouth shut and thoughtful. It added up to a sturdy, cool professional who thinks ahead and then kills you without slipups when it's his job to do so and he has the edge.

Good soldiers stay alive by being unsentimental and having a quick eye for the main chance. There was no time to chew it over. That quirky peek into the man's nature showed me our only long-shot hope, and without a pause for thought I did the hardest thing I've ever done. I grabbed a bag by the bottom, and with a snap of the arm that forced open its drawstrings, I flung its whole contents into the air behind us. I groaned as I did it, looking back. The pearls sped earthward in a glistering black clot, scattering slowly, seeming to swarm as they fell like bees do before hive-making. Our speed and theirs made the jewels flee the faster from sight, and I still see them sometimes in memory, a thousand black stars, tumbling down through the wide blaze of noon.

If betrayal of his Queen was on the soldier's mind before, I do not know. Perhaps if he'd caught us and had the whole two thousand, the habit of loyalty would have stayed firm and he would have smoothly completed his mission. But seeing the pearls there, stark and dazzling in the sky, and knowing that they could be his or they could be who knew whose—it shocked him into realizing the wealth he was pursuing. If he did not follow them down, and finished the chase, they would be leagues behind, and he might never find them. Almost without hesitation, he reined his mount into a dive.

It had to be a whole thousand, you see, for some would be lost, and there must be enough even so to purchase swift escape and a new life. The Queen would eventually work a spell of recall on the mount he rode, and in the meantime he could use it to his advantage. Luck go with the man, I bear him no grudge! Still, as I say, I see them tumbling, tumbling, those thousand dazzling jet-black pearls, sometimes in memory.

Ah well! Having a share of a full thousand would simply have meant more squandering to do. The soldier was a career man, a maker of plans and investments, and is probably cherishing his coffers right now, and dreading thieves. For me, it was work enough to rid myself of the five hundred I came away with. Think—I did it in two years! Surely, that's a feat as great as any involved in the winning of those black beauties!

The End of the Story

❧

Clark Ashton Smith

THE FOLLOWING NARRATIVE WAS FOUND AMONG THE papers of Christophe Morand, a young law-student of Tours, after his unaccountable disappearance during a visit at his father's home near Moulins, in November, 1798:

A sinister brownish-purple autumn twilight, made premature by the imminence of a sudden thunderstorm, had filled the forest of Averoigne. The trees along my road were already blurred to ebon masses, and the road itself, pale and spectral before me in the thickening gloom, seemed to waver and quiver slightly, as with the tremor of some mysterious earthquake. I spurred my horse, who was woefully tired with a journey begun at dawn, and had fallen hours ago to a protesting and reluctant trot, and we galloped adown the darkening road between enormous oaks that seemed to lean toward us with boughs like clutching fingers as we passed.

With dreadful rapidity, the night was upon us, the blackness became a tangible clinging veil; a nightmare confusion and desperation drove me to spur my mount again with a more cruel rigor; and now, as we went, the first far-off mutter of the storm mingled with the clatter of my horse's hoofs, and the first lighting flashes illumed our way, which, to my amazement (since I believed myself on the main highway through Averoigne), had inexplicably narrowed to a well-trodden footpath. Feeling sure that I had gone astray, but not caring to retrace my steps in the teeth of darkness and the towering clouds of the tempest, I hurried on, hoping, as seemed reasonable, that a path so plainly worn would lead eventually to some house or chateau where I could find refuge for the night. My hope was well-founded, for within a few minutes I descried a glimmering light through the forest-boughs, and came suddenly to an open glade, where, on a gentle eminence, a large building loomed, with several litten windows in the lower story, and a top that was well-nigh indistinguishable against the bulks of driven cloud.

'Doubtless a monastery,' I thought, as I drew rein, and descending from my exhausted mount, lifted the heavy brazen knocker in the form of a dog's head and let it fall on the oaken door. The sound was unexpectedly loud and sonorous, with a reverberation almost sepulchral, and I shivered involuntarily, with a sense of startlement, of unwonted dismay. This, a moment later, was wholly dissipated when the door was thrown open and a tall, ruddy-featured monk stood before me in the cheerful glow of the cressets that illumed a capacious hallway.

'I bid you welcome to the abbey of Perigon,' he said, in a suave rumble, and even as he spoke, another robed and hooded figure appeared and took my horse in charge. As I murmured my thanks and acknowledgments, the storm broke and tremendous gusts of rain, accompanied by ever-nearing peals of thunder, drove with demoniac fury on the door that had closed behind me.

'It is fortunate that you found us when you did,' observed my host. ''Twere ill for man and beast to be abroad in such a hell-brew.'

Divining without question that I was hungry as well as tired, he led me to the refectory and set before me a bountiful meal of mutton, brown bread, lentils and a strong excellent red wine.

He sat opposite me at the refectory table while I ate, and, with my hunger a little mollified, I took occasion to scan him more attentively. He was both tall and stoutly built, and his features, where the brow was no less broad than the powerful jaw, betokened intellect as well as a love for good living. A certain delicacy and refinement, an air of scholarship, of good taste and good breeding, emanated from him, and I thought to myself: 'This monk is probably a connoisseur of books as well as of wines.' Doubtless my expression betrayed the quickening of my curiosity, for he said, as if in answer:

'I am Hilaire, the abbot of Perigon. We are a Benedictine order, who live in amity with God and with all men, and we do not hold that the spirit is to be enriched by the mortification or impoverishment of the body. We have in our butteries an abundance of wholesome fare, in our cellars the best and oldest vintages of the district of Averoigne. And, if such things interest you, as mayhap they do, we have a library that is stocked with rare tomes, with precious manuscripts, with the finest works of heathendom and Christendom, even to certain unique writings that survived the holocaust of Alexandria.'

'I appreciate your hospitality,' I said, bowing. 'I am Christophe Morand, a law-student, on my way home from Tours to my father's estate near Moulins. I, too, am a lover of books, and nothing would delight me more than the privilege of inspecting a library so rich and curious as the one whereof you speak.'

Forthwith, while I finished my meal, we fell to discussing the classics, and to quoting and capping passages from Latin, Greek or Christian authors. My host, I soon discovered, was a scholar of uncommon attainments, with an erudition, a ready familiarity with both ancient and modern literature that made my own seem as that of the merest beginner by comparison. He, on his part, was so good as to commend my far from perfect Latin, and by the time I had emptied my bottle of red wine we were chatting familiarly like old friends.

All my fatigue had now flown, to be succeeded by a rare sense of well-being, of physical comfort combined with mental alertness and keenness. So, when the abbot suggested that we pay a visit to the library, I assented with alacrity.

He led me down a long corridor, on each side of which were cells belonging to the brothers of the order, and unlocked, with a large brazen key that depended from his girdle, the door of a great room with lofty ceiling and several deep-set windows. Truly, he had not exaggerated the resources of the library; for the long shelves were overcrowded with books, and many volumes were piled high on the tables or stacked in corners. There were rolls of papyrus, of parchment, of vellum; there were strange Byzantine or Coptic bibles; there were old Arabic and Persian manuscripts with floriated or jewel-studded covers; there were scores of incunabula from the first printing-presses; there were innumerable monkish copies of antique authors, bound in wood or ivory, with rich illuminations and lettering that was often in itself a work of art.

With a care that was both loving and meticulous, the abbot Hilaire brought out volume after volume for my inspection. Many of them I had never seen before; some were unknown to me even by fame or rumor. My excited interest, my unfeigned enthusiasm, evidently pleased him, for at length he pressed a hidden spring in one of the library tables and drew out a long drawer, in which, he told me, were certain treasures that he did not care to bring forth for the edification or delectation of many, and whose very existence was undreamed of by the monks.

'Here,' he continued, 'are three odes by Catullus which you will not find in any published edition of his works. Here, also, is an original manuscript of Sappho—a complete copy of a poem otherwise extant only in brief fragments; here are two of the lost tales of Miletus, a letter of Pericles to Aspasia, an unknown dialogue of Plato, and an old Arabian work on astronomy, by some anonymous author, in which the theories of Copernicus are anticipated. And, lastly, here is the somewhat infamous *Histoire d'Amour*, by Bernard de Vaillantcoeur, which was destroyed immediately upon publication, and of which only one other copy is known to exist.'

As I gazed with mingled awe and curiosity on the unique, unheard-of treasures he displayed, I saw in one corner of the drawer what appeared to be a thin volume with plain untitled binding of dark leather. I ventured to pick it up, and found that it contained a few sheets of closely written manuscript in old French.

'And this?' I queried, turning to look at Hilaire, whose face, to my amazement, had suddenly assumed a melancholy and troubled expression.

'It were better not to ask, my son.' He crossed himself as he spoke, and his voice was no longer mellow, but harsh, agitated, full of a sorrowful perturbation. 'There is a curse on the pages that you hold in your hand: an evil spell, a malign power is attached to them, and he who would venture to peruse them is henceforward in dire peril both of body and soul.' He took the little volume from me as he spoke, and returned it to the drawer, again crossing himself carefully as he did so.

'But, father,' I dared to expostulate, 'how can such things be? How can there be danger in a few written sheets of parchment?'

'Christophe, there are things beyond your understanding, things that it were not well for you to know. The might of Satan is manifestable in devious modes, in diverse manners; there are other temptations than those of the world and the flesh, there are evils no less subtle than irresistible, there are hidden heresies, and necromancies other than those which sorcerers practise.'

'With what, then, are these pages concerned, that such occult peril, such unholy power lurks within them?'

'I forbid you to ask.' His tone was one of great rigor, with a finality that dissuaded me from further questioning.

'For you, my son,' he went on, 'the danger would be doubly great, because you are young, ardent, full of desires and curiosities. Believe me, it is better to forget that you have ever seen this manuscript.' He closed the hidden drawer, and as he did so, the melancholy troubled look was replaced by his former benignity.

'Now,' he said, as he turned to one of the book-shelves, 'I will show you the copy of Ovid that was owned by the poet Petrarch.' He was again the mellow scholar, the kindly, jovial host, and it was evident that the mysterious manuscript was not to be referred to again. But his odd perturbation, the dark and awful hints he had let fall, the vague terrific terms of his proscription, had all served to awaken my wildest curiosity, and, though I felt the obsession to be unreasonable, I was quite unable to think of anything else for the rest of the evening. All manner of speculations, fantastic, absurd, outrageous, ludicrous, terrible, defiled through my brain as I duly admired the incunabula which Hilaire took down so tenderly from the shelves for my delectation.

At last, toward midnight, he led me to my room—a room especially reserved for visitors, and with more of comfort, of actual luxury in its hangings, carpets and deeply quilted bed than was allowable in the cells of the monks or of the abbot himself. Even when Hilaire had withdrawn, and I had proved for my satisfaction the softness of the bed allotted to me, my brain still whirled with questions concerning the forbidden manuscript. Though the storm had now ceased, it was long before I fell asleep; but slumber, when it finally came, was dreamless and profound.

When I awoke, a river of sunshine clear as molten gold was pouring through my window. The storm had wholly vanished, and no lightest tatter of cloud was visible anywhere in the pale-blue October heavens. I ran to the window and peered out on a world of autumnal forest and fields all a-sparkle with the diamonds of rain. All was beautiful, all was idyllic to a degree that could be fully appreciated only by one who had lived for a long time, as I had, within the walls of a city, with towered buildings in lieu of trees and cobbled pavements where grass should be. But, charming as it was, the foreground held my gaze only for a few moments; then, beyond the tops of the trees, I saw a hill, not more than a mile distant, on whose summit there stood the ruins of some old chateau, the crumbling, broken-down condition of whose walls and towers was plainly visible. It drew my gaze irresistibly, with an overpowering sense of romantic attraction, which somehow seemed so natural, so inevitable, that I did not pause to analyze or wonder; and once having seen it, I could not take my eyes away, but lingered at the window for how long I knew not, scrutinizing as closely as I could the details of each time-shaken turret and bastion. Some undefinable fascination was inherent in the very form, the extent, the disposition of the pile—some fascination not dissimilar to that exerted by a strain of music, by a magical combination of words in poetry, by the features of a beloved face. Gazing, I lost myself in reveries that I could not recall afterward, but which left behind them the same tantalizing sense of innominable delight which forgotten nocturnal dreams may sometimes leave.

I was recalled to the actualities of life by a gentle knock at my door, and realized that I had forgotten to dress myself. It was the abbot, who came to inquire how I had passed the night, and to tell me that breakfast was ready whenever I should care to arise. For some reason, I felt a little embarrassed, even shamefaced, to have been caught day-dreaming; and though this was doubtless unnecessary, I apologized for my dilatoriness. Hilaire, I thought, gave me a keen, inquiring look, which was quickly withdrawn, as, with the suave courtesy of a good host, he assured me that there was nothing whatever for which I need apologize.

When I had breakfast, I told Hilaire, with many expressions of gratitude for his hospitality, that it was time for me to resume my journey. But his regret at the announcement of my departure was so unfeigned, his invitation to tarry for at least another night was so genuinely hearty, so sincerely urgent, that I consented to remain. In truth, I required no great amount of solicitation, for, apart from the real liking I had taken to Hilaire, the mystery of the forbidden manuscript had entirely enslaved my imagination, and I was loth to leave without having learned more concerning it. Also, for a youth with scholastic leanings, the freedom of the abbot's library was a rare privilege, a precious opportunity not to be passed over.

'I should like,' I said, 'to pursue certain studies while I am here, with the aid of your incomparable collection.'

'My son, you are more than welcome to remain for any length of time, and you can have access to my books whenever it suits your need or inclination.' So saying, Hilaire detached the key of the library from his girdle and gave it to me. 'There are duties,' he went on, 'which will call me away from the monastery for a few hours today, and doubtless you will desire to study in my absence.'

A little later, he excused himself and departed. With inward felicitations on the longed-for opportunity that had fallen so readily into my hands, I hastened to the library, with no thought save to read the proscribed manuscript. Giving scarcely a glance at the laden shelves, I sought the table with the secret drawer, and fumbled for the spring. After a little anxious delay, I pressed the proper spot and drew forth the drawer. An impulsion that had become a veritable obsession, a fever of curiosity that bordered upon actual madness, drove me, and if the safety of my soul had really depended upon it, I could not have denied the desire which forced me to take from the drawer the thin volume with plain unlettered binding.

Seating myself in a chair near one of the windows, I began to peruse the pages, which were only six in number. The writing was peculiar, with letter-forms of a fantasticality I had never met before, and the French was not only old but well-nigh barbarous in its quaint singularity. Notwithstanding the difficulty I found in deciphering them, a mad, unaccountable thrill ran through me at the first words, and I read on with all the sensations of a man who had been bewitched or who had drunken a philtre of bewildering potency.

There was no title, no date, and the writing was a narrative which began almost as abruptly as it ended. It concerned one Gerard, Comte de Venteillon, who, on the eve of his marriage to the renowned and beautiful demoiselle, Eleanor des Lys, had met in the forest near his chateau a strange, half-human creature with hoofs and horns. Now Gerard, as the narrative explained, was a knightly youth of indisputably proven valor, as well as a true Christian; so, in the name of our Savior, Jesus Christ, he bade the creature stand and give an account of itself.

Laughing wildly in the twilight, the bizarre being capered before him, and cried:

'I am a satyr, and your Christ is less to me than the weeds that grow on your kitchen-middens.'

Appalled by such blasphemy, Gerard would have drawn his sword to slay the creature, but again it cried, saying:

'Stay, Gerard de Venteillon, and I will tell you a secret, knowing which, you will forget the worship of Christ, and forget your beautiful bride of tomorrow, and turn your back on the world and on the very sun itself with no reluctance and no regret.'

Now, albeit half unwillingly, Gerard lent the satyr an ear and it came closer and whispered to him. And that which it whispered is not known; but before it vanished amid the blackening shadows of the forest, the satyr spoke aloud once more, and said:

'The power of Christ has prevailed like a black frost on all the woods, the fields, the rivers, the mountains, where abode in their felicity the glad, immortal goddesses and nymphs of yore. But still, in the cryptic caverns of earth, in places far underground, like the hell your priests have fabled, there dwells the pagan loveliness, there cry the pagan ecstasies.' And with the last words, the creature laughed again its wild unhuman laugh, and disappeared among the darkening boles of the twilight trees.

From that moment, a change was upon Gerard de Venteillon. He returned to his chateau with downcast mien, speaking no cheery or kindly word to his retainers, as was his wont, but sitting or pacing always in silence, and scarcely heeding the food that was set before him. Nor did he go that evening to visit his betrothed, as he had promised; but, toward midnight, when a waning moon had arisen red as from a bath of blood, he went forth clandestinely by the postern door of the chateau, and followed an old, half-obliterated trail through the woods, found his way to the ruins of the Chateau des Faussesflammes, which stands on a hill opposite the Benedictine abbey of Perigon.

Now these ruins (said the manuscript) are very old, and have long been avoided by the people of the district; for a legendry of immemorial evil clings about them, and it is said that they are the dwelling-place of foul spirits, the rendezvous of sorcerers and succubi. But Gerard, as if oblivious or fearless of their ill renown, plunged like one who is devil-driven into the shadow of the crumbling walls, and went, with the careful groping of a man who follows some given direction, to the northern end of the courtyard. There, directly between and below the two centermost windows, which, it may be, looked forth from the chamber of forgotten chatelaines, he pressed with his right foot on a flagstone differing from those about it in being of a triangular form. And the flagstone moved and tilted beneath his foot, revealing a flight of granite steps that went down into the earth. Then, lighting a taper he had brought with him, Gerard descended the steps, and the flagstone swung into place behind him.

On the morrow, his betrothed, Eleanor des Lys, and all her bridal train, waited vainly for him at the cathedral of Vyones, the principal town of Averoigne, where the wedding had been set. And from that time his face was beheld by no man, and no vaguest rumor of Gerard de Venteillon or of the fate that befell him has ever passed among the living. . . .

Such was the substance of the forbidden manuscript, and thus it ended. As I have said before, there was no date, nor was there anything to indicate by whom it had been written or how the knowledge of the happenings related had come into the writer's possession. But, oddly enough, it did not occur to me to doubt their veridity for a moment; and the curiosity I had felt concerning the contents of the manuscript was now replaced by a burning desire, a thousandfold more powerful, more obsessive, to know the ending of the story and to learn what Gerard de Venteillon had found when he descended the hidden steps.

In reading the tale, it had of course occurred to me that the ruins of the Chateau des Faussesflammes, described therein, were the very same ruins I had seen that morning from my chamber window; and pondering this, I became more and more possessed by an insane fever, by a frenetic, unholy excitement. Returning the manuscript to the secret drawer, I left the library and wandered for a while in an aimless fashion about the corridors of the monastery. Chancing to meet there the same monk who had taken my horse in charge the previous evening, I ventured to question him, as discreetly and casually as I could, regarding the ruins which were visible from the abbey windows.

He crossed himself, and a frightened look came over his broad, placid face at my query.

'The ruins are those of the Chateau des Faussesflammes,' he replied. 'For un-told years, men say, they have been the haunt of unholy spirits, of witches and demons; and festivals not to be described or even named are held within their walls. No weapon known to man, no exorcism or holy water, has ever prevailed against these demons; many brave cavaliers and monks have disappeared amid the shadows of Faussesflammes, never to return; and once, it is told, an abbot of Perigon went thither to make war on the powers of evil; but what befell him at the hands of the succubi is not known or conjectured. Some say that the demons are abominable hags whose bodies terminate in serpentine coils; others that they are women of more than mortal beauty, whose kisses are a diabolic delight that consumes the flesh of men with the fierceness of hell-fire. . . . As for me, I know not whether such tales are true; but I should not care to venture within the walls of Faussesflammes.'

Before he had finished speaking, a resolve had sprung to life full-born in my mind: I felt that I must go to the Chateau des Faussesflammes and learn for my-self, if possible, all that could be learned. The impulse was immediate, over-whelming, ineluctable; and even if I had so desired, I could no more have fought against it than if I had been the victim of some sorcerer's invultuation. The pro-scription of the abbot Hilaire, the strange unfinished tale in the old manuscript, the evil legendry at which the monk had now hinted—all these, it would seem, should have served to frighten and deter me from such a resolve; but, on the con-trary, by some bizarre inversion of thought, they seemed to conceal some delec-table mystery, to denote a hidden world of ineffable things, of vague undreamable pleasures that set my brain on fire and made my pulses throb deliriously. I did not know, I could not conceive, of what these pleasures would consist; but in some mystical manner I was as sure of their ultimate reality as the abbot Hilaire was sure of heaven.

I determined to go that very afternoon, in the absence of Hilaire, who, I felt instinctively, might be suspicious of any such intention on my part and would surely be inimical toward its fulfillment.

My preparations were very simple: I put in my pockets a small taper from my room and the heel of a loaf of bread from the refectory; and making sure that a little dagger which I always carried was in its sheath, I left the monastery forthwith. Meeting two of the brothers in the courtyard, I told them I was going for a short walk in the neighboring woods. They gave me a jovial '*pax vobiscum*' and went upon their way in the spirit of the words.

Heading directly as I could for Faussesflammes, whose turrets were often lost behind the high and interlacing boughs, I entered the forest. There were no paths, and often I was compelled to brief detours and divagations by the thickness of the underbrush. In my feverous hurry to reach the ruins, it seemed hours before I came to the top of the hill which Faussesflammes surmounted, but probably it was little more than thirty minutes. Climbing the last declivity of the boulder-strewn slope, I came suddenly within view of the chateau, standing close at hand in the center of the level table which formed the summit. Trees had taken root in its broken-down walls, and the ruinous gateway that gave on the courtyard was half-choked by bushes, brambles and nettle-plants. Forcing my way through, not without difficulty, and with clothing that had suffered from the bramble-thorns, I went, like Gerard de Venteillon in the old manuscript, to the northern end of the court. Enormous evil-looking weeds were rooted between the flagstones, rearing their thick and fleshy leaves that had turned to dull sinister maroons and purples with the onset of autumn. But I soon found the triangular flagstone indicated in the tale, and without the slightest delay or hesitation I pressed upon it with my right foot.

A mad shiver, a thrill of adventurous triumph that was mingled with something of trepidation, leaped through me when the great flagstone tilted easily beneath my foot, disclosing dark steps of granite, even as in the story. Now, for a moment, the vaguely hinted horrors of the monkish legends became imminently real in my imagination, and I paused before the black opening that was to engulf me, wondering if some satanic spell had not drawn me thither to perils of unknown terror and inconceivable gravity.

Only for a few instants, however, did I hesitate. Then the sense of peril faded, the monkish horrors became a fantastic dream, and the charm of things unformulable, but ever closer at hand, always more readily attainable, tightened about me like the embrace of amorous arms. I lit my taper, I descended the stair; and even as behind Gerard de Venteillon, the triangular block of stone silently resumed its place in the paving of the court above me. Doubtless it was moved by some mechanism operable by a man's weight on one of the steps; but I did not pause to consider its modus operandi, or to wonder if there were any way by which it could be worked from beneath to permit my return.

There were perhaps a dozen steps, terminating in a low, narrow, musty vault that was void of anything more substantial than ancient, dust-encumbered cobwebs. At the end, a small doorway admitted me to a second vault that differed from the first only in being larger and dustier. I passed through several such vaults, and then found myself in a long passage or tunnel, half blocked in places by boulders or heaps of rubble that had fallen from the crumbling sides. It was very damp, and full of the noisome odor of stagnant waters and subterranean mold. My feet splashed more than once in little pools, and drops fell upon me from above, fetid and foul as if they had oozed from a charnel. Beyond the wavering circle of light that my taper maintained, it seemed to me that the coils of dim and shadowy serpents slithered away in the darkness at my approach; but I could not be sure whether they really were serpents, or only the troubled and retreating shadows, seen by an eye that was still unaccustomed to the gloom of the vaults.

Rounding a sudden turn in the passage, I saw the last thing I had dreamt of seeing—the gleam of sunlight at what was apparently the tunnel's end. I scarcely know what I had expected to find, but such an eventuation was somehow altogether unanticipated. I hurried on, in some confusion of thought, and stumbled through the opening, to find myself blinking in the full rays of the sun.

Even before I had sufficiently recovered my wits and my eyesight to take note of the landscape before me, I was struck by a strange circumstance: Though it had been early afternoon when I entered the vaults, and though my passage through them could have been a matter of no more than a few minutes, the sun was now nearing the horizon. There was also a difference in its light, which was both brighter and mellower than the sun I had seen above Averoigne; and the sky itself was intensely blue, with no hint of autumnal pallor.

Now, with ever-increasing stupefaction, I stared about me, and could find nothing familiar or even credible in the scene upon which I had emerged. Contrary to all reasonable expectation, there was no semblance of the hill upon which Faussesflammes stood, or of the adjoining country; but around me was a placid land of rolling meadows, through which a golden-gleaming river meandered toward a sea of deepest azure that was visible beyond the tops of laurel-trees. . . . But there are no laurel-trees in Averoigne, and the sea is hundreds of miles away: judge, then, my complete confusion and dumbfoundment.

It was a scene of such loveliness as I have never before beheld. The meadow-grass at my feet was softer and more lustrous than emerald velvet, and was full of violets and many-colored asphodels. The dark green of ilex-trees was mirrored in the golden river, and far away I saw the pale gleam of a marble acropolis on a low summit above the plain. All things bore the aspect of a mild and clement spring that was verging upon an opulent summer. I felt as if I had stepped into a land of classic myth, of Grecian legend; and moment by moment, all surprise, all wonder as to how I could have come there, was drowned in a sense of ever-growing ecstasy before the utter, ineffable beauty of the landscape.

Near by, in a laurel-grove, a white roof shone in the late rays of the sun. I was drawn toward it by the same allurement, only far more potent and urgent, which I had felt on seeing the forbidden manuscript and the ruins of Fausses-flammes. Here, I knew with an esoteric certainty, was the culmination of my quest, the reward of all my mad and perhaps impious curiosity.

As I entered the grove, I heard laughter among the trees, blending harmoniously with the low murmur of their leaves in a soft, balmy wind. I thought I saw vague forms that melted among the boles at my approach; and once a shaggy, goat-like creature with human head and body ran across my path, as if in pursuit of a flying nymph.

In the heart of the grove, I found a marble place with a portico of Doric columns. As I neared it, I was greeted by two women in the costume of ancient slaves; and though my Greek is of the meagerest, I found no difficulty in comprehending their speech, which was of Attic purity.

'Our mistress, Nycea, awaits you,' they told me. I could no longer marvel at anything, but accepted my situation without question or surmise, like one who resigns himself to the progress of some delightful dream. Probably, I thought, it was a dream, and I was still lying in my bed at the monastery; but never before had I been favored by nocturnal visions of such clarity and surpassing loveliness.

The interior of the palace was full of a luxury that verged upon the barbaric, and which evidently belonged to the period of Greek decadence, with its intermingling of Oriental influences. I was led through a hallway gleaming with onyx and polished porphyry, into an opulently furnished room, where, on a couch of gorgeous fabrics, there reclined a woman of goddess-like beauty.

At sight of her, I trembled from head to foot with the violence of a strange emotion. I had heard of the sudden mad loves by which men are seized on beholding for the first time a certain face and form; but never before had I experienced a passion of such intensity, such all-consuming ardor, as the one I conceived immediately for this woman. Indeed, it seemed as if I had loved her for a long time, without knowing that it was she whom I loved, and without being able to identify the nature of my emotion or to orient the feeling in any manner.

She was not tall, but was formed with exquisite voluptuous purity of line and contour. Her eyes were of a dark sapphire blue, with molten depths into which the soul was fain to plunge as into the soft abysses of a summer ocean. The curve of her lips was enigmatic, a little mournful, and gravely tender as the lips of an antique Venus. Her hair, brownish rather than blond, fell over her neck and ears and forehead in delicious ripples confined by a plain fillet of silver. In her expression, there was a mixture of pride and voluptuousness, of regal imperiousness and feminine yielding. Her movements were all as effortless and graceful as those of a serpent.

'I knew you would come,' she murmured in the same soft-voweled Greek I had heard from the lips of her servants. 'I have waited for you long; but when you sought refuge from the storm in the abbey of Perigon, and saw the manuscript in the secret drawer, I knew that the hour of your arrival was at hand. Ah! you did not dream that the spell which drew you so irresistibly, with such unaccountable potency, was the spell of my beauty, the magical allurement of my love!'

'Who are you?' I queried. I spoke readily in Greek, which would have surprised me greatly an hour before. But now, I was prepared to accept anything whatever, no matter how fantastic or preposterous, as part of the miraculous fortune, the unbelievable adventure which had befallen me.

'I am Nycea,' she replied to my question. 'I love you, and the hospitality of my palace and of my arms is at your disposal. Need you know anything more?'

The slaves had disappeared. I flung myself beside the couch and kissed the hand she offered me, pouring out protestations that were no doubt incoherent, but were nevertheless full of an ardor that made her smile tenderly.

Her hand was cool to my lips, but the touch of it fired my passion. I ventured to seat myself beside her on the couch, and she did not deny my familiarity. While a soft purple twilight began to fill the corners of the chamber, we conversed happily, saying over and over again all the sweet absurd litanies, all the felicitous nothings that come instinctively to the lips of lovers. She was incredibly soft in my arms, and it seemed almost as if the completeness of her yielding was unhindered by the presence of bones in her lovely body.

The servants entered noiselessly, lighting rich lamps of intricately carven gold, and setting before us a meal of spicy meats, of unknown savorous fruits and potent wines. But I could eat little, and while I drank, I thirsted for the sweeter wine of Nycea's mouth.

I do not know when we fell asleep; but the evening had flown like an enchanted moment. Heavy with felicity, I drifted off on a silken tide of drowsiness, and the golden lamps and the face of Nycea blurred in a blissful mist and were seen no more.

Suddenly, from the depths of a slumber beyond all dreams, I found myself compelled into full wakefulness. For an instant, I did not even realize where I was, still less what had aroused me. Then I heard a footfall in the open doorway of the room, and peering across the sleeping head of Nycea, saw in the lamplight the abbot Hilaire, who had paused on the threshold. A look of absolute horror was imprinted upon his face, and as he caught sight of me, he began to gibber in Latin, in tones where something of fear was blended with fanatical abhorrence and hatred. I saw that he carried in his hands a large bottle and an aspergillus. I felt sure that the bottle was full of holy water, and of course divined the use for which it was intended.

Looking at Nycea, I saw that she too was awake, and knew that she was aware of the abbot's presence. She gave me a strange smile, in which I read an affectionate pity, mingled with the reassurance that a woman offers a frightened child.

'Do not fear for me,' she whispered.

'Foul vampire! accursed lamia! she-serpent of hell!' thundered the abbot suddenly, as he crossed the threshold of the room, raising the aspergillus aloft. At the same moment, Nycea glided from the couch, with an unbelievable swiftness

of motion, and vanished through an outer door that gave upon the forest of laurels. Her voice hovered in my ear, seeming to come from an immense distance:

'Farewell for a while, Christophe. But have no fear. You shall find me again
if you are brave and patient.'

As the words ended, the holy water from the aspergillus fell on the floor of
the chamber and on the couch where Nycea had lain beside me. There was a
crash as of many thunders, and the golden lamps went out in a darkness that
seemed full of falling dust, of raining fragments. I lost all consciousness, and
when I recovered, I found myself lying on a heap of rubble in one of the vaults
I had traversed earlier in the day. With a taper in his hand, and an expression of
great solicitude, of infinite pity upon his face, Hilaire was stooping over me. Beside him lay the bottle and the dripping aspergillus.

'I thank God, my son, that I found you in good time,' he said. 'When I returned to the abbey this evening and learned that you were gone, I surmised all
that had happened. I knew you had read the accursed manuscript in my absence,
and had fallen under its baleful spell, as have so many others, even to a certain
reverend abbot, one of my predecessors. All of them, alas! beginning hundreds
of years ago with Gerard de Venteillon, have fallen victims to the lamia who
dwells in these vaults.'

'The lamia?' I questioned, hardly comprehending his words.

'Yes, my son, the beautiful Nycea who lay in your arms this night is a lamia,
an ancient vampire, who maintains in these noisome vaults her palace of beatific
illusions. How she came to take up her abode at Faussesflammes is not known,
for her coming antedates the memory of men. She is old as paganism; the Greeks
knew her; she was exorcised by Apollonius of Tyana; and if you could behold her
as she really is, you would see, in lieu of her voluptuous body, the folds of a foul
and monstrous serpent. All those whom she loves and admits to her hospitality,
she devours in the end, after she has drained them of life and vigor with the diabolic delight of her kisses. The laurel-wooded plain you saw, the ilex-bordered
river, the marble palace and all the luxury therein, were no more than a satanic
delusion, a lovely bubble that rose from the dust and mold of immemorial death,
of ancient corruption. They crumbled at the kiss of the holy water I brought
with me when I followed you. But Nycea, alas! has escaped, and I fear she will

still survive, to build again her palace of demoniacal enchantments, to commit again and again the unspeakable abomination of her sins.'

Still in a sort of stupor at the ruin of my new-found happiness, at the singular revelations made by the abbot, I followed him obediently as he led the way through the vaults of Faussesflammes. He mounted the stairway by which I had descended, and as he neared the top and was forced to stoop a little, the great flagstone swung upward, letting in a stream of chill moonlight. We emerged, and I permitted him to take me back to the monastery.

As my brain began to clear, and the confusion into which I had been thrown resolved itself, a feeling of resentment grew apace—a keen anger at the interference of Hilaire. Unheedful whether or not he had rescued me from dire physical and spiritual perils, I lamented the beautiful dream of which he had deprived me. The kisses of Nycea burned softly in my memory, and I knew that whatever she was, woman or demon or serpent, there was no one in all the world who could ever arouse in me the same love and the same delight. I took care, however, to conceal my feelings from Hilaire, realizing that a betrayal of such emotions would merely lead him to look upon me as a soul that was lost beyond redemption.

On the morrow, pleading the urgency of my return home, I departed from Perigon. Now, in the library of my father's house near Moulins, I write this account of my adventures. The memory of Nycea is magically clear, ineffably dear as if she were still beside me, and still I see the rich draperies of a midnight chamber illumined by lamps of curiously carven gold, and still I hear the words of her farewell:

'Have no fear. You shall find me again if you are brave and patient.'

Soon I shall return, to visit again the ruins of the Chateau de Faussesflammes, and redescend into the vaults below the triangular flagstone. But, in spite of the nearness of Perigon to Faussesflammes, in spite of my esteem for the abbot, my gratitude for his hospitality and my admiration for his incomparable library, I shall not care to revisit my friend Hilaire.

THE MAN WHO LOVED THE VAMPIRE LADY

BRIAN STABLEFORD

*A man who loves a vampire lady may not die
young, but cannot live forever.*

—WALACHIAN PROVERB

I T WAS THE THIRTEENTH OF JUNE IN THE YEAR OF OUR
Lord 1623. Grand Normandy was in the grip of an early spell of warm weather,
and the streets of London bathed in sunlight. There were crowds everywhere,
and the port was busy with ships, three having docked that very day. One of the
ships, the *Freemartin*, was from the Moorish enclave and had produce from the
heart of Africa, including ivory and the skins of exotic animals. There were rumors, too, of secret and more precious goods: jewels and magical charms; but
such rumors always attended the docking of any vessel from remote parts of the
world. Beggars and street urchins had flocked to the dockland, responsive as ever
to such whisperings, and were plaguing every sailor in the streets, as anxious for
gossip as for copper coins. It seemed that the only faces not animated by excitement were those worn by the severed heads that dressed the spikes atop the
Southwark Gate. The Tower of London, though, stood quite aloof from the
hubbub, its tall and forbidding turrets so remote from the streets that they belonged to a different world.

Edmund Cordery, mechanician to the court of the Archduke Girard, tilted
the small concave mirror on the brass device that rested on his workbench, catching the rays of the afternoon sun and deflecting the light through the system of
lenses.

He turned away and directed his son, Noell, to take his place. "Tell me if all
is well," he said tiredly. "I can hardly focus my eyes, let alone the instrument."

Noell closed his left eye and put his other to the microscope. He turned the wheel that adjusted the height of the stage. "It's perfect," he said. "What is it?"

"The wing of a moth." Edmund scanned the polished tabletop, checking that the other slides were in readiness for the demonstration. The prospect of Lady Carmilla's visit filled him with a complex anxiety that he resented in himself. Even in the old days, she had not come to his laboratory often, but to see her here—on his own territory, as it were—would be bound to awaken memories that were untouched by the glimpses that he caught of her in the public parts of the Tower and on ceremonial occasions.

"The water slide isn't ready," Noell pointed out.

Edmund shook his head. "I'll make a fresh one when the time comes," he said. "Living things are fragile, and the world that is in a water drop is all too easily destroyed."

He looked farther along the bench-top, and moved a crucible, placing it out of sight behind a row of jars. It was impossible—and unnecessary—to make the place tidy, but he felt it important to conserve some sense of order and control. To discourage himself from fidgeting, he went to the window and looked out at the sparkling Thames and the strange gray sheen on the slate roofs of the houses beyond. From this high vantage point, the people were tiny; he was higher even than the cross on the steeple of the church beside the Leathermarket. Edmund was not a devout man, but such was the agitation within him, yearning for expression in action, that the sight of the cross on the church made him cross himself, murmuring the ritual devotion. As soon as he had done it, he cursed himself for childishness.

I am forty-four years old, he thought, *and a mechanician. I am no longer the boy who was favored with the love of the lady, and there is no need for this stupid trepidation.*

He was being deliberately unfair to himself in this private scolding. It was not simply the fact that he had once been Carmilla's lover that made him anxious. There was the microscope, and the ship from the Moorish country. He hoped that he would be able to judge by the lady's reaction how much cause there really was for fear.

The door opened then, and the lady entered. She half turned to indicate by a flutter of her hand that her attendant need not come in with her, and he withdrew, closing the door behind him. She was alone, with no friend or favorite in tow. She came across the room carefully, lifting the hem of her skirt a little, though the floor was not dusty. Her gaze flicked from side to side, to take note of the shelves, the beakers, the furnace, and the numerous tools of the mechanician's craft. To a commoner, it would have seemed a threatening environment, redolent with unholiness, but her attitude was cool and controlled. She arrived to stand before the brass instrument that Edmund had recently completed, but did not look long at it before raising her eyes to look fully into Edmund's face.

"You look well, Master Cordery," she said calmly. "But you are pale. You should not shut yourself in your rooms now that summer is come to Normandy."

Edmund bowed slightly, but met her gaze. She had not changed in the slightest degree, of course, since the days when he had been intimate with her. She was six hundred years old—hardly younger than the archduke—and the years were impotent as far as her appearance was concerned. Her complexion was much darker than his, her eyes a deep liquid brown, and her hair jet black. He had not stood so close to her for several years, and he could not help the tide of memories rising in his mind. For her, it would be different: his hair was gray now, his skin creased; he must seem an altogether different person. As he met her gaze, though, it seemed to him that she, too, was remembering, and not without fondness.

"My lady," he said, his voice quite steady, "may I present my son and apprentice, Noell."

Noell bowed more deeply than his father, blushing with embarrassment.

The Lady Carmilla favored the youth with a smile. "He has the look of you, Master Cordery," she said—a casual compliment. She returned her attention then to the instrument.

"The designer was correct?" she asked.

"Yes, indeed," he replied. "The device is most ingenious. I would dearly like to meet the man who thought of it. A fine discovery—though it taxed the talents of my lens grinder severely. I think we might make a better one, with much care and skill; this is but a poor example, as one must expect from a first attempt."

The Lady Carmilla seated herself at the bench, and Edmund showed her how to apply her eye to the instrument, and how to adjust the focusing wheel and the mirror. She expressed surprise at the appearance of the magnified moth's wing, and Edmund took her through the series of prepared slides, which included other parts of insects' bodies, and sections through the stems and seeds of plants.

"I need a sharper knife and a steadier hand, my lady," he told her. "The device exposes the clumsiness of my cutting."

"Oh no, Master Cordery," she assured him politely. "These are quite pretty enough. But we were told that more interesting things might be seen. Living things too small for ordinary sight."

Edmund bowed in apology and explained about the preparation of water slides. He made a new one, using a pipette to take a drop from a jar full of dirty river water. Patiently, he helped the lady search the slide for the tiny creatures that human eyes were not equipped to perceive. He showed her one that flowed as if it were semiliquid itself, and tinier ones that moved by means of cilia. She was quite captivated, and watched for some time, moving the slide very gently with her painted fingernails.

Eventually she asked: "Have you looked at other fluids?"

"What kind of fluids?" he asked, though the question was quite clear to him and disturbed him.

She was not prepared to mince words with him. "Blood, Master Cordery," she said very softly. Her past acquaintance with him had taught her respect for his intelligence, and she half regretted it.

"Blood clots very quickly," he told her. "I could not produce a satisfactory slide. It would take unusual skill."

"I'm sure that it would," she replied.

"Noell has made drawings of many of the things we *have* looked at," said Edmund. "Would you like to see them?"

She accepted the change of subject, and indicated that she would. She moved to Noell's station and began sorting through the drawings, occasionally looking up at the boy to compliment him on his work. Edmund stood by, remembering how sensitive he once had been to her moods and desires, trying hard to work out now exactly what she was thinking. Something in one of her contemplative glances at Noell sent an icy pang of dread into Edmund's gut, and he found his more important fears momentarily displaced by what might have been anxiety for his son, or simply jealousy. He cursed himself again for his weakness.

"May I take these to show the archduke?" asked the Lady Carmilla, addressing the question to Noell rather than to his father. The boy nodded, still too embarrassed to construct a proper reply. She took a selection of the drawings and rolled them into a scroll. She stood and faced Edmund again.

"We are most interested in this apparatus," she informed him. "We must consider carefully whether to provide you with new assistants, to encourage development of the appropriate skills. In the meantime, you may return to your ordinary work. I will send someone for the instrument, so that the archduke can inspect it at his leisure. Your son draws very well, and must be encouraged. You and he may visit me in my chambers on Monday next; we will dine at seven o'clock, and you may tell me about all your recent work."

Edmund bowed to signal his acquiescence—it was, of course, a command rather than an invitation. He moved before her to the door in order to hold it open for her. The two exchanged another brief glance as she went past him.

When she had gone, it was as though something taut unwound inside him, leaving him relaxed and emptied. He felt strangely cool and distant as he considered the possibility—stronger now—that his life was in peril.

When the twilight had faded, Edmund lit a single candle on the bench and sat staring into the flame while he drank dark wine from a flask. He did not look up when Noell came into the room, but when the boy brought another stool close to his and sat down upon it, he offered the flask. Noell took it, but sipped rather gingerly.

"I'm old enough to drink now?" he commented dryly.

"You're old enough," Edmund assured him. "But beware of excess, and never drink alone. Conventional fatherly advice, I believe."

Noell reached across the bench so that he could stroke the barrel of the microscope with slender fingers.

"What are you afraid of?" he asked.

Edmund sighed. "You're old enough for that, too, I suppose?"

"I think you ought to tell me."

Edmund looked at the brass instrument and said: "It were better to keep things like this dark secret. Some human mechanician, I daresay, eager to please the vampire lords and ladies, showed off his cleverness as proud as a peacock. Thoughtless. Inevitable, though, now that all this play with lenses has become fashionable."

"You'll be glad of eyeglasses when your sight begins to fail," Noell told him. "In any case, I can't see the danger in this new toy."

Edmund smiled. "New toys," he mused. "Clocks to tell the time, mills to grind the corn, lenses to aid human sight. Produced by human craftsmen for the delight of their masters. I think we've finally succeeded in proving to the vampires just how very clever we are—and how much more there is to know than we know already."

"You think the vampires are beginning to fear us?"

Edmund gulped wine from the flask and passed it again to his son. "Their rule is founded in fear and superstition," he said quietly. "They're long-lived, suffer only mild attacks of diseases that are fatal to us, and have marvelous powers of regeneration. But they're not immortal, and they're vastly outnumbered by humans. Terror keeps them safe, but terror is based in ignorance, and behind their haughtiness and arrogance, there's a gnawing fear of what might happen if humans ever lost their supernatural reverence for vampirekind. It's very difficult for them to die, but they don't fear death any the less for that."

"There've been rebellions against vampire rule. They've always failed."

Edmund nodded to concede the point. "There are three million people in Grand Normandy," he said, "and less than five thousand vampires. There are only forty thousand vampires in the entire imperium of Gaul, and about the same number in the imperium of Byzantium—no telling how many there may be in the khanate of Walachia and Cathay, but not so very many more. In Africa the vampires must be outnumbered three or four thousand to one. If people no longer saw them as demons and demi-gods, as unconquerable forces of evil, their empire would be fragile. The centuries through which they live give them wisdom, but longevity seems to be inimical to creative thought—they learn, but they don't *invent*. Humans remain the true masters of art and science, which are forces of change. They've tried to control that—to turn it to their advantage—but it remains a thorn in their side."

"But they do have power," insisted Noell. "They *are* vampires."

Edmund shrugged. "Their longevity is real—their powers of regeneration, too. But is it really their magic that makes them so? I don't know for sure what merit there is in their incantations and rituals, and I don't think even *they* know— they cling to their rites because they dare not abandon them, but where the power that makes humans into vampires really comes from, no one knows. From the devil? I think not. I don't believe in the devil—I think it's something in the blood. I think vampirism may be a kind of disease—but a disease that makes men stronger instead of weaker, insulates them against death instead of killing them. If that *is* the case—do you see now why the Lady Carmilla asked whether I had looked at blood beneath the microscope?"

Noell stared at the instrument for twenty seconds or so, mulling over the idea. Then he laughed.

"If we could *all* become vampires," he said lightly, "we'd have to suck one another's blood."

Edmund couldn't bring himself to look for such ironies. For him, the possibilities inherent in discovering the secrets of vampire nature were much more immediate, and utterly bleak.

"It's not true that they *need* to suck the blood of humans," he told the boy. "It's not nourishment. It gives them . . . a kind of pleasure that we can't understand. And it's part of the mystique that makes them so terrible . . . and hence so powerful." He stopped, feeling embarrassed. He did not know how much Noell knew about his sources of information. He and his wife never talked about the days of his affair with the Lady Carmilla, but there was no way to keep gossip and rumor from reaching the boy's ears.

Noell took the flask again, and this time took a deeper draft from it. "I've heard," he said distantly, "that humans find pleasure, too . . . in their blood being drunk."

"No," replied Edmund calmly. "That's untrue. Unless one counts the small pleasure of sacrifice. The pleasure that a human man takes from a vampire lady is the same pleasure that he takes from a human lover. It might be different for the girls who entertain vampire men, but I suspect it's just the excitement of hoping that they may become vampires themselves."

Noell hesitated, and would probably have dropped the subject, but Edmund realized suddenly that he did not want the subject dropped. The boy had a right to know, and perhaps might one day *need* to know.

"That's not entirely true," Edmund corrected himself. "When the Lady Carmilla used to taste my blood, it did give me pleasure, in a way. It pleased me because it pleased *her*. There *is* an excitement in loving a vampire lady, which makes it different from loving an ordinary woman . . . even though the chance that a vampire lady's lover may himself become a vampire is so remote as to be inconsiderable."

Noell blushed, not knowing how to react to this acceptance into his father's confidence. Finally he decided that it was best to pretend a purely academic interest.

"Why are there so many more vampire women than men?" he asked.

"No one knows for sure," Edmund said. "No humans, at any rate. I can tell you what I believe, from hearsay and from reasoning, but you must understand that it is a dangerous thing to think about, let alone to speak about."

Noell nodded.

"The vampires keep their history secret," said Edmund, "and they try to control the writing of human history, but the following facts are probably true. Vampirism came to western Europe in the fifth century, with the vampire-led horde of Attila. Attila must have known well enough how to make more vampires—he converted both Aëtius, who became ruler of the imperium of Gaul, and Theodosius II, the emperor of the east who was later murdered. Of all the vampires that now exist, the vast majority must be converts. I have heard reports of vampire children born to vampire ladies, but it must be an extremely rare occurrence. Vampire men seem to be much less virile than human men—it is said that they couple very rarely. Nevertheless, they frequently take human consorts, and these consorts often become vampires. Vampires usually claim that this is a gift, bestowed deliberately by magic, but I am not so sure they can control the process. I think the semen of vampire men carries some kind of seed that communicates vampirism much as the semen of humans makes women pregnant—and just as haphazardly. That's why the male lovers of vampire ladies don't become vampires."

Noell considered this, and then asked: "Then where do vampire lords come from?"

"They're converted by other male vampires," Edmund said. "Just as Attila converted Aëtius and Theodosius." He did not elaborate, but waited to see whether Noell understood the implication. An expression of disgust crossed the boy's face and Edmund did not know whether to be glad or sorry that his son could follow the argument through.

"Because it doesn't always happen," Edmund went on, "it's easy for the vampires to pretend that they have some special magic. But some women never become pregnant, though they lie with their husbands for years. It is said, though, that a human may also become a vampire by drinking vampire's blood—if he knows the appropriate magic spell. That's a rumor the vampires don't like, and they exact terrible penalties if anyone is caught trying the experiment. The ladies of our own court, of course, are for the most part onetime lovers of the archduke or his cousins. It would be indelicate to speculate about the conversion of the archduke, though he is certainly acquainted with Aëtius."

Noell reached out a hand, palm downward, and made a few passes above the candle flame, making it flicker from side to side. He stared at the microscope.

"*Have* you looked at blood?" he asked.

"I have," replied Edmund. "And semen. Human blood, of course—and human semen."

"And?"

Edmund shook his head. "They're certainly not homogeneous fluids," he said, "but the instrument isn't good enough for really detailed inspection. There are small corpuscles—the ones in semen have long, writhing tails—but there's more . . . much more . . . to be seen, if I had the chance. By tomorrow this instrument will be gone—I don't think I'll be given the chance to build another."

"You're surely not in danger! You're an important man—and your loyalty has never been in question. People think of you as being almost a vampire yourself. A black magician. The kitchen girls are afraid of me because I'm your son—they cross themselves when they see me."

Edmund laughed, a little bitterly. "I've no doubt they suspect me of intercourse with demons, and avoid my gaze for fear of the spell of the evil eye. But none of that matters to the vampires. To them, I'm only a human, and for all that they value my skills, they'd kill me without a thought if they suspected that I might have dangerous knowledge."

Noell was clearly alarmed by this. "Wouldn't. . . ." He stopped, but saw Edmund waiting for him to ask, and carried on after only a brief pause. "The Lady Carmilla . . . wouldn't she . . . ?"

"Protect me?" Edmund shook his head. "Not even if I were her favorite still. Vampire loyalty is to vampires."

"She was human once."

"It counts for nothing. She's been a vampire for nearly six hundred years, but it wouldn't be any different if she were no older than I."

"But . . . she did love you?"

"In her way," said Edmund sadly. "In her way." He stood up then, no longer feeling the urgent desire to help his son to understand. There were things the boy could find out only for himself and might never have to. He took up the candle tray and shielded the flame with his hand as he walked to the door. Noell followed him, leaving the empty flask behind.

Edmund left the citadel by the so-called Traitor's Gate, and crossed the Thames by the Tower Bridge. The houses on the bridge were in darkness now, but there was still a trickle of traffic; even at two in the morning, the business of the great city did not come to a standstill. The night had clouded over, and a light drizzle had begun to fall. Some of the oil lamps that were supposed to keep the thoroughfare lit at all times had gone out, and there was not a lamplighter in sight. Edmund did not mind the shadows, though.

He was aware before he reached the south bank that two men were dogging his footsteps, and he dawdled in order to give them the impression that he would be easy to track. Once he entered the network of streets surrounding the Leathermarket, though, he gave them the slip. He knew the maze of filthy streets well enough—he had lived here as a child. It was while he was apprenticed to a local clockmaker that he had learned the cleverness with tools that had eventually brought him to the notice of his predecessor, and had sent him on the road to fortune and celebrity. He had a brother and a sister still living and working in the district, though he saw them very rarely. Neither one of them was proud to have a reputed magician for a brother, and they had not forgiven him his association with the Lady Carmilla.

He picked his way carefully through the garbage in the dark alleys, unperturbed by the sound of scavenging rats. He kept his hands on the pommel of the dagger that was clasped to his belt, but he had no need to draw it. Because the stars were hidden, the night was pitch-dark, and few of the windows were lit from within by candlelight, but he was able to keep track of his progress by reaching out to touch familiar walls every now and again.

He came eventually to a tiny door set three steps down from a side street, and rapped upon it quickly, three times and then twice. There was a long pause before he felt the door yield beneath his fingers, and he stepped inside hurriedly. Until he relaxed when the door clicked shut again, he did not realize how tense he had been.

He waited for a candle to be lit.

The light, when it came, illuminated a thin face, crabbed and wrinkled, the eyes very pale and the wispy white hair gathered imperfectly behind a linen bonnet.

"The lord be with you," he whispered.

"And with you, Edmund Cordery," she croaked.

He frowned at the use of his name—it was a deliberate breach of etiquette, a feeble and meaningless gesture of independence. She did not like him, though he had never been less than kind to her. She did not fear him as so many others did, but she considered him tainted. They had been bound together in the business of the Fraternity for nearly twenty years, but she would never completely trust him.

She led him into an inner room, and left him there to take care of his business.

A stranger stepped from the shadows. He was short, stout, and bald, perhaps sixty years old. He made the special sign of the cross, and Edmund responded.

"I'm Cordery," he said.

"Were you followed?" The older man's tone was deferential and fearful.

"Not here. They followed me from the Tower, but it was easy to shake them loose."

"That's bad."

"Perhaps—but it has to do with another matter, not with our business. There's no danger to you. Do you have what I asked for?"

The stout man nodded uncertainly. "My masters are unhappy," he said. "I have been asked to tell you that they do not want you to take risks. You are too valuable to place yourself in peril."

"I am in peril already. Events are overtaking us. In any case, it is neither your concern nor that of your . . . masters. It is for me to decide."

The stout man shook his head, but it was a gesture of resignation rather than a denial. He pulled something from beneath the chair where he had waited in the shadows. It was a large box, clad in leather. A row of small holes was set in the longer side, and there was a sound of scratching from within that testified to the presence of living creatures.

"You did exactly as I instructed?" asked Edmund.

The small man nodded, then put his hand on the mechanician's arm, fearfully. "Don't open it, sir, I beg you. Not here."

"There's nothing to fear," Edmund assured him.

"You haven't been in Africa, sir, as I have. Believe me, *everyone* is afraid—and not merely humans. They say that vampires are dying, too."

"Yes, I know," said Edmund distractedly. He shook off the older man's restraining hand and undid the straps that sealed the box. He lifted the lid, but not far—just enough to let the light in, and to let him see what was inside.

The box contained two big gray rats. They cowered from the light.

Edmund shut the lid again and fastened the straps.

"It's not my place, sir," said the little man hesitantly, "but I'm not sure that you really understand what you have there. I've seen the cities of West Africa— I've been in Corunna, too, and Marseilles. They remember other plagues in those cities, and all the horror stories are emerging again to haunt them. Sir, if any such thing ever came to London. . . ."

Edmund tested the weight of the box to see whether he could carry it comfortably. "It's not your concern," he said. "Forget everything that has happened. I will communicate with your masters. It is in my hands now."

"Forgive me," said the other, "but I must say this: there is naught to be gained from destroying vampires, if we destroy ourselves, too. It would be a pity to wipe out half of Europe in the cause of attacking our oppressors."

Edmund stared at the stout man coldly. "You talk too much," he said. "Indeed, you talk a *deal* too much."

"I beg your pardon, sire."

Edmund hesitated for a moment, wondering whether to reassure the messenger that his anxiety was understandable, but he had learned long ago that where the business of the Fraternity was concerned, it was best to say as little as possible. There was no way of knowing when this man would speak again of this affair, or to whom, or with what consequence.

The mechanician took up the box, making sure that he could carry it comfortably. The rats stirred inside, scrabbling with their small clawed feet. With his free hand, Edmund made the sign of the cross again.

"God go with you," said the messenger, with urgent sincerity.

"And with thy spirit," replied Edmund colorlessly.

Then he left, without pausing to exchange a ritual farewell with the crone. He had no difficulty in smuggling his burden back into the Tower, by means of a gate where the guard was long practiced in the art of turning a blind eye.

When Monday came, Edmund and Noell made their way to the Lady Carmilla's chambers. Noell had never been in such an apartment before, and it was a source of wonder to him. Edmund watched the boy's reactions to the carpets, the wall hangings, the mirrors and ornaments, and could not help but recall the first time *he* had entered these chambers. Nothing had changed here, and the rooms were full of provocations to stir and sharpen his faded memories.

Younger vampires tended to change their surroundings often, addicted to novelty, as if they feared the prospect of being changeless themselves. The Lady Carmilla had long since passed beyond this phase of her career. She had grown used to changelessness, had transcended the kind of attitude to the world that permitted boredom and ennui. She had adapted herself to a new aesthetic of existence, whereby her personal space became an extension of her own eternal sameness, and innovation was confined to tightly controlled areas of her life— including the irregular shifting of her erotic affections from one lover to another.

The sumptuousness of the lady's table was a further source of astonishment to Noell. Silver plates and forks he had imagined, and crystal goblets, and carved decanters of wine. But the lavishness of provision for just three diners—the casual waste—was something that obviously set him aback. He had always known that he was himself a member of a privileged elite, and that by the standards of the greater world, Master Cordery and his family ate well; the revelation that there was a further order of magnitude to distinguish the private world of the real aristocracy clearly made its impact upon him.

Edmund had been very careful in preparing his dress, fetching from his closet finery that he had not put on for many years. On official occasions he was always concerned to play the part of mechanician, and dressed in order to sustain that appearance. He never appeared as a courtier, always as a functionary. Now, though, he was reverting to a kind of performance that Noell had never seen him play, and though the boy had no idea of the subtleties of his father's performance, he clearly understood something of what was going on; he had complained acidly about the dull and plain way in which his father had made *him* dress.

Edmund ate and drank sparingly, and was pleased to note that Noell did likewise, obeying his father's instructions despite the obvious temptations of the lavish provision. For a while the lady was content to exchange routine courtesies, but she came quickly enough—by her standards—to the real business of the evening.

"My cousin Girard," she told Edmund, "is quite enraptured by your clever device. He finds it most interesting."

"Then I am pleased to make him a gift of it," Edmund replied. "And I would be pleased to make another, as a gift for Your Ladyship."

"That is not our desire," she said coolly. "In fact, we have other matters in mind. The archduke and his seneschal have discussed certain tasks that you might profitably carry out. Instructions will be communicated to you in due time, I have no doubt."

"Thank you, my lady," said Edmund.

"The ladies of the court were pleased with the drawings that I showed to them," said the Lady Carmilla, turning to look at Noell. "They marveled at the thought that a cupful of Thames water might contain thousands of tiny living creatures. Do you think that our bodies, too, might be the habitation of countless invisible insects?"

Noell opened his mouth to reply, because the question was addressed to him, but Edmund interrupted smoothly.

"There are creatures that may live upon our bodies," he said, "and worms that may live within. We are told that the macrocosm reproduces in essence the microcosm of human beings; perhaps there is a small microcosm within us, where our natures are reproduced again, incalculably small. I have read. . . ."

"I have read, Master Cordery," she cut in, "that the illnesses that afflict humankind might be carried from person to person by means of these tiny creatures."

"The idea that diseases were communicated from one person to another by tiny seeds was produced in antiquity," Edmund replied, "but I do not know how such seeds might be recognized, and I think it very unlikely that the creatures we have seen in river water could possibly be of that character."

"It is a disquieting thought," she insisted, "that our bodies might be inhabited by creatures of which we can know nothing, and that every breath we take might be carrying into us seeds of all kinds of change, too small to be seen or tasted. It makes me feel uneasy."

"But there is no need," Edmund protested. "Seeds of corruptibility take root in human flesh, but yours is inviolate."

"You know that is not so, Master Cordery," she said levelly. "You have seen me ill yourself."

"That was a pox that killed many humans, my lady—yet it gave to you no more than a mild fever."

"We have reports from the imperium of Byzantium, and from the Moorish enclave, too, that there is plague in Africa, and that it has now reached the southern regions of the imperium of Gaul. It is said that this plague makes little distinction between human and vampire."

"Rumors, my lady," said Edmund soothingly. "You know how news becomes blacker as it travels."

The Lady Carmilla turned again to Noell, and this time addressed him by name so that there could be no opportunity for Edmund to usurp the privilege of answering her. "Are you afraid of me, Noell?" she asked.

The boy was startled, and stumbled slightly over his reply, which was in the negative.

"You must not lie to me," she told him. "You *are* afraid of me, because I am a vampire. Master Cordery is a skeptic, and must have told you that vampires have less magic than is commonly credited to us, but he must also have told you that I can do you harm if I will. Would you like to be a vampire yourself, Noell?"

Noell was still confused by the correction, and hesitated over his reply, but he eventually said: "Yes, I would."

"Of course you would," she purred. "All humans would be vampires if they could, no matter how they might pretend when they bend the knee in church. And men *can* become vampires; immortality is within our gift. Because of this, we have always enjoyed the loyalty and devotion of the greater number of our human subjects. We have always rewarded that devotion in some measure. Few have joined our ranks, but the many have enjoyed centuries of order and stability. The vampires rescued Europe from a Dark Age, and as long as vampires rule, barbarism will always be held in check. Our rule has not always been kind, because we cannot tolerate defiance, but the alternative would have been far worse. Even so, there are men who would destroy us—did you know that?"

Noell did not know how to reply to this, so he simply stared, waiting for her to continue. She seemed a little impatient with his gracelessness, and Edmund deliberately let the awkward pause go on. He saw a certain advantage in allowing Noell to make a poor impression.

"There is an organization of rebels," the Lady Carmilla went on. "A secret society, ambitious to discover the secret way by which vampires are made. They put about the idea that they would make all men immortal, but this is a lie, and foolish. The members of this brotherhood seek power for themselves."

The vampire lady paused to direct the clearing of one set of dishes and the bringing of another. She asked for a new wine, too. Her gaze wandered back and forth between the gauche youth and his self-assured father.

"The loyalty of your family is, of course, beyond question," she eventually continued. "No one understands the workings of society like a mechanician, who knows well enough how forces must be balanced and how the different parts of a machine must interlock and support one another. Master Cordery knows well how the cleverness of rulers resembles the cleverness of clockmakers, do you not?"

"Indeed, I do, my lady," replied Edmund.

"There might be a way," she said, in a strangely distant tone, "that a good mechanician might earn a conversion to vampirism."

Edmund was wise enough not to interpret this as an offer or a promise. He accepted a measure of the new wine and said: "My lady, there are matters that it would be as well for us to discuss in private. May I send my son to his room?"

The Lady Carmilla's eyes narrowed just a little, but there was hardly any expression in her finely etched features. Edmund held his breath, knowing that he had forced a decision upon her that she had not intended to make so soon.

"The poor boy has not quite finished his meal," she said.

"I think he has had enough, my lady," Edmund countered. Noell did not disagree, and, after a brief hesitation, the lady bowed to signal her permission. Edmund asked Noell to leave, and, when he was gone, the Lady Carmilla rose from her seat and went from the dining room into an inner chamber. Edmund followed her.

"You were presumptuous, Master Cordery," she told him.

"I was carried away, my lady. There are too many memories here."

"The boy is mine," she said, "if I so choose. You do know that, do you not?"

Edmund bowed.

"I did not ask you here tonight to make you witness the seduction of your son. Nor do you think that I did. This matter that you would discuss with me—does it concern science or treason?"

"Science, my lady. As you have said yourself, my loyalty is not in question."

Carmilla laid herself upon a sofa and indicated that Edmund should take a chair nearby. This was the antechamber to her bedroom, and the air was sweet with the odor of cosmetics.

"Speak," she bade him.

"I believe that the archduke is afraid of what my little device might reveal," he said. "He fears that it will expose to the eye such seeds as carry vampirism from one person to another, just as it might expose the seeds that carry disease. I think that the man who devised the instrument may have been put to death already, but I think you know well enough that a discovery once made is likely to be made again and again. You are uncertain as to what course of action would best serve your ends, because you cannot tell whence the greater threat to your rule might come. There is the Fraternity, which is dedicated to your destruction; there is plague in Africa, from which even vampires may die; and there is the new sight, which renders visible what previously lurked unseen. Do you want my advice, Lady Carmilla?"

"Do you *have* any advice, Edmund?"

"Yes. Do not try to control by terror and persecution the things that are happening. Let your rule be unkind *now*, as it has been before, and it will open the way to destruction. Should you concede power gently, you might live for centuries yet, but if you strike out . . . your enemies will strike back."

The vampire lady leaned back her head, looking at the ceiling. She contrived a small laugh.

"I cannot take advice such as that to the archduke," she told him flatly.

"I thought not, my lady," Edmund replied very calmly.

"You humans have your own immortality," she complained. "Your faith promises it, and you all affirm it. Your faith tells you that you must not covet the immortality that is ours, and we do no more than agree with you when we guard it so jealously. You should look to your Christ for fortune, not to us. I think you know well enough that we could not convert the world if we wanted to. Our magic is such that it can be used only sparingly. Are you distressed because it has never been offered to you? Are you bitter? Are you becoming our enemy because you cannot become our kin?"

"You have nothing to fear from me, my lady," he lied. Then he added, not quite sure whether it was a lie or not: "I loved you faithfully. I still do."

She sat up straight then, and reached out a hand as though to stroke his cheek, though he was too far away for her to reach.

"That is what I told the archduke," she said, "when he suggested to me that you might be a traitor. I promised him that I could test your loyalty more keenly in my chambers than his officers in theirs. I do not think you could delude me, Edmund. Do you?"

"No my lady," he replied.

"By morning," she told him gently, "I will know whether or not you are a traitor."

"That you will," he assured her. "That you will, my lady."

He woke before her, his mouth dry and his forehead burning. He was not sweating—indeed, he was possessed by a feeling of desiccation, as though the moisture were being squeezed out of his organs. His head was aching, and the light of the morning sun that streamed through the unshuttered window hurt his eyes.

He pulled himself up to a half-sitting position, pushing the coverlet back from his bare chest.

So soon! he thought. He had not expected to be consumed so quickly, but he was surprised to find that his reaction was one of relief rather than fear or regret. He had difficulty collecting his thoughts, and was perversely glad to accept that he did not need to.

He looked down at the cuts that she had made on his breast with her little silver knife; they were raw and red, and made a strange contrast with the faded scars whose crisscross pattern still engraved the story of unforgotten passions. He touched the new wounds gently with his fingers, and winced at the fiery pain.

She woke up then, and saw him inspecting the marks.

"Have you missed the knife?" she asked sleepily. "Were you hungry for its touch?"

There was no need to lie now, and there was a delicious sense of freedom in that knowledge. There was a joy in being able to face her, at last, quite naked in his thoughts as well as his flesh.

"Yes, my lady," he said with a slight croak in his voice. "I had missed the knife. Its touch . . . rekindled flames in my soul."

She had closed her eyes again, to allow herself to wake slowly. She laughed. "It is pleasant, sometimes, to return to forsaken pastures. You can have no notion how a particular *taste* may stir memories. I am glad to have seen you again, in this way. I had grown quite used to you as the gray mechanician. But now. . . ."

He laughed, as lightly as she, but the laugh turned to a cough, and something in the sound alerted her to the fact that all was not as it should be. She opened her eyes and raised her head, turning toward him.

"Why, Edmund," she said, "you're as pale as death!"

She reached out to touch his cheek, and snatched her hand away again as she found it unexpectedly hot and dry. A blush of confusion spread across her own features. He took her hand and held it, looking steadily into her eyes.

"Edmund," she said softly. "What have you done?"

"I can't be sure," he said, "and I will not live to find out, but I have tried to kill you, my lady."

He was pleased by the way her mouth gaped in astonishment. He watched disbelief and anxiety mingle in her expression, as though fighting for control. She did not call out for help.

"This is nonsense," she whispered.

"Perhaps," he admitted. "Perhaps it was also nonsense that we talked last evening. Nonsense about treason. Why did you ask me to make the microscope, my lady, when you knew that making me a party to such a secret was as good as signing my death warrant?"

"Oh Edmund," she said with a sigh. "You could not think that it was my own idea? I tried to protect you, Edmund, from Girard's fears and suspicions. It was because I was your protector that I was made to bear the message. What have you done, Edmund?"

He began to reply, but the words turned into a fit of coughing.

She sat upright, wrenching her hand away from his enfeebled grip, and looked down at him as he sank back down upon the pillow.

"For the love of God!" she exclaimed, as fearfully as any true believer. "It is the plague—the plague out of Africa!"

He tried to confirm her suspicion, but could do so only with a nod of his head as he fought for breath.

"But they held the *Freemartin* by the Essex coast for a full fortnight's quarantine," she protested. "There was no trace of plague aboard."

"The disease kills men," said Edmund in a shallow whisper. "But animals can carry it, in their blood, without dying."

"You cannot know this!"

Edmund managed a small laugh. "My lady," he said, "I am a member of that Fraternity that interests itself in everything that might kill a vampire. The information came to me in good time for me to arrange delivery of the rats—though when I asked for them, I had not in mind the means of using them that I eventually employed. More recent events. . . ." Again he was forced to stop, unable to draw sufficient breath even to sustain the thin whisper.

The Lady Carmilla put her hand to her throat, swallowing as if she expected to feel evidence already of her infection.

"You would destroy me, Edmund?" she asked, as though she genuinely found it difficult to believe.

"I would destroy you all," he told her. "I would bring disaster, turn the world upside down, to end your rule. . . . We cannot allow you to stamp out learning itself to preserve your empire forever. Order must be fought with chaos, and chaos is come, my lady."

When she tried to rise from the bed, he reached out to restrain her, and though there was no power left in him, she allowed herself to be checked. The coverlet fell away from her, to expose her breasts as she sat upright.

"The boy will die for this, Master Cordery," she said. "His mother, too."

"They're gone," he told her. "Noell went from your table to the custody of the society that I serve. By now they're beyond your reach. The archduke will never catch them."

She stared at him, and now he could see the beginnings of hate and fear in her stare.

"You came here last night to bring me poisoned blood," she said. "In the hope that this new disease might kill even me, you condemned yourself to death. What did you do, Edmund?"

He reached out again to touch her arm, and was pleased to see her flinch and draw away: that he had become dreadful.

"Only vampires live forever," he told her hoarsely. "But anyone may drink blood, if they have the stomach for it. I took full measure from my two sick rats . . . and I pray to God that the seed of this fever is raging in my blood . . . and in my semen, too. You, too, have received full measure, my lady . . . and you are in God's hands now like any common mortal. I cannot know for sure whether you will catch the plague, or whether it will kill you, but I—an unbeliever—am not ashamed to pray. Perhaps you could pray, too, my lady, so that we may know how the Lord favors one unbeliever over another."

She looked down at him, her face gradually losing the expressions that had tugged at her features, becoming masklike in its steadiness.

"You could have taken our side, Edmund. I trusted you, and I could have made the archduke trust you, too. You could have become a vampire. We could have shared the centuries, you and I."

This was dissimulation, and they both knew it. He had been her lover, and had ceased to be, and had grown older for so many years that now she remembered him as much in his son as in himself. The promises were all too obviously hollow now, and she realized that she could not even taunt him with them.

From beside the bed she took up the small silver knife that she had used to let his blood. She held it now as if it were a dagger, not a delicate instrument to be used with care and love.

"I thought you still loved me," she told him. "I really did."

That, at least, he thought, might be true.

He actually put his head farther back, to expose his throat to the expected thrust. He wanted her to strike him—angrily, brutally, passionately. He had nothing more to say, and would not confirm or deny that he did still love her.

He admitted to himself now that his motives had been mixed, and that he really did not know whether it was loyalty to the Fraternity that had made him submit to this extraordinary experiment. It did not matter.

She cut his throat, and he watched her for a few long seconds while she stared at the blood gouting from the wound. When he saw her put stained fingers to her lips, knowing what she knew, he realized that after her own fashion, she still loved him.

THE LAST GRAVE
OF LILL WARRAN

MANLY WADE WELLMAN

THE SIDE ROAD BECAME A RUTTED TRACK THROUGH THE pines, and the track became a trail. John Thunstone reflected that he might have known his car would not be able to travel the full distance, and in any case a car seemed out of place in these ancient and uncombed woods. A lumber wagon would be more in keeping; or a riding mule, if John Thunstone were smaller and lighter, a fair load for a mule. He got out of the car, rolled up the windows, and locked the door. Ahead of him a path snaked through the thickets, narrow but well marked by the feet of nobody knew how many years of tramping.

He set his own big feet upon it. His giant body moved with silent grace. John Thunstone was at home in woods, or in wilder places.

He had dressed roughly for this expedition. He had no intention of appearing before the Sandhill woods people as a tailored and foreign invader. So he wore corduroys, a leather jacket that had been cut for him from deer hides of his own shooting, and a shabby felt hat. His strong-boned, trim-mustached face was sober and watchful. It did not betray excitement, or any advance on the wonder he expected to feel when he finished his quest. In his big right hand he carried a walking stick of old dark wood.

"Yep, yep," the courthouse loafers at the town back on the paved road had answered his questions. "Lill Warran—that's her name, Lill, not Lily. Not much lily about her, nothin' so sweet and pure. She was a witch, all right, mister. Sure she was dug out of her grave. Nope, we wasn't there, we just heared about the thing. She was buried, appears like, in Beaver Dam churchyard. And somebody or several somebodies, done dug her up outa there and flung her body clear of the place. Old-time folks believe it's poison bad luck to bury a witch in church ground. You do that and leave her, you might's well forget the church 'cause it won't be blessed no more. Ain't saying we believe that personal; it's country belief."

But the courthouse loafers had not denied the belief in the necessity of digging up a witch. One or two of them contributed tales of Lill Warran. How she was no dry, stooped, gnarled old crone, but a "well-growed" woman, tall and fully and finely made, with a heavy massive wealth of black hair. She wore it knotted into a great loaf at her nape, they said, and that hair shone like fresh-melted tar. Her eyes, they said, were green as green glass, in a brown face, and her mouth—

"Huh!" they'd agreed to Thunstone. "You've come a far piece, and it's like you seen a many fine-looking women. But, mister, ain't no possible argument, you seen Lill Warran and that red mouth she had on her, you'd slap a mortgage on your immortal soul to get a kiss of it."

And the inference was, more than one man had mortgaged his immortal soul for a kiss of Lill Warran's mouth. She was dead now. How? Bullet, some said. Accident, said others. But she was dead, and she'd been buried twice over, and dug up the both times.

Gathering this and other information, John Thunstone was on the trail of the end of the story. For it has been John Thunstone's study and career to follow such stories to their end. His story-searches have brought him into adventures of which only the tenth part has been told, and that tenth part the simplest and most believable. His experiences in most cases he has kept to himself. Those experiences have helped, perhaps, to sprinkle gray in his smooth black hair, to make somber his calm, strong face.

The trail wound, and climbed. Here the wooded land sloped upward. And brush of a spiny species grew under the pines, encroaching so that John Thunstone had to force his way through, like a bull in a swamp. The spines plucked at his leather-clad arms and flanks, like little detaining fingers.

At the top of the slope was the clearing he sought.

It was a clearing in the strictest sense of the word. The tall pines had been axed away, undoubtedly their strong, straight trunks had gone to the building of the log house at the center. And cypress, from some swamp nearby, had been split for the heavy shingles on the roof. All around the house was bare sand. Not a spear of grass, not a tuft of weed, grew there. It was as naked as a beach by the sea. Nobody moved in that naked yard, but from behind the house came a noise. *Plink, plink,* rhythmically. *Plink, plink.* Blows of metal on something solid, like stone or masonry.

Moving silently as an Indian, John Thunstone rounded the corner of the log house, paused to make sure of what was beyond, then moved toward it.

A man knelt there, of a height to match John Thunstone's own, but lean and spare, after the fashion of Sandhills brush dwellers. He wore a shabby checked shirt and blue dungaree pants, worn and frayed and washed out to the blue of a robin's egg. His sleeves were rolled to the biceps, showing gaunt, pallid arms with sharp elbows and knotty hands. His back was toward Thunstone. The crown of his tow head was beginning to be bald. Before him on the ground lay a flat rectangle of liver-colored stone. He held a short-handled, heavy-headed hammer in his right hand, and in his left a narrow-pointed wedge, such as is used to split sections of log into fire wood. The point of the wedge he held set against the face of the stone, and with the hammer he tapped the wedge butt. *Plink, plink.* He moved the point. *Plink.*

Still silent as a drifting cloud, Thunstone edged up behind him. He could see what the gaunt man was chiseling upon the stone. The last letter of a series of words, the letters irregular but deep and square:

HERE LIES

LILL   WARRAN

TWICE BURIED AND TWICE DUG UP

BY FOOLS AND COWARDS

NOW SHE MAY

REST IN PEACE

SHE WAS A ROSE OF SHARON

A LILY OF THE VALLEY

John Thunstone bent to read the final word, and the bright afternoon sun threw his shadow upon the stone. Immediately the lean man was up and his whole body whipped erect and away on the other side of his work, swift and furtive as a weasel. He stood and stared at John Thunstone, the hammer lowered, the lean-pointed wedge lifted a trifle.

"Who you?" the gaunt man wheezed breathily. He had a sharp face, a nose that projected like a pointed beak, with forehead and chin sloping back from it above and below. His eyes were dark, beady, and close-set. His face was yellow and leathery, and even the whites of the eyes looked clouded, as with biliousness.

"My name is John Thunstone," Thunstone made reply, as casually as possible. "I'm looking for Mr. Parrell."

"That's me. Pos Parrell."

Pos . . . It was plain to see where the name suited the man. That lean, pointed snout, the meager chin and brow, the sharp eyes, looked like those of an opossum. A suspicious, angry, dangerous opossum.

"What can I do for you?" demanded Pos Parrell. He sounded as if he would like to do something violent.

"I want to ask about Miss Lill Warran," said Thunstone, still quietly, soothingly, as he might speak to a restive dog or horse. "I see you're making a gravestone for her." He pointed with his stick.

"And why not?" snapped Pos Parrell. His thin lips drew back from lean, strong teeth, like stained fangs. "Ain't she to be allowed to rest peacefully in her grave some time?"

"I hope she will," said Thunstone. "I heard at the county seat about how she'd been dragged out of her grave at the churchyard."

Pos Parrell snorted. His hands tightened on hammer and wedge. "Now, mister, what almighty pick is it of yours? Listen, are you the law? If you are, you just trot your law back to the county seat. I'm not studying to hear any law. They won't let her stay buried at Beaver Dam, I've buried her here, and here she'll stay."

"No," Thunstone assured him. "I'm not the law."

"Then what are you? One of them reporters from the newspapers? Whatever you are, get off my place."

"Not until we've talked a bit, Mr. Parrell."

"I'll put you off. I got a right to put you off my place."

Thunstone smiled his most charming. "You do have the right. But could you put me off?"

Pos Parrell raked him with the beady eyes. "You about twice as big as me, but—"

He dropped the hammer. It struck the sand with a grim thud. He whipped the lean wedge over to his right hand, holding it daggerwise.

"Don't try that," warned Thunstone, and his walking stick lifted in his own hand.

Pos Parrell took a stamping stride forward. His left hand clutched at the tip of Thunstone's stick, the wedge lifted in his right.

But Thunstone drew back on the stick's handle. There was a metallic whisper. The lower part of the stick, clamped in Parrell's grasp, stripped away like the sheath of a sword, revealing a long, straight skewer of gleaming blade that set in the handle as in a heft. As Parrell drove forward with his wedge, Thunstone delicately flicked the point of his sword cane across the back of Parrell's fist. Parrell squeaked with pain, and the wedge fell beside the hammer. Next instant Parrell was backing away hurriedly. Thunstone moved lightly, calmly after him, the sword point quivering inches from Parrell's throat.

"Hey!" protested Parrell. "Hey!"

"I'm sorry, but you'll have to listen to me."

"Put that thing down. I quit!"

Thunstone lowered the point, and smiled.

"Let's both quit. Let's talk."

Parrell subsided. He still held the hollow lower length of the stick. Thunstone took it from him and sheathed his blade.

"You know what?" said Parrell, rather wearily. "That's about the curiousest place I ever seen a man carry a stab weapon."

"It's a sword cane," explained Thunstone, friendly again. "It was made hundreds of years ago. The man who gave it to me said it was made by Saint Dunstan."

"Who was that?"

"He was an Englishman."

"Foreigner, huh?"

"Saint Dunstan was a silversmith," Thunstone told Parrell. "This blade in my stick is made out of silver. Among other things, Saint Dunstan is said to have twisted the devil's nose."

"Lemme see that thing again," Parrell said, and again Thunstone cleared the blade. "Huh!" grunted Parrell. "It got words on it. I can't make 'em out."

Thunstone's big finger tapped the engraved lettering. *"Sic pereant omnes inimici tui, Domine,"* he read aloud. "That means, 'So perish all thine enemies, O God.'"

"Bible words or charm words?"

"Perhaps both," said Thunstone. "Now, Parrell, I want to be your friend. The people in town are pretty rough in their talk about you."

"And about Lill," said Parrell, so faintly that Thunstone could hardly hear. "But I loved her. Lots of men has loved her, but I reckon I was the only one loving her when she died."

"Tell me," urged Thunstone.

Parrell tramped back toward the cabin, and Thunstone followed. Parrell sat on the door sill and scuffed the dirt with his coarse shoes. He studied the back of his right hand, where Thunstone's skilful flick of the silver blade had raised a thin wale and shed a drop of blood.

"You know, you could have hurt me worse if you'd had a mind," he said.

"I didn't have a mind," Thunstone told him.

Again the shoes scuffed the sand. "I prized up my door stoop stone to make that marker for Lill's grave."

"It's a good one."

Parrell gestured to the edge of the clearing. There, in the shade of the pines, showed a mound of sand, dark with fresh digging, the size and shape of a body.

"I buried her there," he said, "and there she'll stay. At the last end, I reckon, she knowed I loved her and nothing could change it."

A rose of Sharon, a lily of the valley. Lill Warran had been no sweet lily, the court house loafers had insisted. Thunstone squatted on his heels.

"You know," he said, "you'll feel better if you talk about it to somebody who will listen."

"Reckon I will."

And Pos Parrell talked.

Later Thunstone wrote down Parrell's story from memory, as a most interesting record of belief in the supernatural, and also belief in a most beautiful and wilful woman.

❮   ❮   ❮

Lill Warran was called a witch because her mother had been one, and her grand-mother had been one. Folks said she could curse pigs thin, and curse hens out of laying, and make trees fall on men cutting them. They wouldn't hear of things like that happening by chance. The preacher at Beaver Dam had sworn she said the Lord's Prayer wrong—"Our Father, who *wert* in heaven." Which meant Sa-tan, who'd fallen from the Pearly Gates, the way it says in the book of Isaiah. No, the preacher hadn't read Lill Warran out of church, but she stopped coming, and laughed at the people who mumbled. The old folks hated her, the children were afraid, and the women suspicious. But the men!

"She could get any man," said Parrell. "She got practically all of them. A hunter would leave his gun, a drinker would leave his bottle of stump-hole whiskey, a farmer would leave his plough standing in the field. There was a many wives crying tears because their husbands were out at night, following after Lill Warran. And Nobe Filder hanged himself, everybody knows, because he was to meet Lill and she didn't come, but went that night to a square dance with New-ton Henley. And Newton grew to hate her, but he took sick and when he was dy-ing he called on her name."

Pos Parrell had just loved her. She never promised to meet him, she tossed him smiles and chance words, like so many table scraps to a dog. Maybe it was as well. Those who were lovers of Lill Warran worshipped her, then feared and hated her.

That, at least, was witch history as Thunstone had read it and researched it. The old books of the old scholars were full of evidence about such seductive en-chantresses, all the way back to the goddesses of dark love—Ishtar, Ashtoreth, Astarte, various names for the same force, terrible in love as the God of War is terrible in battle. To Thunstone's mind came a fragment of the Epic of Gil-gamesh, lettered on a Chaldean tablet of clay five millennia ago. Gilgamesh had taunted Ishtar's overtures:

> *Thou fellest in love with the herdsman*
> *Who ever scattered grain for thee,*
> *And daily slaughtered a kid for thee;*
> *Thou smotest him,*
> *Turned him into a wolf. . . .*

"It didn't prove nothing," Parrell was protesting. "Only that she was easy to fall in love with and hard to keep."

"What did she live on?" asked Thunstone. "Did her family have anything?"

"Shucks, no. She was orphaned. She lived by herself—they've burned the cabin now. People said she knew spells, so she could witch meat out of smokehouses into her pot, witch meal out of pantries onto her table."

"I've heard of people suspecting that of witches," nodded Thunstone, careful to keep his manner sympathetic. "It's an easy story to make yourself believe."

"I never believed it, not even when—"

Parrell told the climax of the sorry, eerie tale. It had happened a week ago. It had to do with a silver bullet.

For silver bullets are sure death to demons, and this was known to a young man by the name of Taylor Howatt, the latest to flutter around the fascinating flame that was Lill Warran. His friends warned him about her, and he wouldn't listen. Not Taylor! Not until there was prowling around his cabin by something that whined and yelped like a beast-varmint—a wolf, the old folks would say, except that wolves hadn't been seen in those parts since the old frontier days. And Taylor Howatt had glimpsed the thing once or twice by moonlight. It was shaggy, it had pointy ears and a pointy muzzle, but it stood up on its two legs, part of the time at least.

"The werewolf story," commented Thunstone, but Parrell continued.

Taylor Howatt knew what to do. He had an old, old deer rifle, the kind made by country gunsmiths as long back as the War with the North. He had the bullet mould, too, and he'd melted down half a silver dollar and cast him a bullet. He'd loaded the deer rifle ready, and listened for several nights to the howls. When the thing came peeking close to an open window, he caught its shape square against the rising moon and fired.

Next day, Lill Warran was found dead on the foot path leading to her own home, and her heart was shot through.

Of course, there'd been a sheriff deputy down. Taylor Howatt was able to claim it was accidental. The people had gathered at Lill's cabin, and there they'd found stuff, they said. One claimed a side of bacon he said had hung in his smokehouse. And another found a book.

"Book?" said John Thunstone quickly. For books are generally interesting properties in stories like the story of Lill Warran.

"I've been told about it by three folks who swore they seen it," replied Parrell. "Me myself, I didn't see it, so I hold I ain't called on to judge of it."

"What did those three people tell you about it?"

"Well—it was hairy like. The cover all hairy and dark, like the skin of a black bear. And inside it had three parts."

"The first part," said Thunstone, "was written with red ink on white paper. The second part, with black ink on red paper. And the third, black paper, written on with—"

"You been talking to them other folks!" accused Parrell, half starting up.

"No. Though I heard the book mentioned at the court house. It's just that I've heard of such books before. The third part of the book, black paper, is written on with white ink that will shine in the dark, so that it can be read without light."

"Then them folks mocking me heard what you heard about the like of the book. They made it up to vex my soul."

"Maybe," agreed Thunstone, though he doubted that the people of the Sandhills brush would have so much knowledge of classical and rare grimoires. "Go on."

The way Parrell had heard the book explained, the first part—red ink on white paper—was made up of rather simple charms, to cure rheumatism or sore eyes, with one or two more interesting spells that concerned the winning of love or the causing of a wearisome lover to depart. The second, the black ink on red, had the charm to bring food from the stores of neighbors, as well as something that purported to make the practitioner invisible, and something else that aided in the construction of a mirror in which one could see faraway scenes and actions.

"And the black part of the book?" asked Thunstone, more calmly than he felt.

"Nobody got that far."

"Good," said Thunstone thankfully. He himself would have thought twice, and more than twice, before reading the shiny letters in the black third section of such a book.

"The preacher took it. Said he locked it in his desk. Next day it was gone. Folks think it went back to Satan himself."

Folks might not be far wrong, thought Thunstone, but did not say as much aloud.

Parrell's voice was wretched as he finished his narrative. Lill Warran had had no kinsmen, none who would claim her body at least. So he, Parrell, had claimed it—bought a coffin and paid for a plot in Beaver Dam churchyard. He and an undertaker's helper had been alone at the burying of Lill Warran.

"Since nobody wanted to be Christian, nothing was said from the Bible at the burying," Parrell told Thunstone. "I did say a little verse of a song I remembered, I always remembered, when I thought of her. This is what it was."

He half-crooned the rhyme:

> *"The raven crow is a coal, coal black,*
> *The jay is a purple blue,*
> *If ever I forget my own fair love,*
> *Let my heart melt away like dew."*

Thunstone wondered how old the song was. "Then?" he prompted.

"You know the rest. The morning after, they tore her up out of the grave and flung her in my yard. I found her lying near to my doorstep, the one I just now cut for her gravestone." Parrell nodded toward where it lay. "I took her and buried her again. And this morning it was the same. There she lay. So let them all go curse. I buried her yonder, and yonder she'll stay, or if anybody says different I'll argue with something more than a law book. Did I do wrong, Mister?"

"Not you," said Thunstone. "You did what your heart told you."

"Thanks. Thank you kindly. Like you said, I do feel better for talking it over." Parrell rose. "I'm going to set up that stone."

Thunstone helped him. The weight of the slab taxed their strength. Parrell drove it into the sand at the head of the grave. Then he looked to where the sun was sinking behind the pines.

"You won't be getting back away from here before it's dark and hard to pick the way. I'll be honored if you stopped here tonight. Not much of a bed or supper doings, but if you'll so be kind—"

"Thank you," said Thunstone, who had been wondering how to manage an overnight stay.

They entered the front room of the little cabin. Inside it was finished in boards, rough sawn but evenly fitted into place. There was an old table, old chairs, a very old cook stove, pans hanging to nails on the walls. Parrell beckoned Thunstone to where a picture was tacked to a wall.

"It's her," he said.

The photograph was cheap, and some slipshod studio artist had touched it up with colors. But Thunstone could see what sort of woman Lill Warran had been. The picture was half length, and she wore a snug dress with large flower figuring. She smiled into the camera, with the wide full mouth of which he had heard. Her eyes were slanting, mocking, and lustrous. Her head was proud on fine shoulders. Round and deep was the bosom into which a silver bullet had been sent by the old deer rifle of Taylor Howatt.

"You see why I loved her," said Parrell.

"I see," Thunstone assured him.

Parrell cooked for them. There was corn bread and syrup, and a plate of rib meat, hearty fare. Despite his sorrow, Parrell ate well of his own cooking. When the meal was finished, Parrell bowed and mumbled an old country blessing. They went out into the yard. Parrell walked slowly to the grave of Lill Warran and gazed down at it. Thunstone moved in among the trees, saw something that grew, and stooped to gouge it out.

"What are you gathering?" called Parrell.

"Just an odd little growth," Thunstone called back, and pulled another. They were the roots called throughout the south by the name of John the Conqueror, great specifics against enchantment. Thunstone filled his pockets with them, and walked back to join Parrell.

"I'm glad you came along, Mr. Thunstone," said Parrell. His opossum face was touched with a shy smile. "I've lived alone for years, but never so lonely as the last week."

Together they entered the house. Parrell found and lighted an oil lamp, and immediately Thunstone felt the impact of eyes from across the room. Swiftly

facing that way, he gazed into the face of the portrait of Lill Warran. The pictured smile seemed to taunt and defy him, and to invite him as well. What had
the man leered at the court house? *You'd slap a mortgage on your immortal soul to get a
kiss.* That picture was enough to convince Thunstone that better men than pitiful, spindling Pos Parrell could find Lill Warran herself irresistible.

"I'll make you up a pallet bed here," offered Parrell.

"You needn't bother for me," Thunstone said, but Parrell opened a battered
old wooden chest and brought out a quilt, another. As he spread them out,
Thunstone recognized the ancient and famous patterns of the quilt work. Ken-
tucky Blazing Star, that was one of them. Another was True Love Fancy.

"My old mamma made them," Parrell informed him.

Parrell folded the quilts into a pallet along the wall. "Sure you'll be all right?
You won't prefer to take my bed."

"I've slept a lot harder than what you're fixing for me," Thunstone quickly assured him.

They sat at a table and talked. Parrell's thoughts were still for his lost love.
He spoke of her, earnestly, revealingly. Once or twice Thunstone suspected him
of trying for poetic speech.

"I would look at her," said Parrell, "and it was like hearing, not seeing."

"Hearing what?"

"Hearing—well, more than anything else it was like the sound of a fiddle,
played prettier than you ever heard. Prettier than I can ever play."

Thunstone had seen the battered fiddle-case on a hand-hewn shelf beside
the door of the rear room which was apparently Parrell's sleeping quarters, but
he had not mentioned it. "Suppose you play us something now," he suggested.

Parrell swallowed. "Play music? With her lying out there in her grave?"

"She wouldn't object, if she knew. Playing the fiddle gives you pleasure,
doesn't it?"

Parrell seemed to need no more bidding. He rose, opened the case, and
brought out the fiddle. It was old and dark, and he tuned it with fingers diffi-
dently skilful. Thunstone looked at him. "Where did you get it? The fiddle, I
mean."

"Oh, my granddaddy inherited it to me. I was the onliest grandboy he had
cared to learn."

"Where did he get it?"

"I don't rightly know how to tell you that. I always heard a foreigner fellow—I mean a sure-enough foreigner from Europe or some place, not just somebody from some other part of the country—gave it to my granddaddy, or either traded it to him."

Thunstone knew something about violins, and judged that this one was worth a sum that would surprise Parrell, if no more than mentioned. Thunstone did not mention any sum. He only said, "Play something, why not?"

Parrell grinned, showing his lean teeth. He tucked the instrument against his jowl and played. He was erratic but vigorous; with training, he might have been brilliant. The music soared, wailed, thundered, and died down. "That was interesting," said Thunstone. "What was it?"

"Just something I sort of figured out for myself," said Parrell apologetically. "I do that once in a while, but not lots. Folks would rather hear the old songs—things they know, like Arkansas Traveller and Fire in the Mountains. I generally play my own stuff to myself, alone here in the evenings." Parrell laid down the instrument. "My fiddle's kept me company, sometimes at night when I wished Lill was with me."

"Did you ever know," said Thunstone, "why we have so many fiddles in the American country localities?"

"Never heard that I recollect."

"In the beginnings of America," Thunstone told him, "frontier homes were lonely and there were wild beasts around. Wolves, mostly."

"Not now," put in Parrell. "Remember that crazy yarn Taylor Howatt told about shooting at a wolf, and there hasn't been a wolf around here since I don't know when."

"Maybe not now, but there were wolves in the old days. And the strains of fiddle music hurt the ears of the wolves and kept them away."

"There may be a lot in what you say," nodded Parrell, and put his instrument back into its box. "Listen, I'm tired. I've not slept fit for a dog these past six nights. But now, with you here, talking sense like you have—" Parrell paused, stretched and yawned. "If it's all right with you, I'll go sleep a while."

"Good night, Parrell," said Thunstone, and watched his host go into the rear room and close the door.

❨   ❨   ❨

Then Thunstone went outside. It was quiet and starry, and the moon rose, half of its disk gleaming pale. He took from his pockets the roots of John the Conqueror, placing one on the sill above the door, another above the front window, and so on around the shanty. Returning, he entered the front room again, turned up the lamp a trifle, and spread out a piece of paper. He produced a pen and began to write:

My Dear de Grandin:

I know your own investigations kept you from coming here with me, but I wonder if this thing isn't more interesting, if not more important, than what you chose to stay and do in New Jersey.

The rumors about Lill Warran, as outlined to you in the letter I wrote this morning, are mostly confirmed. Here, however, are the new items I've uncovered:

Strong evidence of the worst type of grimoire. I refer to one with white, red and black sections. Since it's mentioned in this case, I incline to believe there was one—these country folk could hardly make up such a grimoire out of their heads. Lill Warran, it seems, had a copy, which later vanished from a locked drawer. Naturally! Or, super-naturally!

Presence of a werewolf. One Taylor Howatt was sure enough to make himself a silver bullet, and to use it effectively. He fired at a hairy, point-eared monster, and it was Lill Warran they picked up dead. This item naturally suggests the next.

Nobody knows the person or persons who turned Lill Warran twice out of her grave. Most people of the region are rather smugly pleased at the report that Lill Warran wasn't allowed rest in consecrated churchyard soil, and Pos Parrell, grief-stricken, has buried her in his yard, where he intends that she will have peace. But, de Grandin, you will already have guessed the truth they have failed even to imagine: if Lill Warran was indeed a were-wolf—and the black section of the grimoire undoubtedly told her how to be one at will—if, I say, Lill Warran was a werewolf . . .

Thunstone sat up in the chair, the pen in his fingers. Somebody, or something, moved stealthily in the darkness outside.

There was a tapping whisper at the screen Pos Parrell had nailed over the window. Thunstone grimly forebore to glance. He made himself yawn, a broad hand covering his mouth—the reflex gesture, he meditated as he yawned, born of generations past who feared lest the soul might be snatched through the open mouth by a demon. Slowly he capped his pen, and laid it upon the unfinished letter to de Grandin. He rose, stretched, and tossed aside his leather jacket. He stopped and pretended to untie his shoes, but did not take them off. Finally, cupping his palm around the top of the lamp chimney, he blew out the light. He moved to where Parrell had spread the pallet of quilts and lay down upon them. He began to breathe deeply and regularly. One hand, relaxed in its seeming, rested within an inch of the sword cane.

The climax of the adventure was upon him, he knew very well; but in the moments to follow he must possess himself with calm, must appear to be asleep in a manner to deceive the most skeptical observer.

Thus determined, he resolutely relaxed, from the toe-joints up. He let his big jaw go slack, his big hands curl open. He continued to breathe deeply and regularly, like a sleeper. Hardest of all was the task of conquering the swift race of heart and pulse, but John Thunstone had learned how to do that, too, because of necessity many times before. So completely did he contrive to pretend slumber that his mind went dreamy and vague around the edges. He seemed to float a little free of the pallet, to feel awareness at not too great a distance of the gates of dreamland.

But his ears were tuned to search out sounds. And outside in the dark the unknown creature continued its stealthy round.

It paused—just in front of the door, as John Thunstone judged. It knew that the root of John the Conqueror lay there, an obstacle; but not an obstacle that completely baffled. Such an herb, to turn back what Thunstone felt sure was besieging the dark cabin, would need to be wolfbane or garlic: or, for what grew naturally in these parts of the world, French lilac. John the Conqueror—Big John or Little John, as woodland gatherers defined the two varieties—was only "used to win," and might not assure victory. All it could do, certainly, was slow up the advance of the besieger.

Under his breath, very soft and very low, John Thunstone began to mutter a saying taught him by a white magician in a faraway city, half a prayer and half a spell against evil enemies:

"Two wicked eyes have overshadowed us, but two holy eyes are fixed upon us; the eyes of Saint Dunstan, who smote and shamed the devil. Beware, wicked one; beware twice, wicked one; beware thrice . . ."

In the next room, Thunstone could hear sounds. They were sounds as of dull, careful pecking. They came from the direction in which, as he had seen, was set the closed casement window of Pos Parrell's sleeping chamber.

With the utter silence he knew how to keep, Thunstone rolled from his pallet, lying for a moment face down on the floor. He drew up one knee and both hands, and rose to his full height. In one hand he brought along the sword cane.

The pecking sound persisted as he slid one foot along the rough planks of the floor, praying that no creak would sound. He managed a step, another, a third. He was at the door leading to the next room.

His free hand groped for a knob. There was none, only a latch string. Thunstone pulled, and the door sagged silently open.

He looked into a room, the dimness of which was washed by light from the moon outside. In the window, silhouetted against the four panes, showed the outline of head and shoulders. A tinkling whisper, and one of the panes fell inward, to shatter musically on the boards below. Something had picked away the putty. A dark arm crept in, weaving like a snake, to fumble at the catch. A moment later the window was open, and something thrust itself in, made the passage and landed on the floor.

The moonlight gave him a better look at the shape as it rose from all fours and faced toward the cot where Pos Parrell lay, silent and slack as though he were drugged.

John Thunstone knew that face from the picture in the room where he had slept. It had the slanted, lustrous eyes, the cloud of hair—not clubbed, but hanging in a great thunder cloud on either side of the face. And the wide, full mouth did not smile, but quivered as by some overwhelming pulse.

"Pos," whispered the mouth of Lill Warran.

She wore a white robelike garment, such as is put on dead women in that country. Its wide, winglike sleeves swaddled her arms, but it fell free of the smooth, pale shoulders, the fine upper slope of the bosom. Now as in life, Lill Warran was a forbiddingly beautiful creature. She seemed to sway, to float toward Parrell.

"You love me," she breathed at him.

The sleeper stirred for the first time. He turned toward her, a hand moved sleepily, almost as though it beckoned her. Lill Warran winnowed to the very bedside.

"Stop where you are!" called John Thunstone, and strode into the room, and toward the bed.

She paused, a hand on the blanket that covered Parrell. Her face turned toward Thunstone, the moonlight playing upon it. Her mocking smile possessed her lips.

"You were wise enough to guess most of me," she said. "Are you going to be fool enough to try to stop what is bound to happen?"

"You won't touch him," said Thunstone.

She chuckled. "Don't be afraid to shout. You cannot waken Pos Parrell tonight—not while I stand here. He loves me. He always loved me. The others loved and then hated. But he loves—though he thinks I am dead—"

She sounded archaic, she sounded measured and stilted, as though she quoted ill-rehearsed lines from some old play. That was in order, Thunstone knew.

"He loves you, that's certain," agreed Thunstone. "That means you recognize his helplessness. You think that his love makes him your easy prey. You didn't reckon with me."

"Who are you?"

"My name is John Thunstone."

Lill Warran glared, her lips writhed back. She seemed as though she would spit.

"I've heard that name. John Thunstone! Shall I not dispose of you, right now and at once, you fool?"

She took a step away from the bed. Her hands lifted, the winglike sleeves slipped back from them. She crooked her fingers, talon fashion, and Thunstone saw the length and sharpness of her nails.

Lill Warran laughed.

"Fools have their own reward. Destruction!"

Thunstone stood with feet apart. The cane lay across his body, its handle in his right fist, the fingers of his left hand clasping around the lower shank that made a sheath.

"You have a stick," said Lill Warran. "Do you think you can beat me away, like a dog?"

"I do."

"You cannot even move, John Thunstone!" Her hands weaved in the air, like the hands of a hypnotist. "You're a toy for me! I remember hearing a poem once: 'A fool there was—'" She paused, laughing.

"Remember the title of that poem?" he said, almost sweetly, and she screamed, like the largest and loudest of bats, and leaped.

In that instant, Thunstone cleared the long silver rapier from its hiding, and, as swiftly as she, extended his arm like a fencer in riposte.

Upon the needle-pointed blade, Lill Warran skewered herself. He felt the point slip easily, smoothly, into the flesh of her bosom. It grated on a bone somewhere, then slid past and through. Lill Warran's body slammed to the very hilt, and for a moment she was no more than arm's length from him. Her eyes grew round, her mouth opened wide, but only a whisper of breath came from it.

Then she fell backward, slack as an empty garment, and as Thunstone cleared his blade she thudded on the floor and lay with her arms flung out to right and left, as though crucified.

From his hip pocket Thunstone fished a handkerchief and wiped away the blood that ran from point to base of the silver weapon forged centuries before by Saint Dunstan, patron of those who face and fight creatures of evil.

To his lips came the prayer engraved upon the blade, and he repeated it aloud: "*Sic pereant omnes inimici, tui, Domine. . . .* So perish all thine enemies, O God."

"Huh?" sleepily said Pos Parrell, and sat up on his cot. He strained his eyes in the dimness. "What you say, Mister? What's happened?"

Thunstone moved toward the bureau, sheathing his silver blade. He struck a match, lifted the chimney from the lamp on the bureau, and lighted it. The room filled with the warm glow from the wick.

Parrell sprang out of bed. "Hey, look. The window's open—it's broke in one pane. Who done that?"

"Somebody from outside," said Thunstone, standing still to watch.

Parrell turned and stared at what was on the floor. "It's Lill!" he bawled in a quivering voice. "Sink their rotten souls to hell, they come dug her up again and throwed her in here!"

"I don't think so," said Thunstone, and lifted the lamp. "Take a good look."

Moving, he shed light down upon the quiet form of Lill Warran. Parrell knelt beside her, his trembling hands touching the dark stain on her bosom.

"Blood!" he gulped. "That's fresh blood. Her wound was bleeding, right now. She wasn't dead down there in the grave!"

"No," agreed Thunstone quietly. "She wasn't dead down there in the grave. But she's dead now."

Parrell examined her carefully, miserably. "Yes, sir. She's dead now. She won't rise up no more."

"No more," agreed Thunstone again. "And she got out of her grave by her own strength. Nobody dug her up, dead or alive."

Parrell stared from where he knelt. Wonder and puzzlement touched his grief-lined, sharp-snouted face.

"Come out and see," invited Thunstone, and lifted the lamp from where it stood on the bureau. He walked through the front room and out of the door. Parrell tramped at his heels.

The night was quiet, with so little breeze that the flame of the lamp barely flickered. Straight to the graveside Thunstone led Parrell, stopped there and held the lamp high over the freshly opened hole.

"Look, Parrell," Thunstone bade him. "That grave was opened from inside, not outside."

Parrell stooped and stared. One hand crept up and wiped the low, slanting brow.

"You're right, I guess," said Parrell slowly. "It looks like what a fox does when he breaks through at the end of his digging—the dirt's flung outward from below, only bigger'n a fox's hole." Parrell straightened up. His face was like sick tallow in the light of the lamp. "Then it's true, though it looks right pure down impossible. She was in there, alive, and she got out tonight."

"She got out the other two nights," said Thunstone. "I don't think I can explain to you exactly why, but night time was the time of her strength. And each time she came here to you—walked or crept all the way. Each time, again, she could move no more when it was dawn."

"Lill came to me!"

"You loved her, didn't you? That's why she came to you."

Parrell turned toward the house. "And she must have loved me," he whispered, "to come to me out of the grave. Tonight she didn't have so far to go. If she'd stayed alive—"

Thunstone started back to the house. "Don't think about that, Parrell. She's certainly dead now, and what she would have done if she'd stayed alive isn't for us to think about."

Parrell made no reply until they had once more entered the front door and walked through to where Lill Warran lay as they had left her. In the light of the lamp Thunstone carried her face was clearly defined.

It was a calm face, a face at peace and a little sorrowful. Yes, a sweet face. Lill Warran may not have looked like that in life, or in life-in-death, but now she was completely dead, she was of a gentle, sleeping beauty. Thunstone could see how Parrell, or any other man, might love a face like that.

"And she came to me, she loved me," breathed Parrell again.

"Yes, she loved you," nodded Thunstone. "In her own way she did love you. Let's take her back to her grave."

Between them they carried her out and to the hole. At its bottom was the simple coffin of pine planks, its lid thrown outward and upward from its burst fastenings. Thunstone and Parrell put the body into the coffin, straightened its slack limbs, and lowered the lid. Parrell brought a spade and a shovel, and they filled and smoothed the grave.

"I'm going to say my little verse again," said Parrell. Standing with head bowed, he mumbled the lines:

> "*The raven crow is a coal, coal black,*
> *The jay is a purple blue,*
> *If ever I forget my own fair love,*
> *Let my heart melt away like dew.*"

He looked up at Thunstone, tears streaming down his face. "Now she'll rest in peace."

"That's right. She'll rest in peace. She won't rise again."

"Listen, you mind going back to the house? I'll just watch here till morning. You don't think that'll hurt, do you?"

Thunstone smiled.

"No, it won't hurt. It will be perfectly all right. Because nothing whatever will disturb you."

"Or her," added Parrell.

"Or her," nodded Thunstone. "She won't be disturbed. Just keep remembering her as somebody who loved you, and whose rest will never be interrupted again."

Back in the house, Thunstone brought the lamp to the table where he had interrupted his letter to de Grandin. He took his pen and began writing again:

I was interrupted by events that brought this adventure to a good end. And maybe I'll wait until I see you before I tell you that part of it.

But, to finish my earlier remarks:

If Lill Warran was a werewolf, and killed in her werewolf shape, it follows as a commonplace that she became a vampire after death. You can read as much in Montague Summers, as well as the work of your countryman, Cyprien Robert.

And as a vampire, she would and did return, in a vampire's travesty of affection, to the one living person whose heart still turned to her.

Because I half suspected all this from the moment I got wind of the story of Lill Warran, I brought with me the silver blade forged for just such battles by Saint Dunstan, and it was my weapon of victory.

He finished and folded the letter. Outside, the moon brightened the quiet night, in which it seemed no evil thing could possibly stir.

LUELLA MILLER

MARY E. WILKINS-FREEMAN

CLOSE TO THE VILLAGE STREET STOOD THE ONE-story house in which Luella Miller, who had an evil name in the village, had dwelt. She had been dead for years, yet there were those in the village who, in spite of the clearer light which comes on a vantage-point from a long-past danger, half believed in the tale which they had heard from their childhood. In their hearts, although they scarcely would have owned it, was a survival of the wild horror and frenzied fear of their ancestors who had dwelt in the same age with Luella Miller. Young people even would stare with a shudder at the old house as they passed, and children never played around it as was their wont around an untenanted building. Not a window in the old Miller house was broken: the panes reflected the morning sunlight in patches of emerald and blue, and the latch of the sagging front door was never lifted, although no bolt secured it. Since Luella Miller had been carried out of it, the house had had no tenant except one friendless old soul who had no choice between that and the far-off shelter of the open sky. This old woman, who had survived her kindred and friends, lived in the house one week, then one morning no smoke came out of the chimney, and a body of neighbours, a score strong, entered and found her dead in her bed. There were dark whispers as to the cause of her death, and there were those who testified to an expression of fear so exalted that it showed forth the state of the departing soul upon the dead face. The old woman had been hale and hearty when she entered the house, and in seven days she was dead; it seemed that she had fallen a victim to some uncanny power. The minister talked in the pulpit with covert severity against the sin of superstition; still the belief prevailed. Not a soul in the village but would have chosen the almshouse rather than that dwelling. No vagrant, if he heard the tale, would seek shelter beneath that old roof, unhallowed by nearly half a century of superstitious fear.

There was only one person in the village who had actually known Luella Miller. That person was a woman well over eighty, but a marvel of vitality and unextinct youth. Straight as an arrow, with the spring of one recently let loose from the bow of life, she moved about the streets, and she always went to church, rain or shine. She had never married, and had lived alone for years in a house across the road from Luella Miller's.

This woman had none of the garrulousness of age, but never in all her life had she ever held her tongue for any will save her own, and she never spared the truth when she essayed to present it. She it was who bore testimony to the life, evil, though possibly wittingly or designedly so, of Luella Miller, and to her personal appearance. When this old woman spoke—and she had the gift of description, although her thoughts were clothed in the rude vernacular of her native village—one could seem to see Luella Miller as she had really looked. According to this woman, Lydia Anderson by name, Luella Miller had been a beauty of a type rather unusual in New England. She had been a slight, pliant sort of creature, as ready with a strong yielding to fate and as unbreakable as a willow. She had glimmering lengths of straight, fair hair, which she wore softly looped round a long, lovely face. She had blue eyes full of soft pleading, little slender, clinging hands, and a wonderful grace of motion and attitude.

"Luella Miller used to sit in a way nobody else could if they sat up and studied a week of Sundays," said Lydia Anderson, "and it was a sight to see her walk. If one of them willows over there on the edge of the brook could start up and get its roots free of the ground, and move off, it would go just the way Luella Miller used to. She had a green shot silk she used to wear, too, and a hat with green ribbon streamers, and a lace veil blowing across her face and out sideways, and a green ribbon flyin' from her waist. That was what she came out bride in when she married Erastus Miller. Her name before she was married was Hill. There was always a sight of 'l's' in her name, married or single. Erastus Miller was good lookin', too, better lookin' than Luella. Sometimes I used to think that

Luella wa'n't so handsome after all. Erastus just about worshiped her. I used to know him pretty well. He lived next door to me, and we went to school together. Folks used to say he was waitin' on me, but he wa'n't. I never thought he was except once or twice when he said things that some girls might have suspected meant somethin'. That was before Luella came here to teach the district school. It was funny how she came to get it, for folks said she hadn't any education, and that one of the big girls, Lottie Henderson, used to do all the teachin' for her, while she sat back and did embroidery work on a cambric pocket-handkerchief. Lottie Henderson was a real smart girl, a splendid scholar, and she just set her eyes by Luella, as all the girls did. Lottie would have made a real smart woman, but she died when Luella had been here about a year—just faded away and died: nobody knew what ailed her. She dragged herself to that schoolhouse and helped Luella teach till the very last minute. The committee all knew how Luella didn't do much of the work herself, but they winked at it. It wa'n't long after Lottie died that Erastus married her. I always thought he hurried it up because she wa'n't fit to teach. One of the big boys used to help her after Lottie died, but he hadn't much government, and the school didn't do very well, and Luella might have had to give it up, for the committee couldn't have shut their eyes to things much longer. The boy that helped her was a real honest, innocent sort of fellow, and he was a good scholar, too. Folks said he overstudied, and that was the reason he was took crazy the year after Luella married, but I don't know. And I don't know what made Erastus Miller go into consumption of the blood the year after he was married: consumption wa'n't in his family. He just grew weaker and weaker, and went almost bent double when he tried to wait on Luella, and he spoke feeble, like an old man. He worked terrible hard till the last trying to save up a little to leave Luella. I've seen him out in the worst storms on a wood-sled—he used to cut and sell wood—and he was hunched up on top lookin' more dead than alive. Once I couldn't stand it: I went over and helped him pitch some wood on the cart—I was always strong in my arms. I wouldn't stop for all he told me to, and I guess he was glad enough for the help. That was only a week before he died. He fell on the kitchen floor while he was gettin' breakfast. He always got the breakfast and let Luella lay abed. He did all the sweepin' and the washin' and the ironin' and most of the cookin'. He couldn't bear to have Luella lift her finger, and she let him do for her. She lived like a queen for all the work she did. She didn't even do her sewin'. She said it made her shoulder ache to sew, and poor Erastus's sister Lily used to do all her sewin'. She wa'n't able to, either; she was never strong in her back, but she did it beautifully. She had to, to suit Luella, she was so dreadful particular. I never saw anythin' like the fagottin' and hem-stitchin' that Lily Miller did for Luella. She made all Luella's weddin' outfit, and that green silk dress, after Maria Babbit cut it. Maria she cut it for nothin', and she did a lot more cuttin' and fittin' for nothin' for Luella, too. Lily Miller went to live with Luella after Erastus died. She gave up her home, though she was real attached to it and wa'n't a mite afraid to stay alone. She rented it and she went to live with Luella right away after the funeral."

Then this old woman, Lydia Anderson, who remembered Luella Miller, would go on to relate the story of Lily Miller. It seemed that on the removal of Lily Miller to the house of her dead brother, to live with his widow, the village people first began to talk. This Lily Miller had been hardly past her first youth, and a most robust and blooming woman, rosy-cheeked, with curls of strong, black hair overshadowing round, candid temples and bright dark eyes. It was not six months after she had taken up her residence with her sister-in-law that her rosy colour faded and her pretty curves became wan hollows. White shadows began to show in the black rings of her hair, and the light died out of her eyes, her features sharpened, and there were pathetic lines at her mouth, which yet wore always an expression of utter sweetness and even happiness. She was devoted to her sister; there was no doubt that she loved her with her whole heart, and was perfectly content in her service. It was her sole anxiety lest she should die and leave her alone.

"The way Lily Miller used to talk about Luella was enough to make you mad and enough to make you cry," said Lydia Anderson. "I've been in there sometimes toward the last when she was too feeble to cook and carried her some blanc-mange or custard—somethin' I thought she might relish, and she'd thank me, and when I asked her how she was, say she felt better than she did yesterday, and asked me if I didn't think she looked better, dreadful pitiful, and say poor Luella had an awful time takin' care of her and doin' the work—she wa'n't strong enough to do anythin'—when all the time Luella wa'n't liftin' her finger and poor

Lily didn't get any care except what the neighbours gave her, and Luella eat up everythin' that was carried in for Lily. I had it real straight that she did. Luella used to just sit and cry and do nothin'. She did act real fond of Lily, and she pined away considerable, too. There was those that thought she'd go into a de-cline herself. But after Lily died, her Aunt Abby Mixter came, and then Luella picked up and grew as fat and rosy as ever. But poor Aunt Abby begun to droop just the way Lily had, and I guess somebody wrote to her married daughter, Mrs. Sam Abbot, who lived in Barre, for she wrote her mother that she must leave right away and come and make her a visit, but Aunt Abby wouldn't go. I can see her now. She was a real good-lookin' woman, tall and large, with a big, square face and a high forehead that looked of itself kind of benevolent and good. She just tended out on Luella as if she had been a baby, and when her married daughter sent for her she wouldn't stir one inch. She'd always thought a lot of her daughter, too, but she said Luella needed her and her married daughter didn't. Her daughter kept writin' and writin', but it didn't do any good. Finally she came, and when she saw how bad her mother looked, she broke down and cried and all but went on her knees to have her come away. She spoke her mind out to Luella, too. She told her that she'd killed her husband and everybody that had anythin' to do with her, and she'd thank her to leave her mother alone. Luella went into hysterics, and Aunt Abby was so frightened that she called me after her daughter went. Mrs. Sam Abbot she went away fairly cryin' out loud in the buggy, the neighbours heard her, and well she might, for she never saw her mother again alive. I went in that night when Aunt Abby called for me, standin' in the door with her little green-checked shawl over her head. I can see her now. 'Do come over here, Miss Anderson,' she sung out, kind of gasping for breath. I didn't stop for anythin'. I put over as fast as I could, and when I got there, there was Luella laughin' and cryin' all together, and Aunt Abby trying to hush her, and all the time she herself was white as a sheet and shakin' so she could hardly stand. 'For the land sakes, Mrs. Mixter,' says I, 'you look worse than she does. You ain't fit to be up out of your bed.'

"'Oh, there ain't anythin' the matter with me,' says she. Then she went on talkin' to Luella. 'There, there, don't, don't, poor little lamb,' says she. 'Aunt Abby is here. She ain't goin' away and leave you. Don't, poor little lamb.'

"'Do leave her with me, Mrs. Mixter, and you get back to bed', says I, for

Aunt Abby had been layin' down considerable lately, though somehow she contrived to do the work.

"'I'm well enough', says she. 'Don't you think she had better have the Doctor, Miss Anderson?'

"'The Doctor,' says I, 'I think *you* had better have the Doctor. I think you need him much worse than some folks I could mention.' And I looked right straight at Luella Miller laughin' and cryin' and goin' on as if she was the centre of all creation. All the time she was actin' so—seemed as if she was too sick to sense anythin'—she was keepin' a sharp lookout as to how we took it out of the corner of one eye. I see her. You could never cheat me about Luella Miller. Finally I got real mad and I run home and I got a bottle of valerian I had, and I poured some boilin' hot water on a handful of catnip, and I mixed up that catnip tea with most half a wineglass of valerian, and I went with it over to Luella's. I marched right up to Luella, a-holdin' out of that cup, all smokin'. 'Now,' says I, 'Luella Miller, *you swaller this!*'

"'What is—what is it, oh, what is it?' she sort of screeches out. Then she goes off a-laughin' enough to kill.

"'Poor lamb, poor little lamb,' says Aunt Abby, standin' over her, all kind of tottery, and tryin' to bathe her head with camphor.

"'*You swaller this right down,*' says I. And I didn't waste any ceremony. I just took hold of Luella Miller's chin and I tipped her head back, and I caught her mouth open with laughin', and I clapped that cup to her lips, and I fairly hollered at her: 'Swaller, swaller, swaller!' and she gulped it right down. She had to, and I guess it did her good. Anyhow, she stopped cryin' and laughin' and let me put her to bed, and she went to sleep like a baby inside of half an hour. That was more than poor Aunt Abby did. She lay awake all that night and I stayed with her, though she tried not to have me; said she wa'n't sick enough for watchers. But I stayed, and I made some good cornmeal gruel and I fed her a teaspoon every little while all night long. It seemed to me as if she was jest dyin' from bein' all wore out. In the mornin' as soon as it was light I run over to the Bisbees and sent Johnny Bisbee for the Doctor. I told him to tell the Doctor to hurry, and he come pretty quick. Poor Aunt Abby didn't seem to know much of anythin' when he got there. You couldn't hardly tell she breathed, she was so used up. When the Doctor had gone, Luella came into the room lookin' like a baby in her ruffled nightgown. I can see her now. Her eyes were as blue and her face all pink and white like a blossom, and she looked at Aunt Abby in the bed sort of innocent and surprised. 'Why,' says she, 'Aunt Abby ain't got up yet?'

"'No, she ain't,' says I, pretty short.

"'I thought I didn't smell the coffee,' says Luella.

"'Coffee,' says I. 'I guess if you have coffee this mornin' you'll make it yourself.'

"'I never made the coffee in all my life,' says she, dreadful astonished. 'Erastus always made the coffee as long as he lived, and then Lily she made it, and then Aunt Abby made it. I don't believe I *can* make the coffee, Miss Anderson.'

"'You can make it or go without, jest as you please,' says I.

"'Ain't Aunt Abby goin' to get up?' says she.

"'I guess she won't get up,' says I, 'sick as she is.' I was gettin' madder and madder. There was somethin' about that little pink-and-white thing standin' there and talkin' about coffee, when she had killed so many better folks than she was, and had jest killed another, that made me feel 'most as if I wished somebody would up and kill her before she had a chance to do any more harm.

"'Is Aunt Abby sick?' says Luella, as if she was sort of aggrieved and injured.

"'Yes,' says I, 'she's sick, and she's goin' to die, and then you'll be left alone, and you'll have to do for yourself and wait on yourself, or do without things.' I don't know but I was sort of hard, but it was the truth, and if I was any harder than Luella Miller had been I'll give up. I ain't never been sorry that I said it. Well, Luella, she up and had hysterics again at that, and I jest let her have 'em. All I did was to bundle her into the room on the other side of the entry where Aunt Abby couldn't hear her, if she wa'n't past it—I don't know but she was— and set her down hard in a chair and told her not to come back into the other room, and she minded. She had her hysterics in there till she got tired. When she found out that nobody was comin' to coddle her and do for her she stopped. At least I suppose she did. I had all I could do with poor Aunt Abby tryin' to keep the breath of life in her. The Doctor had told me that she was dreadful low, and give me some very strong medicine to give to her in drops real often, and told me real particular about the nourishment. Well, I did as he told me real faithful till she wa'n't able to swaller any longer. Then I had her daughter sent for. I had begun to realize that she wouldn't last any time at all. I hadn't realized it before, though I spoke to Luella the way I did. The Doctor he came, and Mrs. Sam Abbot, but when she got there it was too late; her mother was dead. Aunt Abby's daughter just give one look at her mother layin' there, then she turned sort of sharp and sudden and looked at me.

"'Where is she?' says she, and I knew she meant Luella.

"'She's out in the kitchen,' says I. 'She's too nervous to see folks die. She's afraid it will make her sick.'

"The Doctor he speaks up then. He was a young man. Old Doctor Park had died the year before, and this was a young fellow just out of college. 'Mrs. Miller is not strong,' says he, kind of severe, 'and she is quite right in not agitating herself.'

"'You are another, young man; she's got her pretty claw on you,' thinks I, but I didn't say anythin' to him. I just said over to Mrs. Sam Abbot that Luella was in the kitchen, and Mrs. Sam Abbot she went out there, and I went, too, and I never heard anythin' like the way she talked to Luella Miller. I felt pretty hard to Luella myself, but this was more than I ever would have dared to say. Luella she was too scared to go into hysterics. She jest flopped. She seemed to jest shrink away to nothin' in that kitchen chair, with Mrs. Sam Abbot standin' over her and talkin' and tellin' her the truth. I guess the truth was most too much for her and no mistake, because Luella presently actually did faint away, and there wa'n't any sham about it, the way I always suspected there was about them hysterics. She fainted dead away and we had to lay her flat on the floor, and the Doctor he came runnin' out and he said somethin' about a weak heart dreadful fierce to Mrs. Sam Abbot, but she wa'n't a mite scared. She faced him jest as white as even Luella was layin' there lookin' like death and the Doctor feelin' of her pulse.

"'Weak heart,' says she, 'weak heart; weak fiddlesticks! There ain't nothin' weak about that woman. She's got strength enough to hang onto other folks till she kills 'em. Weak? It was my poor mother that was weak: this woman killed her as sure as if she had taken a knife to her.'

"But the Doctor he didn't pay much attention. He was bendin' over Luella layin' there with her yellow hair all streamin' and her pretty pink-and-white face all pale, and her blue eyes like stars gone out, and he was holdin' onto her hand and smoothin' her forehead, and tellin' me to get the brandy in Aunt Abby's room, and I was sure as I wanted to be that Luella had got somebody else to hang onto, now Aunt Abby was gone, and I thought of poor Erastus Miller, and I sort of pitied the poor young Doctor, led away by a pretty face, and I made up my mind I'd see what I could do.

"I waited till Aunt Abby had been dead and buried about a month, and the Doctor was goin' to see Luella steady and folks were beginnin' to talk; then one evenin', when I knew the Doctor had been called out of town and wouldn't be round, I went over to Luella's. I found her all dressed up in a blue muslin with white polka dots on it, and her hair curled jest as pretty, and there wa'n't a young girl in the place could compare with her. There was somethin' about Luella Miller seemed to draw the heart right out of you, but she didn't draw it out of *me*. She was settin' rocking in the chair by her sittin'-room window, and Maria Brown had gone home. Maria Brown had been in to help her, or rather to do the work, for Luella wa'n't helped when she didn't do anythin'. Maria Brown was real capable and she didn't have any ties; she wa'n't married, and lived alone, so she'd offered. I couldn't see why she should do the work any more than Luella; she wa'n't any too strong; but she seemed to think she could and Luella seemed to think so, too, so she went over and did all the work—washed, and ironed, and baked, while Luella sat and rocked. Maria didn't live long afterward. She began to fade away just the same fashion the others had. Well, she was warned, but she acted real mad when folks said anythin': said Luella was a poor, abused woman, too delicate to help herself, and they'd ought to be ashamed, and if she died helpin' them that couldn't help themselves she would—and she did.

"'I s'pose Maria has gone home,' says I to Luella, when I had gone in and sat down opposite her.

"'Yes, Maria went half an hour ago, after she had got supper and washed the dishes,' says Luella, in her pretty way.

"'I suppose she has got a lot of work to do in her own house to-night,' says I, kind of bitter, but that was all thrown away on Luella Miller. It seemed to her right that other folks that wa'n't any better able than she was herself should wait on her, and she couldn't get it through her head that anybody should think it *wa'n't* right.

"'Yes,' says Luella, real sweet and pretty, 'yes, she said she had to do her washin' to-night. She has let it go for a fortnight along of comin' over here.'

"'Why don't she stay home and do her washin' instead of comin' over here and doin' *your* work, when you are just as well able, and enough sight more so, than she is to do it?' says I.

"Then Luella she looked at me like a baby who has a rattle shook at it. She sort of laughed as innocent as you please. 'Oh, I can't do the work myself, Miss Anderson,' says she. 'I never did. Maria *has* to do it.'

"Then I spoke out: 'Has to do it!' says I. 'Has to do it! She don't have to do it, either. Maria Brown has her own home and enough to live on. She ain't beholden to you to come over here and slave for you and kill herself.'

"Luella she jest set and stared at me for all the world like a doll-baby that was so abused that it was comin' to life.

"'Yes,' says I, 'she's killin' herself. She's goin' to die just the way Erastus did, and Lily, and your Aunt Abby. You're killin' her jest as you did them. I don't know what there is about you, but you seem to bring a curse,' says I. 'You kill everybody that is fool enough to care anythin' about you and do for you.'

"She stared at me and she was pretty pale.

"'And Maria ain't the only one you're goin' to kill,' says I. 'You're goin' to kill Doctor Malcom before you're done with him.'

"Then a red colour came flamin' all over her face. 'I ain't goin' to kill him, either,' says she, and she begun to cry.

"'Yes, you *be!*' says I. Then I spoke as I had never spoke before. You see, I felt it on account of Erastus. I told her that she hadn't any business to think of another man after she'd been married to one that had died for her: that she was a dreadful woman; and she was, that's true enough, but sometimes I have wondered lately if she knew it—if she wa'n't like a baby with scissors in its hand cuttin' everybody without knowin' what it was doin'.

"Luella she kept gettin' paler and paler, and she never took her eyes off my face. There was somethin' awful about the way she looked at me and never spoke one word. After awhile I quit talkin' and I went home. I watched that night, but her lamp went out before nine o'clock, and when Doctor Malcom came drivin' past and sort of slowed up he see there wa'n't any light and he drove along. I saw her sort of shy out of meetin' the next Sunday, too, so he shouldn't go home with her, and I begun to think mebbe she did have some conscience after all. It was only a week after that that Maria Brown died—sort of sudden at the last, though everybody had seen it was comin'. Well, then there was a good deal of feelin' and pretty dark whispers. Folks said the days of witchcraft had come again, and they were pretty shy of Luella. She acted sort of offish to the Doctor and he didn't go there, and there wa'n't anybody to do anythin' for her. I don't know how she *did* get along. I wouldn't go in there and offer to help her—not because I was afraid of dyin' like the rest, but I thought she was just as well able to do her own work as I was to do it for her, and I thought it was about time that she did it and stopped killin' other folks. But it wa'n't very long before folks began to say that Luella herself was goin' into a decline jest the way her husband, and Lily, and Aunt Abby and the others had, and I saw myself that she looked pretty bad. I used to see her goin' past from the store with a bundle as if she could hardly crawl, but I remembered how Erastus used to wait and 'tend when he couldn't hardly put one foot before the other, and I didn't go out to help her.

"But at last one afternoon I saw the Doctor come drivin' up like mad with his medicine chest, and Mrs. Babbit came in after supper and said that Luella was real sick.

"'I'd offer to go in and nurse her,' says she, 'but I've got my children to consider, and mebbe it ain't true what they say, but it's queer how many folks that have done for her have died.'

"I didn't say anythin', but I considered how she had been Erastus's wife and how he had set his eyes by her, and I made up my mind to go in the next mornin', unless she was better, and see what I could do; but the next mornin' I see her at the window, and pretty soon she came steppin' out as spry as you please, and a little while afterward Mrs. Babbit came in and told me that the Doctor had got a girl from out of town, a Sarah Jones, to come there, and she said she was pretty sure that the Doctor was goin' to marry Luella.

"I saw him kiss her in the door that night myself, and I knew it was true. The woman came that afternoon, and the way she flew around was a caution. I don't believe Luella had swept since Maria died. She swept and dusted, and washed and ironed; wet clothes and dusters and carpets were flyin' over there all day, and every time Luella set her foot out when the Doctor wa'n't there there was that Sarah Jones helpin' of her up and down the steps, as if she hadn't learned to walk.

"Well, everybody knew that Luella and the Doctor were goin' to be married, but it wa'n't long before they began to talk about his lookin' so poorly, jest as they had about the others; and they talked about Sarah Jones, too.

"Well, the Doctor did die, and he wanted to be married first, so as to leave what little he had to Luella, but he died before the minister could get there, and Sarah Jones died a week afterward.

"Well, that wound up everything for Luella Miller. Not another soul in the whole town would lift a finger for her. There got to be a sort of panic. Then she began to droop in good earnest. She used to have to go to the store herself, for Mrs. Babbit was afraid to let Tommy go for her, and I've seen her goin' past and stoppin' every two or three steps to rest. Well, I stood it as long as I could, but one day I see her comin' with her arms full and stoppin' to lean against the Babbit fence, and I run out and took her bundles and carried them to her house. Then I went home and never spoke one word to her though she called after me dreadful kind of pitiful. Well, that night I was taken sick with a chill, and I was sick as I wanted to be for two weeks. Mrs. Babbit had seen me run out to help Luella and she came in and told me I was goin' to die on account of it. I didn't know whether I was or not, but I considered I had done right by Erastus's wife.

"That last two weeks Luella she had a dreadful hard time, I guess. She was pretty sick, and as near as I could make out nobody dared go near her. I don't know as she was really needin' anythin' very much, for there was enough to eat in her house and it was warm weather, and she made out to cook a little flour gruel every day, I know, but I guess she had a hard time, she that had been so petted and done for all her life.

"When I got so I could go out, I went over there one morning. Mrs. Babbit had just come in to say she hadn't seen any smoke and she didn't know but it was somebody's duty to go in, but she couldn't help thinkin' of her children, and I got right up, though I hadn't been out of the house for two weeks, and I went in there, and Luella she was layin' on the bed, and she was dyin'.

"She lasted all that day and into the night. But I sat there after the new Doctor had gone away. Nobody else dared to go there. It was about midnight that I left her for a minute to run home and get some medicine I had been takin', for I begun to feel rather bad.

"It was a full moon that night, and just as I started out of my door to cross the street back to Luella's, I stopped short, for I saw something."

Lydia Anderson at this juncture always said with a certain defiance that she did not expect to be believed, and then proceeded in a hushed voice:

"I saw what I saw, and I know I saw it, and I will swear on my death bed that I saw it. I saw Luella Miller and Erastus Miller, and Lily, and Aunt Abby, and Maria, and the Doctor, and Sarah, all goin' out of her door, and all but Luella shone white in the moonlight, and they were all helpin' her along till she seemed to fairly fly in the midst of them. Then it all disappeared. I stood a minute with my heart poundin', then I went over there. I thought of goin' for Mrs. Babbit, but I thought she'd be afraid. So I went alone, though I knew what had happened. Luella was layin' real peaceful, dead on her bed."

This was the story that the old woman, Lydia Anderson, told, but the sequel was told by the people who survived her, and this is the tale which has become folklore in the village.

Lydia Anderson died when she was eighty-seven. She had continued wonderfully hale and hearty for one of her years until about two weeks before her death.

One bright moonlight evening she was sitting beside a window in her parlour when she made a sudden exclamation, and was out of the house and across the street before the neighbour who was taking care of her could stop her. She followed as fast as possible and found Lydia Anderson stretched on the ground before the door of Luella Miller's deserted house, and she was quite dead.

The next night there was a red gleam of fire athwart the moonlight and the old house of Luella Miller was burned to the ground. Nothing is now left of it except a few old cellar stones and a lilac bush, and in summer a helpless trail of morning glories among the weeds, which might be considered emblematic of Luella herself.

. . . TO FEEL ANOTHER'S WOE

CHET WILLIAMSON

I HAD TO ADMIT SHE LOOKED LIKE A VAMPIRE WHEN KEVIN described her as such. Her face, at least, with those high model's cheekbones and absolutely huge, wet-looking eyes. The jet of her hair set off her pale skin strikingly, and that skin was perfect, nearly luminous. To the best of my knowledge, however, vampires didn't wear Danskin tops and Annie Hall flop-slacks, nor did they audition for Broadway shows.

There must have been two hundred of us jammed into the less than immaculate halls of the Ansonia Hotel that morning, with photo/résumés clutched in one hand, scripts of *A Streetcar Named Desire* in the other. John Weidner was directing a revival at Circle in the Square, and every New York actor with an Equity card and a halfway intelligible Brooklyn dialect under his collar was there to try out. Stanley Kowalski had already been spoken for by a new Italian-American film star with more *chutzpah* than talent, but the rest of the roles were open. I was hoping for Steve or Mitch, or maybe even a standby, just something to pay the rent.

I found myself in line next to Kevin McQuinn, a gay song-and-dance man I'd done Jones Beach with two years before. A nice guy, not at all flouncy. "Didn't know this was a musical," I smiled at him.

"Sure. You never heard of the Stella aria?" And he sang softly, "I'll never stop saying Steh-el-*la* . . ."

"Seriously. You going dramatic?"

He shrugged. "No choice. Musicals these days are all rock or opera or rock opera. No soft shoes in *Sweeney Todd.*"

"*Sweeney Todd* closed ages ago."

"That's 'cause they didn't have no soft shoes."

Then she walked in holding her P/R and script, and sat on the floor with her back to the wall as gracefully as if she owned the place. I was, to Kevin's amusement, instantly smitten.

"Forget it," he said. "She'd eat you alive."

"I wish. Who is she?"

"Name's Sheila Remarque."

"Shitty stage name."

"She was born with it, so she says. Me, I believe her. Nobody'd *pick* that."

"She any good?"

Kevin smiled, a bit less broadly than his usually mobile face allowed. "Let's just say that I've got twenty bucks that says she'll get whatever part she's after."

"Serious?"

"The girl's phenomenal. You catch *Lear* in the park last summer?" I nodded. "She played Goneril."

"Oh *yeah.*" I was amazed that I hadn't recalled the name. "She *was* good."

"You said good, I said phenomenal. Along with the critics."

As I thought back, I remembered the performance vividly. Generally Cordelia stole the show from Lear's two nasty daughters, but all eyes had been on Goneril at the matinee I'd seen. It wasn't that the actress had been upstaging, or doing anything to excess. It was simply (or complexly, if you're an actor) that she was so damned *believable.* There'd been no trace of *acting*, no indication shared between actress and audience, as even the finest performers will do, no self-consciousness whatsoever, only utterly true emotion. As I remembered, the one word I had associated with it was *awesome.* How stupid, I thought, to have forgotten her name. "What else do you know about her?" I asked Kevin.

"Not much. A mild reputation with the boys. Love 'em and leave 'em. A Theda Bara vampire type."

"Ever work with her?"

"Three years ago. *Oklahoma!* at Allenberry. I did Will Parker, and she was in the chorus. Fair voice, danced a little, but lousy presence. A real poser, you know? I don't know what the hell happened."

I started to ask Kevin if he knew where she studied, when he suddenly tensed. I followed his gaze, and saw a man coming down the hall carrying a dance bag. He was tall and thin, with light-brown hair and a nondescript face. It's hard to describe features on which not the slightest bit of emotion is displayed. Instead of sitting on the floor like the rest of us, he remained standing, a few yards away from Sheila Remarque, whom he looked at steadily, yet apparently without interest. She looked up, saw him, gave a brief smile, and returned to her script.

Kevin leaned closer and whispered. "You want to know about *Ms.* Remarque, *there's* the man you should ask, not me."

"Why? Who is he?" The man hadn't taken his eyes from the girl, but I couldn't tell whether he watched her in lust or anger. At any rate, I admired her self-control. Save for that first glance, she didn't acknowledge him at all.

"Name's Guy Taylor."

"The one who was in *Annie?*"

Kevin nodded. "Three years here. One on the road. Same company I went out with. Used to drink together. He was hilarious, even when he was sober. But put the drinks in him and he'd make Eddie Murphy look like David Merrick. Bars would fall apart laughing."

"He went with this girl?"

"Lived with her for three, maybe four months, just this past year."

"They split up, I take it."

"Mmm-hmm. Don't know much about it, though." He shook his head. "I ran into Guy a week or so ago at the *Circle of Three* auditions. I was really happy to see him, but he acted like he barely knew me. Asked him how his lady was—I'd never met her, but the word had spread—and he told me he was living alone now, so I didn't press it. Asked a couple people and found out she'd walked out on him. Damn near crushed him. He must've had it hard."

"That's love for you."

"Yeah. Ain't I glad I don't mess with women."

Kevin and I started talking about other things then, but I couldn't keep my eyes off Sheila Remarque's haunting face, nor off the vacuous features of Guy

Taylor, who watched the girl with the look of a stolid, stupid guard dog. I wondered if he'd bite anybody who dared to talk to her.

At ten o'clock, as scheduled, the line started to move. When I got to the table, the assistant casting director, or whatever flunky was using that name, looked at my P/R and at me, evidently approved of what he saw, and told me to come back at two o'clock for a reading. Kevin, right beside me, received only a shake of the head and a "thank you for coming."

"Dammit," Kevin said as we walked out. "I shouldn't have stood behind you in line, then I wouldn't've looked so un-macho. I mean, didn't they *know* about Tennessee Williams, for crissake?"

When I went back to the Ansonia at two, there were over thirty people already waiting, twice as many men as women. Among the dozen or so femmes was Sheila Remarque, her nose still stuck in her script, oblivious to those around her. Guy Taylor was also there, standing against a wall as before. He had a script open in front of him, and from time to time would look down at it, but most of the time he stared at Sheila Remarque, who, I honestly believe, was totally indifferent to, and perhaps even ignorant of, his perusal.

As I sat watching the two of them, I thought that the girl would make a stunning Blanche, visually at least. She seemed to have that elusive, fragile quality that Vivien Leigh exemplified so well in the film. I'd only seen Jessica Tandy, who'd originated the role, in still photos, but she always seemed too horsey-looking for my tastes. By no stretch of the imagination could Sheila Remarque be called horsey. She was exquisite porcelain, and I guess I must have become transfixed by her for a moment, for the next time I looked away from her toward Guy Taylor, he was staring at me with that same damned expressionless stare. I was irritated by the proprietary emotion I placed on his face, but found it so disquieting that I couldn't glare back. So I looked at my script again.

After a few minutes, a fiftyish man I didn't recognize came out and spoke to us. "Okay, Mr. Weidner will eliminate some of you without hearing you read. Those of you who make the final cut, be prepared to do one of two scenes. We'll have the ladies who are reading for Blanche and you men reading for Mitch first. As you were told this morning, ladies, scene ten, guys six. Use your scripts if you want to. Not's okay too. Let's go."

Seven women and fifteen men, me and Guy Taylor among them, followed the man into what used to be a ballroom. At one end of the high-ceilinged room was a series of raised platforms with a few wooden chairs on them. Ten yards back from this makeshift stage were four folding director's chairs. Another five yards in back of these were four rows of ten each of the same rickety wooden chairs there were on the stage. We sat on these while Weidner, the director, watched us file in. "I'm sorry we can't be in the theater," he said, "but the set there now can't be struck for auditions. We'll have to make do here. Let's start with the gentlemen for a change."

He looked at the stage manager, who read from his clipboard, "Adams."

That was me. I stood up, script in hand. Given a choice, I always held book in auditions. It gives you self-confidence, and if you try to go without and go up on the lines, you look like summer stock. Besides, that's why they call them readings.

"Would someone be kind enough to read Blanche in scene six with Mr. Adams?" Weidner asked. A few girls were rash enough to raise their hands and volunteer for a scene they hadn't prepared, but Weidner's eyes fell instantly on Sheila Remarque. "Miss Remarque, isn't it?" She nodded. "My congratulations on your Goneril. Would you be kind enough to read six? I promise I won't let it color my impressions of your scene ten."

Bullshit, I thought, but she nodded graciously, and together we ascended the squeaking platform.

Have you ever played a scene opposite an animal or a really cute little kid? If you have, you know how utterly impossible it is to get the audience to pay any attention to you whatsoever. That was exactly how I felt doing a scene with Sheila Remarque. Not that my reading wasn't good, because it was, better by far than I would have done reading with a prompter or an ASM, because she gave me something I could react to. She made Blanche so real that I had to be real too, and I was good.

But not as good as her. No way.

She used no book, had all the moves and lines down pat. But like I said of her Goneril, there was no *indication* of acting at all. She spoke and moved on that cheapjack stage as if she were and had always been Blanche DuBois, formerly of Belle Rêve, presently of Elysian Fields, New Orleans, in the year 1947. Weidner didn't interrupt after a few lines, a few pages, the way directors usually do, but let the scene glide on effortlessly to its end, when, still holding my script, I kissed Blanche DuBois on "her forehead and her eyes and finally her lips," and she sobbed out her line, "Sometimes—there's God—so quickly!" and it was over and Blanche DuBois vanished, leaving Sheila Remarque and me on that platform with them all looking up at us soundlessly. Weidner's smile was suffused with wonder. But not for me. I'd been good, but she'd been great.

"Thank you, Mr. Adams. Thank you very much. Nice reading. We have your résumé, yes. Thank you," and he nodded in a gesture of dismissal that took me off the platform. "Thank you too, Miss Remarque. Well done. While you're already up there, would you care to do scene ten for us?"

She nodded, and I stopped at the exit. Ten was a hell of a scene, the one where Stanley and the drunken Blanche are alone in the flat, and I had to see her do it. I whispered a request to stay to the fiftyish man who'd brought us in, and he nodded an okay, as if speaking would break whatever spell was on the room. I remained there beside him.

"Our Stanley Kowalski was to be here today to read with the Blanches and Stellas, but a TV commitment prevented him," Weidner said somewhat bitchily. "So if one of you gentlemen would be willing to read with Miss Remarque . . ."

There were no idiots among the men. Not one volunteered. "Ah, Mr. Taylor," I heard Weidner say. My stomach tightened. I didn't know whether he'd chosen Taylor to read with her out of sheer malevolence, or whether he was ignorant of their relationship, and it was coincidence—merely his spotting Taylor's familiar face. Either way, I thought, the results could be unpleasant. And from the way several of the gypsies' shoulders stiffened, I could tell they were thinking the same thing. "Would you please?"

Taylor got up slowly, and joined the girl on the platform. As far as I could see, there was no irritation in his face, nor was there any sign of dismay in Sheila Remarque's deep, wet eyes. She smiled at him as though he were a stranger, and took a seat facing the "audience."

"Anytime," said Weidner. He sounded anxious. Not impatient, just anxious.

Sheila Remarque became drunk. Just like that, in the space of a heartbeat. Her whole body fell into the posture of a long-developed alcoholism. Her eyes blurred, her mouth opened, a careless slash across the ruin of her face, lined and bagged with booze. She spoke the lines as if no one had ever said them before, so any onlooker would swear that it was Blanche DuBois's liquor-dulled brain that was creating them, and in no way were they merely words that had existed on a printed page for forty years, words filtered through the voice of a performer.

She finished speaking into the unseen mirror, and Guy Taylor walked toward her as Stanley Kowalski. Blanche saw him, spoke to him. But though she spoke to Stanley Kowalski, it was Guy Taylor who answered, only Guy Taylor reading lines, without a trace of emotion. Oh, the *expression* was there, the nuances, the rhythm of the lines and their meaning was clear. But it was like watching La Duse play a scene with an electronic synthesizer. She destroyed him, and I thought back, hoping she hadn't done the same to me.

This time Weidner didn't let the scene play out to the end. I had to give him credit. As awful as Taylor was, *I* couldn't have brought myself to deny the reality of Sheila Remarque's performance by interrupting, but Weidner did, during one of Stanley's longer speeches about his cousin who opened beer bottles with his teeth. "Okay, fine," Weidner called out. "Good enough. Thank you, Mr. Taylor. I think that's all we need see of you today." Weidner looked away from him. "Miss Remarque, if you wouldn't mind, I'd like to hear that one more time. Let's see . . . Mr. Carver, would you read Stanley, please." Carver, a chorus gypsy who had no business doing heavy work, staggered to the platform, his face pale, but I didn't wait to see if he'd survive. I'd seen enough wings pulled off flies for one day, and was out the door, heading to the elevator even before Taylor had come off the platform.

I had just pushed the button when I saw Taylor, his dance bag over his shoulder, come out of the ballroom. He walked slowly down the hall toward me, and I prayed the car would arrive quickly enough that I wouldn't have to ride with him. But the Ansonia's lifts have seen better days, and by the time I stepped into the car he was a scant ten yards away. I held the door for him. He stepped in, the doors closed, and we were alone.

Taylor looked at me for a moment. "You'll get Mitch," he said flatly.

I shrugged self-consciously and smiled. "There's a lot of people to read."

"But they won't read Mitch with *her*. And your reading *was* good."

I nodded agreement. "She helped."

"May I," he said after a pause, "give you some advice?" I nodded. "If they give you Mitch," he said, "turn them down."

"Why?" I asked, laughing.

"She's sure to be Blanche. Don't you think?"

"So?"

"You heard me read today."

"So?"

"Have you seen me work?"

"I saw you in *Annie*. And in *Bus Stop* at ELT."

"And?"

"You were good. Real good."

"And what about today?"

I looked at the floor.

"Tell me." I looked at him, my lips pinched. "Shitty," he said. "Nothing there, right?"

"Not much," I said.

"She did that. Took it from me." He shook his head. "Stay away from her. She can do it to you too."

The first thing you learn in professional theater is that actors are children. I say that, knowing full well that I'm one myself. Our egos are huge, yet our feelings are as delicate as orchids. In a way, it stems from the fact that in other trades, rejections are impersonal. Writers aren't rejected—it's one particular story or novel that is. For factory workers, or white-collars, it's lack of knowledge or experience that loses jobs. But for an actor, it's the way he looks, the way he talks, the way he moves that make the heads nod yes or no, and that's rejection on the most deeply personal scale, like kids calling each other Nickel-nose or Fatso. And often that childish hurt extends to other relationships as well. Superstitious? Imaginative? Ballplayers have nothing on us. So when Taylor started blaming Sheila Remarque for his thespian rockslide, I knew it was only because he couldn't bear to admit that it was *he* who had let his craft slip away, not the girl who had taken it from him.

The elevator doors opened, and I stepped off. "Wait," he said, coming after me. "You don't believe me."

"Look, man," I said, turning in exasperation, "I don't know what went on between you and her and I don't care, okay? If she messed you over, I'm sorry, but I'm an actor and I need a job and if I get it I'll *take* it!"

His face remained placid. "Let me buy you a drink," he said.

"Oh Jesus . . ."

"You don't have to be afraid. I won't get violent." He forced a smile. "Do you think I've *been* violent? Have I even raised my voice?"

"No."

"Then please. I just want to talk to you."

I had to admit to myself that I *was* curious. Most actors would have shown more fire over things that meant so much to them, but Taylor was strangely zombielike, as if life were just a walk-through. "All right," I said, "all right."

We walked silently down Broadway. By the time we got to Charlie's it was three-thirty, a slow time for the bar. I perched on a stool, but Taylor shook his head. "Table," he said, and we took one and ordered. It turned out we were both bourbon drinkers.

"Jesus," he said after a long sip. "It's cold."

It was. Manhattan winters are never balmy, and the winds that belly through the streets cut through anything short of steel.

"All right," I said. "We're here. You're buying me a drink. Now. You have a story for me?"

"I do. And after I tell it you can go out and do what you like."

"I intend to."

"I won't try to stop you," he went on, not hearing me. "I don't think I could even if I wanted to. It's your life, your career."

"Get to the point."

"I met her last summer. June. I know Joe Papp, and he invited me to the party after the *Lear* opening, so I went. Sheila was there with a guy, and I walked up and introduced myself to them, and told her how much I enjoyed her performance. She thanked me, very gracious, very friendly, and told me she'd seen me several times and liked my work as well. I thought it odd at the time, the way she came on to me. Very strong, with those big, wet, bedroom eyes of hers eating me up. But her date didn't seem to care. He didn't seem to care about much of anything. Just stood there and drank while she talked, then sat down and drank some more. She told me later, when we were together, that he was a poet.

Unpublished, of course, she said. She told me that his work wasn't very good technically, but that it was very emotional. 'Rich with feeling,' were the words she used.

"I went to see her in *Lear* again, several times really, and was more impressed with each performance. The poet was waiting for her the second time I went, but the third, she left alone. I finessed her into a drink, we talked, got along beautifully. She told me it was all over between her and the poet, and that night she ended up in my bed. It was good, and she seemed friendly, passionate, yet undemanding. After a few more dates, a few more nights and mornings, I suggested living together, no commitments. She agreed, and the next weekend she moved in with me.

"I want you to understand one thing, though. I never loved her. I never told her I loved her or even suggested it. For me, it was companionship and sex, and that was all. Though she was good to be with, nice to kiss, to hold, to share things with, I never loved her. And I know she never loved me." He signaled the waiter and another drink came. Mine was still half full. "So I'm not a . . . a victim of unrequited love, all right? I just want you to be sure of that." I nodded and he went on.

"It started a few weeks after we were living together. She'd want to play games with me, she said. Theater games. You know, pretend she was doing something or say something to get a certain emotion out of me. Most of the time she didn't let me know right away what she was doing. She'd see if she could get me jealous, or mad, or sullen. Happy too. And then she'd laugh and say she was just kidding, that she'd just wanted to see my reactions. Well, I thought that was bullshit. I put it down as a technique exercise rather than any method crap, and in a way I could understand it—wanting to be face-to-face with emotions to examine them—but I still thought it was an imposition on me, an invasion of my privacy. She didn't do it often, maybe once or twice a week. I tried it on her occasionally, but she never bit, just looked at me as if I were a kid trying to play a man's game.

"Somewhere along the line it started getting kinky. While we were having sex, she'd call me by another name, or tell me about something sad she'd remembered, anything to get different reactions, different rises out of me. Sometimes . . ." He looked down, drained his drink. "Sometimes I'd . . . come and I'd cry at the same time."

The waiter was nearby, and I signaled for another round. "Why did you stay with her?"

"It wasn't . . . she didn't do this all the time, like I said. And I *liked* her. It got so I didn't even mind it when she'd pull this stuff on me, and she knew it. Once she even got me when I was stoned, and a couple of times after I'd had too much to drink. I didn't care. Until winter came.

"I hadn't been doing much after the summer. A few industrials here in town, some voice-over stuff. Good money, but just straight song and dance, flat narration, and no reviews. So the beginning of December Harv Piersall calls me to try out for *Ahab.* The musical that closed in previews? He wanted me to read for Starbuck, a scene where Starbuck is planning to shoot Ahab to save the Pequod. It was a good scene, a strong scene, and I got up there and I couldn't do a thing with it. Not a goddamned thing. I was utterly flat, just like in my narration and my singing around a Pontiac. But there it hadn't mattered—I hadn't had to put out any emotion—just sell the product, that was all. But *now,* when I had to feel something, had to express something, I couldn't. Harv asked me if anything was wrong, and I babbled some excuse about not feeling well, and when he invited me to come back and read again I did, a day later, and it was the same.

"That weekend I went down to St. Mark's to see Sheila in an OOB production—it was a new translation of *Medea* by some grad student at NYU—and she'd gotten the title role. They'd been rehearsing off and on for a month, no pay to speak of, but she was enthusiastic about it. It was the largest and most important part she'd done. Papp was there that night, someone got Prince to come too. The translation was garbage. No set, tunics for costumes, nothing lighting. But Sheila . . ."

He finished his latest drink, spat the ice back into the glass. "She was . . . superb. Every emotion was real. They should have been. She'd taken them from me.

"Don't look at me like that. I thought what you're thinking too, at first. That I was paranoid, jealous of her talents. But once I started to think things through, I knew it was the only answer.

"She was so loving to me afterward, smiled at me and held my arm and introduced me to her friends, and I felt as dull and lifeless as that poet I'd seen her with. Even then I suspected what she'd done, but I didn't say anything to her about it. That next week when I tried to get in touch with the poet, I found out he'd left the city, gone home to wherever it was he'd come from. I went over to Lincoln Center, to their videotape collection, and watched *King Lear.* I wanted to see if I could find anything that didn't jell, that wasn't quite *right.* Hell, I didn't know what I was looking for, just that I'd know when I saw it."

He shook his head. "It was . . . incredible. On the tape there was no sign of the performance I'd seen her give. Instead I saw a flat, lifeless, amateurish performance, dreadfully bad in contrast to the others. I couldn't believe it, watched it again. The same thing. Then I knew why she never auditioned for commercials, or for film. It didn't . . . *show up* on camera. She could fool people, but not a camera.

"I went back to the apartment then, and told her what I'd found out. It wasn't guessing on my part, not a theory, because I *knew* by then. You see, I *knew*."

Taylor stopped talking and looked down into his empty glass. I thought perhaps I'd made a huge mistake in going to the bar with him, for he was most certainly paranoid, and could conceivably become violent as well, in spite of his assurances to the contrary. "So what . . ." My "so" came out too much like "sho," but I pushed on with my question while he flagged the waiter, who raised an eyebrow, but brought more drinks. "So what did she say? When you told her?"

"She . . . verified it. Told me that I was right. 'In a way,' she said. 'In a way.'"

"Well . . ." I shook my head to clear it. ". . . didn't she probably mean that she was just studying you? That's hardly, hardly *stealing* your emotions, is it?"

"No. She stole them."

"That's silly. That's still silly. You've still got them."

"No. I wanted . . . when I knew for sure, I wanted to kill her. The way she smiled at me, as though I were powerless to take anything back, as though she had planned it all from the moment we met—that made me want to kill her." He turned his empty eyes on me. "But I didn't. Couldn't. I couldn't get angry enough."

He sighed. "She moved out. That didn't bother me. I was glad. As glad as I could feel after what she'd done. I don't know *how* she did it. I think it was something she learned, or learned she had. I don't know whether I'll ever get them back or not, either. Oh, not from *her*. Never from her. But on my own. Build them up inside me somehow. The emotions. The feelings. Maybe someday."

He reached across the table and touched my hand, his fingers surprisingly warm. "So much I don't know. But one thing I do. She'll do it again, find someone else, *you* if you let her. I saw how you were looking at her today." I pulled my hand away from his, bumping my drink. He grabbed it before it spilled, set it upright. "Don't," he cautioned. "Don't have anything to do with her."

"It's absurd," I said, half stuttering. "Ridiculous. You still . . . show emotions."

"Maybe. Maybe a few. But they're only outward signs. Inside it's hollow." His head went to one side. "You don't believe me."

"N—no . . ." And I didn't, not then.

"You should have known me before."

Suddenly I remembered Kevin at the audition, and his telling me how funny and wild Guy Taylor had gotten on a few drinks. My own churning stomach reminded me of how many we had had sitting here for less than an hour, and my churning mind showed me Sheila Remarque's drunk, drunk, perfectly drunk Blanche DuBois earlier that afternoon. "You've had . . ." I babbled, ". . . how many drinks have you had?"

He shrugged.

"But . . . you're not . . . showing any *signs* . . ."

"Yes. That's right," he said in a clear, steady, sober voice. "That's right."

He crossed his forearms on the table, lowered his head onto them, and wept. The sobs were loud, prolonged, shaking his whole body.

He wept.

"There!" I cried, staggering to my feet. "There, see? See? You're *crying*, you're *crying!* See?"

He raised his head and looked at me, still weeping, still weeping, with not one tear to be seen.

When the call came offering me Mitch, I took the part. I didn't even consider turning it down. Sheila Remarque had, as Kevin, Guy Taylor, and I had anticipated, been cast as Blanche DuBois, and she smiled warmly at me when I entered the studio for the first reading, as though she remembered our audition with fondness. I was pleasant, but somewhat aloof at first, not wanting the others to see, to suspect what I was going to do.

I thought it might be difficult to get her alone, but it wasn't. She had already chosen me, I could tell, watching me through the readings, coming up to me and chatting at the breaks. By the end of the day she'd learned where I lived, that I was single, unattached, and straight, and that I'd been bucking for eight years to get a part this good. She told me that she lived only a block away from my building (a lie, I later found out), and, after the rehearsal, suggested we take a cab together and split the expense. I agreed, and the cab left us out on West 72nd next to the park.

It was dark and cold, and I saw her shiver under her down-filled jacket. I shivered too, for we were alone at last, somewhat hidden by the trees, and there were no passersby to be seen, only the taxis and buses and cars hurtling past.

I turned to her, the smile gone from my face. "I know what you've done," I said. "I talked to Guy Taylor. He told me all about it. And warned me."

Her face didn't change. She just hung on to that soft half smile of hers, and watched me with those liquid eyes.

"He said . . . you'd be after me. He told me not to take the part. But I had to. I had to know if it's true, all he said."

Her smiled faded, she looked down at the dirty, ice-covered sidewalk, and nodded, creases of sadness at the corners of her eyes. I reached out and did what I had planned, said what I had wanted to say to her ever since leaving Guy Taylor crying without tears at the table in Charlie's.

"Teach me," I said, taking her hand as gently as I knew how. "I'd be no threat to you, no competition for roles. In fact, you may need me, need a man who can equal you on stage. Because there aren't any now. You can take what you want from me as long as you can teach me how to get it back again.

"Please. Teach me."

When she looked up at me, her face was wet with tears. I kissed them away, neither knowing nor caring whose they were.

The Canal

❦

Everil Worrell

P

AST THE SLEEPING CITY THE RIVER SWEEPS; ALONG ITS left bank the old canal creeps.

I did not intend that to be poetry, although the scene is poetic—somberly, gruesomely poetic, like the poems of Poe. Too well I know it—too often have I walked over the grass-grown path beside the reflections of black trees and tumble-down shacks and distant factory chimneys in the sluggish waters that moved so slowly, and ceased to move at all.

I shall be called mad, and I shall be a suicide. I shall take no pains to cover up my trail, or to hide the thing that I shall do. What will it matter, afterward, what they say of me? If they knew the truth—if they could vision, even dimly, the beings with whom I have consorted—if the faintest realization might be theirs of the thing I am becoming, and of the fate from which I am saving their city—then they would call me a great hero. But it does not matter what they call me, as I have said before. Let me write down the things I am about to write down, and let them be taken, as they will be taken, for the last ravings of a madman. The city will be in mourning for the thing I shall have done—but its mourning will be of no consequence beside that other fate from which I shall have saved it.

I have always had a taste for nocturnal prowling. We as a race have grown too intelligent to take seriously any of the old, instinctive fears that preserved us through preceding generations. Our sole remaining salvation, then, has come to be our tendency to travel in herds. We wander at night—but our objective is somewhere on the brightly lighted streets, or still somewhere where men do not go alone. When we travel far afield, it is in company. Few of my acquaintance, few in the whole city here, would care to ramble at midnight over the grass-grown path I have spoken of; not because they would fear to do so, but because such things are not being done.

Well, it is dangerous to differ individually from one's fellows. It is dangerous to wander from the beaten road. And the fears that guarded the race in the dawn of time and through the centuries were real fears, founded on reality.

A month ago, I was a stranger here. I had just taken my first position—I was graduated from college only three months before, in the spring. I was lonely, and likely to remain so for some time, for I have always been of a solitary nature, making friends slowly.

I had received one invitation out—to visit the camp of a fellow employee in the firm for which I worked, a camp which was located on the farther side of the wide river—the side across from the city and the canal, where the bank was high and steep and heavily wooded, and little tents blossomed all along the water's edge. At night these camps were a string of sparkling lights and tiny, leaping campfires, and the tinkle of music carried faintly far across the calmly flowing water. That far bank of the river was no place for an eccentric, solitary man to love. But the near bank, which would have been an eyesore to the campers had not the river been so wide—the near bank attracted me from my first glimpse of it.

We embarked in a motor-boat at some distance downstream, and swept up along the near bank, and then out and across the current. I turned my eyes backward. The murk of stagnant water that was the canal, the jumble of low buildings beyond it, the lonely, low-lying waste of the narrow strip of land between canal and river, the dark, scattered trees growing there—I intended to see more of these things.

That week-end bored me, but I repaid myself no later than Monday evening, the first evening when I was back in the city, alone and free. I ate a solitary dinner immediately after leaving the office. I went to my room and slept from seven until nearly midnight. I wakened naturally, then, for my whole heart was set on exploring the alluring solitude I had discovered. I dressed, slipped out of the house and into the street, started the motor in my roadster and drove through the lighted streets.

I left behind that part of town which was thick with vehicles carrying people home from their evening engagements, and began to thread my way through darker and narrower streets. Once I had to back out of a cul-de-sac, and once I had to detour around a closed block. This part of town was not alluring, even to me. It was dismal without being solitary.

But when I had parked my car on a rough, cobbled street that ran directly down into the inky waters of the canal, and crossed a narrow bridge, I was repaid. A few minutes set my feet on the old tow-path where mules had drawn river-boats up and down only a year or so ago. Across the canal now, as I walked upstream at a swinging pace, the miserable shacks where miserable people lived seemed to march with me, and then fell behind. They looked like places in which murders might be committed, every one of them.

The bridge I had crossed was near the end of the city going north, as the canal marked its western extremity. Ten minutes of walking, and the dismal shacks were quite a distance behind, the river was farther away and the strip of waste land much wider and more wooded, and tall trees across the canal marched with me as the evil-looking houses had done before. Far and faint, the sound of a bell in the city reached my ears. It was midnight.

I stopped, enjoying the desolation around me. It had the savor I had expected and hoped for. I stood for some time looking up at the sky, watching the low drift of heavy clouds, which were visible in the dull reflected glow from distant lights in the heart of the city, so that they appeared to have a lurid phosphorescence of their own. The ground under my feet, on the contrary, was utterly devoid of light. I had felt my way carefully, knowing the edge of the canal partly by instinct, partly by the even more perfect blackness of the water in it, and even holding fairly well to the path, because it was perceptibly sunken below the ground beside it.

Now as I stood motionless in this spot, my eyes upcast, my mind adrift with strange fancies, suddenly my feelings of satisfaction and well-being gave way to something different. Fear was an emotion unknown to me—for those things which make men fear, I had always loved. A graveyard at night was to me a charming place for a stroll and meditation. But now the roots of my hair seemed to move upright on my head, and along all the length of my spine I was conscious of a prickling, tingling sensation—such as my forefathers may have felt in the jungle when the hair on their backs stood up as the hair of my head was doing now. Also, I was afraid to move; and I knew that there were eyes upon me, and that that was why I was afraid to move. I was afraid of those eyes—afraid to see them, to look into them.

All this while, I stood perfectly still, my face uptilted toward the sky. But after a terrible mental effort, I mastered myself.

Slowly, slowly, with an attempt to propitiate the owner of the unseen eyes by my casual manner, I lowered my own. I looked straight ahead—at the softly swaying silhouette of the tree-tops across the canal as they moved gently in the cool night wind; at the mass of blackness that was those trees, and the opposite shore; at the shiny blackness where the reflections of the clouds glinted vaguely and disappeared, that was the canal. And again I raised my eyes a little, for just across the canal where the shadows massed most heavily, there was that at which I must look more closely. And now, as I grew accustomed to the greater blackness and my pupils expanded, I dimly discerned the contours of an old boat or barge, half sunken in the water. An old, abandoned canal-boat. But was I dreaming, or was there a white-clad figure seated on the roof of the low cabin aft, a pale, heart-shaped face gleaming strangely at me from the darkness, the glow of two eyes seeming to light up the face, and to detach it from the darkness?

Surely, there could be no doubt as to the eyes. They shone as the eyes of animals shine in the dark, with a phosphorescent gleam, and a glimmer of red! Well, I had heard that some human eyes have that quality at night.

But what a place for a human being to be—a girl, too, I was sure. That daintily heart-shaped face was the face of a girl, surely; I was seeing it clearer and clearer, either because my eyes were growing more accustomed to peering into the deeper shadows, or because of that phosphorescence in the eyes that stared back at me.

I raised my voice softly, not to break too much the stillness of the night.

"Hello! who's there? Are you lost, or marooned, and can I help?"

There was a little pause. I was conscious of a soft lapping at my feet. A stronger night wind had sprung up, was ruffling the dark waters. I had been over-warm, and where it struck me the perspiration turned cold on my body, so that I shivered uncontrollably.

"You can stay—and talk awhile, if you will. I am lonely, but not lost. I—I live here."

I could hardly believe my ears. The voice was little more than a whisper, but it had carried clearly—a girl's voice, sure enough. And she lived *there*—in an old, abandoned canal-boat, half submerged in the stagnant water.

"You are not *alone* there?"

"No, not alone. My father lives here with me, but he is deaf—and he sleeps soundly."

Did the night wind blow still colder, as though it came to us from some un-seen, frozen sea—or was there something in her tone that chilled me, even as a strange attraction drew me toward her? I wanted to draw near to her, to see closely the pale, heart-shaped face, to lose myself in the bright eyes that I had seen shining in the darkness. I wanted—I wanted to hold her in my arms, to find her mouth with mine, to kiss it. . . .

With a start, I realized the nature of my thoughts, and for an instant lost all thought in surprize. Never in my twenty-two years had I felt love before. My fancies had been otherwise directed—a moss-grown, fallen gravestone was a dearer thing to me to contemplate than the fairest face in all the world. Yet, surely, what I felt now was love!

I took a reckless step nearer the edge of the bank.

"Could I come over to you?" I begged. "It's warm, and I don't mind a wet-ting. It's late, I know—but I would give a great deal to sit beside you and talk, if only for a few minutes before I go back to town. It's a lonely place here for a girl like you to live—your father should not mind if you exchange a few words with someone occasionally."

Was it the unconventionality of my request that made her next words sound like a long-drawn shudder of protest? There was a strangeness in the tones of her voice that held me wondering, every time she spoke.

"No, no. Oh, no! *You must not swim across.*"

"Then—could I come tomorrow, or some day soon, in the daytime; and would you let me come on board then—or would you come on shore and talk to me, perhaps?"

"Not in the daytime—*never* in the daytime!"

Again the intensity of her low-toned negation held me spellbound.

It was not her sense of the impropriety of the hour, then, that had dictated her manner. For surely, any girl with the slightest sense of the fitness of things would rather have a tryst by daytime than after midnight—yet there was an inference in her last words that if I came again it should be again at night.

Still feeling the spell that had enthralled me, as one does not forget the presence of a drug in the air that is stealing one's senses, even when those senses begin to wander and to busy themselves with other things, I yet spoke shortly.

"Why do you say, 'Never in the daytime'? Do you mean that I may come more than this once at night, though now you won't let me cross the canal to you at the expense of my own clothes, and you won't put down your plank or drawbridge or whatever you come on shore with, and talk to me here for only a moment? I'll come again, if you'll let me talk to you instead of calling across the water. I'll come again, any time you will let me—day or night, I don't care. I want to come to you. But I only ask you to explain. If I came in the daytime and met your father, wouldn't that be the best thing to do? Then we could be really acquainted—we could be friends."

"In the nighttime, my father sleeps. In the daytime, *I* sleep. How could I talk to you, or introduce you to my father then? If you came on board this boat in the daytime, you would find my father—and you would be sorry. As for me, I would be sleeping. I could never introduce you to my father, do you see?"

"You sleep soundly, you and your father." Again there was pique in my voice.

"Yes, we sleep soundly."

"And always at different times?"

"Always at different times. We are on guard—one of us is always on guard. We have been hardly used, down there in your city. And we have taken refuge here. And we are always—always—on guard."

The resentment vanished from my breast, and I felt my heart go out to her anew. She was so pale, so pitiful in the night. My eyes were learning better and better how to pierce the darkness; they were giving me a more definite picture of my companion—if I could think of her as a companion, between myself and whom stretched the black water.

The sadness of the lonely scene, the perfection of the solitude itself, these things contributed to her pitifulness. Then there was that strangeness of atmosphere of which, even yet, I had only partly taken note. There was the strange, shivering chill, which yet did not seem like the healthful chill of a cool evening. In fact, it did not prevent me from feeling the oppression of the night, which was unusually sultry. It was like a little breath of deadly cold that came and went, and yet did not alter the temperature of the air itself, as the small ripples on the surface of the water do not concern the water even a foot down.

And even that was not all. There was an unwholesome smell about the night—a dank, moldy smell that might have been the very breath of death and decay. Even I, the connoisseur in all things dismal and unwholesome, tried to keep my mind from dwelling overmuch upon that smell. What it must be to live breathing it constantly in, I could not think. But no doubt the girl and her father were used to it; and no doubt it came from the stagnant water of the canal and from the rotting wood of the old, half-sunken boat that was their refuge.

My heart throbbed with pity again. Their refuge—what a place! And my clearer vision of the girl showed me that she was pitifully thin, even though possessed of the strange face that drew me to her. Her clothes hung around her like old rags, but hers was no scarecrow aspect. Although little flesh clothed her bones, her very bones were beautiful. I was sure the little, pale, heart-shaped face would be more beautiful still, if I could only see it closely. I must see it closely— I must establish some claim to consideration as a friend of the strange, lonely crew of the half-sunken wreck.

"This is a poor place to call a refuge," I said finally. "One might have very little money, and yet do somewhat better. Perhaps I might help you—I am sure I could. If your ill-treatment in the city was because of poverty—I am not rich, but I could help that. I could help you a little with money, if you would let me; or, in any case, I could find a position for you. I'm sure I could do that."

The eyes that shone fitfully toward me like two small pools of water intermittently lit by a cloud-swept sky seemed to glow more brightly. She had been half crouching, half sitting on top of the cabin; now she leaped to her feet with one quick, sinuous, abrupt motion, and took a few rapid, restless steps to and fro before she answered.

When she spoke, her voice was little more than a whisper; yet surely rage was in its shrill sibilance.

"Fool! Do you think you would be helping me, to tie me to a desk, to shut me behind doors, away from freedom, away from the delight of doing my own will, of seeking my own way? Never, never would I let you do that. Rather this old boat, rather a deserted grave under the stars, for my home!"

A boundless surprize swept over me, and a positive feeling of kinship with this strange being, whose face I had hardly seen, possessed me. So I myself might have spoken, so I had often felt, though I had never dreamed of putting my thoughts so definitely, so forcibly. My regularized daytime life was a thing I thought little of; I really lived only in my nocturnal prowlings. Why, this girl was right! All of life should be free, and spent in places that interested and attracted.

How little, how little I knew, that night, that dread forces were tugging at my soul, were finding entrance to it and easy access through the morbid weakness of my nature! How little I knew at what a cost I deviated so radically from my kind, who herd in cities and love well-lit ways and the sight of man, and sweet and wholesome places to be solitary in, when the desire for solitude comes over them!

That night it seemed to me that there was but one important thing in life—to allay the angry passion my unfortunate words had aroused in the breast of my beloved, and to win from her some answering feeling.

"I understand—much better than you think," I whispered tremulously. "What I want is to see you again, to come to know you, and to serve you in any way that I may. Surely, there must be something in which I can be of use to you. All you have to do from tonight on for ever, is to command me. I swear it!"

"You swear *that*—you do swear it?"

Delighted at the eagerness of her words, I lifted my hand toward the dark heavens.

"I swear it. From this night on, for ever—I swear it."

"Then listen. Tonight you may not come to me, nor I to you. I do not want you to board this boat—not tonight, not any night. And most of all, not any day. But do not look so sad. I will come to you. No, not tonight, perhaps not for many nights—yet before very long. I will come to you there, on the bank of the canal, when the water in the canal ceases to flow."

I must have made a gesture of impatience, or of despair. It sounded like a way of saying "never"—for why should the water in the canal cease to flow? She read my thoughts in some way, for she answered them.

"You do not understand. I am speaking seriously—I am promising to meet you there on the bank, and soon. For the water within these banks is moving slower, always slower. Higher up, I have heard that the canal has been drained. Between these lower locks, the water still seeps in and drops slowly, slowly downstream. But there will come a night when it will be quite, quite stagnant—and on that night I will come to you. And when I come, I will ask of you a favor. And you will keep your oath."

It was all the assurance I could get that night. She had come back to the side of the cabin where she had sat crouched before, and she resumed again that posture and sat still and silent, watching me. Sometimes I could see her eyes upon me, and sometimes not. But I felt that their gaze was unwavering. The little cold breeze, which I had finally forgotten while I was talking with her, was blowing again, and the unwholesome smell of decay grew heavier before the dawn.

She would not speak again, nor answer me when I spoke to her, and I grew nervous, and strangely ill at ease.

At last I went away. And in the first faint light of dawn I slipped up the stairs of my rooming-house, and into my own room.

I was deadly tired at the office next day. And day after day slipped away and I grew more and more weary; for a man can not wake day and night without suffering, especially in hot weather, and that was what I was doing. I haunted the old tow-path and waited, night after night, on the bank opposite the sunken boat. Sometimes I saw my lady of the darkness, and sometimes not. When I saw her, she spoke little; but sometimes she sat there on the top of the cabin and let me watch her till the dawn, or until the strange uneasiness that was like fright drove me from her and back to my room, where I tossed restlessly in the heat and dreamed strange dreams, half waking, till the sun shone in on my forehead and I tumbled into my clothes and down to the office again.

Once I asked her why she had made the fanciful condition that she would not come ashore to meet me until the waters of the canal had ceased to run. (How eagerly I studied those waters! How I stole away at noontime more than once, not to approach the old boat, but to watch the almost imperceptible down-drift of bubbles, bits of straw, twigs, rubbish!)

My questioning displeased her, and I asked her that no more. It was enough that she chose to be whimsical. My part was to wait.

It was more than a week later that I questioned her again, this time on a different subject. And after that, I curbed my curiosity relentlessly.

"Never speak to me of things you do not understand about me. Never again, or I will not show myself to you again. And when I walk on the path yonder, it will not be with you."

I had asked her what form of persecution she and her father had suffered in the city, that had driven them out to this lonely place, and where in the city they had lived.

Frightened seriously lest I lose the ground I was sure I had gained with her, I was about to speak of something else. But before I could find the words, her low voice came to me again.

"It was horrible, horrible! Those little houses below the bridge, those houses along the canal—tell me, are they not worse than my boat? Life there was shut in, and furtive. I was not free as I am now—and the freedom I will soon have will make me forget the things I have not yet forgotten. The screaming, the reviling and cursing! Fear and flight! As you pass back by those houses, think how you would like to be shut in one of them, and in fear of your life. And then think of them no more; for I would forget them, and I will never speak of them again."

I dared not answer her. I was surprized that she had vouchsafed me so much. But surely her words meant this: that before she had come to live on the decaying, water-rotted old boat, she had lived in one of those horrible houses I passed by on my way to her. Those houses, each of which looked like the predestined scene of a murder!

As I left her that night, I felt that I was very daring.

"One or two nights more and you will walk beside me," I called to her. "I have watched the water at noon, and it hardly moves at all. I threw a scrap of paper into the canal, and it whirled and swung a little where a thin skim of oil lay on the water down there—oil from the big, dirty city you are well out of. But though I watched and watched, I could not see it move downward at all. Perhaps tomorrow night, or the night after, you will walk on the bank with me. I hope it will be clear and moonlight, and I will be near enough to see you clearly—as well as you seem always to see me in darkness or moonlight, equally well. And perhaps I will kiss you—but not unless you let me."

And yet, the next day, for the first time my thoughts were definitely troubled. I had been living in a dream—I began to speculate concerning the end of the path on which my feet were set.

I had conceived, from the first, such a horror of those old houses by the canal! They were well enough to walk past, nursing gruesome thoughts for a midnight treat. But, much as I loved all that was weird and eery about the girl I was wooing so strangely, it was a little too much for my fancy that she had come from them.

By this time, I had become decidedly unpopular in my place of business. Not that I had made enemies, but that my peculiar ways had caused too much adverse comment. It would have taken very little, I think, to have made the entire office force decide that I was mad. After the events of the next twenty-four hours, and after this letter is found and read, they will be sure that they knew it all along! At this time, however, they were punctiliously polite to me, and merely let me alone as much as possible—which suited me perfectly. I dragged wearily through day after day, exhausted from lack of sleep, conscious of their speculative glances, living only for the night to come.

But on this day, I approached the man who had invited me to the camp across the river, who had unknowingly shown me the way that led to my love.

"Have you ever noticed the row of tumble-down houses along the canal on the city side?" I asked him.

He gave me an odd look. I suppose he sensed the significance of my breaking silence after so long to speak of *them*—sensed that in some way I had a deep interest in them.

"You have odd tastes, Morton," he said after a moment. "I suppose you wander into strange places sometimes—I've heard you speak of an enthusiasm for graveyards at night. But my advice to you is to keep away from those houses. They're unsavory, and their reputation is unsavory. Positively, I think you'd be in danger of your life, if you go poking around there. They have been the scene of several murders, and a dope den or two has been cleaned out of them. Why in the world you should want to investigate them—"

"I don't expect to investigate them," I said testily. "I was merely interested in them—from the outside. To tell you the truth, I'd heard a story, a rumor—never mind where. But you say there have been murders there—I suppose this rumor I heard may have had to do with an attempted one. There was a girl who lived there with her father once, and they were set upon there, or something of the sort, and had to run away. Did you ever hear *that* story?"

Barrett gave me an odd look such as one gives in speaking of a past horror so dreadful that the mere speaking of it makes it live terribly again.

"What you say reminds me of a horrible thing that was said to have happened down there once," he said. "It was in all the papers. A little child disappeared in one of those houses, and a couple of poor lodgers who lived there, a girl and her father, were accused of having made away with it. They were accused—they were accused—oh, well, I don't like to talk about such things. It was too dreadful. The child's body was found—*part* of it was found. It was mutilated, and the people in the house seemed to believe it had been mutilated in order to conceal the manner of its death; there was an ugly wound in the throat, it finally came out, and it seemed as if the child might have been bled to death. It was found in the girl's room, hidden away. The old man and his daughter escaped, before the police were called. The countryside was scoured, but they were never found. Why, you must have read it in the papers, several years ago."

I nodded, with a heavy heart. I *had* read it in the papers, I remembered now. And again, a terrible questioning came over me. Who was this girl, *what* was this girl, who seemed to have my heart in her keeping?

Why did not a merciful God let me die then?

Befogged with exhaustion, bemused in a dire enchantment, my mind was incapable of thought. And yet, some soul-process akin to that which saves the sleepwalker poised at perilous heights sounded its warning now.

My mind was filled with doleful images. There were women—I had heard and read—who slew to satisfy a blood-lust. There were ghosts, specters—call them what you will, their names have been legion in the dark pages of that lore which dates back to the infancy of the races of the earth—who retained even in death this blood-lust. Vampires—they had been called that. I had read of them. Corpses by day, spirits of evil by night, roaming abroad in their own forms or in the forms of bats or unclean beasts, killing body and soul of their victims—for whoever dies of the repeated "kiss" of the vampire, which leaves its mark on the throat and draws the blood from the body, becomes a vampire also—of such beings I had read.

And, horror of horrors! In that last cursed day at the office, I remembered reading of these vampires—these undead—that in their nocturnal flights they had one limitation—*they could not cross running water.*

That night I went my usual nightly way with tears of weakness on my face—for my weakness was supreme, and I recognized fully at last the misery of being the victim of an enchantment stronger than my feeble will. But I went.

I approached the neighborhood of the canal-boat as the distant city clock chimed the first stroke of twelve. It was the dark of the moon and the sky was overcast. Heat-lightning flickered low in the sky, seeming to come from every point of the compass and circumscribe the horizon, as if unseen fires burned behind the rim of the world. By its fitful glimmer, I saw a new thing: between the old boat and the canal bank stretched a long, slim, solid-looking shadow—a plank had been let down! In that moment, I realized that I had been playing with powers of evil which had no intent now to let me go, which were indeed about to lay hold upon me with an inexorable grasp. Why had I come tonight? Why, but that the spell of the enchantment laid upon me was a thing more potent, and far more unbreakable, than any wholesome spell of love? The creature I sought out—oh, I remembered now, with the cold perspiration beading my brow, the lore hidden away between the covers of the dark old book which I had read so many years ago and half forgotten!—until dim memories of it stirred within me, this last day and night.

My lady of the night! No woman of wholesome flesh and blood and odd perverted tastes that matched my own, but one of the undead! In that moment, I knew it, and knew that the vampires of old legends polluted still, in these latter days, the fair surface of the earth.

And on the instant, behind me in the darkness there was the crackle of a twig, and something brushed against my arm.

This, then, was the fulfilment of my dream. I knew, without turning my head, that the pale, dainty face with its glowing eyes was near my own—that I had only to stretch out my arm to touch the slender grace of the girl I had so longed to draw near. I knew, and should have felt the rapture I had anticipated. Instead, the roots of my hair prickled coldly, unendurably, as they had on the night when I had first sighted the old boat. The miasmic odors of the night, heavy and oppressive with heat and unrelieved by a breath of air, all but overcame me, and I fought with myself to prevent my teeth clicking in my head. The little waves of coldness I had felt often in this spot were chasing over my body, yet they were not from any breeze; the leaves on the trees hung down motionless, as though they were actually wilting on their branches.

With an effort, I turned my head.

Two hands caught me around my neck. The pale face was so near that I felt the warm breath from its nostrils fanning my cheek.

And, suddenly, all that was wholesome in my perverted nature rose uppermost. I longed for the touch of the red mouth, like a dark flower opening before me in the night. I longed for it—and yet more I dreaded it. I shrank back, catching in a powerful grip the fragile wrists of the hands that strove to hold me. I must not—I must not yield to the faintness that I felt stealing over me.

I was facing down the path toward the city. A low rumble of thunder—the first—broke the torrid hush of the summer night. A glare of lightning seemed to tear the night asunder, to light up the universe. Overhead, the clouds were careering madly in fantastic shapes, driven by a wind that swept the upper heavens without causing even a trembling in the air lower down. And far down the canal, that baleful glare seemed to play around and hover over the little row of shanties—murder-cursed, and haunted by the ghost of a dead child.

My gaze was fixed on them, while I held away from me the pallid face and fought off the embrace that sought to overcome my resisting will. And so a long moment passed. The glare faded out of the sky, and a greater darkness took the world. But there was a near, more menacing glare fastened upon my face—the glare of two eyes that watched mine, that had watched me as I, unthinking, stared down at the dark houses.

This girl—this woman who had come to me at my own importunate requests, did not love me, since I had shrunk from her. She did not love me—but it was not only that. She had watched me as I gazed down at the houses that held her dark past, and I was sure that she divined my thoughts. She knew my horror of those houses—she knew my new-born horror of *her.* And she hated me for it, hated me more malignantly than I had believed a human being could hate.

And at that point in my thoughts, I felt my skin prickle and my scalp rise again: could a *human being* cherish such hatred as I read, trembling more and more, in those glowing fires lit with what seemed to me more like the fires of hell than any light that ought to shine in a woman's eyes?

And through all this, not a word had passed between us!

So far I have written calmly. I wish that I could write on so, to the end. If I could do that, there might be one or two of those who will regard this as the document of a maniac, who would believe the horrors of which I am about to write.

But I am only flesh and blood. At this point in the happenings of the awful night, my calmness deserted me—at this point I felt that I had been drawn into the midst of a horrible nightmare from which there was no escape, no waking! As I write, this feeling again overwhelms me, until I can hardly write at all—until, were it not for the thing which I must do, I would rush out into the street and run, screaming, until I was caught and dragged away, to be put behind strong iron bars. Perhaps I would feel safe there—perhaps!

I know that, terrified at the hate I saw confronting me in those redly gleaming eyes, I would have slunk away. The two thin hands that caught my arm again were strong enough to prevent that, however. I had been spared her kiss, but I was not to escape from the oath I had taken to serve her.

"You promised, you swore," she hissed in my ear. "And tonight you are to keep your oath."

I felt my senses reel. My oath—yes, I had an oath to keep. I had lifted my hand toward the dark heavens, and sworn to serve her in any way she chose. Freely, and of my own volition, I had sworn.

I sought to evade her.

"Let me help you back to your boat," I begged. "You have no kindly feeling for me, and—you have seen it—I love you no longer. I will go back to the city—you can go back to your father, and forget that I broke your peace."

The laughter that greeted my speech I shall never forget—not in the depths under the scummy surface of the canal—not in the empty places between the worlds, where my tortured soul may wander.

"So you do not love me, and I hate you! Fool! Have I waited these weary months for the water to stop, only to go back now? After my father and I returned here and found the old boat rotting in the drained canal, and took refuge in it; when the water was turned into the canal while I slept, so that I could never escape until its flow should cease, *because of the thing that I am*—even then I dreamed of tonight.

"When the imprisonment we still shared ceased to matter to my father—come on board the deserted boat tomorrow, and see why, if you dare!—still I dreamed on, of tonight!

"I have been lonely, desolate, starving—now the whole world shall be mine! And by *your* help!"

I asked her, somehow, what she wanted of me, and a madness overcame me so that I hardly heard her reply. Yet somehow, I knew that there was that on the opposite shore of the great river where the pleasure camps were, that she wanted to find. In the madness of my terror, she made me understand and obey her. I must carry her in my arms across the long bridge over the river, deserted in the small hours of the night.

The way back to the city was long tonight—long. She walked behind me, and I turned my eyes neither to right nor left. Only as I passed the tumble-down houses, I saw their reflection in the canal and trembled so that I could have fallen to the ground, at the thoughts of the little child this woman had been accused of slaying there, and at the certainty I felt that she was reading my thoughts.

And now the horror that engulfed me darkened my brain.

I know that we set our feet upon the long, wide bridge that spanned the river. I know the storm broke there, so that I battled for my footing, almost for my life, it seemed, against the pelting deluge. And the horror I had invoked was in my arms, clinging to me, burying its head upon my shoulder. So increasingly dreadful had my pale-faced companion become to me, that I hardly thought of her now as a woman at all—only as a demon of the night.

The tempest raged still as she leaped down out of my arms on the other shore. And again I walked with her against my will, while the trees lashed their branches around me, showing the pale under-sides of their leaves in the vivid frequent flashes that rent the heavens.

On and on we went, branches flying through the air and missing us by a miracle of ill fortune. Such as she and I are not slain by falling branches. The river was a welter of whitecaps, flattened down into strange shapes by the pounding rain. The clouds as we glimpsed them were like devils flying through the sky.

Past dark tent after dark tent we stole, and past a few where lights burned dimly behind their canvas walls. And at last we came to an old quarry. Into its artificial ravine she led me, and up to a crevice in the rock wall.

"Reach in your hand and pull out the loose stone you will feel," she whispered. "It closes an opening that leads into deep caverns. A human hand must remove that stone—your hand must move it!"

Why did I struggle so to disobey her? Why did I fail? It was as though I *knew*—but my failure was foreordained—I had taken oath!

If you who read have believed that I have set down the truth thus far, the little that is left you will call the ravings of a madman overtaken by his madness. Yet these things happened.

I stretched out my arm, driven by a compulsion I could not resist. At arm's length in the niche in the rock, I felt something move—the loose rock, a long, narrow fragment, much larger than I had expected. Yet it moved easily, seeming to swing on a natural pivot. Outward it swung, toppling toward me—a moment more and there was a swift rush of the ponderous weight I had loosened. I leaped aside and went down, my forehead grazed by the rock.

For a brief moment I must have been unconscious, but only for a moment. My head a stabbing agony of pain, unreal lights flashing before my eyes, I yet knew the reality of the storm that beat me down as I struggled to my feet. I knew the reality of the dark, loathsome shapes that passed me in the dark, crawling out of the orifice in the rock and flapping through the wild night, along the way that led to the pleasure camps.

So the caverns I had laid open to the outer world were infested with bats. I had been inside unlit caverns, and had heard there the squeaking of the things, felt and heard the flapping of their wings—*but never in all my life before had I seen bats as large as men and women!*

Sick and dizzy from the blow on my head, and from disgust, I crept along the way they were going. If I touched one of them, I felt that I should die of horror.

Now, at last, the storm abated, and a heavy darkness made the whole world seem like the inside of a tomb.

Where the tents stood in a long row, the number of the monster bats seemed to diminish. It was as though—horrible thought!—they were creeping into the tents, with their slumbering occupants.

At last I came to a lighted tent, and paused, crouching so that the dim radiance which shone through the canvas did not touch me in the shadows. And there I waited, but not for long. There was a dark form silhouetted against the tent; a rustle and confusion, and the dark thing was again in silhouette—but with a difference in the quality of the shadow. The dark thing was *inside* the tent now, its bat wings extending across the entrance through which it had crept.

Fear held me spellbound. And as I looked, the shadow changed again, imperceptibly, so that I could not have told *how* it changed. But now it was not the shadow of a bat, but of a woman.

"The storm, the storm! I am lost, exhausted! I crept in here, to beg for refuge until the dawn!"

That low, thrilling, sibilant voice—too well I knew it!

Within the tent I heard a murmur of acquiescent voices. At last I began to understand.

I knew the nature of the woman I had carried over the river in my arms, the woman who would not even cross the canal until the water should have ceased utterly to flow. I remembered books I had read—*Dracula*—other books, and stories. I knew they were true books and stories, now—I knew those horrors existed for me.

I had indeed kept my oath to the creature of darkness—I had brought her to her kind, under her guidance. I had let them loose in hordes upon the pleasure camps. The campers were doomed—and through them, others. . . .

I forgot my fear. I rushed from my hiding-place up to the tent door, and there I screamed and called aloud.

"Don't take her in—don't let her stay—nor the others, that have crept into the other tents! Wake all the campers—they will sleep on to their destruction! Drive out the interlopers—drive them out quickly! *They are not human—no, and they are not bats!* Do you hear me?—do you understand?"

I was fairly howling, in a voice that was strange to me.

"She is a vampire—they are all vampires. *Vampires!*"

Inside the tent I heard a new voice.

"What can be the matter with that poor man?" the voice said. It was a woman's, and gentle.

"Crazy—somebody out of his senses, dear," a man's voice answered. "Don't be frightened."

And then the voice I knew so well—so well: "I saw a falling rock strike a man on the head in the storm. He staggered away, but I suppose it crazed him."

I waited for no more. I ran away, madly, through the night and back across the bridge to the city.

Next day—today—I boarded the sunken canal-boat. It is the abode of death—no woman could have lived there—only such an one as *she.* The old man's corpse was there—he must have died long, long ago. The smell of death and decay on the boat was dreadful.

Again, I felt that I understood. Back in those awful houses, she had committed the crime when first she became the thing she is. And he—her father—less sin-steeped, and less accursed, attempted to destroy the evidence of her crime, and fled with her, but died without becoming like her. She had said that one of those two was always on watch—did he indeed divide her vigil on the boat? What more fitting—the dead standing watch with the undead! And no wonder that she would not let me board the craft of death, even to carry her away.

And still I feel the old compulsion. I have been spared her kiss—but for a little while. Yet I will not let the power of my oath draw me back, till I enter the caverns with her and creep forth in the form of a bat to prey upon mankind. Before that can happen, I too will die.

☾   ☾   ☾

Today in the city I heard that a horde of strange insects or small animals infested the pleasure camps last night. Some said, with horror-bated breath, that they perhaps were rats. None of them was seen; but in the morning nearly every camper had a strange, deep wound in his throat. I almost laughed aloud. They were so horrified at the idea of an army of rats, creeping into the tents and biting the sleeping occupants on their throats! If they had seen what I saw—if they knew that they are doomed to spread corruption—

So my own death will not be enough. Today I bought supplies for blasting. Tonight I will set my train of dynamite, from the hole I made in the cliff where the vampires creep in and out, along the row of tents, as far as the last one—then I shall light my fuse. It will be done before the dawn. Tomorrow, the city will mourn its dead and execrate my name.

And then, at last, in the slime beneath the unmoving waters of the canal, I shall find peace! But perhaps it will not be peace—for I shall seek it midway between the old boat with its cargo of death and the row of dismal houses where a little child was done to death when first *she* became the thing she is. That is my expiation.

ACKNOWLEDGMENTS

GRATEFUL ACKNOWLEDGMENT is made to the following for permission to reprint their copyrighted material:

"The Insufficient Answer" by Robert Aickman, copyright © 1951 by Robert Aickman. Reprinted by permission of the agent for the author's Estate, JABberwocky Literary Agency, P. O. Box 4558, Sunnyside, NY 11104-0558.

"The Scent of Vinegar" by Robert Bloch, copyright © 1994 by Robert Bloch. Reprinted by permission of the author's Estate and the author's agent, Ricia Mainhardt.

"Sometimes Salvation" by Pat Cadigan, copyright © 1995 by Pat Cadigan. Reprinted by permission of the author.

"The Brotherhood of Blood" by Hugh B. Cave, copyright © 1932 by the Popular Fiction Publishing Company. Reprinted by permission of the author.

"I Vant to be Alone" by Barbara D'Amato, copyright © 1995 by Barbara D'Amato. Reprinted by permission of the author.

"Nellie Foster" by August Derleth, copyright © 1933 by the Popular Fiction Publishing Company. Reprinted by permission of the agent for the author's Estate, JABberwocky Literary Agency, P. O. Box 4558, Sunnyside, NY 11104-0558.

"The Man Who Loved the Vampire Lady" by Brian Stableford, copyright © 1988 by Brian Stableford. Reprinted by permission of the author.

"The Last Grave of Lill Warran" by Manly Wade Wellman, copyright © 1951 by the Popular Fiction Publishing Company. Reprinted by the Executrix for the author's Estate, Frances Wellman.

". . . To Feel Another's Woe" by Chet Williamson, copyright © 1989 by Chet Williamson. Reprinted by permission of the author.

"The Canal" by Everil Worrell, copyright © 1927 by the Popular Fiction Publishing Company. Reprinted by permission of Jeanne Eileen Murphy.